"ELLIOTT'S SURE-HANDED AND SEDUCTIVE
BLEND OF EXOTIC LOCALES, COMPLEX
interstellar politics, intriguing cultures, realistic
romance, and wonderfully realized characters is
addictive. I want my next fix!''
— Jennifer Roberson,
author of *The Chronicles of the Cheysuli*
and *The Novels of Tiger and Del*

"JARAN is an impressive first novel of interstellar
empires and primitive cultures . . . a very strong
debut.''
— *Locus*

"Sweeps the reader along like a wild wind across the
steppes. Tell Kate to write faster—I want to read the
whole saga NOW!''
— Melanie Rawn,
author of the *Dragon Prince*
and *Dragon Star* trilogies

"A new author of considerable talent . . . a rich
tapestry of a vibrant society on the brink of epic
change.''
— *Rave Reviews*

"A bright new talent . . . complex politics . . . a
wonderful, sweeping setting . . . reminds me of C. J.
Cherryh.''
— Judith Tarr

"Well-written and gripping. After all, with a solidly
drawn alien race, galactic-scale politics, intrigue,
warfare, even a crackling love story, all set in a
fascinating world that opens out onto a vast view of
interstellar history—how could anyone resist?''
— Katharine Kerr

Other Novels by
KATE ELLIOTT
available from DAW Books:
Crown of Stars:
KING'S DRAGON
PRINCE OF DOGS
THE BURNING STONE
CHILD OF FLAME*
CROWN OF STARS*

The Novels of the Jaran
JARAN
AN EARTHLY CROWN
HIS CONQUERING SWORD
THE LAW OF BECOMING

&

with Melanie Rawn and Jennifer Roberson
THE GOLDEN KEY

*forthcoming in hardcover from DAW Books

AN EARTH
CROWN

THE SWORD OF HE
BOOK ONE

KATE ELLIO

DAW BOOKS,
DONALD A. WOLLHEIM
375 Hudson Street, New Yor
ELIZABETH R. WOL
SHEILA E. GILB
PUBLISHER

This book is dedicated to my brother,
Karsten,
because he keeps bothering me to dedicate
a book to him,
and because it was meant to be dedicated
to him all along,
for reasons he knows best.

ACKNOWLEDGMENTS

I would like to thank the San Jose Repertory Theatre, and in particular John McCluggage and the cast and crew of the Spring 1992 production of Noel Coward's *Hay Fever,* for graciously allowing me to attend rehearsals. If I got anything right about acting and theater, it's because of them, and because of additional comments by Carol Wolf, Nancy E. Bottem, and Howard Kerr. Exaggerations and inaccuracies are my own.

I would also like to thank Edana Vitro, for photocopying above and beyond the call of duty, and the many readers who made excellent comments on the early drafts.

AUTHOR'S NOTE

THE SWORD OF HEAVEN is a single novel being published in two parts. The author sometimes refers to it as a novel in five acts with one intermission.

"Barbarus hic ego sum,
qui non intelligor illis."

    —OVID
      (Here I am a barbarian,
      because men understand me not.)

"I can take any empty space
and call it a bare stage.
A man walks across this empty space
whilst someone else is watching him,
and this is all that is needed
for an act of theatre to be engaged."

    —PETER BROOK,
     The Empty Space
     Atheneum (New York, 1968)

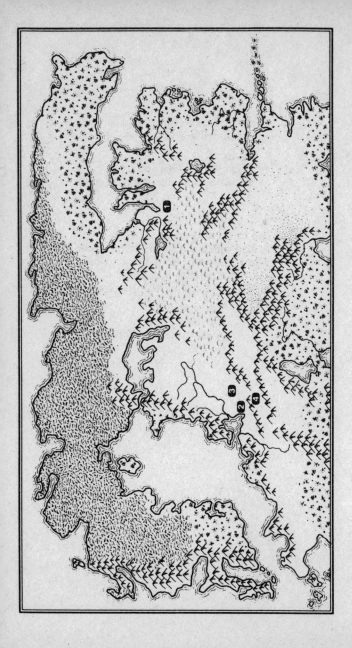

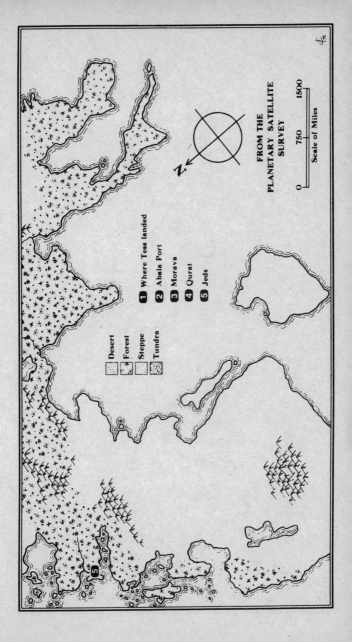

FROM THE
PLANETARY SATELLITE
SURVEY

Scale of Miles
0   750   1500

1 Where Tess landed
2 Abala Port
3 Morava
4 Qurat
5 Jeds

Desert
Forest
Steppe
Tundra

PROLOGUE

"Nature that framed us of four elements,
Warring within our breasts for regiment,
Doth teach us all to have aspiring minds:
Our souls whose faculties can comprehend
The wondrous architecture of the world:
And measure every wandering planet's course,
Still climbing after knowledge infinite,
And always moving as the restless spheres,
Wills us to wear ourselves and never rest,
Until we reach the ripest fruit of all,
That perfect bliss and sole felicity,
The sweet fruition of an earthly crown."
—MARLOWE
Tamburlaine The Great

The rider left the great sprawl of tents that marked the main camp of the nomad army just as the sun set. Dusk washed his scarlet shirt gray, and with only the gibbous moon to light him, he soon faded into the dark of night, the susurration of his horse's passage through the high grass marking his progress. Near midnight, he came to another, smaller camp, and here he changed horses and went on. By dawn, he was within sight of the low range of hills where lay the farthest outposts of the *khaja*, the settled people.

One hand's span after sunrise, he rode through a village. Fields spread out around the huts. Green shoots wet with dew sparkled in the soft light of morning. The khaja stopped in their tasks and stared at him, a lone *jaran* warrior armed with a saber and a lance, passing through their midst as if their presence was beneath his notice. None spoke, or moved against him.

A cluster of jaran tents stood in neat lines outside the leveled sod walls that had once protected the village. A single rider emerged from the encampment and rode out to meet him.

The traveler reined in his mount and waited, leaning forward over the horse's neck to whisper in its ear as it fretted at the tight rein. Then, sitting back, he lifted a hand. "Well met," he said as the young rider from the encampment pulled up beside him. "I am Aleksi Soerensen. I've come from the main camp, with a message for the Gathering of Elders. You're one of Grekov's riders, aren't you?"

"I'm Feodor Grekov. His sister's son. *Soerensen?*" Grekov hesitated, raising a hand to brush a lock of blond hair off of his forehead. He pronounced the name awkwardly.

"Yes," Aleksi agreed, politely but without a smile.

"You're the orphan that Bakhtiian's wife adopted," said Feodor. He examined Aleksi with what appeared to be common curiosity. "It's said you have a fine hand for the saber."

Aleksi was disconcerted. He had not grown used to the respect, and the protection, his adopted sister's name granted him. "I had a fine teacher."

Feodor did not press the matter. "If you've come from the main camp, then your news must be important. I'll get you a new mount, and ride with you myself, if you need a guide."

"It's safe enough for the two of us from here on into the hills?"

"We have patrols running through all these hills. There are a few khaja bandits left, but nothing more. These khaja aren't real fighters. Soon they'll all be subject to us, as they should be." Feodor grinned. "And I'd like to go, anyway. It will be something to tell my children."

"Ah. You've a little one?"

Grekov flushed. "Not yet."

"But you've a woman in mind for a wife, I take it."

"I—" Feodor hesitated. "A man can't help looking," he said at last. Aleksi heard the bitterness in his voice clearly.

"I'd like to marry," Aleksi agreed, feeling suddenly and surprisingly sorry for Grekov, who ought to have had an easy life, being nephew of a tribal warleader and nephew to its headwoman. And since the unnamed young woman in question had no choice in marriage, Aleksi could only guess that the obstacles arose from Grekov's elders. "But I suppose I never will."

"Of course, as an orphan—but surely you've standing enough now, since Bakhtiian's wife has adopted you into her tent."

"Adopted me by her customs, not by ours. Or a bit by both, I suppose. Still, you may be right. I hope so."

"Gods," said Feodor, "there's enough trouble in the world without worrying about women." And that sealed their comradeship. Aleksi felt a bit overwhelmed by how easy it was, when you had a respectable name, a sister, a place in a tribe. "Come on," Feodor added, "we'll get you a new mount and something to eat, and then be on our way." He led Aleksi into camp and introduced him round as if he was just another young soldier like himself and the rest of the riders. A short time later, the two young men rode out in charity with each other.

By midday they reached the butte known to the jaran as *khayan-sarmiia*, Her Crown Fallen from Heaven to Earth. Once, the stories said, this range of hills was known only to the jaran tribes, but in recent generations a few khaja settlements had crept out across the plains from settled lands in the south and west to pollute the holy ground where the Sun's Crown had come to rest on the earth.

At the base of the hill, an army waited. Countless soldiers, in their tens and hundreds and thousands, gathered to acclaim the man who would lead them against their ancient enemies. Aleksi and Feodor left their horses with the army and hiked up the trail that ascended the steep hillside. The wind began to buffet them. Soon both were breathing hard, despite their youth, because they were not used to so much hard walking.

At last, the path leveled and gave out onto a plateau from whose height they could see the shifting mass of the army below, the rolling spread of hills, and a few distant wisps of smoke that marked khaja villages. Far to the south, past the flat haze of plain, a suggestion of bluer haze marked the southern mountains. To the north and east lay only the vast golden plains that blended at the horizon into the equally monotonous blue of the sky. West, though they could not see it from here, lay the sea.

They admired the view for as long as it took to get their breath back. But of far greater interest was the gathering now taking place on the plateau itself.

A single tent had been set up at the southern end of the plateau, a great tent whose sides shook in the wind that scoured the summit. Between the northern end, where the two young men stood on an escarpment of rock, and the tent lay a broad stretch of ground smoothed by generations of wind and storm. On this ground, on the earth itself, some on blankets, some on pillows, sat the assembled commanders and elders of the thousand tribes of the jaran.

At the very back sat the younger men, commanders of a hundred riders each; many now wore the scarlet shirts, brilliant with embroidery on the sleeves and collar, that had come to be the symbol of the jaran army, though a few still wore the colors of their own tribe. In front of them sat a sea of elders, some ancient and frail, some elderly but robust, female and male both.

At the very front sat the *etsanas* of the thousand tribes, each headwoman flanked by the *dyan,* the warleader, of her tribe. Most of the women were elderly, though a few were young. They wore their finest clothing, bright silk blouses beaded with gold and silver under calf-length tunics. Striped, belled trousers swelled out underneath. Jeweled headdresses and necklaces and torques and bracelets adorned them, and their hand mirrors hung free of their cases, face out in the glare so that they reflected the light of the sun. So many wore tiny bells that a faint tinkling chime could be heard, underscoring the rush of wind and the solemn proceedings.

The dyans, too, wore their finest shirts, twined animals or interlaced flora embroidered with lavish detail on the sleeves and capped with epaulets fastened on their shoulders. Each man wore sheathed at his belt a saber and most held a lance, so that the gathering resembled a sea of bright colors tipped with metal.

In a semicircle before the awning that stretched out from the tent sat ten women and eight men, the women on fine silken pillows and the men beside them on woven blankets: the etsanas and dyans of the Ten Eldest Tribes, the first tribes of the jaran. The men held their sabers, unsheathed, across their knees. Each woman gripped a staff from whose tip hung a horsetail woven with ribbons and golden harness, the symbol of their authority.

"Two dyans missing," said Feodor Grekov in a low voice to Aleksi. Aleksi glanced at him, and Grekov cocked his head toward the assembly. "Of course, Bakhtiian himself is the dyan of the Orzhekov tribe. But Sergei Veselov never arrived. I heard that he's ill."

"That's the news I brought," said Aleksi. "Sergei Veselov is dead. He died two days past."

"Who will become dyan, then? Arina Veselov's brother sits beside Bakhtiian, but everyone knows it isn't fitting for a brother and sister to act as etsana and dyan together."

"Sergei Veselov has a son, still, who could claim the position," said Aleksi slowly, not much interested in the Veselov tribe's troubles. He stared at the tent and at the small figures clustered underneath the awning.

"I don't think I've heard of him. Is he here?"

"No."

"Perhaps he doesn't know his father is dead. Perhaps he doesn't want to be dyan."

Aleksi shrugged. "I met him once, a long time ago. I don't know if he'd want the position." He added, under his breath: "Or if he did, if they would let him take it." Then he caught in his breath, because he had seen, under the awning, a woman dressed in man's clothing, the red shirt and black trousers and boots, armed with a saber.

Feodor Grekov made a tiny, strangled noise in his throat. "That's her, isn't it?" he asked. "That's Bakhtiian's niece."

Aleksi, with some disappointment, realized that the woman soldier's coloring was as dark as her uncle's. Where was Tess?

Six men and one woman, soldiers all, sat under the awning. In front of them, on a single pillow at the edge of the awning, half under the awning, half out under the open sky, sat the man on whom all attention was fixed. Ilyakoria Bakhtiian absorbed the force of their regard effortlessly. And yet, even at such a distance, Aleksi felt Bakhtiian's presence so strongly that it was as if Bakhtiian was standing right next to him.

"Come on," he said to Feodor, and he led the other man around the fringe of the assembly. No one paid them any mind. At the tent, etsanas and dyans came up in pairs to pledge their loyalty to Bakhtiian's war, and to be pledged to, his allegiance to their tribe, in return.

When they were about fifteen paces from the tent, off to the side, Aleksi stopped Feodor with a touch to the elbow, settled down on his haunches, and waited.

Ilyakoria Bakhtiian sat cross-legged on a square pillow embroidered with stylized horses intertwined, galloping, racing. His expression was composed, but intent. One open, one curled into a loose fist, his hands lay as still as if they were carved in stone, in contrast to the restless, passionate intelligence that blazed from his eyes. To his right, propped up on a little stand of wood, rested a carved wooden staff somewhat longer than a man's arm.

After an endless time, sun and wind beating down on them, only the Ten Eldest Tribes had yet to speak. There was a silence. The tinkling of bells whispered like the murmuring of the gods, watching over them. From somewhere in the middle of the assembly, Aleksi heard the soft droning chant of priests, intoning the endless cycle of the gods: Mother Sun and Father Wind, Aunt Cloud and Uncle Moon, Sister Tent and Brother Sky, Daughter Earth and Son River, Cousin Grass and Cousin Rain. Here and there in the crowd Aleksi identified the glazed stare of a man or a woman who was memorizing each word to pass on to the tribes. Even one of Bakhtiian's personal commanders, Josef Raevsky, had that vacant expression on his face, although he was a soldier and not a Singer.

Abruptly, Bakhtiian rose.

"Ah," breathed Aleksi, realizing what Bakhtiian meant to do. He glanced at Feodor, to see if his companion also appreciated the coming gesture on Bakhtiian's part. But Grekov was staring like any besotted fool straight at Bakhtiian's niece. The woman shifted slightly and glanced their way, and immediately Grekov's gaze dropped and he stared down at the ground.

Like an echo of his niece, Bakhtiian shifted his attention from the assembly and turned his head to look straight at Aleksi. Even knowing that most of the audience must have turned as well, to see what was attracting

Bakhtiian's attention, Aleksi could not feel their stares at all. Bakhtiian's overwhelmed everything else.

Aleksi stood up. He did not fear Bakhtiian, but he respected him, and he was grateful to him for never once objecting to the way in which Aleksi had become a member of his tribe. Aleksi valued Bakhtiian's protection almost as much as he valued that granted him by his new sister. Bakhtiian gestured with his left hand, and his niece jumped to her feet and walked briskly over to Aleksi. Feodor Grekov climbed hastily to his feet as well. He kept his gaze fixed on his boots.

"Aleksi," said Nadine by way of greeting, "You've come from camp."

"Sergei Veselov is dead."

"Ah," she replied. Then she grinned, and Aleksi grinned back, liking her because he knew that she had the same kind of reckless, bold heart as he did. And because she had never cared one whit that he was an orphan. "Trouble will come of that, I trust." She sounded satisfied, as if she hoped the trouble would come soon, and in an unexpected and inconvenient manner. "Well met, Feodor," she added. "I missed you."

Then she spun and strode back to the tent. She knelt beside one of the seven commanders under the awning. Anton Veselov's fair complexion flushed red first, and then he paled. Bakhtiian turned right round and considered them, but he said nothing. After a moment, Veselov rose and walked out the side of the awning and around to the semicircle. The youngest etsana shifted to let the soldier sink down beside her. He drew his saber and laid it across his knees: his authority as the new dyan of his tribe.

"The gods will look askance at *that*," murmured Feodor.

"There's no other man in the line to give it to," said Aleksi, but he also felt uncomfortable, seeing a sister and brother sitting together in authority over a tribe.

Bakhtiian waited for the stir to die down. Aleksi settled back into a crouch to wait, and Feodor slid his gaze back to Nadine Orzhekov. As if she felt his gaze, she looked back over her shoulder at them. A smile—or a smirk—quirked her lips up. Feodor flushed. He collapsed ungracefully beside Aleksi, looking pale and staring hard

at his hands. Bakhtiian's niece sat down in her place and
did not look their way again.

The wind blew. The assembly was silent. The sun's
disk slid down toward the western horizon.

A flame winked. Aleksi blinked, staring at the tent,
and discovered where Tess had been all along. The tent
flap that covered the entrance to the interior had been
tied up just enough to let an observer hidden inside watch
without being seen. Now, with a lantern lit at her side,
Tess Soerensen was visible to him. Her head bent, as if
she was tired, or too burdened to bear up any longer.
Bakhtiian's khaja wife, sitting silent in her tent as her
husband declared war on all khaja people. Aleksi felt a
vise grip his heart, in fear for her, and for himself. What
if she left him here, to return to her brother's lands?

Then, with a grin, he relaxed. Her right arm moved,
a slight movement but one he recognized. She was *writing*. It was a foreign word, and a khaja thing to do, recording words and events with these scrawls she called
letters, as if she hadn't the memory to recall it all properly, in her heart. Which she had often, and cheerfully,
admitted that she had not. She glanced up. She was staring at someone: at Ilya Bakhtiian? No.

Aleksi followed the line of her sight and he saw that
she was staring at the sky, at, in fact, the only star bright
enough to show yet in the twilight sky. She often stared
at the heavens that way, as if they held an answer for her,
as if she sought something there, like a singer who seeks
the heart of a song in the gods' lands. Oh, yes, he knew
she held some secret inside her, a secret that her own
husband did not guess at. What it was, he had not yet
divined, but Aleksi had spent most of his life watching
people, interpreting their slightest action, their simplest
words, because until this last four months he had only
his powers of observation and his undeniable skill with
the saber to keep him alive. Tess Soerensen was not like
other people, not like her adopted people the jaran, certainly, but not like the khaja either. She was something
altogether different, betraying herself not in obvious,
grand ways, but in the subtle, tiny things that most people overlooked.

Tess's gaze fell from the star and settled on her husband. She loved him in a way that was, perhaps, a bit

unseemly for a woman of the tribes. But Tess wasn't jaran; like Aleksi, she was an outsider. Suddenly she glanced to one side and spotted Aleksi, and grinned, swiftly, reassuringly. And went back to her writing.

"I will protect you," Aleksi muttered under his breath. He loved her fiercely, as only a brother can love a sister, the oldest bond between a man and a woman and the most important one. She had saved his life, had taken him into her tent, had given him the security he had not had since he was a tiny child. Perhaps her other brother, the khaja prince who lived far to the south, loved her more: Aleksi doubted it. Perhaps Bakhtiian loved her more, but it was pointless to measure oneself against Bakhtiian. Bakhtiian was not like other men. He belonged, not to himself, but to the jaran, to his people, and if his passions were greater than other men's, so, too, were his burdens and his responsibilities.

Bakhtiian moved. He walked, lithe as any predator, across the gap between his pillow and the semicircle of elders, and knelt in front of his aunt.

"With your permission, my aunt," he said. She did not speak, but simply placed her palm on his hair and withdrew it again. He rose and walked to the other end of the crescent, to kneel before the etsana of the eldest tribe, Elizaveta Sakhalin. He kept his eyes lowered, as befitted a modest man.

The elderly woman regarded him evenly.

At last, Bakhtiian spoke.

"When Mother Sun sent her daughter to the earth, she sent with her ten sisters, and gifted them each with a tent and a name. The eldest was Sakhalin, then Arkhanov, Suvorin, Velinya, Raevsky, Vershinin, Grekov, Fedoseyev, and last the twins, Veselov and Orzhekov. Each sister had ten daughters, and each daughter ten daughters in turn, and thus the tribes of the jaran were born. This summer we begin our ride against the khaja lands." Now he lifted his eyes to look directly at her, though she was his elder, and a woman. "Of the ten elder tribes, who will come with me?"

Sakhalin rose. She was a tiny woman, well past her childbearing years, and strength radiated from her. She examined her nephew first, then each of the other nine etsanas and their warleaders in turn. Each man went forward and laid his saber in front of Bakhtiian's pillow. Each woman unbound the horse-tail from her staff and bound it, in turn, to the staff resting beside Bakhtiian's pillow. Nine sabers, ten horse-tails. The priests' chanting droned on, a muted counterpoint. The standard atop the tent, a plain gold banner, fluttered wildly.

"Bakhtiian," Sakhalin said, which meant *He-who-has-traveled-far*. "All will come." She raised him up and released him, and he walked back to the pillow and sank down onto it. He took the staff into his hands and held it, weighing its strength. Then he lifted his gaze to the endless blue sky.

Sakhalin turned to survey the assembly. She stretched out her arms to the heavens. "Mother Sun and Father Wind be our witness," she said, and though she did not seem to raise her voice, it carried effortlessly across the plateau. "All will come."

A great shout rose, shattering the stillness.

"Ja-tar!" they cried. "To ride!"

Elizaveta Sakhalin sat down, and a hush fell.

Yaroslav Sakhalin rose, dyan of the eldest tribe, and he walked forward and took his saber from the ground and held it out. Its blade winked in the torchlight.

"Where will you lead us?" Sakhalin asked.

Bakhtiian did not answer. His gaze had taken on a distant cast, as if he were looking at something not there, some place, some person, some vision that only he could see.

"Leave him," said Elizaveta Sakhalin. "We must leave him here to talk to the gods." It took half the night for them all to negotiate the narrow trail down to the camp below, leaving Bakhtiian alone above.

A day passed and Bakhtiian did not come down from the height.

Neither did he the next day.

But at dawn on the third day, smoke rose from the hill, billowing up into the sky. "He's offered the tent to the gods," his aunt said approvingly. In orderly groups, elders and dyans, commanders and etsanas, gathered at the base where the path twisted up the hillside. Aleksi stuck close to Tess and so gained a vantage point right at the front.

Soon enough they saw a single figure, red shirt, black

trousers, black boots, a saber swaying at his hips, walking down the path. He gripped the horse-tail staff in his left hand. Seeing the crowd, he halted. First, he sought out his wife's figure in the throng. He stared at her as if to make sure she was real and not a spirit. Aleksi could not otherwise read Bakhtiian's expression. But then, Aleksi was never entirely sure of what Bakhtiian felt about anything, as if the sheer force of the emotions welling off Bakhtiian served to hide his true feelings.

At last Bakhtiian lifted his gaze to stare at the assembly spread out, waiting for him. Here at the front, the elders, the women, the commanders, stood and watched. Farther back, many of the young men of the army had already mounted, holding their restless mounts on tight reins.

Bakhtiian's face was lit, illuminated by the gods themselves, or by some trick of the morning sunlight, Aleksi could not be sure which. He raised the horse-tail staff and, with that small gesture, brought silence. Then he drew his saber.

"West," he said. So calmly did he raise the fire that would scorch the khaja earth. "West to the sea."

ACT ONE

"He that plays the king shall be welcome."
—SHAKESPEARE,
Hamlet

CHAPTER ONE

"Look here my boys, see what a world of ground
Lies westward from the midst of Cancer's line,
Unto the rising of this earthly globe,
Whereas the sun declining from our sight,
Begins the day with our antipodes. . . .
And from th'Antartique Pole, eastward behold
As much more land, which never was descried,
Wherein are rocks of pearl, that shine as bright
As all the lamps that beautify the sky,
And shall I die and this unconquered?"

In the hush of audience and air alike, Diana moved quietly around to the back of the second balcony to watch the final minutes of the Company's final performance on Earth. *Tamburlaine the Great. Who, from a Scythian Shepheard by his rare and wonderful Conquests became a most puissant and mighty Monarch, And (for his tyranny, and terror in War) was termed, The Scourge of God. Divided into two Tragical Discourses.* Somehow, the two plays seemed ironically appropriate for a repertory company that was about to leave the civilized worlds and spend a year on the last planet in known space where humans still lived in ignorance of their space-faring brothers and sisters.

Next week the entire Company, together with Charles Soerensen and his party, would board a spaceliner that would take them to the Delta Pavonis system and the Interdicted world, Rhui. Owen and Ginny had founded the Bharentous Repertory Company in order to give themselves room to experiment with the theater they loved. This would be their greatest experiment fulfilled: bringing theater to unlettered savages who had not the slightest sheen of civilization to pollute their first experience of drama.

Amyras knelt before his dying father Tamburlaine. "Heavens witness me, with what a broken heart And damned spirit I ascend this seat. . . .''

Diana sighed. Hal always overplayed this part, doubtless as revenge against his parents. But it didn't matter. Gwyn played Tamburlaine so very finely that she never tired of watching him. She leaned her arms along the wood railing that set off the back row of seats from the balcony aisle and watched as Zenocrate's transparent hearse was rolled in. Tamburlaine's final speech: she let herself fall into it.

"Now eyes, enjoy thy latest benefit. . . . For Tamburlaine, the Scourge of God must die." He died. Tears wet Diana's cheeks. Another set of arms slid onto the railing and, startled, she glanced to that side.

The man standing there smiled at her. He looked familiar and, in any case, she recognized the kind of smile he was giving her. Men enough, and a few women, came to the Green Room to court a pretty, golden-haired ingenue.

Hal said Amyras's final lines. The play ended. The audience rose, applauding enthusiastically, as the players came forward to make their bows.

"Shouldn't you be up there?" asked the man casually.

"You're Marco Burckhardt!" exclaimed Diana. "I thought you looked familiar."

"Wit as well as beauty." Marco placed his right hand over his heart and bowed to her. "I hope my reputation has not preceded my name."

Diana laughed. " 'Come, Sir, you're our envoy—lead the way, and we'll precede.' And it's appropriate, too, you know. You've been on Rhui. You're coming with us, aren't you?"

"With Charles," he agreed. He looked out over the house, over to one of the boxes where a sandy-haired man of middle height stood applauding with his companions and the rest of the audience. As if he were just any other playgoer. Which, of course, he emphatically was not.

Marco swung his gaze back to Diana, and he smiled, deliberately, invitingly. "But now that I have met you, golden fair, I need no other inducement to travel so far."

Diana felt a little breathless. In his own way, Marco

Burckhardt was a legend. "Is it true that you've explored most of the planet? Rhui, that is. All alone, and without any aids whatsoever? Not even a palm slate or a fletchette rifle or any modern weaponry? And by only the primitive transportation they have on planet? That you've almost been killed?"

Marco chuckled. "I do carry an emergency transmitter, but I've never used it. And this scar—" He took her hand and lifted it to touch, like a caress, the pale line that wrapped halfway around his neck. "You have soft skin," he murmured.

Diana traced the smooth line of the scar, the sunroughened skin on either side, and then lowered her hand back to the railing. "Is that the only one?" she asked, a little disappointed. Beyond, on the stage, Gwyn and Anahita—Tamburlaine and Zenocrate—came forward to take their final bows. A few in the audience were already filtering out of their seats. Charles Soerensen and his companions had not moved, which surprised her, since most VIPs left immediately and by a side entrance otherwise reserved for cast and crew.

"Not the only one," said Marco, "but I can't show you the others in such a public place."

Diana smiled. "I'm almost convinced, but not quite. Is that the closest you've ever come to death?"

Marco looked away from her, not into the distance, precisely, but at the stage, at Gwyn, in his armor and holding spear and sword, the Scythian shepherd turned conqueror. "No. I could run faster than the people chasing me, that time. The time I came closest to death, there was neither room nor opportunity to run. Did the Company deliberately choose this play as their final performance?"

"What do you mean?" Gwyn and Anahita retreated into the wings, and the audience broke off their applause and burst into a stream of talk and movement. A few young men had rushed down to the stage, to try to bully or plead their way into the back, to court Anahita and Quinn and Oriana—and herself, of course—and a few to court Hyacinth. In his box, Charles Soerensen was entertaining visitors, as if he had the knack of turning any space into a sort of political Green Room. Conversation flowed over and around Diana and Marco, broken into snippets and phrases and abrupt scenes.

"—there just aren't many actors who can make the change from the vids to the theater successfully, though I'll admit you're right about Gwyn Jones. He was superb. But take their Zenocrate. Just a little overdone all around. I suppose they took her on for the publicity—"

"—did you see Charles Soerensen? No, there, you fool. You didn't know he'd be at the performance tonight? It was all over the net—"

"—and Rico was in a rare fury, too, when he discovered the two of them kissing backstage. Imagine, he'd been boasting for the last year that he'd bed her, but nothing came of it. And then it turns out that his sister has been sleeping with her all along."

Diana laughed, and then clapped a hand over her mouth, stifling it. Marco raised one eyebrow and shifted his shoulder so that the two young men—dressed in the gaudy gold-threaded robes that were the most recent fashion at the universities—could not see her past his body.

"It's all right," she murmured. "They won't recognize me without my stage makeup."

"—and what do you suppose Soerensen is up to now, eh? He got the Chapalii merchant house, and what a coup that was, too. Just like laughing in the faces of those damned chameleons. And now he's going off to that primitive world—what is it? Rhui, yes, that's it. Something's going on, I tell you. A man like Soerensen has deep plans. I'd wager my own children that we'll see some kind of action soon against the Empire."

"Is it true?" asked Diana, watching Marco as he tracked this last speaker with his gaze out the balcony exit.

"Is what true?"

"That Soerensen's sister is alive, and on Rhui."

His attention snapped back to her. "Where did you hear that?"

"Oh, we all know it. In the Company. Even after the Protocol Office made the official announcement of her death, Soerensen never confirmed it or denied it. And he never adopted a new heir. Isn't that his right, by Chapalii law? And anyway, why else would Soerensen let us travel to Rhui? He took so much trouble to restrict the planet from all outside contact to begin with. And why would he come along with us? Really, you must give us some credit for intelligence."

"Infinite credit, fair one. It sits beside your infinite beauty."

"Can beauty be infinite?"

"Only in Keats. What else have you heard?"

"About the sister? Nothing. About Rhui—well, we're going to a city called Jeds, first. Soerensen styles himself Prince there, so we'll be under his protection. Not that any of the natives will know where we're really from. After some time there, then there's a chance we'll be going out into the bush, into the really primitive areas. Owen says that we might be traveling with nomads. Doesn't that sound romantic?"

Marco looked amused. "You aren't scared, going off like this to be thrown in among savages? With no modern weaponry to protect yourself?"

"Certainly not. This is the most exciting thing I've ever done. I've never had a moment's danger in my life. I auditioned for the Company because I loved the risks Owen and Ginny were taking with theater, and with the traditions of theater. And this! Well, I suppose Jeds will be much like any city, only dirtier and primitive. But taking the theater out to these barbarian nomads—that's going to be a real adventure!" She felt flushed, and she knew she was declaiming. But what did it matter? Non-actors always seemed to expect her to talk that way off-stage as well as on, and it was true how she felt, and she felt it so deeply.

Marco watched her, looking, perhaps, a little wistful. "I wish I'd known you when Charles and I started all this," he said softly. "I think you would have come with me, the first of us to set foot on Rhui."

She stared, entranced by the green of his eyes. "I would have," she said, sure that at this moment it was true. Though she knew he must be as old as her biological father, he did not look ten years older than her, an attractive man made handsome as much by the suppressed air of wildness about him as by any pretensions to beauty. A man who knew adventure, who knew real danger, who had felt death close at hand and looked it in the face. Her own life had been so—*safe*.

"Goddess, you're young," he said, and broke the spell.

Diana blushed, but she chuckled. "That's put me in my place." She laid a hand on the railing, a self-conscious pose, and looked down from this great height onto the stage. "Oh. That's what you meant, isn't it? About choosing these plays for our farewell performance. Tamburlaine was a nomad. Do you suppose the nomads we're going to travel with have a Tamburlaine among them?"

She said it lightly, but Marco's lips pressed together, and his gaze shifted from her down to the distant figure that was Charles Soerensen. Soerensen was speaking easily with several people that even from this height Diana recognized, the Director of the Royal Academy, the prime minister of the Eurasian States, a respected vid journalist, the assistant stage manager, an usher—he was a university student majoring in xenobotany—who had once made a pass at her, and one of the clerks from the box office who had brought her two children to meet The Great Man. A sudden swirl of movement in the box steadied and stilled to reveal one of the tall, thin alien Chapalii. The creature bowed to Soerensen, offering him the delicate crystal wand in which the Chapalii conveyed important messages from one noble to another.

"I must go," said Marco. "May I escort you down?" He offered her his elbow, and Diana placed her fingers on his sleeve. The contact overwhelmed her, and she could suddenly think of nothing to say. Walking this close to him, down the carpeted stairwell that led to the lobby, she could not imagine why he should be interested in her at all, except, of course, that she was young, pretty, and blonde. This man had explored a wild and dangerous world, alone most of the time, and he was the confidant and right hand of the most important human alive.

"Shall I introduce you?" Marco asked suddenly, and too late Diana realized she was being steered to the box from which Charles Soerensen had watched the play.

How could she refuse? She calmed her suddenly erratic breathing by force of habit and let him lead her there.

A cluster of people walked toward them down the corridor. A moment later they were swept into the retinue.

"There you are, Marco," said Soerensen. He held the crystal wand in his left hand. It shimmered and glinted under the hall lights.

"Charles, I've brought one of the actors to meet you. This is Diana Brooke-Holt, of the repertory company."

"Ah." Soerensen stopped. "M. Brooke-Holt. I'm

honored to meet you." He looked ordinary enough, but his stare was intense: Diana felt as if she were being recorded, measured, and filed away against future need.

However much she wanted to collapse into a gibbering heap, she knew how to present a collected exterior. She extended her right hand, and he shook it. "The honor is mine," she said, careful to give the words no earth-shattering sentiment, only simple politeness.

"You played Zabina, did you not?" he asked.

"Yes."

"She comes to a rather bloody end."

Diana chuckled. "Yes, she does, poor thing. But I suppose that I've always felt more sorry for Zenocrate."

He looked suddenly and acutely interested. "Why is that?"

"Because once Tamburlaine had marked her out as his, she didn't really have much choice but to fall in love with him, did she? Not that he coerced her as much as—" She shrugged, and was abruptly aware that both Soerensen and Marco regarded her intently, as if she were revealing some long-sought-after secret to them. She faltered, realizing that the entire retinue had stopped to listen, some with polite interest, some with no interest at all, but none with the piercing attention of the two men. With an effort, she gathered together the shredding fabric of her self-confidence and drew herself up. "A man like that would be hard to resist," she finished, with dramatic flourish.

"Bravo," said Marco, *sotto voce*.

Soerensen smiled. "But I particularly enjoyed your performance as Grusha in the Brecht play. I look forward to seeing what Owen and Ginny come up with for their next experiment. If you'll excuse me." He nodded, collected the attention of his retinue with unconscious ease, and went on his way.

Marco lingered. "I must go," he said again, although he made no move to follow the others.

"I must, too," she replied. "Really."

"I'll see you on the ship, perhaps."

"Oh, we'll be rehearsing the whole way out. Owen and Ginny are rather dragons about that, when they're developing new material."

"Then in Jeds."

She smiled and finally disengaged her fingers from his elbow. "If there's time."

"In Jeds? Believe me, you'll have plenty of time in Jeds."

"For what? Sight-seeing, I suppose. I'm bringing a journal with me, real paper, bound, and pen and ink, to write down what I see."

"Pen and ink?"

"Rhui *is* an interdicted world. What isn't there already, we aren't to bring."

"Golden fair, you astonish me." He took her hand in his and bent to kiss it, his lips lingering longer on her skin than was, perhaps, warranted by the briefness of their acquaintance.

Diana withdrew her hand from his grasp and blew him a kiss as she retreated through one of the double doors that led into the house. " 'And if thou lovest me, think no more of it.' "

Marco laughed, delighted. "Do all actors quote?" he called after her.

But she let the door swing and click shut behind her without answering him.

"Di! There you are." From the stage, Yomi called out to her. "Double time, girl. No loitering. Where've you been?"

Diana walked swiftly down the aisle and up the steps onto the stage.

"Ah hah!" said Yomi, coming to meet her. "Isn't that Marco Burckhardt standing up there in the VIP box? Watch your step, Di. He's a notorious womanizer, that one is. So they say. Don't dive into water if you can't swim."

"I can swim," retorted Diana, affronted.

"Certainly, my dear. Come on. The meeting's ready to start. Anahita is howling about the lighting for the curtain call. And she was furious that Gwyn got called out alone. As for Hal—"

Diana followed Yomi out stage right. She risked one final look back, to see Marco standing in the box that Soerensen and his party had inhabited. He leaned with his hands on the railing, watching her go.

CHAPTER TWO

Under the circumstances, any human might have forgiven Charles Soerensen for taking a private aircar rather than using public lanes like everyone else. Any human except Charles himself. On Earth, in human space—what had once been human space—Charles never took advantage of the privileges granted him by his rank as a duke in the Chapalii Empire, as the only human elevated above subject status in the convoluted hierarchy by which the alien Chapalii governed the races and stellar systems they had absorbed into their empire. They never used the word *conquered*.

"Chattel," said David ben Unbutu to Marco Burckhardt. They took up stations on either side of Charles on the levitated train that in three hours would take them across the Atlantic Ocean from Portsmouth to North America. David braced himself for the shift as the train jolted forward. Marco, of course, seemed not to notice the transition at all. Charles was sitting down, crystal message wand laid across his knees, still talking with the prime minister of the Eurasian states. She was headed to Quito Spaceport in South America, and Charles had taken the opportunity to ask her to travel with him for part of the journey.

"Who's chattel?" Marco asked. "Shall we sit down?"

"I'm too nervous to sit," said David, although he was not surprised when Marco sat anyway, across from Charles. Four benches ran the length of the car, arranged in two pairs facing in toward each other, split by a central aisle. David stood where the inner bench gapped to allow access to the aisle. Charles and the prime minister sat with their backs to the windows, windows which, on this side of the car, showed programming, not ocean.

"Look." Marco pointed to one of the flat screens.

"There's that interview with Owen Zerentous again." He took on an affected accent. " 'Ginny and I have been interested for some time in theater as the universal medium, in theater's use of ritual and ceremony as a way to access the common essence of humanity.' You know, I think Zerentous believes what he's talking about."

"Maybe he's even right. But you've never been interested in theater, Marco. Or at least, only in the ornamentation thereof."

Marco grinned. "A man can't help looking, especially at women who are as pretty as Diana Brooke-Holt. What did you mean by chattel?"

David glanced at the Chapalii steward standing four seats down from him, on the other side of Charles. Of course, a steward would not sit—could not—in the presence of nobility. All along the car passengers sat at their ease, watching the screens, reading from flat screens, dozing, knitting; an adolescent drew a light sculpture in the air with a pen, erased it with an exasperated wave of a hand, and began again. Human passengers. They had noted Charles's presence. How could they fail to? They all knew who he was; they all recognized him. Many had acknowledged him, with a terse word, with a nod, to which he had replied in like measure. Now they left him his privacy, except for one very young child who wandered over and sat in a seat two down from the prime minister, small chin cupped in small hands, watching their intent conversation with a concerned expression.

"I don't know what I meant," said David, "except that sometimes I think we're just chattel to them—to the Chapalii."

"I don't think they think in such economic terms. I think their hierarchy is more like a caste system than a class system, but how do we know if human theory explains it, anyway? Why are you nervous?"

David sat down. The bench shifted beneath him, molding itself to his contours. "Why should Duke Naroshi send Charles a summons wand? What authority does Naroshi have to summon Charles? He doesn't outrank him."

"As far as we know he doesn't. Maybe the length of time you've been duke matters, in which case Naroshi would outrank Charles. But Naroshi is in fealty to the princely house which has nominal control of human space. Of Earth.''

"That's true. And it was Naroshi's agent who was on Rhui, with Tess.''

"David.''

David looked around, suddenly sure that everyone was looking at him, but, of course, no one was. He dropped his voice to a whisper. "But wouldn't that imply that Naroshi is seeking some kind of information with which to discredit Charles? Especially now that Charles has pulled off a rather major coup within the Chapalii political scene, by taking over the Keinaba merchant house?''

"Not yet finalized, I might add.''

"Not yet? Lady's Tits, Marco, Charles spent long enough at the Imperial palace. Almost two standard years, he spent there. I thought it *was* finalized, all legal, with the emperor's approval.''

"The emperor approved it, but he didn't—oh, what is that phrase? Tess translated it so neatly. 'Seal the braid of fealty.' ''

David sighed and sagged back against the seat. "It's all too convoluted for me. I'm just an engineer.'' Marco chuckled. They had known each other for so long now, he and Marco and Charles, that they spoke as much with what they didn't say as with what they did. David levered out an armrest, tilted his head back, and shut his eyes. The conversation between Charles and the prime minister continued across from him like a murmuring counterpoint. They were talking about Rhui.

The whole thing *was* far too convoluted for David's taste. He liked something he could get his hands on, something concrete, malleable, something that had answers that were correct based on fixed laws. Not something that was mutable. David hated politics. He'd never liked history much, either. That's why he had gone into classical engineering—the design and construction of three-dimensional, utilitarian structures like buildings and bridges and transport facilities.

Everything he knew about the Chapalii made him anxious. They didn't follow the rules. Humanity had discovered spaceflight and then discovered cousin humans on neighboring worlds. Earth and their cousin humans on Ophiuchi-Sei-ah-nai had formed the League, a kind of

parliament of space-faring humanity. Then, human ex-
ploration ships had run into Chapalii protocol agents,
representatives of the Chapalii Empire; soon after, the
emperor had simply co-opted League space as part of his
dominion. But their rule was benign; some people even
called it enlightened, and certainly the Chapalii did not
begrudge sharing some—if not all—of their technological
expertise with their subject races.

But were humans ever content with being ruled? Not
really. Charles Soerensen led a rebellion against the Empire that failed. But instead of arresting him and executing him, the Chapalii ennobled him. They made him a
duke. The emperor granted him two stellar systems as
his fief, one of them the newly-discovered system Delta
Pavonis—discovered, that is, to possess two habitable
worlds. The planet Odys was ravaged by Chapalii mod-
ernization; Rhui was interdicted by Charles's order, an
order that the emperor agreed to despite the fact that the
interdiction closed off access to Rhui's abundant natural
resources. Just as it closed off access to Rhui's native
population.

And that was the other thing that bothered David.
That's what Tess Soerensen had found out; she had discovered ancient Chapalii buildings on Rhui. The half-
mythical Chapalii duke, the Tai-en Mushai, had built a
palace on Rhui. He had seeded the planet with humans
from Earth. It must all have happened long, long ago,
millennia ago in the human span of years, or so Charles
and his experts guessed, though they knew nothing for
certain. Even so, how could the Chapalii have lost track
of these buildings? How could they have lost track of an
entire planet?

David did not like equations that didn't add up.

And now Charles was going with a small party to Rhui,
to find Tess and to investigate these ancient remnants of
a Chapalii presence on Rhui. David supposed he was
looking forward to going to visit an interdicted world
where the living conditions would be, at best, primitive.
At any rate, he'd be happy to see Tess again.

The prime minister left them at Staten Island, and they
transferred to a secured line in to Manhattan, which had

been razed and rebuilt by the Chapalii and was now a
private Chapalii enclave, barred to most humans.

David had once gone to an exhibit detailing the history
of Manhattan. Certainly the Chapalii era Manhattan was
by far the most impressive and beautiful architecturally,
seen from across the river: a mass of monuments and
parks, pierced at the center by a single tower of adaman-
tine grace and astonishing height.

At the ducal palace of the Tai-en Naroshi Toraokii,
they disembarked from the secured line into an atrium
domed with tangled vines about thirty meters over their
heads. Animals shrieked and called in the greenery, but
they only caught glimpses of birds and long-limbed creatures rustling through the leaves. Water sheeted down in
a semicircle all along the far wall; indeed, the misting
waterfall *was* the far wall of the atrium. Charles headed
out across the floor, which was a tangle of ponds,
streams, parquetry decks, and marble stepping stones
carved into the shape of Chapalii glyphs. Avocets and
herons dotted the shorelines. A grebe swam past and
dove, vanishing from their sight in one instant and popping up seconds later a meter ahead.

David saw no passage through the huge curtain of water, but Charles walked steadily toward it, picking his
way along the labyrinthine paths until the three men and
the Chapalii steward came to the wall of water. Charles
lifted the crystal wand. The waterfall parted.

David gaped. It simply parted, by no agency he could
see. Water still rained down over their heads, but an invisible barrier forced it to either side, allowing them access to whatever lay within. Charles led the way. The
steward followed him, and David went next, letting
Marco take the rearguard.

What lay within proved to be a hall as vast as a cathe-
dral. Their footsteps echoed as they crossed the hall's
expanse to a far door. They passed through the door into
a garden lined with columns and thence into a marble-
fronted basilica that transmuted, surprisingly, into an octagon, a two-storied building with a mosaic floor and
somberly glowing mosaic walls portraying austere, gaunt
figures. Within the greater octagon, almost floating inside it, stood an interior octagon of double arches. Within
the central octagon two couches sat on the mosaic floor.

On one couch, a figure reclined. It sat up, seeing their party. Charles marched them under one of the arches—banded with three colors of stone—and sat himself down on the couch opposite their host. David and Marco placed themselves behind him. The steward crossed to stand beside Tai Naroshi.

The two dukes regarded each other in silence. Tai Naroshi looked like all other Chapalii: pale as ice with a wisp of yellow hair; tall, thin, humanlike in his symmetry, but not human at all. He wore a robe of palest orange that seemed to drape itself artistically around his form, according to his movements, by some unrelated gravitational field.

Charles placed the wand across his knees.

They waited.

Then, to David's astonishment, a mist steamed up under one of the arches and coalesced into three seated figures: Owen Zerentous, Ginny Arbha, and an interviewer. They looked so real that they could have been there in person, except that they had appeared so abruptly.

"We ought all to remember," Owen was saying, "that the line between barbarism and civilization is fluid. Ritual is a constant in all human society. Theater is simply a more refined, and perhaps even a more confined, elaboration of primitive ritual events. Certainly my use of the word 'primitive' is a subjective response based on our bias against pretechnological culture."

Naroshi raised one hand, and the figures froze. They then passed through a rapid succession of expression and angles, as if their conversation was accelerated. Naroshi lowered his hand, and the interview continued.

"To find cultures that have never seen theater before," Owen said, clearly in answer to a question. "*Human* cultures, that is. We haven't seen that for centuries on Earth, or in any of the human cultures in the League, for that matter. Does theater work as a ritual for any human culture? Even one grown and bred on a planet other than our own? Are these aspects of the human condition, are the emotions that theater engenders, universal to our genetic coding? And if they are, where does the real translation take place: in the words, or in the gestures? In the letter, or in the spirit? That's what we're going to Rhui to find out."

Still talking the figures imploded into mist and evaporated.

"Tai Charles," said Naroshi, acknowledging his visitor.

"Tai Naroshi," said Charles, with the exact same lack of inflection, acknowledging his host.

"You undertake a journey," said Naroshi.

"I am honored by your interest," said Charles.

"Rhui is a primitive world. Certainly it is not a planet where any civilization can be found."

"It is interdicted," agreed Charles, and David had to wonder what Charles was thinking, what message he meant Naroshi to read from this colorless conversation. *It is interdicted, and I know damn well you sent agents down onto Rhui in direct defiance of that interdiction.*

"Yet still you intend to travel there."

In the muted light within the interior octagon, David could still detect fleeting colors chasing themselves across the white skin of the steward, colors that reflected his emotions as he listened to this conversation between the two noblemen. But the duke, Naroshi, remained as pale as frost. No hint of color tinted his skin. Were the high nobility genetically superior or simply taught techniques from an early age with which to control the shadings of their skin? No human knew.

"Still I intend to travel there."

"With these others, some of whom are artisans."

Rather than replying, Charles simply inclined his head.

"May I hope that you will still consider my sister for the design of the mausoleum for your sister?"

"Tai-en, I have just returned from the palace. Indeed, from the presence of the emperor himself. I have not yet considered what I intend to do to honor my sister."

"Ah," said Naroshi, and paused. David strained to see if any color stained the duke's face, but he could discern none. On the distant walls, color shifted along the mosaics, moving subtly along the wall and lightening and darkening the images in slow waves. "The Keinaba house. I am surprised that you would take in a dishonored house."

"Yes," agreed Charles. "I did not know that you were

interested in theater." He extended a hand and gestured in the direction of the arch under which Owen and Ginny had, for that brief time, appeared.

"Many of us are interested in Rhui, Tai-en. I am not alone in my interest in such a rich planet."

"No," agreed Charles, "I do not suppose you are." From this angle, David could only see the back of Charles's head; he could not observe his expression, and he could not hear any emotion in his voice. Silence followed the remark. The two dukes seemed to have reached a stalemate.

Into their silence, a humming rose, soft, implacable. The air began to shimmer. The wand laid over Charles's knees shone all at once with a brilliant light, picked up a high-pitched overtone from the hum, and quite simply dematerialized.

Both dukes stood up at once.

Naroshi spoke a curt command to the steward, and the Chapalii servant turned on his heel and hurried away. But even as the steward crossed under the double arches, the arches themselves vanished. The air shimmered, melding, blending; the whole huge chamber melted away and the grand architecture was overwhelmed by another locale.

The change occurred over seconds—minutes, perhaps—but it was hard to keep track of time when you were floating in immaterial space, in a shifting void. David caught a glimpse of the mosaic wall, of a hollow-eyed man draped in robes splintered by a sudden bright light, and then it, too, was gone. They stood in a chamber so vast that David could not see walls but felt the presence of still air enclosing him. In such space there ought to be a breeze, some sense of the air being alive; there was not.

He stood on a silver floor that shaded to translucence and then became transparent, and he stared down, dizzy with vertigo, at an expanse of towers and avenues laid out so far below that this floor must have been hundreds of meters above the ground. Darkness swept over and swallowed the city below like a wave and David could only mark each tower now by the single light at its tip. Or were they now stars? Was he standing above space itself, staring down into the vast deeps? He tilted his head back, to look up, and got dizzy, felt the galaxy whirl around him. Staggered a little, steadying himself with a touch on Marco's arm.

Now he felt like the floor was moving, or that he was; he couldn't be sure which. Only the two dukes appeared stable to his eyes. He fixed on Charles.

The air shone in front of Charles, took on weight and coalesced into matter. A braid of silver fire hung in the air. David saw the shift as gravity grabbed hold of its substance. The air stilled. The braid fell. But Charles caught it before it could touch the floor. David saw how heavy it must be by the way it weighted down Charles's arm. "Seal the braid of fealty."

At that instant David understood. The braid of silver was the emperor's seal. And he had delivered it to Charles in order to seal with imperial approval Charles's act of taking the Keinaba merchant house into the Soerensen ducal house. But where had it come from? How had it reached them? There *had* been nothing there; Charles now held a silver braid that undeniably possessed mass and volume. The problem, the possibilities, made David's head whirl. He just stood there and let the chamber reel around him and after a moment, as he forced himself to focus on the silver braid in Charles's hand, the world stopped moving.

The stars vanished. Now they stood in a glade carpeted by perfectly manicured pale orange grass; probably not grass at all, but that was what it looked like. Twenty-one white-barked trees ringed them. Slender trunks shot up, endlessly up, to a kaleidoscopic canopy so high above that David could not measure it. Beyond, impossibly high, he saw the faint spires of towers.

Naroshi stood opposite Charles. Against the stark white trees, Naroshi's complexion bore the barest tinge of blue, so pale that in any other surroundings David would not have noticed it. Blue was the color of distress. Clearly, Naroshi was not happy to be here—wherever *here* was.

Charles faced Naroshi across the pale grass, and Marco and David flanked Charles. David wondered if they really had been somehow transported into the imperial presence—into the *emperor's* presence—or if this was just an incredible projection. If he stepped forward, would he

bang into the couch? He felt it the safer option not to
move at all.

"I thank you," said Charles into the silence, hefting
the braid in his hand. "I ask permission for myself and
some companions to visit the planet where my sister and
heir has ceased to exist, so that we may suitably mourn
her, without interruption."

Marco glanced sidewise at David and winked. Yes,
clearly that last little qualifier was aimed at Naroshi. But
Marco's ability to remain unawed in the most awe-
inspiring circumstances gave David heart. He winked
back. Against the purity of the white bark of the trees,
Naroshi's complexion shaded in the slightest degree from
blue to green, the color of disapproval.

The humming stopped. David had not really noticed it
until it ceased. Then he was aware of its absence, and as
abruptly as a light is switched from light to dark, they
stood in the octagonal chamber again. Mosaics glowed
on the far walls, seen through the double arches. The
images flowed, as if the figures stirred, but David could
not be sure if they really moved or if he was still recovering from the whirling of the stars.

A pink scarf lay draped over Charles's shoulders. Pink
was the color of approval. For a moment, Charles simply
stood there. Then he lifted his free hand to touch the
scarf, to check its color. His chin shifted, just a little,
but David knew him well enough to know that he was
pleased. He bowed, low, to the precise degree by which
a duke honors the emperor, dipping to touch one knee to
the floor. Then he straightened and regarded Naroshi in
silence.

In this light, David could discern no slightest tint of
color in Naroshi's pallid complexion. "I will watch your
progress with interest," said Naroshi.

Charles inclined his head in acknowledgment, but said
nothing more.

The steward reappeared and led them out the way they
had come. By unspoken consent, the three men did not
talk at all until they left the secured line on Staten Island
and transferred to a lev-train that would take them back
to London. Charles sank into a seat. He draped the silver
braid across his thighs. It was as heavy as gold, and as
supple as the finest silk. David and Marco sat on either

side of him. It was the old pattern from their university days: Marco on the right, David on the left.

" 'I'll be watching you,' " mused Charles as he stared out the window at the gray ocean. "But is Naroshi for me or against me?"

Marco shrugged. "Does our concept of dualism even apply to the Chapalii? Maybe he's for you *and* against you."

"I hate equations that don't add up," muttered David.

CHAPTER THREE

As soon as Yomi called the break, Diana fled the rehearsal space.

"And if Hyacinth keeps flinging himself all over the stage like that, I'm going to scream!" Anahita proclaimed.

"I don't think she's got more than one tone to play Titania with," muttered Quinn to Hal. "If she's going to go on like that for the whole trip shut up in this boat, then *I'm* going to scream."

Hal pulled a hand through his hair, tousling it, and heaved a great sigh. "What an awful day. I feel further from this scene than I ever did."

Gwyn stared at the plain wooden floor, and by the way his right hand turned up and then down, Diana could see that he was still thinking about the scene they had just rehearsed, a scene from Shakespeare's *A Midsummer Night's Dream*. Phillippe was massaging Hyacinth's shoulders and Hyacinth was, of course, smirking. Owen and Yomi had lapsed into a cabal, heads together over the table that was the only furniture in the space. Ginny sat in a chair, keying furiously into a notepad.

"Di?" called Hal. "Do you want to go to dinner?"

Then the door closed behind her, and she was mercifully free of them. What a bad day it had been. The tempo ran slow and they kept clumping together in the ensemble scene. She was beginning to feel claustrophobic. That was one thing she liked about Chapalii ships: they built their passageways wide, even if they were a strikingly ugly shade of orange and heated right to the level of sticky hot. She waited outside the door while a pack of human university students swarmed by her, chattering and giggling, ignoring her except for one red-haired young woman who threw her a startled and surprisingly vindictive glance; then a trio of alien *nar* skittered by, flicking their secondary dwarf wings at her in polite acknowledgment. She answered with a brief bow and set off in the opposite direction, toward the dining hall.

It still surprised Diana that Charles Soerensen ate his meals in the regular dining hall, along with all the other passengers. All the non-Chapallii passengers, of course; the Chapallii themselves remained in segregated quarters. He had somewhere developed the ability to sit at a different table every meal while making it seem as if he was as much graced by his tablemates' presence as they were by his. Marco Burckhardt sat on his right. Marco looked up, saw her, and smiled.

Don't do it, she told herself fiercely as she picked up her meal. Twenty steps later she stopped beside Marco's chair.

At least he didn't stand up. "Golden fair, please, sit down." Marco had the ability to look at you as if you were the only object in the world of interest to him.

She sat down. Her heart pounded in an annoying yet gratifying way.

"You've met Charles, of course," said Marco. "This is David ben Unbutu, and this is Suzanne Elia Arevalo."

Soerensen greeted her with polite interest, David with evident good nature, and Suzanne with a pitying glance. Then Soerensen, Suzanne, and the two mining engineers they sat with fell back into a heated discussion about the ratio of volume to cost in the transport of metals in the Dao Cee system from the asteroid belt to the processing plants orbiting the planet Odys.

"How is rehearsal?" Marco asked.

"Slow. A little frustrating today. Owen says you've actually met the nomadic people we're going to be traveling with, once we've left Jeds. What are they like?"

He rested his chin on one hand, tilted his head to the side, and regarded her with amusement. "What do you imagine they'll be like?"

Diana laughed. "Don't think I'll fall for this trap. Gorgeous clothes, of course, and beautiful jewelry. Dashing horses. Stern men and shy women who possess honor and simple dignity in equal measure. I suppose they'll have weapons. And lots of dirty but sweet-faced children."

"Yes, I think you covered most of the clichés," he said approvingly, and she laughed again, half from relief and half because the whole scene between them was so transparent, without losing any of its intensity.

A hush fell over the hall. Marco's attention jerked away from her. A Chapalii dressed in the pale tunic and trousers of the steward class stood in the far doorway, holding a gold wand in his hands.

Soerensen rose. "Excuse me," he said to others at the table. "Suzanne." She rose as well, and together they collapsed their trays, deposited them in the sort bin, and walked over to the door. Soerensen received the gold wand from the steward, and after a brief conversation with the alien, he and Suzanne left the hall. At once conversation flooded back along the tables.

David ben Unbutu, unruffled at being abandoned, went back to his meal. The engineers begged pardon and left. Marco glanced at the strip on the back of his left hand. "Ah," he said. He returned his attention to Diana. "My heart, it grieves me to part from you, but I must go." He lifted her hand to his lips, brushed a kiss there, and hurried out of the hall.

Don't watch him go. Even as she thought it, she wrenched her gaze away from Marco's back only to find David ben Unbutu watching her with a wry smile on his face. Instantly, she blushed.

"Sorry," said David. "I noticed your necklace. Are you a Trinitarian, or is it just a family heirloom?"

She lifted a hand to touch the necklace, with its intertwined star, book, and cross. "I was brought up in the worship, yes," she replied. How kind of him to change the subject.

"Have you visited the chapel on board? It's very . . . quiet. I'm going there now."

Diana smiled, a softer smile than the one she had offered to Marco Burckhardt. She felt like an idiot, sitting down by Burckhardt only to be deserted; probably he had gone off on Soerensen's business. Probably David ben Unbutu understood her plight. "Oh," she said, noticing the four short, beaded braids hanging from his coarse black hair down the back of his neck to dangle over the collar of his tunic. "You're Orthodox."

"Orthodox Judaeo-animist," he agreed with a chuckle.

"Our village is one of the last pockets of Trinitarian animism left in western Africa, and, of course, there's a long history of engineers in our family because of it."

Behind them, through the other doors, a horde of actors swept into the dining hall.

Diana jumped up, collapsing her tray over the uneaten food. "I'd love to see the chapel."

Along the red curve passageway, down a slow lift to yellow core, and they came to the Three Faiths chapel. Diana expected it to be untenanted at this time of ship's cycle, but someone had arrived there before them. David tried to stop her in the door, but he was too slow.

Diana had never thought of Marco Burckhardt as a particularly religious sort of person. But there he sat on a back bench of the chapel. Diana was skilled at reading the nuances of body language. The slight sound of their entrance had alerted Marco to their presence, but his red-haired companion remained oblivious, as well she might, being locked in so tight an embrace.

"Oh, Goddess, Marco," said David emphatically, and with no little disgust. "Have you no respect?"

The companion took her time in allowing him to break off the kiss. Without turning to look, Marco said, "but David, dear David, we all choose our own ways of worship."

"Let's just go," Diana murmured.

"I will not," said David, showing an unexpected stubborn streak, "surrender this divine ground to your earthly pleasures, Marco."

Red-Hair leaned away from her conquest and rested her weight on a hand, cupping the curve of the ivory bench. She preened, and when she saw Diana, the smile that tipped her lips was positively triumphant.

Marco got a startled look on his face, and he turned to look directly at them. "Oh, hell," he said, seeing Diana. He covered his face with a hand. That he was sorry to be caught by *her* did not make her feel any better. She felt mortified.

But Marco wasn't the sort of man who slinks away from confrontation; he lowered his hand, and Diana had to admire his nerve. He bent forward and whispered to Red-Hair. He had a loose-limbed grace, tall and big-framed, trim, but not slender, the kind of man who is comfortable in his body. Behind him, the stark white walls of the chapel set off the scene, framing the woman's red hair and Marco's purple shirt so boldly that Diana could, for a moment, only think that the two colors clashed.

"You will note," said David in a low voice, "that this is not in fact a circular room, but an oval. It's shaded so subtly with the carpet and a slight difference in hue in the white walls that it's hard to tell." He made a noise in his throat. "As if you care. But it's a marvelous room."

Red-Hair heaved a great, dramatic sigh—overdone, of course—and oozed up to her feet. She flung a scornful glance toward Diana and exited stage left, through an otherwise invisible door that whisked open just as she reached it and shut into the seamless wall behind her.

"Don't retreat," whispered David. "And never on holy ground."

They went in. The ceiling lofted into a dome, paling to a soft white glow at the crown. It made Diana think of standing inside an egg, nested and safe. Marco met them by the altar, which stood in the center of the room, ringed by benches.

"Well," he said, "that looked bad."

"Yes," said Diana, desperate to put a bold face on, "it did. Now I recognize her. She's a university student. Isn't she a little young for you?" Then cursed herself inwardly for saying it, since she and Red-Hair were probably much of an age.

David rolled his eyes and shook his head. It was so quiet in the chapel that Diana could hear the beads on his name braids as they clacked together.

But Marco only laughed. "Hoist with my own petard."

" 'For 'tis the sport to have the engineer hoist with his own petard: and it shall go hard. But I will delve one yard below their mines, and blow them at the moon.' "

He loved it, of course. She knew he would. He caught one of her hands and lifted it to his lips, which were cool and soft. "Golden fair, my heart is yours forever."

"If I were you," said David, sounding more amused than disgusted now, "I'd leave before you dig yourself in any deeper."

Marco released her hand. "I'd better go see if Charles needs me," he said, and he winked at Diana and left, that fast. Leaving her breathless and embarrassed and warm.

David moved away from her, walking over to sit down on a bench. She felt all at once that she didn't have to make any excuses to David, that he wouldn't judge her. Marco had a reputation; he didn't apologize for it or even try to hide it. So why, when she sat down herself and closed her eyes, was his the first image that came to her mind? But after a while, the peace of the chapel seeped into her, and she let the silence wash over and envelop her, the silence through which the Divine spoke to each individual.

"David!" A sharp whisper.

Diana started. Suzanne Elia Arevalo hurried into the room, striding over to stand beside David, who lifted his head and regarded her quizzically.

"Charles needs you. You can't imagine—" She broke off and looked straight at Diana. "Oh, hell," she swore. "I need another woman anyway. Diana—that's right, isn't it?" Suzanne had a brisk, competent air about her. Diana felt impelled to stand up, like a soldier awaiting orders. "Are you free? I don't know how long it will take."

"I'm free for the evening," Diana admitted.

"Good! Then come along."

"You might explain—" protested David, but he followed meekly in her wake, and Diana was far too curious to be left behind.

As they hurried down the yellow curve, Suzanne spoke in a hushed voice. "That wand, the request, came from a Chapalii lord who is on board with his family. Well, his wife and retinue, in any case. It turns out that his firstborn child—or male child, it must be, since it's to be his heir—is about to be born. And under Chapalii law the birth of an heir must be witnessed by a noble of higher rank. Well, Charles is the only duke on board—so. . . . Here."

They came to a pink lift, which halfway through its rise turned flat white on all its walls. It opened onto a threshold of granite columns. The scent of cloves and cinnamon hung in the air, smothering, and the heat swallowed them. Diana broke into a sweat. Four stewards waited at the threshold. Their pale skin bore tints of colors, bewildering in their variety. Under their escort, the three humans proceeded forward. Diana stared around, but here in the sacrosanct Chapalii halls she saw nothing that looked different: just the sickly-orange walls. They crossed two intersections and came to a broad white seam. One side opened. The stewards gestured to David to go through, and followed after.

Suzanne laid a hand on Diana's arm. "We don't go with him. There's a separate place for the females."

"But why—?"

"—are we here?" Now they waited alone in the corridor. Suzanne leaned back and looked down one curve, then the other, and touched the brooch at her shoulder. She swung her shoulder slowly back and forth, taking in the entire scene—scanning it, maybe—not that the scene itself was much to look at. "Charles has Marco and David attending him, and evidently they want two females to balance the two male attendants. I don't know. Parity? Harmony? Hostages? How should I know? Have you ever seen a Chapalii female?"

"Of course not! I thought they were all in seclusion, or something. Purdah."

Suzanne took her hand off the brooch. "Neither have I, and I, my dear, have seen a damn sight more of the Chapalii than most people. And no human has ever witnessed the birth of a Chapalii child. Ah."

The other side of the seam opened. A rush of cooler air swept over them, mingling with a scent like nutmeg and a charge in the air that sent prickles down Diana's back. She tried to shake it off, but it coursed down through her and made tiny sparks at her feet as she and Suzanne stepped onto the black-tiled floor of the chamber within.

A riot of color greeted them, so profuse that it made Diana dizzy. Animals and plants in garish hues intertwined like lovers clutched together in an endless embrace. A beaded curtain of plain black stone cut off one side of the chamber. Suzanne and Diana stood alone in the room. The curtain twitched, stirred in a musical rustling, and stilled. A voice spoke in what Diana assumed must be Chapalii, and was answered by a second voice that had in it the reedy musicality of a woodwind.

Diana stared around, stared at the curtain, stared at the walls. The strange scent pricked against her constantly, and a distant sound like falling water played in the background. She was numb with excitement and at the same time out of breath and yet again cold, as if one part of her brain had detached itself from her body in order to survey her surroundings without emotion. *This* was an adventure, and it seemed to her that, like a prologue that grabs your interest, it boded well for the play to follow.

No one came through the curtain, though. Suzanne did not touch her brooch. One wall faded to black, became translucent, and there, in a white chamber, sat an egg.

Diana gasped. Then she looked again, realizing that she merely called it an egg because it was egg-shaped and white, because humans like to label things as familiar things; it could be anything, organic, metal, plastic, an incubator, a womb, or something altogether out of her experience. At the far end of the white chamber, Soerensen appeared between two figures: one a Chapalii lord, the other so swathed in robes that Diana could not see one single millimeter of skin nor even the suggestion of eyes or a face.

Suzanne's whole body was canted toward the window, as if she wished mightily to press herself up against it in order to get a better look, but dared not move. Chills ran up Diana's spine. A seam appeared in the smooth surface of the oval. The lord ventured forward, hesitant, and Soerensen came with him, close enough that Diana could judge by his height that the egg was about a meter tall—just over half as tall as he was. The duke had a peculiar expression on his face, as if the air smelled bad in the white chamber and he had to endure it. The robed figure glided around to the other side of the egg. The curtain stirred and rustled back to silence. She saw no sign of Marco or David.

The top half of the container sheened from white into a glowing translucence. Through it, Diana caught a glimpse of a tiny object squirming. Soerensen edged closer to the egg. His eyes widened as he watched something within. The Chapalii lord moved closer to him and spoke, and Soerensen started. He extended both hands. Diana detected the slightest hesitation, and then Soeren-

sen placed both hands, palms down, onto the glowing
surface of the egg.

"Marking it," Suzanne said under her breath, evidently unable to contain herself. "He's sealing the act of
witness, that the heir is alive and viable. *Can you see
it?*" The older woman was wound so tight that Diana
could feel her exhilaration, like waves roiling off her that
struck and eddied with Diana's own excitement.

At the touch of Soerensen's hands, the top surface of
the container dissolved into a swell of steam and then
nothing. He bent at the waist, almost overbalanced, and
together, as one, the three of them—the duke, the lord,
and the robed figure—bent down to examine what lay
within. The beaded curtain rustled and the woodwind
voice spoke a long phrase, so musical that it seemed
more like a melody than a sentence. Suzanne winced.

"What—?" Diana began softly, but Suzanne only
waved her away impatiently.

"Damn, hell, *chaib*," she hissed, whispering, "but I
can't understand them."

The Chapalii lord straightened. He held in his hands a
small, white, wriggling thing, an exact, miniature version
of himself. That brief glimpse they gained; then the robed
figure fluttered forward and the child was restored to the
egg. Soerensen retreated. A glow domed the empty crown
of the egg, solidified, and sealed off the container again.
A seam shut. The wall darkened and became the frieze
of animals and plants. Another seam opened, this one
leading into the passageway.

"I think we're being asked to leave," said Suzanne,
and then she said something more, in Chapalii, but there
was no response from behind the curtain.

Sparks flashed around Diana's feet as she crossed back
into the passageway. The seam shut behind them, leaving
the two women alone in the corridor. Suzanne let out a
great sigh. Her face shone; she looked replete with satisfaction. Diana felt weak in the knees, but she also
floated, so amazed, so elated by what she had just experienced that she hardly needed to touch the ground in
order to walk.

"Which reminds me," said Suzanne suddenly, "before they get back, and because you look like a sensible
girl. Let me give you some advice about Marco." The

older woman might as well have slapped her, for all that the friendly tone of the words stung Diana, for all that they brought her hard down to earth. "He's not arrogant, he doesn't count coup. He just likes women. He never sets out to deliberately hurt anyone, but he lives rather at the mercy of his . . . appetites. It's the same urge that makes him go exploring. He just can't stand to see virgin ground go untouched. He just has to see what lies over the other side of the hill. He's charming and attractive, and he is sincere, in his own way. Just don't think that you're going to be any different than the other ones—that's the trap." Then she shrugged. "Sorry. I'm sure you didn't want to hear that. Just remember that we were all at university—that we were your age—well before you were born."

Before Diana could respond, the other seam opened and Marco and David and Soerensen emerged, escorted by four stewards. A tangible scent of sulfur wafted from the duke. Marco blinked at Diana, offered her a smile, and then walked on with the Chapalii escort, clearly preoccupied by this major turn of events. Diana followed the others meekly, endured their taut silence in the lift that shaded to pink and dumped them off in the passenger levels, and then escaped to make her own way back to the stateroom she shared with Hal and Quinn and Oriana.

"You smell funny," said Hal as she came in.

Quinn looked up from the game of Go they were playing. "Where've you been? Off assignating with the intrepid explorer? Oh, don't think we haven't noticed him nosing around."

"Oh, be quiet," snapped Diana. She flung herself down on the bunk and stared at the wall. "I just witnessed the birth of a Chapalii lord's heir."

Oriana snorted, and Hal and Quinn laughed. "That's good," said Quinn. "Try another one."

Diana buried her head in her arms and wished that they would arrive on Rhui, and at the city of Jeds, as quickly as possible. But then she smiled to herself. What did she care if they believed her or not? She knew what she had witnessed. And this was only the beginning of the adventure.

CHAPTER FOUR

David came out to the battlements of the palace to get away from the audience room. He couldn't stand stuffy rooms, and he particularly disliked the obsequiousness with which the Jedan nobles treated Charles. Not that Charles seemed to like it, mind, but it grated on David after a while. He leaned against the sea wall, letting the spray mist his face and hair, and pulled his cloak around himself to ward off the cold. Clouds hung low over the crowded harbor of Jeds, off to his left. Beyond the harbor, the city crawled up and down the hills like a rank animal—or at least, that was how David always thought of it. They had been here two months now, and he saw no reason to change his opinion.

He slipped his sketchpad out from under his cloak and opened it to the page he had just been working on: a sketch of Charles seated in the audience hall, with Marco at his right and two Jedan guards behind him.

"Oh, hello, David."

He turned to greet Diana Brooke-Holt. She also wore a cloak, but it billowed up from her shoulders, lifted by the wind, lending her entrance a dramatic flair. "Coming out to take the air?"

But her gaze went immediately to the sketchpad. "You drew that! That's wonderful!"

David shrugged. He was always embarrassed when people admired his sketching, because he knew he had a dilettante's skill, not a true artist's. But Diana's interest was infectious.

"Is there more?" Without really asking for permission, she flipped the pages back. "That's the north front of the palace. Look how wonderful the architectural details are. You're really good."

"Thank you," murmured David.

She paused too long on a study of Marco, got a self-conscious look on her face, and hastily turned to another page. "You can record the expedition this way, can't you? Out in the open."

"It's true," he agreed, and then she turned another page and there found—herself.

"Oh," she said.

"Do you like it?" asked David, feeling violently shy all of a sudden.

Diana did him the honor of studying the sketch for some moments in silence. But then she got a grin on her face, and she struck a pose and pressed a palm to her chest. " 'Oh, wonderful, wonderful, and most wonderful wonderful! and yet again wonderful! and after that, out of all whooping!' "

David laughed. "Which reminds me. How is the acting business in this town?"

She laughed in turn. "We're a great success. A sold-out house every night. Lords and merchants showering the actresses with gifts, flowers and jewels and gowns and expensive baskets of fruit. Poor Yomi has to tag and catalog and return the nonperishable items." She rested her back against the stone and brushed her golden hair back away from her face. The sun, behind her, set into the bay, casting a golden-red echo across the waters, staining the clouds pink. Was she unconscious of the effect she caused, of the way any man might linger to watch her, to wonder? Diana had a bright face, full of warmth, and the cut of her tunic and skirt, while conservative, lent her figure a pleasing grace. David was not surprised that Marco—in the limited free time that they'd had—put himself in her way. Not that he'd had any success, that David had heard of. But there is pleasure given freely and with a whole heart between friends, and there is a subtle form of coercion that some people see fit to call romance. David did not believe in romance, but he suspected that Diana did. Diana grinned at him; was she aware of the way his thoughts were tending? She was, in some ways, quite as young as she looked, but David did not think she was a fool. "And Hyacinth fell in love with some dark-eyed, perfumed young lordling, if that's what they call them. He managed to sneak out every night for two weeks before Yomi caught him at it and slapped a curfew on him.''

"And he obeyed it?"

"Only because she threatened to tell Soerensen."

"Ah," said David. "I'm sorry I haven't had time to attend any of the performances. How is the experiment going?"

She turned her shoulders just enough so she could see both him and the sunset. Light spilled out over the bay, chopped by the waves into splinters. Jeds fell into shadow, and the distant hills marking the east grew quite black. Stars began to fill the darkening sky.

"Shakespeare plays well. We've done a condensed repertory schedule: *A Midsummer Night's Dream; King Lear; The Tempest; Peer Gynt; Caucasian Chalk Circle; Oedipus Rex; Berenice*. Ginny's translated some; others we've done in the original. I don't know. Maybe Owen is right. Maybe some human emotions and gestures *are* universal. They certainly communicate to these people, and they know nothing of Earth.''

At times like this, David was reminded that he was talking with a fellow professional. He wondered if Marco ever saw this side of Diana, or if he only saw that she was pretty, that she had a warm, attractive personality and the ability to listen. "How *do* you memorize all those lines?'' he demanded.

She rolled her eyes. "I refuse to answer that question. Why doesn't Charles Soerensen ban debt-slavery in Jeds?"

"Debt-slavery?"

"Haven't you been in the city at all? Owen has already been approached by three brothel owners and two wealthy merchants to buy my debt from him, because they want to own me, you can imagine what for. It's been the same for Oriana and for Quinn and Anahita. And Hyacinth, of course. He holds the record: he's had four brothel owners, three merchants, and eight veiled gentlewomen bargaining through stewards try to buy him. Owen kept trying to tell them that we weren't slaves until Yomi finally told him just to tell them that we aren't for sale.''

"Oh, my," said David, amused and horrified at the same time.

"Of course, we found it funny at first," she went on,

her expression darkening. "But the native girls and boys aren't so lucky." She hesitated, and David had a sudden premonition whose name was going to come next to her lips. "Marco took me down into the town last week. It had never occurred to me that they might look them over and sell them off like furniture. Those poor girls looked so terrified, and one actually—" She choked on the next words, faltered, and lapsed into silence.

The waves beat on the rocks below. Faintly, from the audience room, David heard the sound of trumpets.

"How can he let it go on, when he could stop it?" Diana demanded suddenly.

"It *is* an interdicted planet." The words sounded weak. "Well," he added apologetically, "if he uses his real strength, it would rip apart the fabric of this society. What right do we have to interfere?"

"What right? It's *wrong,* what they do. It's wrong for those children."

David sighed. "Diana, someone is always going to be hurt. I know that Charles is well aware of the contradictions inherent in his situation."

"You're a fool for going, Charles. Let the company go, and I'll go with them. Send Cara, if you must. But don't go yourself. It can't be perceived as anything but a threat. You forget, I've met him."

Like conspirators, David and Diana both froze. David wondered if this was how an actor felt, who has forgotten to exit and so, inadvertently, is stuck out on stage for the next scene, in which he does not belong. Diana pressed herself closer against the wall, as if she could sink into the stone and thus hide herself. The voices, accompanied by footfalls, came closer.

"It is time for Tess to return," said Charles, sounding cool. "It has been four years, Marco. *Four years,* since she left Earth. I would have come sooner, but how was I to know it would take two years to finalize the Keinaba alliance? Damned chameleons. One needs the patience of Job to deal with them."

Marco chuckled. "Which you have. I'd much rather deal with barbarians. Quick to anger, quick to friendship. Not this years-long game playing the Chapallii love. Years? Hell. Decades-long, centuries, for all we know of them. Still, I say you're better off letting me talk to Tess first.''

The footfalls ceased. The curve of the wall, and the twilight, still hid them from the two men. Alone, David would just have gone to join the others, but Diana looked utterly embarrassed. And anyway, he was curious about the tenor of their conversation.

''No.''

''Charles—''

''No. In any case, the rendezvous is already arranged. We sail in two weeks. Baron Santer will act as regent until my return. I'll leave him the scepter of office, although I'll keep the signet ring and the prince's chain just in case he gets ambitions. Tess will meet us at Abala Port in about six weeks.''

''And?''

''And the Company can travel on into the interior with the jaran, if that's still their wish.''

''And you?''

''We'll see.''

''Yes, we'll see because you have every intention of turning straight round and coming back here with Tess, don't you? *Merde*, Charles, don't do anything rash.''

Charles laughed, short and sharp. ''When was the last time you've known me to do anything rash?''

''A damned long time ago, as you well know. Let me say it this way. You're getting used to things going your way. This may not be your choice to make.''

''Tess has a duty—''

''Yes, I know all about her duty, and I'm sure she does as well. In any case, it's not Tess I'm thinking of now. In the words of that ancient song, I think an irresistible force is about to meet an immovable object, and I'm sure as hell going to get out of the flash zone.''

''I'll think about it,'' said Charles Soerensen. David was shocked to hear such coldness in his voice; this was Charles, who always listened, who could always be counted upon to be open-minded. Diana clutched a fistful of cloak in one hand. Footfalls sounded again, but moving away from them, and they were left in silence but for the sea surging below and the distant sound of carriages leaving the palace.

"Curiouser and curiouser," said a woman's voice beside them.

David gasped, starting round. Diana sagged back against the wall.

"I beg your pardon. I didn't mean to startle you." The woman smiled.

"Cara!"

"Oh, not you," said Cara Hierakis dismissively. "I meant Diana."

"Dr. Hierakis," said Diana in a small voice. She glanced guiltily toward the right and then back. "Oh. I. . . ."

"Yes, we were all eavesdropping, weren't we?"

"Speak for yourself," said David, affronted. "We came here by accident."

"Oh, not on purpose, I know," said the doctor mildly. "Or at least, not on your part, Diana."

"Thank you," said David, but he laughed.

"Is she really alive?" Diana asked. "Terese Soerensen, that is? We heard rumors, but I didn't know if they were true."

"Yes, she's alive."

Whenever he heard Tess mentioned, just that simple fact set against the official announcements proclaimed by the Chapalii Protocol Office, David felt a warm glow start up inside him. Tess *was* alive, and he would be seeing her soon.

"But why did she come to Rhui?" Diana asked. "Oh, I know I shouldn't ask, but. . . ." She trailed off, and David turned to look at Cara Hierakis because it was a question he had never gotten a satisfactory answer to.

Cara laughed. The breeze off the bay stirred her black hair and she squinted out at the distant islands that rimmed the western horizon like glass beads shot through with the last red fires of the sun. The barest trace of crows-feet showed at her eyes. Her face looked not young, yet not old, that mature mask that most humans between the age of forty and ninety now wore: ageless, smooth, and healthy. That David himself wore, although it was by now an ancient joke that folks with the darkest skin stayed the youngest looking for the longest time; there was not four months in chronological age between

Charles and David and Marco, but people often mistook
David for younger.

"But," echoed Cara, smiling at Diana. "You'll ask
anyway. I must say you're looking pert, David, after that
impossibly boring audience and ceremony."

"I left."

"Of course. You could. Tess is doing linguistics research, Diana."

"Linguistics research? That seems so mundane, somehow. I thought maybe she was kidnapped by a dark
warrior and swept off into a life filled with hardship and
passionate lovemaking. Oh, well."

There was a pause. David chuckled.

Cara regarded Diana with an expression of amused in-
dulgence. "And a bastard every year? Or do you suppose
she was married in some primitive ceremony?"

"Oh, certainly," said Diana with conviction, pushing
herself away from the wall. "Barbarians are prudes,
aren't they? Of course there was a ceremony. She's probably scarred for life."

David laughed.

"How long have you been an actor?" Cara asked.

Diana smiled in a way that showed her dimples to perfection. David sighed and shook his head, feeling very
old. "My first performance was at age four as the
changeling in *A Midsummer Night's Dream*."

"That must explain it," said Cara, but David knew
her well enough to see that she liked Diana. "In any
case, Tess is gifted with languages, and I suspect she saw
Rhui as an excellent laboratory to study human evolution
in parallel to our own."

"Like Owen?"

"Perhaps. It's not a bad analogy."

"You have a laboratory here, too, don't you? A medical one."

"Yes." Cara cast a glance at David.

"She's studying aging," he said.

But Cara was only angling for an opening, since it was
her favorite subject. "As grateful as we may be for the
longevity treatments the Chapalii gave us, allowing us to
live out our full one hundred and twenty year life spans
with good health and a long period of relative youth, I
suspect there's something we're missing. Something they

didn't tell us, or something, perhaps, that they don't know."

"What do you mean?"

David had seen Cara's lecture mask before. It slipped firmly into place now. "Aging is a two part process. One is a breakdown of the vitality and regenerative abilities of the tissues and the metabolic system, that's what the Chapalii treatments deal with. But the other is a genetic clock that switches off the organism at a set time. We're still stuck at one hundred and twenty years. I think we can do better." The mask slipped off, and she suddenly looked cautious. "Perhaps. We'll see."

"It's a delicate and peculiar issue," put in David, since Cara had left him his opening. "We don't talk about it much."

"Oh," said Diana. The sea faded into darkness behind them, and the massive bulk of the palace rose against the stars. "Is that why you have your laboratory down here, on an interdicted planet? Where the Chapalii aren't allowed?"

What need to reply? The wind coursed along the parapet and the sea dashed itself into foam on the rocks below. The fecund moon lay low, bordering the hills. A shoe scraped on stone, and Marco emerged from around a curve of wall. He smiled at Diana and leaned casually against the wall beside her.

To David's surprise, it was Diana who broke the silence. "But, Dr. Hierakis, are the Rhuian humans really the same species as we are?"

David almost laughed, seeing how disconcerted Marco looked, as if he thought that once he arrived, Diana would not be able to think of anything but him.

"Oh, yes," said Cara. "By all the biological laws we know. Identical." She appeared about to say something else, but did not.

"But how?" Diana asked. "That should be impossible."

Though it was night, the moon lent enough light to the scene so David could still read their expressions. Marco gazed soulfully on Diana, and David thought she was aware of his gaze on her. Cara sighed and shifted to stare out to sea, imposing the kind of silence on the little group that betrays knowledge hard-won and dangerous to share.

"Oh," said Diana. She looked disappointed, but resigned to her fate. "It's a state secret. I understand."

Marco chuckled. "Fair one." He caught one of her hands in his. "Had you agreed to marry me yet?"

"You hadn't asked me yet," Diana retorted, extricating her hand from his. Then she lowered her eyes from his face and looked quickly away.

Oh, dear, thought David. He looked at Cara. Cara looked at him. The signs of infatuation were easy enough to read. And she *was* young, and susceptible.

"I hear you're doing *The Tempest* tonight," said Cara. "Do you suppose you could find a seat for me? I've always loved that play."

"Goodness," said Diana, sounding a bit strained as she said it. "I really must go. I'm sure we can find you something, Doctor, if you'd like to come with me. The duke's—the *prince's*—box is always vacant, unless he's attending. If you think he'd like to go."

"Ah," said Cara in a dangerous voice. "I'm sure he'd *love* to attend tonight."

They made their good-byes. They left. Marco began to walk after them.

"Marco," said David softly, "she is an intelligent and sensitive young woman, and I stress the word, 'young.' Stop playing with her. It's cruel, above all else."

Marco spun. "Et tu, Brute? Hell, I had a lecture from Suzanne before she left to go back to Odys. Is this some kind of conspiracy? I think she's old enough to know her own mind."

"Maybe she just strikes us all as more vulnerable than the others. She's terribly romantic."

"Well, so am I," Marco snapped. "I suggest you let the subject drop." He propped his elbows up on the battlements and glared out at the bay, striped in darkness and moonlight. But then again, Marco was always short-tempered when he was in full pursuit.

"I've said everything I intend to say. For whatever good it will do. When do Maggie and Rajiv and Jo get in?"

"Tomorrow," said Marco grumpily. "And don't forget Ursula."

"Ow." David winced. "I had. Well, I've lived through worse."

"Or the next day," Marco added, evidently determined to be perverse. "It depends on the weather. They're marking time in orbit now."

"Why did you tell Charles that an irresistible force is about to meet an immovable object? What does that have to do with Tess?"

Marco fixed a brooding stare on David. "Don't say I didn't warn him."

"My goodness," said David, "you certainly make me look forward to *this* expedition."

Marco only grunted. Then he lapsed into a silence from which, David knew, he could not be coaxed. David decided to see if he could go wangle a chair in the prince's box, to see tonight's performance of *The Tempest*. Somehow, a play about being shipwrecked on a lost and primitive island seemed appropriate to the moment.

CHAPTER FIVE

Jiroannes Arthebathes was at Eberge when he received the courier from his uncle ordering him to leave three-quarters of his retinue and all of his women and their attendants at the northern villa of the Great King's fourth cousin.

His personal secretary, Syrannus, read the letter to him. Jiroannes grabbed the parchment out of Syrannus's hands and spoke the words to himself. " '. . . It has come to our attention that the presence of women in your party would be a hindrance to our negotiations. Therefore, nephew, I feel it wise for you to travel with only twenty guardsmen, two grooms, three slave-boys, and your personal secretary. Be so good as to obey my wishes.' "

Jiroannes had learned to swear fluently at the palace school for boys; he did so now. "This is humiliating! And well he knows it, too. He would never travel with such a paltry escort."

"Surely, eminence, your uncle would not demand such privations of you without good reason."

"How can he expect that I will be granted any respect at all, even by such barbarians as these jaran, coming to them with a mere six servants? And no women! Their *Bakhtiian* will think me the merest lordling. Surely my uncle understands that as the ambassador of the Great King, may his name resonate a thousand years, I must present a dignified retinue. Savages are only impressed by force, size, and gold. They will think Vidiya is some trifling princedom." He snorted and glanced around his chamber. True, he was far out in the provinces, but the Great King's fourth cousin had imported the finest carved furniture from the port of Ambray, and the cunning designs woven into the upholstery of the couch attested to the skill of his slaves. Though it was also true that the tile inlaid into the floor had flaws and inferior color, and the beads of the door curtain were painted wood, not glass. "How can the jaran respect us as the most civilized of peoples, as well as the most powerful, if the Great King's ambassador arrives with a train of servants that any concubine might own? Feh."

Syrannus said nothing, but he extricated the delicate parchment from his lord's smooth, dark hands and rolled it up with the reverence due any communication from the person of a great lord and King's Companion of Vidiya.

"And I showed laudable restraint, I would have thought," Jiroannes went on, although in a more subdued tone of voice. "I brought only three of my concubines."

"Eminence, perhaps your most honored lord uncle has obtained information that forces his hand in this?"

"I know. I know." It was too much, really, to have to endure a year in circumstances of the utmost coarseness, ambassador to these jaran, and now to have to maintain himself as a Vidiyan ought with so few servants. "I doubt if these barbarians can even recognize such markers of status."

"I think, eminence, that it would not do to underestimate them. Eight kingdoms and four principalities have already fallen to their onslaught. Why else would the Great King, may his name endure a thousand years, bother to negotiate with their prince?"

"Four kingdoms and eight principalities. Let us not exaggerate their power. Surely, if it came to war between us, you don't think these barbarians have the slightest chance to win?"

"One hears tales, eminence. The more savage the man, the less honor and the Everlasting God's tenets will stay his hand. They say this Bakhtiian violated a holy temple and its ten virgin priestesses. That he massacred an entire town out in the wilderness, five thousand men, women, and children, even the cattle, leaving only the smoking ruins of the buildings and bloodied corpses for the scavengers. They say jaran men are so proud that they won't touch any women but their own, that they call foreign women 'dogs.' They ride covered in their own blood, and they can't walk, since they sit on horseback from childhood on."

Jiroannes stroked his beard, amused. "I hope you do not believe all these superstitious tales, Syrannus. I have also heard it said that they scorn the bow and arrow because it is a woman's weapon. Can you imagine? Thinking a woman could shoot? It is nonsense, and you'd do well not to believe such stories."

"Still, eminence, your most honored uncle must have had good reason to give you this order."

"Yes. I have never doubted my uncle's judgment. And it *was* undoubtedly my uncle's influence that convinced His Imperial Majesty to grant me this mission."

"It is true, eminence, that five other young men of good family vied for the position. To succeed with such an important assignment will assure you higher standing at court."

"Yes. And a hope of moving into the Companion's Circle." Jiroannes sank back onto the silken couch and snapped his fingers. His Tadesh concubine padded forward from the corner and knelt at the foot of the couch to massage his feet. "And if I fail, I will spend the rest of my life in the provinces." He considered the papered walls trimmed with gold leaf, the arched windows looking out over the gardens, sere and brown with winter, and the beaded curtain that concealed this room from the rest of the honored guest suite. Wooden beads, indeed!

"Certainly, eminence, the rewards for succeeding will be great. Your most honored uncle has already begun negotiations, I believe, for your suit for the hand and dowry of the daughter of this house."

"Yes. The daughter of the Great King's fourth cousin. That would be sweet indeed."

"With such a connection to the royal family, eminence, surely a Companion's Sash would be guaranteed you."

Jiroannes did not reply. He watched the Tadesh. Her hands, stroking his feet and ankles, were strong and assured. She was a foreign girl, from the Gray Eminence's lands across the sea. He had paid a ridiculously high price for her. She was not a beauty, certainly, but exotic as any foreigner is, and in any case she knew the five fabled arts of seduction and the five erotic dances of Tadesh. He could tell, by her lowered eyes and the set of her chin, that she knew he was studying her. She did not smile. She never did.

"Syrannus," he said abruptly. "There is a slave-boy about her size. Go get his clothing."

"Your eminence?"

"His clothing."

Syrannus looked troubled. "Your eminence, surely, if your most honored uncle said—"

"Are you questioning me?"

Syrannus bowed. "Of course not, your eminence, but in my position as a tutor for many years in the palace school, from which your eminence so graciously elevated me to become your secretary, I beg leave to remind you that while your high spirits and rebellious nature made you a favorite among the tutors at the school, it would not perhaps be wise to go against your uncle's orders."

"I can cut the girl's hair." The concubine's hands halted for a moment, then resumed their rubbing. "With short hair, and loose clothing, she will pass well enough for a boy. By my ancestors, Syrannus, surely my uncle cannot expect me to endure an entire year without female companionship? The First Prophet himself warns against such privations. It is simply too much. She will go in the slave-boy's place. My uncle will not know of it, and the barbarians will neither notice nor care."

Syrannus hesitated. At last, he bowed and left the room. The curtain parted, whispering, to let him through, and with a jangle of beads settled back into place.

Jiroannes sighed. "Something to drink, Samae." The concubine rose and padded in her slippers to the far table and brought him back a cup of melted fruit sorbet. He liked to watch her. She had an unconscious grace, and her slim hips swayed in an enticing manner. He did not think she did it on purpose. She had yet to show the least interest in him, except to perform her duties as ordered and with exacting perfection.

She knelt beside the couch and lifted the cup up to him. He took it, and drank. She wore two layers of cloth, an outer silken gown slitted cunningly to reveal the sheer silk garment beneath and the white curves of her body. The sorbet cooled his throat, but not his ardor.

"My sash," he said.

She undid the complex knot that bound his sash and

unwound him from its confines. The emerald cloth studded with jewels and precious stones fell to the floor in a heap. Even as she slid his trousers and blouse off, he was thinking as much of his ambitions as of the expert ministrations of her hands: endure this one year, negotiate a successful treaty with this Bakhtiian, secure Vidiya's borders and perhaps even arrange some diplomatic marriages—the Great King had a daughter by his fifth wife he was willing to offer to the Bakhtiian, and surely this nomad prince had some female in his family to offer the Great King or his heir in turn—and then. . . .

Samae paused in her stroking while Syrannus came in, deposited the boy's clothing in a neat pile at the foot of the couch, and left. As the beaded curtain settled back into place, she dabbed oil on her hands and began again.

Then he could marry well and gain the honor of wearing, instead of a gaudy, jeweled sash, the plain white silk granted only to the Companions. With such a prize within his reach, he could almost look forward to the coming year.

Manifest of the Soerensen Expedition
Compiled by Margaret O'Neill, Assistant to C. Soerensen

Personnel:

Charles Soerensen
Dr. Cara Fel Hierakis
Margaret O'Neill
David ben Unbutu
Ursula el Kawakami
Rajiv Caer Linn
Joanna Singh

The Bharentous Repertory Company:

Ginnaia Lac Arbha	Owen Zerentous
Seshat Onn	Dejhuti Joldine
Anahita Liel Apphia	Gwyn Jones
Helen Angiras	Jean-Pierre Dasas
Diana Brooke-Holt	Henry Bharentous
Madelena Quinn	Hyacinth
Oriana Vuh Catanya	Phillippe Navarone
Yomi Applegate-Hito	Joseph Applegate-Hito

Partial Manifest of Goods:

22 Hou-Kohl palm slates
1 Ananda-Cray Modeler
1 Ananda-Cray
   demiModeler
1 Grousset solar mini
1 Xi-Dela portable
   cookery
10 two-capacity canvas
   tents
3 ten-capacity canvas tents
23 canvas cots
4 folding tables
23 folding chairs
23 wilderness thermal
   blankets
4 dishpans
25 sets: knives, forks &
   spoons
25 sets: mugs, plates &
   bowls
3 chopping boards
3 kettles
3 ladles
1 water purifier
axes & shovels
soap

thermal mitts
2 frying pans
clothespins
rope
portable platform
4 free-standing screens
10 carpets
scrubbing pads & towels
1 fire extinguisher
3 buckets
1 portable efficiency: WC
   and shower
7 crates belonging to Dr.
   Hierakis (uninspected)
5 crates of misc. props
   and costumes: see
   Company manifest for
   Interdiction allowance
misc. personal items, ltd.
   to 2 carry bags per
   person (12 kg. ea.)
100 gallons of water
emergency transmitter
5 Minimax solar cells
10,000 bags of tea

CHAPTER SIX

A peremptory knock sounded on the door behind Diana. She glanced up, startled, and lost hold of the inkwell just as the ship rolled steeply. The inkwell slid off the table and fell to the floor. Diana swore and ducked under the table to grab for it. It spun in a furious circle, spewing ink, and then rolled with the tilt of the floor toward the bunk. Diana swore again, more heated words this time, bumped her head on the top of the table, and saw a booted foot catch the inkwell, stopping it neatly before it could roll under the lip of the bunk.

"Such language," admonished the owner of the foot.

She crawled out from under the table. "Hello," she said, surveying Marco Burckhardt with remarkable calm. Somehow, her anger at the mess counteracted her fluttering heart.

He grinned at her and bent to retrieve the inkwell. "It's a messy business. Writing with pen and ink. Palm slates are much more convenient."

"This *is* an interdicted planet." She took the inkwell from him, stoppered it, and used a rag to mop up the spilled ink. "Thank you." Out in the passageway she heard the voices of the rest of the party as they packed and readied to leave.

Marco examined the room—Hal's three duffel bags, open, with clothing and interesting odds and ends strewn over the lower bunk; Diana's two little carry bags on the upper bunk, tied and neat and ready to go. "Where's your roommate?"

"Out throwing up over the stern one final time, I think."

"Ah, he was one of the really sick ones."

"And an actor, you know. Think of it as a farewell gesture."

"If you're ready, I can get you on the first boat going in to the harbor."

"Can you?" Diana clapped her hands together and clasped them at her throat. "That would be marvelous! Here, I'm ready to go right now." She closed the journal, laced it shut with a leather cord, and stuffed it into the side pouch of one of her bags.

"May I carry those for you?"

"No, I'm fine. Well, if you insist, you may take one." She handed him the bag without the journal in it, hoisted the other in her left hand, and followed him out of the cabin and down the passageway, dodging actors and their gear.

A brisk wind blew on deck, and though it was cold, it was clear, the sun a fine golden disk in the purpling-blue sky. A shoal of harbor boats crowded up against the ship's low-slung hull. Dr. Hierakis stood supervising the loading of her mysterious selection of crates and barrels into the forward boat. Charles Soerensen appeared from his cabin. He swung two bags—no heavier, Diana judged, than her own—over the rail and dropped them the two meters. They landed next to a meter-square crate. He climbed down the ladder, into the boat.

"Hello, Marco. Coming with us?" Margaret O'Neill, Soerensen's assistant, appeared at the railing beside them. She glanced at Diana, at Marco, grinned, and then hid her mouth behind one hand.

"But of course, my flame-haired vixen. I could not bear to be parted from you even for so short a time. Do you know Diana?"

"Of course I know Diana. We spent a companionable two days together at the beginning of the voyage, throwing up over the stern."

Diana smiled but could think of no reply. Maggie treated Marco with a casual irreverence that Diana could only marvel at, and certainly could not hope to imitate.

Without asking, Marco took Diana's second carry from her grip and slung both bags down into Charles Soerensen's waiting hands. A gaudy gold ring flashed on the duke's right forefinger. Looking up, Soerensen caught Diana's gaze on him and he nodded in greeting. Diana blushed and waited to descend into the boat until Maggie and Marco had gone before her. The boat rocked on the wind-whipped water. Dr. Hierakis secured the last of her crates and then sat. As one of the boatmen poled them free of the ship, Diana could not resist turning to wave to the handful of actors who had by now arrived on deck. Four sailors began the steady stroke of the oars, and the boat headed in to the docks, leaving the rest to follow in its wake.

A line of red rimmed the dockside. It had a shimmering, restless texture like, Diana thought, a festival decoration or some religious iconography. But as they neared the shore, she realized that it was a long line of figures—of men mounted on horses. There were many, many—perhaps a thousand—along the wharf, three deep and snaking in lines up into the town. Each and every one of the mounted men wore a similar costume: a brilliant scarlet shirt and black trousers and boots. The oars beat rhythmically as the boat scudded across the harbor, closing, and Diana saw that the riders were armed with sabers, and that most of them held long spears, some with pennants tied up near their heads, snapping in the breeze.

"They're armed!" she exclaimed. "We're rowing straight into them."

Soerensen shaded his eyes with one hand to stare. One of the rowers spoke rapidly in a foreign tongue.

Marco listened and nodded, and then translated for the others. "He says the barbarians came into town two days since, that they came to wait for the Prince of the far city, which is Charles, of course."

"Of course," Maggie echoed, glancing sharply at Soerensen. If he was paying attention to this conversation, he did not show it.

"He says," Marco continued, beginning to smile, "that it's the Bakhtiian's own private guard, his picked troops, and that Bakhtiian himself is with them."

"But isn't he the conqueror?" Maggie demanded. "The king? Why would he be here?" But Marco fell silent as the boat slipped in among pilings and the sailors tied her up to a pier.

Soerensen disembarked without taking his packs. The others scrambled after him. The little party walked at a brisk pace up the pier to the waiting guard. This close, the riders were even more impressive—each horsed and seated magnificently, a long line of men, fair and dark, set off by the intense red of their shirts. Soerensen moved with an impatient, clipped stride.

Maggie dropped back beside Diana and whispered, "He'll see his sister Tess at last. It's all he's been speaking of." Soerensen slowed, surveying the line, and halted at the end of the pier, faced with the barbarians. Diana and Maggie stood behind him, Marco and Dr. Hierakis on either side of him.

First there was silence. Diana scanned the line for any sign of the sister, but she saw only men. Each one in turn, those close enough for her to look at, cast down his eyes, as if they had some taboo about looking on a stranger. Then, to the far right of the line, a rider appeared, flanked by two others.

"Enter, the king," said Diana under her breath.

Soerensen lifted a hand in greeting, but as the three riders neared, he lowered it. All three were men, and the one in the fore rode a splendid black horse. The trio halted in front of Soerensen, and the dark-featured man on the black horse dismounted and handed the reins to one of his companions. Then he examined his audience, making no immediate move to come forward. He wore the brilliant clothing of his people with impeccable neatness, and he had that air of utter authority that comes from having one's will obeyed instantly.

Marco made a hiss of amazement. "That's him," he said in a voice pitched low, for Soerensen's ears. "That's Bakhtiian."

"Of course it is," whispered Diana. "Only kings or actors make entrances like that."

Soerensen did not acknowledge either comment. "I don't believe it," said Maggie.

Marco glanced back over his shoulder and shook his head. "No, really. I met him once. He's not a person I would forget."

"I confess I thought a great conqueror would be taller." Maggie said it in a low voice, but the conqueror's gaze flashed her way for an unreadable instant.

"For God's sake," said Marco, "you're damned well taller than everyone else in this party as it is, Maggie."

Diana could not help herself, *Tamburlaine* was so fresh in her mind. " 'His looks do menace heaven and dare the gods, His fiery eyes are fixed upon the earth, As if he has devised some stratagem.' '' She faltered, because he moved.

He walked forward with easy grace and halted in front of Soerensen. There was a pause. This close, Diana felt compelled to stare at him. He was not handsome, exactly, but rather one of those people who attracts the eye as much by force of will as by physical perfection. He was exceedingly well-proportioned and his features were precise, marked especially by a pair of dark, passionate, and impatient eyes. Of course he had a scar, a white line running diagonally from one high cheekbone almost to his chin, doubtlessly suffered in a battle, or a brawl, or perhaps in an assassination attempt. Diana realized that she was holding her breath and staring, and she let air out deliberately and breathed in again.

In Jeds, the natives bowed to Soerensen as one would to a prince. Bakhtiian inclined his head, as one equal greets another. "I am Bakhtiian," he said. In Rhuian, the language of Jeds.

Soerensen returned the nod and replied in the same language. "Charles Soerensen."

"I give you greetings."

"And blessings in return."

What their true feelings were, Diana could not guess through the mask of politeness they wore. Soerensen had always been an enigma to her, a rather pale man with sand-colored hair who showed humor readily and never gave the slightest inkling of how he felt at having been turned from a failed revolutionary leader into the only human duke in the massive and labyrinthine Chapalii Empire. Most people she could read, she could get a sense of, but Soerensen was a blank.

The two men studied each other, but what they made of that examination did not show on their faces.

At last Bakhtiian spoke. "I have arranged that we leave morning after next, for our camp some ten days ride inland. That will give your party a day to organize their goods on the wagons we've brought for the journey."

After a beat of silence, Soerensen said, "Where is my sister? I expected that she would be here to greet me." His face maintained its mask of politeness, but the air changed quality, as if charged by a net of electricity.

Bakhtiian's expression did not change, but everything

else about him did, the indefinable shift of his posture utterly transforming the message his body carried. He moved his left foot slightly. His left hand strayed to his saber hilt, and he brushed the tip of the golden hilt with his thumb. "She is at the camp," he said, in a tone that meant: *and* that *is that*.

Soerensen blinked, once. When he spoke, it was without inflection. "She told me, in a letter, that she would meet me at the port."

"She may well have," replied the conqueror of half a dozen kingdoms and principalities, "but she could not come." He removed his hand from his saber hilt and began to turn away, to lead the group up into town, since the matter was now obviously settled.

Soerensen did not move. "Why is that?" he asked, as easily as if he were commenting on the weather.

Half turned away, Bakhtiian froze, paused, and swung back. The force of his stare, antagonistic and unforthcoming, would have cowed any other man. He did not reply.

"Why could she not come?" repeated Soerensen.

For an instant, Bakhtiian looked taken aback that a living being questioned his authority. For an instant only. "Because she could not leave camp."

For the first time, a sudden, intense energy radiated off of Soerensen. Abruptly, Diana saw in him the man who had dared to challenge humanity's alien masters. He was powerful, and frightening. His jaw tightened; his lips thinned; he took in a breath.

The storm was about to hit. The charge of emotion washed over her like fire. She burned with it, fear and exhilaration together. Marco took a step back, putting a hand out to push Diana back behind him. Maggie gasped. Without thinking, Diana reached out to grasp Maggie's hand. Maggie glanced at her, pale skin flushed with alarm, and neither let go. The scarlet-shirted riders nearest the group stirred, and horses minced under tense hands.

Dr. Hierakis stepped forward into the breach. "I am sorry to hear that she is ill," she said with astonishing smoothness. "However, we had better be sure we have accommodations for the next two nights, since the rest of our party are coming in from the ship and will need to be directed as to where they can stow their baggage.''

Soerensen said nothing, but as quickly as it had shone forth, his light was buried again. Evidently he approved of the doctor's intervention. But Bakhtiian's response was more startling: she looked directly at him, as one does when addressing a person, and he immediately dropped his gaze away from hers and stepped back. ''Of course,'' he said obediently. ''I have arranged for two inns for your party. I hope they will be adequate.''

''I am sure they will be.'' She seemed taken aback by Bakhtiian's sudden deference.

Marco looked astounded. Maggie let go of Diana's hand and nervously straightened her tunic. Diana was not sure where she ought to look, like an actor with no lines, on stage but not given direction. She felt a wee bit disappointed.

''I am Doctor Hierakis, by the way,'' Hierakis added. ''And may I introduce Diana Brooke-Holt and Margaret O'Neill . . .'' With stunning aplomb, Bakhtiian gave a curt but gracious bow to each of the women in turn, like any accomplished courtier, managing to acknowledge them fully without looking either in the eye. ''This is Marco Burckhardt.''

But now Bakhtiian looked up, directly at Marco. A smile appeared and vanished on his lips so quickly that Diana was not sure she had actually seen it. ''We have met.''

Marco's smile was more ghostly than humorous. ''Indeed.'' He inclined his head. Bakhtiian swept their group with a comprehensive gaze, looked out past them at the ship, and with a terse command to his two attendants, he turned and began the long walk up the hill into town. Soerensen did not hesitate but followed, and by some unspoken communication the two men paced their speed so that within five steps they walked together, if not in harmony. Dr. Hierakis paused only long enough to check Marco, Diana, and Maggie in turn, and then she hurried after them—doubtless, Diana thought, to make sure no blood was spilled.

''Mary Mother of God,'' said Maggie as soon as the two men were out of earshot. The two men who had served as Bakhtiian's escorts waited patiently, hands light on their horses's reins. "Where did you meet him, Marco?"

"It's a long story. Tupping hell, I thought we were done for."

"He spoke perfect Rhuian." Diana glanced up at the two escorts, and when they flicked their gaze away from her, she knew that they were trying very hard not to stare at her. If in a cosmopolitan city like Jeds, where trade was commonplace to ports an ocean voyage away, the contrast between her pale and flawless complexion and Oriana's coal-black skin had been the cause of much comment, she could well imagine that this company of visitors would look doubly exotic to these northerners. "How did he learn to speak such perfect Rhuian? And that bow!"

"Very easily." Marco grinned. "He was educated at the university in Jeds."

"You're joking," said Maggie.

"No, actually, I'm not. But don't worry, Diana. From my previous experience—nothing extensive, I might add—I can make a shrewd guess that it's all surface gloss. He's as barbaric as you please underneath. At least, *I* wouldn't cross him."

"Coming from you, Marco," said Maggie tartly, "and having seen the scars you have, I do not find that one bit reassuring."

Marco shrugged, and he grinned up at the two waiting riders. Hesitantly, they grinned back at him.

Diana sighed with pleasure. Until this journey, her childhood dream of having a true adventure had seemed unattainable. Marco Burckhardt glanced back at her, and he winked. She folded her hands together, in front of herself, and smiled, feeling a delicious sense of antici-pation.

CHAPTER SEVEN

News traveled like the wind. For many reasons did the khaja fear the jaran armies, and for this reason as much as any. No matter how quickly khaja princes or khaja towns sent messages or made alliances or maneuvered troops to stem the jaran tide, more quickly still did the jaran respond. It was as if the wind itself was the ally of the nomads, a silent, swift messenger on whom the horsemen alone could rely.

At midday a jaran rider came galloping out of the north into sight of a town. The sod walls here had been too high to level; they had been breached at frequent intervals instead, and by the main gate a troop of some hundred horsemen rode drills in the flat space beyond the remains of the two wooden gate doors, which had been thrown down and partially burnt.

The harness of the messenger's horse shook with bells, and the sound, as well as the lance tipped with a gold pennant borne by the rider, alerted the garrison. Within moments, a second rider emerged from the tents of the garrison leading a saddled horse. The men met at the edge of the drilling ground.

"Vanya!"

The garrison soldier pulled up and helped the messenger swing his saddlebags onto the new mount. "Feodor Grekov! What brings you here?"

"Sibirin sent me. A message for Nadine Orzhekov."

"Oho! I'll wager I know what it concerns, and I wish you luck when you deliver it."

"What, she *is* here, then?"

"No, just left with her jahar for Basille. That's the khaja town where they're to collect the barbarian ambassador and bring him back to camp."

Feodor shook his head, fair hair stirring in a breeze that curled down from the heights. "Her jahar?"

"Orzhekov's jahar."

"That's not who I meant—"

"I know who you meant." Vanya grinned, an engaging smile made no less merry by the fact that his right eye was scarred shut by an old wound. "As I said, I wish you luck. She was in a foul mood."

"Nadine?"

"Oh, *Nadine*, is it, now? When did you leave off addressing her as *tsadra?*"

Feodor blushed.

Vanya laughed again. "Still that way with you? I won't tease you, then. Why don't you just mark her and be done?"

"Would you?"

"Gods, no! She's too good with that saber. No, Orzhekov has been full of mischief since she got here. She has the khaja Elders dancing this way and then that, with her clever words. It's not *her* who's in the foul mood." A red-shirted man appeared, on foot, at the gate, and hallooed toward them, waving. "You'd better go on," said Vanya, sobering. "You can catch them in two spans." The transfer completed, Vanya took the reins of the blown horse.

"Gods," said Feodor. His blush had faded. "Why did Sibirin send *me?*"

Vanya grinned again. "Oh, he knows Orzhekov has an eye for you, that's it. He thinks it will soften the blow."

"Gods," murmured Feodor.

Nadine Orzhekov called her jahar to a halt as soon as the scouts brought word that a messenger had been sighted following them. "Look," she said to Tess Soerensen as the rider came in, flanked on either side by scouts, "it's Feodor Grekov. He must have come all the way from the main camp. I wonder what he wants."

"You know damn well what he wants," said Tess irritably. "Sibirin sent him to take me back."

"You can't know that," protested Nadine, but her eyes lit with unholy glee. "You don't suppose Bakhtiian got back already?"

"I hope so." The surge of anger that coursed through

Tess at the mention of *his* name was so strong that it shocked her. Gods, where had it all come from?

"Tess. Tess." Nadine shook her head. "For shame." But her expression belied the words, and she chuckled. "Poor Feodor. He looks terrified."

Feodor's escorts peeled away from him and galloped off from the troop, leaving him to approach Nadine and Tess alone. The other riders, all men, watched surreptitiously but with piercing interest as Feodor drew his horse up beside the two women. Tess felt sorry for him because she knew Nadine would treat him badly. Nadine possessed her own stores of hidden anger.

"Well met, Grekov," said Nadine. "What brings you here?"

He kept his eyes lowered. "Sibirin sent me. With a message."

"Ah, a message," said Nadine wisely, drawing out the pause by fiddling with the closes on the leather pouch strung in front of her saddle. She reached inside, pulled out a rolled-up bundle of yellow parchment, examined it without opening it, and then replaced it.

Tess sighed heavily beside her and said, in Rhuian, "Oh, let the poor man out of his misery, Dina."

Feodor glanced up at her words, hearing their tone but not knowing their meaning, and looked away again as her gaze settled on him.

"You're losing your sense of humor, Tess," replied Nadine in Rhuian.

"Never that!"

Nadine grinned. She turned back to Feodor. "Well enough, Grekov," she said in *khush,* the language of the jaran. "I can guess what your message is. I suppose you're to return to camp with Tess?"

"Yes."

"Then you'll have to stay with us."

He was surprised enough to look straight at her, eyes widening. "But Sibirin said—"

"*Yetra,* Niko Sibirin does not order me."

"But Bakhtiian himself ordered—"

"Bakhtiian," said Tess viciously, before she knew she meant to say it, "can go to hell."

Feodor's expression of surprise glazed over, freezing an instant from pure shock, and then he shook it off and addressed Nadine again. As if, thought Tess wryly, what she had just said was beyond response. "Forgive me, tsadra. But Sibirin said that I was to bring your cousin—" He glanced from under lashes at Tess, who knew that her brown hair and green eyes did not resemble Nadine's black hair and eyes at all. "—back to camp before Bakhtiian returned from the coast. And not to return without her."

"I won't force her to go back now. She doesn't intend to go back until I do. There you are. Will you come with us, then?"

"I have no choice."

Nadine dismissed him with a shrug and signaled the troop to ride. Feodor turned his horse aside to fall in with the ranks as they started forward. Tess looked back to see the young man staring at Nadine. Everyone knew he was in love with her.

Were her own feelings so transparent? With one hand, she traced the curve of her mirror. It took no great skill to see that she had married into an impossible situation, that the confrontation that was bound to come was of her own making. Mostly she was angry at herself; sometimes she felt as if she was constantly holding up that mirror and staring at her own flaws, and she was getting a little tired of it.

"Brooding?" asked Nadine, mocking her, but Tess laughed in reply because she knew Nadine showed affection by being caustic.

And abruptly, the thought triggered in Tess an upwelling of the love, of the heart's warmth, she felt for her family—for Sonia and Katerina and Ivan and Kolia, for Niko and Juli, for Irena Orzhekov, for Nadine; for Aleksi, the brother she had adopted. And, God damn him to hell, for Ilya.

"I shouldn't have done it," said Tess when Nadine halted her jahar in sight of the township of Basille. "I shouldn't have come with you."

"Losing your nerve?"

Tess chuckled. "What do you think? But perhaps the dramatic gesture wasn't the wisest one."

"It will certainly get Ilya's attention, though."

"Damn it, it was just one last thing too many. Yaro-

slav Sakhalin himself picked me out. He told both Bakhalo and Zvertkov that he wanted me in his jahar. You
know what an honor that is! And then before I was ever
consulted, Ilya goes around behind my back and tells
Sakhalin that I'm to be left where I am: still in training.
Still in reserve. He never lets me out of camp except if
I'm with him or maybe, maybe, on a safe scouting expedition with Ilya's picked thousand and Aleksi at my
right hand.''

Nadine looked at Tess's scarlet shirt and black trousers, and then at her own, similar except in the stiff
leather shoulder pieces and the pattern of quilting and
embroidery running up the sleeves. ''It's true,'' she
mused, ''that Sakhalin is not the kind of dyan to pick
you out in order to curry favor with Ilya. He chose you
on your merits, nothing else.''

''Thank you.''

''Still angry? It *was* an honor.''

''An honor I'm never to receive the fruits of.''

''Do you want to fight in battle that much?''

Tess regarded her companion with a rueful smile. Behind Nadine's left ear, where her black hair pulled away
into a waist-long braid, began the scar that followed parallel to the line of the braid, all the way down. Nadine's
bronze helmet hung from her saddle and her lamellar
cuirass was tied on behind, although most of her men
wore cuirasses or scale girdles and belts. But then, Nadine preferred to keep her reputation for being reckless.

''No, not that much,'' Tess admitted. ''But you know
as well as I do that I can't just have the privileges of my
position. I have to accept the dangers as well.''

''Otherwise,'' said Nadine, slipping easily from khush
into Rhuian, ''you're just a player in a masquerade. All
show.''

''Yes, all show. I don't care to live that way. And I'm
not jaran. So I don't have to. Ilya keeps forgetting that.''

''You're wrong, Tess. He's never forgotten it. That's
why he wouldn't let you go to the coast with him.''

Tess went pale with anger, and her fingers clenched,
and unclenched, on her reins. Zhashi shied sideways,
and settled. ''The business with Sakhalin was inexcus-
able,'' she said in a voice made low by fury. ''But to

refuse me the journey to the coast to meet Charles—!''
She broke off.

Nadine watched for a few moments the interesting
spectacle of Tess Soerensen too angry to speak. Then she
lifted a hand to signal the jahar forward at a walk. Rather
than looking at Tess, Nadine examined the timbered palisade that surrounded Basille, noting its gaps and its open
gates and the sudden blur of activity at the gates when
the approach of two hundred horsemen was noted by its
guards.

''He's afraid,'' she said softly. Tess did not reply. Perhaps she had not heard her. Perhaps she did not—or could
not—understand what Nadine knew to be true. ''Off the
fields!'' she shouted at two idiot stragglers, and she led
them along a dirt track that wound in toward town.

Out in the fields, workers breaking the ground in preparation for the spring ploughing raised their caps to stare,
while others scattered back across the furrowed earth to
find safety in hovels and behind low carts. A string of
watchers appeared on what still remained of the palisade
of Basille.

Nadine regarded these signs pensively. ''Poor things.
They hadn't a chance, you know, when they brought out
their pitiful army against Veselov's ten thousand with my
jahar and Mirsky's jahar in reserve. After the first day
they saw it was useless and negotiated a surrender. They
would have done better to close their gates and try to
wait out a siege. We weren't very good at sieges that first
year.''

Tess chuckled. ''You spent one year too many in Jeds,
Dina. Are you sorry for them, now?''

Nadine shrugged. ''What the gods have brought them,
they will have to endure. Still, it's true enough. One year
too many in Jeds marks you, just like any good jaran
woman is marked for marriage.''

''Like you aren't.'' Tess touched the scar that ran diagonally from cheekbone to jaw on her left cheek.

Nadine smiled, unmarked. ''Gods, it's no wonder he
married you. He would never have married a jaran
woman, not after the years he spent in Jeds. Sonia and
Yuri—that's why they only spent a year there. They didn't
want to be changed. Or couldn't be.''

''Poor Yuri. It's probably just as well he died. He

would have hated this. Three years of war—one battle after the next. So much killing. He would have hated it.''

Nadine examined Tess reflectively—the hair and eyes no color ever seen in jaran-born; a good rider, for a khaja; and she could fight, it was true. Nadine recalled the cousin she had last seen years before, that gentle boy Yuri. It was true he had hated fighting—could do it, but hated it. Tess was good, probably better than Yuri had ever been, but she lacked the love of the art itself, she lacked the indifference to killing: and to be a truly good fighter one must have both of those traits in moderation, or one in excess. Good timing, and a fine eye for distance: those were Tess's skills.

Tess watched her, one lip quirked up in ironic salute. ''Judged and found wanting?''

''Your skills aren't at issue, Tess. Just remember, there are only five women I know of in Bakhtiian's army. Before you came, not one woman rode to battle. It's no dishonor to you to choose not to ride now.''

The set of Tess's mouth tightened. ''It's not such a simple choice for me. It never was.''

Nadine sighed. Poor Tess, always agonizing over what was the right thing to do. She changed the subject. ''Would Yurinya have hated it? I never knew him that well. We weren't of an age, and anyway, he was so quiet.''

''Unlike you.''

''Judged and found wanting?'' retorted Nadine. Tess grinned. ''The entire coast subject to his uncle's authority? Half the southern kingdoms that border the plains? We ride into a town now that gives us tribute so that we'll never again attack them. One more season of campaigning and we'll either all be dead or we'll see the other half recognize us as their kind protectors, and we'll seal alliances with the Vidiyan Great King and the Habakar king, and—gods, Tess, and then we'll be free to ride north and east along the Golden Road.''

''Yuri would have hated it,'' muttered Tess.

''Ilya is a fool,'' said Nadine. ''He believes what he says, that it's our duty to conquer them so that all jaran will be safe from the khaja forever. Gods, what nonsense.''

''Are you going to tell him?''

"Why bother? You're the only person I know of who has the slightest chance of changing his mind—even my mother couldn't have done it. We all know what happened to Vasil Veselov when he tried. But you could, Tess. Maybe. Are you going to try?"

Tess looked away. "How can I?" she asked in a low voice. "This is what makes him what he is."

Nadine had long ago made a pact with herself not to think too deeply about her uncle. She loved him; how could she not? She hated him, because it was his fault that her mother and little brother had died. And in between, tangling it all up, the harness of duty that constrained her, her duty to her family, and the memory of her mother—the most wonderful person in all the tribes—telling her that of all men, it is to your own brothers and your mother's brothers that you owe the deepest part of your affection.

"Good," she said, mocking herself more than Tess. "I wouldn't want you to change his mind about his wild sweep of conquest. Gods, I'd be bored if I didn't have this to do." And the specter of boredom, of having too much time to think, was the worst one of all. "Look. There's a party assembling at the main gate. The ambassador must have arrived before us. He'll have had time to worry." She lifted a hand to sign for the troop to spread out, leaving them room to maneuver. The horsemen shifted position with that absolute mastery of riding that each one had, having been practically bred and raised in the saddle. Feodor looked their way, and averted his gaze when he realized she had noticed him.

"He's in love with you, you know," said Tess suddenly.

"Our ambassador? He hasn't even met me, Tess. How can he be in love with me?"

"Feodor."

"Oh, him." She did not bother to look at him. "For a sweet, modest jaran man, he's a bit too obvious about it for my taste. And the gods know, after three years in Jeds I came to appreciate sweet, modest jaran men."

"Did you?"

Even the broken, pitiful walls of Basille reminded her enough of Jeds that she was stricken with a longing to return there—now, this instant. "Of course I did. I loved that city. I could easily have forsaken the plains for Jeds, except I'm too much jaran to live in a place where only one group of women can make advances to men—women who get paid to do so. Paid! It made me heartsick. They're barbarians, these khaja. I didn't want barbarians as my lovers. It's the only reason I came back.'' She meant the comment to be light; the force of it surprised even her. Tess, kind Tess, made no reply.

At the gates of Basille, a party had indeed gathered. As they neared, Nadine could distinguish between two styles of dress, and she saw that a certain, delicate distance separated two groups of people—a group of men dressed in plain, dull cloth, and a smaller group arrayed in golds and purples and jade greens made the more vivid by the muted garb of their neighbors.

"It appears," said Nadine in Rhuian, "that Basille's elders can scarcely wait to pass their visitors on to us." She lifted a hand and the jahar halted, a semicircle ringing the gate out of archer's range. She glanced at her riders and smiled. Solemn, austere, with an arrogance that frightened khaja everywhere. Why, jaran riders had such contempt for all khaja that they did not even bother to touch khaja women. Was that what khaja thought? She had often wondered, but never found the opportunity to ask.

"Grekov. Yermolov." Her voice carried clearly into the silence. "Will you attend?" And softer: "Tess?"

"Assuredly."

The four of them rode forward. The crowd at the gate watched, stilled either by fear or by anticipation.

"Lord," said Tess, "look there on the steps. Is that our ambassador? From the vast and fabled empire of Vidiya?"

Nadine shifted her gaze self-consciously from the blond head of Feodor Grekov, who had come up with Yermolov on her left, to the low stairway that led up to the night portal in an intact portion of the palisade. "Gods. He's young. And is that supposed to be his retinue—what, six besides himself? Only four hands of guardsmen? He can't be very important if that's the lot. Ilya won't be pleased if he thinks he's being snubbed."

They halted equidistant between the steps and the group of elderly men marked with the heavy chains and pentangles of the town's stewards. There was silence. Nadine waited.

A young man stood on the steps, utterly and obviously foreign by his purple and green striped overtunic and huge, belled trousers of cloth of gold, by the odd sculpting of his dark beard and mustache, and by the white turban that concealed his hair. He lifted one manicured hand. An older man, less flamboyantly dressed, stood one step lower; he coughed, preparing to speak. Both their gazes stopped briefly on the two women and flicked away again as quickly, dismissing them.

After a moment the older man addressed Feodor Grekov in rough, but serviceable, Rhuian. "I am Syrannus, bond servant to the Most Honorable Jiroannes Arthebathes, ambassador from His Imperial Majesty, Honor of the People, Great King of All Vidiya, may his name be sung for a thousand years. We place ourselves and the rest of our party in your hands, sir, as you are to be our escort to the court of the Bakhtiian."

Feodor looked at Nadine and shrugged. Nadine sighed and urged her mount two paces forward. "I am Nadine Orzhekov. I am the leader of the party that will escort the Most Honorable—" She let the syllables roll off her tongue. "—Jiroannes Arthebathes and his—ah—retinue to the camp of Bakhtiian."

"But—" sputtered Syrannus. For an instant he looked like a man trapped by starving wild animals. Basille's elders whispered among themselves.

"*You* lead my escort?" said the ambassador suddenly, curt and doubting. "A woman? Perhaps one of these men will verify this outrageous assertion." He waved toward Grekov and Yermolov.

"Since they don't speak Rhuian, they can't." Nadine grinned, enjoying his indignation.

"*You* are the only one in your party who speaks Rhuian?" demanded the ambassador. "That is absurd."

"Not the only one," conceded Nadine. "This woman, Terese Soerensen, speaks not only Rhuian but Taor and, I believe, a few words of Vidyan as well."

At this unfortunate juncture, especially given the appalled looks on the faces of Jiroannes Arthebathes and his servant Syrannus, Tess started to laugh.

CHAPTER EIGHT

"David," said Marco, "you *will* come sit through this banquet with me. I refuse to endure hours of rancid food and city elders sucking up to Charles and Bakhtiian all by myself."

"Maggie is going," said David.

"Maggie," said Maggie tartly, "is serving an official function. I'm going to be the wine pourer for His Nibs and Attila the Hun."

David groaned. "Are you for me or against me? You're no help."

But there was nothing for it. He could see by the look on Marco's face, and by the light in Maggie's eyes as she laughed silently at him, that he was doomed to sit through the state dinner and audience that the barons and elders of the town of Abala Port were holding for the man who had conquered them, Ilyakoria Bakhtiian, and the prince who was his chosen guest.

"As long as I don't have to act as food taster," he muttered, "although with that army in this town, I don't think I'd try to poison anyone."

"You wouldn't try to poison anyone anyway," said Maggie. She rummaged through her carry bag and drew out a clean tunic and the only skirt she possessed. She went on talking as she changed, letting her old clothes drop into a heap on the slatted floor of their tiny inn room. "Owen Zerentous has asked permission to hold an impromptu performance at the end of the banquet, or after the formal audience. Evidently the city elders have some cases they need tried, some people accused of crimes, that they're going to bring before Bakhtiian."

"Trial by personal whim?" asked Marco.

"You said yourself he was educated at the university in Jeds," retorted Maggie. "He must have some concept

of justice. Damn it! Where'd that brassiere go?'' She upended the contents of her bag onto her cot. David, from
his cot, hooked a dark toe through the brassiere strap
and hoisted the garment up into the air. ''Where'd you
find that?'' she demanded.

''On the floor, where most of your clothes eventually
come to rest.''

She snatched it from him with a mock growl and put
it on, then a linen shirt, and then her tunic and skirt. The
room was crowded in part because it was small, but
mostly because neither Maggie nor David could bring
themselves to sleep on the straw-filled mattress that
served as the room's bed. They had set up their traveling
cots instead, one on each side; a tiny aisle led to the
door, where Marco stood with his arms folded, surveying
the mess.

''Shall we go? It can't smell any worse there than it
does here.''

''Just because we're over the stables,'' said Maggie
with a laugh. ''And where are *you* sleeping, may I ask?''

''You may not.''

''Marco! You're frightening me.''

That teased the shadow of a grin from him. David
sighed and rose, pulling his sketchpad out of his carry
bag. He brushed two flealike bugs off his sleeve and five
earwigs off the sketchpad, and ran his other hand along
the ends of his hair and through his name braids. ''I'm
just sure they're crawling all over me. It *can't* be worse
in the town hall.''

But it was. It was rank. Marco didn't seem to notice
that it was only a thin layer of fresh rushes that covered
the floor; that underneath lay a mat of ancient straw and
other, happily nameless substances, which had created a
kind of fetid loam. It squished. Incense burned in racks
along the walls, set up between the windows, and lanterns were set at intervals along the tables. Rank and
cloying at the same time. Quite a feat, David thought, to
produce two such opposite effects in one chamber.

Charles walked in front of them, together with Bakhtiian. David hung back with Marco, who waited in his
turn for the actors. But in the end, the actors sat at a side
table and David and Marco ended up on the dais, at the
very end of the long beamed table—which was actually

three tables shoved together—which seated the guests of honor. The actors were in fine form, being boisterous in an engaging fashion, and the city elders were disgustingly obsequious.

"Have you noticed," said Marco in a whisper, "how Bakhtiian has picked out two boys, there, to eat with him, to share the food from his plate? Honoring them, because they're both sons of important men in town. But it also ensures that no one attempts to poison him."

David hadn't noticed. There was a clump of something stuck to the bottom of his shoe, and he was trying to scrape it off. The food thrust in front of him looked unappetizing in the extreme, except for the bread. He didn't trust the water, and the wine had a vinegary-flavor. If this was the best Abala Port could do, then it must not be a very wealthy town.

"I think this is real gold leaf on this plate," said Marco, poking at it with his knife. A laugh burst up from the actors' table, and Marco looked up at once, caught Diana's eye, and smiled winningly at her.

"How has Tess managed to endure these conditions for four years?" David demanded of his plate. "This is appalling."

"Maybe she's as much of a slob as Maggie and you are. Maybe she doesn't care."

"She *isn't* a slob. Or at least, she wasn't."

"What? As an eleven-year-old in Jeds? But wait." Marco eased his attention back from Diana and propped his chin on one hand to regard David with interest. "You weren't in Jeds then. How could you know? Oho!"

David cursed under his breath. Trust Marco to know him well enough to read him.

"You're blushing under that attractive black complexion of yours, David my boy," said Marco in his most annoyingly superior manner. "Out with it."

"Damn it. Listen. If you breathe a word of this to Charles, I'll have your head. And then where will you be with handsome young actresses?" He leaned forward and peered down the table toward Charles, but Charles was deep in conversation with an old man in a pale blue gown trimmed with silver fur who wore a ring on each finger and a heavy bronze medallion on the end of a gold necklace. Charles's own finery paled in comparison—his signet ring and the chain of office draped down over a painted silk tunic—and the barbarian king looked positively spartan, dressed without any ornamentation at all except the embroidery that ran down the sleeves of his simple red shirt. He wore his curved sword; no one else in the room bore a weapon except his own personal guards: ten at the door and two standing behind him on the dais.

"Do you remember when I taught that seminar at the university in Prague?"

"Oh, yes." Marco's eyes narrowed. "Tess was attending the university at Prague then, wasn't she? In fact, I rather have it in mind that Charles encouraged you to take the position so that you could keep an eye on her."

David found he could not speak the words, especially since it was the one secret he had ever kept from Charles and Marco.

"You had an affair with her!"

"Marco! Hush. And in any case, I wouldn't call it an *affair*. We grew fond of each other. True, we shared a bed, but we shared a friendship, too."

"What was she like? I confess I haven't seen her since the year she left for university."

David smiled. In his heart, he felt her presence as an honest and pleasing warmth. She was a good person, an amiable companion, and a fine intellect, though she suffered from insecurity; as well she might, since she was Charles Soerensen's little sister and heir, whether she liked it or not. "She was chubby."

Marco choked on a hunk of bread. "How unromantic of you! Chubby!"

"Well, it's true. She was."

"And then?"

"My seminar ended, and I left. Later I heard she got engaged to another student, but evidently it didn't work out, which I've often suspected is why she left for Rhui so suddenly." And perhaps even why she had stayed there; Tess was insecure enough that David also suspected she might nurse a wound like that for years, especially to hide it from Charles.

"David, you see me at a loss for words. You see me rendered speechless. I am astounded. Amazed."

"Oh, shut up."

Marco laughed and picked at his meat with his knife, trying in vain to find a strip that wasn't spiced to death. Liveried men lit torches and placed them in racks alongside the incense burners, adding a fine, stinging smoke to the brew. Charles laughed at something Bakhtiian said—although David could not imagine a man who looked as hard and dangerous and uncivilized as Bakhtiian did having a sense of humor—and, like a nervous echo, the city elders laughed as well. Maggie, looking serene, poured more wine for the two men. Cara, sitting down at the other end of the table with Jo and Rajiv, stifled a yawn under one hand.

"And just think," said David, "these conditions must be advanced compared to the way the nomads must live. Poor Tess. Whatever do you suppose possessed her to stay there? Sheer intellectual curiosity? Is the fieldwork too good to let go?"

Marco put down his knife. "Oh," he said, as if God itself had just granted him a revelation. "David. . . ."

"And don't you dare tell Charles!"

Marco blanched. "But, David—"

"Give me your word!"

Marco laughed abruptly, an odd note in his voice. "Hell. I swear it. It lends one a warm feeling to think about these youthful indiscretions, doesn't it?"

Marco was definitely acting strangely all of a sudden. "You talk about it like it was in the past, and meant to stay that way."

"It always is, David. In the words of the immortal Satchel Paige, 'Don't never look back. Something might be gaining on you.' "

"Marco, did you eat something that affected your brain? No doubt there are molds aplenty in this food. Or is that lovely young actress just addling it?"

"I'm just saying that Tess may have changed, and you should . . . go slowly when you see her again. And not expect too much."

"Hah! Odd sort of advice, coming from you. You sound positively auntly, Marco."

There was a sudden commotion at the far end of the hall. A woman screamed. A jaran soldier stumbled against a chair, tripping backward over it, and sprawled onto the floor. Like a wave rushing in, five men, swords drawn, plunged forward up the central aisle toward the dais. Marco jumped to his feet. David gaped.

For an instant, nothing and no one moved except for the five armed men, who ran toward the head table with death in their eyes and a sudden scrambling of guards at their backs.

Bakhtiian was on his feet before David realized he had moved. He grabbed the table and heaved it up and forward, and it crashed over onto its side. Plates and glasses and half-eaten food and the dregs of wine spilled onto the steps and clattered onto the floor. His saber was already in his hand in the span of time it took Charles to blink.

David sat there stunned with his food in front of him while an attack was waged not six paces away. Marco knocked over his own chair in his haste to get to Charles. Men shrieked.

"Aleksi!" shouted Bakhtiian as the first of the assassins leapt up the steps. A dark young man in a red shirt jumped over the upended table and cut down the first man so quickly that David did not even see the blow. Jaran soldiers closed in from the other end of the hall. A guard flung himself past David from behind and engaged the nearest assassin. The young man called Aleksi twisted his saber around another man's sword, sending it flying, and with a cut that seemed born of the first one disarmed a second man by disabling his arms with wicked-looking slices. One man left—

And then Aleksi suddenly sprang around and flung a cut back at Bakhtiian, who ducked away from it while at the same time shoving over Charles's chair. Charles landed in a heap, Bakhtiian in a crouch, and Marco tackled from behind the old baron who had sat beside Charles this whole time. From whose robes had appeared an ugly looking short sword, which Aleksi had knocked away.

David had not yet moved from his chair. All of the actors except Owen and the leading man, Gwyn Jones, were cowering under their table. Diana stood beside Jones. She gripped the edge of her chair, staring with bright eyes at Marco, who was sitting on top of the old baron, looking furious.

Now, two assassins were left. The one nearest David had been driven back into a circle whose boundaries were

delineated in red: the scarlet shirts of the jaran guard.
One lay quivering in a heap; one lay prostrate; one
sobbed, clutching his bleeding arms against his chest.
The two remaining clutched hard at their deadly-looking
long swords.

Bakhtiian rose. "Aleksi, take them," he ordered with
astounding calm.

Aleksi nodded without expression and stepped forward, and the others made way for him. The elders and
other barons on the dais clumped into a frightened group.
Cara had already run down to Charles, and she helped
him to his feet. Marco stayed sitting on the old baron.

And the most horrifying thing of all was that it was
beautiful to watch. Barbarian he might be, but he was an
artist with the sword. Two of them, against one of him,
with such different weapons, but there was no doubt what
the outcome would be. The knowledge made the two assassins desperate. Aleksi looked as cool as a man out for
an evening stroll. One of his comrades shouted something in a joking voice, and Aleksi actually cut down one
man with a swift slice along his face and chest, paused
beside his comrade long enough to grab a saber in his
other hand, and turned back to face the last man.

"And you realize, of course," said Ursula el Kawakami, appearing in all her unwonted splendor beside David, "that he's already at a distinct disadvantage, using
that saber on foot against long swords. That's a cavalry
weapon. Amazing."

Aleksi used one of the sabers to distract the poor man
and neatly hamstrung him with the other. The man
screamed out in pain and collapsed to the floor. There
was a moment's pause. The assassins were all disarmed.

Then everyone in the hall turned to look at Bakhtiian.
He sheathed his saber, and the scraping sound it made
in the hush sent an atavistic shiver down David's back.
At once, the barons and elders of Abala Port flung themselves on the floor in an obscene frenzy of groveling.

But Bakhtiian ignored the nobles of Abala Port. He
delivered a stinging rebuke to his guards, in his own language. They did not grovel. They looked ashamed.

At the door, a pack of jaran soldiers appeared, and
they quickly entered the room under the command of an
expressive young man and moved out to take control of

the hall, to drag the prisoners aside, to move the heavy
tables off the dais, to thoroughly search every man in the
room save those of Charles's party.

And when that was all accomplished, Bakhtiian said
something more. One by one the original guards came
forward, all but the two who had stood on the dais, and
each man laid his saber at Bakhtiian's feet, disarming
himself. The intensity of their shame was painful to
watch.

"Goddess Above," whispered David, "must it be
done so publicly?" Had he remembered that Ursula was
standing there, he would not have said it aloud.

"Of course it must be done publicly. It's a lesson for
everyone." The dishonored guards filed from the hall.
"What do you think he'll do to the prisoners?" She
sounded breathlessly excited. Aroused, even, David
thought with a shudder. "And to those terrified towns-
men?"

Marco slipped back beside them, no longer needed at
the front. "Now we're about to see what justice means
to the conquered," he whispered. They waited. Bakhtiian waited. The silence stretched out until it was a vis-
ceral thing, agonizing to endure.

One of the townspeople finally found enough courage
to rise to his knees. "Please believe," he stammered,
"that we knew nothing of this."

Bakhtiian glanced at him as if at an afterthought. "I
assume, Baron," he said in a cold voice, "that you have
laws by which you judge such cases here."

"Of course! Of course!" Their fear was almost as humiliating to see as their desperate attempt at appease-
ment. "The punishment for treason is death."

"Then by your own laws shall they be judged." He
lifted his chin, and the prisoners were led away.

"The sentence shall be carried out at once," said the
baron, and he snapped an order to a younger man, who
hurried out of the hall on the heels of the prisoners. A
richly-dressed old woman wept noisily in the corner.

Bakhtiian found his chair and sat down in it. He looked
at Charles. Charles raised one eyebrow and sat down
next to him. Cara remained standing behind Charles, but
she did not touch him, although David could tell she

wanted to. Her hand hovered over his shoulder, veered toward his sleeve, and settled, twitching, at her waist.

"Sit!" said Bakhtiian impatiently to the barons and elders. "You said you had other cases you wished to bring before me."

David realized that his rump hurt, from sitting so still, from being so tensed up. Maggie crept over to them and Marco put an arm around her. She was so white that her freckles stood out like blazons. The actors had crept out from under their table and they stood in a tableau, clutching one another. Not one eye left Bakhtiian for more than a second, except perhaps for Charles, who looked thoughtful and not at all cowed. None of them dared move as, one by one, prisoners were led in, their crimes recited aloud, and Bakhtiian begged to judge and sentence each one.

But in every case he deferred to the elders of the town, to their own laws, and placed the judgment squarely back on them according to their own customs. Despite himself, David was impressed by Bakhtiian's restraint. Especially since some of their own people had just tried to murder him.

Last of all an unremarkable young man was brought forward. He had a big nose, rheumy eyes, and he looked young and frightened. The baron sighed and relaxed, as if he knew the worst was over.

"This young man is accused by Merchant Flayne of raping his daughter, and although the usual punishment is that he must marry the girl, he's but an apprentice in a neighboring shop, and she *was* out walking at night by herself, and there is another merchant who has agreed to marry her despite—" He broke off because Bakhtiian stood up.

Stood up and took the three steps down to the accused with deliberate slowness. Glass rasped under his boots. Faced with Bakhtiian's devastating stare, the accused dropped to his knees, clasped his hands together, and began to plead in the local dialect.

"And is it true?" asked Bakhtiian in a voice so soft that David could barely hear him. "Did he force her?"

"He has confessed to the deed. It's the sentence that concerns us—"

Bakhtiian drew his saber and killed the young man.

Cut him through the throat so quickly that it was done before anyone realized he meant to do it.

Charles stood up, right up out of his chair. Bakhtiian stared at the corpse and took a step up to avoid the pool of blood growing, flooding broken bits of glass and plate on the floor. He flicked a glance back at the dais. Slowly, slowly, Charles sat down. One of the actresses gave a great shriek and fainted. Bile swelled in David's throat, and he clapped a hand to his mouth and fought against it, gulping, feeling it poison his tongue and burn his lips.

"David," whispered Marco, and David felt Marco's hand press into his back. "Breathe slowly. Breathe slowly."

Bakhtiian turned to regard the baron. "Is there anyone else?"

The baron could not speak for a long while. He held one hand to his breast, and his eyes bugged out, staring. "None, lord," he stuttered. "No more." No more to be judged, did he mean? Or was it a plea for no more of this harsh and merciless justice? That was no justice at all, no law, but only the tyrant's whim.

Bakhtiian turned to look at Charles. "Will you accompany me?" he asked, and David could not tell if it was a request or an order.

"I'd better wait for my own people, who are a trifle discomposed," said Charles. How could he remain so self-possessed? The calm mask he wore for an expression only added to David's dismay.

"He's cool," muttered Maggie.

"Oh, come now, what did you expect?" hissed Ursula with disgust. "Frankly, I think it was a just execution."

Bakhtiian inclined his head, to acknowledge Charles's decision. "Then if you will excuse me," he said, distinctly to Charles, not to anyone else. He swept from the hall, his guards behind him. The young man named Aleksi lingered behind, and David saw him slip a folded piece of parchment into Charles's hands. Then he, too, was gone, and they were left with the weeping actors, the shell-shocked townsfolk, and the dead man.

CHAPTER NINE

They huddled together in the common room of the inn they shared. None of them wanted to be there, but neither did they want to go up to their filthy rooms. Owen stared at the fire, and Diana just knew that he was playing the awful scene back through his mind, gleaning ideas from it that he would eventually turn around and use in the theater.

"Cold-blooded bastard," muttered Hal beside her. "Mom's no damn better. Look at her." Ginny sat next to Owen. For the journey, she had given up her slatepad and taken up a real paper notebook, but the result was the same: she jotted down notes and revised scenes in every spare second given to her.

Anahita lay prostrate on a bench, moaning softly. Hyacinth fanned her, and Phillippe massaged her feet. Seshat and Dejhuti sat off by themselves, and Helen and Jean-Pierre argued about how best to take the wine stain out of his white linen tunic. Joseph sat with one arm around Oriana and the other around Quinn, talking quietly to them. Yomi just watched over them all.

"What do you think, Gwyn?" Hal asked Gwyn Jones.

Gwyn appeared to ponder the question, but Diana could see right away that he didn't care what Hal thought of the cavalier reaction of his parents to that horrible scene. "I think I've never seen someone handle a sword that well," he said softly. "That young man is an artist."

Hal rolled his eyes in disgust, heaved himself to his feet, and went over to sit beside Quinn.

"I think he expected sympathy," said Diana.

Gwyn shrugged. "Di, I can't change what happened. Why dwell on it?"

"What do you mean, that he's an artist? Who?"

"The young man who did most of the fighting. He was brilliant."

"How would you know? Or do you mean to say those weren't simulated, all those fight scenes from the samurai interactives you did?"

Gwyn smiled, but not too much, since laughter would have been out of place. "Not simulated at all. I got into those vids because I was a martial artist. I only got interested in acting afterward. And lo, came here."

"Are you sorry? After tonight?"

"No. Are you?"

She almost chuckled, had to stifle it. "That I'm an actor? Never. Coming here with Owen and Ginny?" She surveyed the common room: the slatted wood floors were warped from age and dampness, the smell of the stables permeated everything, and the food was pretty bad. "But look how respectfully he treated Charles Soerenson. I can't think *we're* in any danger. Not really."

"Just the rest of this world, evidently," murmured Gwyn.

"Yes," Diana mused. She stood up. "I'm going outside."

He put a hand on her sleeve. "Diana, I'm not sure I'd do that. This isn't Earth, you know. Don't forget the testimony of the baron—I don't think it's safe for people to walk around by themselves at night."

But then the door opened, and Marco came in. He looked flushed from the night air. He found her immediately with his gaze. Ten meters between them, but it might as well have been one. She could feel him as if he already had his arms around her, as if they were already alone. The rush of feeling washed over her like a swoon.

Marco laid a hand on the door latch, opened it, and went back outside. She took a step toward the door.

"Have a pleasant night," said Gwyn.

She blushed, but she didn't look back. Her hand trembled as she lifted the latch, but she knew now that the die was cast. She slipped outside, and he was waiting for her. She stood there, in the cold night air, not one meter from him, but she did not move closer, because the anticipation was sweet enough to savor.

"Diana," he said, his voice low and a little rough.

And she had the satisfaction of seeing that he shook, too; that he wanted her as much as she wanted him.

"Marco!" The voice shattered the finespun web of intimacy. It was like being slammed into a brick wall.

"Marco! Damn it!" Maggie jogged up to them. "Back to Charles, you idiot."

"Maggie, I'll thank you to stay out of my—"

"Your what? Your affairs?" Maggie looked so angry that Diana thought she might burst. "After what just happened that you can even think about—"

"Maggie, I didn't ask your opinion—"

"That's not what I meant." The narrow streets of Abala Port were empty but for two jaran horsemen riding patrol far down this street, menacing black shapes against the ramshackle angles of the buildings. "I meant that any person who thinks with their brain instead of their genitals would realize that this is not the time to—well, how can we know what the customs are among the jaran? Do you intend to take that chance? And anyway, Charles wants you back right now."

"Marco!" That was David's voice, from down the street.

"Hell," said Marco under his breath. He cast an anguished glance at Diana. "You have my profoundest apologies, golden fair," he said, and then he left, hurrying away down the street toward the inn where Soerensen and his group were staying. He passed David without pausing to speak to him.

David stopped beside Maggie and Diana. "What was that all about?" Then he looked at Diana. Then he looked at Maggie. Diana wanted nothing more at that moment than to shrink into the ground and die. "Never mind," said David. "Listen, Mags, not Rajiv. Please. He gets up at dawn every morning. He'll say, 'But, David, should you not be putting your tools into better order?' "

"I always knew you only tented with me because I'm a slob," retorted Maggie, but there was so much anger still hanging on her that she sounded irritated, not amused. "I'm sorry, Diana. I really am. I really, really am."

"It's all right," said Diana in a small voice. Maybe the ground would open up and swallow her.

"We can't know *what* they consider a crime so serious

that it warrants summary execution. So you see why I had to send Marco away?''

"I see why," Diana choked out. And she did, truly. They could not afford to offend their hosts, not now; probably, given the look on Bakhtiian's face as he killed that man, not ever. But every part of her that had been set spinning by Marco's entrance, by the promise of what was to come next, ached for release.

"Shall we go in?" asked Maggie, sounding impatient, or maybe she was just feeling embarrassed for Diana.

"I'd better go back to Charles," said David. "Just don't put me in with Rajiv." He ran back into the night.

"Christ!" said Maggie with disgust. "Shall we get this over with?" She led the way. The heat of the fire blasted them as they came back into the common room. Gwyn, seeing Diana, raised his eyebrows but did not comment.

"Owen, Ginny. The rest of you. Please, may I have your attention?" Maggie did not have the natural authority of, say, Suzanne Elia Arevalo, but her agitation lent her a snappish air, and, in any case, everyone in the company was desperate for some sort of distraction. They quieted and regarded her with the kind of attention that only actors—trained to listen—and lovers usually grant a speaker. "Charles Soerensen just sent me down here with a new decree. No more mixed rooming, unless you possess a legal marriage certificate. Girls with the girls. Boys with the boys. That sort of thing. I've been sent to reassign places."

"Well, I don't mind boys with the boys," said Hyacinth.

"Oh, be quiet," snapped Quinn.

"I can't believe it!" Hal threw a look at his parents that he would have done better to save for a farce. "Have we retreated to the Dark Ages? Are a man and a woman rooming together automatically having sexual relations as well? Will adulterers be stoned?"

"You may as well save your sarcasm for later, Henry," said Ginny mildly. Then a thought occurred to her, and she scribbled something down on her notepad.

"Well, obviously Ginny and I can continue to share a tent," said Owen, "as well as Yomi and Joseph, and Seshat and Dejhuti. No one would contest that, I think."

"I'm *not* going to share a tent with Helen just because we were married once," said Jean-Pierre.

Anahita let Hyacinth raise her up. She swept her beautiful black hair away from her face and back over her shoulder and gave a great sigh. "It's true," she said breathlessly, "that Gwyn and I aren't married, but we share a spiritual bond. Surely that should be enough."

"I'll tent with Jean-Pierre," said Gwyn.

"I don't want Hal," said Hyacinth.

"Thank the Goddess," muttered Hal. "This is so stupid. Di and I have been rooming together forever."

"Gwyn! How can you say such a thing?" Anahita sagged back into Hyacinth's arms. She even managed to wipe a tear from her eye. "How can you reject me at a time like this?"

"I *told* you it was a mistake to come here," Helen said to Jean-Pierre. "Savages!"

"No more than you, my darling," replied Jean-Pierre with a sneer, which sent Helen into a full flood of scathing retort. Oriana flinched, jumped up, and went over to the counter to get something to drink.

"Please," said Yomi, in her best Stage Manager voice, "I know we're all upset, and with good reason, but we must help this run smoothly." For once it didn't work. Arguments broke out all over.

Diana sat down, closed her eyes, and let the squabbling surge around her. The draft from the fireplace did not work efficiently, so smoke parched the air. Her throat was sore. But at least it all served to bring her back to earth. And they needed to squabble right now, to let off steam. After awhile Quinn sat down beside her and whispered into her ear.

"It's you and me, sweetheart. Ori and I tossed up, and she lost. She has to go room with that strange woman in Soerensen's party who's the military historian. Ursula, that's it. And Hal is going off with Rajiv Caer Linn. He's some kind of computer modeling expert, I guess. Rebel Hal is thrilled he doesn't have to room with the actors, and Maggie thought it was funny because it left David ben Unbutu as the only person without a tentmate. And Hyacinth—"

"Oh, Quinn," said Diana, opening her eyes. "I don't really care who Hyacinth rooms with. Do you?"

Quinn laughed. It was the first honest laugh Diana had heard for hours, and it heartened her immensely. "Do you think it was a mistake to come here?" Quinn asked, serious again.

"Not one bit," said Diana. "That doesn't mean I'm not a little scared, but don't you think we can learn more here than we ever would playing for the same safe crowds on Earth?"

Quinn shuddered. "I don't know. *Safe* sounds very attractive to me right now."

Diana shook her head stubbornly. "Not to me."

CHAPTER TEN

"Most honored uncle," said Jiroannes Arthebathes into the clear chill of the night. He waited, after those three words, for the pen of his personal secretary, Syrannus, to complete the required list of titles and honorifics with which a nephew was obliged to address a noble and powerful uncle in the Great King's court.

After some minutes, during which the careful scritching of his pen blended with the low popping of the fire, Syrannus paused and lifted his eyes. At his right hand burned a lantern, casting light over the parchment laid on a board across his knees. The thin veins of his lined hands showed constricted and blue in the muted illumination. The lettering those elderly hands had produced was sinuously beautiful.

Jiroannes cast it a cursory glance, expecting nothing less. "Now some opening pleasantries, a synopsis of the journey since Eberge, with perhaps an anecdote or two—but leave off at the difficult part."

As Syrannus began to write again, Jiroannes lifted one hand. His concubine padded forward and gave him a cup of bitter, hot tea before kneeling in silence behind his chair. When Syrannus at length finished, the younger man read the words and nodded. "Very well. Now." He sighed, twisting the ends of his mustache between thumb and forefinger. "How can I introduce this subject without offending him? 'I was shocked—' No. What impossible barbarians these jaran are. I suppose all their women go about unveiled and in men's clothing."

"Surely not, eminence," interposed Syrannus. "Do not forget that Her Most Benevolent Highness, the Princess Eriania, is allowed by Her Most Gracious Brother privileges which all other women would never desire. Perhaps these females also have an exalted position of some kind. Their boldness is indeed shameful and certainly humiliating for them, but they are discreet.''

"Discreet? Not a word I would have chosen. If you mean they don't display themselves like the whores one sees at ports—that may be true, but this woman, Nadine Orzhekov, shows such a complete lack of true womanly modesty, of that humility which is proper in a female, that she disgusts me far more than any prostitute. Samae. More tea.'' The concubine rose and took the cup away. "But perhaps we misinterpret Bakhtiian's motives. Perhaps he meant these two women to be an offering to me. Certainly the Orzhekov woman is not at all to my taste, but the other one—I have seen her gaze on me once or twice. Should I take that as an invitation? It would be a pleasant diversion from Samae, and she is certainly attractive—''

"Your eminence,'' hissed Syrannus, warning.

A figure appeared at the edge of the tent. At Syrannus's nod it moved forward into the light and resolved into a dark-haired young woman. "Your eminence,'' she said, but the tone mocked him.

Jiroannes eyed her with vast dislike. He had quickly ceased trying to spare her womanly virtue by not looking at her directly, since he was sure she had none. "To what do I owe the honor of this late visit?'' he asked, neither rising nor honoring her with a title.

Nadine Orzhekov gave the barest of smiles, and he had the satisfaction of knowing that the slight was not lost on her. "As commander of your escort, I feel it my duty to warn you—no, to *inform* you about some jaran customs that may seem strange to you.''

"Indeed. Has some special occasion brought on this generosity?''

"Indeed,'' echoed Nadine. "I understand, your eminence, that you come from a society very different from ours. I even know a little about it, having read of Vidiya at the university in Jeds. Because of that knowledge, I have endured your rudeness to me, but if you persist in expecting the women of the jaran to act as Vidiyan women do, and in scorning them because they do not, I can assure you that Bakhtiian will have nothing to do with you or your mission. You had better learn to be polite, since I doubt you'll ever learn proper deference. Otherwise you will be sent home a failure.'' She paused. Behind her, hidden by darkness, a musician played a melancholy tune on a high-pitched pipe.

Jiroannes, lips tight, said nothing. Syrannus looked shocked.

"I will venture a more personal observation," added Nadine, noting her speechless audience with what Jiroannes knew was malicious satisfaction, "because I'm not the only one to have noticed it. If I were you, I would not watch Terese Soerensen as if I were measuring her to see if she would fit in my bed."

It was too much to bear, such insolence. "Certainly I may look at whom I please!"

"In fact," she went on, ignoring his words as if they were a child's outburst, "you would be well served to moderate the way you look at jaran women in general. It isn't *becoming* in a man to stare." Then, having said it, she had the effrontery to grin.

"Are you quite finished?" he demanded.

She shrugged. "We have tribute to collect, so we must return to the main camp roundabout. We'll be some days before we arrive there." She hesitated as the concubine came back to the edge of the circle of light furnished by Syrannus's lantern. Her dark eyes met Samae's almond-shaped ones for the barest instant, and then Samae placed the cup into Jiroannes's waiting hand and retreated to kneel behind his chair.

Nadine's mouth had pulled tight, and Jiroannes was gratified to see that she felt compelled for whatever reason to suppress her anger. He hoped the act caused her pain. "I thought," she said, her anger betrayed by the hoarseness of her voice, "that a message was sent that you only bring men."

Jiroannes dismissed Samae's presence with an airy wave of his free hand. "She is dressed as a boy. Surely that will suffice."

"Only a fool would take her for a boy."

Now he stood. "And for what reason am I expected to answer to you?" *A mere woman!* "In any case, she is nothing. Only a slave, if you know what that is."

Her voice dropped, softening with an emotion he did not recognize. "I know what a slave is. Send her back to your lands, eminence. I will provide an escort for her."

"No." It came out petulant, but he was furious by now. "I will not."

For a moment she stared, most brazenly and contemptuously, at him. Then she turned on her heel and left, without a word or a sign or the merest polite valediction. His hands shook. He touched the tea to his lips, coughed, and threw it down so that the hot liquid spattered the rug.

"Fresh-brewed tea, girl! I do not expect this swill!" The concubine started up and, retrieving the cup, hurried away. "Syrannus. I am too tired to compose. Write what you see fit. I cannot possibly explain this to my uncle. He would never believe me. Samae!" She appeared out of the small tent pitched next to his. "Attend me." He stormed over to his tent, paused, watching her. She inclined her head, acquiescing, and lifted the veil that draped down over her shoulder up and across her face, concealing all but her coal-black eyes.

Satisfied, he went into the tent. She followed him, but at the tent flap she hesitated and looked back, out into the darkness of the jaran camp, her eyes glittering in the lantern light, her expression hidden by the veil. Syrannus had begun to write, the precise flow of his hand right to left, left to right, across the white page, filling it in with his supple calligraphy. The flap sighed down behind her as she went in. Syrannus wrote on, blowing on his hands now and again to warm them. Out in the darkness, by a far campfire, a man sang, a wistful melody that wound itself round the chill air and somehow seemed to soften it.

CHAPTER ELEVEN

The first two days, heading away from the port with their escort, Diana endured the jolting of the wagons and watched, with careful interest, the landscape and the jaran riders. On the afternoon of the third day, when they halted for the night, she left Quinn to set up their tent and ventured out to patrol the outskirts of the ring of tents that marked out Soerensen's party.

Soon enough she came across a strange and remarkable sight. The great lord of the plains, conqueror of one kingdom, three princedoms, and uncounted lesser territories, sat in front of his small tent and embroidered a pattern onto the sleeve of a red shirt. At a tent pitched across from him, equally intent, sat another man, but David ben Unbutu held in his hand not a needle but a pencil. As the one stitched, the other sketched. Diana settled down beside David and observed.

Bakhtiian was a perfect subject, since he scarcely moved except for the shifting of his wrists and hands. Diana would have thought him oblivious to them, except for the one time she lifted her eyes to study him and found him staring directly at her. It was so disconcerting that she jerked back and David, startled, fudged a line on the sketch. But when Diana's eyes met Bakhtiian's, he averted his gaze immediately. Just like, she thought inconsequently, the shy heroine in a Victorian melodrama. The comparison struck her as so incongruous that she smiled.

"Are you admiring David or his drawing?" said a voice above her. "I wasn't aware that you actors had interests off the stage."

Diana did not look up for a moment, because she knew she was blushing. She waited, a beat, a second beat, for the heat to fade from her cheeks. Then she looked up over her shoulder. "Hello, Marco. In fact, I'm admiring David's subject."

Marco crouched beside Diana, and she could feel the heat, the weight, of his body next to hers. His sleeve brushed her arm. "You've caught exactly the set of his mouth, David," he said, studying the sketch from this vantage point.

David grunted, but did not otherwise reply.

"A passionate mouth," intoned Diana. "Made for kisses."

"Made for kisses?" Marco laughed abruptly, and she forced herself to look straight at him, to meet his gaze, feeling bold and breathless together. Thinking of what had almost come about between them. But Marco looked, if anything, a little annoyed. "Have you forgotten our little banquet at Abala Port? I find it hard to imagine a man responsible for so much violence and killing as *kissing*."

Evidently he was still angry about Soerensen's decree. "I haven't forgotten it. But it's not hard for me to imagine *him*, that flesh and blood person sitting there, kissing. It can be hard sometimes to separate an actor from a role offstage. Onstage it's impossible, or it should be. Do you suppose he's onstage or off right now?"

"Do you think it's a role, the great conqueror?"

"I don't know," said Diana. "I gave up a long time ago trying to decide whether we're ever ourselves or are only playing roles. And who could tell which the role was, the passionate kisser or the ruthless conqueror? Maybe they both are roles. Or maybe they're both true. Can't two contradictory things exist inside one person?"

"Are they necessarily contradictory?" Marco leaned forward again, examining the sketch. His shoulder brushed hers, and his hand caught itself, straying, on her thigh. "David, David, David. Have I ever told you how much I admire your ability to draw?" David grinned and flashed a look toward Marco, there on the other side of Diana. As if he knew that Marco was using the entire episode as a way to cozy up to her.

Diana flushed, well aware of Marco's hand on her leg.

"Look at that," Marco continued, ignoring these undercurrents. Diana doubted he was unaware of them. "Like the pattern on the shirtsleeve. That kind of thing

fascinates me. Those elements add depth to our understanding of a culture. Is this pattern symbolic? Individual? Related to a clan, if indeed these people have clans.
Even the material of their tents has a pattern. Are the two
related? There are so many things to record, and words
can only record so much. Even Maggie's photography
can't record everything. It misses that essence.''

''Do I detect a note of disapproval for Maggie's photography?'' David asked without looking up. ''She's ab-
surdly careful about it, and in any case, her equipment
is all disguised.'' He examined his sketch and penciled
in a few more lines of the interwoven spiral pattern embroidered on the sleeve of the shirt the great conqueror
wore.

''This *is* an interdicted planet,'' Diana said.

Marco took his hand off her thigh, as if the comment
made him remember prudence. ''The truth is, I've never
been able to risk anything covert, traveling the way I have
these past years. And I've no hand for sketching, so I've
missed recording much of what I've seen. Now I'm so
accustomed to traveling that way that I never bothered to
request any such equipment for this trip. I'm not sure I
want to, anyway. What if one of the natives discovers
it?''

''But, Marco,'' said Diana, ''you traveling all that time
broke the quarantine. Certainly the Bharentous Repertory Company having spent three months in Jeds and
now coming out here is a contamination, isn't it?''

''Yes, it is.''

''You don't approve, do you?'' Diana fell silent and
together they watched as David, with economy and grace,
used a few simple lines to expand the pattern that flowed
down the shirtsleeve in his sketch. ''I think it's a road,''
she said suddenly. ''A winding road.''

''What is? The evolution of cultures?'' Marco examined the sprawl of camp around them, the tidy expanse
of tents losing color as the afternoon light deepened into
dusk. ''I suppose Charles would say so, that no culture
is pure, that it is always adulterated by contact with any
other culture, as it must be. That our contact with it, if
we're careful and discreet, will be scarcely more contam-
inating than that. But I'm not sure I agree. There's a
stronger force behind us. Broader knowledge. Won't that

take its toll?'' Sitting on his haunches, the deep tan of
his skin set off by the blanched gold of his linen tunic,
he appeared to Diana not much more civilized than the
jaran riders themselves.

''I think she meant the pattern on his shirt,'' said David dryly. ''Artist's fancy, I guess.''

''How old do you suppose he is?'' Diana asked.

''Who can tell?'' said Marco. ''Not too old, I'd
judge.''

''I never saw naturally aged people until Jeds,'' Diana
confided.

''The commonplace made quaint,'' said Marco drily. He
set his chin on a fist and pondered the distance.

Embarrassed, Diana turned her attention back to David and watched as he finished filling in the sleeve of the
right arm. Across the camp rang a low, trembling sound,
like a muffled gong being struck. The great conqueror
did not even look up, but Marco rose.

''There's supper. Are you coming?''

David shook his head without looking up. ''I just want
to finish this while there's still light.''

Diana was torn between accepting Marco's escort and
her real fascination with watching David work. After all,
it wouldn't do for Marco Burckhardt to think that she
hung on his every word. ''I'll be there in a bit. Save
some for me.''

He hesitated as if taken aback at her refusal. But he
recovered quickly. ''You have my word on it, golden
fair.'' Marco left.

David sketched for a few minutes undisturbed. Red-
shirted men moved back and forth between tents. Laughter swelled in a distant corner. A man's voice, a pleasant
baritone, sang a simple song in a language she had identified as khush, the native tongue. Farther away, identi-
fiable only because she knew the voice so well, Diana
heard Henry Bharentous shouting at someone, but she
could not make out his words. Prince Hal rebelling again.
Beside her, David held the sketch out at arm's length to
scrutinize it.

The model moved. Rose, lithe as any wild predator.
Diana felt his movement. David lowered his sketch to
see Bakhtiian walking straight toward them. David re-

coiled, nearly falling back down onto the ground, and almost dropped the sketch. Began to scramble to his feet.

"No," whispered Diana urgently. "Keep sitting, keep still. Stillness doesn't startle them."

She held her place, and David, looking ashen under his dark complexion, sat still beside her. Bakhtiian halted before them. There was a moment's uncomfortable silence. Then Bakhtiian crouched, far enough away from them that he couldn't touch either of them if he reached out. "I beg your pardon," he said in his perfect Rhuian. "We haven't been introduced. I am Ilyakoria Bakhtiian."

In the first instant, she realized that David had gotten the eyes wrong. This close, she saw the depth of the intensity, of the sheer, driven force in them. "I'm Diana Brooke-Holt," she said, and her voice spurred David on.

"David ben Unbutu." It came out in a rush. "I'm sorry. I should have asked your permission to draw you, but—" He hesitated.

"Here," said Diana, breaching the sudden silence. She took the pad out of David's hands. "It's very fine. Would you like to see it?"

Addressed by her, Bakhtiian lowered his eyes. "I was hoping I would be allowed to look at it." Crouched thus beside her, eyes cast almost bashfully to the ground, he seemed much less threatening.

She handed the pad to him. There was silence but for the distant sounds of the camp settling in to dusk and the impending night.

Diana rose, and David drew in a breath and rose as well. After a moment, Bakhtiian stood up. "You must know how good you are," he said finally, directly, to David. He gave the sketchbook back to David, holding it as if it was something he considered valuable. "You have great talent. Is this your profession?"

"No, I'm an engineer." David look taken aback by Bakhtiian's politeness.

"Ah—and you?" His gaze shifted for the briefest moment to Diana's face.

"I'm one of the actors in the repertory company." She faltered. "Do you know what that is?"

For a terrifying moment she thought she had offended

him. The corner of his mouth tugged up, softening his expression. "Yes," he said gravely.

"You speak excellent Rhuian," she said impulsively.

"Thank you," he replied, still grave.

She had a brief hallucination that he was suppressing laughter, dismissed it.

He turned back to David, regarding him with obvious respect. "Perhaps you would be willing to undertake a commission."

"A commission!"

"That is the right word, isn't it?"

"Yes. I was just startled."

"Perhaps you would undertake a commission to draw my wife."

David's mouth dropped open. Diana pinched him in the leg. "I would be honored," he said in a constrained voice.

"The honor is mine," Bakhtiian replied, as formal and impeccable as if he were a noble of Jeds and not a man who had killed in cold blood. "When we've arrived at the main camp, we can discuss the arrangements further. Now, if you will excuse me." He inclined his head and left them.

David swore under his breath.

"Well," said Diana.

"In case you're wondering," said David, "the answer is no. I'm not brave. Not at all. Not one bit. And especially not after seeing him execute that man."

"But then why did you sit here and draw him? You must have known that would attract his attention."

"I know. I know. But I couldn't resist, seeing him sitting there. What an image." He examined the sketch with a frown.

" 'But, sure, he's proud; and yet his pride becomes him,' " murmured Diana.

David sighed and closed the sketchpad carefully. "Thanks for your support, by the way. Goddess, I hope his wife is a good subject. I'd hate to do anything that antagonized him. Shall we go eat?"

CHAPTER TWELVE

"He doesn't like me," said Charles Soerensen.

Cara Hierakis had knelt next to him to lace up her boots. She did not bother to look up. "What possible reason would he have not to like you?" When Charles did not reply, she answered herself. "Perhaps he considers you a threat to his power. I just don't understand why all the mystery about Tess. I feel that there is something I'm missing."

She waited expectantly. A misting rain fell, though they remained dry here under the awning. Charles merely shifted in his chair, moving one arm to rest on the padded armrest. "I just wish he weren't so cursed polite all the time," he said.

"Yes, he was well brought up, wasn't he? I like him."

Charles stood up. Cara glanced up at him, then stood as well, turning.

Bakhtiian, flanked by four of his men, approached them. The rain let up just as the sun came out, casting a glow on the cluster of monochromatic khaki-colored canvas tents that housed Charles's party and the Company. Beside the central tent, two of the actors crouched by the fire pit, rubbing their hands together to warm them over the bright lick of flame while they waited for the kettle to boil. About twenty paces away, two of Bakhtiian's riders watched this display with perplexed interest.

Bakhtiian did not give the scene a second glance. He paused outside the awning of Charles's tent, and when Charles nodded, he stepped under the awning, leaving his attendants behind. First he inclined his head to Dr. Hierakis: only then did he turn his attention to Charles.

"We must move quickly today. My scouts have brought me word that a force of armed men, mercenaries, is marching to meet us. Some of my riders will help your party break camp and load your wagons and then guide you along the swiftest route toward our main camp while the bulk of my troop engages the enemy. I would not want you in any danger.''

Watching Bakhtiian's face, Cara wondered if he meant the comment to be sarcastic, but she could read no insincerity in his expression or his tone.

Charles studied him a moment in silence. "Obviously," he said, "your strength as an army is mobility. Will your opponent be equally mobile?"

"They're mostly foot soldiers. We've already encircled them. They should pose no threat to your people, but it would be safer for you to travel farther out onto the plains."

"I will see to it that my party understands," Charles replied, "but I wonder if it could be arranged for a member of my party to observe the battle?"

Bakhtiian blinked. "*Observe* the battle?" he asked, as if the idea of observing a battle was so fantastic that it had to be repeated to actually take form.

"She studies war," Charles explained.

"Ah," said Bakhtiian. "The one who walks like a man." Then he glanced swiftly at Hierakis, and said, "I beg your pardon."

"No offense taken," replied Cara, torn between amusement and apprehension. The thought of a battle worried her. How could it not? She had lived in Jeds long enough to know the sorts of ugly wounds that swords and spears and arrows produce in human flesh. But more worrisome was this constant undercurrent of sparring between the two men, as if there, too, a battle loomed, but neither general was yet willing to commit his forces.

Charles fought to suppress a smile and finally gave up. "Yes. That would be Ursula. Can it be arranged?"

"Yes." Bakhtiian glanced over his shoulder and spoke words in khush. One of his attendants jogged away. "Is there anyone else who would like to—observe?" he asked.

"I would," said Charles.

Bakhtiian did not reply for a moment, as if waiting for Hierakis to apply as well. When she did not speak, he nodded curtly. "I will arrange it. Now, if you will excuse me." He left, attendants in tow.

"Charles, why in hell do you want to watch men killing each other? Ursula will be faint for the chance to see
this, and since she has as much sensibility as a grave
digger, it doesn't concern me, but you—?"

"Cara, my dear, Tess has trained to fight in this man's
army. I want to see what she's let herself in for."

"Lady bless us," responded Cara, suddenly enlightened. "You don't suppose she was *wounded*, do you?
That would explain why she didn't come to meet us—"

"I'll go roust Ursula." Charles left her without waiting for her to finish.

Used to his abruptness, Cara merely knelt and laced
up her other boot. Then, glancing once at the actors by
the fire, whose numbers had tripled, she slipped into
Charles's tent. Since he had so little baggage, it took her
very little time to find the folded parchment square that
the young jaran rider named Aleksi had delivered to
Charles at the end of that awful banquet. She flicked the
brooch at her collar so that it bled light into the dark
interior. Tess's writing! She began to read.

"Dear Charles, I apologize for not coming to meet
you, although why I'm apologizing I don't know, when I
had every intention of riding to the port but was forestalled by Ilya, who compounded the offense by forbid-
ding me to leave camp until he returns with you and your
party. Despite the fact that I have trained for over three
years, he refuses to let me fight. While this may be an
act you applaud, you cannot understand how it under-
mines what I am, and the entire fabric of my relationship
to the jaran. If he did, in fact, marry me because—"

Cara had to stop reading for ten entire ten seconds,
just absorbing this astounding fact. From outside, she
heard a wagon draw up, and the lowing of beasts. She
forced herself to read again.

"If he did, in fact, marry me because I am different,
then he is doing everything in his power now to absorb
me into his world entirely, however much he does it unconsciously. But then, Ilya is such a—" Here Tess had
scratched out several words with such a thick stroke that
Cara could not puzzle them out. "I will not let that happen."

A sudden lance of natural light interrupted her. Charles
walked in. He paused, one hand still on the tent flap,

holding it open. She touched her brooch, and the slim beam of light vanished.

He regarded her quizzically. ''What's that?''

''Tess's letter to you.''

''You might have asked.''

''If I'd asked, you would simply have hidden it better. I've known Tess almost as long as you have, Charles. You might have shared this with me. *Married!* To Bakhtiian!''

Charles smiled. ''It gives me such pleasure to see you astonished, Cara, because it happens so rarely. Let me remind you that under Chapalii law a woman who marries loses all connection to her birth status and takes on her husband's status entirely. Given that the natives of Rhui, again under Chapalii law, qualify as wildlife—not even as intelligent life—that puts Tess's position as my heir rather in jeopardy. As it were.''

''You can scarcely think I'd trumpet this marriage to Chapalii Protocol. And in any case, you never contested her death declaration, so it seems to me that it's a moot point.''

He let the tent flap down, drowning them in dimness. ''Tess's marrying can never be a moot point. I didn't contest the declaration, but neither did I acknowledge it. That leaves her fate open to change.''

''And frees your hand to play your cards when you will. Still, there are rumors enough floating around that Tess is not dead, but in hiding.''

''Yes, and that serves our purpose as well. We humans understand rumors, and Chapalii do not.''

There was a silence, broken at last by Cara. ''Do you know, Charles, I'm a little hurt. Marco must know.''

''Of course, but only because he guessed. And he swore not to tell *anyone,* for the same reasons. If only I know, then it can go no farther, no matter what the persuasion.'' In the gloom of the tent, his voice carried with a mildness that was, Cara knew, deceptive.

But she still felt hurt. ''Have I ever told you that the one thing I most dislike about you is this tendency you have to hoard information? You may smile, since you've heard it a hundred times, but you must start trusting others.''

She had long since grown used to his silences. This

one was rueful. He got that funny little half smile on his face and crossed the room to her. "My love, I trust you entirely." He embraced her, and they stood for a while that way. Finally, he eased himself away from her and kissed her lightly on the cheek. "It's the Chapalii I don't trust. Please recall that they murdered my parents."

"I haven't forgotten it. Goddess, how could I? Still—"

He chuckled and released her hands. "I yield. It's now time that you know the whole of it. Read the rest."

"I appreciate your openness," she said dryly, and she flicked on her brooch light and scanned the page.

"Now I regret letting Aleksi remove the contraceptive patch in my left arm. Not entirely, because Ilya wants children so badly, but I had hoped—it sounds incredibly ridiculous to me now to say that I had hoped to have some experience, to have acquitted myself well as a fighter, before being bound to camp by pregnancy."

"Pregnancy!" For the first time since beginning this journey, Cara felt real alarm, the pound of adrenaline, warmth flushing her skin. "But the incompatibilities! It could be lethal!"

"Now you see why I brought you, Doctor."

"But wasn't she told—?"

"How old was Tess when she lived in Jeds with us?"

She shook her head, having to count back years and calculate. "Ten? Twelve? She was a child."

"Too young to get the lecture all the adults working on Jeds have received. And neither you nor I ever expected her to return so precipitously."

"Or so secretly. Much less marry. She's just a little girl. I never thought she would grow up." She shook herself with disgust. "How I hate it when I don't think."

Charles smiled, a quirk of the lips. "We are here now. There's no reason Tess can't come home with us, when we leave. That will put her out of danger."

"Charles. Charles. You can't possibly believe that it will be so easy. Married! There's a very good reason. You've met him."

It was too dark to read his expression, but his mouth tightened, and his lashes shadowed his eyes. "We shall see," he murmured. "I must go."

Light flashed and vanished, and she was alone. "Goddess," she swore. Still, what if it could be done? One

Earth woman and three Rhuian women had gotten pregnant by men from the *other* planet and all of them had died, inevitably, from antigenic reactions caused by incompatibilities between Earth and Rhuian humans. But one of the babies had lived. Surely with proper monitoring, with complete studies of both parents, a pregnancy could be brought to term successfully. Think how much she could learn from it! The rate of mutation, the alterations the Chapalii had made within the DNA of the Earth population moved to Rhui, the changes, the adaptations, that had come about by themselves on Rhui which could be measured in contrast to Earth's template—indeed, the development of a fetus molded of both worlds—all of this could be measured and quantified in such a controlled experiment. Added to what she had already learned, to her studies of the fundamental process of human development and aging—

But this was *Tess*. She recoiled from her own thoughts, shook herself, and read on.

"By the way, don't be concerned about Aleksi's involvement. He has a peculiar, detached way of looking at things, having been orphaned at an early age and only admitted into our tribe because of my friendship and because he has quite simply the best hand for the saber that anyone in recent memory has possessed, and he guessed soon after we met that I had come from a place not only different, but different in a way that passed the understanding of most of the jaran—even of Ilya. He is truly my brother in every sense of the word (except the biological). I trust him completely, and you should, too. He will deliver this letter to you. Also, when you arrive at the main camp, if I'm not there, do not worry. I may be riding out with a group that is going to escort a southern ambassador to our camp. I will be back soon after you arrive. Bakhtiian does not know this (of course), so don't be concerned if he gets furious. He has a hard time containing his emotions and he hates having his will thwarted, but he won't let his anger at me prejudice his dealings with you. Safe journey. Love, Tess."

"Safe journey, indeed," Cara muttered. She folded the parchment and tucked it back neatly into the pocket of the shirt in which she had found it, squaring off the corners. Then she went outside.

David had weeks since been granted the unofficial post of camp leader, a position he warranted due to his previous experience of camping expeditions on Earth and to his ability to work in harmony with Yomi Applegate-Hito, whose authority over the day to day routine of the Company not even Charles dared contest. By the time Cara ventured outside, David had already begun directing the striking of camp. Most of the actors and all of the rest of Charles's immediate party rolled up tents and loaded wagons with commendable haste. Next to one of the wagons, reclining soporifically on a canvas chair, Anahita Liel Apphia sat with one hand cast up over her eyes, as if the sudden turn of events had exhausted her nerves. One of the young male actors—Cara could not recall his name, but Narcissus would have been appropriate—knelt beside her, patting her cheeks with a damp cloth. Beyond them, the big tent fluttered and sagged and with a gushing sigh collapsed. Beneath the canvas, a single figure struggled to free himself from inside. Cara hurried over and lifted the material enough to help him out; it was the leading man, Gwyn Jones.

"May I help?" she asked.

He smiled. Gwyn was a fairly young man, his features interesting rather than handsome; he had a quiet intensity that never, except when he was on stage, erupted into dramatics. "Please," he said. He glanced briefly toward Anahita and her companion. Diana had stopped next to the pair and seemed to be making a speech. "Di!" Gwyn called. She turned and, when he waved at her, jogged over to them.

"We need a hand here." Gwyn indicated Cara and himself. He bent to straighten one corner of the big tent.

"Well, I must say," said Diana to Cara, seeing that Gwyn was inclined to ignore her, "that I'm disgusted with Hyacinth that he would cater to *her* whims rather than do something useful." Expecting no reply, and receiving only Cara's enigmatic smile, she strode around to another corner and pulled it tight.

Hal Bharentous arrived and, with four of them, the folding went quickly. As Diana and Gwyn rolled the canvas up and tied it, and Hal collected and bound up the poles, Cara allowed herself a moment to step back and watch while she wound the guidelines up.

"Doctor," said a voice behind her. "I see you observe as well. Everything we watch, everything we do, becomes part of the work. And all work feeds the exercise that becomes the theater, the actual performance of which is only another, if more polished, exercise."

Cara turned. "M. Zerentous."

Owen Zerentous gave the briefest nod in acknowledgment, but his attention remained fixed on his actors. "There can be no separation between work and life. Like the rehearsal, the journey itself is a discovery."

"Dad," said Hal, half hidden by the bound poles, "I don't think Dr. Hierakis is interested in your theories."

"But of course she is," said Zerentous. "She is a research scientist, an act of creative performance that binds her close in spirit to every other artist. Are you not, Doctor?"

Cara was saved a reply by the sudden eruption of an altercation over by the wagons, where Madelena Quinn was attempting to physically drag Hyacinth away from his station by Anahita. Zerentous' interest, and his focus, shifted so thoroughly away from her that Cara felt as if he had left her before he took one step away.

"Well," she said to no one as Zerentous strode away to observe this newest scene.

Gwyn Jones glanced up at her. "Yes," he said, following the direction of her gaze, "but you must forgive him much. He's a genius."

"Tell that to the army that's approaching when they ride, swords drawn, into a camp we haven't broken yet," muttered Hal.

"Good Lord," said Diana, trying to hoist one end of the rolled up tent. "This thing weighs a ton."

David ran up, his skin sheened with sweat. "This is down? Good. If you can load this into the fourth wagon—there—then all we've got is the bedding and carries, and we can get started."

Hal and Gwyn and Di hoisted the rolled up tent between them and lugged it over to the wagons. Cara tarried behind. "I certainly don't understand why actors must travel with so much luggage."

David grinned. "I hadn't noticed that you travel lightly, Doctor."

Cara picked up the bundle of poles. "Have I ever told you how much I detest impertinent young men, David?"

"Many times. Here, I'll take those, and if you'll roll up that rug, we'll be finished here."

"You seem damned cheerful. Aren't you nervous? With battles looming in the near distance."

David shrugged as they began to walk. "I've never been scared of threats I can't see. It's a form of blindness, I suppose. It's why I went into engineering. It's all there, right in front of you. Yomi!" he called, diverted by the appearance of the Company stage manager. "I'll give you five minutes. Then we're going." Yomi nodded, and then, with characteristic efficiency, she rounded on the group that had gathered by Anahita and dispersed it ruthlessly.

David proved as good as his word. In five minutes, the first wagon jolted forward, and in succession, the rest followed its lead. David sat next to the driver of the lead wagon, and Cara, as usual, began the day by walking briskly alongside. Like all the drivers, this one was an elderly but hale jaran man who spoke no language but khush. Nevertheless, he and David had formed a friendly partnership, linked by a shared even temperament and, Cara suspected, the simple fact of both being male.

Cara walked for an hour. The grass was damp from rain, and the sun slipped in and out from behind the clouds, so that the cast of light over the land brightened and dulled by turns. Finally, she swung up into the back of the wagon as it trundled along at an even and unslacking pace. She had conceived the greatest respect for the beasts that drew it, thick-shouldered, bovine animals that could walk for hours without rest. This day they did not even pause at midday, but it was only mid-afternoon when a new rider, an older man whose blond hair was bleached white with age, galloped up from behind and spoke to the lead driver. Their course altered; within half an hour the little train snaked around a low rise and came to a halt by a swampy pond ringed by scrub trees and a scatter of dense bushes.

Cara climbed down and surveyed the terrain. Already the drivers unloaded the wagons with unseemly haste despite Anahita's shrieks of anger. First one wagon, then a second and third, and more, trundled out, leaving the party stranded by the pond.

"David," said Cara, "I think you'd better get all those tents up. And get—ah, there you are, M. Applegate."

"What in heaven's name is going on?" Yomi asked. She cast a disgusted glance back toward the handful of actors clustered around Anahita, and a puzzled one toward the stream of wagons heading away from them. "Are we being abandoned?"

Now others came up to join the discussion: Joanna Singh, Rajiv, Maggie, and Marco. The actors had by now split into two groups: those milling around Anahita, and those with Diana and Gwyn, who were already unrolling the Company tent.

Cara caught Marco's glance, and nodded. "We'll need all the tents up, fires, as many open fires as you can get going, and I want to start boiling water now."

"Oh, hell," said David, as if he had just figured out what was going on. "I'll do what I can, but I can't stand the sight of blood."

"Then we'll put you in charge of preparations," said Marco. "With Jo and Rajiv and Maggie. Start by gathering brush. Cara, will you need attendants?"

"You certainly, Marco. Anyone else who can stand it. The rest will have to fetch and carry." She watched as Anahita collapsed onto a chair set up for her by Hyacinth. "Or else stay out of the way."

David and Joanna and Rajiv and Maggie left.

"I beg your pardon, Dr. Hierakis," said Yomi. "But I'm still confused. What's going on?"

"We're about to receive the wounded."

"Ah," said Yomi. "From the battle. I'll go tell the actors. I'm sure they can help out." She left.

Cara sighed. "So blithely. She hasn't an inkling, Marco, of what we're about to see."

"They chose to come here. Now they have to face the consequences of that choice. If they can't endure it, let them go home."

Cara snorted. "You're not very compassionate today, are you, Marco?"

"I save my compassion for where it will do the most good. It's all very well to spout this nonsense about the universality of theater, but it's still nothing more than a holiday for them. We'll see how they like a dose of the painful truth.''

"My, you're bitter today.'' But she followed his gaze and saw that he was looking toward Diana Brooke-Holt, watching her as she and Hal and Gwyn extended the poles and lifted the canvas weight of the Company tent. "Ah. Test of fire for the sweet young thing?''

Marco started, glanced at her swiftly, and grunted in annoyance as he turned on his heel and stalked away in the direction of the pond.

"Well!'' Cara considered his back as he strode off toward David and Maggie, who were gathering brush. "What does that mean?'' But Marco's affairs did not concern her now. She went to assemble her medical kit.

CHAPTER THIRTEEN

When the first riders were sighted, coming in toward the camp, Diana felt sick with fear. She hoisted two buckets of water from the pond and lugged them over to the ring of campfires. Dr. Hierakis was swearing fluently in Rhuian about the lack of containers in which to boil water. At the far end of the pond a single tent had been set aside for Anahita and anyone who wanted to languish there with her, a total of five of the actors and none of Soerensen's party.

The riders glinted in the sun as they pulled up a respectful distance outside of camp. They wore, over their scarlet shirts, segmented body armor with scaled tasses hanging down to cover their legs to the knees. A few wore helmets, although most had slung their helmets on leather straps over their saddles. Altogether, they presented a formidable picture, and there were only fifty of them.

Diana stared, realized she was staring, and picked up the two empty buckets to make a trip back to the pond.

"Diana! Can you help me over here?" It was Gwyn, setting up the Company's screens into a square.

She hurried over. "What is this?"

"The doctor wants an outdoor surgery. Tie that there—"

Diana watched the riders from her vantage point. "It doesn't look as if this group has any wounded, or as if they're even going to come into our camp—" She broke off as Dr. Hierakis and Marco strode across the grass to the group of waiting jaran. Their gestured conversation was fascinating to watch, since it was obvious that no one spoke a common language. Soon enough Owen wandered over to study them.

"Excuse me." Diana whirled, to see David and Maggie carrying a long, rectangular table. They brought it inside the screens and set it down. David stepped back to examine it. "Well, it was the best I could cobble together."

Out by the riders, the doctor and an older jaran man had reached some kind of agreement. They walked together back to the tents, and behind them, walked—or limped—a number of the riders. As they came closer, Diana could see that they were indeed wounded: one man had an arrow sticking out of his thigh, broken off; another had blood seeping from his right side; a third had a bloody strip of cloth tied around his left eye.

"Marco, get my kit. Maggie, where's Jo? I want her to stay in my tent and run sterilization on my instruments, so we'll need someone—one of the actors, say— to fetch and carry. That should be easy enough for them. David, we'll need another table, the wagons will be showing up by dusk. Can you find—yes, leave Rajiv in charge of the water; perhaps one of the actors can help you." Dr. Hierakis caught Diana staring at her.

Diana felt like she was being considered by an expert. She shifted uneasily and glanced at the elderly jaran man next to the doctor. He had a kindly face—for a savage— and, meeting her gaze, he smiled at her and nodded.

"Of course," said Dr. Hierakis abruptly. "If you think you can stand it, Diana, you can take water—boiled water, of course—to the wounded who are waiting to be treated. Goddess knows, they'll be thirsty enough, and a pretty face will likely do them as much good as the drink. Can you manage it, do you think?"

It did not sound precisely like a challenge, but Diana became aware all at once that Marco Burckhardt had paused and was looking at her. "Certainly," she said, hoping there was no betraying quaver in her voice.

"Good," said the doctor. "Tell Rajiv what you're about, and get some cups. And a spoon, perhaps, for the worst of them."

But the cup sufficed, Diana quickly discovered. Of the fifty riders who had come in, at least three-quarters had some kind of injury that clearly kept them from fighting but not from riding. They settled in on the ground, waiting patiently as Marco and a young dark-haired rider performed triage and sent the worst-injured up to the privacy of the screens. Quinn got a cup, too, and they took water

to each rider in turn. Diana soon suspected that many of
these men could have gotten water for themselves but
were content to wait in order to receive it from her hands.

The few older men, lined, sun-weathered, with silver
in their hair, smiled directly at her and spoke a few words
which she guessed to be some kind of thank you. The
young ones never looked her in the eye, or if they did,
not for more than an instant. But it was obvious that their
apparent shyness did not stem from disgust. Quite the
opposite, if anything; many times she turned only to see
a young man blush and look away from her.

By the time they finished with the first group, a second
group had ridden in. Things went much the same. The
afternoon sun spread a layer of warmth along the ground,
but it was shallow, and Diana knew that when night came,
so would the cold. What if it rained again? Did these
men even have blankets?

A second surgery had been set up in the Company tent,
and Diana watched as Dr. Hierakis, now with two elderly
jaran riders flanking her, walked into the tent. She had
rolled up the sleeves of her tunic. Blood spattered the
yellow fabric. Behind her, Maggie carried two unlit
lanterns.

"Here." Diana knelt beside a young man with corn-
flower blue eyes and fair hair. One shoulder piece dangled, cut away, and underneath it his scarlet shirt was
damp. "You must be thirsty. Where are you wounded?"

An instant later she realized that the red shirt was doubly red, damp with blood not water, and that he was pale
as much from pain as from complexion. He smiled at
her, and looked away as quickly. He lifted his good arm
and took the cup from her and drank, still not looking at
her. But his body was canted toward her, not quite leaning, but yearning. He was pretty, not tall, and his shyness made him seem sweet to her.

She felt a sudden rush of affection and felt foolish all
at once. "Goddess, I suppose that hurts like hell," she
went on, secure in the knowledge that he could not understand a word she was saying. "And you have the most
beautiful eyes. Do all you *jaran* men have such gorgeous
eyes?"

He blushed—clear to see, on his fair skin—and handed
her back the cup.

"Careful, golden fair. The words may be Greek to him, but the intent is plain."

Diana flushed and rose, casting a last sympathetic glance at the young rider before she turned to confront Marco Burckhardt.

Then he smiled, disarming her. "But the good doctor was right. He looks better already." He knelt beside the young rider. *"Te chilost?"* The rider made a gesture with his good arm, speaking a few words. "Ah," replied Marco. *"Pleches voy?"* The rider replied in a stream of words, but Marco only shook his head.

"Do you know their language? Did you know it before?" Diana asked, loitering.

"No. I'm learning it bit by bit. Very useful." He glanced up at her. "Try asking *nak kha tsuva*. That means, 'how are you called,' more or less."

That was definitely a challenge. Diana tried the words out in her head, and then turned to the young rider. *"Nak kha tsuva?"* she asked.

The rider grinned. "Anatoly Sakhalin." He repeated the question back at her.

"Diana Brooke-Holt." She hesitated, glancing at Marco. "I'm glad he's not badly hurt, at least."

Marco had his little red knife out and was trimming the shirt away from the shoulder. "What makes you think that?"

Diana looked around them, at the men waiting patiently on the ground, some silent, some joking; one older man whose left arm hung limply and at an awkward angle sang a cheerful tune in a pleasant baritone. "They rode here, for one. And they aren't—"

Marco peeled away the silk of the shirt. Skin came off with it. He dropped the bloody remains beside the broken shoulder piece. The shoulder had been crushed—by what, Diana could not imagine, except that bone gleamed white under pulped tissue. She gasped. Nausea and dizziness swept over her in waves. Anatoly Sakhalin shut his eyes. He paled to white with pain.

"Because they aren't complaining?" Marco asked. "Well, they're only savages you know, they don't feel it like we do. He needs to go directly to surgery. I think the good doctor can manage something with this. Otherwise he'll die when gangrene sets in. Could you fetch someone to help him over?''

He was mocking her. Through her horror at the sight of the gaping, splintered wound and her compassion for the young rider's pain, she knew that Marco Burckhardt scorned her, that he scorned all the actors.

''I'll do it.'' She knelt without waiting to hear more, leaving her cups and leather canteen on the grass, and slipped her left arm around the young man's waist. His eyes snapped open and he glanced at her and then, with an immense effort, he pushed himself to his feet. Swayed a little once there, with his good arm around her shoulders, but she steadied him. Marco stood up also. He looked, well, angry more than anything.

Diana ignored Marco and started off toward the screens. After about ten steps she felt dampness on her thigh and looked down to see blood leaking out of a rent in the rider's black trousers. By the time they reached the surgery, the young man's eyes were half-shut and most of his weight hung on her, but his right arm, gripping her right shoulder, was strong. Gwyn appeared at a gap between screens.

''Goddess, Diana. Here, let me help.'' Together they half-carried Sakhalin in and lifted him onto the table. Blood spattered the grass around. Gwyn's tunic was dappled with red.

''What's this?'' demanded Dr. Hierakis, pushing Diana away. Diana moved, only to be stopped by Anatoly himself. He clutched her wrist in his right hand. ''Ah. Crushed shoulder, some splintering of the joint, dirt embedded; speared and trampled, I'd say. Thigh wound—that's superficial. Here, Klimova, you see how the tendon—'' Dr. Hierakis went on, explaining in Rhuian to her jaran companion as she doctored the wound. He watched, soaking in her techniques although he did not understand her words. But Diana lost track of the diagnosis. Anatoly Sakhalin had crept his hold up from her wrist onto her hand, and he held on to her as if she was his lifeline. While the doctor probed and poked and cleaned and moved things and took a needle and thread to him, he stared at Diana, his eyes locked on hers. She did not look away, as much because he so urgently needed her to fix on as because she did not want to see what the doctor was doing. Blood leaked out from the wound to trickle along Anatoly's neck. His throat worked convulsively. His skin shaded from white to gray, and the black of pupil eclipsed the brilliant blue of his eyes. His grip crushed her fingers. A moment later, his eyes rolled up and he went limp.

She stood frozen until she realized his chest still rose and fell. She released his hand.

"Thank you, Diana," said Dr. Hierakis. "Perhaps you'd do better here in the surgery. They're stoic enough, but I must say this boy's done the best of the lot."

Diana felt like her head was attached by only a string to her neck. In an instant, she would be floating. She stared at the young rider, the blood, the pale curve of his lips, the blond mustache above his mouth and the clean-shaven line of his jaw. It stank here, of blood and wounds and pain.

"Diana," said Gwyn calmly, "you'd better sit down."

She sat down. Her vision blurred, dimmed, and focused again. Goddess, she would have fainted in another second. She took an even deeper breath, another, in and out, clearing her head. When it was safe, she looked up. Dr. Hierakis's jaran companion, the old man, bound up the shoulder wound.

"Move him off," said the doctor to Gwyn. "Who's next?" She glanced down at Diana, who sat at her feet. "Move, Diana. You're in the way."

Gwyn and, to Diana's surprise, Hal got their arms under the unconscious Anatoly and lifted him as gently as they could off of the table, carrying him away—to one of the tents, probably. Marco appeared, helping in a young man mutilated by a gash that had peeled the skin away from his cheekbone. Bone gleamed. It was horrifying.

"Where do you want me?" Diana climbed to her feet. "I'll do whatever you think is best."

Dr. Hierakis did not even glance at her. Diana felt—knew—that she had been judged and found wanting. An attendant who fainted at the least sign of pain was of no use in the surgery. "You're doing very well with the water, Diana," she said, though she certainly could not know how well Diana was doing, with all her efforts concentrated in the surgery. "Now, Klimova, you see here how the epidermis and facial muscle has—"

Diana retreated. Marco followed her, but she avoided him, gathering her canteen and cups back and starting down the line. A new group of riders had come in. She asked their names, one by one, as she gave them the precious water to drink.

Later, much later, she heard the wagons trundling in before she saw them. Belatedly, she realized that David was hanging lanterns from all the tent poles, that it was getting dark, well into twilight. The wagons rolled past: one, two . . . ten in all.

Diana hurried over to where they had halted, sure that these men would be parched, having fought all day and then jolted over the ground for such a distance. Out here, men had stripped off their armor and most of them clustered around the horses. A group broke off to assist with the wagons. At the head of the line, Marco and his young jaran associate leaned over the slats and peered at the wounded lying within. Diana ran up to the last wagon just as two men slung the first wounded man off.

She winced. How could they be so casual with him? Even if he was unconscious. . . . They carried the rider past her, not a meter from her. He was dead. Fair hair hung down, trailing toward the grass. His face, so young, was unmarked. But the spark was gone. Whatever had animated him was fled, leaving only a shell.

Diana stared after him. She felt cold and hot all at once. He was dead.

"Diana?" The voice was tentative, and frightened.

Diana turned. "Quinn?"

"I . . . I can't do this anymore. I'm sorry. It's just . . . it's just too awful." Quinn caught in a sob. Her brown hair hung, tangled, loose over her shoulders, and dirt streaked her forehead. Lines of tears trailed down her cheeks. "Oh, Goddess. Look at them." Then she spun and ran.

Diana knew where Quinn was headed without having to look: to the tent at the other end of the pond, where Anahita held her court, away from the horror that the camp had become. At the second wagon, Marco Burckhardt paused to stare toward them, to stare after Madelena Quinn, retreating from the ugliness of death.

Diana was suddenly furious. What right had he to judge them? Was he better than them, for having spent so many

years on this barbaric planet? Because he had seen death
before, because he could shrug it off now, did that give
him license to despise them for their innocence? Marco
was still watching her. Waiting. Seeing if she passed the
test, which was no test at all except that he wanted it to
be one. A man moaned, sobbing in pain. Goddess, these
were the men too injured to ride. Another man was carried past her while she stood, hesitating; another man
who was dead. She took two steps, three, then four, to
the side of the wagon.

A man lay there, on his back. His chest rose and fell,
rasping. An arrow protruded from his eye.

If she thought about it, she would scream. She knew
it. But she was damned if she would give Marco Burckhardt the satisfaction of seeing her give up. And oh, sweet
Goddess, the pain they were feeling. It tore at her, it
hurt, to see them suffer.

She unscrewed the canteen and poured some water into
the cup. Spooning it out, she got some through the lips
of the man with the arrow in his eye—he was still partially conscious—and then she moved on to the next
wagon.

As long as she didn't think, she could manage her job.
Each canteen went a long way, because these men were
so badly hurt that mostly a spoon or two, fed through
their dry lips, was all they could take. At some point she
must have gone through all ten wagons, but by then two
more wagons had come trundling in. About a third of the
men were dead. They were carried away and set down in
the grass. Some of the least injured jaran men carried
brush out into the grass and laid out a circle of tinder;
for what, she could not imagine. Funeral rites? She dismissed the thought as quickly as it came, knelt by a rider
propped up on his saddle, and lifted the cup to his lips
for him to drink.

"Nak kha tsuva?" she asked him. He managed the
barest of smiles and whispered his name so softly that
she couldn't make it out, but by that smile, she suddenly
understood that he would probably live, although blood
stained his abdomen and his right leg was sheared
through to the bone.

She rose and went on to the next man. And the next.
Ran out of water and trudged across to get more from

Rajiv. The moon was up. Its light cast hazy shadows on
the pale expanse of grass and the monstrous angles of
the tents. A man screamed in pain. A moment later the
scream cut off, abruptly. A million stars blazed in the
black sky.

Crossing back to the three new wagons that had just
come in, she strayed past the field of the dead. Several
jaran men rifled the dead bodies, but in a reverent way
that made her understand that this was part of their culture, removing the silk shirts, unbuckling belts, rolling
up tassetted armor, collecting sabers.

She got to the new wagons just as Marco did. Halted
opposite him, staring in at six men thrown together on
the floor. One was dead. She could recognize the dead
ones instantly by now. Marco leaned in and pulled aside
armor and cloth, looking for wounds, gauging their se-
riousness. They looked mutilated, all of them.

"This one, to surgery now. *Stanai.*" Marco's jaran
associate spoke to some waiting men. They lifted the
wounded man gently from the wagon and carried him off
toward the tents. "He can wait. He can wait. This one,
stanai." Marco paused by the sixth man, a young rider
with black hair. His eyes were closed. His breathing came
in liquid bursts, blood bubbling and sucking on his chest;
a trickle of blood ran out of his mouth. Marco probed
under armor for the wound. Then he shook his head. The
young rider's eyes opened, and he looked up at the sky
and then at the men surrounding him. He spoke, weak
words but clear.

Marco shook his head again, but he said nothing.

"Shouldn't he go straight to surgery?" Diana demanded. All the riders started, shifting to look at her and
then away.

"Lungs," said Marco. "He won't last another hour.
If he's conscious at all, now, it's only because he's in
shock and can't feel the wound."

"But you can't just leave him—"

Marco shrugged and went on to the next wagon. Riders carried the other wounded men away, and lifted out
the dead one, leaving the black-haired boy alone in the
wagon. He watched them, but he said nothing more.

He knew he was dying.

Diana started to cry. Tears trickled down her face. The

worst thing she could do was to cry; it weakened all her defenses, it was idiotic. There was nothing she could do for him, nothing anyone could do.

Then he saw her. His face lit with wonder. *"Elinu,"* he said, and he smiled.

Fiercely, Diana wiped the tears from her cheeks. She slung the canteen over her shoulder and crawled into the wagon. Getting her hands under his shoulders, she lifted him up and cradled his head in her lap. His eyes were clear, perfectly clear, as he stared up at her.

"Nak kha tsuva?" she asked.

"Arkady," he whispered. His breath rattled in his throat. "Arkady Suvorin." He said something more, words she did not know, but that one word again, elinu. She faltered. What else could she do but stare at him, and he at her. What use? She wanted to cry, but that would do neither of them any good. She grasped, and found the first leading role she had played, as an ingenue. And said it to him:

" 'Dost thou love me? I know thou wilt say 'Ay;' And I will take thy word.' " He gazed at her, rapt, as she went on with the lines, every fiber of her being concentrated on him. What else could she do, but ease him in his dying? " 'Therefore pardon me, And not impute this yielding to light love, Which the dark night hath so discovered.' "

But he was dead by then, slipped silently away. He lay still. His chest neither rose nor fell, and a last drop of blood congealed on his chin. But his face was at peace.

"Bravo," said Marco softly, from so close beside her that she would have jumped if she weren't so bitterly exhausted.

She stared at the dead man, his slack face, his dark hair.

"You're braver than I thought," said Marco. He made it sound like an apology.

" 'I have no joy of this contract tonight,' " she said in a low voice. She lifted the dead boy's head off her lap and laid him down on the wagon floor. Stood up, brushing off her trousers and shaking out her knee-length tunic. Picked up the cup. Marco came around to the end of the wagon and caught her by the waist before she could clamber down, swinging her down, holding her. She felt

the flush all along her neck, up into her cheeks. One of
his hands rested at the small of her back, pressing her
into him, against his chest and his hips. His breathing
was unsteady, and he bent his head and kissed her lightly
on the lips. Lightly, but he shook with some extreme
emotion, desire for her, certainly, and perhaps even sorrow or rage at his night's task.

"The other wounded—" She squirmed away, but he
held her.

"No more. It's quiet. They're taken care of, or they're
dead."

Out here, the two of them stood alone with the dead,
those left in the wagons and those laid out in neat lines
in the grass.

"I love you," said Marco.

Diana wedged her hands in between them and shoved
him away. "Don't patronize me, you bastard," she
screamed, and then wrenched away from him and ran
back to camp, not caring who stared.

Campfires ringed the cluster of tents. She slowed,
coming to her senses. Or at least, coming to a sense of
her dignity again. Her breathing came in short bursts,
ragged, and she impatiently wiped another tear away from
the corner of her mouth. Wiped at her nose with the back
of one hand. The canteen sloshed against her right hip.
She was gripping the cup so hard that her fingers ached,
and then she realized that the fingers ached as well from
the grip of the young rider, Anatoly Sakhalin.

As if the name, rising to her thoughts, was a talisman,
she saw him. He sat inclined against a saddle, his face
illuminated by firelight, talking to a man crouched beside
him. He glanced her way, marking her movement, but
his glance caught on her and his entire body tensed as he
recognized her. The man next to him shifted and looked
her way. Bakhtiian.

As if with a will of their own, her feet took her over
to them, and she knelt beside Anatoly Sakhalin.

"We were just talking of you, my lady," said Bakhtiian in Rhuian. His face glowed in the firelight, as if the
heavens, even in the dark of night, could not bear to leave
him unilluminated. "I am grateful, to you and to the
others, for your work here today. I think I would have
lost many more riders without your help."

Diana blushed and looked at her hands, which rested on her knees. She could feel Anatoly Sakhalin's gaze on her like a weight, pressing against her. Bakhtiian said something, short but not unkind, to the young man, and she looked up to see Anatoly avert his gaze from her.

"It's Dr. Hierakis you should thank," said Diana finally, finding her voice again.

"She is a great healer. There is much she can teach those of my people who are also healers. This young man, for instance, will keep the use of his arm, and since he is one of my promising young commanders, I am pleased."

The young man had his left arm in a sling, bound against his chest, but the fingers of his left hand played with a necklace of golden beads draped around his neck, rolling the beads around and around against his palm. Now he spoke, quiet words to Bakhtiian. Bakhtiian raised his eyebrows, looking half amused and half quizzical, and turned back to Diana.

"Anatoly asks that I tell you that he is the eldest grandchild of Elizaveta Sakhalin, who is the—" He hesitated. "—I'm not sure how this would translate. She is the *etsana*, the woman who speaks for her tribe, of the eldest tribe of the jaran, the Sakhalin. He rides with my jahar until he gains enough experience to be awarded a jahar of his own. Which will be soon. Anatoly acquitted himself well today, leading the left flank in on the charge that broke their ranks."

"What is a *jahar?*" At the sound of her voice using a familiar word, Anatoly brightened.

"A group of riders. Not my entire army, you understand, but a smaller group within it."

"I understand. But I never heard what happened at the battle." She hesitated. Was it even proper to ask such a thing? Bakhtiian seemed so mild, crouched here next to her. She knew the pose must be deceptive.

He smiled. "It seems that all khaja women are fascinated with war."

"If I shouldn't ask—" She broke off. Goddess, what if she had violated some kind of taboo?

"It is not my part," said Bakhtiian cryptically, "to dictate to a woman what she should and should not do. As it happened, they were all on foot, a mercenary group

hired by the port towns along the coast, with too few
archers to do any proper damage.'' Diana could not re-
press a shudder, thinking of the wounded men she had
seen. ''They had spears, too, and their captain seems
intelligent enough. He seems inclined to shift his loyalty.''

''To shift his loyalty? To *you?*''

''As I said, he seems intelligent enough.''

''But could you trust such a man? And his troops?''

''A commander uses the tools he is given. It is up to
him to use them where they will be strongest. Now, if
you will excuse me, I have other riders to visit.'' Bakhtiian spoke a few more words to Anatoly Sakhalin and
then, nodding once at Diana, rose and left them. Anatoly
lifted his head to watch Bakhtiian go. His expression betrayed the fierceness of his loyalty. Then he dropped his
gaze to Diana, and then away, to stare at the fire.

Diana sighed. Suddenly, she realized how achingly
tired she was. The barest gleam of light tinged the horizon. Soon it would be dawn.

Anatoly said something in khush to her, softly. There
was no one else at this fire. Beyond, other fires sparked
and burned, but she felt wrapped in a cocoon here, she
felt, strangely enough, safe. She felt so completely un-
threatened, sitting beside a man she barely knew, a barbarian, above all else, who had yesterday fought in a
battle that would have sickened her to see, that she could
not be sure if it was exhaustion that gave her a false sense
of security or if indeed he posed no threat to her. The
idea seemed ludicrous. He sat there, saber lying on the
ground beside him, fingers playing with his necklace.

Out in the darkness, two people strolled by, talking in
Anglais. A woman's voice: ''It was textbook, I tell you.
The left flank charged in and just within bowshot turned
tail and retreated in the most ragtag flight you've ever
seen, and, of course, the damned fools took after them,
thinking they'd scared them off. I saw someone—I believe it was the captain of the mercenary troop—trying
to pull them back into line, but they charged after the
left flank and then, of course, got slammed by a second
charge from the jaran center. Beautifully done, and who-
ever commanded the jaran left flank had his timing and
distance down to the penny. 'When opponents open a

doorway, swiftly penetrate it.' That's Sun Tzu. And they use the spears effectively enough as impact when they hit the line, but I can't fathom why none of these riders use bow and arrow.''

"I'm glad you enjoyed yourself, Ursula.'' That was Maggie, sounding tired and hoarse. "We saw the uglier end of it here.''

"Aha, do I detect the superior voice of civilization lurking in your tone?''

They faded off into the camp. A man moaned, and a woman spoke gentle words. Farther away, someone chopped wood. The rhythmic hacking soothed Diana's nerves. It was such an ordinary sound.

"Diana.'' She glanced up, startled, to see Anatoly looking at her. On his lips, her name sounded exotic and yet tentative. Somehow he had slipped the golden bead necklace off from around his neck and now he held it out in his right hand, offering it to her. He said words to her in khush, grimaced as if frustrated by their inability to understand each other, and then spoke again. A handful of syllables said quietly the first time, then repeated with vehemence.

The words were meaningless to her, but said with an intensity that people reserve for a heartfelt "Thank you,'' or "You're beautiful.'' Or, "I love you.'' The words Marco had mocked her with, that she wished she had not heard. And here sat this one, and she wished so desperately that she could understand him.

She burst into tears. Finally, after all the long hours wearing away at the wall she had constructed in order to go on this hellish day, it took only this to shatter her. She choked down her sobs and looked up at him. With the tips of his fingers, he brushed the tears off of her cheeks and touched his wet fingers to his lips, savoring their precious substance. No man had ever made as simple a gesture as this for her; layers of polished words, of fresh, expensive flowers, or sophisticated holowraps weeping of desire unfulfilled and hearts pining away; but never anything this artless and this sincere.

He said something more to her and then, to her horror, struggled up to his feet.

"Anatoly! No, you shouldn't get up.'' She jumped to her feet.

He wasn't listening to her. He dipped his head, to get the necklace back on.

She stopped him. "No." She took it from him and settled the gold beads around her own neck. His face lit in an astonished smile, and he recalled himself and looked away.

He waved toward the tents, pillowed his head on his hand, mimicking sleep. Motioned that way, but did not touch her. He began to walk, so she had to follow. He limped badly, but he refused help. He led her to Dr. Hierakis's tent, and here he paused beyond the awning, in the half-gloom heralding dawn. Under the awning, Charles Soerensen sat with Dr. Hierakis and David and Marco, conferring by lantern light. Marco glanced up. His gaze froze on Diana for an instant, moving to her chest, where the necklace dangled, gleaming. Darted to Anatoly Sakhalin, and then he looked away, lips tight, his expression shuttered.

Anatoly spoke to her in a low voice and motioned toward the tent and made the pillowing gesture again. Diana nodded and, as if that satisfied him, he caught her gaze for a piercing instant, and then turned and limped away.

Diana took in a deep breath and walked under the awning. "Doctor, is there somewhere I can sleep?" she asked.

Dr. Hierakis did not even look up. "Yes, dear. In my tent. Maggie and Jo are already in there. Just be careful of the equipment."

Diana did not look at Marco, kept her gaze away from him as she slipped past the little group and pushed the tent flap aside to go in.

"Diana? Here's a stretch of ground, and a thermal blanket."

"Maggie. Goddess, I'm tired. What are you doing?"

"Just trying out this new program." Maggie lay on her side. A thin slate gleamed on the tent floor, its screen lit with letters and numbers. "It's a fairly primitive translation program from an abstract of the khush language sent to us by His Nib's sister."

"Oh." Diana lay down. She stared at the dark canvas ceiling above. Perhaps she was simply too tired to sleep. "Maggie. What does *elinu* mean?"

"Hmm." The sound of light tapping. " 'Angel.' 'Spirit.' Wait, there's a longer description here. 'The Sun's daughters are *elinu* and they come down from the heavens to men and women who have died in battle or in childbirth—' That's egalitarian of them, I should say. '—to raise them up to Heaven.' There's a cross reference to—'' Maggie went on.

Diana shut her eyes. "Arkady Suvorin," she whispered, so that she would not forget his name. But somehow, she doubted she ever could. Yet it was not his face she saw, drifting down into sleep, nor even Marco's, but Anatoly Sakhalin's, staring at her while he lay on the surgery table, holding on to her as if she alone secured him to the earth.

CHAPTER FOURTEEN

Orzhekov liked to maintain a leisurely pace, preferring to save her riders' strength for battle. Not for her the constant, restless driving pace endured by those riders favored enough—or cursed enough, some men muttered—to ride with Bakhtiian's chosen thousand, or with those commanders eager to emulate Bakhtiian. It was one reason that men sought a place in her jahar. For another, she knew how to think fast and well when trouble rode in, and her jahar had invariably taken low casualties in the past three years. She was famous for being reckless on her own behalf and conservative when it came to the riders under her command. That she was a woman, and Bakhtiian's niece, counted for less than the chance to see the plains and one's wife and children again.

So it caused no comment that Orzhekov's looping sweep of towns along the lands tributary to Bakhtiian took longer than it might have, given a hastier commander. Indeed, it took so long that word reached them when they were still a day's ride from the main camp that Bahktiian had already returned from his mysterious trip to the coast with a host of barbarians in tow.

A number of the men dug out a fire pit near the commander's small traveling tent and loitered there, hoping to glean additional information by proximity. Hobbled horses grazed on the outskirts of the little camp. Orzhekov stood outside her tent, talking with Tess Soerensen and Soerensen's brother, Aleksi, who had joined up with them in late afternoon with the news.

"That one, Aleksi, he rides with Bakhtiian's jahar, doesn't he? But I heard he hasn't even a family name. How'd he get so honored?"

"He's Soerensen's brother, you fool. She adopted him three years past."

"But he's an orphan, Leonid. I heard his whole tribe was killed, that it was a plague sent by the gods. That only he and a sister lived, and she died soon after. You'd think even a khaja woman would know better than to take in someone as cursed as all that—"

"Hush, you idiot. Have you ever seen him fight? He'd take your ears and your balls off before you even drew your saber."

In the low round of laughter that followed this sally, Feodor Grekov strolled up to the fire and some of the men moved aside to make room for him.

"Grekov. Haven't you any news for us?"

"Why should I have any more news than you, Yermolov?"

Several of the riders chuckled. Feodor flushed. "Well," said Leonid with a grin, "you've shared her tent more than one night this trip. She must say something."

Conscious of Orzhekov's proximity, a few men offered suggestions, in low voices, of what their commander might say.

From her tent, Nadine had turned to watch Feodor Grekov settle down by the fire. She raised her voice and called over to her riders. "If you men haven't anything better to do but sit and gossip around the fire, you can give the horses some extra grain. We've a hard ride in the morning, and an early start."

The men grumbled, but they all rose.

"Just like a woman," said Leonid good-naturedly. "If they think you're giving their lover a hard time, then they work you to death." But he gave Feodor a friendly slap on the shoulder as he left.

Nadine watched the riders disperse and then turned back to Tess. "If you'll excuse me, I'd better go prepare our ambassador. We'll reach camp by mid-afternoon, and if he doesn't want to destroy his embassy completely, he has a couple of hard truths to learn about the jaran."

"Dina, if you don't mind me saying so—"

"I probably will, but you'll say it nevertheless, so go on."

Tess rubbed her hands together and blew on them, then

slid her gloves out from under her belt and pulled them on. "You're just putting his back up."

"I invite you to try. You've a worse temper than I do."

"Do I, indeed?" Tess glanced at Aleksi, who winked at her. She sighed. "Only where Ilya is concerned, and it hasn't done me a damn bit of good yet. I'll speak with the ambassador."

Nadine stared past Tess at the elaborate flagged awning that Jiroannes's servants had set up, as they did every evening, precise in their work. The tent entrance always faced southeast, toward the lands of the Great King. From this angle, they saw the back of Jiroannes's head where he sat in his carved and padded chair. One of the Vidiyan guardsman stood next to him, holding a lantern to cast light on the parchment Jiroannes read. "I wish you luck. May I watch?"

"Aleksi and I will go. You may listen, but stay in the shadows. He doesn't like you, Dina, so I'd rather he not see you."

Nadine gave a sarcastic snort. "As you command, Soerensen." But she did not wait to watch them go, rather walked out toward the horses.

"She's moody," said Aleksi.

"Dina is always moody. How did Charles seem? You got the letter to him?"

"Yes. He doesn't look like you."

"No, that's true enough." She pulled off her gloves and tucked them back into her belt.

"You're nervous, Tess."

She rubbed her hands together and started to jerk the gloves back out, then stopped herself, looking rueful. "Damn it. Yes, I am."

"He didn't seem frightening to me, though he's a great prince."

"You didn't grow up being the only heir to the prince, Aleksi. I know he's not happy that I stayed here."

"But, Tess, you're a woman, you're of age. Where you stay is surely your own choice."

If only it were. Or at least, if only it were so easy. He cocked his head to one side, waiting; Aleksi always knew when to wait and when to speak. He read her better, in many ways, than Ilya did, because Aleksi never layered any emotions on top of hers. But she was in too strange a mood tonight to nurse her anger at Ilya. She sighed finally and said nothing. Instead, she walked out onto the grass in a loop that would bring her by a roundabout way to Jiroannes's cluster of tents.

"Bakhtiian is furious that you left camp," said Aleksi.

Tess shrugged. "I'm not afraid of Ilya."

"But you are afraid of your own brother." He flicked at his chin with one finger, considering the stars. "I don't understand the khaja," he said at last. "And you even less."

"What do you mean by that?" It was his turn to shrug, and Tess chuckled. "Tell me about the battle."

"Some of the elders of the coast towns hired a mercenary force to waylay us. They did as well as they could, being khaja, but of course it was hopeless for them. Anatoly Sakhalin did a brilliant job of executing the charge and flight. He was wounded, but he says that one of the khaja women—" Aleksi switched for a moment to Rhuian. "—one of the actresses—saved him from being carried away by the angels. He gave her a necklace."

"Oh, dear. What happened to the mercenaries?"

"Bakhtiian sent the captain to occupy Barala, the principal of the towns that hired him. He's to execute the elders, collect tribute, send half to Bakhtiian and keep half for himself. Bakhtiian is going to send Suvorin's jahar out to patrol that line of coast for the summer and perhaps into the winter as well."

"Suvorin, eh? Ilya doesn't much like Suvorin, so doubtless that will keep Suvorin busy and out of trouble." Tess halted.

The square Vidiyan tents rose like blots of darkness some thirty paces before them. A Vidiyan guardsman sat on a rug to the left of the cluster of tents, polishing a silver tray and a set of silver dishes. The scent of aromatic herbs drifted to them on the breeze, swelling with the steam from a kettle perched on a fire of red-hot coals. The woman—the slave—knelt behind her master's chair. Her hands lay perfectly still on her thighs, and her gaze seemed fixed on her hands. She did not move.

What kind of a world have I chosen to live on? Tess thought. Yet it was no different from what Earth had been, with the same cruelties and the same kindnesses and the same hopes. And whatever else the jaran might be, they were her family. She took in a deep breath and let it all out in one huffing blow. "Now, Aleksi. You are to be silent and still."

"As still as that one?" He nodded toward the slave.

"Lord. I wonder what she thinks of, sitting there. Silent in any case. I'm going to be respectful, which is what this boy needs, I think. In order to be able to allow himself to hear what I'm saying."

"You're never respectful to Bakhtiian."

"Gods, if I was as respectful to Ilya as the rest of you are, he'd become insufferable. Shall we?" She walked forward around the outskirts of the camp and halted at the farthest fringe of awning. Aleksi followed two paces behind her.

Tess stood there, patient, until Syrannus rose and approached her. If Jiroannes was aware that she was there, he showed no sign of it. He kept reading.

"I thank you for recognizing me," said Tess to Syrannus, in Rhuian. "I ask for permission for myself and my companion to enter, and to speak with His Eminence." The final words, Jiroannes's title, she spoke in Vidyan, and that did make Jiroannes glance up in surprise. He lowered his gaze as swiftly, still pretending to ignore her, but the line of his mouth tightened.

"Please." Syrannus gestured for her to step onto the carpet. "If you will wait."

The old man looked nervous, and when he turned to hurry over to his master's chair, he wiped his hands on his black sash as if he were wiping sweat from his palms. The two men spoke together. Jiroannes handed Syrannus the parchment and the servant rolled it up carefully and called a second guardsman over to take it away. The first guardsman shifted position, angling the lantern light to include a patch of ground before the chair.

Syrannus hurried back to Tess and gestured her forward. She crossed the outer carpet and inclined her head respectfully to Jiroannes. "May the Great King live many years, and his affairs prosper, and your fortunes follow his," she said, still in Vidyan.

Jiroannes hesitated. From what little Tess knew of Vidyan, she had now put him in a position from which he had either to greet her respectfully in return or else insult her deliberately.

At last, he spoke. "May your name dwell a thousand years in the heart of the Great King." He did not stand. Neither did she kneel. After a moment, he signed to Syrannus, and the old man brought a stool.

Tess sat. It was parity, of a sort. "I hope, your eminence, that you will forgive my speaking in Rhuian, since I do not speak your language well enough to converse in it."

"Where did you learn it? Surely you have not visited the Great King's lands?"

"No, to my sorrow I have not. But I always seek to learn new languages."

"Ah." He appeared satisfied that some piece of a puzzle known only to himself had just fallen into place. "You are an interpreter."

Tess suppressed her grin. "Yes," she agreed, realizing just then the best tack to take with him. "But I am also a khaja—a foreigner—traveling with the jaran. In this, you and I are alike. Originally, I came from Jeds."

Now he looked interested. "Jeds is a great city. The Great King has exchanged royal gifts with his cousin the prince of Jeds, and we have sent envoys there in the past. Indeed, a Jedan merchant admitted to the palace school taught me and the other young nobles Rhuian, since the Great King deemed it an important language to learn for those of us aspiring to become envoys and ambassadors."

"Perhaps, your eminence, you will kindly allow me to tell you a few things I have learned in my years with the jaran. I have every hope that your mission will succeed. Certainly I hope to avoid war between Bakhtiian and your Great King."

He prickled, definitely, but he did not dismiss her. "How did you come to be with the jaran?" he asked at last. "Are you a slave?"

For an instant, Tess allowed herself the pleasure of imagining how Nadine would react to such a remark, directed at any jaran woman. But then, Nadine would never make a good ambassador. "Your eminence, I am married to Bakhtiian."

He blinked. In the cast of light from the lantern, his narrow face bore an almost demonic look, framed by the white cloth bound around his head and his pointed black beard.

But Jiroannes came from a polygamous culture. She could be any junior wife, of marginal importance, except perhaps that she was khaja and an interpreter.

"I beg your pardon, your eminence," Tess added. "I did not make myself clear. I am Bakhtiian's only wife. I am also the sister of the prince of Jeds."

There was silence; a long silence, as the poor boy absorbed the full meaning of her simple declaration. "Your grace," said Jiroannes at last, reluctantly but with a kind of fascinated horror. He stood up.

"Please, your eminence. Do sit down." He sat. She considered his chastened face. Doubtless the knowledge that the Jedan prince had already deemed Bakhtiian and his jaran hordes dangerous enough to offer a marriage alliance to them made a formidable impact on the Vidiyan ambassador. Not to mention insulting her by calling her a slave. Lord, he really was quite young, and probably as spoiled and self-absorbed and isolated a young noble as she herself had been, growing up as the only sibling of the great hero of humanity, Charles Soerensen.

"Your grace, I beg pardon for any rudeness you may have received on my behalf."

"You are forgiven."

"Certainly I would be honored to listen to your wisdom concerning these jaran barbarians."

How quickly they came to an accord, civilized cousins thrown in with the savages. Tess allowed herself a smile, and then she began, gently but firmly, to make him begin to understand how different things were with the jaran.

The slave-girl still knelt behind Jiroannes's chair. Could the girl understand Rhuian? She did not move. She might have been carved from stone, so still was she. Tess realized that she wasn't particularly angry with Jiroannes for keeping a slave. Disgusted. Resigned, knowing that the institution could not be erased with a wave of her hand. One had to work slowly. That's what Charles would say. She winced internally. Who was acting like Charles now?

At last she took her leave. Jiroannes rose and bowed to her, then escorted her personally to the edge of the carpet. She walked out onto the grass with Aleksi and just stood there, breathing in the air. The wind brushed her hair. Stars filled the night sky, brilliant with promise. Over by Nadine's tent, the fire pit had long since smoldered into coals. On a far rise, an edge of darkness against the darker sky, the tiny figure of a scout blotted out stars. Horses stood scattered beyond the camp, some staked, some hobbled. A few tents had been set up, but most of the men slept on the ground, dark lumps wrapped in blankets.

"I love the plains," said Tess in a low voice, letting the sky and the sweep of ground envelop her. "It's so open here."

"Look there."

Tess followed the line of Aleksi's gaze to see a man pause beside Nadine's tent and then duck inside. "Grekov, again? He's in love with her. She'll never have him, though."

"But women have no choice in marriage," Aleksi objected.

"Jaran women don't, it's true. But Nadine is no longer truly jaran. Jeds marked her too well." Tess's gaze flicked over the Vidiyan encampment and halted on the slender form of the ambassador, watching—what? But it was clear enough what he was watching. He, too, stared at Nadine Orzhekov's tent. A moment later his slave-girl approached him and knelt at his feet. He retreated inside his own tent. She followed.

"Sonia's not going to like this," Tess said, to no one in particular, to the stars, perhaps. And why should Sonia like it? That she would not was one of the reasons that Tess could love her so well.

"Aren't you going to sleep?" asked Aleksi.

She shook her head. "I can't sleep. I think I'll walk for a while."

"I'll walk with you, then."

And Tess was glad of his company.

The night wind came up, swelling and ebbing around them, sighing through the grass in waves. Above, stars shone. Men slept below. The deep silence that lay here was otherwise complete and, in its immensity, liberating.

CHAPTER FIFTEEN

The first day, Yomi told the actors to stay within their little enclave of tents and on no account to venture out into the confusion of the jaran camp. Ever the slave driver, Owen led them in a round of exercises until midday and after lunch put them to work setting up the screens and the carpets and the portable platform at the edge of the enclave. He had chosen the space carefully. The ground sloped up here, providing a natural amphitheater. He fussed over the placement of the screens, of the carpets, of the platform, until he drove all the actors crazy. Yomi finally sent them to supper.

Diana escaped to the enclave bordering the Company's cluster of tents, that of the Soerensen party. To her eye, Charles Soerensen's tent had also been set up carefully, facing the outskirts of the jaran camp as if inviting envoys to visit this acre of earth that he claimed as his by right of possession. Dr. Hierakis's large tent stood beside his, more a companion than an attendant, and behind them the smaller tents of his party formed a semicircle around the back, enclosing a patch of ground as a kind of private courtyard.

Here she found David and Maggie, crouching beside a fire pit dug into the earth.

"It's cold today," said Maggie as Diana came up, "but at least it didn't rain. Hello there, Diana. I heard you all hooting and howling over yonder. What on earth were you doing?"

"Vocal exercises. I hope we didn't spook anyone." Diana glanced past the straight edge of Soerensen's tent toward the vast camp sprawled beyond.

"Oh, they already think the good doctor is some kind of otherworldly visitor."

"Good Lord," muttered David.

"I didn't mean it like that," added Maggie. "Not literally, that is. She's been very careful to make sure that all the medicine she does is technologically within their limits. There's an entire conclave of old men and women in the doctor's tent right now. I gather that they were tremendously impressed by her healing skills after that battle five days ago."

Diana shivered. She knelt beside the fire and gratefully accepted a mug of hot tea from David. That afternoon and night seemed surreal to her now. She could almost believe it had never happened, except that they had had to repack the wagons and convey some of their goods on horseback in order to leave room in the wagons for the wounded who could not ride. "Gwyn said that only one man died on the trip here."

"Two, I think," said David. "But one of them Cara called a courtesy death. You acquitted yourself well, Diana, that night." He shuddered. "I couldn't have done what you did. I hate blood."

"Handsome necklace." Maggie reached out and traced her fingers over the gold beads. "I'll bet these are solid gold. Do you know what this is worth for the metal alone?" Diana blushed. Maggie grinned. "Ah, going native already, are you? I hear the young man who gave this to you is one of their nobility. Or at least, of an important family. I'm not sure our concept of nobility is quite the right word."

Diana studied the steam rising out of her mug. It rose into the air and dissipated, wafted into nothingness by the cold breeze. She had not seen Anatoly Sakhalin since that night, and by now he was probably swallowed up in the jaran camp. Never to be seen again. "It seems like once Bakhtiian and his army—his soldiers—got back to us, that we weren't allowed anything to do with the wounded. Except for Dr. Hierakis, of course."

"Can you blame them? We are foreigners, after all. Perhaps they have some kind of taboo. Or perhaps they just prefer to take care of their own. Why should they trust us?"

Marco ducked out from the back entrance to Soerensen's tent and glanced up. Diana saw him register her presence, she even caught his eye, but he turned around and slipped back inside the tent. As if he was avoiding her. Which he was. Which he cursed well ought to. "Did you ever find out what the big fire was that they lit after we left?"

"Oh, you mean from the pond? A cremation pyre. They burn their dead."

David shuddered again. "Just heaped them on and burned them. Why did I come? Or did I ask that already?"

Maggie laughed. "A thousand times. Don't repeat yourself, David, you'll get boring."

"I wonder what they think of us," Diana mused.

"They think you're an angel," said Maggie, and laughed again when Diana turned red. "Which seems ironic enough, when you think of it."

"When will we be allowed to go out into their camp?" David asked. "I'd like to do some drawing."

"I don't know," admitted Maggie, "but I imagine His Nibs is going to be cautious."

"Very cautious," echoed David. "What's going on out there?"

Diana rose with the other two and followed them out alongside Dr. Hierakis's tent. Under the awning of her tent, Dr. Hierakis sat cross-legged on a pillow surrounded by about twenty women and men of various ages, mostly elderly.

Diana stared. She had not yet seen a jaran woman. They looked, well, rather ordinary. They wore long tunics dyed in bright colors over striped trousers and soft leather boots. Some wore simple beaded headpieces draped over their braided hair; others wore a round fur cap shaped like the men's helmets. The men here wore gold or blue shirts, not red, and there was less embroidery on their shirts. A few men in the scarlet worn by the soldiers loitered in the background. One man was seated in the middle, his back to Diana and her companions, and he was clearly the object of the conversation: his shirt lay at his hips, revealing a handsome expanse of bare back. An older silver-haired jaran man was crouched beside him, drawing patterns on his shoulder that traced the line of his scars and injuries.

"Look," said Diana, nodding toward the silver-haired man. "He speaks Rhuian, too. If you listen to the interchange between him and Dr. Hierakis, you can tell he's translating for the others. I wonder where an old man like that learned Rhuian.''

''Lady in Heaven,'' said David in a hushed voice. ''It can't be.'' He sounded so odd that Diana turned to him in alarm. But he was looking beyond her, beyond the gathering under the doctor's awning, beyond Soerensen's tent, toward the outskirts of the jaran camp.

Three jaran soldiers came cantering around the outer fringes of the vast encampment. An instant later, Diana realized that although they all were dressed in the red shirts and black trousers of the jaran soldier, two were female. The man was the one called Aleksi. Of the women, one had the black hair and olive complexion of those of the jaran who were dark, but the other had, not blonde hair and a fair complexion, but something in between. They pulled up thirty meters in front of Soerensen's tent and dismounted. The brown-haired woman was half a head taller than her female companion, as tall as the male, as tall as many of the jaran men; as tall as the women in Soerensen's party. She wore a saber at her belt and carried herself with the kind of unconscious authority of those who are used to an exalted position in life.

''Tess!'' The exclamation came, unexpectedly, from Dr. Hierakis. She stood up abruptly, disrupting her conference.

As if on cue, the entrance to Soerensen's tent swept aside and Soerensen walked out, deep in conversation with Marco. He took two steps, glanced toward the doctor and the more distant clump that was Diana and David and Maggie, and stopped. For a beat, he did nothing. Then he looked straight up, along the converging lines of their sight, at his sister.

''Charles!'' The name burst out of Terese Soerensen as if by accident. She clapped her hands over her mouth in a gesture that looked utterly spontaneous and after a moment lowered them. She had the kind of stupid grin on her face that afflicts people who are overwhelmingly nervous and excited together. A few words passed between her and her companions; then she ran forward and hugged her brother.

He, too, was smiling. They separated, and Tess turned to greet Marco. She laughed at him and slapped him with some amusement on the chest. He grinned. Diana could

not hear what they were saying. Dr. Hierakis waded
around the sea of healers and put out her arms.

This time, Tess Soerensen's smile looked more confident and more genuine. She embraced Dr. Hierakis
firmly, and her smile as they parted was easy and cheerful. Skilled as Diana had become at reading body language, she could tell that the doctor's greeting was
warmer than Charles Soerensen's; not more heartfelt,
perhaps, but less constrained.

"My God, she's different," breathed David.

"Well well well," said Maggie.

"She's . . . she's . . .''

"I'd never heard she was quite that handsome as a girl.
I always heard she was shy, awkward, and headstrong.
But then, I've never met her, and by the time I signed on
with His Nibs, she was at university and then absconded
to Rhui.''

"Reserved, not shy," corrected David, still gaping.
Tess Soerensen glanced their way, and her eyes rounded
suddenly, recognizing David. She hesitated, then waved
him over.

"Invited to the presence," said Maggie.

"Damn you, Mags. Come with me. I'm not doing this
alone. You, too, Diana.''

"Cold feet?" Maggie asked.

"You cold-hearted bitch. Mags, please.''

Maggie chuckled. "Well, come on, then, Diana. Our
womanly presence will support the poor besotted fool.''

" 'What passion hangs these weights upon my tongue?
I cannot speak to her, yet she urg'd conference.' ''

"Lord," moaned David. But he straightened his
shoulders and set off to cross the gap. Maggie followed,
grabbing Diana by the wrist and tugging her along behind. The jaran healers sat quietly, patiently, and watched
this little scene with interest. The silver-haired man
smiled at Diana as she passed. The next instant, she realized that the young man sitting in the center, just now
struggling to get back into his shirt, was Anatoly Sakhalin. As his head emerged through the collar, he glanced
up, saw her, and averted his gaze from her as swiftly as
if her presence stung him. Maggie dragged her to a stop
behind David, and she had to wrench her attention back
to the matter at hand.

"David!" Tess Soerensen was saying. "What are you doing here? Did Charles drag you along?"

It took Diana a moment to figure out what was strange about her speech: the cadences of her Anglais were slightly altered, as if she had not spoken it for some time.

"I had sufficient inducements," replied David. "I'm interested in ancient engineering, after all. Tess, you haven't met Maggie O'Neill."

"Honored," said Tess Soerensen, shaking Maggie's hand.

"Likewise," replied Maggie with her usual aplomb. "I'm Charles's assistant, recorder, and official historian. This is one of the actors, Diana Brooke-Holt."

Diana smiled at Tess Soerensen. Tess had fine green eyes and a sincere smile, but nothing of her brother's quietly formidable bearing. "Honored," Diana said, feeling all at once that she might like this woman and not feeling at all overawed by her. "I understand you're doing linguistics fieldwork here, M. Soerensen."

"Tess, please." Soerensen blinked, looking confused for a moment. She glanced at her brother and immediately an expression of comprehension flashed over her features. "Of course," she said, sounding a little simpleminded. "My linguistics research. Of course. And you're one of the—actors?"

"The Bharentous Repertory Company," put in Dr. Hierakis. "Surely you've heard of them, Tess. They've come along to do some fieldwork themselves."

"Of course I've heard of them. I saw them in Berlin, performing the *Mahabharata*. I don't recall if you were with them then." She considered a moment and as if by habit glanced back toward her two jaran companions, still waiting fifty paces out. "Oh, hell," she said under her breath.

Charles Soerensen was a quiet man, holding his power in reserve, hoarding it, concealing it from a power greater than his own—the power of the Chapalii Empire. Waiting for a chance to strike again, to free humanity from the yoke of the alien Empire. Even his entrances, such as the one Diana had just witnessed, were subtle, small entrances, perfectly timed but not showy, and never ostentatious.

From the camp, entering stage left, came an altogether

different kind of leader. He walked with only two attendants, and yet the two could as well have been one hundred, they endowed him with so much state.

Bakhtiian looked furious. His fury radiated so far that even though Diana could barely distinguish his features, she could read anger in every line of his body.

"Excuse me," said Tess, turning to leave.

"Where are you going, Tess?" asked her brother quietly.

Tess cast a rueful grin back over her shoulder. "To head him off at the pass."

"No," said Charles.

Tess halted as if she had been pulled short by a rope. She did not move at all for a moment, then she spun back. "Charles, let me go." She sounded—angry? scared? shocked?—Diana could not tell.

"We will wait here," he replied calmly.

Tess dropped her chin and stared at the ground, for all the world like a scolded child.

Bakhtiian paused for long enough beside Aleksi and the female soldier to add them to his train. Their obedience, like Tess's to her brother, was absolute and immediate. Bakhtiian advanced on Soerensen's tent. Diana looked behind, to see the jaran healers and Anatoly Sakhalin watching also.

With curt politeness, Bakhtiian halted five paces outside the awning of the tent and inclined his head toward Charles Soerensen. "I trust you have set up your camp to your satisfaction," he said in Rhuian. He did not look at Tess Soerensen. No, it was more than that. He was forcefully not looking at her, as if the action of not looking at her was as deliberate as if he had chosen to look at her.

"Indeed, we have," replied Charles Soerensen. "It is a good stretch of ground, and suitable to our purpose here. The actors are especially pleased with the terrain, since it provides them with a natural amphitheater."

"I hope my people will be able to enjoy their performances soon. We will have a proper celebration to honor your arrival at our camp tomorrow evening. I would be pleased to escort you and any of your party around our camp tomorrow morning, if it pleases you. Now, if you will excuse me, there are military matters which I must discuss with my generals.''

He took one step back, turned, and then turned back. "Soerensen?'' he said, to Tess. It meant: of course you will attend me as well. Now.

Standing with one foot on, one foot off, the carpet, at the edge of the awning, Tess stood equidistant between the two men. Everyone was watching her. They were waiting for her decision.

She lifted her chin finally, clearly aware that she was the focus of all attention. She looked angry and embarrassed and irresolute and even slightly amused. But she did not say anything. The silence stretched out until it became painful.

Soerensen waited. Bakhtiian waited. In fact, Diana realized, they were both waiting for Tess to capitulate to them, knowing that she could not capitulate to both. In a sudden rush of insight, of compassion, Diana realized that Tess could not make that decision. Not now, at any rate. What had led her to wear jaran clothing and ride with jaran soldiers Diana did not know. What led Bakhtiian to order her around as if she were one of his people was also a mystery. Even if Tess wanted to disobey her brother's deceptively mild command, Diana was not sure that she could.

Murmuring rose in the huddle of jaran healers only fifteen paces to their backs. Marco Burckhardt slipped a hand inside his belt, reaching for something. David took an impulsive step forward, blindly trying to protect— Tess? Or Charles? Anatoly Sakhalin appeared to the side, stepping into the group flanking Bakhtiian. Although his arm still rested in a sling, he wore a saber. His good hand brushed its hilt.

Things were going to get ugly very quickly. Battle lines had been drawn, and if someone didn't intervene—well, Diana now knew what the aftermath of a battle looked like. And neither Bakhtiian nor Soerensen looked ready or willing to back down.

So Diana did the first thing that came to mind. She gave a gasp, flung the back of her left hand up to her forehead, and collapsed to the carpet in a faint.

CHAPTER SIXTEEN

In the confusion, Tess escaped. She backed up, spun, and sprinted for her horse, which had been left with reins dangling to wait for her return. Bracing her left foot in the stirrup, she swung on and urged the mare away. She shook with rage and self-disgust.

How dare they reduce her to a pawn? How dare they try to force her to choose between them? And, oh God, she hated herself for letting them. She had just stood there, gaping like an idiot, paralyzed. Charles had not changed, not one bit, and she was still terrified of him. And Ilya! She thought her heart might well burst with anger.

She was out of sight of camp by now, and she slowed the mare to a halt and dismounted to lean against her shoulder. Zhashi nuzzled her cheek and then nosed at her belt, trying to pry her shirt loose.

"Stop that, you miserable beast," Tess said with affection. "I don't have anything for you." She rubbed Zhashi's forehead with her knuckles and then found a tangled stretch of mane and combed it free with her fingers. Distracted, she fished in her pouch and brought out a length of ribbon, which she braided into Zhashi's mane. Zhashi submitted to this attention with the patience of the vain.

It was soothing work. The bitter truth was, she was still running away. She was still afraid to face Charles. And Ilya—

"The other bitter truth is, Zhashi, that I love him too much. He's been gone for a month, and when I saw him walking across to us, it was like seeing the sun rising. Lord, I sound like any love-sick adolescent. But he's so beautiful." Zhashi snorted in disgust and bent her head to rip up a clump of grass. "Oh, certainly not more beautiful than you, my dear. How could I ever have said such a thing?'' Tess chuckled, then sobered, tying off the ribbon. ''Oh, Zhash, I don't know what to do.''

Zhashi resumed grazing. The indistinct gold of the plain extended without interruption to the sharp line that separated grass and sky. Thin strings of cloud laced one half of the sky, trailing down below the horizon. The wind blew—the wind always blew here—whipping the tall grass into a frenzy. At the horizon, she could see the amorphous mass of a herd of horses, out grazing. The sun hung a handsbreadth above the horizon, sinking, and the moon already shone, pale, in the deepening blue of the sky.

She had to go back, of course. She mounted and headed back toward camp, back toward Charles's encampment. An hour or two with Charles, then back to her own tent for the reunion with Ilya. That ought to satisfy both of them, as a beginning.

But as she came into sight of camp, a rider intercepted her. It was Ilya. She considered for an instant trying to avoid him, but it was undignified, for one thing, and for the other, he could outride her without thinking about it, and he was mounted on his stallion, Kriye. She pulled up instead and waited.

Kriye began to prance, showing off for Zhashi as Bakhtiian reined him in beside Tess. With a ruthless tug on the reins, Bakhtiian brought the black to an abrupt halt. ''Damned horse,'' Bakhtiian muttered. Then he looked up at her.

More than any other feature, it was his eyes that Tess loved. They burned. They were lit, pervaded by an intensity that was perhaps, just perhaps, a little mad. Obsessed, at the very least, but no more so than Charles was obsessed. Charles just hid it better.

''Tess.'' His voice sounded hoarse. He reached out and took hold of her left hand, gripping it tightly.

''Oh, Ilya,'' she said impulsively. ''I missed you.''

From her hand, it was but a turn of the wrist for him to take hold of her reins and commandeer them for himself. Zhashi minced, objecting to this kidnapping. ''You're coming with me,'' said Ilya, and started back for camp, leading Zhashi.

"Damn you." Tess went red. "Give me back my reins."

"You're coming with me."

"I won't have you leading me through camp like this."

He did not reply. His trail led away from the distant Soerensen enclave, around the fringe of tents. But she saw quickly enough what he was doing. Vladimir and Anatoly Sakhalin stood waiting at the edge of camp to receive the horses. Tess was damned if she'd make a scene in front of them. She dismounted, handed Zhashi over to Sakhalin, and hoped like hell that the chestnut mare would kick him.

Then she relented. Seeing Anatoly's arm in a sling reminded her too bitterly of Kirill Zvertkov, who had never regained use of his injured arm. "What happened?" she asked Anatoly.

"Speared and trampled," he said cheerfully. He wiggled the fingers of his left hand. "But you see, the prince's healer says I'll be free of this sling in a hand of days."

"Ah. Dr. Hierakis looked at you. I'm glad." She smiled at the young man, whom she liked well enough, except for his doglike devotion to Bakhtiian. "But then again," she remarked aloud, walking alongside Ilya into the darkening expanse of camp, "they're all besotted with you."

He had a good grip on her wrist, but he walked so close to her that anyone passing them might not mark that he was forcing her to go along with him. "Not all of them," he replied. "I'm sending Suvorin and his jahar to the coast. His sister's son died in the battle. I'm keeping his son with my thousand, now."

"A hostage for Suvorin's good behavior."

"It's a great honor, to ride with my jahar."

"It's a great honor to ride in any of the first rank jahars. Like Yaroslav Sakhalin's jahar. Those that are allowed to, that is."

His fingers tightened convulsively on her wrist, but he did not rise to the bait. Fuming, Tess kept silent. They walked the rest of the way without saying one single word. At last they came to the clearing in the center of camp that housed her tent. Its colors had already gone dull in the deepening twilight. The golden banner of the army that graced its peak fluttered and sank in the dying wind. No one accosted them here, as if the camp had been emptied out before their arrival. Around the great tent in a crescent stood the other tents of the Orzhekov family, those who remained here with the army: Sonia's tent, Nadine's tent, Aleksi's little tent and those of a few female cousins. At the very edge of the crescent stood the tent of Juli Danov and her husband Nikolai Sibirin, bridging the gap between the tents of the Orzhekov family and those surrounding the center of camp who were of the Orzhekov tribe. Beyond them, in the same kind of clusters, spread the tents of the other tribes of the first rank, Sakhalin and Grekov, Suvorin and Arkhanov, Velinya and Raevsky and Vershinin and Fedoseyev. And beyond them, their daughter tribes, and their daughters' daughter tribes, the army of the jaran.

Three figures waited under the awning of Tess's tent. Ilya did not let go of her even after they crossed onto the carpet. "Out," he said to the occupants.

Sonia Orzhekov rose. Her blonde hair was braided with ribbons and beads, giving her a festive look, but her normally cheerful expression was stern. "Cousin," she said to Ilya, "I expect better manners from you."

"I beg your pardon, cousin." He bent at once and kissed her on either cheek, and for an instant his expression softened. "Where are the little ones?

"Well away," said Sonia ominously.

"Then," he said stiffly, "if you please, I would like a word alone with my wife."

Sonia crossed over to Tess and gave her adopted sister a hug. "Well," she said, "I'm glad to see you home safely, at any rate." She flashed a glance back at Bakhtiian, but did not elaborate on her statement. "Come along, Aleksi." Aleksi followed her away.

Nadine rose as well, heading after them.

"You'll stay," said Ilya abruptly. "I want your report."

Nadine halted and turned to face her uncle. "You don't really want my report. You're just exacting vengeance because I took Tess with me despite what you wanted."

"Orzhekov, you are a jahar leader because of your skill, not because you are my niece. I expect you to behave accordingly. Now, your report."

Like her uncle, Nadine had the ability to make her face go still, revealing no emotion. In a tight voice, she delivered her report of their journey.

"And the ambassador?" Ilya asked. "Where is he now?"

"I installed him in the northeastern corner with the other foreign embassies. May I make a suggestion?"

"You may."

"When you receive him, I suggest you put the fear of the gods into him."

"Ah," said Ilya, looking for an instant thoughtful rather than angry. "I understand. You may go."

"Thank you." With a curt nod, Nadine left.

"That certainly was both comprehensive and enlightening," said Tess in Rhuian, drawling slightly. "I have nothing to add to her edifying report. Now, I'll join Nadine." She did not move, however, because he still had hold of her wrist.

In khush, without looking at her, he said: "I haven't given you permission to leave."

"Haven't you? I wasn't aware that I required your permission to leave."

Now he turned. "I expressly told you not to leave camp."

"Yes, you did, and it finally occurred to me that since you won't trust me as a soldier, then I might as well act as your wife. And by the gods, Ilya, as your wife, you have no authority over me whatsoever." She twisted her wrist in his hand and jerked herself free of his grip. But as she started away, he caught her arm. "People are staring," she snapped.

"Let them stare." He flung his other arm around her waist and with no warning dragged her bodily backward and into the tent. Pressed this close against him, she could feel that he was shaking. Inside, two lanterns burned, casting a glow across the interior: the table and chair, khaja work, to one side, where she wrote; an empty bronze cauldron with a smaller cauldron nested inside; a small bronze stove with two handles; a wooden chest carved with stylized horses; a standing cabinet with hinged doors, another piece of khaja work; and the tapestry that concealed the sleeping area.

"One month it has been," he said, his voice so low

that Tess knew he was in a rage. "You didn't even greet me."

"My God. You're jealous."

"You disobeyed my direct orders not to leave camp."

"You refused to let me go to the coast with you, to meet Charles. Gods, Ilya, what did you expect me to do?" Standing this close to him, she felt her anger ebb. "Did you really think I'd wait meekly for you to return?" For an instant, she thought he was going to smile. But to her surprise, he let go of her and strode over to the table, sitting down in the chair. He regarded her from this uncharacteristic seat, glowering at her. Fine, then, if he didn't want a truce. Tess was more than happy to continue the argument.

"You didn't tell me that your brother holds me in such contempt," he said at last.

That took her off guard. "*What* are you talking about?"

"What am I to think? He is a great prince, and he comes attended with a handful of assistants, only one of whom is a soldier—and she a woman—and, by the gods, a company of actors. Is this the kind of state he keeps? Does he think my power so trivial that he fears me not at all? What if I chose to kill him, claim Jeds for myself through my marriage with you, and march south? Oh, I know it's a long journey overland, through many khaja princedoms, and I would never attempt it with the army I have now—but what is ten years to me, Tess? If I kill him now, and consolidate my power here, what is to stop me from marching on Jeds and conquering all the lands between?"

Even when she knew an ambush was coming, she was never prepared for it, because he always attacked from an entirely different position than the one she expected. Damn him. What could she say? What *should* she say? What he read in her silence she didn't know. In any case, he went on.

"Why should he put himself in my power in this way? He doesn't fear me. Does he think I am incapable of desiring to have what is his? That my awe of Jeds is so great that I fear him? That your influence with me will stop me from harming him?"

"But why should you kill him?" Tess asked at last,

her voice perfectly calm because she was still too surprised by this sudden confession to know what to make of it. "What good would it do you?"

He stood up, pushing himself up with one hand on the table. It rocked slightly, and then he lifted his hand and crossed to Tess in five strides. "Unless he never meant to come out on the plains at all," he said quietly. "We have nothing to negotiate. Jeds is too far away and I am young in my power. In time, certainly, but I can just as well ride north and east along the Golden Road. What if he brought no entourage because he never meant to leave his ship? If you had come with me to the coast, he could have put you on board the ship and sailed south."

Which was perfectly true. Trust Ilya to have seen it. Trust Charles to have made the point clear without ever stating it aloud. And leaving her to deal with it. "But what about the actors, then?" she asked, knowing the question was a flanking action.

"The actors," said Ilya, with the merest quirk of a smile, "are all mad, clearly. But like all entertainers, they must know they are welcome anywhere. Like all singers-of-tales, they are given both the favor and the protection of the gods. I will do them no harm."

"And meanwhile, you have offered me a grave insult. How dare you have so little respect for my dignity that you would lead my horse as if I was a child and then drag me by main force back through camp like that?"

He looked taken aback by this direct attack. He looked a little embarrassed. "Tess." He placed his hands on her shoulders and slid them up to cup her face in his palms. He swayed toward her.

"Don't think this will work," she murmured, and then she leaned into him and kissed him, running her hands from his belt up the smooth silken line of his back. The hard knot of his belt buckle pressed against her, and she had to shift her hips slightly to keep her saber hilt from tangling with his sheathed knife.

He broke off the kiss and sighed, gathering her into him, and kissed her along the line of her jaw up to her right ear. "If he takes you away from me," he whispered, as softly as an endearment, "then I promise you that I *will* destroy Jeds."

Tess stiffened in his embrace and slid her hands around

to his chest, bracing herself away from him. He let go of her. "What if I decide to leave of my own free will?"

So many expressions chased themselves across his features that it took her a moment to recognize the one that lay underneath all the others. He was afraid. Ilya was afraid of losing her.

He threw his arms around her, enclosing her, and yanked her tight against him. "By the gods, I will stop you."

"How?"

He did not answer in words. Words contained the least part of the language they spoke to one another. The heat of his hands burned on her skin. Tess traced the line of his beard, traced his lips, with her fingers. Her hands ranged down to the clasp of his belt, and she eased it away and let it drop onto the soft pile of carpets.

"Tess," he said again, hesitant.

Tess got her hands under his shirt and slid them up, over his chest, teasing the nipples and then, when he was breathless, steering him backward through the curtain into the sleeping alcove. By shifting her foot, she tripped him, and he tumbled down onto the heap of silken pillows, pulling her with him. Astride him, she eased off his shirt, and let him unbuckle her belt and thrust it away. She captured his hands and pressed them against her.

"Promise me," she said. "Promise me you will not threaten my brother."

"Damn you." He was angry, still, but he was also laughing. "It gains me nothing, now, to kill him, and you know it."

"Then it costs you nothing to promise me. He is your ally, Ilya, you must believe that."

He shifted his hips beneath her and used the toe of one boot to pry off the other. "He cares nothing for me, Tess, except that I married you."

"That isn't true."

"Isn't it? Then tell me he would have come here, that he would even send an embassy to the jaran, if you weren't here."

"Jeds is far away—"

"Gods, Tess," he said, exasperated. With an expert twist, he freed his hands and flipped her over, so that he lay on top of her. He found the tip of her braid and undid it, loosening her hair until it lay free, spread out on the pillows.

"You haven't promised me yet," she said stubbornly.

He sat back with a great sigh and took off his other boot. She lay still on the pillows, watching him in the soft light of the lanterns. He kept his black hair cut short, a fashion that had spread among his soldiers, and he was obsessive about keeping his beard neat and trimmed. Whether by accident or by design, the lantern light haloed him, giving him a haze of light, as if the gods had long since marked him as their own. Which they had, according to the beliefs of his own people.

"I promise you that I will not threaten your brother as long as you stay with me," he said.

"Ilya!" It was her turn to be exasperated.

"We're negotiating, my wife. Now it is your turn to make a counteroffer."

She sat up and took off her boots, and regarded him. Oh, she was still angry with him, but right now, it didn't matter. She laughed. "I'll consider it. Now, my husband, I think it time to remind you that you have been gone for a month, and you have certain obligations to your wife that you have not yet fulfilled."

"Most willingly," he murmured. "Gods, Tess, I missed you." He sank down with her into the soft bed of pillows.

Later, lying quiet, she stroked his hair while he kissed her fingers, one by one.

"We'll make a child," he said, and because it was habitual with him, it came out more an order than a request. "Do you know, by the time Niko was my age he was a grandfather." Then, content for now, he sighed and nestled his face against her neck, tangling himself in with her and, as he often did, he fell asleep immediately.

A grandfather. The word looped over and over in her thoughts as she lay still, staring at him. Thirty-seven—not old at all. But here, if he lived another thirty years, it would be a miracle. Whereas she could expect to live another eighty or ninety years: the thought of living in a universe without him in it—she winced away from even thinking about it.

She sought out the silver in his hair, but there was not

enough yet to show up in the dim light, not enough to lighten his black hair. He had sun-weathered skin, but like all the jaran, the wrinkles came late and slowly. She traced the scar on his cheek—the scar of his marriage to her—and farther down, to one on his shoulder, along his chest to the flat line of his abdomen, to his hips. Easing out from under his arm, she pulled away from him and covered him with a thick quilt of fur. He slept, undisturbed by these attentions.

But the signs were beginning to show: cuts, superficial wounds that did not heal as quickly, wrinkles at the corners of his eyes. He would grow old, truly old, and she would still be young.

She dressed, braided her hair, and went outside. It was dark now and most of the camp was quiet. In the direction of the Sakhalin encampment some kind of carousing was going on, doubtless in celebration of Anatoly Sakhalin's elevation to a command of his own.

Under the light of lanterns hung from the awning of her tent, Sonia sat with Nadine. She was sewing together two strips of woven cloth, with Nadine aiding her.

"Well, well," called Sonia as Tess ducked under her awning. "So you survived that, did you?"

"Damned arrogant bastard," said Tess, bending to give Sonia a kiss. "It's good to be back."

Sonia chuckled. "You should have greeted him first, Tess."

"I can't believe you say that, Sonia. Of all people."

Sonia grinned. "Oh, not for his sake, or even his dignity, Tess. You must think of the rest of us, although I trust he'll be in a better humor when he wakes."

"He ought to be. Where *are* the children?"

"I sent them off to the Sakhalin celebration."

"Aren't you going yourself?"

"Mother warned me that I mustn't defer to Mother Sakhalin *too* much."

"Oho," said Tess, "very clever, then, to send the children but not yourself. Now, if you'll excuse me, I need to return to my brother."

"I hear that Anatoly Sakhalin has fallen in love with one of the actors," said Sonia. "Perhaps you'll look her over for me."

Tess shrugged. "I don't know who you mean."

"Yes, you do," said Nadine suddenly. "The one who fainted. Well timed, you know, from a tactical point of view."

"Good Lord. What would Anatoly Sakhalin want with a khaja wife, anyway?"

Both Sonia and Nadine laughed. "My dearest Tess," said Sonia with a grin, "he wants to be like Ilya, of course."

"Gods." Feeling that this expressed everything that was left to express, Tess took her leave and walked back through camp to her brother's enclave.

Here it was not quiet. Coming up on the two sets of tents pitched just beyond the army, Tess recognized with a shock the life of a society that was at once familiar and distant to her, after four years on Rhui. Day and night were equal to these people. Even though here they had to rely on lantern light, still they did not put aside their activities with the sunset and begin again with sunrise. She paused in the gloom outside the ring of light, watching.

Under Charles's awning sat Charles and Cara and David—those three she knew from before. Maggie sat with them, and a handful of others she had not met. As she watched, a trio walked in from the side, laughing and talking in voices trained to carry: a few of the actors, evidently. Tess marked out Diana, the young golden-haired actress; she was pretty, of course, but more than that, she seemed to carry light with her wherever she went. Rather like Ilya, however ironic that might be, except that Diana shone with sweetness and a fine, generous spirit, not with stark power.

Tess felt a presence move at her back and she turned to see a man approaching her. He was tall and bulky—not fat, not at all, but much bigger than jaran men.

He halted beside her, crossing his arms on his chest. "The Tess I knew wouldn't have spotted me coming."

"Hello, Marco. I didn't get a chance to greet you properly, before. I wanted to thank you for your letter." She chuckled. "How long ago that seems. 'Your dear old uncle Marco,' indeed. I always thought you didn't much like children."

"I never know what to do with them," he replied curtly. She glanced at him, curious, but he was looking at the group under the awning. He was looking at Diana. "Is it true that you're married to him?" he asked without taking his eyes from the young actress.

"Yes, it's true. Didn't Charles tell you?"

"He didn't tell anyone, but I guessed, and he didn't deny it. Cara only found out five days ago, because she read the letter you wrote to Charles."

"Of course. He wouldn't want the Chapalii to know, since by their laws a female upon marriage takes her husband's status. And since Rhui has no intelligent life, by Chapalii measure, that would mean I had descended to the level of horses and wolves. That's why Charles told them the fiction that I'm out here doing linguistics research, isn't it?"

Now Marco turned to look at her. "Tess, didn't you know that according to the Chapalii Protocol Office, you're dead?"

She laughed, short and surprised, put her hand to her throat, and lowered it again. "Am I, really? But then—?"

"Then what? Charles did not protest the announcement, so in fact you're officially dead and only a few of his intimates and now, of course, the Bharentous Company, know the truth."

"But, Marco—" She felt a surge of hope and lifted her cold hands to suddenly hot cheeks. "That means he's free to adopt. He's not bound to our blood tie any longer, and he can adopt someone else as his Chapalii heir." It was like a cord bound around her heart had been cut through, freeing her. "That means he doesn't need me anymore."

"I wish it was that easy. The cylinder from the Morava site is a priceless piece of information for our side, Tess, but it's configured awkwardly and we've got to have the parameters of the system installed at Morava in order to get at its deep structure. Those damned chameleons don't have any standard programs. It's all in the interrelationship of systems. If Rajiv can't crack it, then we'll have to bring in one of the Keinaba experts."

"Keinaba? You mean the Chapalii merchant house? How can you bring them in here, or to Morava?"

"They're Charles's now. They transferred their house pledge to him. It's all proper and affirmed by the emperor himself. It's a long story, anyway."

"What does that have to do with his adopting a new heir?"

"He's holding you in reserve, Tess. You're the ace up his sleeve. Charles didn't make the proclamation that you were dead. Another Chapalii duke did."

"Oh, hell. Charles is jumping feet first into court intrigue, isn't he? If he needs to discredit this other duke, then he'll produce me, and—there you are—public shame. The Tai-en will have to leave court and perhaps even be stripped of his title."

Marco shook his head. "Tess, you amaze me. You speak their language better than any human I know, and you seem to understand how they work. Don't you see that Charles can't afford to lose you?"

"Lose me, or my expertise?"

"There's no difference."

She stared at the gathering under the awning, at these outlandish alien beings, large of limb and clothed in gaudy, foreign clothing. They laughed, and the pitch of their voices as they spoke was strange to her, producing exotic sounds and disorienting syllables. Then she realized that they were speaking Anglais and that she could understand them perfectly well.

"Marco," she demanded, "why are you talking to me in Rhuian?"

"I didn't want to startle you. Do you want to go in now?"

"No. But I will anyway."

"Lamb to the slaughter," said Marco in Anglais.

Tess snorted in disgust and walked in. Charles noted her immediately, of course, and stood up. Formally, he introduced her to Rajiv and Joanna and Ursula, and Maggie introduced her to the two other actors, Gwyn Jones and Hal Bharentous. A moment later, Tess realized that Marco had not followed her in. She glanced out into the darkness, but could not see him, lurking or otherwise. She sat down on a camp stool and wondered what in hell she was going to say to these people.

"You're looking well, Tess." David sat down beside her. He smiled, awkward, and Tess was so thankful for the sight of a familiar and unthreatening face that she smiled warmly back at him. "You're looking very—" He hesitated. "Very well. Very different."

"Thank you, David. It's been a long time. You're looking well yourself. Lord, it sounds strange to hear myself speaking Anglais after all this time."

"How do you like it out here?"

He was kind, really, to make this kind of small talk, to try to set her at ease. But David had always been kind, and Tess recalled his sojourn at Prague, their six-months-long love affair with fondness for what he had given her: confidence that she was attractive in and of herself. Without him, she might have spent her whole life believing that any least bit of attention paid her was only on account of Charles. He had recalled her to the self-respect she'd had as a child; for that, she would always be grateful to him.

". . . and how did you get that scar?" David asked and, daringly, lifted a hand to touch her cheek. Tess had a sudden, vivid memory of the time they'd taken one of the ducal shuttles into Earth orbit and tried to make love in freefall. He met her gaze and she knew, immediately, that they were thinking the same thing. They both laughed.

"Sojourner warned us, didn't she?" Tess said. "But we refused to follow her instructions. How is she, anyway? Do you know?"

"She's doing very well. Handfasted to an aspiring young diplomat named Rene Marcus Oljaitu. After she finished her dissertation two years ago, she talked Charles into letting her and Rene apprentice to the Keinaba house."

"Well. Good for Sojourner. Firsthand xeno experience, and they'll be the first humans placed directly inside a Chapalii house, even if it is only a merchant house."

"Don't underestimate the Keinaba, Tess." Charles placed a stool beside her and sat down. "They're one of the richest merchant houses in the Empire."

"But, Tess," said David, "you never did tell me how you got that scar. In a battle?"

Others stood around them. Of course, she was the curiosity of this little gathering, the center, the focus. They'd had each other on the long journey, and now they had her. "No, it's—" She hesitated. How to tell them: it's what the men do when they marry their wives? Thrust in among her own people, she recalled her own reaction when she first found out about the mark of marriage. It was barbaric. It was mutilation.

What would they think of her, knowing that she had allowed herself to be mutilated? What did they think of her in any case, sitting here with her jaran clothes and her long hair braided in jaran style, looking quite jaran, except for her brown hair and green eyes and her unusual height, for a woman? Like an actor, desperately trying to live a role not meant for her.

"It's nothing," she said finally. Charles was looking at her approvingly. What did *he* think? That she knew better then to jeopardize his position, and her own, by revealing a marriage that would ruin her status within the Empire and perhaps cause him to face ridicule and shame? Shame, which was fatal. Or could he even imagine what the scar represented? That she had marked—mutilated—her own husband, quite against jaran custom, in return?

She didn't belong with these people anymore, these people from her impossibly distant past.

"May I please?" Maggie dislodged David from his seat. "Tess, look at this." She handed Tess a flat rectangle, smooth of surface, curved at its edge. "I took the abstract you wrote for Charles and applied a rather primitive translation program to it. For khush, you know."

Tess stared at the computer slate in her hand. An illegal slate, brought downside, brought with the party. Of course Charles did not fear Ilya. He must have weapons with him, just as Cha Ishii and his Chapalii party had hidden weapons with them, four years ago, when they had made their illicit journey together across the plains with Bakhtiian and his jahar.

Then a word caught her eye. "That's wrong." She tapped a few keys, and found the program structure, and recoded a few lines. "No, it's fine, Maggie, but you're right, it's a primitive program for this kind of translation work. And the abstract I sent to Charles was limited in and of itself, since I had to hand-write it. And it was a preliminary draft, in any case, and very rough."

"Here, my dear." Cara Hierakis leaned in and offered Tess a cup half-filled with some dark liquid. "I brought a good supply of Scotch with me. Will you have some?"

"Scotch?" Oh yes, Scotch.

"I suppose," said Ursula, drifting by on the edge of the conversation, "that they drink fermented mare's milk out here."

Tess blinked. "At festivals. How did you know? They call it—" She took a sip of the scotch, made a face, and huddled back over the computer slate, seduced by its promise. "Oh, if I only had a modeler, I could compile a full translation model in all media, networked through . . . Hell, through Rhuian, Anglais—not Chapaliian, of course, the Protocol Office doesn't let you interlink Chapaliian—Ophiuchi-Sei."

"But we do have a modeler with us," said Maggie.

"You do! This is wonderful!" At that moment, Tess glanced up to see that everyone was beaming at her in relief, as if they had only now been reassured that the poor misguided thing had been rescued from the barbarians intact.

At that moment, Tess decided to get drunk.

CHAPTER SEVENTEEN

That Charles seemed willing to sit by and watch his sister drink herself into oblivion appalled David. There she sat, the center of attention, tossing off the Scotch as if it were water. What drove her he did not know, but he recognized well enough the desperation the action stemmed from.

He sidled over to Diana, who was talking to Jo Singh and Rajiv on the outskirts of the group. She glanced his way, excused herself, and met him on the edge of the carpet.

"Diana, you seem skilled at creating diversions—"

She looked past his shoulder at Tess. Tess was laughing at something Cara had said even while her hand groped for her cup again. "I can see that an exit is called for."

"Bless you, Diana. Did anyone ever tell you that you're a angel?" She flushed abruptly and, to his surprise, looked embarrassed and unhappy. "I'm sorry. My stupid tongue."

"No, it's not your fault. But David, she looked so marvelous riding in on that horse, so . . . . so competent and adventurous and confident. Did you hear the way she lit into Maggie's program? Nicely, of course, but it's clear she's brilliant with languages."

David chuckled. "The Rhuian complex we all learned from was written by her at the age of twenty-one."

Diana's eyes widened. "Is that true? I've never learned a language faster than through that matrix. It made the connections so obvious. But then why is she—" She hesitated, and David could see that she very much wanted not to say anything negative about Tess Soerensen. He glanced back to see Tess shift on her stool and almost overbalance and fall off. Cara steadied her and shot Charles a meaningful glance, but Soerensen ignored her.

"I don't know. But I remember when I won top honors from middle college and the accelerated slot to apply to the Tokyo School of Engineering—which is the most competitive, the best of the best—and they threw a big party for me at my village. I felt like a fraud, because I hadn't worked as hard as the other kids in my region and the ones at Yaounde College. All their praise sounded cheap because I knew the truth even if they didn't. So I got drunk."

"That's funny. I got admitted on my first audition at nineteen to the Royal Shakespeare Academy in London."

"That's young, isn't it?"

"Very young, these days, and I always felt guilty about it. Some people accused me of having connections, but I didn't. But then, I never wanted to do anything but theater, and lots of them had already spent time in the holos. Still." Diana considered the party under the awning. A clot of actors had invaded, and since at least three of them—Hyacinth, Anahita, and Jean-Pierre—were already drunk, Tess did not stand out so painfully.

"Oh, I don't mean to say that she feels like a fraud, or feels guilty, but that she feels something, and that it's driving her to this. If you can—"

"Pull focus off of her, that's what you want, of course."

"Yes, that sounds right. Then I'll ease her out and take her back to wherever it is she sleeps."

Diana sighed. "I wonder what her life is like, with the jaran."

David snorted. "Dirty, cold, and harsh. Don't get any wishful illusions here."

"They don't seem so barbaric to me."

"After what we've seen? The wounded? And Bakhtiian executing that man for rape?" David gazed out at the camp beyond, at the tents and the occasional fire, stretching out so far on either side that he could not see the end of it. He had good night vision and as he stared, he saw a single figure crouched in the gap between Soerensen's enclave and the jaran camp, watching them. He felt cold up and down his back and then shook his head, impatient. Of course they would watch Soerensen's camp. Why shouldn't they?

"It's all right." Diana laid a hand on his elbow, a brief warmth, and removed it again. "I'll go. Do your part, but you'll have to be quick. What I have in mind won't last long."

She eased back into the throng and before David realized what she was about, she had started a loud argument with Anahita about somebody named Grusha. Anahita at any time was a formidable presence. Drunk, she was uninhibited, and David marveled as Diana applied just the right words to manipulate Anahita into dragging Charles into the argument.

David circled around and came up to Tess from behind. Cara still stood there, hovering like a protective mother. When she saw David she looked relieved. He put his hands on Tess's shoulders.

"Come on, Tess," he said in a low voice. "Time to go home." Cara helped him lift her up and steer her out from under the awning and into the covering darkness between the two large tents. Tess stumbled on the level ground and swore in a foreign language.

"You're drunk," said David.

"I know," she said.

"Let me help you back to your—to wherever you sleep."

She shook her head violently, tripped over her own feet, and would have fallen if David hadn't caught her. "No. No. I don't want them to see me like this." She went on, sounding angry, but she had lapsed into khush, and he couldn't understand her.

"Cara, your tent?"

Cara frowned. "I have equipment out that's not in place yet. Put her in your tent, and you sleep in mine."

"Cara, we are both adults. I think we can manage to *sleep* together without—"

"David. May I remind you that we are in a foreign land, whose customs we do not know?"

"Lady in Heaven. She's not one of them. If it was some young jaran woman . . . all right. All right. I'll tuck her primly in and retire to your tent. Or Charles's, if it comes to that. Or wherever it is Marco sleeps. I suppose you're right, although I can't imagine why they

would care and how they would know.'' Then he recalled
the distant sentry. ''Or, anyway, why they would care.
She's a foreigner, too, after all.''

''David.''

''I'm going.'' He led the unprotesting Tess to his tent,
going on a brief side trip to their portable toilet, which
they were using until he could devise something more
permanent. For an instant, listening outside the tiny
square tent, he thought he was going to have to give Tess
instructions on how to use the thing, but she emerged at
last, staggering and catching onto him for balance.

He tried to talk to her. She did not reply. He was not
entirely sure she understood him. She seemed morose
more than anything, but at least she was not crying. David hated crying drunks. He helped her inside his tent,
sealed her up inside the sleeping pouch, and retreated.

By the time he got back to Charles's tent, the party
had moved on. He could hear its remains over in the
Company enclave. Hyacinth was singing an obscene song
in his grating falsetto, with one of the women—Oriana,
perhaps—providing the contralto descant.

Charles and Marco sat alone under the awning, in
darkness. ''Well?'' Charles asked when David appeared.

''I'm disgusted.'' David chose not to sit down.

''Yes,'' said Charles. ''I don't remember Tess getting
drunk habitually when she was at the university, and she
certainly wasn't particularly happy there.''

''Not with her,'' snapped David. ''With you. You just
sat by and let it happen.''

Charles arched an eyebrow. ''It is not my part to dictate Tess's behavior.''

Marco made a noise in his throat, a short, caustic
laugh. ''Just her life.''

''Do I scent a mutiny?'' Charles asked good-naturedly.

Marco sighed and leaned back in his chair, balancing
it on the back two legs. ''No. You're right, of course.
You can't afford to lose her.''

''What the hell are you two talking about?'' David
demanded. ''Why would you lose Tess?''

''Where is Tess?'' Charles asked.

''In my tent, sleeping it off.''

Marco slammed down his chair. ''David, you'd better
move her. Here, or into Cara's tent.''

"Cara wouldn't take her. I'd hate to wake her up."

"No, it's fine," said Charles. "You can sleep here, David."

"Charles." Marco stood. "I don't think this is a good idea, unless you deliberately want to set up your authority against his."

"But I do, Marco. That's just the point. Within our encampment, we will act according to our laws. It is only once we step outside it that we acknowledge theirs. Once their laws penetrate our world, then we *have* lost Tess. Don't you see?"

"So you'll make a point of it now. And what about our poor David?"

"Yes," broke in David, bewildered. "What about poor David? What are you talking about? What do jaran laws have to do with losing Tess?" He paused. "And furthermore, why are you even bothering to jockey power with Bakhtiian? He's nothing. He's not even important."

Marco cast a measured glance at the jaran encampment. "Try telling that to the people whose countries he's overrunning. Or to him, for that matter."

"You know what I meant. I meant compared to the Chapalii Empire. To space. You haven't answered my question."

Marco tucked his hands into his belt and whistled softly.

Charles pulled off his gloves and stood up. "Tess is married to Bakhtiian, under jaran law. Now, I'm going to bed." He went inside. The tent flap slithered down after him.

"Sit down," said Marco congenially. "You look awful."

David sat down. He stared blankly at the night sky, at the stars. He could even trace a few constellations. Then he jumped to his feet. "She's sleeping in *my* tent!"

Marco laid a hand on his arm and, firmly but inexorably, sat David back down again. "Don't you see? Charles wants to make it clear that Tess is one of us, not one of them. Let her stay."

"With me as the sacrificial victim? No thank you."

"Goddess, David, do you think for a minute Charles has any intention of letting anyone in his party get hurt?

How is Bakhtiian to know it's your tent she's sleeping in, anyway? Or that she's sleeping here at all?''

"Why didn't you tell me!" David demanded.

"Sorry, I was under oath. I really am sorry, David."

Easy for him to say. "His wife." David formed the words as if they were alien, and taboo. "His wife."

"Go to bed," said Marco kindly, and left him.

David slept soundly and without dreams, but he woke at dawn. He crept out of Charles's tent into the quiet of their camp. Beyond, the jaran camp was full of life. He went to use the portable and to wash: inside the little tent, beside the commode, he had rigged up a sterilizing and recycling unit for wash water. The water was bitterly cold, and he wandered outside into the cold dawn to pace out the size block he would need to set up the solar minis. How to disguise them? What water source was the jaran camp using? How did they remain supplied? Was this a permanent camp, or did it move?

Ursula el Kawakami came up, looking revoltingly awake at such an early hour.

"What do you think, Ursula?" he asked. "Do you think this is their permanent camp? Or that they move?"

"Of course they move. 'They commonly feed many flocks of cows, mares, and sheep, for which reason they never stay in one place.' That's Marco Polo. And this can't be the entire army, although I'll get a better sense of their numbers when we tour the camp today. Foodstuffs and fodder for the animals alone would deplete any one area within weeks. Days, perhaps. This is a good site, though. Well chosen. Good grassland for the herds, and a river about half a mile to the south. Can you mock me up a map so I can get an estimate of how close we are to the settled agricultural lands to the south? My sense is that Bakhtiian has control over the western seaports and is consolidating his control over the southern borderlands now."

David chuckled. "In other words, I shouldn't build anything permanent here."

Ursula surveyed the square tent that the actors called The Necessary. "Certainly I think this is elaborate enough. It isn't as if we're on some kind of safari vacation on Tau Ceti Tierce, after all. This *is*—"

"—an interdicted planet." David settled his left hand on the back of his neck and contemplated the ring of canvas tents belonging to Soerensen's party. His four tiny name braids, dangling from the nape of his neck down to brush his shoulder blades, tickled his knuckles. "Yes, I know. Well, if you'll excuse me . . ." He escaped from Ursula's uncomfortable presence and walked over to his tent to see if Tess was awake.

She was. She was lying on her stomach with the heels of her palms cushioning her eyes.

"Hello, Tess." He crawled into the tent and knelt beside her.

"I have a headache," she said without moving her hands. But her Anglais was precise and clear. "Where am I?"

"In my tent. Oh, ah, this is David."

She made a disgusted noise in her throat. "I know it's David. What am I doing here? Never mind, I know the answer, and I would be churlish not to thank you for taking care of me. I must have made a fool of myself."

"A bit. Luckily some of the actors were drunk, so you weren't alone. And you were among friends."

"Thank you. So reassuring." Tess slid her hands away from her eyes and flinched, even though the only light in the tent came through the open flap. "Lord, how late is it?"

"It's early. Just after dawn."

She wiggled out of the bag, pausing to let him unseal it for her, and got herself up on her knees. Considered. "Well, the damage isn't too bad. My head pounds, but I don't feel sick to my stomach."

"Small favors. Tess." He hesitated, wanting to ask her if it was true, and instead sealed up the sleeping pouch and rolled it up into a neat cylinder.

"Plumbing," said Tess suddenly, not appearing to notice his unease. "Civilized plumbing. That's what I remember from last night. Where is it?" She clambered out of the tent and stood. David hurried out behind her. "That's what I miss more than anything. And hot showers. They're remarkably clean, you know, the jaran, and practical about it, but still. . . ."

She went on, but David did not hear her next words. She had her back to her brother's tent. She could not see the little embassy that waited outside Charles's awning. But the embassy could see Tess and David.

Eight people. All jaran. Three soldiers whose faces David recalled from the journey from the coast. The silver-haired man who had been at the healer's conference yesterday. Three women, two young, one elderly. And Bakhtiian.

Who had just seen Tess and David emerge from the same tent.

"What's wrong, David?" Tess asked. She turned.

David was calculating ground. About twenty meters separated Bakhtiian from him. How quickly could a man cover that ground?

"Oh," said Tess. "That's right. The tour. Of course you don't want to miss it. Here, wait a minute." She trotted off to the necessary.

David would have stared after her. He was appalled that she would desert him. But he had to keep his eye on the group. He had to keep his eye on Bakhtiian. A man who practiced summary execution for rape. . . . Perhaps they hadn't noticed. But they had. Of course they had. Even now, while they waited for Charles to come out, different individuals within the group glanced over at him and away. One of the women grinned. But Bakhtiian was not looking at him. Perhaps by some astounding piece of good luck, Bakhtiian had not noticed.

Tess jogged back up to him. "Are they still there? Oh, good. Come on." She dragged him over to Charles's tent.

Charles had just come outside, with Cara and Marco, and the actors had gathered in a clump, looking excited. Ursula, Jo, Maggie, and Rajiv waited as well.

"I have brought with me," Bakhtiian was saying to Charles, "as many of my people as speak Rhuian, so that we can have sufficient translators. Six in all. That includes Tess, of course. If you prefer to go as a single group, that is acceptable."

"Did you have another suggestion?" Charles asked politely.

Bakhtiian nodded. "A large group does not see as much as a small group. If you divide your party into six groups, each to go with a translator, then you can move quietly and with more ease through the camp."

And by splitting them up, David thought, he could

isolate the man he thought had just slept with his wife. He began to wipe his hands on his trousers, realized that would make him look nervous, and stopped. He'd stay in camp—but then he *would* be isolated, and easy prey.

Next to him, Tess said under her breath: "He's showing off. He's going to let the jaran charm Charles and the rest of you. Which they'll do, given the chance to meet them as individuals. He'd never do this for any other foreign embassy. Those get full state, to cow them into submission."

"—and I would be honored to escort you personally," Bakhtiian finished, still speaking to Charles.

"The honor is mine," replied Charles smoothly. "And the others?"

As smoothly, without any fanfare, Bakhtiian transferred his gaze from Charles to David. If a look had the physical edge of a saber, if a wish, an emotion, could manifest instantaneously into an act, then David ben Unbutu would have been dead at that moment. He knew it without a doubt.

Bakhtiian looked away. "As you wish," he said graciously to Charles.

"The bastard," muttered Tess. "Still trying to keep Charles and me apart. Excuse me, David." She stalked off to stand next to Charles.

The silver-haired man appeared next to David at the same time Cara Hierakis did. "I am Nikolai Sibirin," he said, in serviceable Rhuian. "We have not been introduced."

David cast a pleading glance at Cara.

"This is David ben Unbutu," said Cara, who already seemed on casual terms with this elderly jaran man. "Niko, I don't know your customs, but I can assure you that Tess was only sleeping in David's tent because she was drunk."

Niko considered David. "Whatever mood she may have been in, I do wish you hadn't been so hasty, young man. Still, please allow me to apologize for Ilya's behavior. He thinks he doesn't show his emotions, but he can't help it. Of course he has no right to be angry, so if you humor him, he'll calm down eventually."

"No right to be angry?" David asked in a small voice.

"But Charles—er, Soerensen—the prince said they are married."

The old man smiled abruptly. "Of course. You khaja are barbarians. Sometimes I forget that. Jaran women may lie with whomever they wish. It is none of men's business."

"But—" David began, utterly confused.

"David," said Cara in Anglais, "leave well enough alone." She turned to Niko. "I had hoped that you might show me through camp, Niko. With your wife." She turned to greet the elderly woman in the group. "Hello, Juli." They kissed each other on the cheek like old friends. Juli responded with a jaran greeting. "David? Are you coming with us?"

"It is my belief," said Niko gently, "that David ought to go with Bakhtiian and the prince." David put a hand to his throat, lowered it, and swallowed. Niko looked him closely in the face and suppressed a grin. "Perhaps not. Would you like to come with us?"

With vast relief, David said yes.

CHAPTER EIGHTEEN

Sonia Orzhekov regarded the khaja Singers with trepidation. Six of them at once! Few things daunted her, raised as an etsana's daughter, cousin to Bakhtiian; there had been death aplenty in her family, but she came from a resilient line, and, the gods knew, there was no point in dwelling on things that had already come to pass. But Singers were touched by the gods, and everyone knew that they were a little crazy—not in a bad way, mind you, but that they looked at the world differently, that the gods spoke through them. Perhaps she should have brought Raysia Grekov with her, for Raysia was a Singer, and also daughter of the etsana of the Grekov tribe. Then, perhaps, Raysia could *translate* for her just as Sonia would translate for these women, these *actors,* as they walked through camp.

But even an etsana's daughter and a cousin of Bakhtiian could not command a Singer, or even summon one. Sonia examined the six women and reminded herself that they were, after all, khaja like Tess, from the country called Erthe, across the seas. Perhaps, like Tess, their gods were distant and silent gods, not so prone to speak through them at awkward times or to give them fits and starts and odd moments of reticence. Certainly they were neither timid nor shy, unlike most khaja women she had come across, unlike the women of Jeds.

"How is it that you are called Tess's sister?" asked the golden-haired one in a friendly manner, the one to whom Anatoly Sakhalin had given a necklace. Diana, that was it.

"My mother adopted her into our tribe, as her daughter, when she first came to us. I'll take you to meet my children."

The one called Helen muttered something in their

tongue to the handsome black-haired woman named Anahita.

"Oh, don't be rude, Helen," whispered Anahita in
Rhuian, but with such emphasis that Sonia wondered if
she had intended that the whisper be heard.

Children of other tribes tagged along behind them as
they walked slowly through camp. The children stared at
the women. That was one thing about these khaja; they
all of them looked different from the others, with skin
ranging from pale to black, with eyes every color and
shape, and so tall! They were all, except for Diana, as
tall as men.

"You seem very young to have children," said the one
called Quinn.

Sonia chuckled. "Tess said much the same thing to
me, when she first came to us. If a woman waits too
many years, then how can she have children at all?"

The coal-black Oriana elbowed Quinn in the side and
hissed something at her in another language. Quinn
flushed; she had a light complexion, easy to see the
changes in, and with her odd red-brown shade of hair,
Sonia reflected, it would be difficult to find dye for cloth
that would look good on her. Still, she wore a fine tunic
neither blue nor green but some shade in between, and
it looked well.

"It's a beautiful weave," Sonia said, nodding at the
tunic. "And a lovely color. Have you weavers in your
mother's tent? Your mother's house, that is. Perhaps you
could show us the secret of the color, if you're willing
to give it up."

The three younger women looked at each other, perplexed. Helen yawned. Anahita examined every man who
came in sight and had obviously lost interest in the conversation. Sonia sighed.

Then, thank goodness, the woman with the funny eyes,
Yomi, chimed in. "I weave," she said. "Perhaps you
could show me your looms."

"How do you make dye for colors?" asked Diana
quickly, and Sonia could not be sure whether she was
truly interested or merely being polite. But then, with
Singers, one never knew.

"This is all so quaint, and charming," said Anahita
suddenly, with a bright, false smile.

"I'm so pleased that it entertains you," replied Sonia sarcastically, and then caught herself. But it had already been done. She had been impolite to a Singer.

Oriana snorted and clapped a hand over her mouth.

"Oh, shut up, Anahita," said Quinn. "Didn't your mother ever tell you to say something nice or nothing at all?"

"In which case she'd never speak," muttered Helen.

"I'm going back to camp," announced Anahita, and she gave them all a withering glare and stalked away.

Gods. Now she had offended a Singer. Sonia stopped walking and took in a breath to apologize to the others, though it was an unpardonable offense.

"I do apologize for her," said Diana. "I don't—we're not—I beg your pardon. That was terribly rude of her."

"Patronizing little bitch," said Quinn. "I wish she hadn't come. And the rest of you do, too, only you won't admit it."

"Girls," said Yomi reasonably, "that's enough. I beg your pardon, Sonia. We've had a long and sometimes trying journey together, and that rather puts people at odds after a while, don't you think?"

"We always travel," said Sonia gently.

Yomi chuckled. "Well, then, perhaps you can offer us some advice."

"Was it not Democritus of your own country who said, 'Well-ordered behavior consists in obedience to the law, the ruler, and the woman wiser than oneself'? Although in the text I read the words were written as, 'the *man* wiser,' but I can only suppose the scribe wrote the word wrong or meant it to be 'Elder.' "

"Who is Democritus?" whispered Quinn.

"I think he was a Greek philosopher," muttered Diana.

"But of course," added Sonia, "it's also true that we have our own quarrels. As do any people, I suppose."

Yomi smiled and wisely guided the conversation back to weaving. In this way they came to the Orzhekov encampment, where Ilya had arrived before them.

Tess stood between her husband and her brother, and Sonia was distracted from her guests by the striking way in which Tess seemed caught between the two men, not mediating but wavering. Oh, it looked very bad, indeed.

A woman must keep peace between her husband and her brother, not make it worse by letting each man pull her in a different direction. Ilya could never accept that Tess might hold her brother first in her heart, that Charles Soerensen had every right to expect his sister to cleave to him and to her mother's tent. But if Tess, khaja that she was, truly wished to stay with her husband and her husband's people, then she damned well ought to tell her brother so straight out and not leave poor Ilya hanging there never knowing what she intended to do. As for Charles Soerensen himself, Sonia simply could not tell if he loved his sister. But he would never have journeyed so far if he did not want her back very badly. For an instant Sonia wished that her mother was here. Irena Orzhekov would know what to do. Ilya deferred to many people, because he had good manners, but there were few who could make him stop dead in his tracks and change his mind. *Mama is one. And I must become another.*

"Bakhtiian is your cousin?" asked Diana into the silence, pulling Sonia back to the Singers with a wrench.

"His mother and my mother are sisters, yes."

"And are they here also?" asked Yomi.

"His mother is dead." Sonia paused one second, flicking her wrist out to deflect the notice of Grandmother Night. "My mother remains out on the plains, the true plains, with the rest of our tribe." She watched as Katya and Ivan and Kolia came running with their cousins to greet Ilya and Tess with hugs and questions. Tess introduced the children to her brother, and Sonia approved of the way in which the prince acknowledged each child in turn.

"Are they all yours?" asked Diana. "What sweet-looking children!" Said with such honesty that Sonia felt at once that she liked this young Singer who had been blessed with beauty as well as song. "May we meet them?"

Ilya, seeing their party come up, guided his on. He had with him as well several others of the prince's party, including a man who stared in the most unseemly fashion at Diana as they left.

"There's Marco Burckhardt," said Quinn in an undertone, and Oriana said, "Oh, don't tease Diana."

Then Marco Burckhardt caught Sonia looking at him
and he smiled at her as if to say that here was a man who
could appreciate a mature and confident woman. Well!
Clearly he was as impudent as Kirill Zvertkov, but then
again, he was khaja, and khaja men did not have very
good manners, on the whole. Still, he had a pleasant way
of admiring a woman. Sonia watched him go, even as he
hastily returned his attention to his party, which had gotten a ways ahead of him.

Leaving, he almost bumped into another man.

Both men halted. A glare flashed between them, like
two stallions who accidentally cross paths, and then
Marco hurried on after his own party. Which left the
other man standing outside the awning of her tent. And
just what *was* Anatoly Sakhalin doing in her camp?

Except she knew the answer. She watched Diana register his presence, watched the Singer's hand as it lifted
to touch the golden necklace and then, self-consciously,
dropped. She watched, with disgust, as Anatoly insinu-
ated himself in with the children and thus was standing
with them when she brought the Singers over to meet
them.

"And these are the children of my family. Mitya and
Galina are Kira's eldest two, and Katerina and Ivan and
Kolia are my own. There are also four girls and two boys
still with the tribe."

"You have more?" Quinn asked, looking astounded.

"No, just those eleven."

"You have eleven children?" asked Yomi.

"My sisters and I have eleven children, yes. Last I
heard, Stassi was pregnant, so soon there will be twelve
again."

"Oh my," said Yomi abruptly, "look at that loom."

Galina led her over to the loom, and at once the girl
and the khaja woman became engrossed, though they
could not speak any words to each other. Truly, weaving
was a common language in and of itself.

Sonia looked back at the others. "Katya! Stop that! It
doesn't come off. Show respect for a Singer."

"It's all right," said Oriana with a laugh, clearly not
minding at all that the children were licking their fingers
and rubbing at her skin. She crouched down and re-

garded them with a grave face. "It comes from being out in the sun too much."

"It does not!" said Katya once her mother had translated. "Does it, Mama? There are other khaja with you who have skin like this. Mama says it's because you're from a place where the sun is hotter. But if that's true, and if all of you are from the same country, then why don't you all have black skin?"

"Good question," said Oriana with another laugh. "Why do you have blonde hair and your uncle—well, I suppose he's not your uncle, but your mother's cousin, so I don't know what that makes him to you—why does he have black hair? My skin is this color because my mother and my father had skin of this color."

Helen regarded the children with resignation. Quinn allowed Ivan to show her every knife and saber that he could find; he was showing off, but at his age, one had to expect it. Mitya, of course, strayed no farther than an arm's length from his hero, Sakhalin. Diana, crouching down, admired little Kolia's first, awkward efforts at embroidery on a torn hank of sleeve. Slowly, slowly, Anatoly sidled over to stand between Sonia and the young woman. When his shadow darkened the sleeve Kolia held, Diana glanced up. Both of them looked away from one another as quickly as a horse bolts from a loud noise.

Anatoly, at least, had enough decorum not to look back down at her. "Please, Cousin Orzhekov," he asked Sonia, keeping his eyes carefully fixed on a neutral spot between the carpet and the tent flap, "could you ask her, for me, what she thinks of the camp?"

Diana's gaze lifted to examine him more boldly now.

"Does your grandmother know where you are?" demanded Sonia in khush. "Your manners are appalling, Sakhalin, and I hope I never see this sort of behavior from you again."

Diana rose to her feet, ruffling Kolia's hair absently. But she looked at Anatoly. "What did he say?" she asked, and hearing her voice he glanced at her, and she smiled at him.

Damn it anyway. It would only encourage Anatoly, but Sonia did not dare refuse to answer a Singer's question. "Anatoly wonders what you think of the camp," she said

in Rhuian. "But he really has to go now." And switched
to khush. "Go on, Anatoly."

Bowing to her superior authority, he left, but reluctantly. Really, his grandmother had spoiled him; it was
deplorable, and yet he *was* at an age when men are most
likely to be brash. A boy would be overawed; an older
man would know better. But at twice twelve years and
just honored with a command of his own, he had come
into the first flush of his power.

"Oh, dear," said Diana quietly. Tentatively, she
touched Sonia on the arm and then smiled and withdrew
her hand. "I hope I haven't done something that offends
you. Or him."

"Of course not! I must apologize for *his* behavior."
*There are some things I will never understand about the
khaja,* Sonia thought, *for all that I have read their books
and lived with them.* Singers who apologized, as if they
could offend anyone but the gods! Women who acted with
the modesty that was really only proper for men!

"Oh," said Diana, bewildered. "Perhaps Tess Soerensen can tell us more about your laws and ways of
doing things."

"A very fine idea," agreed Sonia, and not just because Diana was a Singer. If these khaja were to travel a
long way with the tribes, maybe it wasn't Raysia Grekov
who needed to translate, maybe it was Tess, who had
grown up in one land and embraced the other, who was
the only one of all of them who truly stood halfway between. "But I had hoped to show you the herds, if you'd
like, or if you'd rather, other parts of the camp."

"Oh, both, if it can be managed," said Yomi, coming
back with Galina. "This is fascinating."

So they went on. Soon enough Sonia saw Anatoly Sakhalin again. Diana saw him, too, and now and again her
gaze would jump away from the group to seek him out.
He dogged them all the rest of the morning, like any
good scout, vanishing when Sonia's attention was turned
directly on him, coming closer when he could, never being so forward that she could in fairness castigate him.
Still, she would definitely have to discuss his behavior
with his grandmother.

CHAPTER NINETEEN

Aleksi sat cross-legged on the table, watching Tess and Sonia where they knelt before the wooden chest.

"This one, then." Sonia draped a cloth-of-gold coat over her arms, displaying it for Tess to examine.

"No. Too gaudy."

"Tess, barbarians are impressed by gaudy things. Gold and riches. Surely this Vidiyan ambassador will recognize that this coat came from the Gray Eminence's lands across the sea and feel fear that such a prince sends gifts to Bakhtiian."

"But Sonia, Nadine brought that coat back from Jeds."

"He doesn't have to know that, does he? Here, what about—"

"No, those are my marriage clothes."

"Yes, and this shade of green does look particularly well on you. This, and the jade headdress. No, the golden one."

"Sonia, I—"

"Or should I go to your brother's encampment and ask if he has any of these ugly clothings the women of his people wear? Are you embarrassed of us, now that your own people have come?"

Tess hung her head and did not reply. Aleksi watched her face. Unlike her brother, Tess had an expressive face that showed emotion clearly. She *was* embarrassed, and this perplexed Aleksi. After all, if the gods meant for the jaran to rule all other peoples, then the jaran would do so. Why should Tess feel shame to be seen as one of the gods' chosen people?

"This is not the Tess I know," Sonia went on. "Of course Jeds is a fine city. Do you forget that I have been there? Perhaps they scorn us because we don't live in stone tents, but I will never forget how filthy everything

was there. Although I admit,'' she added, in a placating
tone of voice, ''that everyone of your brother's party
seems clean.''

Tess clapped a hand over her mouth and her shoulders
shook. She was laughing. ''Oh, Sonia.'' She reached out
and hugged the blonde woman. ''I'm not ashamed of
you. I just—'' She hesitated, then shrugged. ''I think too
much.''

''You worry too much,'' retorted Sonia. ''These khaja
don't teach their daughters to become women. You had
no mother or aunt to give you a tent, but must live beholden to your brother and now your husband. Why do
you think I stayed in Jeds only a year, though Ilya wanted
me to stay longer? I know we have no university here,
no books, no writing, but still, they are the barbarians,
not us.''

''But Sonia,'' said Aleksi, ''the women of Soerensen's
party aren't like other khaja women, any more than Tess
is. They don't veil their faces when they see us and avert
their eyes. They wear proper clothing, even if it is ugly,
and they walk with pride and not fear.''

''That is true. But they're from another country, the
country where Tess's mother was born.''

''*Erthe,*'' said Aleksi, trying the unfamiliar sound out
on his tongue.

Tess leaned over the chest and lifted out the jade headpiece, weighing it in her hands. ''Dr. Hierakis came from
Erthe, as well as the acting company. Women are—well,
women own their own tents there. But so do men.''

''Yes, and from what you've told us, they don't seem
nearly as barbaric as the people of Jeds.'' Sonia lifted
out the gold headpiece and laid it down on the green
tunic. ''This looks better, Tess. I'd like to visit there
someday.''

''It's a long voyage. A very long voyage.'' Tess placed
the jade headdress back inside the chest and settled back
on her heels. ''No, you're right, Sonia. Even though I
didn't precisely need my brother's consent to marry, still,
I married without it.''

''If you have the courage to make a decision, then you
must learn to have the courage to stand by it. Perhaps
Ilya's power doesn't seem so impressive to your brother
now. In ten years, he will be happy to have such a brother

by marriage. You must tell him you are thinking ahead. It is an advantageous alliance.''

''For whom?''

''Come now, Tess. I have been to Jeds. I have ridden in the countryside and gone even as far as the city of Filis, where another prince rules. Your brother is rich and his merchants sail to the ends of the world, and he is a prince to be reckoned with, but Ilya's army is larger. Much larger. And it will grow.'' Sonia shook out the calf-length tunic and a pair of belled, striped trousers and then rummaged in the chest until she found a wide belt inlaid with cloissoné and gold. ''Now, Aleksi. Out.'' Her own festival clothing lay draped over the chair, a tunic of vivid blue that matched her blue eyes and a headpiece of gold and gems. ''We must dress. You might see if Galina needs a hand with the children.''

Aleksi gave each woman a brotherly kiss on the cheek and retired from the fray. At Sonia's tent, her niece Galina sat with those few Orzhekov children who remained with the main army. Sonia had kept her three children with her, and Niko and Juli had two grandchildren with them. Other children, like Galina and her brother Mitya, were old enough to do adult work but not old enough yet to marry or to ride in the army.

''We saw the barbarians today.'' Galina greeted Aleksi with a kiss on the cheek. She looked much like her aunt and her mother, with a merry, round face, fair hair, and cerulean blue eyes. ''Aunt Sonia brought five of them by. One of them had skin that was black. Really,'' she added, as if afraid that Aleksi wouldn't believe her. ''Wasn't it, Katerina?''

''It was,'' agreed Katerina, Sonia's eleven-year-old daughter who, at two years younger than her cousin, was her shadow and champion. ''We thought maybe she had painted it on, so we rubbed it, but it didn't come off.''

''Then Aunt Sonia scolded you for being rude,'' finished Galina. ''But the woman didn't mind. She was tall, too, taller than a man. And one of the other women had chestnut hair, like a horse has.'' She stifled a giggle under a hand. ''And another one had funny eyes, like . . .'' She grimaced, searching for a comparison.

''Like this,'' said seven-year-old Ivan. putting his index fingers on either side of his eyes and pulling the lids tight. All of the children burst into laughter.

"I liked her, though," said Katerina. "Her name was *Yomi*. She knows how to weave," she added, since this skill obviously placed the woman in a different, and superior, class from the others. "But they didn't have any men with them. Is it true their men act like women?"

"What do you mean?" asked Aleksi. "I escorted four of the men around the camp, and they seemed like men to me. They were very polite."

Katerina considered the question seriously, screwing her mouth up. She was a pretty girl, having inherited her looks from her grandfather, but she had as well the same vital intelligence that animated Sonia's otherwise undistinguished features. "They say khaja men use bows and arrows to fight other men with and that they haven't any manners toward women. And that they own their own tents, and they even say that the women don't own tents at all. How can that be?"

"You forgot the angel," said Mitya suddenly. He sat on a pillow at the back of the awning, too old to include himself in the younger children's activities but too young, at fifteen, to be an adult. Like most boys his age, he spent a small part of his day helping his grandmother, mother, or aunt and the rest of it with the adult men, doing chores, learning to fight, caring for the horses and the herds, and generally tagging along. Right now he was polishing one of Bakhtiian's sabers.

"What angel?" Aleksi asked. He knelt and helped four-year-old Kolia straighten his tunic and belt it with a girdle of gold plates.

"Anatoly Sakhalin's angel."

"Mitya," retorted Galina in a disdainful voice, "she is not Sakhalin's angel. And he showed bad manners, too, in following them around."

Aleksi settled down on his haunches, satisfied that he was about to get some good gossip. He loved these children, who had accepted him readily once they saw that the adults of their tribe acknowledged Tess's adoption of him. Although he had been Tess's brother for three years now, he still preferred the children's company to that of adults. They said what they thought, and they were not embarrassed by the fact that he had once been an orphan.

Like the foreign woman's coal-black skin, his peculiar status interested them more than it revolted them. "He followed Sonia and her party around camp?"

"Yes," said Galina. "That's what Aunt Sonia said. When they got here, he got Mitya to invite him in so that he could talk to her. She was very embarrassed by his behavior, as any woman would be. She flushed all red."

"Sonia did?" Aleksi asked, astounded.

"No, no," said Katerina. "The angel. *Diana*. But Sonia refused to translate for him so he just had to stand there. But he kept looking at her," she finished with disgust.

"He never looked at her straight," said Mitya.

"Oh," said Galina, "you're always defending him."

Mitya flushed at his little sister's superior tone of voice. "And why not? I want to ride in *his* jahar when I'm old enough. He's the best rider of all the young men."

"Mitya, everyone knows that Aleksi is the best rider. No one is as good with the saber as he is. Isn't that true, Aleksi?"

Aleksi grinned. "Anatoly is a good commander, and he deserves the command Bakhtiian gave him, though he's young to be granted such an honor."

"But you wouldn't ride in his jahar, would you?" asked Katerina, looking pleased with her sly question.

"Katya, I ride in Bakhtiian's own thousand. Why should I want to ride in anyone else's?" The girls laughed, and Mitya appeared mollified.

Sonia came out of Tess's tent. "Are you children still here?" she called. "Galina, Mitya, take them and go. Mother Sakhalin will have plenty for you to do before you start serving."

Galina and Katerina rounded up the little ones and marched them off. Mitya lingered. "Would you like to walk with me?" Aleksi asked the boy, and Mitya's face brightened, since this was clearly exactly what he had hoped for. The chance to stroll around camp beside the man everyone knew was the best saber fighter since the legendary Vyacheslav Mirsky, who had died of old age six years ago. . . . Aleksi chuckled. Then he felt a pang of regret. He had never enjoyed such simple pleasures as a boy. No friends, no companions. Alone— He shut it off. No use thinking about it, no use remembering. He lived in the Orzhekov camp now. "Come on, then."

"Oh, wait," said Mitya. "Aunt Sonia," he called, "what shall I do with the saber?"

She had already gone back into Tess's tent, but came out again. "Here, give it to me." She took it, smiled at Aleksi with the warmth that she seemed to have an endless supply of, and carried the precious weapon back inside.

Aleksi walked on, and Mitya matched his pace to the older man's. Already he was Aleksi's height and would probably grow taller still. Now he was gangly and uncoordinated, coltish in an endearing way. It was a stage Aleksi had never gone through, so while he felt sympathy for the boy, he could not quite understand him. However awkward Mitya might be, he had time to grow and an enviable position to grow into. Grandson of Irena Orzhekov, who was etsana of the Orzhekov tribe, Mitya was thereby related to Ilyakoria Bakhtiian himself; his mother, Kira, and Ilya were cousins. The boy wore a golden torque around his neck and golden braces at his wrists and, like his little cousin Kolia, a belted girdle of golden plates. A heavy enough burden, Aleksi supposed, made doubly so by the fact that Mitya's father was a respected smith. It was no wonder that Mitya admired Anatoly Sakhalin, a young man with equally important relatives who had managed to gain respect on his own account and not simply because of whom he was related to.

They wandered through the late afternoon bustle of the camp. A child ran behind a wall of captured shields, hiding from her playmates. A blacksmith's forge smoked, and two soot-stained, sweating men pounded out lance heads. Their strokes beat out a rhythm to the late afternoon. Two adolescent boys repaired bridles, and they waved at Mitya as he walked by. A group of women turned carcasses on spits over four large fires. The smell of the meat was tantalizing. Fat dripped and blazed on the coals.

"He must be very powerful," Mitya said suddenly.

"Who?"

"The prince of Jeds. Tess's brother. The ambassadors that come to us have greater retinues, and they bring gifts. What is an actor, anyway?"

"I'm not sure," Aleksi admitted. "They tell stories, I think, but with their bodies, not with words and a song. Perhaps they will perform tonight."

But they did not. On the circle of ground separating the inner group of tents from the outer ring, blankets were laid and awnings set up in a great ring. At the southwest of this compass a single wagon sat upended and shorn of its wheels, covered with leather drawn tight with ropes and laden with pillows. Before it, on the ground, lay carpets under an awning of golden silk. Large square pillows embroidered with flying birds or galloping horses littered the carpets, seating for the feasters. Now, waiting, the pillows were empty, except for a single figure sitting under the center of the awning, writing painstakingly in a book. He glanced up and saw Aleksi and Mitya and beckoned them over.

'Mitya," he said, "surely Mother Sakhalin is expecting you." Mitya murmured a few unintelligible words and retreated. Bakhtiian watched the boy flee. "His father says he'll never be a blacksmith, so I hope he shows some promise for command. Here, Aleksi, sit down, if you please."

Even Bakhtiian's polite requests sounded like orders, but Aleksi was used to it. He sat down and nodded toward the book lying open on Bakhtiian's right knee. "You're writing." Aleksi could read, with effort, and he could make letters, but the gift of reading and writing with ease eluded him, though Tess encouraged him to practice every chance she got.

"Yes." Bakhtiian contemplated the open book, a page filled with neat lines in his precise script. His eyes moved over the last line, and Aleksi watched as his lips moved ever so slightly, forming the words he had written.

"That's Tess's book," said Aleksi abruptly, recognizing the pattern of marbling on the leather binding as Bakhtiian closed it.

"Yes. She began to record our campaign three years ago. I write in it as well. You see." He rifled through the pages. "It's almost filled. We'll have to start a second book." He glanced at Aleksi, looked away, out at the near ring of tents, where women and men and children prepared the feast, and then back at Aleksi again. "Is Tess still angry?" he asked.

Aleksi considered the question. Whatever else Bakhtiian might be, he was fair, and when he asked a question he wanted a straightforward answer whether or not that answer was flattering to himself. "I expect she's still angry at you. I wouldn't have advised that you try to keep her away from her brother while you showed him around camp."

Bakhtiian snorted. "And I did not, as it turned out. But perhaps it was for the best. Because she walked with us, he saw how well-loved she is and how much she has become jaran." Then he hesitated. His fingers played with the clasps on the book. "This David ben Unbutu—" He trailed off.

"She has said nothing of him."

"Ah," said Bakhtiian, meaning by that comment nothing Aleksi could fathom. Then he looked up, and his whole face changed expression. It lit, like a smoldering fire that bursts into flame. He smiled.

Aleksi glanced that way to see Tess and Sonia approaching. Sonia looked glorious, the brilliant blue of her tunic studded with beads of every color and gold plates lining the sleeves. Her headdress of gold and silver chains linked and braided over her blonde hair shifted as she walked. Golden crescent moons dangled to her shoulders; tiny bronze bells shook with her stride. The wealth gained in three summers of war adorned her, and she was by no means the vainest woman of the tribes. Beside her, Tess's wedding clothes looked subdued, although they had been rich enough at the time.

But Bakhtiian had eyes for no one but his wife. The force of his regard was both comprehensive and unnerving. A jaran man respected his wife; that went without saying. But to love her so openly, so entirely, so exclusively, that provoked criticism. It was not good manners. Except in Bakhtiian, who was beyond such criticism.

Bakhtiian rose and walked out to greet his wife. He took her hand and even, daringly, kissed her on the cheek, there in the open. Sonia raised her eyebrows, disapproving, but she said nothing.

"Aleksi." Bakhtiian released his wife's hand and turned to Aleksi as he strolled up. "If you could tell Mother Sakhalin that Tess and Sonia and I are going now to escort the prince here. Perhaps Raysia Grekov can be persuaded to sing.''

Sonia chuckled. ''Yes, and if any man can persuade Raysia to sing, it is you, Aleksi.''

Aleksi's cheeks flamed with heat. How he hated it when anyone drew attention to him. Raysia Grekov was not just a singer, but a Singer, a shaman, a poet, touched by the gods with the gift of telling the old tales and singing new ones. That she admired his ability with the saber was a running joke: like to like, both touched by the gods. But she was the daughter of the etsana of the Grekov tribe, niece of their dyan, and while her cousin Feodor might hope to marry Bakhtiian's niece Nadine, with such relatives, she certainly could not look upon Aleksi as anything but a casual lover.

''Oh, don't tease him,'' said Tess, mercifully, and Aleksi escaped Sonia's scrutiny and went to find Mother Sakhalin.

He did not seek out Raysia Grekov, but by the time he returned to the feasting ground, the meal was well under way. Bakhtiian sat with Charles Soerensen to his right and Cara Hierakis to his left, honoring her, Aleksi noted, as if she were the consort of a prince as well as a great healer. Mother Sakhalin sat between Dr. Hierakis and Marco Burckhardt, and Sonia sat on the other side of Burckhardt, flirting with him outrageously. Tess sat on Charles's right, and next to her, Qures Tinjannat, the ambassador from the king of Habakar lands who also happened to be a philosopher. Next to him, Niko Sibirin, and so on, foreigner mixed in with jaran. The newest ambassador was not here, but, of course, he had not yet been formally received.

Aleksi prowled the back, sidestepping serious children bearing wooden platters mounted on broad bases that they set down in front of their elders. Young men from the army assisted. Aleksi steadied Kolia as the little boy stumbled over an uneven patch of ground; he was clutching a bronze cup filled with water, taking it to Bakhtiian.

''Yes,'' Bakhtiian was saying to Soerensen, ''but when Sister Casiara wrote of the idea of precedence, she included the idea of legal precedence as well.''

''You were establishing a legalistic precedence, then,

when you wrote the letter to the coastal ports west of here and claimed that they had violated the peace by attacking a party of jaran?''

"My envoys." Bakhtiian nodded, took the cup from Kolia, and patted the little boy on his golden head before sending him away. "Envoys are sacrosanct. Is it not thus in all civilized countries?''

Soerensen smiled, received from Galina a platter heaped with steaming meats and a few precious slices of fruit, and set the platter carefully on the carpet. "This is a clever design.'' He unhooked the spoon that dangled from the platter's lip. "Since you have no tables. You're well-read, Bakhtiian. Whatever made you decide to travel to Jeds and study there?''

Aleksi crouched, watching the two men. They were alike, in many ways, and underneath the uneasy truce they seemed to be honoring, he thought that perhaps they actually respected one another.

Bakhtiian drew his gaze away from the other man and stared, as he often did when confronting his destiny, at the sky. Twilight lowered over them. Anatoly Sakhalin and Feodor Grekov led two lines of young men along the length of awnings, lighting lanterns at each pole. About thirty paces in front of Bakhtiian, out on the grass, Nadine supervised the building of two stacks of wood, side by side, twin bonfires.

"I desired to know the world," Bakhtiian said at last, glancing past Soerensen to Soerensen's sister, who was deep in conversation with the Habakar philosopher, "and I had heard that Jeds cradled the finest university, where one could learn.''

"Know the world?" asked Soerensen, sounding curious and not at all accusatory. "Or conquer it?''

"If I know the world, then it will be mine.''

Soerensen studied the other man. The prince had an ordinary face, similar to his sister's only in the high cheekbones and blunt chin, but like a well-made saber, his edge was clean and sharp. "You say that with conviction, but without avarice.''

"I want only to lead my people to the destiny that the gods have granted us. Surely that is not so different from what you want for your people, for Jeds.''

As the sky purpled to dusk, a single star appeared, the

bright beacon of the evening star. Soerensen considered it, as if it contained some answer for him, and then regarded Bakhtiian with a steady gaze. "Not so different. I want to go to Morava. The place Tess visited when she first came here."

"It's north from here, out on the true plains. The ancient home of the *khepelli*. Is it true the khepelli wish to overrun these lands, to conquer them and drive we humans off them?"

"We *humans?* What has Tess told you of the Chapalii?" Soerensen pronounced it differently, but it was clearly the same word.

Bakhtiian's smile was tight and sardonic. "Tess has told me many things, Soerensen. Which of them I can believe, and which I cannot, I have not yet divined."

A chuckle escaped from Soerensen quite spontaneously. "My sympathies," he said, and the comment sounded sincere enough to Aleksi's ears.

"But it is true enough, is it not," continued Bakhtiian, pressing this point, "that the khepelli are *zayinu*. The ancient ones. I don't know the word in Rhuian. Not demons. Not spirits."

"*Elves,*" said Cara Hierakis from the other side, startling both mēn. "Of course. Ancient ones with powers unknown to humans." Then she said something in their foreign tongue to Soerensen.

"Can it be arranged?" asked Soerensen. "I must see Morava."

Bakhtiian's expression had shuttered, becoming opaque and unreadable. "Is that why you came? Are the khepelli so dangerous?"

"You know why I came," said Soerensen quietly. Neither man looked toward Tess. "But it is true that the khepelli are dangerous. To both of us."

"I will consider this," said Bakhtiian, and he turned to Dr. Hierakis and began to discuss wounds and medical procedures with her. Tess ceded her conversation with the philosopher to Niko and leaned toward her brother. They began to talk, rapidly and in their language. For a time, Aleksi listened. Tess had taught him Rhuian, but not the other tongue, the language of Erthe. He was beginning to be able to pick out words and meanings, but he could not string them together yet into meaningful sentences. But they were talking about the khepelli and the shrine of Morava, that much he could discern. Anatoly Sakhalin lit the lanterns directly in front of Bakhtiian and passed on, smiling at his grandmother, pausing before Sonia and glancing once, quickly and with dislike, toward Marco Burckhardt, then going on. Soon enough he would reach the carpets where the actors sat.

Aleksi snagged a platter of meat from Mitya and retreated to the solitude of the wagon to eat. Beyond, Raysia Grekov began to sing, accompanying herself on a bowed lute. She sang the tale of how the daughter of Mother Sun came down to the earth from Highest Heaven and how the legendary dyan Yuri Sakhalin fell in love with her and followed her into the heart of demon country.

"Where the rocks littered the earth, where the mountains touched the paths of father wind, there she bore the child. Where the heat of her mother's hands scorched the soil, where the demons swarmed at twilight, there she brought forth the child. He heard its cry on the wind, but he could not find them."

As Aleksi always did, he lost himself in her voice. She sang so sweetly, and with such power, that it was no wonder that the gods had drawn her up to Heaven once because of their desire to hear her sing. When they came to move the wagon, he jumped, startled, and kicked over the platter, spilling the scraps onto the grass.

"What are you doing there, Aleksi?" asked Nadine. "Here, give us a hand."

Standing, he saw that the world had changed. Raysia was still singing, and a knot of people clustered around her, sitting and kneeling: the actors, mostly, listening intently. Bakhtiian was standing off to one side, talking with Dr. Hierakis and Niko Sibirin. Charles Soerensen and Tess and the Habakar philosopher, together with Elizaveta Sakhalin, were off on the other side, leaving the central carpet clear.

Aleksi helped Nadine and a few of the men from her jahar hoist the wagon and carry it onto the carpet and set it down. Nadine tossed six pillows onto it and then, with reverent care, received the horse-tail standard which Mitya had brought from the camp and laid it on the pillow embroidered with birds that Bakhtiian always sat on.

"Shall I go get him, Uncle?" Nadine called to Bakhtiian.

"You're sounding cheerful," said Aleksi. "Who are you going to get?"

"Jiroannes Arthebathes," said Nadine. "May he rot in hell." She grinned.

Bakhtiian waited until Raysia Grekov had finished her song. Then he lifted a hand in assent, and Nadine hurried off, her soldiers at her heels.

Immediately the two bonfires were lit, and in their roar and glare, a sudden change transformed the scene. The older man and woman who headed the Company herded their actors off to one side, placing them behind a group of commanders who appeared from the right. Soerensen collected his party and retreated a discreet distance to the left. There they could watch but remain outside the action.

Bakhtiian helped Elizaveta Sakhalin up onto the overturned wagon and settled her onto one of the pillows. Sonia followed her, then Tess, then Niko Sibirin, and then old Mikhail Suvorin, the most senior of the dyans currently with the main army. Bakhtiian balanced the horse-tail staff across his knees. They waited. At last the ambassador and his party arrived, halting beyond the twin bonfires.

Aleksi saw the glitter of armor in the Vidiyan ambassador's retinue: his guard. There was a pause. Past the shifting height of fire he saw Nadine explaining something to an older man and a younger one. The younger one, dark and bearded and dressed in wildly colorful clothing, bore himself arrogantly, by which Aleksi deduced he was the ambassador. But his bearing melted a bit when Nadine gestured him forward. To pass between the two fires, to reach Bakhtiian.

The hesitation was checked. One of the guards transferred a small chest into the hands of the older foreigner, and thus burdened, the old man followed his master forward. The fire beat on them. Aleksi could see it by the way the ambassador leaned first away from the one fire and then away from the other, caught between both, purified by their raging heat, by the furnace pressure of their light. The old man staggered after him.

The softer glow of lanterns lit them when they halted

before Bakhtiian. The old man dropped the chest more
than set it down, and he knelt, head bowed, as if glad of
the excuse to rest. The young one stood, looking angry
and impressed together, and trying to hide it.

Bakhtiian regarded him evenly. From his seat on the
wagon, he stared eye-to-eye with the ambassador. The
very plainness of Bakhtiian's clothing, red shirt embroidered on the sleeves, black trousers and boots, merely
added to his dignity, compared to the ambassador's gaudy
costume. Some men did not need to display their power
by displaying wealth. Like Soerensen, it occurred to
Aleksi very suddenly. None of the prince's people wore
gold, none wore weapons, and yet their bearing reeked
of natural confidence.

At last, cowed by Bakhtiian's stare, as fierce a pressure
as the fires through which he had passed, the ambassador
dipped to one knee.

"I am Jiroannes Arthebathes," he said in queerly accented Rhuian, fluid and blurred on the consonants. "I
bring you greetings from your cousin the Great King of
Vidiya, and these gifts, which he hopes you will graciously accept." He gestured, and the servant struggled
forward with the chest. Jiroannes's gaze flicked to Tess,
and his eyes widened as he recognized her. Then he
turned his attention back to his servant.

The chest was not just wooden, but cunningly carved
and set with enameling and strips of gold into the wood.
The servant opened the clasp and removed silver dishes,
an amazingly lifelike bird made of bronze, two tiny jade
horses, a collar of gold embossed with tiny human figures, a bolt of sheer white silk, and an arrow plated with
gold and fletched with black feathers.

Bakhtiian looked them over impassively but did not
touch them. Then he gestured, and the children, with
proper solemnity, came forward and took away everything except the arrow. That Bakhtiian considered at
length and in silence, and at last he lifted it up and leaned
back to present the arrow to Elizaveta Sakhalin. "The
Great King must be complimenting your prowess in hunting, Mother Sakhalin," he said. The old woman snorted,
amused and skeptical, but she took the arrow and placed
it over her knees.

Jiroannes looked outraged, and then he bowed his head to stare with seeming humility at the ground.

"You are welcome to our camp," said Bakhtiian, at last addressing the young ambassador directly. "I will send for you when it is time." He glanced around, caught Aleksi's eye, and gestured for him to escort the ambassador away. Then he turned to talk to Niko, as if the affair was of no more interest to him.

Leading Jiroannes away by a roundabout route, Aleksi had leisure to wonder what the young man was thinking. Nadine joined him, the Vidiyan guard marching obediently at her back, and they conducted the silent ambassador back through camp to the distant envoys' precinct. From here, the noise of the celebration, now in full flower, reached the dark clot of tents only as faint music and fainter laughter, like a distant roar of a mountain cataract to a man trudging through the night on a desert track. Out in the deep plains, where winter met summer like a blast of snow hitting fire, where spring existed for a week, for a scant month at most, such extremes were commonplace. To these envoys, cast out to the fringe of camp, their lives dependent very much on the whim of the jaran, such contrasts must prove unsettling.

"Ilya was too lenient," said Nadine to Aleksi as they left, walking back to the celebration. "The man was insufferable. He was angry. He showed it in his back, in the way he stood. He showed too little respect."

"Bakhtiian will make him wait. Then he'll get nervous."

"It could be." Nadine sounded peevish. "He has a slave."

"What is a *slave?*"

"Never mind. Look, the dancing has started."

At the celebration, they were dancing on the ground around the two bonfires. The angel was dancing with Anatoly Sakhalin. He was, shyly and modestly, showing her the steps to one of the simpler partner dances. But most of the other actors were out dancing as well, partnered with jaran men and jaran women. The dance ended and another started. Aleksi saw Tess dancing with her husband. Sonia, of all people, had somehow persuaded Soerensen out, and it appeared that Soerensen was a quick learner and adept enough to dance well. The angel was still dancing with Anatoly Sakhalin.

"Someone had better talk to him," said Nadine, voicing Aleksi's thoughts out loud.

"Surely his grandmother will speak to him," said Aleksi. "She's very pretty."

"She's beautiful," said Nadine. "She is also khaja. Look how the other man, Marco Burckhardt, look how he glares at them."

The dance ended. The angel strolled out of the ring of light with Sakhalin. She held her head cocked slightly to one side, looking at him with a provocative smile on her lips as he spoke to her. Surely she could not understand what he was saying. But perhaps the *words* did not matter.

A moment later, before they could vanish into the gloom, Elizaveta Sakhalin appeared and called to her grandson. His head jerked up and he halted, hesitated visibly, and finally, reluctantly, slowly, he retreated to his grandmother's side. The angel watched him go and with an unfathomable shrug of her delicate shoulders, she walked on out into the night, alone.

"And *that*," said Nadine, "is that. Excuse me, Aleksi. I've a sudden urge to dance." She broke away from him and strode straight toward the distant figure of Feodor Grekov.

Aleksi sighed and wandered on. He paused to watch Raysia Grekov where she sat on the now vacant wagon, playing simple songs for the amusement of a swarm of jaran men and two of the foreigners: Margaret O'Neill and the actor Gwyn Jones. The copper-haired foreign woman had her right hand on her belt buckle, and she kept toying with it, as if she was nervous. In contrast, her left hand held the bronze medallion around her throat with deliberate steadiness, canting the medallion's onyx eye so that it faced the singer. Beside Raysia, a young man played a low accompaniment on a drum. As Aleksi listened, he caught a fainter counterpoint, a vocal one, distant, whispering on the breeze. He lifted his chin and tilted his head, sounding for direction, and drifted out into the night.

Stars blazed above. Out beyond the awnings, the angel was cursing at Marco Burckhardt. Aleksi stopped stock-still, astonished. Burckhardt had his hands on her. He held her in a tight grip, one hand on each of her shoulders, and each time she spit words at him, he replied in an equally angry voice.

They were not married. Nor were they related by blood. If anything, Marco Burckhardt was as interested in her as Anatoly Sakhalin was. But no jaran man would stand by and see a woman handled like this, by a man who was neither husband nor brother.

Before Aleksi could come forward, before he could even speak to warn them, another figure burst onto the scene, materializing from the direction of the celebration. Diana gasped. Burckhardt whirled.

Anatoly Sakhalin drew his saber.

"No!" Diana cried in Rhuian. "Don't hurt him!" She cast herself between the two men. There was silence. Diana took four steps forward. "Anatoly, please, put away your sword."

Anatoly lifted the saber to rest on her cheek. She froze, and her face went white from shock and fear. Marco shifted. In an instant, he would lunge—"

"Stop!" shouted Aleksi. He sprinted forward.

In that moment, with Marco hesitating, Anatoly marked Diana, cutting a line on her cheek diagonally from her cheekbone almost to her chin. Blood welled from the cut. Slowly, she lifted her hand to touch her skin. Lowering it, she stared at her fingers. They were covered with blood. She swayed. Then she collapsed to her knees.

Aleksi hit Marco broadside and slammed him backward before he could do something rash. A knife spun out of Marco's grip and Aleksi pounced and grabbed it before Marco could react.

Anatoly had sheathed his saber. Now he stared at Diana with concern. He knelt beside her and put his good arm, comforting, firm, around her shoulders. At his touch, she screamed and scrambled away from him, panting.

"Damn you," said Marco from the ground.

Aleksi offered him a hand. Surprised, Marco took it and let Aleksi pull him up. Marco took a step toward Diana, but Aleksi held him back. "Don't go to her," Aleksi said.

Anatoly climbed to his feet and fixed a threatening stare on Marco, keeping himself between Marco and Diana. He rested his good hand on his saber hilt.

"What do you mean?" Marco demanded. "My God."

"He's marked her," Aleksi explained patiently.

"I can see that," said Marco caustically. "What kind of savages are you, anyway?"

"You're upset." Aleksi put a hand on his shoulder just to make sure he didn't bolt. "He's marked her for marriage. But I suppose you khaja don't do that."

Diana threw her head up. "What did you say?" she gasped. Left hand still pressed against her cheek, she rose unsteadily to her feet, flinched away from Anatoly's awkward offer of help, and circled him warily to come stand next to Marco. But when Marco reached toward her, she jerked away from him as well. "What do you mean, he marked me for marriage?" she demanded of Aleksi.

"When a man chooses a woman, he marks her. To show he means to marry her."

"That's barbaric," said Marco.

"What about the woman's choice, then?" Diana asked.

Aleksi shook his head. "But marriage is not a woman's choice. Someday you'll hear Raysia sing the tale of Mekhala, and how horses came to the jaran. You see—" He hesitated, finding words in this foreign tongue of Rhuian and placing them together in a form that would make sense to these people. "—when Mekhala beseeched the wind spirit for the horses that would set her people, that would set the jaran, free, he agreed only on the condition that she marry him. But in those days, before the jaran had horses, women chose both lovers and husbands. And so the wind spirit said, 'I will give you horses, but you must give me the choice of your husbands, and a woman may never choose her husband again.' And the women agreed that this was a fair trade for the gift of horses. So that women may still choose their lovers, but no longer their husbands. But this was long ago, in the—" He faltered, running up against concepts he had no words for in Rhuian. "In the long ago time."

Marco looked appalled. Diana gaped, looking as if she was still in shock.

"Aleksi," said Anatoly in khush. "What are you telling her?"

What a fool. But, of course, Aleksi was not about to say that to Mother Sakhalin's grandson. "She didn't know what you were doing." He glanced at the other man, but Anatoly's expression showed only stubborn resolve. "She thought you were trying to kill her."

Anatoly flushed, but he said nothing. He glared at Marco.

"But Tess Soerensen has a mark like this on her cheek," said Diana suddenly in a low voice. "And so does Bakhtiian. That means she *is* married to him." She glanced sidelong at Anatoly Sakhalin and then away. "So why can't I, if I love him?"

"God help us," Marco said. It was an oath Aleksi recognized, because it was an oath Tess used it. "Diana, you can't begin to go along with this—"

"I can do what I want," said Diana emphatically. She tossed her hair out of her face and walked over to Anatoly. He started, looking at her, and she tilted his chin down and kissed him on the mouth.

Marco swore.

"What in hell is going on?" The first person to arrive from the direction of the celebration was Dr. Hierakis. "Diana, come here. Goddess help us, child, what has happened to you?" The doctor lifted a hand to trace the cut on Diana's cheek. A moment later Charles Soerensen appeared, and behind him, Tess and Bakhtiian.

"Oh, God," said Tess. Then in khush: "Anatoly, have you gone out of your mind?"

"This is your work, then?" Bakhtiian demanded.

Anatoly held his ground under that devastating stare. "Yes. I marked her."

"Gods. You will come with me, young man. We will see what your grandmother has to say about this."

Anatoly did not move. He was tense, but determined. "It is a man's choice, in marriage."

"She is not jaran, Anatoly," said Tess.

He glanced at her, and she smiled slightly, ironically, since neither was she jaran. Then he returned his gaze to Bakhtiian. "If she wishes to be rid of the marriage, she can do so, but I am content."

"Tess," said Charles in a calm voice, in Rhuian, "what is going on?"

"He wants to marry me," said Diana suddenly. "This is the way they get married."

"Ah," said Charles. He studied his sister a moment, and Tess flushed and lifted a hand to brush the scar on her cheek, then lowered it again self-consciously. "I understand this is sudden, Diana. Such an action is not binding on you."

"No," she said stubbornly. "I want to marry him."

Marco muttered something.

"Marco, really," said Dr. Hierakis in Rhuian. "There's no need for such language."

Burckhardt's hands were clenched into rigid fists, and he looked so angry that Aleksi wondered how long he could maintain his composure.

"That is your choice, of course," said Charles to Diana. If he was shocked by her pronouncement, he did not show it. "But surely, Bakhtiian, the matter can be waived for some days so that the young woman can think it over."

"I don't need to think it over—"

"Diana," said Tess in a friendly but firm voice, "you will, by custom, have nine days to think it over. If you really want to go through with this, then you must go into seclusion for nine days, after which you will be reunited with this man and become husband and wife."

"Fine."

"What is she saying?" asked Anatoly in khush, a little desperately.

"You young fool," said Bakhtiian, also in khush. "Come along. I don't envy you the tongue-lashing you are about to receive from your grandmother. Perhaps I'll let Niko in on it as well. If your uncle Yaroslav was here. . . ." He trailed off, letting the thought go unfinished. With a gesture, he indicated that Anatoly precede him. "Your grace," he said to Soerensen, "perhaps you would be part of this council as well."

"Of course. I'll follow in a moment." He nodded, and Bakhtiian left.

"Diana, Cara, perhaps you'll come with me," said Tess. She led the two women off on the long walk to the Soerensen enclave.

Aleksi, silent, did not move. By now the others had forgotten him. He had that gift, to stand so still, to draw so little attention to himself, that it was as if he was invisible.

"Marco," said Soerensen softly.

"Leave me alone." Marco did not even look at the other man. He was not looking at anything, exactly, but at some sight, some vision, some pain, that only he could see.

Soerensen sighed, but he honored the request, and left quietly.

Aleksi dared not move. *He doesn't want me here.* And Aleksi felt an odd feeling: He felt ashamed because he had intruded on another man's anguish.

Bells tinkled softly. A golden vision appeared out of the gloom: Sonia, laden with an ornamentation that lent grace to her features and a glow to her expression. A single glance she spared for Aleksi, a brief tilt of her chin in acknowledgment of his presence. Crescent moons spun and danced at her shoulders. She halted beside Marco Burckhardt and settled a hand on his sleeve.

"Come," she said. That was all. Without a word, he went with her. The bells faded.

But Aleksi still heard the bells. Distant, but growing louder. A shout came from the far ring of tents. Another shout followed, and a lantern, two lanterns, sprang to life. They bobbed and swayed, approaching over the grass. Two horses with two riders, but only the foremost rider rode upright. The second lay over his mount's neck, hugging it from exhaustion. Men on foot trailed after them, a group that swelled in size and volume.

Aleksi ran to meet them.

"Where is Bakhtiian?" shouted the lead rider. "Gods, man, there's been treachery from those khaja swine."

The man lying over the second horse looked unconscious. The horse was blown and scarcely in better condition than its rider, though it did not look wounded. A broad strip of bloodied cloth was wrapped around the rider's head, obscuring his face, and more cloth bound his ribs and his left thigh. He slipped. Aleksi grabbed him and steadied him on the horse.

Bakhtiian came running, Sibirin behind him. "Bring the horse up to the carpet," someone called, and they arrived there, a ragtag procession, at the same time Bakhtiian did.

Bakhtiian halted for one instant. A look of rage suffused his face. Then he came forward and tenderly swung the wounded man down from the horse, laying him on the pillows. The movement opened the wound in his thigh, but the blood leaking onto the fine embroidery did not seem to bother Bakhtiian.

"Josef! Niko, go get the healer. Dr. Hierakis. Grekov, see to the horse."

Now that the rider was lying on his back, Aleksi could see that it was indeed Josef Raevsky, Ilya's finest general, a man who could have been dyan of his own tribe but who gave it over into his brother's hands many years ago in order to pledge himself to Bakhtiian and Bakhtiian's cause. The worst blood stained the cloth bound over his eyes.

"Ilya." Raevsky had some life yet.

"Who did this? The rest of your party?"

"The Habakar king," Raevsky gasped. "Treachery. Honored us as envoys and then at the feast, fell on us." He panted. His face was gray. "Left me alive, to deliver this." His hand fluttered feebly. A crumpled scroll was tucked into the sheath of his saber. His saber—was gone.

Bakhtiian removed the scroll and unrolled it. Scanned it. His lips were pressed so tight that they had lost all color. His eyes burned. " 'So that you will understand that you must fear me, and set no foot on my ground, I have shown you my power. But because I am merciful as well as strong, I have left one alive to tell the tale.' "

Sibirin came up with Dr. Hierakis in tow, and Bakhtiian shifted aside to make room for her. She knelt beside Raevsky and stripped the cloth bandages away. Her face was intent, impassive.

"It looks like they burned the eyes out." She ran a finger down the bridge of Raevsky's nose. "How far did he come?"

Bakhtiian shrugged. "It's about ten days' ride to the border. Much much farther to the royal city."

"Incredible," she said curtly. "Make me a litter to bear him to my tent. If you wish him to live, do it quickly." She rose. "I will be waiting there." And left, striding out into the darkness.

"Do as she says," said Bakhtiian. He stayed kneeling beside Raevsky until men came with a litter and bore him away. Then he rose. Glanced around, at the men waiting on his word. "You," he said to the rider who had come in with Raevsky. "What is your name?"

"Svyatoslav Zhulin, with Veselov's jahar."

"You will return south, then, with this message. I want Veselov and Yaroslav Sakhalin to drive into Habakar territory. Then the king will begin to understand that he must fear us." He glanced down at the pillow that rested against his boots, at the bright stain drying between the two birds of prey. "Then he will understand our power. Aleksi." His voice had the temper of the finest steel, decisive, cold, and sharp. "You will bring the Habakar philosopher to me. Now."

"Are you going to kill him?" someone asked, angry, wanting revenge.

"Of course not! We respect philosophers and envoys *here*. But I will inform him myself of this treachery. In the end, he may prove a valuable ally. Aleksi?"

Aleksi nodded and retreated, heading for the foreign envoys' enclave. Behind, he could hear Bakhtiian's crisp voice issuing more orders. The spring's campaign was beginning.

ACT TWO

"Some good I mean to do
Despite of mine own nature."

—SHAKESPEARE,
King Lear

CHAPTER TWENTY

From the ridge that bounded the valley on the northeast, black-shirted riders watched the battle raging below.

"They'll be routed by nightfall," said the black-haired man who sat on his horse at the fore of the group, next to its leader.

"Sooner, Yevgeni," replied the leader. "Look there. The center is breaking. And there: do you see the general's standard? It's wavering."

Yevgeni spat. "The coward. He's running."

The leader of the band watched as a clot of riders broke away from the back of the khaja army and raced for the western hills. He was fair, with golden hair and a strikingly handsome face. "Bring the woman up here, Piotr," he ordered, and a moment later Piotr returned. With him came the woman, a girl, more like, with a baby strapped to her back. She clutched the reins of a mountain pony, and she gave the battle below the briefest glance before fastening her gaze on what interested her most: the fair-haired man.

He gestured toward the retreating riders below. "Do you know where they're heading? What path they'll take?" he asked, speaking khush slowly.

She tore her gaze from his face and studied the valley and the swell of hills that marked the western boundary. Near a lake, a city lay smoking and battered, and it was past these ruins that the riders fled. "That way," she replied, pointing to a gap in the hills. Her khush was faltering, but comprehensible. "A road leading to the pass."

"Is there a good spot for an ambush?"

She looked back at the band: about one hundred horsemen in black, all with sabers, a few with lances. "With arrows, yes." She ran her left hand over the quiver that

hung from her belt along her thigh. "With swords. . . ."
She shook her head. "It is narrow."

"I want that general," said the leader.

"Vasil, are you mad?" asked Yevgeni. "Let the khaja
pig go, that's what I say. What does he matter? He'll be
a worse burden on the khaja king alive than dead."

Vasil glanced at the riders in his group and then down
at the jaran army driving through the khaja infantry in
the valley below. Evidently the bulk of the army had not
yet realized that its leader had deserted it. "I need a
prize."

Yevgeni shook his head. "I don't understand you,
Vasil. Your father was dyan of your tribe's jahar. It's a
fair enough claim, if you want it back. But your cousin
has been dyan now for—what?—three years? He may
contest you."

"Anton is Arina Veselov's brother," said Vasil.

"That's bound to cause trouble, two so close making
decisions."

"And knowing Anton and Arina as I do, because of
that, they'll be glad to give the command over to me. It
isn't my cousins I have to convince. Viaka." He turned
to address the girl. "We must go, quickly. Can you lead
us?"

"It is a bad place for swords," she insisted. "There
are others of my family who will come, if we can stay in
the heights and shoot down. Then perhaps you can overcome your enemy. They have fine armor."

Grumbling arose from the men closest. "Archery . . .
arrows in battle . . . it's dishonorable."

"Come now," said Vasil scornfully. "Surely you men
don't believe I'd ever suggest such a thing against an
honorable man of the tribes? But these are khaja. What
does it matter if arrows are used against them? They have
killed enough jaran men with arrows. And these khaja
villagers have agreed out of their own free will to accompany us."

Yevgeni snorted. "Out of the will of their headman's
daughter, who's bedding with you." The girl started
around and glared at him. Then she flushed. She was an
unremarkable young woman, scrubbed clean, with her
brown hair tied back and bound with a net of tiny golden
beads strung on a bronze wire. She wore a girdle of iron

plates around her waist, and a golden embossed pectoral hung from around her neck, covering her upper chest: it was more armor than any of Veselov's riders had.

Vasil smiled. "Yevgeni, my love," he said softly, "are you jealous?"

Yevgeni flushed with anger. "You have no right to say such a thing to me," he said in a fierce undertone. "I have never asked anything of you, Veselov, except first a place in Dmitri Mikhailov's jahar and now, a place with your arenabekh."

"Forgive me," said Vasil, his voice as smooth as silk, "but I do not like to be questioned. Do you understand?"

"I understand."

Vasil surveyed his riders. He pitched his voice to carry to the back ranks. "We're going to bag a prize, boys. We will take some khaja archers with us. If there are any of you who can't stomach their presence, then you may stay behind."

No one moved. Vasil shifted his gaze to the girl. She gazed at him as much with avarice as with love. "Then we can go," he said to her. "And swiftly."

She urged the pony forward and the band set out, riding on twisting paths down off the ridge and through the steep hills. At a narrow crossroads, the party of villagers joined them. A woman took the baby from Viaka and vanished up the trail. The rest went on. The villagers were mounted on sturdy ponies, each man—and a few young women—armed with bow and arrows and a long knife. Only Viaka spoke khush well, and she used this skill and Vasil's deference to her to bully the older khaja men, who clearly objected to her authority.

She led them along a narrow road cut through the hills. They rode two abreast, with Viaka and Vasil at the fore and the bulk of the villagers at the rear. At last the road dipped down into a gully and gave out onto a wider road that led up toward the pass. Here, they found signs of the city's death: A burned out wagon and seven corpses, three of them children, littered the roadside.

Yevgeni moved up beside Vasil and sniffed the stench in the air with distaste. "Arrows. Do they kill their own children?"

"These are Farisa," said Viaka. "As are my people.

We ruled this land once, until the King's grandsire rode here with an army, in my grandfather's father's time. He killed our prince and became prince himself. It was his army attacked the city, not yours, and killed these people. Those who escaped ran to the hills. We do not love the King.''

Vasil lifted a brow, questioning. ''So that is why your father agreed to help us? I thought all the khaja were alike. Where is the site for the ambush?''

They rode down and came to a curve in the road that was shielded by a rocky ridge. Vasil concealed his riders behind the ridge. Viaka sent archers up the steep cliffs on either side, where they hid behind boulders and underbrush. Then they waited.

After a time, the ring of harness and the pound of hooves drifted to them on the clear air. No voices carried: it was a silent flight. Vasil's face bore a curious stillness as he listened, as if this skirmish signaled the beginning of a momentous campaign.

Sudden shrieks echoed off the cliffs. Shouts and a scream blended with the terrified neighing of horses.

''Forward!'' cried Vasil. He led the charge.

The jaran riders came around the curve and smashed straight into the panicked troop. Already demoralized from the battle, they scattered under the archers' fire, half fleeing back down the road, half ahead into the jaran charge.

Next to Vasil, Piotr lowered his lance and with the weight and speed of his horse behind the thrust, he toppled a heavily armored rider from the saddle. The khaja warrior screamed as a man in the second rank cut him down. The charge drove through the khaja ranks and Vasil shouted for half the jahar to go on, after the retreating remnants. Fifty riders headed down the pass. Behind, the archers let loose a new stream of arrows into the group that had just survived the charge. Then Vasil wheeled his horse around along with his remaining fifty men and hit the disintegrating troop from the rear, trampling some, killing the rest.

Yevgeni and Piotr cornered a man in a golden surcoat, and when the man saw that he was surrounded and defeated, he dropped his weapons and began to plead in a language none of them could understand. Vasil rode up and stared at him: an older man with a grizzled beard, dark eyes and skin, and fine gilded armor.

"Yevgeni," said Vasil, "take twenty riders and help Georgi mop up the others." Yevgeni rode away.

The mountain people scrambled down from the heights and scurried among the bodies, gleefully stabbing those still alive and looting the dead.

"Is this the general?" Vasil asked when Viaka came up beside him on her pony.

She shrugged. "How should I know? All these Habakar bastards look the same to me. His armor is rich enough."

"Then you shall have it, my dear. Piotr, strip him."

The man protested, at first. Piotr grabbed his left hand and cut off his little finger, and after that, the man submitted in silence. Until Yevgeni returned with seventy riders, a few of whom were wounded, and two captives. The first of the captives was a stalwart man in a fine brocaded surcoat who endured many bleeding wounds stoically. The second was an adolescent boy without a trace of beard on his face, tall but clearly young and terrified. He, too, wore a gold surcoat and gilded armor. When the Habakar general saw him, the old man broke out in a storm of weeping and struggled away from his captors to embrace the boy.

"They force children to ride into battle, too," said Yevgeni, pulling his mount up beside Vasil. "It's barbaric. But the boy seemed important, so we let him live."

"The other man?"

"He fought courageously to defend the child."

"Bind his wounds, then, after you've stripped him of his armor. Leave the boy in his, though, or they'll never believe we found such a child fighting."

The old man, stripped down to his linen tunic and hose, broke away from the boy and threw himself at Vasil's feet, babbling in his khaja tongue. Vasil sighed and looked around for Viaka, but she was kneeling, running her hands over the golden surcoat and the fine armor with a gleam of lust in her eyes. She glanced up, and when she saw that Vasil was watching her, her face flushed with pleasure and she rose and came over to him, glancing back frequently as if to make sure her new armor was not being stolen by one of her villagers. She halted beside Vasil and listened to the old man, then spat on him.

"He says he will gladly give you anything you please, as long as you spare the boy," she said to Vasil. "He says his name is Yalik anSiyal, and he is a great nobleman and the leader of this army. The boy is his son."

Vasil smiled. Not gloated, not quite, but he felt entirely pleased with himself. "We'll ride, then. I have what I need."

"I'm coming with you." Viaka's gaze up, at him seated splendidly on his mount, was worshipful as well as possessive.

Vasil chuckled. "My dear, you are wealthy now. You don't need me."

"My father will only take these things from me once you are gone and give them to my brothers. I would gladly become your wife. My father would not protest."

Yevgeni laughed under his breath. "He'd be glad enough to be rid of her," he said softly.

"I am married," said Vasil quietly.

She gestured impatiently. "I do not ask to be your chief wife. But surely you have a place for a secondary wife."

"Savages," muttered Yevgeni.

"Yevgeni, get the men ready. We must go." Vasil put out a hand and took Viaka's, holding it a moment. "My dear, however much I might wish it, it is impossible." Then he released her hand and reined his horse away. Piotr bundled the general onto his horse and tied him there, stringing the boy's mount on behind. Viaka simply stood, staring at them. One of the villagers, an old man who had protested the most at the girl's usurpation of authority, grinned vindictively as the riders mounted and rode away.

Vasil did not even glance back, although Yevgeni did. "You cold bastard," he said to Vasil. He laughed. "Gods, these khaja can't even keep their own tents in order. How can they expect to resist Bakhtiian's army?"

"We are not part of Bakhtiian's army yet."

"I still don't understand," said Yevgeni, "how you can expect Bakhtiian to take us in, now that we're arenabekh, and then agree to let you become dyan of the

Veselov tribe, after we rode with the last dyan who tried to kill him.''

"There is a great deal you don't understand, Yevgeni. There is a great deal no one understands. But I am determined to have my way, this time." He glanced back as Piotr cantered up from the rear. "What is it?"

"The girl. She's following us."

"Let her follow. I'm no longer concerned with her."

Yevgeni snorted. "Meaning you don't need her anymore."

Vasil did not answer. He picked up their pace, and they made good time down to the valley, riding past the ransacked city by late afternoon. A contingent of armored riders, hailing them, met them by an outstretched arm of ruined wall.

"Halt! I hadn't heard of arenabekh in these parts. Where's your leader?" This from their captain, a beautiful young man whose handsome face was marred by scars along the jaw and across the ridge of his nose. "Vasil! Gods, I thought you were dead! Everyone thought so."

Vasil smiled. "But I am not dead, Petya, as you see."

"But these are arenabekh, Vasil!"

"It's true that I've proven myself as a dyan by leading these men. Now I've returned. How is my sister? Have you any children yet?"

Petya flushed. "You must know that Vera is disgraced. It isn't—it isn't anything to speak of here."

"Then forgive me for speaking of it. Have you any news of my wife?"

"Karolla is well. Your cousin Arina took her in."

A gleam lit Vasil's fine blue eyes. "And my children? They are well also?"

The tight line of Petya's mouth relaxed slightly. "They are well. They are sweet children. Everybody loves them."

"Of course. You're outfitted differently—all that armor. You look like khaja soldiers."

"Things have had to change." Petya regarded the older man warily. "Why are you here, Vasil?"

"Even arenabekh may return to the tribes, if their etsana agrees to it. I heard that my father died. I have come to claim the position that is rightfully mine. Can you take me to Anton? He is here, is he not? I saw the Veselov standard.''

"He is here." Petya hesitated. Then, as if he could find no excuse to refuse, he motioned to the riders under his command and they turned and escorted Vasil and his men back along the valley. Corpses speckled the grass and the fields, fleeing soldiers who had been cut down and left to die. An overturned cart blocked the road, but the riders simply rode around it, not bothering to move it. Vegetables spilled out from its bed, bruised or flattened by the impact. In a far field, a crowd had been herded together under the watchful eyes of a group of riders.

"You have prisoners," Petya studied the two men and the boy in the middle of Vasil's jahar. "We were just heading up into the hills to see if we could catch the general of this army. He fled the battle."

"I have him. That one, there, and his son."

"Ah. Sakhalin will be pleased."

"Yaroslav Sakhalin leads the army? Bakhtiian isn't here?''

Petya's brows drew down in confusion. Then he laughed. "You didn't think this was the entire army, did you? We're only the vanguard. Bakhtiian is coming soon with the main army. We are as plentiful as the birds, and as strong as the winter wind."

"Then it is true," said Vasil thoughtfully. "Bakhtiian will conquer all the khaja lands."

"Did you ever doubt it?" Petya blinked up at Vasil, looking naive and perplexed and utterly assured all at once. "Did you ever doubt that he could do it?"

Vasil did not reply. Instead, Yevgeni leaned forward. "Excuse me," he said politely to Petya. "But if you are with the Veselov tribe—do you know—I have a sister. She was with me, before, with Mikhailov, and I never heard what had happened to her. Perhaps you've heard of her. Her name is Valye Usova."

"I don't know her," Petya confessed. "I'm sorry. But Arina Veselov might, or Irena Orzhekov. After Mikhailov died, those two etsanas oversaw what became of the women and children who were left behind." He hesitated again, visibly, his open face betraying doubt. "Vasil. Are you certain you will be welcome? You followed Mikhailov, after all. You tried to kill Bakhtiian. He has no reason to forgive you.''

''No reason except what lies in his heart,'' said Vasil, so low that only Petya heard him.

Petya's face became a flood of emotions that he suppressed with difficulty. ''Then it's true, the things Vera said about you.'' He spoke quietly and, because it was in his nature, deferentially.

Vasil snorted. ''Vera is a snake, Petya, which I think you ought to know by now, being married to her as long as you have been. She says only what she pleases, to strengthen her own position.''

''She no longer has a position. The etsanas stripped her of all rank. Arina argued against it, but Orzhekov and the elders insisted. Vera does menial work for Varia Telyegin, who treats her kindly enough, though she's nothing but a servant now.''

Vasil laughed. ''I am amazed. She endures such treatment?''

''What choice does she have?'' Petya asked bitterly.

Vasil turned his head smoothly to stare at Petya. ''And after everything, after the way she treated you, after she betrayed your trust, you still love her?''

Petya pressed his lips together and turned his face away, refusing to answer.

''Here is the main army,'' said Yevgeni. A scout hailed them, and Petya led them around its mass to the northwest, where they came to a ring of horses and a knot of men standing talking together.

''Ah, there you are, Petya,'' called a middle-aged man, dark featured and with a pleasant, open face. ''What did you catch?'' His gaze skipped over Vasil, wrenched back, and he blanched, as though he had seen a ghost. ''Vasilley,'' he said hoarsely. ''I thought I would never see you again.'' Then, transformed as if by the rising sun, his face lit with joy. ''You damned bastard, where have you been?''

Vasil dismounted and strode forward. The two men embraced. ''Anton.'' Vasil's tone was fervent. ''How I've missed you, you more than anyone, for all the kindness you ever showed me. You look well. I'm glad to see it.'' He disengaged himself from Anton and turned to regard the other five men, who watched this reunion with interest. His gaze quickly fastened on the man who stood with quiet command to the far right. "You are Yaroslav Sakhalin?"

Sakhalin nodded, acknowledging the question. "You are Sergei Veselov's son Vasil? It would take a greater man than I not to be astonished by your sudden appearance here, and so many years after you vanished and were presumed dead." He examined Vasil with an intent, intelligent gaze. He carried himself easily, with the relaxed authority of a man who knows he is both important and competent. He was a man at the height of his maturity, older than Vasil and Anton, but not yet old—old enough to have a married daughter and a nephew just elevated to his own command, and yet young enough to be a dangerous fighter still. His gaze settled on Anton, reading the dyan's face, and then returned to Vasil. "What brings you back to us, Veselov?"

Vasil did not speak immediately. His own men stirred restlessly in their saddles. Petya looked worried, gnawing at his lower lip. In the end, in the silence, it was amazingly enough Anton Veselov who spoke.

"But, of course, if you just heard of your father's death, then you must have returned to claim the jahar. You are dyan by right, if the etsana and the elders agree to the election."

"But you are dyan, Anton," said Sakhalin without expression. "Bakhtiian himself approved your election. I am sure no one will protest if you petition to keep your position."

Anton looked surprised. "You know yourself, Yaroslav, that it isn't proper for a brother and sister to act together in authority over a tribe. They're too close. There was simply no one else to take the position. And now there is." He nodded at Vasil.

"I have led these arenabekh for three years," said Vasil quietly, "and I have brought khaja prisoners that I feel sure Bakhtiian wants."

"Arina will wish it also," added Anton, "that her cousin become dyan." Vasil flashed him a smile.

Sakhalin's lips twitched up. "Then the question becomes, will Bakhtiian wish it? Very well, Veselov. It is no business of mine. You may take your case to Bakhtiian

himself.'' He looked beyond the two men, at Vasil's jahar. ''Who are these khaja you have with you?''

''The general of the army you just defeated, Sakhalin.
As well as his son. The third is an honorable soldier who
fought courageously in defense of the boy.''

''You do me a service, then, in bringing them to me.''

''I meant them for Bakhtiian, begging your pardon.''

Sakhalin chuckled. ''Did you, indeed? You may take
them to him, then, and save me the bother. Anton, you
will have to go as well, but I can't afford to lose your
riders. Have your captains report to me, until you—''
Here a glance spared for Vasil. ''—or your cousin returns.''

''As you wish, Yaroslav,'' replied Anton. He gave
Vasil a slap on the arm and a grin, and then mounted
and rode away with Petya and his troop to give the orders.

''You seem to inspire loyalty, Veselov,'' said Sakhalin,
whether with sarcasm or admiration it was impossible to
tell. He was distracted by a scout riding in. ''What
news?''

''We've rounded up every khaja we could find in the
valley and on the nearby slopes. There's few enough
women and children—they've either fled or been slaughtered by their own army, I don't know which. What shall
we do with the men?''

''Sort out those who have some skill, artisans and
blacksmiths. Kill the rest.'' Sakhalin turned back to
Vasil. ''You'd best be on your way at dawn, Veselov.
Bakhtiian is assembling the army, and he won't want any
confusion about his commanders, not on this campaign.
We'll be driving on through the pass in the morning. The
heart of the kingdom lies beyond these mountains.'' Then
he turned to the man at his right, dismissing Vasil, and
began to discuss supplies and fodder for the horses on
the mountain crossing.

The finest blush crept onto Vasil's cheeks, but he
turned and walked with a careless stride back to his horse.
''We'll set up camp here,'' he said to Yevgeni, ''and go
on in the morning.''

They found a quiet spot, distant from the ruined city
and the slaughter going on there. The men built a few
fires, including one set aside from the rest for Vasil. He

sat before the fire, brooding. Bringing out his *komis* cup, he poured the pungent drink out of a flask and into the cup, and drank. By the other fires, his men laughed and sang songs and gambled, relaxed now as they had not been for a long time. Still, there was no assurance that Bakhtiian would not punish them: they were arenabekh, after all, men who had left the tribes for their own reasons, or been cast out. Some had no families to return to, and others, no hope that their tribes would want them back. But with the jaran tribes united, they had no future anywhere else. Vasil licked a spot of the fermented milk off of his lips and smiled. He knew Bakhtiian's weak spots, and he knew how to exploit them. It came down to one thing in the end. It always had. What he wanted, he intended to have.

CHAPTER TWENTY-ONE

"Diana, you don't have to go through with this."

Diana stared at her hands, refusing to look up. After nine days sequestered in the Company's camp, rehearsing every day and then staying behind when the others went out to explore the jaran encampment, she had grown used to her colleagues coming back to harangue her, to get her to change her mind, and in some cases to ridicule her for going native. But the more they tried to budge her, the more her resolve hardened.

Now it was early morning of the day she was to marry, and Yomi had appeared at her tent at dawn with Tess Soerensen in tow. And left the two women there together.

Diana stared at her pewter bracelet and heard Tess sigh. "Diana, are you even sure why you're doing this?"

Diana looked up. "You did it. You married Bakhtiian."

Tess chuckled. "Not on my second day in camp, I didn't. Although it's true enough the tribe welcomed me in as soon as I arrived, and adopted me only days after that. You must think of Anatoly as well. Have you considered what it would be like to stay here, after your Company goes back to Earth?"

Diana twined her fingers together and fastened her gaze on her knuckles.

"Or what it will be like for him if you leave?"

She pressed her lips together. She could feel the heat burning in her cheeks. "Isn't it better that we—even if I go, isn't it better that we have shared something together than nothing?"

"If by something you mean you want to have sex with him, I must tell you that you don't need to be married to him to do *that*."

"But—" Diana felt all at sea, confused and hurt at

once. "But why did he mark me, then? I thought all barbarians were prudes, that you had to be married or else it was—taboo or something. Bakhtiian killed a man, back at the port—"

"For rape."

"You approved of it? The execution, I mean."

"I wasn't there. You can't make assumptions about these people, Diana." She hesitated. Diana braced herself. She knew what was coming, and she was determined to resist it. But instead, Tess took her off guard. "I've asked my sister Sonia Orzhekov and Anatoly's grandmother Elizaveta Sakhalin to come to you this afternoon before the celebration. I hope you will listen closely to what they say."

Which would be yet another attempt to talk her out of the marriage. "I've learned a little khush," said Diana defensively. "You think I'm a fool for doing this, don't you?"

Tess smiled ruefully. "That would be rather like the pot calling the kettle black, don't you think? It's easy to act on impulse, and much harder to think about what the consequences might be. But the consequences will show up sooner or later, and then you must prepare yourself to deal with them."

"I love him," said Diana stubbornly, as much to convince herself as to convince Soerensen. Then she recalled the intense blue of his eyes, the piercing sweetness of his gaze, and she flushed.

"Love is a compelling reason," said Tess quietly, "if indeed what you're feeling is love. But you don't even know him. You've never exchanged one word with him that wasn't translated through someone else."

"That doesn't mean I can't love him!" But, Goddess, what if Tess was trying to tell her that it was *Anatoly* who wanted free?

Tess sighed and rose. "Just remember, Diana, that love is never the only reason. I'll go now. Yomi said to tell you that rehearsal will start early this morning."

Diana flung her head up and jumped to her feet. "Oh, Goddess! If I'm late, Owen will have my head on a platter."

"Yes. I heard that the company will be doing its first

performance tonight. What have they chosen to perform?''

Diana shook her head as she pulled a tunic on over her shirt. "We've been rehearsing some of Ginny's reductions of Shakespeare. Keeping the content without the verbiage and—well, reducing the story to its most basic components and mixing in some of the dell'Arte conventions of telling a story without words, or at least that the words in and of themselves don't have to be understood to understand the story. Owen has us working with gesture primarily, and tone and intonation. It will be fascinating to see how well it carries over.''

"I'm sure it will be," Tess replied tonelessly. The two women parted, and Diana ran over to the rehearsal area. Luckily she was not the last one to arrive. Hyacinth jogged up at her heels. His white-blond hair was in disarray and he held his belt in his right hand, fastening it as he halted beside her.

"Why are you late?" Diana demanded as they walked together through the screens and arrived to find the others assembled around the raised platform on which they usually rehearsed.

Hyacinth winked at her. He had delicate features and perfect lips, and eyelashes to die for.

Diana snorted. "Male or female?"

He grinned. "Both. Together."

Diana laughed, choked it off, and flushed suddenly. "I hope you know what you're doing," she said in a whisper, aware that half the company was watching them.

"Oh, Mother's Tits, Diana," said Hyacinth with disgust. "I may be gorgeous, but I'm not stupid. I've had days to watch how things go in the jaran camp. They invited me, not the other way around. I'm discreet, as were they." Then he leaned down and nibbled at her right earlobe. "And as you know," he said softly, "I'm very good."

Diana shoved him away, fighting back a smile. "I hope you're keeping track. At the rate you go, you'll sleep your way through half the camp before we leave."

"Only half? I'm wounded by your lack of faith. Look, here come Owen and Ginny. Phillippe and I have a bet running—I say we'll do *Lear,* and he says we'll do *Tempest.* What do you think?''

"Anything but *Dream,*" Diana muttered.

Hyacinth giggled. "Two men in love with the same woman. Too close for comfort, eh?"

"Shut up!" she hissed, furious that she was so transparent, and especially to Hyacinth, who was not only promiscuous but a notorious gossip.

Owen mounted the platform and surveyed his troops. "We'll do our final run-through this morning and then move the stage to the performance ground. You'll have the afternoon off, but I want everyone back at—" He checked the back of his hand to read the transparency strip, but all such physical evidence of their off-world origin had been left behind on the ship that had brought them here. "Ah." He glanced around, perplexed. Ginny sat hunched over her notebook. His gaze settled on Yomi.

"Sunset is at 1900 Standard. Meet at 1800 hours."

"As Yomi says. Now." He paced from one end of the platform to the other, as if measuring it, studied the scattering of clouds in the sky, and motioned to Hyacinth. "Puck. We'll walk the awakening scene first and then go back to the beginning."

Hyacinth smiled charmingly. "But you haven't told us what we're doing yet."

Owen blinked. *"A Midsummer Night's Dream,* of course. Come, come. We haven't much time. I'm a little concerned about the division between our world and the faery world. But one must assume that all human cultures have some understanding of a spirit world, of a world coterminous with our own. I believe that the mythic element must touch all human cultures, that it is there that we must seek our initial contact."

At first Diana felt weak all over. Then she was furious. What would they think? What would Anatoly think? It was like a slap in the face, like making fun of something that was serious, not a lark. "You can't!" she blurted out. "Owen, you can't do it."

Owen blinked at her, looking bewildered. "Can't do what?" he asked. Anahita tittered.

"You can't make me play that part. It's . . . it's . . ." She clenched her hands into fists and found that she was too upset to go on.

"But it's perfect. Love's misunderstandings. Weddings. A comedy. It will play to the audience, and we will find a bridge across which we can communicate.''

Hyacinth coughed into his hand, hiding his smug grin. ''Poor Owen. I'm having no problem in communicating.''

Unexpectedly, Hal spoke up. ''Di's right, Dad. Considering what happened with Burckhardt, isn't it a bit inappropriate? What if the natives take it as an insult?''

Owen regarded first Diana, and then Hal, with a penetrating gaze. His usual vagueness sloughed off him like a duck shedding water from its back. ''I hear your reservations. But. I am right in this. Now. Hyacinth, shall we begin?''

''I refuse,'' said Diana, before she realized she meant to say it. ''I refuse to play Helena. You're asking me to insult my . . . my . . .'' The word was hard to say, but she forced herself to say it. ''My husband.''

''Ooooh,'' said Anahita. ''My, my. Aren't we the little queen today?''

''Anahita,'' said Gwyn in a soft voice. ''Shut up.''

Everyone else was watching Owen. Owen scratched at his black hair, frowning a little. Then he clambered down from the platform and walked over to stand in front of Diana. She wanted to take a step back, but she did not. He pulled at his lower lip, studying her with his dark eyes.

''Are you a member of this Company?'' he asked finally.

She swallowed, but she met his gaze. ''Yes.''

His voice dropped. In an undertone that could not be heard five feet from them, but carried clearly to her, he said, ''Then do as I say. It is your choice, Diana. You are free to go, if that is what you wish. Although I would hate to lose you, that goes without saying. Now, will you play the part?''

Her hands were still tightly fisted. She lowered her gaze away from him. Of course she was out of line, disputing with him in this way. Of course she was free to go. She had always been free to go, as were any of them. ''I'm not free to go, and you know it,'' she said in a whisper, because it was true. She was an actor. Her whole life had led her to this. ''Yes.'' She could not look up at him. She felt their stares like a weight on her. ''I'll play.''

"Good." He said it curtly but not without sympathy, and then turned and hopped back up on the platform.

"From Puck's entrance," said Yomi.

"Sorry," muttered Hal, with a lift of his chin motioning toward his father.

"Thanks," she said, and took her place. And forced everything else out of her mind, to concentrate on her part: Helena, scorned by Demetrius—Demetrius, who together with Lysander loves Hermia—until out in the enchanted wood, by the mistaken conjurings of Puck, both Demetrius and Lysander forget their love for Hermia and compete for Helena's affections.

They broke at noon, and Diana went and sat in the big Company tent while the others trooped off to assemble the stage and screens over in the jaran camp. Joseph was assembling food for the company. He had a fire going outside, with a huge kettle full of soup set on a tripod over it. Inside, he frowned at the solar-powered oven that sat disguised as a chest in one corner of the tent. "We'll need more flour soon," he said. "And I don't know how to requisition it. Otherwise we'll have to give up bread."

"And you make the most wonderful bread, Joseph." Diana propped her chin on her fists and stared at the canvas wall. The filaments that led up to the solar strips sewn into the ceiling blended into the canvas fabric, lending the barest sheen to the fabric if the light struck it right. "I hate being confined to camp like this."

"It's a good lesson," said Joseph thoughtfully.

"What is?"

"Well, marriage, a legal or spiritual partnership of whatever kind, is restrictive in that you must think of another person and not only of yourself and your desires. You are no longer as free as you once were, responsible only for yourself. Not that I think that that's necessarily the meaning these people give this custom of seclusion— I wouldn't presume to know that—but it's one lesson to be gained, nevertheless. Is there someone outside?" He ducked his head out the flap and then turned back to look at Diana, a quizzical look on his face. "I believe they've come to see you."

He disappeared outside, and Diana heard a brief exchange. She stood up. Joseph reappeared. "Go on," he said. Then he smiled. "And good luck."

"You don't think I'm a fool?" she asked, because Joseph and Yomi were the rock on which the company was laid, the solid foundation that held everything together, and she trusted their judgment.

"We're all fools sometimes," said Joseph cheerfully. "But foolishness is one of the saving graces of our lives. Go on. I can't have them in here. The bread's about to come out."

She pushed past the entrance flap and blinked to adjust to the sunlight. Sonia Orzhekov and Anatoly's grandmother waited for her outside. Elizaveta Sakhalin was a tiny woman, quite old, but Diana felt cowed by her presence nevertheless.

Sonia smiled graciously and took Diana's hands in hers. "I hope you will allow us to have a talk with you."

"Of course." Diana dared not refuse. She felt like a giant, towering over Sakhalin, and yet she felt as well at a complete disadvantage.

"Will you come with us, then?" Sonia asked, with a kind smile. "We discovered that you have no tent of your own, so we took the liberty of bringing one with us, which we set up out here."

"Out here" lay just beyond the Company's encampment and not quite within the jaran encampment. "That's very diplomatic," said Diana, seeing that the colorful tent was sited to belong to both camps, and yet to neither—the meeting of two independent tribes. "And generous, too. It's a beautiful tent." Which it was, striped in four colors on the walls. The entrance flap bore a pattern of beasts intermingled, twined together.

"You must thank Mother Sakhalin," said Sonia. "She has gifted you the tent. Here, now, come inside. We sent Anatoly out of camp for the day, knowing we would bring you here, but you really ought to be inside until sunset." Sonia pulled the tent flap aside and gestured for Diana to precede her. Diana hesitated, and then motioned to Sakhalin to go in first. That brought the first softening of the old woman's features, but the smile was brief. She ducked inside, and Diana followed her. There was room to stand up, but barely, and the walls sloped steeply down from the center. Sonia came in last. She showed Diana how to sit on the large pillows that covered half the rug that made up the floor of the tent.

"I spoke to Mother Yomi," said Sonia as she, too, sank down onto a pillow. "She agreed that you might wait out the rest of the day in seclusion here, as is fitting. She said some preparations were necessary for your performance tonight, but one of the other women of your Company will come by to help you."

"Thank you," said Diana, aware that Elizaveta Sakhalin was studying her with a frown on her face. "I . . . I hope that you will tell me anything I need to know, about . . . about . . ."

Sonia grinned. Her eyes lit, a trifle mischievously, perhaps, and Diana felt suddenly that here she had an ally, not an enemy. "As for what to do with Anatoly, I think you need no instruction from me." Diana flushed and twisted her bracelet around her wrist. "As for the rest— well—first Mother Sakhalin wishes to ask you a few questions." She spoke a few words in khush to Sakhalin, and then the grilling began.

Elizaveta Sakhalin wished to know about Diana's family. Were they important? Wealthy? Had they any skills to pass on to her new husband's family? Did they own horses? How many tents made up the family? Only after Diana had stumbled through this inquisition, scrambling to answer the questions truthfully without revealing anything about where she really came from, did Sakhalin's questions narrow in on Diana herself. Did she have any particular skills to bring to the marriage? Any marriage goods? What was an actor? Was it like a Singer?

In fact, it was clear that Elizaveta Sakhalin thought her grandson was marrying beneath himself, that he had fallen in love with a pretty face, marked Diana on a whim, and now was going to marry a woman who had nothing but her looks and her curious status as an actor to recommend her. And she *had* nothing. Diana stared at her hands as silence descended, and she realized it was true. To these people, she had no knowledge and no skills that made a woman valuable, and no family except the Company, here.

"Well," said Sonia apologetically, "Tess came from an important family in her own right. You mustn't mind Mother Sakhalin's disappointment, Diana. You must understand that the Sakhalin tribe is the Eldest of all jaran tribes, and she the headwoman of that tribe, so of course—''

''So of course she expected her grandson to marry a woman of higher rank,'' said Diana bitterly. If only they knew what an honor it had been for Diana to be accepted into the Bharentous Repertory Company, or how many actors she had beaten out for the place. It was absurd; millions of people knew her name, millions had seen her perform, on stage or watching through holo links, and this old woman, this barbarian of a tribe that didn't even know the rest of the universe existed, thought she wasn't good enough to marry her grandson.

''Diana,'' said Sonia firmly, taking one of Diana's hands in her own, ''I understand that actors are Singers, that they are gifted by the gods with their art. But Mother Sakhalin believes that jaran Singers are the only true Singers—that can't be helped. Most jaran care nothing for khaja ways, and why should they? But I can see that you are a woman who thinks well of herself and has a position she is proud of. I have been in khaja lands, and I know you are a Singer. Still, you are not in your land now, and Mother Sakhalin is worried about her grandson. Who is, I might add—'' She shifted her head so that she could wink at Diana without Sakhalin seeing. ''—since she can't understand me, her favorite grandchild. Make him happy, and she will come to love you.''

A rush of gratitude overwhelmed Diana. Impulsively, she reached out and took Sonia's other hand in hers. ''I thought you came to try to talk me out of the marriage.''

Sonia looked puzzled. ''It is Anatoly's choice, and while I might think that choice was rash, I cannot now interfere. Not even his grandmother can interfere.''

''I . . . I thought—'' Now she glanced at Mother Sakhalin's stern face, and then away, because the old woman terrified her. ''I thought perhaps Anatoly no longer wanted to marry me. That you came to tell me that. It isn't—as if we know one another very well. He might have had second thoughts.''

Sonia laughed and squeezed Diana's hand reassuringly. ''Men never have second thoughts. Anatoly, like most young men who have gotten what they want, has been infuriatingly well-mannered for the past nine days.''

If the rug had been yanked out from under her feet,
Diana could not have felt more unstable. It really *was*
going to happen. "But I don't know—that is, what is
expected of a wife here? What do I do?"

Sonia sighed and released Diana's hands. "How like
Tess you are. I begin to think you khaja women are hopeless. But perhaps that is because you have servants or
slaves to do all the work for you."

"We don't have slaves!" Diana broke off. She could
not begin to imagine what these jaran women must do,
every day, to keep their families fed and sheltered and
clothed and healthy. Her world and their world barely
intersected, and in their world, she was as ignorant as a
baby. "I hope you will help me understand what things
I need to do." She hadn't the faintest inkling of what she
was getting into.

Sonia shook her head. "You need a woman of the
tribes to help you, to treat you as a sister. I can't offer,
because I have too many responsibilities as it is. But
perhaps . . ." She turned to Sakhalin and the two women
had a rapid conversation in khush. Diana could not understand a word they were saying, could not even recognize any of the khush words she had so laboriously
learned from the program on Maggie's slate. "That is
settled, then," said Sonia finally, nodding her head with
a satisfied look on her face. Even Sakhalin looked mollified. "The tribes are moving. The main army leaves
tomorrow, and our camp moves as well. We will meet
up with Arina Veselov and her tribe, and I will ask her
to take you in. That will do, I think. You'll like Arina. I
think you must be of an age, you two. She and her husband know Tess well, too, so they will understand about
your khaja ways. But you'll have to learn khush, although
I believe Kirill has learned some Rhuian these past three
years. Is that acceptable to you, Diana?"

"To me, yes." Pitched into this unknown sea, Diana
was not sure she could swim. "But I'll—you'll—Arina
Veselov will have to speak to Owen and Ginny first. I
need their permission for any drastic change in my circumstances. I have my duties to the Company."

Sonia repeated this speech to Sakhalin, and the old
woman voiced her approval of Diana's deference to her
elders. "Mother Sakhalin says that until we meet up with

the Veselov tribe, you and Anatoly may consider the Sak-halin camp your own.''

''But isn't that his family? Wouldn't he live there any-way?''

Sonia cocked her head to one side. She wore her hair in four braids, each bright with ribbons woven in the hair, and her head was capped by a beaded net of gold that hung in strands down to frame her face. ''When a man marries, he goes to his wife's kin to live. Tomorrow, if you wish, you may move your tent into your people's encampment, and Anatoly will move there as well.''

Except that inside the encampment lay concealed the forbidden technology that they used every day. ''But—''

''Or you may wait, if you wish, and see what agree-ment you and Mother Yomi reach with Arina Veselov.'' Sonia stood and shook out her skirts and helped Elizaveta Sakhalin to rise. Diana got hastily to her feet and went to hold the entrance flap aside. ''If there is any wedding finery that you wish to borrow,'' said Sonia, pausing be-fore she left, ''let me know.''

''That much I think we can manage,'' said Diana, and then realized how snappish she sounded. ''But thank you.'' She smiled sincerely at the other woman. Sonia smiled back. Sakhalin did not smile. The two women took their leave.

Diana let the tent flap fall back into place, leaving her in the gloom of the tent. She sat down, then threw herself out along the pillows, and sighed. What *was* she doing here, anyway? What did she think she was doing? And here she was, stuck in the tent with nothing to do. Of course, she could walk out any time she wanted. She did not have to go through with the marriage. Everyone said as much; she knew as much. But when it came right down to it, she could not bring herself to hurt Anatoly by publicly repudiating the marriage in such a fashion, not when Sonia had just said that he still desired it. And she absolutely refused to give Marco Burckhardt the sat-isfaction of knowing that he was right.

''Diana?'' It was Joseph. ''I brought some of your things. And a camplight for the tent. And some food.'' The tent flap rustled aside and he stuck his head in. ''Here you are.''

''Bless you, Joseph. How kind you are.''

He grinned. "I'll send Anahita by later to help you with your makeup and costume."

"Monster." She laughed, feeling suddenly heartened. "Don't you dare. Go on, you must be busy back at camp."

" 'I go, I go; look how I go; Swifter than arrow from the Tartar's bow.' Lady knows, I've heard that line enough times." He retreated to her applause.

She ate a little and then took out her journal and wrote. "My dear Nana, I'm not sure how to explain this to you . . ."

Quinn interrupted some time later. "Diana." She crawled in. "What a gorgeous piece of weaving. Where did you get this? Oh, from his grandmother. My, my. Now *there's* a formidable woman, even though she barely comes up to my shoulder. You must have charmed her."

"She doesn't like me."

"Surely not."

"Well, I don't know whether she likes me, but she certainly doesn't approve of me. Did you bring everything?"

"Mirror. Kit. Gown. Seshat sent baubles, for afterward—after the performance, for whatever they do for a ceremony. She thought you ought to sparkle, even though we don't have the kind of gold they do. Those women do weight themselves down with it, don't they?"

Diana fingered the gold bead necklace that Anatoly had given her. "I suppose it's a marker of status." Which she sorely lacked. "Oh, well. Let's get ready."

They were old hands at putting on makeup. That accomplished, they changed into the simple gowns that Joseph had designed to fit the greatest range of plays, using smaller accessories to give them character and place. It was dusk when they emerged from the tent and walked over to the encampment where the others had gathered.

Yomi counted them off. "In two more minutes, Hyacinth will be late," she proclaimed. One minute and fifty five seconds later, Hyacinth appeared. He had highlighted his eyes with black pencil and tied various odds and ends—scraps of material, beads, bracelets strung together—to his tunic to lend him an air of being subtly different from the rest, of being a spirit from that parallel world that intersects our own.

Owen looked them over and nodded, satisfied. "I hope you are ready, because now we see."

"Where's Ginny?"

"She's at the house already, helping the audience settle in."

They marched, a ragtag troop, through the quiet dusk of the jaran camp. The walk seemed to last forever to Diana, past the dark hulking tents, past smoldering campfires, toward the murmur of voices, toward the people gathered on the ring of empty ground in front of which their stage sat. She caught a glimpse of the audience as they came up behind the screens: a huge mass of bodies, uncountable, waiting for them rather like a predator waits for its prey. She recognized no individual faces; it was too dim for that. The stage was lit by lanterns. One screen without its fabric center had been set on stage, to form a doorway through which the players could pass from one scene, or one world, to the next. No other scenery existed, only the players and what they gave to their audience.

Yomi called the five minute warning. Gwyn and Anahita shook out their tunics, preparing to enter. Joseph stood ready at stage left with their changes of costume, since they were doubling parts. Owen vanished around the stage to go sit in the house. The play began.

Diana was aware of the audience only as an intent, listening beast, but the beast was theirs. The force of its concentration was like a pressure on them, faltering here and there when the scene passed its understanding, then snapping back, fixed and tangible.

Though the night was cool, Gwyn was sweating from the exertion of playing two major roles. But he was magnificent, as always: his Theseus was martial and strong, his Oberon utterly unlike, ethereal and just slightly spiteful. Even the audience could not confuse the two, though they were played by the same man. As for Anahita— well—Diana had always thought she played Hippolyta too stridently and Titania as a hair-brained twit, but she was powerful, nevertheless.

The lovers fled to another part of the forest. Love became confused, and then was righted at last. The audience did not laugh once, but their attention did not waver.

Puck gave his final speech and extinguished half of the lanterns. Exit.

Dead silence.

Behind the screens, Diana looked at Hal and Hal looked at Gwyn and Gwyn shrugged. A rustling noise carried to them.

"They're all standing up," said Yomi.

Gwyn chuckled suddenly. "Who ever said they'd know how to applaud?" he asked. He wiped sweat from his forehead and shook the moisture off his hand.

Owen appeared, looking intent and excited. "Di, where are you? Come on, come on."

"Come on where?" she asked, shrinking back.

"The rest of you, too, up on the stage—this isn't a bow, they won't understand that—but don't you see? We can cement the link. We can complete the circle in their minds. The masque of a wedding followed by an actual wedding. Come, Diana."

"Owen, wait," said Joseph. With economical skill, he stripped the makeup from Di's face and then adorned her with the costume jewelry Seshat had brought. "That will do. You may go."

Owen grabbed Diana's wrist and dragged her away, back around the screens. By the time they got to the front, the other actors had filed onto the stage and formed themselves into a neat semicircle. The audience was standing, murmuring now, but Diana saw that their silence, their rise to their feet, was their way of showing respect for what had just been given them. A clot of people stood at the foot of the platform, but only one of them mattered. Her heart began to pound. He stared at her, and he looked nervous, worried even. Owen released her ten paces from Anatoly, and she halted.

Anatoly wore the brilliant red shirt of the jaran riders, embroidered in a fantastic pattern down the sleeves and along the collar. Gold-studded epaulets shone on his shoulders. Gold braid lined the rim of his black boots. He wore two necklaces at his throat and gold bands on each wrist, and his saber's hilt glinted in the lantern light. A belt of gold plates girdled his wrist. Then his grandmother stepped forward and addressed a long speech to Owen. It had the cadence of poetry.

Tess Soerensen stepped forward into the gap between

the two pairs. She turned to Owen. "Elizaveta Sakhalin presents to you her grandson, who, in accordance with the traditions of the people, has come to bow to the parents and the relatives of the bride and to ask to be taken in to your camp as husband to this woman. He brings with him a string of fine horses, he brings his armor and his weapons, and he brings his skill at fighting. To his bride he brings a new set of bow and arrows. His family brings these presents for the bride's family: wine and milk, dry fruit, meat, and a silk scarf to bind your camps together. They bring also blessings to this young couple, for their happiness and well-being." She paused, and then with an open hand gestured to Owen.

He smiled. Diana realized abruptly that Owen had rehearsed this all along and simply not told her, or possibly anyone else, about it. He lifted a hand and Joseph appeared, bearing gifts in his hands: foodstuffs, clothing, a carved chess set. Diana felt cold and hot all at once, and because she did not know where else to look, she looked at Anatoly. His gaze, on her, was intense, and she clung to it as to a lifeline.

"'More strange than true,' " Owen began, and in his pleasant baritone, he reeled off the entire speech.

Tess's lips quirked up as he finished. "How am I supposed to translate that?" she asked.

"In whatever way it is most appropriate."

Tess spoke at length, her phrases cadenced as Sakhalin's had been, a ritual that was generations old. Gifts were brought forward and exchanged. Tess beckoned Diana forward, and then Anatoly, and then she retired. Anatoly put out his hands. Diana took them, clutched at them. They were warm and strong. Elizaveta Sakhalin and Owen came forward and bound the silk scarf around their clasped hands. More words were spoken. Then, sparking, a huge fire burst into flame out on the flat of ground beyond. Two drums beat out a rapid rhythm, and pipes came in with a melody. Under the concealing silk, Anatoly twined his fingers in with hers and stroked her palms with his thumbs. The caress lit fires all along her, and she swayed toward him, wanting nothing more at that moment than to be alone with him.

"Anatoly," said his grandmother, scolding. He stopped what he was doing, but his entire face lit with a smile, a smile that was meant for Diana only, intimate, exultant. Daring much, Diana tilted her head up and kissed him, briefly, on the lips. He whispered words into her ear, another caress, and then pushed back and unwound the scarf from around their hands and tied it around her waist like a belt. Then he turned and left her, walked over to his family and a moment later Sonia Orzhekov had taken him out to dance. Diana gaped after them.

"Diana." Appearing abruptly beside her, Bakhtiian bowed. His presence was as powerful as the fire's. "It is traditional for a new bride to dance on her wedding night. I hope you will excuse my immodesty in asking you to dance."

"Of course," she said, wondering what on earth he meant. But it quickly became apparent to her that she was not meant to spend any time with Anatoly at all, during this celebration. She caught glimpses of him, dancing with other women, speaking with men out on the fringes of the celebration, glancing her way, once, his gaze catching on her, his smile, and then he was drawn away by someone else.

The actors emerged, pale without their makeup, to congratulate her. She danced. She felt confused and disoriented, but she went from one instant to the next and tried not to think beyond that.

"Well," said Anahita, coming up beside her much later. "I see that Marco Burckhardt isn't at the celebration. I haven't seen him all day. What do you think of that?"

"I think you're just jealous he was never interested in you," Diana snapped.

"Bravo," said Gwyn softly behind her as Anahita flounced away. "Congratulations, Diana."

"Thank you. Owen made a spectacle out of it, didn't he?"

"Owen can't help himself. But I assure you that it was impressive."

"Did he have it rehearsed all along? How did he know to bring presents? Where did he get them? Why didn't he tell me?"

Gwyn chuckled. "I think you were part of the experiment. As for the rest, Owen always does his research.

You ought to know that, Diana. If you hadn't provided this wonderful opportunity for him, he'd have had to invent it. Ah, here comes your husband. I'll leave you now." He kissed her on the cheek and retreated.

Anatoly strode toward her, looking purposeful. His grandmother and several members of his family walked at his heels. A moment later Owen and Ginny arrived, together with Yomi and Joseph.

Yomi hugged Diana. "I hope you're ready," Yomi murmured. "We've come to escort you to your tent."

All at once Diana could not move. In a few minutes, she would be alone with a man she barely knew, with a man she could scarcely even communicate with. She stood rooted to the ground. The others moved away, but she could not lift her feet, could not follow them. She had made a terrible, stupid mistake. She knew that now, knew it bitterly, and hated herself for knowing it.

Anatoly turned back. His eyes narrowed as he examined her. He put out his hand, offering it to her. Diana took in a big breath and laid her hand in his.

They walked through camp. No one spoke. The silence weighed on her, counterpointed by the music and singing coming from the celebration behind, which still played on. So she spoke:

> "You that choose not by the view
> Chance as fair and choose as true!
> Since this fortune falls to you,
> Be content and seek no new.
> If you be well pleas'd with this
> And hold your fortune for your bliss,
> Turn you where your lady is
> And claim her with a loving kiss."

Anatoly smiled and squeezed her hand. Joseph grinned. They left the jaran camp behind and came to her tent, set out in the middle, isolated, lonely. There Owen and Ginny kissed her, Yomi and Joseph hugged her, and they left. Anatoly's family left, leaving with them two sets of saddlebags, a rolled up blanket, a leather flask and two cups. Diana stood alone with her new husband in a gloom lit only by the single lantern set on the ground beside them. He did not move, but only watched her.

She hesitated, and then bent to pick up the lantern and pushed the entrance flap aside, and ducked into the tent. A moment later, he followed her in, carrying his worldly goods in his arms. He knelt and set them carefully in one corner, then rose.

She just stood there, the lantern heavy in her hand. His pale hair seemed lighter by contrast with the shadows in the tent. His lips moved, forming soundless words. Gently, he took the lantern from her and hung it from a loop on the center pole.

"Anatoly." She dug for words, khush words, to speak to him, but they had all evaporated.

"Diana—" He said a whole sentence, but it was meaningless to her, nothing but sounds strung together.

They stood a moment in awkward silence. He lifted one hand to trace the scar on her cheek. His fingers slid to trace her lips, and she kissed them, and his other hand sought her hips, to draw her closer to him, and she slid one arm around his back and caught her other hand in his hair. . . .

Then, as quickly as that, she discovered that in fact they did speak the same language.

CHAPTER TWENTY-TWO

At the edge of the firelit glow cast by the roaring bonfire, Ilya Bakhtiian halted beside his wife where she stood in the gloom. Tess glanced up at him, then back out at the camp.

"They left, then?" asked Bakhtiian.

"Who, Anatoly and Diana? Yes." She turned to face him, watching him as he watched her, measuring. Her lips quirked up. "No stranger than you and I."

"Perhaps. But I doubt it. She will leave him." Once, he would have hesitated to touch her in public, since it was unseemly. Now he lifted his hands without the least self-consciousness to cup her face and stare at her, searching. "I love you," he said, and that was all, although it was a question.

"What would you do if I left?"

His lips drew out, tightening, and his face went taut. He dropped his hands from her face and grasped her hands instead. "You will not. I forbid it."

"You can't forbid it."

"No." The admission was shattering, wrung from him. "I cannot. But if I could, I would."

"The ambassador from Vidiya has a slave. A woman."

Now she had gone too far. "How dare you compare me to that pompous, overdressed boy?" he demanded. "How dare you even suggest that I have made such a thing of you?"

"To make you think, damn you."

"Then go. You are free to choose." He was so angry that he was shaking. "We ride south tomorrow. I can leave a jahar to take you to the coast with your brother, if that is what you wish. What I wish, you know well enough."

"Oh, Ilya." She embraced him suddenly. He was

tense, stiff, but his anger could not sustain itself when she showed the least sign of her love for him. She felt him relax against her, and he sighed into her hair.

"Damn you," he muttered.

"Come with me."

"Where?" He drew his head back and frowned at her, suspicious.

She chuckled. "No, not to Jeds. To see my brother, now."

"Why?"

"To tell him the truth. That I don't intend to leave the jaran. Not now, at any rate. Not this year."

He was still frowning. "When, then?"

"When you die, damn you. Now stop bothering me and come with me."

He laughed, surprised, and hugged her tightly. "We have an old tale," he whispered into her ear, "about a woman who poisoned her husband because she wanted to marry another man."

Tess smiled and pressed into him, returning the embrace. "If you can find me another man to marry, then I'll consider it." She broke free of his grasp and pushed him away. "Now, you'll come with me, and you'll stay quiet while I talk with Charles."

"Yes, my wife," he said meekly, and he walked with her across camp to Soerensen's encampment. At the gap, they passed about fifty paces away from the little tent that sat on the grass between both camps. Bakhtiian fought down a smile and he stopped Tess with a hand on her shoulder, and bent and kissed her. The night shielded them. "After," he murmured, releasing her.

"Don't distract me. You don't know how hard it is for me to do this."

Under the awning of Charles's tent, Marco Burckhardt sat with a thin tablet on his lap. Charles sat next to him, staring at something on his hand. Two lanterns lit the two men, one to either side of them, and from the slightly askew flap of Dr. Hierakis's tent, a steady glow could be seen coming from the interior. Then both men looked up, saw Tess, saw Bakhtiian, and Marco collected something from Charles's hand and took it and the slate back into the tent before Tess and Ilya reached the awning.

Charles stood up. Cara emerged from her tent, glanced

at the converging lines, and walked over to stand next to
Charles. Marco reappeared from the tent.

"They're hiding something from me," Bakhtiian muttered, and he glanced at Tess to see what her reaction
was. Tess flushed, but he could not see the color of her
skin in the darkness, so she was safe.

"How long will the carousing go on?" Cara asked
with a smile as she motioned them to come in under the
awning.

Bakhtiian acknowledged her first, with a nod, and then
Charles, and last Marco. "As long as they wish. The
army rides south tomorrow. They'll earn this celebration
tonight."

"The poor child won't have much of a honeymoon,
then," said Cara. "But I saw that she was safely put to
bed a little earlier. Where are you going, Marco?"

"Out to carouse," he said curtly. He excused himself
and left.

They watched him go. Charles's expression was unreadable. Cara shook her head. Bakhtiian arched his
brows, looking puzzled. "He doesn't seem like the kind
of man Sonia would take to her bed." He glanced at
Charles, as if to gain corroboration from the other man,
and Tess was struck by how clearly he treated Charles as
an equal. There were many men, men of the jaran in
particular, whom he treated with respect, but there was
no question of where the ultimate authority lay. No question but here: Ilya did not defer to Charles—he did to
women, of course; that was so deeply engrained in him
that Tess doubted he would ever lose the habit—but neither did he attempt in the slightest to command him.

"Sonia likes a challenge," said Tess.

"Is that where he's been at night?" Charles asked. "I
had wondered."

"And you didn't ask?" Tess spoke the words and an
instant later realized how sarcastic they sounded. "I have
to talk to you," she said quickly, to cover her embarrassment and to get it over with. This was something best
done quickly, before she lost her nerve. Somehow, seeing Anatoly and Diana escorted off into the night to their
tent had made her determined to talk to Charles now,
however much she wanted to put it off.

"Please sit," said Charles. Cara and Tess sat down

next to each other, in chairs. Ilya hesitated. "I have pillows," said Charles suddenly, "and something I brought for you from Jeds." He vanished into the tent, emerging with two large pillows and a velvet bag. He tossed the pillows onto the ground so that the two men could sit side by side and on the same level.

Ilya's lips twitched, and then he smiled. "Well done," he said, and sat down. Charles sat down beside him, opened the velvet bag, and drew out two objects: a book and a clock.

He gave Ilya the clock first. It had a simple design, a white unnumbered face framed with mahogany; a spring door in the back opened to reveal the mechanical workings.

"This is different," Ilya said, "than the clocks I saw in Jeds."

"The lines and hands mark out the hours of the day."

"Like a khaja wall marks out land," said Ilya, glancing up at Tess. Then, turning back to Charles, "Its simplicity lends it beauty."

Charles offered him the book and, of course, he took it. Ilya never could resist a book. He ran his hands along the leather binding in a way that was almost amorous, and then turned it to the title page and then to the text. He gave a short bark of laughter. " 'Being convinced that the human intellect makes its own difficulties—' " He closed the book and handed it up to Tess. "True enough words," he said to Charles.

"*The New Organon*. Francis Bacon," read Tess. "Charles!" Both men looked up at her expectantly. She stroked one arm of her chair, tracing the patterns in its carved wood with her fingers. "Charles," she said again, and lapsed into silence. A book and a clock—the one by a philosopher who had helped develop the scientific method, the other, well, Ilya himself had compared a device that measures time in artificial increments to the walls that interrupt the natural flow of the land. These were the worst weapons Charles could have brought; and he knew it, and she knew it.

Cara rescued them from the uncomfortable silence. The doctor leaned down to rummage in a cloth bag crumpled at the base of her chair and drew out a mass of yarn, and began to knit.

Ilya's face lit with interest. "That is like weaving. May I ask what it is you're doing?"

"It's called knitting. The women of your people don't knit? Who did the marvelous embroidery on your shirt?"

He tilted his head to one side, looking pleased and a little shy. "I did."

"*You* did?" Cara laughed. "Well. That ought to teach me not to make unwarranted assumptions. What were you going to say, Tess? Would you like something to drink? Some Scotch, perhaps?"

"I don't think so—"

"Certainly." Ilya cut across her refusal. "We would be honored." He shot her an admonishing glance. Sharing food and drink was one of the two fundamental courtesies that bound the jaran tribes together.

"Perhaps you'd like to come with me," said Cara, to Ilya.

"No. I want Ilya to stay here." His presence was both the spur and the anchor, forcing her to go forward, keeping her stable. She clutched the book in both hands. "And you, too, Cara. It's no long speech. It's very little, really, it's very simple. I'm not going back."

Charles rested his elbows on his knees and leaned forward. "You're not going back where?"

"To Jeds, with you, when you go back. When you leave." She burned with heat. She knew it, could feel the flush on her face, could feel her pulse pounding. "It's only fair to tell you, so you don't keep thinking . . . that maybe I will. That I'm going back. I know that's what you came for. But I can't go. Not now."

"Why is that?" Charles's voice was cool, neutral.

Ilya sat straight, his chin lifted in triumph, and he looked at Tess, not at his rival, as if, having won, he could now dismiss him.

Why did she have to defend herself like this? And why must she do it so damned badly? "Because I love him," she said in Anglais.

"Love is a compelling reason," said Charles in Rhuian, and Ilya shifted his gaze to Charles. "But alone it is not always sufficient. I think it isn't all that is keeping you here."

"What do you mean by that?" demanded Ilya. Whatever ease had existed between the two men at the beginning

of the conversation vanished, evaporating in the heat of
Ilya's question.

"Ilya," said Tess.

"I'm getting the Scotch," said Cara, "and I expect
you two to behave yourselves until I get back." She rose
and strode off to her tent.

Charles raised his eyebrows. His gaze caught on Bakhtiian's, and a moment later the two men smiled stiffly at
each other.

"Serves you right," muttered Tess. Cara returned with
the bottle of Scotch and four sturdy glass tumblers. Ilya
held up the one she gave him and turned it, watching the
light splinter and catch in the crystal.

"This is beautiful." He lowered the glass so that Cara
could pour a splash of the liquor into it. With the others,
he lifted it and drank. Tess lowered her glass and watched
him, saw his eyes round at the potency of the alcohol.
He choked back a cough and took another sip, cautiously
this time.

Cara chuckled. "Now," she said, "you *will* come with
me, Bakhtiian. I have a few things to show you, and
some questions to ask about your army's medical logistics."

Ilya looked at Tess, and she sighed and nodded. He
rose and obediently followed Dr. Hierakis.

"It's an interesting culture," said Charles, watching
them go. "And rather admirable, in its way."

"Yes, well," she replied sarcastically, "Francis Bacon will soon put an end to that."

"You don't approve?"

"He'll never use the clock. They just don't think that
way."

"Doubtless," said Charles, sounding sardonic in his
turn, "in the Great Chain of Philosophic Being, their
culture ranks far above our own."

Stung, she tossed the book with purposeful disregard
onto Ilya's pillow. It landed next to the clock. "You know
it's ridiculous to compare cultures in that fashion."

He looked serious all at once, and Tess did not know
what to make of his expression. "Tess, I have faith in
you that you would not have stayed with the jaran if they
were savages."

But his sympathy made her feel worse. She curled her

hands around the tumbler and stared at the Scotch, swirling it around in the glass. ''They're killing a lot of people, Charles. Lots of people. Hordes of them.''

''As will I, if I lead another rebellion against the Chapalii Empire. That's my choice, isn't it?''

Tess set the glass down on the rug. She could hear Cara talking softly behind her, and Ilya's softer replies. ''Charles.'' She wrapped her fingers together, unwound them, and let them fall to her lap. ''You made a choice to make a cause the center of your life. I can't live that way. Someday I'll come to the end of my life and when I look back, I know what measure I'll make of how well I lived. That measure is in the lives I lived beside.''

''But someone must live for the cause. Or else we remain slaves. Well-treated slaves, it is true, but slaves nevertheless.''

''You're right, of course. I never said I wouldn't do my part. But you've given up everything else for your work and I can't—I won't—do that. Otherwise my life is a desert—nothing.'' She hesitated, not wanting to hurt him, to judge him, but he merely watched her, unfathomable. ''If anything of me lives on after I'm dead, it will be my linguistics work, and, I hope, children as well.''

''You've thought about this a great deal.''

She steepled her hands and rested her lips on her thumbs, then raised her head to look at him again. ''I've torn at myself. Half of me says that I must give myself entirely to your work, that it's my duty to you, my duty to humanity, that's most important. It's a litany that runs through my head. But what use would it be for me to sacrifice myself for that? I'm not a leader. I'm not like you. Or like Ilya, for that matter. I don't want to be a leader, I'm not cut out to be one. I can contribute in other ways. I will. But I won't give up my family to do so.'' She said it with passion, and only a moment later realized how it must sound to him.

''As I've given up mine?'' he asked, and she could not tell if he was hurt, angry, or amused.

''I don't fault you, Charles. I never said that. You're doing what you have to do. I don't think there's anything else you could do. Like Cara—her research is the heart of her life. Everything else is a hobby.''

"Including me?"

Tess bent down to pick up the tumbler and drained it in one gulp. The heat of it seared her throat, but the burning gave her courage. "Including you. That knife cuts both ways. It's why the two of you are so well-matched."

Now Charles did smile, and Tess relaxed slightly. "I see my baby sister has grown up."

"I'm a little older. Not much."

"And yet, you married a man who has dedicated his life in the same way I have dedicated mine."

"Yes." Her smile was sardonic. "The prince's sister must marry a prince. There was another man I fell in love with, another man of the jaran, but I would never have married him. Once I met Ilya . . ." She shrugged. "In the end, I suppose it was inevitable."

"How old is he?"

"By their calendar, which runs in twelve year cycles, he's thirty-seven." She gave an ironic nod toward the clock. "However accurate their time-keeping is."

"But, nevertheless, well into the prime of his life. He'll die, Tess."

It was like being slapped. All she could do was try to hit back. "Are you willing to wait him out? Knowing he'll die soon enough and then you can get me back?"

"I meant," he said mildly, "that he'll die sooner than you will, barring any accidents. Much sooner."

She twisted her hands together and glanced back at Dr. Hierakis's tent. Cara and Ilya stood talking together outside the tent, and as if he felt her gaze, Ilya turned their way, looking at her as he always looked at her, so intently, so intimately, that her own feelings rose fiercely to meet his across the gap. With an effort, she turned back to Charles. "Don't you think I know that?" she asked bitterly. "Don't you think I remember that every damn morning? And every night, after he's fallen asleep?"

"I'm sorry," said Charles, but whether for her pain or for the specter of Ilya's premature death, by their standards, she could not be sure.

Cara and Ilya returned. "But surely you'll ride with the army," Ilya was saying. "There is so much more you can teach my healers."

"I don't know. Charles?" Cara sat down again, but Ilya remained standing.

"I need to go to the shrine of Morava," said Charles.

Ilya's gaze flicked from Charles to Tess and back to Charles. "I can send a small jahar with you, if you wish to ride north now. Then you can follow us south, if you will, or return to the coast and sail back to Jeds, if that is your desire."

"I need to take Tess with me to the shrine."

"That is impossible."

Charles stood up. "Of course it is not impossible. I need her to translate."

"I remind you that you are in my camp." Ilya's voice dropped and its very mildness was threatening.

Charles smiled.

Tess had a horrible premonition that Charles was about to say something rash—something like, *I remind you that you are on my planet*—and she jumped to her feet and placed herself between the two men. "Stop it. Damn you two, stop it. I'll make my own choice. Sit down."

Neither sat. No one spoke. Tess did not know what to say, so she simply stood there, feeling the force of them one on each side. Like Jiroannes through the bonfires, she felt the pressure of their attention on her, the force of their equally strong personalities brought to bear on her, and she was caught in the middle. If she had ever thought for an instant that these two men could compromise, then she had been sorely mistaken.

"Someone's coming," said Cara.

Ilya turned. A man ran toward them. He halted beyond the carpet, outside the awning's overhang. "Bakhtiian. A messenger has come in from Sakhalin."

"I'll come." Ilya nodded at Dr. Hierakis. "Doctor. If you'll excuse me."

"Of course."

"Tess?" He put out his hand.

She did not move. "I'm not done here yet. I'll come along in a while."

He froze, tensing, then jerked himself around and strode off with the soldier, vanishing into the darkness.

"Tess," said Charles, "sometimes I think I would be doing you a service simply to take you forcibly out of here."

"Don't you dare! You're no better than him, you're just a damned sight cooler about it. And if you're so damned righteous, then why are you flouting your own interdiction laws?"

"I beg your pardon?"

"Francis Bacon. Or had you forgotten so quickly? And you let the Bharentous Repertory Company come here. However much you claim to be preserving Rhuian cultures, you're already corrupting them."

Charles blinked, looking surprised at the vehemence of her attack. "Tess, inevitably Rhui's interdiction will be lifted. In a cautious way, I'm trying to prepare for that."

"Gods, you've already thought about it. You're doing it on purpose. Do you have a timetable set, too? When do the sea gates open?" She was so angry that tears came to her eyes.

His voice cooled to a chill. "If I hadn't intervened, Rhui would have been raped. Which do you prefer? Quick and ugly, or giving them a chance to meet the change on their own terms?"

"Oh, hell," said Tess, wiping at her eyes. "I'm sorry."

"Charles." Cara stood up. "I want to talk to Tess a bit, alone, and take a few tests. If you'll excuse us."

He muttered a word under his breath, then turned and stalked into his tent.

"That's one thing that always encourages me about humanity," said Cara, taking Tess's arm and leading her across to her tent, "that in the midst of all our nobility we can be so incredibly foolish. And petty. And otherwise damned asses."

"Thank you."

Cara snorted, amused. "The comment wasn't actually meant for you, my dear." She guided Tess into the tent and snapped her fingers. A light flicked on, hidden in the ceiling. Cara pushed through into the back compartment of the tent, where a diagnostic table stood next to a counter laid out in neat lines with a field laboratory, a lacework of metal and plastine and glass. "Now. We have some serious discussing to do, my girl, and I need to do a full diagnostic on you. Sit."

Tess sat obediently on the table. "Cara, is it too late? Can you give Ilya treatments to make him live longer?"

Cara turned from the counter and regarded Tess. Something lit in her face and was, as quickly, smothered. "Ah," she said, and turned back without replying, busying herself with the equipment.

"But can you?" Tess demanded.

"I've had to relearn a good deal about the human life span, a great deal we've forgotten these last one hundred years, now that we live out a full one hundred twenty years, all of us. Did you know, Tess, that with their year being longer than ours, Rhuians normally live longer lives than Earth humans did before the advent of decent medicine in the twenty-first century? I once thought they were some kind of amazing parallel evolution."

"But the cylinder I got at the shrine of Morava—"

"Yes. It proved that they are descendants of Earth, brought thousands of years ago from Earth to Rhui by the Chapalii duke, the Tai-en Mushai, to populate this planet. One wonders if he killed off some developing intelligent indigenes in order to make room for our kind. But in any case, he altered the humans he brought. He made them more—efficient."

"But they still age more rapidly than we do."

"Indeed. Bakhtiian can expect to live another thirty or forty years, all else being equal, but you can expect to live another ninety, and you won't age appreciably for a long long time. As in the old folktales of elves and humans, we would seem eternally young to them."

"Then you're saying there's nothing you can do?" Her voice caught with fear and grief.

"This planet, and whatever the Mushai's engineers did to them, has altered their chemistry from ours. The techniques given us to extend our lives might work for them, but they might not. It would be . . . experimental, Tess. Risks go together with experiments."

"Oh, God. But I'm so scared of losing him. Or of him getting old while I'm still young."

"There is another question. Ought I to interfere? It would clearly breach the interdiction."

"Which Charles has already breached."

"Yes. But knowledge works slowly, and Bakhtiian, my

dear, may well change the face of this continent very
quickly indeed. How long do we want it to go on?''

"It doesn't matter, does it?'' Tess asked bitterly.
"Either way, we play god. Either way, we choose for
Rhui.''

"That is the burden of greater knowledge. But there
are two other factors, Tess. One only Charles knows of,
and now you: there are clues, here on Rhui, that there
may be a way to alter the human life span, to extend it
past the one hundred twenty years given us by the Chapalii, to double it or more. I intend to break the code. I
believe that I'm close to doing so. In fact, with your
cooperation, I need some subjects from the jaran, although I've had some luck studying them since I arrived
here.''

"The wounded,'' said Tess under her breath. "God,
that's cold, Cara.''

"If I save them as well, why not let them benefit all
of us? Lie down, I'm going to take some blood and run
the scanner over you.'' Tess lay down. "I want Bakhtiian. Perhaps I'll make you a trade: let me examine him,
take tissue and blood from him, and I'll see what I can
do about some kind of basic serum to retard his aging.''
Her expression grew distant. "And if I can manage it,''
she said, more to herself than to anyone, "it will mean
I possess Rhui's code.''

It was an odd, unsettling experience, to see Cara wear
the look that Ilya wore when he contemplated lands he
did not yet control.

"But don't answer me now,'' added Cara, crashing
back to earth. "I can't quantify the risks for you, only
say that there will be risks. I can't predict how his chemistry will react. You'll feel a pinch here; that's the needle. Now breathe normally and lie still.''

Tess shut her eyes. A low hum filled her ears. A breath
of air puffed on her face and drifted down over her body,
followed by the slight tingle of some kind of pressure
and field. "I'll risk it. I have to. Though I don't know
how you can study Ilya without betraying all this.''

"Shhh. Don't move. Tess.'' Her voice lowered, becoming grave. "There's a more serious problem. Why
did you remove your implant? To get pregnant, I know.
But it's too risky. I have four recorded deaths, three many

years ago and one recent, of women who died in childbirth from a reaction to the—well, once it was an Earth
woman who got pregnant by a Rhuian male and died, in
the others it was the opposite. It's an antigenic reaction
to blood types and antibodies that no longer mesh well.
I don't want you to get pregnant, Tess. No, one more
minute.''

The silence drew out.

''There, we're done.''

Tess pushed herself up. ''But Cara—''

''No, I have no recorded instances of women who survived cross breeding.''

''What about the children?''

''In one instance the child lived, because I arrived
immediately after birth.''

''Then there must be—''

''Tess, as soon as a woman gets pregnant, she is in-
undated with hormonal changes. My research shows that
the risk is immediate and acute. I suppose—'' She broke
off.

''What?''

''You did start puberty here, on Rhui. That might—''

''That might what? God, Cara, you must know how
badly Ilya wants children.''

''What about what you want?''

Tess hung her head, and her voice shook. ''I want
something of him, after he's dead. But that's only part of
it. I never thought about children before. There was never
any urgency in it. But I *want* children with him, Cara.
Can't you understand that?''

''Since I have no children of my own?''

''I didn't mean it as an accusation.''

Cara finished transferring blood from one tube to another and pressed a few buttons, and then came to sit on
the table beside Tess. She put an arm around Tess, and
Tess felt safe with her. Tess trusted her. ''Tess, I will
study the matter. When did you take the implant out?''

''Three months ago.''

''That should give us time. It usually takes a year until
ovulation resumes. Meanwhile, I want you to take some
of this rather primitive birth control method I have with
me. Goddess, child, I will take no chances with you. Do
you understand that?''

"But, Cara—"

"No. No chances with you. I'll run a fuller test on you once I've gone through these preliminary results, and once I do a study of Bakhtiian, I'll see if I can make any kind of prediction based on blood type and other factors. That's as far as I'll go, Tess. If you won't promise me now to use this contraception, then I will forcibly insert an implant in you where you can't dig it out. Do you understand me?"

There was no compromise in Cara's voice, and little enough hope. Tess's throat felt all choked, and a moment later she felt the rush of tears. She buried her face in her hands to cover the tears, to hide them. She squeezed her eyes, as if that could stop them, but the devastation she felt was stronger than her self-control.

"Oh, Tess." Cara wrapped both arms around her and held her as if she were a child. "I'm sorry."

A foot scuffed at the entrance. "Cara? Tess?" It was Charles. Tess looked up in time to see him push the inner hanging aside and stand there in the gap, watching her. "Ah. You've told her about the dangers of pregnancy, haven't you?"

"You're glad of this, aren't you?" Tess broke out of Cara's embrace and jumped to her feet. "Well, it doesn't matter. I won't leave him anyway."

Charles stiffened. "I hope you think better of me than that."

Tess stared at him, smitten with the sudden and astonishing realization that he actually cared what she thought of him. That it mattered to him.

A beep sounded, low and brief, from the counter behind them.

"What the hell?" muttered Cara. She slipped off the table and hurried around to the counter.

"I'm sorry, Charles," said Tess slowly. "I didn't mean it. You aren't petty."

"Thank you." He chuckled. "But don't overestimate me, Tess. Sainthood is a heavy burden to bear. However, I don't think my pettiness extends to *that*." He hesitated. "Knowing what it means to you."

The words came hard to him. She could hear that and it touched her that he would open up to her like this.

"Charles," she began tentatively, "I know—we've always been far apart in years, but—"

"Oh. Shit." Cara turned. In the glare of artificial light, she looked grim, angry, and scared. "Damn you, girl. What have you done?"

Tess looked at Charles, but he simply shrugged, puzzled. "What have I done?" she asked.

"This alters things considerably," said Cara. "Clearly, whatever else may happen, I'm not leaving your side for the next nine months."

Tess went white and sank down onto the table, clutching at the edge with her hands to steady herself.

"What's going on?" asked Charles. An instant later, his face altered as the realization hit him. "But surely, if it's so dangerous—Cara!" The expression of helplessness on his face looked totally out of place. "Perhaps a surgical abortion—"

"No!" yelled Tess, even as she realized she might have no choice.

Cara shook her head. "No. We'd still have an antigenic reaction to deal with."

"She's all I have left, Cara," he said, his voice so low that Tess barely heard him. She didn't know how to respond; Charles wasn't supposed to be so vulnerable.

"I'm well aware of that, Charles," said Cara coolly, as if she were offended. "I think it would be safer if I instead applied my skills and some testing to bring her safely to term."

The vulnerability in Charles's expression vanished, smoothing into the mask worn by a duke in the Empire. "Very well," he said, and he left the tent.

CHAPTER TWENTY-THREE

Jiroannes paced from one edge of the carpet to the other, turning with precise anger at the very fringed border, right before he would otherwise step out onto the grass, and then stalking back to the other side. Above him, the awning sighed lazily in the breeze.

"What are they doing?" he demanded of Syrannus. "Obviously they are breaking camp. Is everyone going? Only some of them?" Off in the distance, a contingent of jaran soldiers rode by, their red shirts gleaming like blood in the early morning sunlight. "Why weren't we told? This is a deliberate insult to me, and thus to the Great King, may his sons multiply to the ends of the earth. It is intolerable. Samae, I *said* that I wanted my green sash now." He cuffed her across the cheek. She dipped her head and vanished with ethereal grace into his tent.

His guards sat watching the upheaval in the jaran camp. Usually they sat at their ease, gambling, polishing their swords and armor, mending blouses and trousers and boots, gossiping among themselves. But now they sat uneasily. Once or twice they glanced his way, and that annoyed him. Didn't they trust him? Did they think he was unequal to this task?

He sank down into his chair and regarded the six gold and jeweled rings that studded his fingers. Anger boiled inside him, at this impossible situation, at these primitive and squalid surroundings, at these savages. And yet, at the same time, deep down inside himself, he was beginning to wonder if it wasn't true: perhaps he was unsuited for the role of an ambassador. Wouldn't a better man have been called before Bakhtiian again and not left waiting here for ten interminable days? Wouldn't an older man have made a better impression in that one brief audience he had been allowed? Had he really lost his temper? Had it showed? Had Bakhtiian scorned him? Or worse, dismissed him as an inexperienced and ridiculous boy?

Samae appeared. She knelt before him, head bowed, her arms extended with the emerald sash laid out across them for his approval. Her coarse black hair was pulled back tightly today, just long enough now to twine the ends into a short braid.

A braid? When had she ever worn a braid? Before he had made her cut it, she had worn it in many exotic styles, but never like this. Where had she gotten such a notion, to wear her hair in a braid? The innovation irritated him. He slapped the sash to the ground.

"No. Not that one. You are impossible." He stood so quickly that he clipped her leg with his stride, and she shrank away from him and then straightened as he paced out to the edge of the carpet again. Another troop of horsemen rode by, heading south. "Syrannus."

"Yes, eminence," Syrannus knelt before him.

"I must know what is going on. What they mean for us to do. Surely they don't intend to leave us here?" But even as he said it, he looked out along the row of tents that housed the other ambassadors and envoys, and he could see that they, too, were striking their camps. Knowledge had been granted them but denied him. Clearly, the snub was deliberate. One set of features leapt to mind immediately: Bakhtiian's arrogant niece was surely responsible for this, influencing her uncle to insult him despite the fact that he was the ambassador of the Great King himself. If she and her uncle only understood the power of the Great King, they would not dare to treat his ambassador in this fashion. Then, as if by thinking of her he made her flesh, he saw her ride past with a troop of about one hundred horsemen, but she neither paused nor looked his way.

"Your eminence," said Syrannus, warningly. The old man stood up. Jiroannes turned.

A boy approached them. Not yet old enough to wear soldier's clothing, still, he wore riches: a blue shirt and gold necklaces and a girdle of golden plates. He bore no trace of beard on his cheek. A child, sent as envoy. Jiroannes was furious, knowing how deep the insult ran, and he began to turn away again, to ignore the boy. But Syrannus put a hand on his elbow, daring much, and in that instant Jiroannes remembered caution, and waited.

The boy was nervous. He halted at the edge of the carpet, not quite under the awning, waiting to be invited in. He stared at Jiroannes, at his clothes, curious, and then recalled himself and straightened his back.

"I am Mitya Orzhekov," he said slowly, in labored Rhuian. "My cousin Bakhtiian sent me to . . ." Here he faltered, as if he had learned his message by rote and forgotten it between there and here.

Abruptly Jiroannes remembered being this age himself. It had not been so very long ago. This child was no mere messenger but a male child of Bakhtiian's own family, sent off on an errand too important to be left to any lackey. He could afford to be generous. "Please." He met the boy's gaze with a friendly smile. "Please come in."

Mitya returned the smile tremulously. "I am Mitya Orzhekov," he said, starting over. "My cousin Bakhtiian sent me to give you this letter." He produced a scrap of parchment from his belt and held it out.

"Eminence," said Syrannus, "he does not understand Rhuian. That was memorized. I can hear it." The old man hesitated, clearly unsure of how his master would react.

The boy's eyes skipped past Jiroannes and settled on Samae. He stared, astonished, and then wrenched his gaze back to the letter, flushing as he fixed his stare on the parchment instead of the slave. He wore his hair short, an affectation of the jaran riders that Jiroannes had yet to comprehend. Surely one test of a man's beauty was in the fineness and length and sheen of his hair. The boy coughed, jerking Jiroannes's attention back to him, and began his little speech again.

"I understand," said Jiroannes, "and I thank you." He took the parchment from the boy and unrolled it. As he read, he was aware of the boy sneaking glances at Samae, as if this child were aware that he ought not to covet another man's property and so was trying to hide his interest. The text itself was unremarkable. The army was riding south, toward the Habakar kingdom. The ambassadors were free to move along with the main camp, which would travel in the army's wake. Bakhtiian had assigned his cousin's son as an escort, and he trusted that the ambassador would treat the boy with the honor he deserved.

"A threat," said Jiroannes, handing the letter to Syrannus, "and a promise. Tell the guards to strike camp. You must learn khush, Syrannus."

"Yes, eminence. I have learned what I can these past days. I will learn more."

Jiroannes motioned the boy in to sit in one of the chairs, and watched as Mitya shifted, trying to find a comfortable seat, as if he were unaccustomed to such a structure. Then he had Samae serve them tea and cakes while they watched the guards strike the camp, everything but the awning and the carpet under which the two sat. Mitya stared, awed by his surroundings, and his gaze flashed again and again toward Samae, and away as swiftly.

When the wagons were loaded, Mitya went away and returned with a string of three horses, one laden, one saddled, and the other barebacked. Jiroannes allowed the boy to introduce him to the saddled chestnut mare, and he saw that this was a fine, elegant horse, a superior creature. At once he coveted her for himself. How fine a gift a herd of such horses would make for the Great King! The boy was proud of her; that was evident. He mounted. Jiroannes mounted his gelding, and they rode.

The entire plain seemed on the move. Troops cantered by them. Lone riders galloped back the way they had come. A belled messenger passed, heading south. Wagons trundled along in the distance. The whole thing seemed like chaos to Jiroannes, but come late afternoon they rolled into a makeshift camp that rose up out of the grass. Jiroannes recognized the tents: this was the same ambassadors' row they had inhabited before, set up in the same order, and Mitya directed them to the far end, as if the order of tents had some meaning, some hierarchy. Mitya left them then, but only to pitch a small tent for himself about one hundred paces outside of Jiroannes's camp, and there he sat, alone, until Jiroannes took pity on him and sent Syrannus to ask him in to dine. The two dined alone, Syrannus and Samae serving them. The boy ate with surprisingly good manners, cleanly and precisely, making no mess. He flushed every time Samae paused beside him. He even rose, after he was finished, as if to help clean up, but Jiroannes motioned him to sit again. One of the guards ventured over with his flute, and he played sorrowful tunes as the light faded and darkness fell.

Mitya rose. He spoke, to Jiroannes first, then to Syrannus.

"Eminence, the boy says that he must go to bed now, as we must rise early and be on our way. He thanks you for the dinner. Or at least, some of these words I recognized, and I believe that is what he said."

Jiroannes rose and watched the boy walk away to the solitude of his tent. Beardless still, but already by his height and his walk half a man.

"Samae." She appeared, sinking to her knees before him. "You will go to the boy tonight." Her head jerked up and for an astonishing instant she stared straight at him. She shook her head roughly. He slapped her. Red burned on the fine pale parchment of her cheek. "I *said* you will go to him," Jiroannes repeated, offended and infuriated by her defiance.

She sat there, head bowed, for long enough that he thought he was going to have to hit her again. Then she rose and padded away across the grass. Jiroannes watched as she paused before the tent. She glanced back, once, to see him looking at her, and then she knelt and a moment later she had vanished into the small tent.

"Was that wisely done, eminence?" Syrannus asked in a soft voice.

"The boy is old enough, clearly, and if she is his first, then the honor is the greater. He admired her but was polite enough not to say so to me. It will make him grateful to me, and he will speak to his cousin of my generosity. So we begin to build a bridge on which to negotiate. Now, since Samae is not here, send Lal to undress me." He went to his tent, but he paused at the entrance to see that Syrannus was still staring out at the little tent, at the campfires glowing around them, at the night and the vivid sky, black splintered with bright stars.

"We shall see," said Syrannus quietly.

In the morning, while Jiroannes sat in his chair as the camp was struck around him, he caught Samae glancing up at the boy. She had paused beside one of the wagons, about to place into the bed the little carved chest that held his jewels and sashes and seals of office; she looked up briefly, toward Mitya saddling his horse. Mitya remained intent on his task. From this distance, Jiroannes could not see the boy's expression, but something in his carriage betrayed a new confidence. Samae seemed unaware that her master watched her. Something touched her lips, something unknown, an expression he did not recognize. For an instant he thought it was a smile, but he dismissed the idea immediately. Samae never smiled. Distaste, probably. Still, he would send her to the boy every now and then. Such generosity would seal their relationship. Content, he allowed the guards to take his chair and bring him his horse. For the first time, he felt confident that his mission would succeed.

CHAPTER TWENTY-FOUR

When Diana woke, she found Anatoly lying on his side, watching her. He smiled and reached out to trace her lips with one finger.

"Good morning, Diana," he said in Rhuian, looking pleased with himself. She repeated the greeting, haltingly, in khush, and he looked even more pleased. He said another sentence in khush, but she had to shake her head because she could not understand him. He cocked his head to one side and tried again, some words meant, perhaps, to be Rhuian. Diana laughed, because they were equally incomprehensible. And yet, she did not feel awkward with him at all. Not that there was much left for her to feel awkward about, after last night.

She smiled at him. The set of his body, his eyes, the curve of his mouth, all revealed what he thought of her. Blankets covered him to the hips; above that, he was bare. His one shoulder was a mass of fresh scars. She ran a hand up his chest and plumbed the curve of his neck and the strong line of his chin. She touched her hand to his mouth.

"Lips," she said. "Eyes. Hand."

He mirrored her. "Lips. Eyes. Hand." Then he repeated them in khush, and went on. "Ears. Nose. Hair. Neck. Shoulder. Arm."

"Ah, none of that yet. Breast, but chest, too. Elbow."

A wicked gleam lit his eyes. He grasped one of her hands and drew it down along his torso, all the way down. *"Pes."*

"Anatoly!" She laughed. "That will hardly help me communicate with the rest of your people." However diffident he may have been before, out in the world, however reserved and modest, here in her bed he was not bashful at all, and anything but modest. The blankets slipped off him as he rolled with her off the pillows and on to the stiff carpet, but he only grinned and said something to her, sharp and passionate, before running his hands down to her thighs—

And then, of course, a man called to them from outside.

Anatoly jerked his head up at the sound. He swore. The voice spoke again, and its tone was clearly apologetic but firm. Anatoly made a great gesture out of a sigh, rolled to his knees, and wrapped a blanket around himself before going to the entrance. Diana scrambled to the pillows and covered herself. Anatoly twitched the entrance flap aside and directed a rude comment at their inopportune visitor. In reply, a long explanation was forthcoming, and Diana watched as Anatoly's shoulders reflected first anger, then resignation, then excitement, and then, last, turning to regard her, some emotion caught between reluctance and eagerness.

He knelt beside her and kissed her lingeringly, sighing against her face. "I love you," he said, first in Rhuian and after, more slowly, in khush. Then he rose, got dressed, strapped on his saber, and left her.

That abruptly. Diana stared at the flap as it rustled down behind him. She was alone. Not to mention that she was utterly bewildered. Listening, she heard horses riding away. She dressed quickly in a tunic, long skirt, and boots, and went outside. Anatoly was nowhere in sight, but the jaran camp was in an uproar. Loaded wagons creaked past. A troop of horsemen rode by. She could not imagine finding Anatoly in such chaos. Besides, she needed to use the necessary. And she desperately wanted to wash.

She walked over to the Company camp, only to find that it, too, was being struck. Although, thank the Goddess, the necessary was still intact: first up, last down. Quinn saw her and yelped in surprise, waving, attracting attention to her, but Diana slipped quickly inside the little tent. Although she lingered there, stripping and washing herself all over, shivering at the cold water, when she finally came out she had an audience.

"Well?" demanded Quinn. Hyacinth had an arm around Quinn, and he was smirking. "Was he any good?" he asked. "Is he circumcised?"

"You ought to know whether they're circumcised, Hyacinth," retorted Diana. "You've slept with more of them than I have. Or so you say."

He giggled.

"Oh, leave her alone," said Hal. "Come on, Diana. Can you help? We've fallen behind. We were supposed to leave an hour ago."

"Where are we going?"

"Didn't he tell you?"

"How could he? We scarcely know any words in common." Then she flushed, remembering the language they did speak.

Hyacinth laughed. "You see, Di, I told you they were easy to communicate with. You're looking satisfied. Where is your blue-eyed paramour, anyway?"

She set her lips together, not wanting to telegraph every least thing about herself to Hyacinth, of all people. "Where's Yomi?" she asked instead.

"Over at Soerensen's camp," said Hal.

"Whatever for?"

"They're working out logistics—oh." He faltered. "You wouldn't have heard. Soerensen is leaving."

"Leaving?"

"We're moving south with the army. He's going north. There's some site out there—"

"Site?"

"I don't know. Something archaeological, I think. Anyway, he's going north, and then I guess his party will meet up with us later." He lifted one hand to stop her protest. "Don't ask me any more questions. That's all I know. Are you going to load your tent in with our wagons, or is some other provision being made for it?"

"I don't know." She shook her head. "I don't know what's going on." Suddenly she missed Anatoly so acutely that it was like a physical pain.

Hal took her by both shoulders and examined her closely, then kissed her on the forehead. "Maybe you'd better go see Yomi. Go on. I'll tell Mom and Dad where you went."

Diana went. Soerensen's enclave no longer existed. All the tents were down except for Dr. Hierakis's tent, and David ben Unbutu supervised while Maggie and Joe and Rijiv and Ursula loaded the wagons. An astonishing number of crates sat beside a line of wagons next to the doctor's tent, and as Diana walked up, the doctor emerged carrying another crate, which she set down carefully beside the rest. The doctor looked up.

"Hello, Diana. I trust you had a sufficiently restless night."

Diana smiled.

"It seems a shame to have to disturb your rest like this. Where is your husband?"

"I don't know."

"Ah," said the doctor, reading something from Diana's expression. She stood up. "Here. Come with me."

Diana followed her to a knot of people standing beyond the wagons. Yomi was there, but she made good-byes and started walking away, then stopped as she caught sight of Diana. "There you are, Diana. I need you now. Will you be loading your new tent in with our wagons? Also—" She paused, seeing the doctor lift a hand.

"I'll send her in a moment," said Dr. Hierakis. "If I may."

"Certainly." Yomi strode away.

Marco was there. He had half turned to look at her, and Diana flushed and bit her lip and kept walking without missing a beat, sticking close to Dr. Hierakis. The others—Soerensen, Tess, Bakhtiian, and the silver-haired jaran man called Niko—all smiled at the same instant, seeing her.

"Ah," said Bakhtiian. He looked embarrassed. "I do apologize for taking Anatoly away like that. But I needed to send him on ahead to his uncle. He should be back soon."

"Oh," replied Diana, feeling stupid, and wondering if they all knew in what condition she and Anatoly had been interrupted this morning. "This afternoon? Or this evening, that's not so bad."

"He means a few days, Diana," said Tess softly. "I'm sorry. Ten, twenty at the most, I should think."

"Twenty days!" To her horror, Diana burst into tears. Abandoned, just like that. Not that Anatoly had had any choice, which almost made it worse. Yet she could not believe that Bakhtiian had sent him off for any ulterior motive—to get him away from her, to get her away from him. She had just begun to feel easy with him, to find a way to talk. Goddess, they would have to start all over again, after twenty days apart. She sniffed hard, trying to stop her tears. Her nose was running.

"Here, Diana." Surprisingly, it was Marco who offered her the handkerchief. She glanced up at him, grateful. He was red in the face, and he would not look at her.

"Well, then," said Soerensen, neatly throwing focus away from her, "it's settled, although I don't like it much."

"I'm sorry, Charles," said Tess. "But I know you understand why I have to travel with the army right now."

Diana looked up, hearing a peculiar note in Tess's voice, something being communicated in the tone, not in the words. Tess was pale, and her husband frowned, resting a hand possessively on her lower back.

Charles looked past her to Dr. Hierakis. "Cara, I'd like Ursula to accompany you. I'll send a messenger if I need anything from you."

"Here is my niece," said Bakhtiian as a contingent of riders came up. "As soon as your wagons are ready, she will escort you north to the shrine of Morava."

Soerensen smiled enigmatically. "You honor me with your choice of escort."

Bakhtiian did not smile. "She is my closest relative. For you, I would do no less."

Like a trade, Diana thought, distracted for a moment from her own pain by the curious dealings going on here. Soerensen took the niece, Bakhtiian took Tess.

"Damn," muttered Marco under his breath, in Anglais, "but they're playing a delicate game, indeed. I can't believe Tess isn't coming with us."

"Do you think he's stopping her somehow?" Diana whispered.

Marco shook his head. "If Charles thought that was true, then he wouldn't stand for it. No, it's been agreed between them. That's what puzzles me." He hesitated. "Diana."

"Are you going, too?" she asked. She hadn't been this close to him since the night Anatoly marked her, since the night Marco had said such awful things to her—and she felt shy, suddenly, wondering if he still thought well of her.

"Yes, with Charles. Diana." He made a movement

toward her but checked it. "I'm sorry. I'm sorry he had to leave so suddenly. I know it must be difficult. It's obvious you care for him. I'm sorry I—expressed myself so poorly, before."

"Stop it," she said under her breath. She stared at her feet. She did not want to think kindly of Marco; that was too dangerous. His booted feet rested on the ground near hers. She saw how they shifted. He murmured something unintelligible—not angry but perhaps despairing, and then he moved away. She forced herself not to look up after him. An instant later, she realized she still clutched his handkerchief.

"Tess, I leave you in the best of hands," said Soerensen. "Cara." Diana looked up to see Soerensen nod at the doctor, and the doctor nod, coolly, back. "Bakhtiian." This farewell was cooler still, reserved, almost disapproving.

Bakhtiian acknowledged Soerensen with an equally reticent nod. Diana would have thought that Bakhtiian would have looked overjoyed that Tess had chosen to go with him rather than with her brother, but he only looked troubled and perplexed. And why was Dr. Hierakis going with the army, not with Soerensen? But Diana knew well enough that she was not in the confidence of any of these people, and so as they parted, she trailed away alone, back toward her tent.

Quinn came jogging to meet her. "Di! Yomi sent me over to help you with your tent and your things. So? Well? What was he like?"

Diana stopped outside the tent. She could not help but smile. "He was sweet."

"But—how else? Come on, Di. The jaran men are so shy, so reserved. Are they that way in bed, too?"

"I'm hardly an expert. You'd have to talk to Hyacinth about that."

"Oh, Hyacinth. You know as well as I do that you can't trust anything he says."

"Then find out for yourself."

"Not if I have to marry one! Begging your pardon."

Diana flushed. "I don't think—Tess Soerensen said that you don't. Have to marry one, that is." She brightened suddenly. "That's one thing I can do, though."

"What? Find out what the rules are for sleeping around? I thought all barbarians were prudes. That's what you say, anyway.'' Then Quinn laughed. ''Oh-ho, Diana. You're blushing.''

Diana flung the tent flap back hastily, distracting Quinn's attention. Light streamed into the interior of the tent, dappling the scattered pillows, the blankets and fur in disarray, some clothing thrown down to one side and left in a heap.

''Well!'' Quinn sounded gratified by this revealing sight.

The pounding of horses startled Diana, coming from close by. She started around. Perhaps it was Anatoly. . . . But the troop cantered past and went on, oblivious to her. She felt helpless. Never in her life had she felt as superfluous as she did now. The jaran were off to war—War! She could not imagine it, except the glimpse she had received that one day, salving the wounded, the day she had met Anatoly. Was this the true measure of the barbarity of the jaran culture? That the men—the soldiers—rode off, leaving their women and children, their families, behind? Did the women always follow in their wake? Was there no true comradeship? She could not imagine her parents, her uncles and aunts—the little clan of a family she had grown up in—separating for such an arbitrary reason, or if they did have to separate, separating on this rigid, artificial line of sex.

''I hate it here,'' said Diana.

''What?'' Quinn had already gone into the tent without asking permission, which offended Diana even more, as if her intimacy with Anatoly had been violated. ''Oh, Di, you don't want to lose this.'' She lifted up the gold necklace. ''And look here.'' She giggled, crouching. ''I see he must have taken off those beautifully decorated boots rather quickly.'' She held up a gold braided tassel, one of the braids that had rimmed Anatoly's black boots.

Diana grabbed the tassel out of Quinn's hand and pressed it against her heart. ''Stop it, Quinn. You can collect my things if you want, but I'll pack his. Do you understand?''

Quinn arched an expressive eyebrow. ''What? Do you love him that much already?''

''Would that be so strange?'' murmured Diana, but Quinn had lapsed into an obscene song by whose rhythm she folded up the blankets, and she did not reply.

CHAPTER TWENTY-FIVE

Vasil stood listening to his cousin Anton boring on about their family and tribe, little details of who had married whom, who had borne a child, and what girls and boys had shown unusual aptitudes for important skills. Such gossip fascinated Anton, whose eldest daughter, just married to a respectable blacksmith, was showing talent for dyeing. Vasil swallowed a yawn and smiled and nodded and Anton happily went on, assuming that Vasil must be hungry for news of the tribe he had deserted many years ago in order to ride with Ilyakoria Bakhtiian.

Anton, Vasil reflected, was the perfect etsana's brother: he could support the headwoman by keeping abreast of all the niggling day-to-day details and so help her in her task of keeping the tribe running smoothly. An etsana's husband needed the same skills and interests, and back when Vasil was still young, less than two cycles of the calendar old, back when Bakhtiian had left the tribes to travel south to that half-mythical city called Jeds, Vasil had considered finding an etsana's elder daughter to marry. Actually, he had found three, any one of whom would have been thrilled to have him. But, gods, he could not stand to hear about other people's affairs, to listen to the petty complaints, the disputes, the women and men droning on and on about their concerns. The three young women in question had gone on to find other husbands, presumably better suited for the task, and Vasil hoped they were happy, when he thought about them at all.

Relief from Anton's recital came in the form of Yevgeni riding in from scout to meet up with the main group as they took their midday rest for the horses. With him rode an entire troop of horsemen, impressively armored. They wore sleeveless, knee-length silk robes, slit for riding, over their armor. Some wore gold cloth, some red, all of it embroidered in black and gold and silver.

"Mount," said Vasil, and he and Anton mounted and rode out to greet them.

"Anton Veselov!" The greeting came from the jahar's captain, a young blond man with a handsome face, very blue eyes, and an ambitious set to his shoulders. "Well met." The young man's glance settled on Vasil a moment, questioning, and then flashed back to Anton. Clearly he thought that this was where the authority lay.

"Well met," said Vasil, forestalling Anton's greeting. "I am Vasil Veselov."

"Well met," replied the young man politely, obviously recognizing nothing special in the name. "I am Anatoly Sakhalin. Yaroslav Sakhalin's nephew and Elizaveta Sakhalin's eldest grandson. Are you one of Anton's kin?"

Vasil was so furious that for a moment he could not speak. How dare this boy not know who he was?

"Vasil is my cousin," said Anton. "Sergei Veselov's son."

"I didn't know Veselov had a son. He died some three years past, didn't he?"

"I just learned of my father's death," said Vasil, cutting in before Anton could say any more. "I decided it was time I reunited with my tribe and take on my responsibilities."

Sakhalin regarded him and his black arenabekh clothing, and suddenly comprehension bloomed in his face. "Ah. Now I recall the story. You must have been one of the men riding with Dmitri Mikhailov. Do you think Bakhtiian will welcome you back?"

Vasil smiled. "Yes. I do. Indeed, I am sure of it."

"Ah," said Sakhalin, and then, to Vasil's disgust, he shifted his attention back to Anton. "We rode past your tribe. You can reach them by sundown if you go at a good pace."

"Where is the main army?" Vasil asked.

The arrogant young pup actually hesitated before answering. "Behind us. We've orders from Bakhtiian to take ahead to my uncle." He said *that* proudly enough, pleased that he had been chosen for such an honor. "Do you have khaja prisoners?"

"Only a Habakar general and his son."

"No doubt Bakhtiian will be pleased. Now, we must be riding on." He made farewells and his troop rode on, south.

Vasil snorted. "A boy in on the intimate counsels of Bakhtiian? Or so he would have it sound."

"He's not much older than Ilya was when he came back from Jeds," said Anton mildly, "and he's ambitious, and he's a Sakhalin, so perhaps it's no surprise that he feels he's important. Though he is young to have a command of his own, and I don't think Bakhtiian gives out such an honor casually. Even to a Sakhalin."

"There's more," said Yevgeni, breaking in. "One of his men told me he's just married a khaja woman, a Singer—no, he had a different word for it. They tell tales, but with their entire bodies and their words . . . well, it was a khaja art, he said. I've never heard of anything like it. What do you think of that? A khaja wife!"

"What of Bakhtiian's khaja wife?" asked Vasil abruptly. "Is she with the tribes still?"

Anton motioned to Yevgeni with a lift of his chin, and the young rider reined his horse aside to leave the cousins some privacy. "Vasil." Anton spoke slowly, weighing his words. "Bakhtiian still has a wife. Perhaps you didn't know that. It's something you might want to keep in mind."

Dear, good Anton—so right-minded and so honest. "My dear cousin," said Vasil ingenuously, "I also have a wife. Have you forgotten that? And two children."

"That's true." Reminded of this, Anton appeared mollified. "And Sakhalin said—"

"Yes. Let us hasten our reunion."

They made good time. It was still light when they came in sight of the wagons and tents marking the Veselov tribe. A scout greeted them, an adolescent boy who flushed bright red when he saw Vasil and called to him by name before he even greeted Anton. Vasil did not remember the boy's name, or whose child he was, but he greeted him warmly nevertheless. The child was gratified to be allowed to lead them in.

"Vasil!"

"Look, it's Vasilley."

"Gods, Veselov, I thought you were dead."

"Where have you come from?"

"Let me get Arina."

Vasil slowed his horse to the barest walk, letting the exclamations, the surprise, the warmth, and, to be sure, the adulation wash over him. Here and there he saw a disapproving grimace, a finger pointed, and he noted who they were; they could be won over later. He did not want speed: he wanted his reunion with Karolla and the children to be blindingly public.

He caught sight of Karolla just before she saw him. She was so very plain—that was the first thing he noticed—and she had certainly grown no better looking in their three years apart. Then a child nudged her and pointed, and she spun around. Her hand covered her mouth, and she went dead pale. Another woman might have burst into tears, might have acted rashly or stupidly or made a scene, but not Karolla. She had far too much courage, combined with a huge portion of common sense. She set down her spindle with dignity and shook out her skirts, then called into her tent. Vasil admired her for that self-control. A moment later, two children appeared.

Vasil pulled up his horse. Gods, they were older. Little Valentin had perhaps doubled in size, and Ilyana was a stunning girl, tall, slender, and serious. Vasil dismounted and walked across the last bit of ground separating them.

"Father!" Yana launched herself at him, and he laughed and crouched down to receive her embrace. She clutched him, hugging herself against him. Not sobbing, never that, not Karolla's child. And she was strong, too, for being so young—about eight winters old. She let go of him and grabbed him by the hand, tugging him. "Come, Papa. Come see Mama. And here is Valentin, but I expect he doesn't remember you."

Vasil let her drag him forward. Karolla was staring at him as if he was a spirit, or an angel. She did not move. So he let go of Yana's hand and took his wife by the waist and, well aware that everyone was watching, embraced her and kissed her rather more intimately than was proper for so public a place. The crowd murmured appreciatively. When he released her, her face shone. A few tears slid from her eyes, but she brushed them back impatiently and turned to call the boy to her.

"Valentin, come greet your papa."

Valentin did not move. His mouth set into a sullen frown and he closed his hands into fists. He stared at his father, and then looked up beyond him. "Uncle Anton!" he exclaimed, and darted past Vasil to greet the other man.

Vasil stiffened. "Give him time," said Karolla. Her hand brushed one of his hands, tightened on it, and then let go.

Ilyana came to hang on his other arm. "Are you going to stay, father? Or are you going away again?"

"Hush, Yana," said Karolla.

"No, it's all right. I have every intention of staying." Karolla bit at her lower lip, and Vasil could see that it was only with an immense effort that she refrained from bursting into tears. "But where is my cousin Arina? She is etsana now, is she not? I must have her permission to enter camp, surely."

"Rather late to get that," said a cool voice behind him.

He spun, and was shocked to see his little cousin Arina looking very composed and at her ease, and prettier than he had ever seen her. She held herself with surprising authority, and next to her stood a man Vasil recognized instantly.

"I am happy to see you, cousin," said Arina formally, "and I am pleased to receive you back into the tribe. This is my husband, Kirill Zvertkov. But I'm sure you know each other."

Zvertkov was a good-looking man, fair-haired, but his appearance was hopelessly marred by one lifeless arm that hung loose at his side, as if it were, like an ill-made saber, a mere dead appendage. In his other, his good, arm, he held a tiny baby, and a child somewhat younger than Valentin peeked out shyly from behind his legs.

"No longer riding with Bakhtiian?" Vasil asked, but smoothly and without glancing at the useless arm.

"No, I am an etsana's husband now," replied Zvertkov, with a touch of ironic pride. Vasil did not recall that Zvertkov's family had ever had high enough standing that Kirill could have expected to marry so well—but perhaps there was more to it than that. So often there was. "And I have other duties as well."

Arina smiled, not disguising her pride in her husband. "Many young men come here to train, to find places in the army, and Kirill is in charge of all of them. He oversees their fighting and what jahar they are assigned to. Since Kerchaniia Bakhalo died, Bakhtiian gave the entire command into Kirill's hands."

One of which was withered and curled up into a clawlike loose fist. "I see you have done well, then," said Vasil kindly, wondering how important Zvertkov was to Bakhtiian.

"If I may?" asked Kirill, looking at his wife.

She nodded. Kirill motioned to Vasil and led him aside. A moment later Anton joined them. The baby whimpered and Kirill shifted it deftly in his arm, and it quieted. Behind them, Arina ruthlessly dispersed the crowd. Karolla, with stunning aplomb, went back to her spinning. Yana trailed after the men, loitering just far enough from them that they would have no reason to shoo her away. Her face was bright with joy. A gorgeous child, she was, prettier than her brother, but only because his features were blemished by his fretful, sullen expression.

"Well, Vasil," said Zvertkov. "I'm surprised to see you."

"I heard my father died."

"It's true, but quite a while back. Don't think, Veselov, that I don't have a good idea of why you've really come back."

Vasil blinked innocently. "Why is that?"

Zvertkov smiled mockingly. "I don't think it's anything we need talk of publicly, do you?" Vasil recalled him as a young and rather foolish man, the kind of overgrown boy who attaches himself to a powerful man out of love and loyalty without having much personality himself. He revised this estimate quickly. Kirill Zvertkov had evidently become a rather more formidable man since they'd last met, and not just because he was now an etsana's husband. "Personally, I'd as soon you were gone for good, meaning no offense to your person, of course. But Karolla has missed you bitterly." He glanced to one side. "As has little Yana there, and for their sake, I'll counsel my wife to let you stay."

Vasil laughed. "I think Arina loves me rather more than you realize."

"I am sure she does, and if this were the times before, I would not be talking to you now. But it isn't. Bakhtiian has changed everything we are."

"Is that why I see khaja weapons in camp?"

"You can't take cities on horseback, Veselov. We have learned that, and other things. We're going to conquer the khaja lands, as the gods have meant us to all along, and nothing will interfere with that. Especially not you."

"What is this, Kirill? Don't forget I knew you when you were young. I always thought your infatuation with Ilya was only a boy's admiration for a stronger man— well, but perhaps I was wrong."

Kirill's lips tightened, and he shifted. The baby mewled. "I don't think you have any power over him anymore, Vasil. Perhaps you've forgotten that he is married."

"I have never forgotten it," said Vasil softly. "But what makes you think I returned because of Bakhtiian? I, too, have married. And now that my father is dead, I am dyan by right."

Now Kirill was startled. "What? Anton—"

Anton shrugged. "What's past is past, Kirill. It's true enough that Vasil is the proper dyan."

And since it was true, Kirill did not reply.

Vasil smiled and nodded. "Excuse me," he said. "My daughter is waiting." The moment he turned away from them, Yana dashed across to grab his arm. Clearly she did not mean to let go, but the weight did not distress Vasil. He kissed her on the brow and mussed her golden hair, and let her lead him back to his wife's tent where Karolla waited, patient, solemn, and just as desperately in love with him as she had been from the very first, when he had marked her in order to make her father, Dmitri Mikhailov, take him into his jahar. He sat down beside her as if he had never been gone and helped her wind yarn.

When Vasil woke the next morning, he could hear Karolla singing softly to herself outside as she went about her work. Occasionally she broke off her song to speak to one of the children, or to someone passing by, and Vasil marveled at how sweet and pleasant her voice was, as if all the beauty had been poured into it instead of into her face.

"Mama, can I go in and wake him up?"

"Yes. Tell him that Arina said that the scouts for the main army have already ridden by."

Vasil was half-dressed in the clothes Karolla had laid out for him by the time Yana got all the way back to the sleeping alcove. "Oh," she said, almost disappointed, "you're already awake."

He kissed her on each cheek. "Not truly awake until I'd seen your sweet face, little one." She beamed. "Here, hand me my saber, will you?" She shyly held it out to him. "Come, take my hand and we'll go outside."

Outside, he greeted Karolla by kissing both of her palms and then by offering to go fetch water. "No, no." She shook her head. "Yana will go with the other girls. You'd better go see Anton and Kirill. The vanguard of the army will be coming by soon. I don't know—Vasil." She hesitated.

Vasil kissed Yana on the forehead and sent her off to her chores. "Karolla, you must never hesitate to tell me what you think. I would be a poor husband if I did not listen to my wife's wisdom."

She blushed with pleasure. "Vasil, if it is your dearest wish to become dyan, then I will support you. Although I have little standing in this tribe—Arina was very generous to take me in at all, and everything I have here I owe to her. I can't go back to my mother's tribe. Not now."

"All the more reason, then, that I become dyan. I don't intend that my wife and children live beholden to others. Once I am dyan, then you are by right a member of this tribe, and you will not be here only on Arina's sufferance."

"Arina has been kind. You must not think she has ever treated us badly."

"What about my sister? I haven't even seen her."

Karolla returned her attention to the copper pot she was scouring clean. "Vera disgraced herself. You must know that."

"Since she did what she did at my bidding, I can hardly consider her fairly treated."

Karolla looked up, angry. "She betrayed her own tribe.

She violated the sanctity of the camp. It is true that I left my mother and my aunts, but I never betrayed them. What you did—trying to kill Bakhtiian—well, you did that at Mikhailov's bidding.''

"Is that what people say?''

Karolla shrugged. "I have long since given up listening to what people say. But if you go to see Anton, you'll see Vera. She serves the Telyegin family now." She glanced away, looking shamed. "Valentin is there.''

"Yes, I had noticed that he wasn't here."

"Don't be angry with him, Vasil. It was a shock, to have you come back so suddenly. He was so young when you left.''

Vasil kissed her on her hair and straightened his saber. "How could I be angry with him, Karolla? He will come to love me.''

"Of course he will,'' agreed Karolla, but Vasil could see that she only half believed it.

"There is one other thing, my love," he said, and he ran a hand down the sleeve of the shirt he had put on this morning. "These are my old clothes. Where did you get them?''

She paled, looking distressed. "Tess Soerensen gave them to me. And your old saber, it is here, too.''

"Is it now?'' he said thoughtfully. He left, pausing first to see if Arina was at her tent, which was sited to one side of his wife's tent, but Arina was out and a young woman he did not recognize told him that she was out with Uncle Marenko looking at the herds. So he strolled across camp, taking his time, greeting any person who greeted him, pausing to ask them questions about how they had been and what they were doing now and ex- claiming over how very tall their children or grandchil- dren had grown. He discovered a few things along the way: that the Veselov tribe was inordinately proud of the fact that of all the tribes, it alone had been chosen by Bakhtiian to shelter those young men who for whatever reason were not part of any official jahar and who were training to find a place in the army. As they told it, Bakh- tiian had insisted that one of his most trusted lieutenants marry their beloved etsana in order to cement the close- ness between the two tribes. And they believed utterly and passionately that the jaran tribes were meant by the gods to conquer the khaja lands, and would do so, led by Bakhtiian.

Vasil had just come within sight of the cluster of tents that marked the Telyegin family when he saw Vera. She was still remarkably handsome, though she wore only a plain blue tunic with neither beading nor embroidery, over striped trousers, and she wore her golden hair in a simple braid with no ornamentation in it at all. She bent over a fire, stirring cloth in a kettle filled with green dye. Her face had flushed red from the heat. She wore only one earring, and that in her left ear, signifying that she was bonded to a family as a servant. One of the Telyegin sisters came out and called something to her, cheerfully and without any sense of nasty glee at Vera's misfortune, and a moment later spotted Vasil. The woman's eyes widened. Vera looked up. She went white.

Vasil strolled over toward her. "Hello, sister—" he began.

She spat at his feet. Then she turned back to her work.

Vasil prided himself on his self-control. He never let anger show unless it was in his interest to do so. Instead, he shrugged and turned toward the other woman—Lydia Telyegin, second daughter of Varia Telyegin and elder sister of Anton's wife Tatyana.

"My apologies," began Lydia.

"No, I should have prepared her. It was a shock to see me, I'm sure." This much he said loud enough for Vera to hear, and then he followed Lydia farther into the family encampment, toward the main tent. "But her husband—is it true that he didn't repudiate her?"

"True enough. But then—" She glanced sidelong at Vasil, and he knew immediately that she was gauging how soon she might decently approach him for a more intimate encounter. "—Petya always had more looks than wit."

"You are looking handsomer than ever, Lydia. But I perceive that your wit has not suffered for it." He watched a hint of red tinge her cheeks and then fade. "Is your mother here? I must pay my respects."

"She is with the army. Bakhtiian called the finest healers to him when he started this campaign."

"So of course she would have been the first called."

Lydia laughed. "Of course. Are you trying to flatter your way back into favor, Vasil?"

"Certainly. But in this case you know as well as I that it is true, so how can it be flattery?"

"Neatly said. Well, a healer has come from the khaja lands, with skills surpassing our own, and they say she is gifting our healers with much of her knowledge. They also say that she is Tess Soerensen's foster mother—"

"Foster mother?"

"Ah." Lydia smiled abruptly, looking horribly pleased with herself. "You have not heard, then? Soerensen's brother has come. The prince of Jeds."

The rush of hope Vasil felt was so powerful that he had to stop walking for a moment. "To take her back to their own lands?"

"No one is sure. But here is Anton. And that is my youngest, Grigory, playing with Valentin."

Vasil greeted everyone, from the frail eldest aunt to the infant great-granddaughter of Varia Telyegin. Valentin slunk away and hid behind one of the tents with several of the children his age. But Vasil was not worried. The only person he had ever failed to charm was Karolla's father, Dmitri Mikhailov, and Vasil had always attributed that to Mikhailov's distrust of his motives. After all, Vasil had once been Bakhtiian's closest companion. Why should he then turn against Bakhtiian and ride with Mikhailov?

"Vasil." Anton rose and greeted him. "You've heard that the main army will ride by shortly. We'll go out to greet them. I'm waiting here for Arina—ah, there she is. Shall we go?"

Graciously, Vasil acquiesced. Arina rode a handsome gray mare, and her husband, a chestnut mare of equally fine breeding. Yevgeni brought Vasil's horse, and instantly, comparing his stolid beast to the elegant creatures the other two rode, Vasil desired one of these other horses—*khuhaylan arabians,* Kirill called them, a breed from over the seas, given in payment to Bakhtiian for his services by a company of foreign priests. Bakhtiian himself had given the two mares to Arina and Kirill on the occasion of his wedding.

"Although," said Arina with a smile, "I still think it

was only as an apology for spoiling our wedding celebration.''

Kirill cast a sidewise glance at Vasil, but said nothing.

Vasil shrugged, unsure of why they thought he would
be in on the joke. ''They are beautiful horses. Have you
any foals of them?''

''Yes,'' said Arina smugly. ''Little Mira was born the
same day as the first colt.'' She smiled at the sturdy tod-
dler who sat up in front of Kirill on his horse, already at
ease in the saddle.

Vasil, who rode beside Kirill, tickled little Mira under
the chin and got her to laugh, and then turned back to
Yevgeni. ''Have they treated you well here? Did you find
any news of your sister?''

Yevgeni's expression was difficult to read, it being so
full of contradictions. ''I found her, Vasil,'' he said in
an undertone. ''She's here. But she's . . . she's training.
She wants to be a rider. To be in the army.''

Vasil had to think hard to remember Valye Usova, and
found that although he could not recall her face, he remembered that she had been a headstrong, difficult adolescent girl who had run away from her tribe in order to
be with her brother. ''Is that so surprising? She left everything to follow you.''

Yevgeni glanced at the group surrounding them and
dropped his voice even lower. ''She says there are other
women in the army. She says that Bakhtiian's wife was
asked by Yaroslav Sakhalin himself to join Sakhalin's jahar.''

''And she did not?''

''How should I know? I'm only repeating what Valye
told me. She says that Bakhtiian's niece has her own
command.''

Vasil snorted. ''That I can believe. You never knew
Nadine. Yevgeni, it's Valye's choice, not yours.''

''But what if no dyan will have her? Our aunt won't
have her back. Valye hated her anyway, and what is she
to do without a tribe?''

Vasil laid a hand on Yevgeni's shoulder. ''Then my
wife will take her in. I promise you.''

All at once, the tension drained out of Yevgeni's face.
''Thank you,'' he whispered.

Vasil mounted and rode with the others along the base

of a long escarpment. At last, Anton greeted a trio of riders coming from the north, and they urged the horses up the slope and came to a halt on a rise that gave them a wide view of the land to the north.

Vasil was not sure what he had expected. Yaroslav Sakhalin's army had seemed enormous to him, though he would never have admitted that. But Sakhalin's command was as nothing to the army marching south now. Rank upon rank of horsemen rode at a steady pace southward, covering half the ground that Vasil could see. Farther, only dust rising along the far horizon now, came some unimaginable mass following hard upon the riders: wagons and more horsemen and the gods knew what else.

"Are all the tribes riding south?" Vasil asked, unable to hide his astonishment.

Arina laughed. "Of course not. Many of the women have gone back out on the plains, although some have stayed with the army."

"There are jahars along the western coast, still," added Kirill, "and every man is granted leave to go back to his tribe, to see his wife and children when he has been gone from them for two winters. This army is, perhaps, half of what Bakhtiian can call on."

"I should never have doubted you," Vasil murmured under his breath.

"I beg your pardon?" asked Arina, but Vasil merely shook his head.

A clot of about twenty riders broke away from the vanguard of the army and speared across the open ground, toward the waiting group. The army itself continued on south, like some inexorable predator bent on its prey. Before he could even make out features, Vasil knew which one was Bakhtiian. He realized that he was clenching and unclenching one of his hands convulsively, and he forced himself to stop and glanced quickly around to see if anyone had noticed. But they were all watching Bakhtiian amidst the other riders as the horses climbed up the slope.

Vasil recognized the proud black stallion that Ilya rode. And Bakhtiian himself: but how could he have changed? He had never changed, except to grow older. The arrogant, dreaming adolescent boy whom Vasil had fallen in love with, those many many years ago, was still there,

and time had only honed his arrogance and made reality
of his dreams, and sharpened his radiant power.

Then Bakhtiian saw him. Their eyes met, and Vasil
smiled.

And Bakhtiian, all unprepared, went rigid with fury.
Gods, he had fire to him. It was like a raging heat that
attracted cold things to it, and the fire burned as fiercely
as ever, for all that Vasil could see. He could not stop
himself smiling from pure joy.

Greetings, smiles, ten different little exchanges begun
and not quite brought to fruition, withered and died in
the blazing heat of Bakhtiian's anger.

Ilya turned to glare at Arina Veselov. "Where did he
come from?" he demanded, his voice rasping and hoarse.
"Who granted him peace to ride among you?"

"I did," said Arina with astounding calm. "You forget, Bakhtiian, that I am the etsana of his tribe, and it is
my right to give him leave to enter it."

He stiffened at the cool assurance of her tone. "And
if I say that I want him gone?"

"How you direct your army is none of my concern."
She lifted her chin slightly. That so slight a woman, and
one still so young, could withstand the force of Bakhtiian's censure was impressive but not surprising. "How
I oversee my tribe is none of yours."

Like a fire banked with ashes, his anger subsided from
its flaring heat and settled into something less blazing
but no less dangerous. "I beg your pardon, Mother Veselov," he replied, formal. Someone coughed. A general
sigh passed around the assembly as its members seemed
to realize that they might relax without seeing bloodshed.
Vasil knew he was still smiling, but he simply could not
help himself. He had forgotten the sheer, breathless elation that the sight of Ilyakoria Bakhtiian had always filled
him with.

Then, ignoring the unsettled problem lingering in their
midst, the riders greeted each other. Arina dismounted
and went to hug a brown-haired woman—yes, it was indeed Bakhtiian's khaja wife. She, too, was one of the
rare people Vasil would never forget: he was not sure
whether he hated or loved her more for what she was to
Ilya. Tess. She walked across to Kirill and smiled up at
Zvertkov.

"She loves him," said Vasil under his breath, and he glanced over to see what Bakhtiian made of this greeting. But Ilya was sitting stock still, moving only with a twitch of his hands here, and here, to keep his restive stallion from walking forward. He was staring at the sky. Otherwise, the movement as the two parties greeted each other excluded him, although he was its center.

"Vasil," said Anton mildly, "Tess Soerensen loves many men, and women as well. She has a generous heart. If you try to stir up trouble there, I think you'll find trouble, but only for yourself."

"I'm only surprised that anyone, loving Bakhtiian, could find room in his heart to love another."

"Ah," said Anton. "As well you might be. If you will excuse me." He reined his horse away to go greet Niko Sibirin.

Vasil cursed under his breath, aware that he had just given himself away. Beside him, Tess Soerensen reached her arms up to take little Mira Veselov down from the saddle, and she turned to look up at Vasil. Behind her, Bakhtiian had shifted his attention to his wife, and his expression, fixed on her with the child in her arms, was painfully naked: no man ought to reveal himself so, not in public, at least.

"Well, Vasil," said Tess. "How like you to come along when you're least expected."

"And least wanted?"

Tess smiled, not entirely kindly. "How is your wife?"

Vasil flushed. "Karolla is well. As are the children. Arina was very kind to them."

"Yes, Arina has indeed been kind to them. But I must say I've always thought Karolla deserving of kindness."

"I have always been kind to her," retorted Vasil, stung by this accusation.

"I am sure you have been. But I can't imagine it was kind to desert her for so long."

"I didn't—" He stopped himself, and then laughed at her expression. "You're cruel as well as clever, Tess. How I've missed you."

Tess's entire face lit up with amusement, and she laughed. "Have you, indeed?"

"Tess!" Bakhtiian had reined his stallion two lengths closer to them, and his expression lowered to fury once again. "The child." Jealous! Ilya was jealous of him for gaining Tess's attention.

Tess swallowed the last of her laughter and carried the child over to her husband. Surprisingly, Mira was not afraid of this grim-faced man in the least. The little girl reached right up to him. Ilya plucked her out of Tess's arms and settled her in the saddle before him, and shot a glance toward Vasil that was filled with such venom that Vasil was immensely heartened.

"Zvertkov." The tone was stiff, but Kirill rode over to Bakhtiian quite cheerfully. "Have you any riders ready for the army?"

"Yes. A whole troop that I recommend you fit entire into one of the commands. They've worked quite well together—boys who came to me three years past, who've grown up here, and two girls."

"Two?"

"One fights well enough." Kirill winked down at Tess. "As well as Tess, I must say."

Vasil saw how Ilya frowned at this comment, how a certain indefinable tension settled around his shoulders, yet Zvertkov seemed immune to it. "And the other?"

"Well, not every man has the gift for fighting, so why should every woman? She'll not get herself into trouble, and she wants nothing else but to ride. Has nothing else. She was with Mikhailov." Kirill glanced back at Vasil and then away. "Also, Veselov brought men with him."

Bakhtiian's gaze jerked to Vasil and then wrenched away. "How many?" He halted, seemed to inhale resolve like air, and turned to hail Arina. "I will end this now," he said. "Mother Veselov. And *you*. Why have you come back, Vasil?"

As if it were warmth, Vasil basked in the intensity of Ilya's regard, let it flow over him and envelop him. "My father is dead. I am dyan by right."

"I do not approve it."

"Whether you approve it or not," said Vasil lightly, "it is not your decision to make."

"Is it not? Anton, come here. Arina, are you determined to allow this man back into your tribe?"

Arina bowed her head. "Even though you disapprove, Bakhtiian, I will allow him back. For his wife's sake. She has suffered enough."

"Even if I ask you to forbid him?"

Her voice was even, and calm. "Even so."

"Very well. I cannot interfere in your decisions. But he will not be a dyan in my army, whether your tribe elects him or not."

"I refuse the command," said Anton. "I bow to the greater wisdom of the gods."

"And in many tribes it would be wrong. But not here. You are my choice, Anton."

Anton, too, bowed his head before Bakhtiian's wrath, but his voice remained mild. "Nevertheless, I refuse."

"As do I," said Arina.

Well, there was no argument against *that.* Ilya sighed and settled back, and Mira reached up to rub her fingers along his trim beard. His expression altered instantly and he smiled at the little girl. "So be it. Kirill, I leave it to you to split up the men he brought with him into other jahars. No two together."

"No!" Vasil started forward and then reined his horse back sharply, coming close to trampling his own cousins. He was furious. "They are my men. They have been loyal to me for three years now."

Bakhtiian smiled coldly. "Exactly. Now they will learn to be loyal to me. As is the rest of this army, Veselov, a fact you had best learn quickly. Now, if you will excuse me." He gave little Mira a kiss on the cheek and handed her back to her father. "Tess. Niko." He gathered his party back together swiftly and with the single-minded purpose characteristic of him. He did not look toward Vasil again, and they rode away, back toward the army streaming past on the plains below.

Arina mounted. So did Anton. With a lift of her chin, Arina signaled something unspoken but understood to her husband, and Kirill took the rest of the party aside, leaving the cousins together.

"Vasil," Arina started, and lapsed into silence.

"You have honored me with your trust," Vasil began. "I will never betray you."

Anton sighed. "Won't you, Vasil? I almost believe you."

Arina looked out at the party of riders approaching the army beyond. "Vasil." Her expression was pained but hopeful. "I was too young, really, to know much of what

went on . . . before . . . between you and Bakhtiian. But
you must see that whatever power you may have had over
him, whatever feelings he may once have had—well, this
isn't anything that ought to be spoken of, as you well
know.''

"Do go on," said Vasil softly.

"The past is gone, Vasil. You can't recapture it." Anton, too, stared out at the army. "Look at that, out there,
and you can see. We have another destiny now. Don't try
to interfere with it. We can only protect you so far. Beyond that—"

"Beyond that, Vasil," said Arina firmly, sounding very
much the etsana, "Bakhtiian will not hesitate to kill you
if you make him angry again. That he has not done so
now is only because of his respect for Anton and me. Do
you understand?''

"I understand."

"Good. Then come, Anton. Vasil. We have much to
do.''

She rode away, and Anton followed her. But Vasil lingered, watching as Bakhtiian's party mingled in with the
vanguard of Bakhtiian's army. "I understand very well,"
he said to himself. "I understand that Ilya is afraid of
me. And that gives me hope.''

CHAPTER TWENTY-SIX

"No," said Owen. "I want more curve in the arms. Both arms. Higher. The gesture represents exultation with yet a hint of supplication. There. Hold that."

Diana thought her arms were going to drop off. She could not keep her mind on the rehearsal. Endless hours jolting along in the back of the wagons as the army moved south, and then not even the comfort of any company that she craved at the end. She was surprised, each evening, at how bitterly she missed Anatoly. She was sick of the company of the other actors, except for Gwyn, but he was usually off watching the natives. He was learning khush quickly, and making himself known and liked, and slowly but surely he incorporated bits of gesture, bits of speech, asides into his acting that blended with Owen's vision and yet always, in their impromptu and brief performances every evening, got the most reaction from the audience that gathered to watch them.

"Now, the expression. That's good, but more of a blankness, Diana."

"That shouldn't be hard," said Anahita in a stage whisper. Hyacinth giggled.

"Smooth the lines of the mouth." As always, Owen worked on, ignoring the comment. Perhaps he didn't even hear it. He fell so far into his work that Diana wondered if he ever thought or talked about anything else, but she had never had the nerve to ask Ginny if that was so.

"You're not with me, Diana," he added chidingly. She hurriedly fixed her thoughts on her mouth, on the droop of her eyelids, on the exact tilt of her chin, and on her arms, lifting toward the heavens.

"Yes! Now hold it."

Her heart bounded, uplifted by his single word of praise. It was for this, and for those moments when the

ensemble work went seamlessly, when the house was
gripped by the spell and the barriers between audience
and players dissolved completely, that Diana worked and
lived.

"Gwyn, enter. Good, but I want more movement in
the shoulders. Yes, there's the gesture."

Since Diana still faced forward with her eyes lifted
toward the cloudy sky, she could not watch Gwyn go into
his *mie*. Drops of rain wet her face. Anahita sneezed
and began to complain about staying out in such bad
weather. If Owen noticed the onset of the drizzle, he
gave no sign of it. Diana's arms ached. She shifted her
gaze down from the thick clouds to her fingers, and set
about memorizing the exact angle and line of each individual digit. Ten of them, one for each day they had been
traveling. One for each day since her husband—the word
was less strange now than it had been before—had left
her.

"Phillippe," said Owen, "the drum beats. Wind demons, your entrance."

The rain fell in double time to the drumbeats. Diana
stood so still that she could practically feel each point,
each moment, that a drop of rain struck her bare skin.
Hyacinth and Quinn, the wind demons, prowled about
her and Gwyn, moving in a sinuous, threatening line.

Owen clapped his hands together twice. "Break."

Yomi said, "You have one hour. Meet back here."

"Yomi, we'll need light. Joseph, can you rig an awning over the stage?" Owen fell into an intense conversation with Joseph about shifting the placement of the
various tents.

Diana shook out her arms and hopped down from the
platform. At the edge of the encampment, about forty
children had clustered together to watch the rehearsal.
Now that it was over, they raced away into the jaran
camp. Late afternoon faded toward dusk.

"I don't want to attempt *Tamburlaine* yet," Owen was
saying to Ginny and Yomi. "We can't know if it will
offend."

"And Marlowe is so damn talky," said Ginny, "especially if you don't know the language. Certainly the
verbiage will lose a great deal in the translation."

"I'm thinking *Caucasian Chalk Circle*. But after we present the folktale."

"Owen," broke in Anahita, who like the rest of the actors had been eavesdropping, "you can't expect us to put up something this new on so little rehearsal?"

"Of course I can. If you wanted safety, Anahita, then why did you come on this trip? I asked Tess Soerensen specifically for a jaran folktale that we might render into a gest and so make it clear to our audience what we mean by our acting. I am still of two minds about the performance of *Dream*. Did it indeed connect? Or were they simply being polite and curious? Certainly they were closest to us for the epilogue, when we drew the parallel from the play into the actual wedding and thus linked the two. But it's by no means clear to me yet even with our impromptus and scenes that they understand what we mean to convey with our craft. What we do here is rather more ephemeral, it seems to me, than their epic singers, who perform a tale over and over again in the same fashion."

"Do you really think it's that different?" asked Gwyn. "Or just different because it's not a medium they communicate by? Anyway, once rehearsal is over, we perform a play the same way every night. That's no different than their epic tales. I like it when we take chances, like this folktale."

"Owen," said Ginny, "I'll finish the cuts on *Caucasian* this evening and then you can see how much physical business you want to substitute for what's left."

"I don't see why we're doing *Caucasian*," said Anahita, making a great physical business of showing her disgust with an overblown sigh and a toss of her curly black hair.

Gwyn winked at Diana.

"The deeply rooted feelings of mother and child, Anahita," said Owen. "Surely that will connect. Now, Yomi, about the—"

"I've got dinner for anybody who wants it," said Joseph, pitching his voice to carry over Owen's. "Hal and Oriana, could you hurry it up and then help me rig this awning?"

The company dispersed. Ginny dragged Owen along toward the big tent, where the food was, although she

did not attempt to interrupt his conversation with Yomi.
Diana lingered. She rubbed her hands over her arms to
dispel the last of the ache but mostly to warm herself.
The army had marched into the hills here, and the elevation brought cold nights.

Gwyn appeared beside her. "Going out?" he asked
softly.

"Do you know," she said suddenly, "that of everyone
I know, Gwyn, I admire you the most. You accomplish
what I've always wanted to accomplish in acting. You
present the part without any self-consciousness—not that
you become it, but that you play it so seamlessly. It's
because your ego is involved with the process itself, with
how well you act to your own satisfaction, to the achievement of that communication, and not with how well and
how much people think of you, and if they give you
enough attention and praise and adulation."

He chuckled. "Thank you. If I'd only wanted adulation, I could have stayed in the interactives. I got enough
of that there to last me a lifetime. I'm not interested in
being noticed or lionized." Then he smiled again, an
almost wolfish grin. "Only in being the best. But don't
tell anyone I confessed that to you."

"You're not afraid to take risks."

"Neither are you, Diana. Don't ever lose that quality.
Once a person stops pushing and growing, she is as dead
in the spirit as if she were dead in the flesh."

Diana smiled in return, but pensively. "I thought I
might—I was introduced by Sonia Orzhekov to the family that has agreed to act as my—well, as my and Anatoly's foster jaran family, I suppose we would say.
Although it's a strange thought, having three families."
When Gwyn looked puzzled, she explained. "My family
at home, the Company, and now Anatoly and whatever
my marriage to him has brought me. But I thought I
might go there now. They said I was welcome any time."

"Do you think I might go with you? Or is it forbidden
for married women to walk about with men who aren't
their relatives?"

"I thought you were going to say, with unmarried men.
Are you married?" She began to walk, out into the jaran
camp. He walked beside her. "Or am I allowed to ask
that question?"

He considered for a moment, serious. "You're allowed," he said finally. "In fact, I am married."

She felt her mouth gape open, and shut it as quickly.
"But then Anahita was telling the truth when she said—"

"Anahita!" Gwyn laughed. "I don't think so. No, the
woman I'm married to is someone altogether different."

Diana wanted to ask more, but his tone did not encourage questions. "Well, we'll tell them you're my
cousin. Which you are, in a manner of speaking, in the
craft. Their camp is in the third circle out from the center, to the northwest."

"Ah, then you've identified the pattern. It's interesting
that they pitch their camp in exactly the same layout, by
tribe and family, every time they set up camp."

"It does make it possible to find your way around. Of
course, the main army must be way ahead of us by now.
There aren't that many men around."

"Once there's a battle, there will be more."

Diana shuddered. "Here, Gwyn, teach me some more
khush words. It's terrible trying to learn a language without a matrix. It's so slow."

"I can't say that I know many more words than you
do, Diana. But here: Tent. Horse. Girl. Boy. Except that
I'm still trying to work out the familial terms. They seem
to have a lot more of them, and more specific ones, than
we do. And more terms defining a woman and what stage
of life she is at than for a man. There's a boy, an adolescent, and then I can't tell whether the shift to 'man' is
defined by a man's getting married or becoming a fighter.
Then when he's too old to fight, he becomes an Elder. If
he lives that long."

"And for a female?"

"I haven't worked that out yet, but I think puberty,
marriage, childbirth, first grandchild, and menopause all
define shifts in a woman's status. But I'm really only
guessing. It's easier for me to learn about the men."

"Do you like to travel?" she asked suddenly.

"Yes."

"I do, for now. But I can see that I'll get tired of it.
Packing up every day and going on at this pace is bound
to pall eventually."

"We're moving pretty fast, for a group of this size. I

can't begin to count the number of wagons, much less the people involved. How do they feed themselves?''

''You haven't seen all those dirty animals being herded alongside? I suppose once you conquer a country, you can expect it to feed you. I don't know. How they get along on a daily basis at all mystifies me. Look, there's the camp.'' She hesitated at the farthest rim of the circle of tents, peering into the camp to see if she could recognize anyone. A woman rose from beside the campfire and came to greet them.

It was Arina Veselov, a pretty young woman whom Diana had liked immediately. Her little daughter tagged at her heels and went to Diana for a kiss. Arina greeted Diana with a kiss on both cheeks and, haltingly, Diana introduced Gwyn as her cousin. Arina gestured for them to come in, to sit, and soon other members of the family gathered, since it was supper time. Children brought them wooden bowls of a watery stew and leather cups filled with pungent milk. Compared to some of the other camps, the proportion of children to women was higher here, as if this tribe had sent fewer of its children out into the safety of the plains.

''Who's that?'' Gwyn whispered, nodding toward a tall, golden-haired man who came into the circle of light attended by a plain woman and a beautiful young girl. The focus of the assembly altered subtly, warping to somehow pull him into the center of attention.

''That's Arina's cousin, Vasil. Isn't he gorgeous?''

''He's a natural charismatic,'' said Gwyn, still softly, and still in Anglais. ''I'll have to make sure that Owen sees him. Owen loves to watch people like him.''

''And people like Bakhtiian. It's funny, though. Charles Soerensen and Bakhtiian are in many ways the same kind of powerful leader, yet outwardly they don't seem at all the same. And this man—Vasil—has the same kind of charisma that Bakhtiian does, but I don't see him leading armies.''

''Not the same kind of charisma,'' murmured Gwyn, thoughtful.

Vasil, noticing their attention, flashed them a smile across the gap. He had a warm smile, intent and encompassing, as if for that instant no thing and no one else was on his mind but the recipient of his smile. Diana smiled back. Gwyn bent his head in acknowledgment.

"Oh, and there's the baby. This is Kirill, Gwyn. He's Arina's husband, and this is the little baby, Lavrenti. May I hold him?" She held out her arms and Kirill, with a smile, transferred the baby to her waiting grasp.

"Goddess, it's small." Gwyn examined the infant. "Are they supposed to be that small?"

"I don't know. I don't know much about babies, and nothing about Rhuian babies."

The infant mewled and hiccuped and gave a little gasping cry and then relaxed. Arina came and knelt beside Diana, and while Diana held the child, Arina dipped a cloth in a cup of warm milk and dribbled the liquid into the baby's tiny mouth. All at once, its lips caught on the cloth and it sucked away for one minute and then sighed and let go and fell asleep.

Diana glanced up in time to see Arina and Kirill look at each other. That glance they shared was despairing. They thought their child was going to die; they knew it. Diana clutched the little bundle closer to her, as if willing Lavrenti her own strength might make the difference. Kirill sighed and moved away to speak to Vasil's wife. His left arm shifted strangely at his side, a dead weight that was only by some fluke attached to his body. Arina sighed as well and wiped a drop of rain off her face. Except the rain had stopped a little while ago. Diana settled the baby into the crook of her left elbow. His tiny head barely reached to her palm. His skin was remarkably clear and pale, stretched, almost translucent, and his tiny lips were perfectly formed, like a pale pink rosebud.

"Look," said Gwyn. "There's the doctor. Have you any idea yet of why she came with us, with the army? I can't imagine why she didn't leave with Soerensen."

"There can only be one reason, Gwyn. See, Tess is with her. She stayed to be with Tess."

Tess's arrival in the camp brought a sudden flare of life to the quiet gathering. Tess kissed the women, hugged children, and seemed to have a separate greeting for each one of the score of people around the fire. Diana watched with interest as Vasil drew himself into her orbit and

promptly became her other half, sharing in her progress
as if he had been part of it all along.

"Scene stealer," she muttered.

Gwyn chuckled under his breath. "Tess Soerensen?"

"You know who I mean."

"Yes, and it was subtly done, too. Very natural.
Wouldn't he be awful to act with? He'd pull focus every
time he came on stage even worse than Anahita does,
and she's shameless."

"Diana! I'm so pleased to see you here." Tess came
up to them. Her entourage now included Arina and Kirill
as well as the doctor and Vasil. "Gwyn. I watched a bit
of your rehearsal of—the one about the woman who saves
the child from the revolution. I quite liked it, although
I'm not sure the jaran will understand a man acting as
Judge in such matters. I'll have to mention that to Owen.
Do you think he'd be willing to change the Judge to a
woman?"

"If you present the case strongly enough," said Gwyn,
"and you think it would enhance the audience's understanding, I suspect he'd be willing."

"Oh, here, Cara." Tess turned and beckoned the doc-
tor forward. Vasil had retreated back one step, watching
these proceedings with a keen eye. "Here's Lavrenti."
She delivered a long comment to Arina in khush, and
Arina glanced at Kirill, bit her lips, and then nodded.
"Diana, let Cara see the baby."

Diana handed the infant over. Dr. Hierakis handled the
child briskly, for all its seeming fragility. "Clearly he's
premature. I'd like to examine him, but I'll want somewhere enclosed and warmer. And you and the mother as
well, to answer questions. Perhaps you can find out who
attended the birth? I'd like to talk to her, too."

Now that the baby was gone, Diana realized how little
its weight had been. She did not feel lightened of any
burden with her arms now empty. Tess spoke in rapid
khush to Arina and Kirill, and then, with a sudden, almost sly smile, turned and addressed an order to Vasil.
The handsome man looked startled, but then he smiled
and spun and walked swiftly away into the darkness. His
golden-haired daughter ran after him, deserting her
mother.

"Karolla Arkhanov and one of the Telyegin sisters at-

tended the birth,'' Tess said to Cara in Anglais. ''I sent
Vasil to fetch Lydia Telyegin. Karolla is here. And,
Cara—'' She hesitated, glancing sidelong at Arina's good-
looking husband. ''Kirill is the one I told you about—
with the injured arm. If there's anything you can do . . .''

''I'll have to diagnose the injury first. But if he's gone
three years with it, it can wait. This baby needs my immediate attention. Come on, then.''

Dr. Hierakis did not even acknowledge the two actors
but merely strode away in the direction of Arina Veselov's tent. Arina walked beside her, looking anxious. Tess
did not move immediately, and Kirill, strangely enough,
lingered beside her. Diana noticed how close he stood to
her, rather closer than mere acquaintances usually stood.

''Diana, I am truly glad you've come to this camp. I
don't know—'' Tess broke off. ''Well, it isn't my part to
give you advice, especially since you haven't asked me
for any.''

''No, please. What were you going to say?''

Tess sighed. She wore, as she usually did, men's clothing—the scarlet shirt and black pants of the jaran riders—
and she wore a saber at her belt. She looked to Diana as
if she fit in easily with the people she had decided to live
among, and somehow Diana could not see herself exist-
ing so entirely within the jaran, so unconsciously at ease.
''You've brought your life with you, Diana, and however
more realistic it might seem to try to keep the two things
apart—that is, Anatoly and the Company—I think you
have to consider finding some way to bring yourself into
his circle, but also him into yours. Otherwise he will feel
that you are deliberately keeping something from him.''
At her side, Kirill watched her intently while she spoke,
although he obviously would have no reason to understand Anglais.

''But I am—we all are keeping things from them.''

''Yes.'' Tess grimaced. ''But we have to do it delicately and we have to try our best to make it seem that
we are not.''

''I think I understand.''

''It won't be easy. Now, I really must go.'' She nodded
at them and walked off to Arina's tent with Kirill.

''Do you think they can save the child?'' Diana asked.

Gwyn blinked once, twice. "We'd better go, Diana. Rehearsal starts in eleven minutes."

"Where did you get that retinal chip implant, anyway?" she asked after they had taken their leave of the family and started back through camp. "My family was never able to afford anything like that, but one of my father's sisters got one when she qualified for the fleet navigation academy."

"Got it in prison," said Gwyn with a grin.

"Oh, I'll certainly believe that." Then she sobered. "But really, Gwyn, do you think they can save the baby?"

"I don't know. On Earth, there would be no question."

"It seems wrong, somehow, knowing how much we could improve their lives and then not doing anything about it. Hiding it from them."

"Who are we to judge what is best?"

Diana sighed. At the Company's encampment, Joseph had rigged an awning over the platform and now he and Yomi hung lanterns out to light the stage. A group of jaran children together with a steadily growing number of their elders gathered about thirty paces from the stage, waiting patiently for the spectacle to begin. Owen had decided early on that letting them watch rehearsal might help them understand the idiom. Diana recognized some of the faces—some of the children came every night— and she waved at them, and they waved back, eagerly, with smiles.

"Now." Yomi called them to order. "We'll start with a run-through, and then go back through the scenes. Anahita and Diana, your entrance."

CHAPTER TWENTY-SEVEN

"Do you think you can save the baby?" Tess asked. She sat in front of a low table that seemed to be made of burnished black wood. But the field projected above the wood belied that illusion: a screen of three dimensions on which Tess manipulated words into a matrix by which a person ignorant of khush could learn the language quickly.

Cara Hierakis sat at a separate console, running analyses of blood samples. "I'm not equipped to run a hospital here. The fact that the baby has survived a month is hopeful. The lungs are the greatest risk, and it shows no severe signs of respiratory distress. It's small and weak. It needs to be kept warm; it needs food—they're doing that now. If I could design an enhanced formula . . . but I'm not equipped for that." She turned in her chair to regard Tess. "Now do you see why I suggested to Charles that we take you back to Jeds?"

Tess stared into the matrix, shifting colors, floating words. Her shoulders tensed, and she did not look around at Cara. "You have to test Ilya."

"That's true. The more I know, the better placed I'll be to act correctly when the time comes. As it will."

"You said yourself that as far as you know the reaction doesn't set in until after delivery."

"As far as I know."

"You also said that you're equipped to give a blood transfusion here."

"I'm equipped for a rough field surgery, yes." Now Tess could hear a certain amusement creeping into Cara's voice. "Let me see if I can reel off the rest of the list. The other baby lived, which implies that it's a medical problem that can be overcome. I took blood from most of Charles's party before they rode north, thus supplying me with a bank. Bakhtiian would make a fuss, and he doesn't yet know you're pregnant anyway.''

"Can't know, Cara. Not for another month or two.''

"Yes, it must be hard for them to diagnose the condition any earlier than ten or twelve weeks' gestation. But what you're really saying, Tess, is that you've weighed the odds and are choosing to believe that I can pull you through under these conditions.''

"I believe in you, Cara. And anyway, you told me that the woman who bore the child who's now living almost survived.''

"Yes. If I'd reached her an hour earlier, I would have saved her as well as the baby.''

Now Tess did turn. In the artificial lights illuminating the interior of the tent, the sharp planes of Cara's face were softened. "Who got her pregnant, anyway? You never told me.''

"None of your business, my dear. But he was no more foolish than you've been. Don't you people stop to consider that life grown on other planets is bound to have certain subtle and possibly lethal differences?''

Tess chuckled. "But they're so *like* us. And they did come from Earth originally.''

Cara smiled suddenly. "That was well done, Tess. Getting that Chapalii cylinder to Charles, with the heart of the Tai-en Mushai's private data banks encoded into it.''

Warmth filled Tess at Cara's words. "Praise from you is rare, indeed. I love having this modeler at my disposal. Besides this matrix, I'm running several programs off the early language data base and seeing if I can find the evolutionary links between Rhuian languages and Earth languages. But my time is so limited.''

"Which I remind you has been your choice all along. You are welcome to return to Jeds any time. Which you won't do. Be that as it may.'' Cara rose and came over to stand beside Tess, resting a hand on Tess's shoulder and peering at her matrix, which rotated slowly on the screen in front of them. "If we can only coordinate our research. . . . I can't yet prove that the Chapalii genetically engineered the humans they transferred from Earth to Rhui, although I *know* they did.''

"How do you know?''

"If you study the history of disease and mortality among humans, which I've done, and then compare the Rhuian humans to Earth models, the Rhuians are too healthy and too long-lived given similar conditions."

"The human mechanism must seem horribly inefficient to the Chapalii," Tess mused. "Naturally they'd tinker with it."

"So speaks the woman who understands them so well. I can't give more than a rough estimate of how long ago it happened. Not less than 5,000, not more than 40,000 years ago. I can't prove it until I understand how they did it."

"And once you understand how they did it—"

"Then their knowledge is my knowledge. I think I'm close to a serum that could well double the human life span."

"Double it? Lord, what would we do with doubled life spans?"

"That's not *my* question. Nor my answer to give. But surely you can find some clues in your language research on the time frame involved."

"Which would also give us insight into the history of the Chapalii Empire, insight that we're denied by the Chapalii Protocol Office. Philology wasn't my specialty, but I'll do my best."

"When do you think that matrix will be done? Translation takes up far too much time for me. There's a lot more basic information I can give the jaran healers on fundamental medical principles, and I'd like to communicate straight to them."

Tess played with the screen, dividing it into three discrete parts and spinning one until a series of pathways arcing away toward an unseen horizon filled one side of the field. "A full-blown matrix would take months to construct, under better conditions than these. What I'm doing is a series of trees. They each contain a finite set, and instead of gaining the language pretty much entire, you simply accelerate the learning curve of what would otherwise be unenhanced acquisition. So you seem to be learning it quickly, and efficiently, but not too damn quickly."

"So they won't become suspicious when we all turn around one day speaking fluent khush? Very neat."

"Cara." Tess glanced up at the older woman. "Why can't Charles see that I'm not the right person to be his heir?"

Cara patted her on the shoulder and walked back to her console. "Charles thinks strategically, Tess, not tactically. Other than that, I can't tell you what's in his mind." From outside, a bell rang once, then twice. "Ah. We have a visitor. Close off the back half, Tess. I'll go see who it is."

Tess spoke two words and the field over the table vanished, leaving only the smooth black surface. Then she drew closed the curtain that screened off the back section of Cara's tent—and the equipment laid out there—and tied it shut. A moment later, the entrance flap to the tent was twitched aside—it, too, tinkled, sewn all along its edge with warning bells—and Cara ducked back inside followed by—

"Ilya!" Tess grinned stupidly and threw her arms around him and kissed him soundly on the lips. "I thought you were days ahead of us."

He glanced at Cara, who watched them with a smile, and disengaged himself from his wife. He frowned. "Has Vasil been bothering you?" he demanded.

Tess blinked. The question surprised her, as did his obvious anger. But she had to think back to recall how much she had seen Vasil over the past days. "I saw him tonight," she began. His expression clouded. She went on hastily. "But only because we went over to the Veselov camp to see Arina and Kirill, and the baby."

"Ah." A pained expression chased the anger off his face. "They have two children already. And Vladi and Elena have a child."

"Ilya." Tess glanced at Cara and then back at her husband. She took his hand between hers and held it tightly. "I feel sure that we will have a child soon, too. Kirill and Arina's new baby isn't strong. It was born early. They may well lose it."

Then he looked ashamed, as if by being jealous of their fortune in having two children where he had none, he had brought misfortune on them. "I hadn't heard. I'll go visit them tonight before I leave."

"You're riding south again tonight?" She lifted one hand to brush a smear of dirt from his face. He had a rather travel-worn look about him, as if he had not rested much during the seven days since she had seen him last. His hair was mussed, and the usually trim line of his beard had grown a little ragged. "Why did you come back?"

"I need more interpreters. I need you."

"I'm not part of the army, Bakhtiian," she said stiffly. "Or had you forgotten that?"

His gaze flicked to Cara and then back to Tess. "Excuse me," he said to Cara. In khush he said, "I do not intend to argue with you in front of another person, Tess. I won't let you ride with Yaroslav Sakhalin's jahar. Not so far away from me."

"And?" she demanded, not feeling much like compromising.

"If you'll excuse me." Cara slipped out of the tent. The bells chimed behind her and then stilled.

"Something your brother said to me—about envoys. Why not have a—a jahar of envoys? *Diplomats,* that's the Rhuian word. Anatoly Sakhalin has married a khaja wife, so I'll put him in command of half the jahar, of those who are primarily fighters, young men who will also learn how to communicate and deal with the khaja. Eventually, we will need governors from their ranks. We'll have to be careful to make sure they marry well, marry a woman who can also learn about khaja ways and who will be willing to live among khaja for some time. That's where you and Josef come in."

"Josef and I? Josef Raevsky?"

"Yes. You know he'll never fight again. How can he, blinded? But with his knowledge—and yours—you two will be my other commanders of this jahar."

"Me?" Tess sank down into the chair that conveniently caught her knees when they sagged beneath her. "Did Charles put you up to this?"

"I would be a fool not to use your skills."

"And keep me out of battle." But somehow, knowing that she was pregnant made her less anxious to prove herself in war. Not to lose her fighting skills, not at all, but the sense of urgency that she had felt before about putting them to the test was eased. And she did have other skills. . . . "I don't know," she said reluctantly. "I might be good at that."

"You already are, in camp. Now you will be my right
hand as well as my heart."

"I don't know," she repeated, but vaguely, already
thinking about what she and Josef could do, building a
kind of diplomatic corps for the jaran, to create—what?
To create an empire. She did not doubt for a moment that
Ilya could—that he would—forge one, the empire of the
jaran. She could be instrumental in seeing not only that
it would last and remain stable, but that it would hold to
the rule of just law, a better rule, perhaps, than that many
of the khaja lands bowed to now. Perhaps. Damn Charles,
anyway. Certainly she could see his hand in this. He was
grooming her to succeed him, by any means he could.

Ilya smiled brilliantly. "Then you will."

Tess had to laugh, because Ilya was so transparently
pleased that his little scheme had worked: he could give
her a place in his army and give her authority of her own
without putting her in the line of fire. She lifted a finger.
"But. I want Aleksi."

"Aleksi! Give up one of my finest fighters—?"

"He's lost in your jahar, Ilya, and he's unlikely to get
a command of his own, even if he wanted one. But if
he's mine, and he chooses a select group of young riders
to be my escort, then I'll have the protection an envoy
deserves, and a group of riders that Josef and I can call
on at need."

"Hmm. Kirill has such a group of young riders. Mis-
fits, most of them, like Aleksi. I'll give them to you.
Now, Sonia has agreed to take Josef into our camp, and
little Ivan will serve as his eyes. It's another five days to
the mountains at this pace. You and Josef can discuss
your plans. When I see you there, you'll tell me what
you and Josef have decided." He had been angry when
he arrived, but Tess could detect no anger in him now,
as if the emotion had evaporated once he had a new out-
let for his energy. He paced to the inside curtain, and
Tess jumped to her feet. If he even twitched it back a
handsbreadth, and saw what lay within. . . .

But he twirled and strode back toward the entrance.
He would never invade the private space of another person's tent. He was jaran, after all. He bent, kissed Tess,
and with no further word left the tent. Tess caught the
flap before it could fall. The bells shuddered and faded.

"Well." From outside, Cara watched Ilya stride away into the night. "What was that all about? Why did he ride back here?"

Tess stepped out beside her and let the tent flap chime closed behind. "There's the obvious answer. A jahar of envoys. You know, Cara, that damned education of his is going to make him a rather different breed of barbarian conqueror. But I don't think that's the complete answer, and I can't put the rest of the puzzle together yet."

Six days brought the huge ungainly mass of the jaran camp into a broad valley at the foot of the mountains. A few fields had survived the invasion, but not many, Tess noted. She rode out with Aleksi, who had come back to take his place at her side, to view the burned city and the refugee town growing up all makeshift and scattered within the city's half-ruined walls. They picked their way along the streets, the troop of fifty riders that Aleksi now commanded in neat lines behind them.

It had rained for the last two days, although this day was clear, and mud spattered their horses' legs and choked the entryways of the hovels built out of what wood and brick remained to the refugees. Mercifully, Tess saw no corpses and no men, either, but many women and hordes of children. A girl with sunken eyes and a swollen belly clutched a rag doll and stared as they rode past her. Two boys picked through the litter of a burned house, seeking treasure. They glanced over their shoulders at the riders, but hunger or familiarity had made them apathetic and they simply went on with their digging.

A thin young woman holding a thin baby looked up at them and then away. Tess wondered if she had tried to sell her body, to trade herself for food for the child, only to find herself scorned and ignored. What else could such a woman do, except scavenge in the ruins? But Tess had seen women working out in the fields; surely some kind of government still existed here.

"Let's go back," she said. They rode back past the row of tents Cara had appropriated for a hospital. Tess waved at Niko and Juli and rode on into the main camp. Aleksi took her mare, and she walked alone to the very center, where she found Ilya scolding Yaroslav Sakhalin's second-in-command.

"Of course we don't want to leave soldiers behind to
regroup and attack us again, but it does us no good to
kill all the farmers as well. Yes, the ones who sow the
ground. Who is to supply our army once we reach lands
where there isn't enough pasture for our herds? In future,
farmers as well as artisans are to be spared. Otherwise,
you did well. Now, all of this take on to Sakhalin, and
tell him to send his nephew back to me. The Habakar
general and his son?" Ilya looked up, saw Tess, and
beckoned her over. "Yes, I will see Veselov now. You
may go." The man signed his obedience and hurried
away.

"What general?" Tess asked. Ilya sat on a pillow below an awning strung out before her tent. "You're looking angry again. I'm beginning to see a pattern here.
This has something to do with Vasil, doesn't it?"

"Would you sit down, please?" Since he sounded so
irritated, she complied, though she didn't feel much like
sitting at the moment after being on horseback all morning. "What can I do, Tess? If I wish to keep the loyalty
of my people, then I must abide by our traditions. If I
abide by our traditions, then I must accept him as dyan
of his tribe."

"Then accept it, Ilya, and send him somewhere far
away. To the coast, as you did Suvorin."

"I don't trust him."

"Then keep him close by, so you can keep an eye on
him."

"That's worse."

"Why?"

His hands lay in tight fists, one on each knee, and he
sat so straight that the line of embroidery on the sleeves
of his shirt stretched unbroken by wrinkles or folds from
shoulder to wrist. His saber rested on the ground to his
left, hilt by his knee, and his horse-tail staff lay to his
right, propped up on its wooden stand. "There he is.
Stay by me."

Vasil approached, flanked by men from the Veselov
jahar. They escorted three men, a bedraggled-looking
older man, a scarred, upright soldier, and a boy dressed
in a rich surcoat who looked to be about Mitya's age.

Vasil made a great show of halting before Ilya and
beckoning the prisoners forward. Ilya neither moved nor

reacted. He was so tense that Tess had to stifle an urge to place a reassuring hand on his thigh.

"I present these prisoners to you, Bakhtiian, as proof of my worthiness to succeed my father as dyan of the Veselov tribe. This is the Habakar nobleman Yalik an-Siyal and his son Qushid anYalik. This captain fought courageously in defense of the boy and for his valor we spared his life."

Ilya examined the prisoners. He did not look at Vasil at all, although Vasil gazed raptly on him. The general abased himself and a moment later the boy did as well. The captain knelt, but no farther did he bend.

"Very well," Ilya said to the air. "I accept them. You are dismissed." Vasil did not move. A few of the Veselov soldiers shifted nervously. "You are dismissed," repeated Ilya in a cold voice.

Tess caught Vasil's eye and nodded her head. Faced with her command, he had no choice but to go. The prisoners remained behind. Once Vasil vanished from sight, Ilya's shoulders relaxed.

"Konstans. Take them away."

"What should I do with them, Bakhtiian?"

"Gods. Confine them somewhere. I'll deal with them later."

"Ilya, I make this suggestion." Tess examined the boy. "It's children his age we can make the best use of. We should start a school, teach him khush. He can act as an interpreter."

The tension brought by Vasil evaporated completely as Ilya considered her words. "He's about Mitya's age. If we make enough links between their people and ours, then when we rule them, we'll rule the better for it. He is yours, Tess."

"Mine!"

"It's your school to establish, as an envoy."

She laughed. "Very well. And leave the brave captain as his bodyguard, perhaps. I don't know what you want to do with the father."

"He fled the field, according to Sakhalin," said Ilya. "Deserted his army."

"Ilya."

He glanced at her. "It would be more merciful to kill

him, I suppose. I'll give him to Mother Sakhalin as a servant. Konstans? Ah, here comes the embassy.''

Konstans led the prisoners away.

''What embassy?'' Tess saw a troop of about twenty horsemen coming through camp, but then they parted to reveal a ragged group of women in their midst. Khaja women. ''Their men all dead or gone,'' said Tess softly. ''Who is left to plead but the women?''

Ilya's gaze flashed her way, but he said nothing. Half the riders dismounted and herded the women forward, careful to keep themselves between the foremost woman and Bakhtiian himself. They let the embassy kneel some twenty paces from the awning. All of the women abased themselves, lowering their foreheads to the ground: all but one. She knelt at the front of the group, and she wore golden armbands and a rich golden surcoat. She bowed her head, but proudly, and it was she who spoke.

''I am named Viaka, daughter of Headman Karst of the Farisa people. We come, we women, to beg mercy of you.'' Her khush was halting, but even when she begged mercy, she did it without meekness.

''How have you learned khush?'' Ilya asked. His eyes narrowed, and he examined the surcoat intently.

''A man of your people taught me.'' She flushed, a stain along her dark skin.

Ilya stood up. ''You say you are a woman of the Farisa people, yet you wear a Habakar nobleman's cloth.''

''It was given—'' Her head jerked up, and she looked angry and defensive, as if she were afraid he would take it from her. ''Fair spoils for my help.''

''*I* command the spoils in this army,'' he said, his voice low but so threatening that the woman collapsed in fear onto the ground, abasing herself with the others.

''Forgive me,'' she said, abasing into the dirt.

''Who gave it to you?'' he demanded.

''A rider. His name was Vasil.''

Ilya swore under his breath. ''Of course,'' he muttered. ''Of course it would be Vasil.'' He turned on his heel and stalked back inside the tent.

No one moved for a moment. Some of the other women glanced up, terrified and yet desperately wanting to know what was going on. Viaka stayed prone in the mud. One of the women had a pack on her back that wiggled suddenly: a baby. Tess sighed. Someone had to dispose of them.

"Come now," she said briskly. "It was ill done, and I think, Viaka, daughter of Headman Karst, that you'd do best to simply give all your spoils back to me. Yes, starting with the tunic. That's right. There you are, Aleksi. Take the coat from her, and the armbands." All the women looked up, gaping at the sight of a woman giving orders and a man taking them from her. "Now. What have you come here for?" Tess was not sure what to expect. Would they ask for blankets? Medicine? Food for their children? Passage to somewhere else?

Viaka, stripped down to a dirty tunic and drab skirt, was too humiliated and frightened to speak. An older woman finally raised her head, regarding Tess with an expression composed mostly of terror and with little enough hope. She spoke in a voice roughened by privation and whatever horrors she might have seen in recent days.

After she finished, Viaka lifted her mouth a handsbreadth from the ground and spoke just loud enough for Tess to hear. "We ask that you spare our lives."

And that was all.

Tess was shocked, down to the core of her being. "Of course you won't be harmed!" she exclaimed, but even as she said it she knew that the harm was already done—that those who survived the summer would have to last out next winter. Perhaps in a year, next spring, those left might hope to build anew. "If you build faithfully and—pay the tribute due to the jaran, then Bakhtiian will treat you justly. Have you—where are your men?"

No one answered her at first. Perhaps they took her silence for a threat, since at last one spoke. "Those of our men the Habakar did not kill are in hiding, princess."

"They've nothing to fear from us!" Tess exclaimed, and then she wondered if it was true.

"Ilya," Tess said that night after they had gone to bed. A single lantern burned, hanging from the center pole. "Who burned the city?"

"The Habakar general, the one taken prisoner. The Farisa ruled here before them, and once we struck into the country the Habakar rulers were willing to devastate the land rather than lose it. The Farisa people are eager to embrace our rule, having suffered under the rule of the Habakar King since their grandparents' time. Or at least, that's what the scouts and some of the artisans left from the city tell us. I have it in mind to recruit Farisa men for an auxiliary unit of foot-soldiers. *Infantry.* We'll need infantry when we besiege the Habakar cities.''

"Would you burn a city to the ground like they did?" The sight of the devastated city and the children picking through its ruins still haunted her.

"If necessary." He said it casually and turned to pull his shirt off over his head. He held a sleeve out in the dim light, examining a fraying edge on the embroidery. "Damn," he said to himself, and he rummaged in his saddlebags to find a needle and yarn to repair the damage.

Light and shadow mixed on his torso, blending him to a pale, sheeny gray. His hair seemed darker even than the shadows, and his saber hilt gleamed, caught at just the right angle by the lantern's glow. Tess propped her chin on her hands and watched him, and he smiled without looking up at her, knowing that she watched him. He was precise with his needlework, pulling out the frayed threads and winding new ones in among them, strengthening the pattern. He was equally precise in finishing off the ends and rolling the needles and yarn back up in their cloth bag and replacing it in the saddlebags.

"Haven't you anything better to do than watch me?" he asked.

She chuckled, and stood, and stripped. "Gods, it's cold." She covered herself with the blankets and fur, and quickly enough he slid in beside her. She yelped. "Your hands are cold!"

He laughed.

A wind stirred the tent. It was a slight shudder, and then Tess heard the distinct sound of a footfall, soft, on the carpet in the outer chamber.

"Kolia, is that you?" said Ilya sternly, but he grinned and shook his head at Tess, who sat up. "Haven't I told you—?"

The hanging parted, and Vasil stepped through into the inner chamber. "Oh, I beg your pardon," he said cheerfully. He looked at Tess, but only briefly and without a trace of lascivious interest in her nakedness. All avid, his gaze fastened on Ilya. "I could join you," he offered.

Tess was so astounded by Vasil's audacity that she gaped at him and did not even attempt to cover herself up. It took her that long to register Ilya's stillness. An instant later, he was out from under the blankets with his saber drawn. Vasil stared at him, drinking in the sight, frozen, unheeding.

All at once Tess realized that Ilya was taking a step forward. One step—it registered, as if at a slower pace than she usually thought, and yet all their movements were slow: Ilya was going to kill him. Right now. No mercy.

She dove in front of him and Ilya had to sidestep to avoid her. He cursed. She jumped to her feet and slapped Vasil across the face as hard as she could. Vasil came back to himself with a snap, and in the instant when his attention was not quite off Ilya and not quite on her, she shoved him backward, back through the slit in the hanging, back into the outer chamber.

"And *stay* out, you damned interfering bastard!" she yelled, hoping that Aleksi would hear.

A moment later, Aleksi's voice came from outside. "Tess?"

"Escort him back to his camp, Aleksi." Her voice shook because she was now breathing so hard, panting. Adrenaline raced through her. Her hands trembled. "Don't tell anyone." Vasil, damn him, hesitated. He gazed at the curtain as if wondering whether to risk going back in, or if Ilya might come out. "Out," she said, "or I'll kill you myself." She grabbed a knife from a sheath hanging along one wall and held it up. "Or don't you believe I could do it? Or better yet, scar that pretty face of yours."

Vasil's gaze leapt to her. He smiled. "You're glorious, my sweet. Especially with no clothes on."

"Get out."

He got out.

Tess spun and went back into the inner chamber. Ilya sat on the floor, saber cast away to one side of the chamber, his face buried in his hands. Tess knelt beside him and embraced him, wrapping her arms around him.

"Ilya? Can you believe he—?" She broke off her laugh. "Ilya!" She might as well not have been there, for all he responded to her. As if he could not bear to look at the chamber, at what he had almost done. "My sweet love, he's gone. I chased him off by threatening to cut up that handsome face of his, which would have served him right and probably made all of our lives a bit easier. But I didn't think it was a good idea to kill him. He's shameless, it's true, but I don't think he's worth killing." She faltered. "Ilya?"

Oh, God, this ran deep. The old wound had just reopened, except—she could see it now—it had never truly healed. So ugly a wound that Ilya would kill to keep it closed.

A worse thought hit her. Was it hatred that had made him want to strike? Or was it fear, that what Vasil so obviously wanted he wanted too and was not, by jaran laws, allowed to have. *I don't want to know.* But she had to know.

"Ilya," she whispered. Broke off. *You and Vasil were lovers once, weren't you?* She could not make herself ask it, not about a person who was that much more beautiful than she ever would be, not about a person he might still love more than he had ever loved her.

"Ilya," she said, and her voice shook on his name. "Come to bed. Please?"

But he would not answer her, nor did he sleep that night.

CHAPTER TWENTY-EIGHT

The retching sound came from the straggle of bushes that edged the road. The line of wagons lurched to a halt, and Diana sighed and exchanged a glance with Arina Veselov. Arina took the reins from Diana and pulled them taut. The animals that pulled the wagons—Diana thought of them as oxen—stood with bovine stupidity and flicked flies from their backs with their tails.

The bushes crackled and Gwyn appeared, pushing through them. "Was that you?" Diana called, amazed at his appearance. Like an echo, the retching sounded again, worse this time, followed by a woman's moan.

Gwyn shook his head. "No. It's Anahita. This is the second day she's been sick. I don't know if she ate something, or if she's just overwrought."

"They stopped the wagons for her?" Diana demanded. Only after they had reached the mountains did Diana realize how truly easy the traveling was on the plains. Now they inched along. At the widest stretches they managed to fit three wagons abreast. Often, negotiating falls of rock on the high pass road, they had to drive single file. It was so damned slow. It was cold at night. Tempers were fraying, and Diana had two days since—four days out from the gate of the kingdom, the burned city—decided to ride during the day with her jaran family rather than with the Company. Arina and Kirill held a tight rein on those of their tribe accompanying the army and, perhaps, the egos they dealt with were not quite as weighty as the ones Owen and Ginny had to cope with.

Gwyn walked over to them. Dust had painted his boots and trousers a monotonous color that could only be termed a color at all by courtesy. His pleasant face was sunburned; dirty gloves encased his hands. He nodded a

greeting to Arina and leaned against wooden slats beside
Diana's feet. "No, I don't know what's holding us up
this time. Anahita just took the opportunity to throw up
in private."

"I'd feel more sympathy for her if she didn't complain
so much."

Gwyn glanced back at the bushes, which were silent
now. He lowered his voice. "Her work is suffering."

"Everybody's work is suffering."

"No. Be honest, Di. We're tired, we're displaced, and
I can see the fatigue and a little fear in Quinn and, say,
Phillippe. But even Hal is doing his usual best. It's only
Anahita who can't stay the course. Tell me the truth.
What do you think of the work you're doing now?"

Diana looked at Arina, feeling guilty about leaving the
other woman out of the conversation, but Arina merely
nodded at her, gave her the reins back, and clambered
down from the wagon to walk back along the line to the
wagon which held her two children. Diana shrugged and
pulled the reins taut. "I think I'm stretching my tech-
nique. I think I'm learning."

"So do I. So do the rest, however grumpy we might
be about these conditions. Anahita shouldn't be here."

"You've never liked her."

"That's true. You should be playing her roles, Diana."

Guilt and joy warred within her. Gwyn Jones was
courting her. Goddess, of course she was ambitious. She
would not have gotten so far so fast unless she was driven.
"I know exactly how I would play Zenocrate," she said
passionately, and then blushed.

He chuckled. "Now that you've seen Tess Soerensen?
Do you suppose Owen will let us play *Tamburlaine*
here?"

"Do you want to take the risk?"

"I don't know. You've spoken with Bakhtiian more
than I have. Do you think he'd take offense at it?"

Up and down the line, oxen bawled. A horse neighed.
A man shouted in khush, and Arina Veselov trudged back
along the line, carrying her infant son bundled in her
arms. A young man in soldier's red and black rode past,
his bay mare kicking up dust.

"I don't know," said Diana. "He might, but maybe

he wouldn't. Here, Arina, give me Lavrenti.'' This last in her halting khush. Arina handed the baby up to Diana and climbed back up onto the seat. Under the beaded design of her bodice were hidden ties, and Arina undid the front right side of her blouse to reveal a swollen breast. Diana handed the baby back and Arina settled Lavrenti against herself. He snuffled for a moment, half asleep, and then abruptly his eyes popped open and he latched on and sucked noisily.

"Oh, look!'' cried Diana. "Look how well he's eating!'' Arina smiled and cradled him a little closer. Ahead, wagons lurched forward and the line began to move again, painfully slow. Diana adjusted the reins, a little nervous.

"They let you drive?'' asked Gwyn, standing back from the wagon.

"A little. On the straight stretches. It's better than just sitting here.''

Anahita appeared from out of the bushes, looking wan and angry. "Gwyn? Gwyn! Where are you?'' Her voice was shrill, and for an instant Diana felt sorry for her. "Damn you, Gwyn. The little slut can take care of herself. I *told* you—'' Gwyn shrugged his apology and hurried back to her.

"That one,'' said Arina, "is full of herself.''

The wagon ahead of theirs jerked forward and Diana clucked at her oxen and flicked the reins up and down and braced for the jolt, and then they were rolling again, up the pass.

That night they camped along the road. Most of them slept in the wagons, and because Mira was fretful, Diana took the little girl back with her to the Company's camp so that she wouldn't disturb her brother's sleep. In the morning Mira had a raging fever. Diana commandeered two of the young men attached to the Veselov tribe, and they carried Mira and Diana on their horses up to the front of the train, to Dr. Hierakis.

"What's this? Hello, Diana. Ah, a fever. Come inside.'' It was not much past dawn. The front wagons were being hitched and readied to go. The doctor took Diana and Mira up onto one of her wagons, which had a roof and walls. "Oh, hell, she's not old enough to tell her parents what really happened. I'll just check with real instruments." She brought out a scanner. Mira watched with wide-eyed interest as the doctor moved it around. "Well, it's nothing unusual, a bad ear infection, but I'm sure it hurts like hell. Get this timed-released capsule into a piece of—of something, bread, sweet, whatever she'll eat. It'll release antibiotics over a ten-day course."

"I shouldn't be doing this, should I? Giving her this special treatment? Bringing her to you?"

The doctor shrugged. "I happen to believe that it's criminal to let people suffer when we could prevent it."

"But—"

The doctor waved her out of the wagon. "Go on. Leave. I don't want to hear the whole litany about the fundamental hypocrisy of our presence here. How's the baby?"

"He seems stronger. He's eating."

"The Goddess is merciful."

Holding Mira in her arms, Diana paused at the back of the wagon. "Doctor, why did you stay? With us, I mean? I thought you would go with M. Soerensen."

"Very romantic of you, I'm sure, my dear, but remember that Charles and I are used to spending more time apart than together. Such is the nature of our work. Now get. We're leaving."

The next day they passed some kind of threshold. Suddenly the streams along the roadbed ran a different way—along with them, and not back the way they came. They had reached the summit. That night at dusk they creaked down onto a plateau, a miraculous place of flat ground and real vegetation. From the height, coming down, Diana saw thousands of fires burning all the way to the horizon, echoing the stars above. At the farthest edge of the horizon, a greater fire burned, spilling smoke and light into the lowering night.

In the morning, they traveled only until mid-morning and then set up camp near a river. An order came down the line to slaughter a tenth of the herd animals. That night Owen decided to give the first performance of the folktale, followed by the Brecht, as an interlude during the feasting.

The mood in the camp was triumphant and yet anticipatory. Diana could tell some event had happened that was gratifying to the jaran, but she was not sure what it was, and it had been days since anyone in the Company had had any contact with Tess Soerensen or any of the handful of jaran who spoke Rhuian. But Owen sent them along to the feasting ground to assemble the platform, and no one stopped them or even commented particularly on their industry.

"We're part of the army," said Diana to Hyacinth and Hal as they lifted one segment of the floor up onto the base and secured it with pegs. "They've accepted us."

"The court jesters," said Hal. He sniffed hard and then wiped his nose on his sleeve. "This air is wreaking havoc with my sinuses. I think the doctor has forgotten us."

"Go home then," said Hyacinth haughtily.

"As if I could. I don't want to anyway. Do you?"

"What? I haven't even slept through a tenth of the camp yet. I've decided that when we get back to Earth I'm going to get a grant to produce an interactive holie called, *Thrust In Among The Savages* or *Discretion is the Better Part of Amour.*"

"You're disgusting," said Hal, laughing.

Diana snorted. "Sure to go down in the annals of literature with that awful holie Quinn acted in two years ago, that historical romance about the early computer industry—"

"What?" asked Hyacinth. "*Access To Love?* That wasn't so bad. At least they researched it accurately. Hal, could you stop laughing and come help me?"

"Hyacinth, how can you say so?" Diana helped them hoist the last segment of floor. "The dialogue was atrocious, and the acting was worse. Quinn was the only decent actor in the piece, except for that man who played her secretary." They dropped the floor into place and slid the pegs in.

Yomi jogged up. "Curtain in two hours. Owen wants as much of the light as possible. Eat your dinner first. Wait, first slide that screen one meter to the right . . ."

When all was settled to Yomi's satisfaction, they returned to their encampment. Diana ate sparingly and then layered her clothing for her double role: a skirt and blouse for the sister of the heroine of the folktale—Anahita took the role of the heroine Mekhala, of course—and a shift

underneath for Grusha in *The Caucasian Chalk Circle*.
She paced out her entrances and exits and some of her
scenes on the ground, walking her stage directions, pausing to murmur the lines under her breath, and walking
on. After a bit, Owen gathered up the Company and led
them over together.

Somehow Owen had arranged on such short notice to
give a command performance. The house was huge,
seated in precise disorder out from the platform. People
stood farther back, too far, really, to hear anything, and
the open air would in any case suck the volume from the
actors' voices, although Joseph had cunningly constructed the screens with chambered skeins that deflected
the sound out into the audience.

Owen did not introduce them. Phillippe came out in
stiff red and gold robes and struck first a bell, then a
pattern on his drums, and then the bell again. The tone
rang loudly and held long—but Diana knew it was augmented by a few tricky electronics built into a strip wound
around the inside lip of the cup. The house stilled. Seshat
led the women in—all but Quinn, who played one of the
wind demons—mourning for their servitude to the khaja.
This was the story of the girl Mekhala, who brought freedom to the jaran by trading her own freedom for the gift
of horses.

The house talked all the way through it. Buzzed, more
like, an intent, aggravating buzz that niggled at Diana's
concentration through the entire piece. Anahita once
dropped out of character and directed an angry glare toward the wings, as if expecting Owen to fix the problem.
At last they finished.

Phillippe rang the bell again and retreated. As soon as
he came through the screens he pulled a face. "What a
disaster!"

"I *said* it would be." Anahita tossed her hair back
over her shoulder. All the actors turned and listened: the
buzz had increased to a dull roar. "But Owen wouldn't
listen to me."

Owen appeared. He had a strange expression on his
face. "Listen up. They want us to do it again."

"Again! And put up with that! You must be—"

"Anahita, shut up. Phillippe, on your cue." Owen retreated. They shrugged at each other and began again.

This time the house was dead silent. It took Diana two scenes into the pastiche to understand: This time they understood what was being told to them. Last time they had been busy figuring it out. The audience absorbed the piece, like a sponge sucking moisture, and the longer it went on, the more exhausted Diana felt, even though her part was only a secondary one. Gwyn sweated buckets again. His wind spirit clothes were damp with it. When they finished, the house gave them silence, as they had that very first time, but this had reverence in it that was above the simple respect for their craft.

Owen was delirious with satisfaction. "We reached them! We reached them!" he said over and over as if all other words had been erased from his memory.

"Go on," said Yomi. "We're canceling the Brecht for tonight. Get back to camp and get clean."

"No. No." Owen intervened before any of the actors could straggle away. "En masse. We go as a troupe. Let no one see us as who we really are. Let them think we have brought the tale to life, that who they saw were the real participants and we only the channel through which they manifested. Let them think there is magic in our craft."

"He's crazy," muttered Hal to Diana as they cut out behind the platform with Owen and Ginny and Yomi and Joseph as escorts. "I think it's dangerous to play with people's superstitions."

Most of the jaran who had watched the performance remained in the area in front of the stage, and because they were well within the camp, no troops of horsemen impeded their progress, although the children raced to see them, providing an additional escort. Soon it would be twilight. A thick plume of smoke rose up on the western horizon, obscuring the sun, reddening the sky.

"We're under Soerensen's protection, Hal," said Diana. "Don't forget that. What do you think that smoke is?"

Hal shook his head, making a wry face. "What do you think it is, Diana? Or are you really that naive?"

But the answer was obvious, if ugly. Something burned, something large, like a town or a city. And the jaran camp celebrated. What else would they be celebrating but a victory? She shuddered. How easily they walked and feasted and watched the strange khaja art called theater. There three young men, two blond, one dark, walked along parallel to the actors, and they laughed and made jokes and recounted stories among themselves. She could imagine it: and how about those ten soldiers I killed? What, only ten? I killed twenty.

What of the wounded? Where were they? Had Dr. Hierakis seen the performance or had she been too busy patching up torn bodies? And the poor city folk, those who were still alive, had no such medical recourse. They could only suffer, or die.

The dissonance felt so strong that it was physical, a stone in her stomach, bile in her throat. These jaran soldiers could avidly watch a performance and think nothing of the battle—or had it been a massacre?—fought only a day, an hour, before. And they could laugh.

One of the blond men made an expansive gesture and turned his head so far to the side that she could see him full in the face. She stopped stock-still, and first Quinn, then Dejhuti, bumped into her.

"Diana!"

She pushed past Hal and ran, heedless of Yomi calling after her, toward the three jaran men. "Anatoly!" she cried.

He halted and stared at her. A second later he averted his gaze. Even when she halted in front of him, he did not recognize her. He glanced at his companions, but they simply shrugged and looked bewildered.

"Anatoly! It's Diana."

He drew back. His double take was so theatrical that she almost laughed, except she could not, because he still did not understand who she was. Exasperated, she grabbed his right hand and pulled his fingers across her left cheek, smearing her makeup. He stared at the residue on his fingers, hesitated, and, more gently, rubbed more makeup from her face. He looked astounded. He was also drunk.

"Go," he said to his companions. "Get." They excused themselves unsteadily and stumbled off.

Diana looked back over her shoulder to the company, but Owen had already herded them on, acquiescing to her defection. She turned back to Anatoly. "When did you get back?" she demanded in Rhuian. "I didn't even know you were in camp, damn you!'' He didn't look as if he had just been in a battle. His clothes were clean and his face newly shaved. She ran a hand along his jawline, but he captured it and drew it away.

"Not here," he said slowly in khush. "We go to our tent. I missed you, Diana.'' Then he grinned his wonderful, captivating grin, and gestured to himself, to his face, his clothes, the gleam of his saber hilt in the fading light. "This . . .'' He considered, using his hands to emphasize his words. "My grandmother—she washed me. She told me to wash.''

"Before you came to see me," said Diana, bemused, and repeated it haltingly in khush.

"You speak khush!" He looked delighted. He took her by the elbow and pulled her along with him, toward their camp. "You were—" The sentence was difficult for her to understand, except for the name of the character she had played. "I think—it is she, there, Mekhala's sister, talking to us.''

"No. It was me.''

"But it was not you. It was her.'' Clearly, he did not comprehend the distinction between acting a part and being a part. Diana chuckled; she had inadvertently achieved what actors in representational theater so valiantly strove for: her audience had believed her. Owen would be so pleased.

"I *became* her. I *acted* her. I don't—'' She broke off, frustrated, but he merely smiled at her. His hand caressed her inner arm, and his breathing shifted, catching, and her breathing changed, too, getting unsteady, and it was still a long walk to their tent.

He sighed and slid his hand off her arm. "I missed you,'' he said again, with more fervor than before.

The faint perfume of smoke and burning tinged the air. "Anatoly. Do you . . . did you . . . fight?''

Anatoly's face lit up. He launched into a long explanation of something Bakhtiian had done—or said—and how that had led to something else and then the horses had done something and something about arrows and sabers; and all in all, Diana was relieved that she only understood a tenth of it.

CHAPTER TWENTY-NINE

Cara Hierakis surveyed her kingdom and was satisfied. Or as satisfied as she could be, given the circumstances. A wagon trundled in, bearing wounded, and three young women—hardly more than girls, really—looked over the wounded under the supervision of elderly Juli Danov and sent the injured men off in various directions to be cared for.

At the edge of the hospital encampment, next to her own tent, appeared a troop of about twenty riders. She recognized Bakhtiian easily from this distance: of all the riders, he alone wore little armor and no gold or other adornment. One city and three towns on this plateau had fallen to the jaran advance in the thirty days since they had arrived here, and the wealth looted from those cities was not hoarded but passed out into the army and the camp to adorn women and men and children. Bakhtiian swung down from his horse and walked across the camp toward her. At the same time, the implant embedded below her right ear pulsed; Charles was trying to reach her. Cara tied her wide-brimmed hat tighter at her chin and waited. The sun glared down. As spring slid into summer, it had grown hot here, hot in the day although still cool at night.

"Doctor." Bakhtiian halted before her, inclining his head with the respect and deference that Cara had not yet grown used to, not from him, at least. His personality was so strong and so forceful that these moments of modesty still surprised and amused her.

"Bakhtiian. Do you bring me news?"

He surveyed the encampment, the ordered busyness, the tents arrayed in neat rows and the pallets of wounded men convalescing in the sun. Cara had worried, at first, about finding enough attendants for the wounded beyond the healers and their apprentices. But for each wounded man brought in, a relative soon appeared to help nurse him.

"Are you sure, Doctor," asked Bakhtiian, "that there is nothing that I can offer you to show how grateful I am for this gift of healing you have brought us?"

"Give me? Whatever might you give me?"

His smile was tight and ironic. Cara saw at once that she had offended him. "Yes, I had wondered that, since we possess nothing, not even with the wealth of these khaja cities, that seems to interest you. Truly, Jeds is as far beyond us as we are beyond these sorry khaja farmers."

"Do you believe that?" Cara asked, startled. She could not read his expression.

"I stand helpless before you, Doctor. I have nothing you want, except for my wife, who was yours to begin with. While you—" He shrugged. "Sometimes I wonder if we have yet seen the tenth of your knowledge. I warn you, I want that knowledge."

"The better to conquer Jeds?"

His expression changed. Now he was amused. "I am not yet ready to contest with Charles Soerensen, Doctor. Be assured of that. Let me conquer this Habakar kingdom first, and consider what to do with the Great King of Vidiya, who is, they say, as powerful as the sun on her rising and as rich as the earth giving forth gold."

Cara could not help but smile. "Very polite of you, Bakhtiian, to give us fair warning."

He laughed and bowed to her as the courtiers did at Jeds. "My respect for you, Dr. Hierakis, is as boundless as the heavens."

"Your flattery is impressive as well. I thank you. Respect from you, Bakhtiian, is respect worth having. Where is Tess?"

"A city many days' ride from here, called Puranan, has sent an embassy to our camp. Tess and Josef Raevsky are speaking with them now, over the terms of surrender."

"You would give them terms?"

"Certainly. If they surrender, we will spare their lives."

"Ah." Cara examined the encampment again, won-

dering if Tess's influence might mitigate the suffering
bound to be visited upon those poor innocent khaja who
were unfortunate enough to live in the line of the jaran
advance.

"I thought to ask, Doctor, if you would have time to
escort me around your hospital?"

"No battles today? No fighting? We've gotten few
enough casualties in today."

"No, although there was a skirmish out to the northwest. Sakhalin's and Grekov's jahars are riding west now,
to the city that lies at the base of the pass. This fortress
controls the road that leads on into the heart of Habakar
territory, and to the royal city."

"Is this fortress the city that wishes to surrender?"

"Not at all. I expect a battle."

The implant continued to pulse, a slow, regular throb.
Charles would know she could not be expected to reply
immediately, and the pulse was not coded to the emergency signal. "I would be pleased to show you around,
Bakhtiian. This way."

What interested Cara most about Ilya Bakhtiian was
the restless intelligence he brought to bear on whatever
person or event or problem came to his attention. He
discussed the treatment of wounds as if he wished to be
a healer himself. He asked each injured soldier he talked
to how he had received his injuries. He asked each soldier's nurse—many of whom were children—how it went
with their family and their tribe. All of them basked under the heat of his attention. His attendants fanned out,
so that each wounded man received at least the reflected
light of Bakhtiian. Cara noted that Kirill Zvertkov had at
some point within the last thirty days been admitted into
this inner circle of advisers who rode constant attendance
on Bakhtiian. She noted as well Kirill's lifeless arm, and
the movement still left him in that injured shoulder.

Midday drifted into afternoon, and afternoon toward
evening, and when Bakhtiian had at last made his rounds
to his satisfaction, Cara invited him to her tent for supper. Of course he could not refuse. She invited Kirill as
well, and the other men vanished out into the camp, to
their own families.

"Here, Galina." Cara called out as they came to the
tent. Sonia Orzhekov had assigned her niece to act as

Cara's chatelaine and to provide the food and other necessities that Cara did not care to make time to provide for herself. The girl appeared from around the corner of the tent, smiling, with a baby on one hip and a companion—a girl about her age—in tow. "Some food, please, my dear."

"Come, give me a kiss, little one," said Bakhtiian. He kissed Galina on each cheek and asked her a few questions in khush that Cara could not quite follow. The girl answered forthrightly enough, without the least sign of being overawed by her formidable cousin. Then she and the other girl—a Sakhalin granddaughter, evidently—hurried off toward the greater sprawl of camp beyond.

"Please, gentlemen, be seated." Cara offered them pillows and Scotch. The Scotch she laced with a low dose of tranquilizer. Then, between her tentative knowledge of khush, Kirill's halting knowledge of Rhuian, and Bakhtiian translating the rest, she got a full description from Kirill of how he had ruined his arm. A skirmish— the Goddess knew these people had seen enough of that kind of thing—and to the best of his knowledge he had been trampled by a horse, and never regained any feeling in his arm or hand, although the shoulder was not entirely immobile.

"You were a damned sight slow getting to us, too, Bakhtiian," said Kirill with a grin. "You ought to have known Mikhailov would try an ambush."

Bakhtiian played with his glass, not drinking as quickly as Kirill. "I should never have split the jahar."

"As if you had any choice. You're not still blaming yourself for Tess getting wounded so badly, are you?" Kirill snorted. "But knowing you, you would be."

"Tess was wounded?" Cara asked, immediately interested, and aware as well that Bakhtiian found the subject painful.

He downed the rest of the glass on one swallow. "She almost died. Niko saved her."

"Her own stubbornness saved her," said Kirill cheerfully. "Or isn't that what you always claimed?"

"Ah, *that* scar." Cara poured more adulterated Scotch into their glasses. "Very impressive. So she's been in a fight, then? Did she handle herself well?"

"Dr. Hierakis," said Kirill, "Tess is perfectly capable in my opinion of riding with the army as a soldier. And I've trained a fair number of young men in the last three years."

"You always take her side against me," said Bakhtiian in a low voice.

"I always will," replied Kirill, lower still and with a remarkably malicious grin.

"Has she—" Bakhtiian stopped, flushed, and drank down the Scotch again. "No, I beg your pardon. It's none of my business."

Kirill laughed. "You're not still jealous, are you? I ought to make you wonder, you damned officious bastard, but I'll have mercy on you this time. The answer is no."

"Here is Galina," said Cara, enjoying this interplay immensely. She received the dishes—meat, of course, and warm milk, and some fruit—and shooed the girl away again. Galina was reluctant to go but obedient, and she left with many glances back over her shoulder. Twilight came. Cara rose to light one lantern, enough to make it seem she was hosting them but yet not too much light. Tonight she did not want too much light. She excused herself for a moment and went inside to get more Scotch. It was precious stuff, but in this case, the ends justified using so much. She also went all the way in to the inner chamber and pressed the code that would alert Ursula that Cara needed her. When she got back outside, Bakhtiian and Kirill were arguing good-naturedly over whether Tess had truly become jaran, or whether she was khaja still.

"Oh, Ilya," said Kirill with disgust, "because you want it to be true doesn't make it true. Tess will always be khaja in her heart. Just ask Arina or Sonia. Or your aunt. If you care to risk their opinion."

"I am not afraid of their opinion," said Bakhtiian. He looked moody and preoccupied. That streak of asceticism that Cara had noted in him before worked to her advantage now. The alcohol and drugs were having a more profound effect on him than on Kirill. She poured them more Scotch. Dusk lowered down, and stars spread across the sky. A few lanterns lit the hospital encampment, but otherwise the single light in their midst haloed them alone, as if the three of them were cut off from the rest of their world, torn apart, melding into some transitional state. An appropriate enough thought, considering what she meant to do.

"How old were you when you went to Jeds?" Cara asked.

He considered this question. "A full cycle of the calendar and four winters had passed. So I was sixteen. My sister married." Bakhtiian paused, as if this event was so weighty that the world needed a moment of silence to absorb it.

"She married a man from the Suvorin tribe. He was the dyan's brother," added Kirill.

"I hated him," said Ilya softly. The words made Cara shudder, they were said so quietly and with such calm venom.

"Whatever happened to him?" Kirill asked. "I never saw him again after she was killed. Gods, we saw him little enough once you returned from Jeds."

"Kirill, I do not care to speak of him."

"As you wish, Bakhtiian," said Kirill with considerable irony. "Is there anyone else you don't wish to speak of?"

Bakhtiian's hand tightened on his glass. "Don't try me too far, Kirill."

"Gentlemen," said Cara mildly, "I do hope you haven't forgotten that I'm here." They both apologized profusely. "But I'm still curious, Bakhtiian, about your time in Jeds. You studied at the university?"

"Yes. I desired knowledge." Desired it very much, by the way his eyes burned when he spoke of it. "I desired to know the world."

"But however did you survive there?"

He shrugged. "At first I sold the things I had brought from the plains: furs, gold, a necklace given to me by—" He broke off before he said the name. "Later, a woman named Mayana took me in."

"Mayana! You don't mean the courtesan!" Cara laughed out of pure astonishment.

"You know her?"

"My dear boy, the entire city knows her. That is—" For once, she found she could not contain her laughter. "—not in the biblical sense—" But, of course, the ref-

erence was entirely lost on Bakhtiian and Kirill. "She is
famous, and justly so, for her beauty, her wit, and her
learning. She was sold into a brothel at the age of ten,
but she bought out her contract through—ah—hard work,
and so gained her freedom. But surely you knew that."

"She was eighteen when we met," he said slowly,
"the same age as I was, and she was still beholden to
the old harridan's tent."

"What is a *courtesan?*" Kirill asked.

Bakhtiian shook his head. "I cannot begin to explain
it to you, Kirill, and it would disgust you in any case.
The khaja are savages. How do you know her, Doctor?
Does the prince know her as well?"

"She is received everywhere. I find her delightful."
But several conversations she had had with the courtesan
fell together in Cara's mind. She leaned forward, feeling
a little giddy and wondering if she herself had drunk too
much Scotch, especially given the work she had to do
tonight. "But surely—it must be—she told me once about
a young man, her barbarian scholar, she called him,
whom she discovered shivering on the street one winter
night. He was a pretty boy, she said, with fire in his eyes,
so she took him back to her room in the brothel and was
astonished to find that he had no experience of women at
all. None, although she always said with that marvelous
smile of hers that he was the quickest student she had
ever tutored. Then it transpired that he was so ignorant
that he didn't know that one paid the woman afterward.
He had no money, only the clothes on his back and seven
books. He had spent all his money on books. So she let
him live in her room in trade for him teaching her to read
and write. It's a lovely little tale. She said she still sends
the man books, by a roundabout route, all the way to the
distant plains, to which he returned a few years later. Is
it true, the story that she raised the money to buy herself
free from her contract in just one night by performing an
erotic dance built around a foreign tale called 'The
Daughter of the Sun'?" She broke off.

Kirill was leaning far forward, almost overbalanced,
staring with glazed fascination at the sight of Ilyakoria
Bakhtiian too mortified to speak.

"I beg your pardon," said Cara.

"Oh, gods." Bakhtiian covered his eyes with a hand. "Does the entire city know about that?"

"But she's become a legend, Bakhtiian. Such stories are known by everyone. Do you mean to tell me that it *is* true? Oh, Goddess, and that it was *you*." Despite his stricken expression, she simply could not stop laughing. "That's simply too rich."

"Ilya," said Kirill. He looked dazed with astonishment. "I've never seen you embarrassed before. So it *is* true that you'd never lain with a woman before you went to Jeds. I never believed it."

Bakhtiian's expression shifted with lightning swiftness from chagrin to anger. He started to rise, collapsed, and glared at Kirill instead, since his legs refused to hold him up. "How dare you mention Vasil's name to me! It is only because I refuse to contest Arina's authority that—"

"But Ilya," said Kirill reasonably. "I never mentioned Vasil's name. You did."

Bakhtiian lapsed into a brooding silence. His eyelids fluttered, down, down, and snapped up. "Kirill. Why is it that you have two children and I have none?"

"Three," Kirill corrected. Luckily, the drink had the effect of making him mellower. "You're forgetting Jaroslav. It's your own damned fault, Bakhtiian. The gods cursed you with getting the woman you wanted. I should have gotten her, you know, but she wouldn't marry me."

"She loved you," said Bakhtiian accusingly.

"She still does. But she loves you more and she always will. Sometimes I wish I could hate you for that, but I don't. Gods, I'm drunk. I beg your pardon, Doctor."

"You are pardoned. Here. Drink this." Obediently, he drank. Cara handed another glass to Bakhtiian, but he turned the glass around and around in his hands and then, clumsily, dropped it. He apologized curtly, trying to pick up the glass, but his hands kept slipping on the smooth surface of crystal. Kirill's head sagged. Cara paced to the edge of the carpet and peered out into the darkness, and there—thank the Goddess—she saw Ursula striding across the ground toward the tent.

"Do you suppose the gods *have* cursed me?" Bakhtiian asked suddenly, softly but clearly. "That I'll never have a child? The gods know it is true, what I offered her—" He stopped speaking abruptly. He had passed out as well, without revealing what he had, in fact, offered to "her," or who she was, or what he had offered it for.

"Ursula. Come quickly."

Ursula halted at the edge of the carpet and surveyed the two men. "Cara—?"

"Help me carry them inside. Quickly, please." Ursula picked up Kirill's limp form in her arms and carried him inside, then came back to help Cara hoist up Bakhtiian. "Bakhtiian on this table. Kirill on the surgery." She sprayed each man with a light anaesthetic mist and trained the monitor on them. Blips appeared in one corner of the computer display, tracking their vital signs. "Now, can you do me a full diagnostic on Bakhtiian? You know the equipment, and I'll need a full blood and tissue sample and an immediate cycle through the physiology matrix. Then I want you to go find Tess, so she can take him back to her tent, and I'll need—hmm."

Ursula surveyed the proceedings with her usual imperturbability. "How will you get this other one back to his camp?"

"Yes, that's a problem. It must be another man, but— no, I must trust Tess in this. Have her bring her brother Aleksi. Are you clear on everything?"

"Yes." Ursula arranged Bakhtiian's limbs on the table and set the scanner on its path. "What *are* you doing, Doctor, if I may ask?"

"Additional subjects for my research. You know about Tess's pregnancy."

"Yes. But what about the other one?"

"I'm doing a favor. And indulging my curiosity." As Cara spoke, she stripped Kirill of his blue overblouse and the fine linen undershirt beneath. Freed from its coverings, his withered arm looked ghastly in the bright light, a horrible deformity compared to the fine, strong lines of the rest of his body. "And seeing if there's anything I can do for this poor boy." She began the sterilization process and set up the sealing walls and fine netting on the surgical table. She set the deep tissue scanner over his shoulder and began to image. "Oh, Ursula, put a callback in to Charles."

Ursula obeyed. Cara studied the pattern emerging on the screen, the shoulder developing shape and texture, rotating to show all angles, the splintered collarbone, the muscles and nerves, the atrophied tissue beginning at *this* point. "Ah, there it is. The lateral, posterior, and medial cords are all damaged. Comprehensive, I must say."

"Can it be repaired?"

"In our hospitals, certainly. Repair on a molecular level, some regrowth, perhaps, but here. . . ." A blip appeared on the console, flashing red and blue in a rhythmic pattern. The bells on the outer entrance flap of the tent rang out as someone swept them aside.

"Cara?" It was Tess. A moment later she ducked into the inner chamber. "Galina said Ilya was here. Do you know where he went—?" She stopped dead and stared.

"Do reply to the console, will you, love?" Cara asked. "Ursula, leave him for a moment and do a full sterilize and come assist me." She laid out tiny instruments along the gleaming surface of the surgery table and made a single, centimeter-long incision just below Kirill's collarbone. Blood welled up and was immediately sucked away into a tiny holding chamber.

Tess started visibly and went to the console. "Reading," she said. Charles's face materialized in the air.

"Hello, Tess," he said. "You are well, I take it?"

"I'm well. Where are you?"

"Bogged down by terrible weather. Nadine keeps apologizing, not that it's any of her fault." He turned his head to one side, showing his profile. "Rajiv, take a location reading. Now." He turned back. "All right. I've got you marked. Is Cara there?"

"Yes."

"But she's busy right now," said Cara loudly, "and I've nothing to report. I'm running tests. Tess can open the field if you wish to observe."

His image smiled. "No, thank you. You know how I hate the sight of blood. I received a full report from Suzanne, filed on Odys, and there is nothing to tell. All is quiet in the Empire. Very well, no further communication unless an emergency. I will call through once we reach the shrine. Off." The image froze.

"Off," echoed Tess. His face vanished, to be replaced by the rotating image of Kirill's injured shoulder. "That's awful," she said, watching it. "Can you fix it?"

"We'll see. Ursula, hand me the probe."

Tess jerked her gaze away from the screen, where strange instruments invaded the image, and she strayed across the chamber to stand beside Ilya. "It's just so undignified, somehow."

"Tess, you may assist or you may leave. In fact, you may go get Aleksi. We need someone to take Kirill back to his tent later, someone who can cheerfully lie and say that Kirill fell while drunk and reinjured his shoulder."

"But what will I tell Aleksi?"

"Tell him whatever you wish, Tess. You know how far he can be trusted. Where do his loyalties lie?"

"He is loyal to me."

"Before all else? Before even Bakhtiian?"

"Yes. He is my brother, after all. And I saved his life. Very well. I can't stand to see Ilya lying there like that." She left. A moment later the bells tinkled, and Cara and Ursula were left alone to their work.

In the morning, tired but pleased with herself, Cara visited Tess's tent. Tess sat outside holding a half-full cup in her hand, eyes half shut. Aleksi lay asleep on a heap of pillows near her feet. He had a sharp, intelligent face that in repose looked more innocent than Cara supposed he really was. Sonia ducked under the awning, greeted Cara, and handed Tess a bowl of fruit, then left again. Kolia ran in and begged for food. Tess laughed and gave him some and chased him off again.

"You're tired," said Cara. "I didn't expect you to come back after you'd put Bakhtiian to bed. Is he up yet?"

"No." Tess picked at the fruit.

"He'll have the devil of a hangover. You didn't have to come back and sit through the entire operation with Kirill."

"I wanted to." Tess looked up at Cara, a desperately hopeful expression on her face that shuttered in almost immediately. "Do you think he'll ever use the arm again?"

"It was very interesting to listen to Bakhtiian and Kirill talk together when they were both drunk. You haven't told me much about the first year you spent here, Tess."

"Kirill is very special to me," said Tess in a low voice.

"So I divined from their conversation. Tess, I just came from the Veselov camp. Kirill's arm is back in a sling, and it's hurting him like hell, which is a good sign, but it will probably be days, even weeks, before we'll know if he can expect to use it again. But as for regaining full use—that you must not expect. If we could take him to a real hospital—''

''I know. I know.'' Tess hesitated and glanced at the entrance flap of her tent, cocked half up so that a slice of the interior was visible: the wooden table and chair, and one corner of a carved chest. ''And Ilya?''

''I'll have to study the results.''

''Cara. What about—? Gods, seeing him lying there I kept thinking that that's what he'll look like when he's dead.'' Her voice dropped to a whisper. ''Can you treat him?''

Yes! Cara wanted to say, because she wanted nothing more than to try. Yet the risks . . . she forced herself to show caution. ''Are you certain this is what you wish, Tess? You must consider the consequences if we succeed, not just for yourself and for him but for everyone.''

''I won't age, not in their life spans. There's nothing I can do about that except learn how to make myself up from the actors, I suppose. Last night—he was still half drunk when I brought him back here—he told me how young I looked. No, he said, 'You look no older than the day I met you.' '' Her lips set tight. Dark circles of exhaustion showed under her eyes, giving her an anguished look. ''I know it's selfish—''

''As well as dangerous.''

''Yes. But he puts himself in danger every day. He could die any day, Cara.''

''As could you.''

''As could any of us, despite our vaunted knowledge. We may live longer, but we're not immortal.''

''And may we never be,'' breathed Cara devoutly.

''But you're—''

''It's true I'd like to extend our life span, but I'm not seeking the philosopher's stone, Tess. The fountain of youth, perhaps, and yet in the end I don't think this physical human form is capable of sustaining eternal life. That's for the next evolutionary stage. Which I hope I won't be around to see.''

Tess set the empty bowl down on the carpet and drained the last of the milk in her mug. ''You're braver than I am, Cara. I can't bear to see him age so quickly. He already looks older than when we met. Gods, I hate it.''

Cara sighed and laid a hand on Tess's shoulder, squeezing it. "I'll do what I can, Tess. Which reminds me, can I do tests on Aleksi as well?"

Tess stared for a long moment at the sleeping Aleksi, then lifted her gaze to watch Sonia busy over at her own tent, Kolia in equal parts hindering and helping her. Ivan sat working with severe concentration on embroidery. Katerina and Galina had gone off together to get water. "I want to save all of them," she said softly.

"And the burden is harder on you knowing that you cannot."

"It isn't right."

"That we leave them in ignorance? But Charles is right in one thing, Tess. If we bring down our gifts en masse, we will obliterate them, their culture, and their lives. Is the trade worth it? For them? For us, even? Perhaps they wouldn't care to live as we live. How can we choose for them?"

"The same argument," said Tess bitterly, "run over and over and over again. Either way, we are right. Either way, we are wrong."

"Do you wish you had never come here, then?"

At that moment, footfalls sounded from inside the tent, followed by a curse. Bakhtiian pushed out from inside, fumbling with the entrance flap, and emerged out under the awning, blinking furiously, bleary-eyed and pale.

"No," said Tess as she rose to greet him.

"Gods," he said. "My head pounds." He stumbled over Aleksi, waking the other man, apologized, and then saw Cara. "Doctor." Even in this condition, he recalled his manners. "I thank you for your hospitality last night." He blinked again, against the sunlight. "I think."

Cara laughed. "Drink as much water as you can, Bakhtiian. I promise you'll feel better in a day or two."

He bowed, then winced at the movement. "You are gracious, as well as wise."

She laughed. "Now, if you'll excuse me."

"Doctor, we'll be marching at dawn tomorrow."

"Ah. Thank you for the warning." She kissed Tess on the cheek and left them.

CHAPTER THIRTY

"Tess," said Aleksi, reining his horse aside and waiting with her as the line of wagons trundled past, "are you pregnant?"

Her startled glance betrayed the truth. "How did you know?"

"You stopped eating *glariss* milk and cheese, but nothing else."

"I can't stomach it. It's strange, though. None of the other food bothers me, just that."

"Does Ilya know?"

"No."

He nodded, understanding her perfectly. "You must be early still. Does Sonia know?"

"No one knows."

"Not even the healer?"

"Yes, she knows."

Aleksi smiled. "You meant, no jaran knows. Does your brother know?"

"Of course he—" She broke off. "How could he know, Aleksi? It's been over twelve hands of days since I've seen him."

"I thought as much," said Aleksi with that maddeningly knowing smile that he had.

Tess pulled a face at him and urged her mare forward as the last of the wagons in this segment of the train passed them by. The wagons climbed steadily through the range of hills, heading for the fortress that blocked the pass that led on into the heart of the Habakar kingdom. The main army had passed this way the day before, and Tess could read the signs of their passage still, here in the vanguard of the great train of wagons and horses and herds that made up the jaran camp as it moved. Such signs had not yet been churned away beneath the oblit-

erating tread of uncounted wheels and hooves and feet.
Riders from Anatoly Sakhalin's jahar, augmented by the
recruits for Bakhtiian's jahar of envoys, rode up and down
the line at intervals, watching the hills, watching for
breakdowns, urging any recalcitrant oxen along with
whips. All in all, the mood of the camp was positive.
They traveled incessantly in any case, Tess reflected; it
was only the change of scenery that made this journey
different. That and the families they had left behind on
the plains.

At a broad stretch of track, she and Aleksi cantered up
alongside the wagons to the head of the train. They passed
the Bharentous Repertory Company, and then the wagons
of the Veselov tribe.

"What's Anatoly doing loitering there?" Aleksi asked,
pointing toward that young man, who held his horse to a
walk abreast of a wagon.

"His wife is driving the wagon," said Tess. "Leave
him be. They have little enough time to spend with each
other."

"I don't think he was pleased when Bakhtiian assigned
him this duty."

"Perhaps not, since there's not much obvious glory in
it. But if he's wise, he'll see the rewards are greater for
him in the long run."

Aleksi shrugged. "Anatoly is ambitious. Perhaps he'll
learn to be patient as well. It was kind of you to insist
the Veselov tribe be allowed to travel in the front ranks,
Tess. I don't think Bakhtiian will approve."

"I did it for the baby's sake." So little, struggling
Lavrenti would not have to breathe the dust of thousands
of wagons. "And for Diana." So she could ride near
Anatoly. Then she forced herself to think of the reason
she felt safe, letting the Veselov tribe ride here with her—
because Vasil and his jahar rode all the way at the back,
with the distant rearguard. Surely that must be far enough
away. And in any case, Ilya was with the army, a day
ahead of them all. She and Aleksi rode on past the Sakhalin wagons and up to the fore, where Bakhtiian's own
tribe led the way, together with the string of wagons belonging to Dr. Hierakis.

"Ah," said Aleksi suddenly, "so that is why the doctor never lets you get far from her."

"Yes. What's that up there? Yevgeni?" She called ahead to one of the red-shirted riders, the dark-haired man who had once ridden with Vasil and who had been permitted to join Anatoly's jahar in order to ride with his sister. He rode back to her. "What's that smoke up ahead? Is it in the hills?"

"Khaja," said Yevgeni.

"Has anyone been sent to investigate?" Aleksi asked.

"Five riders," replied the young man.

Aleksi nodded at him. "Ride back and find Anatoly Sakhalin and send him forward. Take a few riders with you, and tell the children to get in the wagons. Send a rider back to the tribe behind us to alert them."

"Do you think we might be attacked?" Tess asked. She lifted a hand to wave at Ursula el Kawakami, who pulled her horse in beside them, looking impressively warlike in a lamellar cuirass and bronze helmet. She was armed with a bow quiver strung along one thigh, a short sword belted at her waist, and a lance balanced in her right hand with its butt braced in a holder strung to the harness along her saddle.

"I'd advise you have the women ready their bows," said Ursula in Rhuian. "In this kind of country, we'll need their range and versatility if there is trouble."

Aleksi considered Ursula, considered Tess, and then turned to Yevgeni. "Have the women ready their bows," he said in khush. Yevgeni glanced back at the smoke rising to the northwest and, with a quick nod, he rode off.

But Yevgeni had barely vanished down the line when his sister appeared, galloping in along the curve of the road ahead. Behind her came another rider with an arrow in his thigh and a riderless horse on a lead tied to his harness. The steep hills framed them, two riders, three horses, fleeing some unseen conflagration.

The alert—a high call in khush—went down the line. Tess strapped her helmet on. "Didn't the army clear the hills?" she demanded, feeling sick with fear—not for herself, but for the children in the wagons. But Aleksi had already ridden forward to order the front rank of riders to spread out. They broke aside to let Valye ride through to Aleksi.

"They've fired the road," she gasped. "Put trees and

debris in the way and lit them. They attacked the scouting party, and we've already lost—''

"What's our ground ahead?" Aleksi interrupted. "And
you, Orlov—'' To the rider wounded in the thigh. "Does
it continue this narrow?''

"No, it broadens out, wide enough for a camp," replied the rider.

"They fired the road just before that," said Valye.
"And there's a troop of them, on foot, behind it. Archers, too."

Aleksi nodded. "Orlov, ride down the line with the
alert. All women ready to fire. We'll break through with
the jahar and then pull the wagons into a square and force
them to come at us."

Orlov cast him an astonished glance at this casual
preparation for bows and arrows in battle, but he pulled
his mount quickly around and headed down the line of
wagons.

"Tess, beside me. Ursula, on her other side. Valye, in
the third rank." He paced his horse alongside Tess's in
the second rank. "We'll pick up speed," he shouted,
"and hit them with our full weight."

Tess glanced back at the wagons, which the troop left
behind as they changed pace and broke as one into a
canter. "But what about the women?" she cried.

Aleksi shook his head. "They'll pick us off if we stay
trapped by the wagons. We need room to maneuver."

The high walls echoed the pounding hooves back at
them. Tess had a moment to wonder what in hell she was
doing here and then they rounded a steep curve and the
hot smell of the fire hit her. Smoke poured up into the
pale blue bowl of the sky. Aleksi shouted something, but
he was so close to her that it only came to her as an
undifferentiated sound. Beside her, Ursula whipped her
horse into a gallop as well. Ahead, a horse faltered, shy-
ing at the smoke, and its rider whipped it forward.

Shouting. An arrow sang by her, so close she felt its
breath. Then they were on the fire. Zhashi jumped over
a tangled heap of smoking brush.

Smoke and heat scorched Tess, choked her. A horse
screamed. Aleksi's lance shuddered, bending, and then
he let it go and was past it. His saber winked in the
sudden glare of sunlight, and Tess saw Ursula, her face

frozen in a rictus grin, throw her lance like a javelin into the crowd of infantry facing them. The first rank of riders hit the khaja soldiers. Some of the jaran riders fell, some were thrown back, but most plowed on through, cutting to each side.

Tess parried a spear, batting it aside with reflexes she had forgotten she possessed, and cut with a sweeping stroke at the bare head of a man standing below her. He staggered back, but there was another man there, and another, and another. Aleksi reined his mare back and like a demon he cut Tess free.

"Stay with me!" he shouted. She whipped Zhashi forward, slicing, back-cutting, whipping one stocky man on her left—dark eyes, bulbous nose—across the cheek, raising a welt of blood, and then lost her whip and the next moment Zhashi raced unhindered out onto a little plateau of ground. Tess jerked the mare hard around, found Aleksi, and formed up beside him. Most of the first rank was gone. Aleksi waved riders forward to fill the gaps.

"Now!" he cried. "Before they have time to regroup!"

They poured back, hitting the khaja soldiers from behind. Men sprinted for the hills. Arrows sprayed down from the heights. Tess caught a glimpse of Ursula, still with that horrible grin; an arrow, fletches quivering, stuck out from her body armor. Zhashi jumped again, over a body, and came down in the center of a skirmish. Tess fought her way to the aid of two jaran riders—no, three: one was Valye, sobbing, saber held rigid and unmoving in front of her. Then she heard Aleksi calling to fall back. She slapped Valye's horse on the rump and she and the other two riders retreated in good order. One of them had snagged the reins of the girl's mount.

They rode out into the little valley.

"You didn't stick by me!" Aleksi shouted, riding up to her with blood on his face and a wild look in his eyes. He looked a little crazy. "Pull back farther, damn you!" he shouted at her. "Out of arrow range."

Then he swore again. They were halved in numbers, and isolated now. Arrows fell and skittered toward them along the ground. The infantry regrouped but did not—

yet—advance, although by Tess's quick estimate the khaja outnumbered them two to one.

"Here, girl, stop that crying," Ursula yelled at Valye, but the girl was almost incoherent with fear, shaking. She had dropped her saber, and it lay in the dirt.

Tess rode over to them. "Ursula, go away. Get that arrow out of your armor. Valye." She said it firmly, but without anger. "Where is your bow?"

A sob, stifled slightly. "I couldn't—I just couldn't— So close . . . so many. . . ."

"Where is your bow?"

"Here." A tear-stained face tilted up toward Tess. Gods, she was young.

"Shoot some of the bastards for me. I know you can do it."

The tears stopped. A sudden light gleamed in Valye's eyes. She pulled her bow from its quiver and nocked an arrow. And let fly. A khaja soldier stumbled and went down. The men cheered, immensely heartened. A barrage of arrows rained down from the heights, but they fell just out of range. The infantry advanced, step by slow step. Valye shot again, and hit. And again, and hit.

With a great shout, the infantry charged. An instant of indecision on Aleksi's part: the khaja center was heavy and thick with soldiers, and if the riders went to either flank, they exposed themselves to archery fire from the hills.

Then he grinned. "Retreat! We'll break back at my command."

They retreated in good order toward the distant end of the little valley. But there, on the road where it wound around a rise, a second group of infantry appeared. Tess heard the khaja shout in triumph at their victory.

And then shout a warning. "Turn!" cried Aleksi. They turned, to see Anatoly and the rest of the jahar charging through the gap and hitting the infantry from the rear. Behind Anatoly, emerging through the smoke, came the first of the wagons.

They charged through and, meeting Anatoly's group, routed the infantry between them. As quickly as wagons came forward far enough out into the valley they halted and with astonishing speed and efficiency, women shouting and cursing, a square formed. With a handful of other riders, Tess chased the retreating khaja, cutting them down from behind, those that did not turn to fight. Just in front of her, a khaja soldier fell with an arrow in his neck. A man shrieked out in pain up in the heights above.

"Fall back!" cried Anatoly. The cry went out.

"Tess!" yelled Aleksi. "Fall back with me!"

In that wild instant, Tess realized that her charge had brought her out to the very edge of the battle, that she was surrounded by khaja soldiers with only Aleksi trailing at her side. A clot of khaja turned on her. She reined Zhashi hard around, slicing with her saber. A thump jarred her helmet, and an arrow fell over Zhashi's withers and tumbled down to the ground. Tess froze, realizing in that second that she had been shot in the head. A man lunged forward, sword raised—and an arrow sprouted from his throat. Like a brilliant, sudden, red germination, another arrow sprouted from the throat of his companion, and the man next to him, and the next one, a lethal flowering. Tess did not wait to see anymore but fled, Aleksi beside her.

There was a gap in the wagons. They rode through it into the eddying calm of the center. Behind, a wagon rolled to close the gap.

"Dismount," said Aleksi in a low voice. Tess dismounted, because she was suddenly so tired that she could not think. "Were you hit anywhere?" he demanded. She shook her head. Her hands shook. Without that helmet, she would have been pierced through the skull. Bile rose in her throat.

"Aleksi, I'm going to be sick."

"Here." He held her by the shoulders while she threw up. A moment later Anatoly appeared, and with him, his grandmother. A moment later Sonia ran up and knelt beside Tess.

"Tess—? Gods!"

"No, I'm all right. Just sick."

"Ah." Sonia rose as quickly. "Mother Sakhalin, come. We need all the women old enough to shoot placed along the wagons. We need to prop up shields for cover. Boys to the herds. Some kind of screen—some wagons upended, I think—for the littlest ones." They hurried off.

"Aleksi," said Anatoly. "Come with me. The women

can hold them off for the time, but I'd like your opinion—
should we sortie out to that other troop before the ones
we routed have time to regroup?''

Aleksi patted Tess on the shoulder and let go of her
and went away. Tess sank back on her heels and groped
for her water flask at her belt. It was punctured, empty.
She stood, feeling dizzy and swept in waves by nausea,
and staggered over to Zhashi. Thank God, the flask on
Zhashi was unharmed. Tess gulped down water and then
cupped water in her hands to let the mare drink. She
raised her head.

Chaos. No, not chaos at all. Herds bleated; a string of
boys pressed the animals into one corner of the square.
The song of bows serenaded her. Sweet-faced Katerina
crouched down beside a limp khaja soldier tumbled in
the dirt and stabbed him up under the palate, making sure
he was dead. Three silver-haired men turned a fourth
wagon up onto its side and herded a troop of little children inside. Tess recognized Mira among their number.
The little girl was sober-eyed, not crying, clutching the
hand of an older child, who carried a baby. There, at the
edge of the wagons, two young women staggered in from
the outside. Each wore a wicker shield bound onto her
back, and between them they carried a jaran man. Tess
saw his lips move and realized that he was alive, though
wounded. They laid him on the ground next to another
injured jaran man, and as they turned and went to run
back out, Tess realized that *they* were Galina and Diana.

Katerina kicked a khaja soldier and unbuckled his helmet and threw it to one side. She glanced up. ''Oh. Aunt
Tess! Can you help me strip these two? And then help
me drag them out of here?''

The man was dead. Thoroughly dead. Perhaps Tess
had killed him herself. Tess felt a haze descend on her
as she stripped his armor, his weapons, anything valuable from him. She and Katya dragged the two dead
bodies over to one side where a considerable pile of the
khaja dead had built up, brought here by other children.

''I think we got all of the ones who were inside the
wagons,'' said Katya, sounding as practical as her
mother.

''You'd better check again,'' said Tess. The girl nodded and trotted off. Tess went back to find Zhashi, but

the mare was gone. Over to one side a set of wagons had been formed into a square within the square, and here the wounded congregated. Young Galina sat on the ground between two men. She held her left arm with her right hand, gripping her arm where an arrow protruded from the flesh. Her face was pale, her lips set tight with pain, but she talked with the men. Cara moved among the wounded: Niko mirrored her over on the other side, and Juli Danov shouted at someone—gods, it was one of the actors, the chestnut-haired girl—who was offering water to the wounded but spilling more than she gave because her hands shook so badly. Gwyn Jones knelt beside a black-haired jaran man, delicately turning an arrow out of his side by easing the unbroken silk of his red shirt back along the twisting path of entry. Farther, at the outer line of wagons, women stood and shot, a rhythmic, deadly pattern.

"Aunt Tess! Aunt Tess!" It was little Ivan, leading Zhashi. "I looked for you. Here is Zhashi."

"Thank you, Vania." Tess let Zhashi blow in her face and watched as the mare's ears pricked up. She kissed Ivan on the cheek. "I want you to go make sure the little children are well. Where is Kolia?"

"But, Aunt Tess, I'm supposed to help with the herds."

"Take care of yourself, then." He ran off.

"Tess!" Aleksi hailed her. He rode over to her. "We're about to make another sortie."

"*Another* sortie?" She swung up on Zhashi more from habit than volition.

"We drove them back once, but they've re-formed again. That crazed woman Ursula says we should let the women hunt them."

"Hunt them?" They trotted across to the far wall of wagons, where the remains of Anatoly's jahar milled, forming up for another attack.

"Hunt them," Aleksi repeated. "Distance, with arrows. She's right, you know. I know Bakhtiian and the other men would never consider archery in battle, but they're wrong. We're not fighting feuds any longer, that it matters as a point of honor. I suggested to Sakhalin that we use archers. They're only khaja, after all."

Tess was greeted by the sight of about fifty mounted

women, bows ready, each with a sheaf of arrows at her back, ready to ride out with the men. They wore their heavy felt coats as protection. Anatoly's little sister rode with them and—to Tess's surprise—Vera Veselov and little Valye Usova.

Anatoly, deep in discussion with Ursula nodded; his face lit with a grin. "Now, you women," he said, and then flushed as if at his own presumption in ordering them about. "You will fire over our heads into their ranks. Once we engage, if there is room, circle them and fire into the rear where most of their archers stand." He waved Aleksi over, and Tess and Aleksi took position in the second rank. Mother Sakhalin yelled out the order to move the wagons: a string of men, boys, girls, and women—some actors among the group, Tess saw—rolled four wagons aside. With a shout, Anatoly led the jahar out at a trot.

The khaja infantry unit had marched close enough to fire arrows into the square. The khaja soldiers jeered and let out a great shout at the appearance of the jaran riders.

The jahar broke into a canter. The women began to shoot. The sky went black with arrows. They broke into a gallop, and then hit the front rank of the khaja fighters and she was too busy to see what became of the women.

Until the khaja line disintegrated in front of her. The soldiers ran. Their entire back had vanished, shot through, decimated with archery fire. Out to either flank, Tess saw the women riding in circles, firing off to their left, cutting down the fleeing soldiers from behind with their devastating fire. The men rode the enemy down and cut them to ribbons. Not many escaped back into the hills.

The jahar re-formed quickly, but it took longer to get the women back in order. They rode a great circle around the wagons, and not one arrow disturbed their circuit. The women ululated in triumph. Tess caught a glimpse of Vera Veselov, her face lit with an expression of uncanny glee, as if she had come to life again after so many years in a daze.

"What have we started?" Tess asked Aleksi.

"By the gods," said Aleksi. His face shone. "So will they all fall before us."

* * *

The first outriders of the segment of wagons that traveled just behind them reached them soon after. These scouts reported that sporadic arrow fire had impeded the progress of the train, but several forays up into the hills had rooted out—killed or chased away—the khaja rebels. Mother Sakhalin ordered the wagons back into line, but there was delay with the wounded, and the road to be cleared behind them, so in the end, with night lowering down on them, they stayed where they were. They built the debris into a pyre and burned the twenty dead, as was fitting. One of the archers had died—a heart-faced young woman whose mother wept because the girl had left no children to follow her. Tess did not watch the pyre burn, but others attended it all night long.

The khaja dead they left lying, except to clear them from the road and the camp. Of the rest, perhaps two-thirds of the fighters had received some kind of wound, although Tess had come through unscathed—this ascertained in a ruthless examination by Cara. Four children had been wounded by arrow fire. Tess was too tired to eat, but Aleksi made her eat anyway, and she slept next to him and the children under one of the wagons.

At dawn, Tess woke thinking at first that she had just had a bad dream, but when she staggered out from under the wagon, it all came back to her, much too clearly. The battle itself—her fighting, the skirmish—was all a blur, except for the man she had whipped across the face and the line of khaja soldiers wiped out by arrows in front of her. But it was the memory of Katerina stabbing the injured khaja soldier that haunted her. So young to be forced to such a horrible act, and the pragmatic nature of the act made it worse in a way: not done with rage, or viciousness, or sadism, but simply because it was necessary, and little Katya was the one available to do it.

Katerina came by at that moment, looking nothing like a murderer. "Aunt Tess, did you see? Part of the army is riding back in. Mama says a scout came in, and that it's Cousin Ilya."

"The scout is Ilya?" Tess felt hazy, a little dizzy.

Katerina's face pulled in concern. "Have you eaten anything?" She put an arm around Tess's waist. "Here, come with me. You're looking very pale. The doctor said to bring you to her anyway. I'll get you something to eat. Wait, here's a bit of cheese.''

It was *glariss* cheese. The sight of it made Tess's stomach turn, and then Katya, all-unknowing, lifted the crumbling, pungent mass up to Tess's face, just to be helpful. It reeked.

"Excuse me," said Tess politely. She clapped a hand over her mouth and ran to get outside the wagons so she could throw up with some privacy. But the run, the adrenaline, the abrupt removal of the awful cheese, shut off some reflex. She fell to her knees, gagged, choked, coughed, but nothing came up. She sat back with her eyes shut and tried to concentrate on anything but the sick feeling in her stomach.

"Tess!"

Of course Ilya would find her like this. She opened her eyes to see him dismiss his entourage and run over to her.

"Dr. Hierakis said you weren't hurt." He sounded angry as he knelt beside her. She sighed and leaned against him and buried her face in his shirt. Thank the gods that he smelled good to her. She took deep breaths, inhaling his scent.

"I'm not hurt," she said into his chest.

He tilted her head up and studied her with a frown. "You look pale. Anatoly says you fought well yesterday." He offered her the praise grudgingly enough. "I know that—" He stopped, grimacing, and she could see what it cost him to go on. "—I have been unfair about this in the past. It's only that I fear to lose you, Tess. But Anatoly needs new riders to make up those he lost in the battle. Archery in battle! Gods." He lapsed into silence and just held her close.

She watched him. He had a slight smile on his face and a distant look in his eyes, a gleam, plotting, thinking, working out how he could use this new development to his advantage. As he would. Ilya would not let tradition hold him back now that the advantages of using mounted archers were so clearly shown, and now that someone else, not him, had been forced to use them for the first time. It was not his innovation; he himself had not broken with tradition. But now that it was done, now that Mother Sakhalin had seen her own granddaughter ride into battle, seen the women used so effectively, seen the devastating effect on a khaja unit larger than their own, Ilya could exploit it.

"So," he said at last, his attention returning to her, "I will put no obstacles in your way if you wish to ride with Anatoly's jahar."

Gods, what he must have gone through to bring himself to this point. "But, Ilya, I have my own jahar. My envoys."

"Yes," he agreed, looking guilty, looking trapped.

She chuckled. "I know you offered that only to get me out of riding in the army."

"That's not the only reason," he exclaimed, looking offended. "It's perfectly true you're well suited to it, but you have always been so determined to ride with the army to fight."

She sighed and stood up, and he stood with her, still holding her. "Yes, well, and I fought. I'll fight again, if I have to. But I've decided that a jahar of envoys is exactly what I want. Eventually, with good enough diplomats, your army won't have to fight at all. Think how many lives that will spare. Ilya, why are you here, anyway?"

He surveyed the field of battle, the square of wagons even now unwinding into the line of march. The last smoke from the pyre dissipated into the cool morning air. "We discovered that a whole unit of khaja soldiers had circled wide around our line and gone back into the hills. Of course we came back, knowing that they might threaten the wagon train. With the line of wagons drawn out so thin along this narrow road, and the rearguard such a distance behind—" He shrugged. "But what were you doing out here, my love?"

"Trying to throw up."

He shook his head, looking perplexed, and cupped her face in his hands. "You aren't well? I was sick the first time I fought in a battle, too."

Tess smiled. "Were you? That gives me hope." She paused and thought back, calculating. She was over two months along, Earth standard. Surely that wasn't too early to know. Aleksi had already guessed. "I'm pregnant."

He let go of her as if she burned him. Then, an instant

later, he hugged her so tightly that she could not breathe. She wheezed. He pushed her back, holding her by the shoulders, and just gazed at her. He was alight. He was radiant. He blazed.

"Oh, God," said Tess, "I'd forgotten how insufferably smug you get when you're happy."

He laughed and kissed her, right out there in the open where anyone could see them. "Oh, Tess." That was all. They just stood there for a while, not needing to say anything more.

Beyond, the first of the wagons lurched forward. "I'd better go," said Tess. "Mother Sakhalin doesn't wait for anyone, including me."

"No. You'll ride with me today."

"Will I?" she asked, trying not to laugh at his autocratic tone.

"Yes, you will. If it pleases you to do so, my wife."

"It pleases me to do so, my husband." They went to find their horses.

CHAPTER THIRTY-ONE

Diana would never have believed that she could sleep so soundly after living through a battle, but she did. She slept snuggled in between Quinn and Oriana, for comfort, under one of the wagons, for safety, and if she dreamed, she did not recall it in the morning. Anatoly spent all night on guard. In the morning they hitched up the wagons and went on as if nothing untoward had happened: nothing except the lingering ash of the funeral pyre and the mound of khaja dead. She was happy to leave it behind.

And yet, handling the reins of the wagon, she felt—not happy, not that, but valiant. She had seen the worst, she had run out into the line of fire with no weapon but only a shield to protect her, and she had saved lives. Terror had racked her, but she had done it anyway. And the worst terror hadn't been on her own account. The worst had been seeing Anatoly ride out of the protective square of wagons straight into the other army. Had she even breathed between the time of watching him ride away and seeing him return?

All day the wagons rolled on through a narrow valley whose heights rose in stark green relief against the hazy blue of the sky. In the late afternoon they drew up in a broad field that bordered a rushing stream, and the word came down the line that they were allowed to set up tents, for the sake of the wounded. Diana delivered her wagon to a Veselov girl and then walked back along the train to find the Company, to see if Owen intended to rehearse tonight. Although surely even Owen would allow them a break after what had happened yesterday.

She had to stop, though, to stare. Green still, the heights, ragged and steep and falling down to the flat bed of the valley through which they rode. In the forty days

since Anatoly had returned, their road had followed this
kind of path: long valleys snaking along river bottoms
through the hills and then a sudden ascent over a pass
only to dip down again into another green valley. The
heat grew stronger each day; perhaps the summer would
soon bake the hills brown, but for now, it was beautiful.
They had been harried a bit, but yesterday had been the
first time a real skirmish had hit the train. Pockets of the
basins were dense with cultivated fields and villages, but
most of it seemed to be pastureland. The only city she
had actually seen had been the ruined Farisa city, but
Anatoly assured her that far greater cities, Habakar cities,
lay ahead of them.

And there he came, leading his horse along the line of
wagons, looking for her.

It was a little embarrassing, how quickly she smiled,
seeing him. It was gratifying, how quickly he smiled,
seeing her. He loved her. He said so every day, and she
believed him. Because it was true. Because a Sakhalin
prince had no cause to lie—that much she had learned
about the jaran and their various tribes—and because Anatoly wasn't the kind of person who needed or wanted to
lie.

He came up to her, glanced around, and thought better
of kissing her in public where anyone could see. But his
eyes kissed her by the very light that shone in them, and
his smile promised more.

"My heart," she said in khush. "You must be tired."

"Not when I see you." Definitely promising more.
"My grandmother wants to see you."

If she had actually tripped and fallen, the sudden
plunge could not have jarred her more. "But I don't want
to see your grandmother," she said without thinking.
The old harridan practically haunted her, asking every
other day at least about supper arrangements and where
Diana's tent was sited in the Company camp. Making
sure her precious grandson was being treated with the
honor he deserved.

"Diana, I know you don't want to see Grandmother—"

"I have *rehearsal* tonight. I can't go."

It took him a moment to process that one through.
They communicated in a hodgepodge of khush and
Rhuian, each gaining more of the other every day, but

they still stumbled now and again. He shook his head.
"No rehearsal. I ask Mother Yomi. Before I find you."

"Today you asked?"

He nodded emphatically. "Now I asked. Diana, I know
you don't want to see Grandmother. She doesn't respect
you as she ought to. But this time, I think you should
go."

Anatoly was impossible to fight with. He always gave
enough ground that she could not stay angry with him,
and yet, he always seemed to get what he wanted.

"Why?" she muttered, but already she knew, and he
knew, that she was going to agree.

"We will eat. No one, not even Grandmother, can say
that you did not act as a good woman in the *yadoshtmi*."

"*Yadoshtmi*. Is that a *battle?*"

"Battle." He thought about it. "No. It was a small
thing. Not a battle."

Not a battle. All at once, she remembered being out
beyond the wagons, she and Galina, dragging in a
wounded jaran soldier, and she had looked to her left in
time to see a man clawing at the arrow in his throat and
reaching toward her in supplication, pleading, for what—
mercy? death? healing? water?—she could not know. And
they had gone on and just left him there. She gasped, it
was so vivid, and covered her face with her hands, but
that only made it worse, because then she saw vultures
picking at the heap of khaja dead and heard the little girl
sobbing over the body of her dead father.

Anatoly moved. He enclosed her in his arms and held
her tight.

"I'm sorry," she mumbled, almost incoherent, because she knew that he would be scolded by his grandmother for such behavior in public should anyone report
the scene.

He only shook his head against her hair. "It's no shame
for you to feel deeply," he murmured into her ear.

"Because I'm a woman?" She said it with anger, because anger was the only place she had to turn to. But
she knew him just well enough by now to hear that his
silence was one of puzzlement, and that dragged her out
of the memory and back to him. She tilted her head back.

He regarded her with a quizzical expression. "No. Because you're a Singer." He wiped away her tears with

his fingers. Then he insisted she mount the horse and he led her back through camp, like a queen or a prisoner, she thought wryly, to his grandmother's tent.

Mother Sakhalin greeted Anatoly with a kiss on each cheek, fondly, and Diana with formidable civility. "You have acted bravely in the yadoshtmi," she said by way of sealing her greeting. "Now you will eat with us."

Not that Diana had any choice in the matter. Anatoly brushed his boot up against hers, a subtle reminder. "Mother Sakhalin," she said, and the tiny old woman fixed her eagle eye on Diana's face. No mercy there for the khaja wounded, Diana thought wildly at random, nor even for her own, those of her own people whom she deemed had crossed over the line of the jaran law. "I thank you for this offer of hospitality." She managed the polite phrase Anatoly had taught her, realized she had gotten it wrong, and braced herself for Mother Sakhalin's disapproval. But Mother Sakhalin merely regarded her a moment longer and then turned to go back inside her tent.

Inside it was huge. The public chamber was easily as large as the Company tent, and behind it, behind a bold tapestry of lions, lay the private chamber which must, judging by the circumference of the tent, be equally as large. Hordes of Sakhalin relatives waited there, seated on pillows and served by an exotic collection of their own children, older jaran men and women, and one old khaja man who looked utterly out of place. Diana could not help but watch him as the meal proceeded, but they treated him no differently than they did the others as far as she could see.

Anatoly sat beside his grandmother. Diana was placed farther down, between Anatoly's younger sister Shura and an old man, and they proved genial companions. They even took it in stride when she paused for a moment of silence to give thanks for the food. They paused with her.

After they had eaten for awhile, the old man, who was some kind of an uncle, took it upon himself to begin the conversation. "In the Orzhekov tribe," he said, "they say you are a Singer."

"I listened to the first song you sang, you and the others," added Shura, a girl of about sixteen who was not as pretty as her brother but equally self-possessed, "and I thought, maybe a Singer of our tribe could learn that tale—make it to a song. Do you understand?"

"Maybe you could make it to a song, Shura," said Diana, thinking it was a wonderful suggestion.

But Shura went red, and Diana was terrified: she had offended her. "I am not a Singer," Shura said, making a little warding gesture with one hand. "There has been no Singer born into the Sakhalin tribe since my grandmother's great-grandmother's time."

Not offended. Shura was scared. "I am the only *actor* in my family," Diana confessed. "These are beautiful tapestries. Who made them?"

With this safe subject, they managed to while out supper time discussing weaving and then the complex thread of relationships within the Sakhalin tribe: who was related to whom, and how, and which cousins had stayed on the plains with Konstantina Sakhalin, Mother Sakhalin's only living daughter, and which had come with Mother Sakhalin to attend the army. That was the oddest thing about Anatoly and Shura: They were in fact orphans. Both their mother—the eldest daughter of Mother Sakhalin—and their father—a Vershinin cousin—were dead, and they had also lost two siblings, and yet they weren't orphans at all except by the strict definition. The Sakhalin tribe was their family and within the tribe itself, this web of cousins and uncles and aunts was so interwoven that it was rather like a blanket that protects you against the cold night. No wonder Tess Soerensen, orphaned and left alone with only a much older sibling who was distracted by huge responsibilities, had fallen in love with the jaran.

"Shura likes you," said Anatoly when they left.

"I like Shura," she replied, and he looked pleased.

They walked back to the Company's encampment. The barest drizzle began, but it was scarcely enough to mist her hair. It was already twilight, and under the awning of the Company tent five actors sat out with lanterns hung around them, staring at slates set on their laps.

Diana put out a hand and stopped Anatoly. She coughed. Hal looked up, saw them, and at once Quinn leapt up to her feet, collected the slates, and took them inside the tent. She came out with Joseph, and he had tea. He beckoned them over.

"Come in, come in," he called. "Don't stand out there in the rain."

Diana cringed. It looked so patently obvious that they were hiding something from Anatoly. She glanced at him, but he simply waited patiently for her to move forward. So she went, and they sat down. Anatoly sat on the carpet; she could not get him to sit in a chair. Joseph offered Anatoly tea first and then poured for the others, and they all tasted it politely and stared at each other: Hal, Quinn, Oriana, Hyacinth, and Phillippe. Joseph retreated back into the tent.

"Where were you?" Quinn asked finally in Rhuian.

"We had supper with the Sakhalin family," said Diana.

Anatoly smiled. There was silence. Hyacinth eyed Anatoly out of the corner of his eye, admiring him, but for once he was on his best behavior and he did not do one outrageous thing.

"Well," said Hal. He looked at Oriana, Oriana looked at Quinn, Quinn looked at Phillippe. Phillippe shrugged and looked at Hyacinth.

"That was a terrible fight," said Hyacinth. "Yesterday."

"*Fight?* Oh. Yes, it is terrible thing that soldiers attack the women and children. But khaja have no honor—" Anatoly broke off, looking chagrined. "I beg your pardon. I do not mean you."

"We know that," said Quinn. "But it was still awful. It was awful to see it. I suppose that's why you train to be a soldier, so you can be used to fighting and not mind it so much. You must have always known that you would be a rider, a soldier."

Anatoly digested this statement and then nodded. "Yes," he said calmly, "I have always known I would be a rider."

"But don't all the men ride?" asked Hal. "Aren't all the men soldiers?"

"All men can fight, yes. Not all are riders. Some man must be the smith. Some speak to the animals. A few are Singers, like you."

"Singers don't ride to war?" Oriana asked.

Anatoly looked perplexed. "What does she ask?" he asked Diana in khush. "I do not understand."

"She asked if Singers don't ride to war because they're Singers."

Now he looked confounded. "Singers do whatever they wish," he said, looking a bit suspicious, as if he thought he was being asked a trick question, "as long as it does not offend the gods' laws."

This brought another silence. "I'm tired," announced Diana, having endured enough gatherings for one evening. She stood up. Anatoly rose as well and bade polite farewells and they left and walked back through the drizzle to her tent.

"Are you really tired?" he asked once they were inside the shelter of the tent. "If it is not fitting that I sit and drink *tea* with the Singers, then I will wait here for you." He sat down and took off his boots and slid back onto the carpet, and watched her.

"Not at all! It's fitting that you sit and drink with them. With us. They just—don't know what to say to you, Anatoly." She knelt in front of him and ran her hands up the elaborate embroidery of his sleeves and hooked her hands behind his neck and rested her forehead against his.

He did not reply for a while. The soft hush of rain serenaded them. "I do not know what to say to them," he admitted. "I am embarrassed that I almost see such sacred objects that only the gods-touched may behold."

What was he talking about? Then she realized: he meant the slates, which Quinn had gathered and hidden away, so that he wouldn't discover that these khaja had magical tools—interdicted technology—in their possession. He didn't know what they were, only that he wasn't to see them; and he didn't even take offense at that. She sighed. He put his arms around her and tilted his head back and kissed her.

One thing led to another, as it so often does.

After all, they were still newly wed. Not quite seventy days, it had been, and of those days, thirty days entire at the beginning he had been gone, and of the rest, he might be gone for two nights or with her for ten, and during the day she only saw him in passing.

He *was* sweet. And she felt utterly safe with him.

She had to laugh a little, afterward, because he really

wasn't anything like she had imagined he would be. She nestled in against him and sighed again, content.

"Diana," he said, "I am glad you sit beside Shura at supper because it is good that you come to love her, but I am sorry that Grandmother does not sit you beside her with the honor that a Singer ought to have."

"I don't mind."

He got that determined look on his face that reminded her that he was, after all, a young prince from a powerful family. "It is not right. She does not yet wish to see that khaja may have Singers as well. The old ways are strong in her, but Tess Soerensen says to her envoys that we must bring new ways into the jaran as well."

"She does?"

"It is difficult," said Anatoly, "like giving a new rider to an old horse. They must each learn the other's gaits."

Diana chuckled and stretched out across him to rummage in her carry bag, searching for her journal. "I like that. And Shura said something to me today that I want to write down, too." She pulled out the journal and rolled back to her side, uncapping the pen, and made a note to ask Ginny about suggesting to a Singer that they make a jaran song out of some of Shakespeare's material.

Anatoly heaved himself up on one elbow and stared at her hand. "What are you doing?" he asked.

"You've seen my journal before."

"I have seen this *book*. But what are you doing?"

"I'm *writing*—" She faltered.

But, of course, Anatoly was illiterate.

"These marks are letters and each letter makes a sound and you put the letters together into words and the words into sentences and—" She trailed off. She was not at all sure that he understood what she was talking about.

"But why do you do this?" he asked.

"Well, to remember things."

"But how can these marks make you remember things? This *paper* could be burned or lost. In your mind, it is always there. It can't be lost."

"But what if you don't know?"

"Then there is another person, a Singer, a healer, an Elder, who will know."

"Well, there are other reasons." Diana did not feel capable of attempting to explain, not right now.

He looked doubtful, as if he weren't sure he believed there *were* other reasons. "Do all khaja do this, or only Singers?" Then he answered himself. "Tess Soerensen *writes*. I have seen her do it. And Bakhtiian has learned. Perhaps I should learn."

For some reason, that pleased her immensely. "If you want to, Anatoly, then I'll teach you."

"Well," he said, as if he couldn't make up his mind. Then he closed his eyes. How tired he must be, having fought in a battle and then stayed up all night and another day. She smoothed his hair back from his face and he smiled without opening his eyes and shifted to snuggle in against her. Inadvertently pressing against her right arm so that she couldn't write. Oh, well. It wasn't that important. She watched him drift off to sleep and she let her own mind find peace in a prayer of silence, as comforting as the warmth of Anatoly's body alongside hers.

And then she recalled that word they had used. She eased away from him and extricated her slate out from under the neatly folded clothes in her other carry bag. Glanced back at him, to make sure he was still asleep.

Yadoshtmi. Not battle. The only translation she could find was: "an annoying fly bite."

CHAPTER THIRTY-TWO

Tess ate little at supper and then excused herself abruptly and left for her own tent, not even wanting her husband's escort. Sonia watched Ilya stare after Tess, and she dismissed the rest of the family and took Ilya back into her private chamber. There he took off his boots, settled down on a pillow, and then proceeded to turn over and over again in his hands the book by the philosopher Bacon which she had taken to read.

She regarded him with amusement. This always happened to men when their wives were pregnant with the first child. "I am sorry, Ilya, to tell you that most women eat poorly, sleep a great deal, and grow irritable when they are first pregnant."

He glanced up at her. He did not want to admit that that was what he was worried about. "I am not an idiot, Sonia," he said, sounding as ill-tempered as if he himself were pregnant.

"No," she agreed. "But you're scared."

She expected him to snap at her for saying it, but instead, he set the book down. "It's true. What if the gods mean to take her from me?"

"Ilya! You must not speak so rashly about the gods. You are no more a Singer than I am, although we have both made long journeys and returned, to talk about what the gods mean to do."

"But the gods granted me a vision."

"That is true," she said with reluctance and with pride. "Perhaps I'm not sure what you ought to be called: not a Singer, and yet not simply a dyan either."

He sighed.

"Mama." It was Katerina. "Mother Sakhalin has come to visit. What shall I do with her?"

"Ah. Chase everyone else away and bring her into the

outer chamber. We will speak with her there. Come, Ilya.''

''Perhaps she wishes only to speak to you, Sonia.''

''If she wishes only to speak with me, then she will say so, Cousin. It is fitting that the dyan of this tribe sit with me to greet another etsana.''

She preceded him into the outer chamber and tidied it up a bit, throwing three pillows down in the center, on the best carpet, next to the little bronze oven chased with does. She surveyed the chamber with a critical eye and decided that it would do, for Mother Sakhalin's visit, to keep things spartan as a reflection of the knowledge that they all were traveling at an army's pace through khaja lands toward a goal of Ilya's making. Certainly the Or-zhekov tribe was by now as rich as the Sakhalin, but compared to the riches of a khaja city like Jeds, they were all of them poor. It was not by such a measure that one judged the jaran. Their wealth lay in greater things, in their horses and their herds, in the beauty of their weaving and the fine tempered steel of their sabers in the multitude of tents that made up each tribe and in the strong children that they bore. Mother Sun succored them, and Father Wind whispered to them, his favorite chil-dren, his secrets. Certainly the khaja had their own se-crets, but they wrote them down in books and then anyone who wished might learn them.

Ilya emerged from the back, having put his boots back on. He was supposed to be riding with the main army, out in front of the wagon train, but for the last three days—ever since Tess's announcement that she was preg-nant—he had stayed with the camp, sticking close by Tess.

''You will have to go back to the army, you know,'' Sonia said to him, and he had no chance to reply since at that moment Katya showed Mother Sakhalin in. Galina followed at her heels—just as she should—with a tray laden with tea and sweet cakes. Sonia watched as Katya settled the etsana onto a pillow and Galina offered her tea, all with the very best manners. Then Sonia sat and Ilya sat, and Galina poured them tea as well, and the two girls retreated to sit by the front curtain, heads bowed. That way they could serve, if need be, but they could also listen and learn about the responsibilities they would take up in time.

Mother Sakhalin began by asking about each Orzhekov child and grandchild. Then Sonia asked in her turn about each Sakhalin child and grandchild.

"I am not sure, however," said Mother Sakhalin finally, "if it is wise to keep Anatoly's jahar with the camp and not with the army."

"I thought it time," said Ilya quietly, "that Anatoly have a command of his own and not simply ride with my jahar. I judge him young enough and intelligent enough to understand what I am trying to do with my new jahar, with my envoys."

"Your envoys, who will go out and learn khaja ways," replied Mother Sakhalin. She frowned as she said it. "But, of course, Anatoly has a khaja wife."

Aha. Sonia could see that the sparks were about to fly.

"*I* have a khaja wife," said Ilya even more quietly.

"Your wife is not at issue here, Bakhtiian," replied Mother Sakhalin, defusing his anger with her tartness, "since we all know her worth. I fear that Anatoly married a woman who has nothing to recommend her but her looks."

"Mother Sakhalin," said Sonia mildly, "whatever else she may or may not have to recommend her, you must agree she acted bravely and saved jaran lives when the train was attacked by the khaja soldiers."

"Hmph." But since it was true, the etsana could not gainsay it. Sonia doubted if Elizaveta Sakhalin would ever accept Diana, but she could not tell if it was the fact that Diana was a khaja woman, that she was of no distinguished family, or simply that Anatoly had not consulted his grandmother in his marriage, that had so set her against the match. "Well," Mother Sakhalin finished, "it is pleasant enough for her, I am sure, to have his devotion now, but she will leave him because she cares nothing for our ways, not truly, and who will comfort him then?" She nodded decisively to show that she did not wish to discuss the matter any further.

Galina rose and lit another lantern and sat back down. The shadows shrank and re-formed into different patterns. From outside, Sonia heard Josef Raevsky telling, in his strong voice, the litany of clouds, and Ivan and some of the other young boys repeating it back to him so that they, too, would learn how to read from clouds and sky and wind and air the patterns of the weather. Mother Sakhalin ate a sweet cake as a prelude to what she intended to say next.

"My granddaughter Shura wishes to fight with the army," she said at last. "She says that if men can fight with the saber, then women ought to be able to fight with the bow."

"We do not use archery in battle," said Ilya. "Everyone knows it is dishonorable to fight from a distance when one ought to face one's enemy eye to eye."

"Dishonorable for men," said Mother Sakhalin, "but women may defend themselves with the bow if it becomes necessary."

"Are you suggesting, Mother Sakhalin," asked Sonia, "that women join the army and fight?" Both Katya and Galina glanced up, looking startled, and then recalled themselves and looked down again.

Mother Sakhalin ate another sweet cake. "I am simply repeating what my granddaughter said to me, and what other girls are saying, who fought in the skirmish three days ago."

"It is true," said Ilya slowly and cautiously, "that archery turned the tide of that battle."

"It is true," agreed Mother Sakhalin, "that our women know how to shoot, as they ought to. It is true that the khaja now fear jaran archers. But I am not sure that the gods will approve. If women leave the sanctity of the tribe, then why should the gods protect our tents?"

"But Mother Sakhalin," said Sonia, "the khaja will not respect the sanctity of our tents."

Mother Sakhalin's sharp eyes rested on Sonia's face for a moment and then flicked over to the two girls, and then to Ilya, "How do you know this?"

"They did not respect the women and children in the Farisa city. They killed the children, and the women, any they could find. Why should they treat jaran children differently?"

"That is true. Then I ask this: What if a girl rides to war before she is married, and she is killed and thus bears no children for her mother's tent? This has already happened. What if a woman with no sisters rides to war, and she is killed, and thus leaves her children with no tent at all? What if a woman rides to war and is captured by the khaja? Will they respect her as a woman ought to be respected, or will they treat her as they would a man?''

Sonia looked at Ilya, but he simply folded his hands in his lap and waited for her. Just like a man! Wait at the side for the women to argue over the difficult points. And yet, he was wise to do so. He knew, and she knew, and Mother Sakhalin knew, that adding archers to his army would only strengthen it. Better that he not push a course of action that benefited him so obviously. Better that he wait and let others make the decision that needed to be made.

''Out on the plains,'' said Sonia finally, ''the old ways protected us. They will protect us still, but to win this war we must learn new ways as well.''

''The old ways made us strong,'' retorted Mother Sakhalin. ''What if the new ways make us weak? What if our grandchildren's children forget the old ways? Then they will no longer be jaran.''

There was a hush, a sudden quiet in the tent, and Sonia felt all at once that the gods were about to speak. Only she did not know how, or where.

''There will always be jaran,'' said Ilya into the silence, his voice filled with an eerie resonance, a conviction, that seemed to emanate from both inside and outside of him at once. ''If we stay as we have been, then we will die, just as a pool dries up in the summer if there is no rain. We must change if we want to live. But we must also remain who we are and who the gods gifted us to be.''

Out of respect for his words, Mother Sakhalin allowed the silence to stretch out before she replied. ''What you ask is difficult, Bakhtiian.''

''*I* do not ask it,'' he said. ''I only tell you what the gods have given me to see.''

Mother Sakhalin snorted, and then she sipped some tea and ate two more sweet cakes. Galina rose and took the teapot and went outside to replenish it. Katya looked thoughtful, sitting with her back to the woven entrance flap where red and black wolves ran over a gold background, twined into each other just as the tribes were wrapped so tightly each around the next that, in the end, they were all of one piece and yet each different.

"I suppose," said the etsana, "that in the end you will have a jahar of archers. You may as well start now."

Ilya inclined his head, acquiescing to her judgment. She rose, made polite farewells, and let Katya show her out. Ilya watched the flame of one of the lanterns, studying it as if some answer lay within the twisting red lick of fire.

"She's right, though," said Sonia reflectively, into the silence. "We can't know how we will change, if it will be better for us, or worse. We can't know what the gods have chosen for us. We can't see what lies ahead, not truly."

He lifted a hand to her shoulder and rested it there, as a cousin might, to show his affection and his respect. "We have already changed, Sonia. It is too late to go back now."

"It is too late," she agreed. The wolves danced in the lantern light, racing toward an unseen prey.

CHAPTER THIRTY-THREE

Sieges were a dull, dirty, and thoroughly unpleasant business. Jiroannes had plenty of time to reflect on this truth as the days dragged on and the camp remained ensconced below the fortress of Qurat without the city showing any signs of surrender. But the food was better: the army foraged, took tribute, pillaged—whatever they wanted to call it—from the lands surrounding, and they were rich enough lands in midsummer to supply jaran needs. There was entertainment, too. He had gone to this *theater* that the foreigners had brought to the army four times now; each time the players had enacted something different. It reminded him of the Hinata dancers of his own land, who paced out in measures and with a drummed accompaniment stories and legends from the Age of Gods. He had even learned to listen to the jaran singers, with their sonorous, exotic melodies and endless tales set to music. With Mitya's tutoring, he could now understand some of the language.

"Your eminence?"

He sighed and set aside the tablet and stylus that lay idle on his lap. He simply did not have anything to write to his uncle that he had not already set down in his last letter twenty days past, when the train had arrived at Qurat. As tedious as the army's constant travel had been, sitting here in one place in these primitive conditions was worse. "Yes, Syrannus?"

"Eminence, if I might have your permission, I would like to send Samae out for water. Half of the guardsmen are down with the flux, and the others are engaged in various work. It would be convenient for me if Samae could go with Lal."

"Lal? Who is Lal?"

"The slave-boy with the scar under his right eye, eminence. Of course I will send a guard along to escort her.''

Jiroannes sighed again and stretched his legs out, resting the heels of his supple boots on the thick carpet. The pillow on the seat of his chair slid beneath him; he braced his elbows on the carved arms. ''Why are you bothering me with this?''

Syrannus hesitated, looking prim for a moment. ''The girl has never been outside of this camp, eminence.''

''Great heavens, Syrannus, I should hope we have allowed her the seclusion which befits her female nature. What woman would want such freedom?'' Then he stopped, because here in the jaran camp, however little they had to do with the jaran themselves on a daily basis, even he could see that the statement was ridiculous. He waved the problem away with his right hand. ''Whatever you think best, Syrannus. I suppose there is no other choice.''

''If you think it wise, eminence. I only suggest it because of necessity.''

''Do what you wish.'' Syrannus bowed and retreated. Because there was nothing else to do, Jiroannes picked up the tablet again. Then, with pleasure, he saw Mitya striding toward his tent. He rose with a smile to greet the boy. ''Well met,'' he said in khush. He bowed with just the right degree of condescension due a prince's cousin, and Mitya echoed the movement, with a grin. He was really quite a likable boy, for a barbarian.

''Here,'' said Mitya, ''do you want to come see the drills? There's a slope from which we can watch.''

Jiroannes had yet to see the jaran riders in action—he had never been near the scene of any of their battles—and in any case, he was bored. A guard saddled his gray gelding and he rode out with Mitya, with two guards as escort behind them. But it was not the jaran riders at all: not the men, at any rate. These were women riding complex drills and firing sheets of arrows at various targets. It was startling, but impressive.

A line of riders watched the maneuvers from a hillside above the flat field on which the archers and their mounts drilled. They greeted Mitya with enthusiasm, and Jiroannes with polite reserve, but shifted to make room for them.

One man, fair-haired and with his left arm in a sling, spoke to an unveiled old crone. By concentrating completely on their conversation, Jiroannes could follow much of it.

"Vera suggested we use prisoners as targets," said the man.

"What a very khaja thing to do," replied the old woman, showing so little respect for this young man's words that Jiroannes was shocked. "If they must die, then let them die quickly and bravely. But then, I have never thought much of the Veselov family, excepting your wife, of course. If we wish these riders to practice on live quarry, a *birbas* would be much more effective. I do not approve of killing prisoners and I have told Bakhtiian so. There is no glory in killing unarmed men,"

"I am in agreement with you there, Mother Sakhalin," replied the man. "But what are we to do with the khaja soldiers, then? If we leave them alive, they will strike at us again."

The old woman turned to glance at Jiroannes, as if finding fault with his presence here, as if *she* had some say in whether or not he could move around camp. But seeing her full in the face, he recognized her suddenly: the old woman who had been sitting next to Bakhtiian that night he had been brought before the jaran prince for the first, and only, time. As much as it galled him to do so out here in public, he inclined his head respectfully toward her, acknowledging her gaze on him. She sniffed audibly and arched a skeptical eyebrow, and turned back to the man at her side.

"We will speak of such things later, Kirill," she said. The group lapsed into silence again. A troop of riders arrived on the field and they began maneuvers as well, sometimes alone, sometimes coordinated with the women. Their dexterity and discipline were exemplary. Although Jiroannes hated to admit it, they rode in formation with more precision than the Great King's own elite cavalry guards. But perhaps young Mitya had more than one motive in bringing him here; perhaps Bakhtiian had encouraged it, to show the Vidiyan ambassador how very formidable his armies were.

But Mitya's motives seemed innocent enough. He cheerfully pointed out the captain of the unit, who was evidently the grandson of the old harridan, and gave a running commentary on the drill that Jiroannes understood perhaps half of. More people came to watch, on foot, an astonishing collection of sizes and coloring and shapes that Jiroannes immediately recognized as the acting troupe: the tall, black-skinned woman stood out anywhere, and the rest were as varied as the slaves owned by his uncle, who had a predilection for the exotic. Even after all these months with the jaran, he was still not used to seeing so many women with their faces naked. He watched the actors, distracted from the drilling below by the beautiful face of a golden-haired young woman. Were they slaves as well? Could he buy her? Or were they, like the Hinata dancers, dedicated to the god and thus sacrosanct?

"Here comes Sakhalin." Mitya sounded disgusted. "It's a little disgraceful, how he shows off that he has a khaja wife."

A young man rode up from below. He stopped to pay his respects to the crone first, but left her quickly and rode over to the actors. The beautiful one rose to greet him, with a smile on her face.

"Do you say," Jiroannes asked, "that these two are married?" He was astounded. But perhaps he had misunderstood the word. More and more, he saw that he understood very little about the jaran. That Bakhtiian had married the sister of the prince of Jeds—that was political expediency, and wise in a ruler. The Great King's third wife was a daughter of the Elenti king. But if this young man was a prince of the jaran, how could he be married to a common entertainer?

"Yes," agreed Mitya, "Mother Sakhalin was not pleased with the marriage, and Anatoly certainly did not consult her, as he should have. But she's very sweet. Diana, that is." He grinned slyly and glanced at the crone, who ignored the spectacle of her grandson publicly flirting with his wife. But soon enough the captain left to go back to his troop, and the actors left, and the crone left, and Jiroannes began to feel restless.

In the distance, a thin line of smoke rose from inside the high walls of Qurat. A sea of tents covered the ground all around the city, a billowing ocean. Beyond the tents, herds of horses grazed, and farther still, herds of other beasts, though these herds grew smaller every day as the forage gave out and they were slaughtered. A long line of khaja slaves trudged by, sacks of grain balanced across their shoulders.

"Oh," said Mitya suddenly, "I was to tell you that you may have an audience this afternoon with Bakhtiian, if you wish it."

If he wished it. Jiroannes flushed half with elation and half with annoyance. To the boy, an audience was evidently a trivial affair. "I am honored that Bakhtiian has deigned at last to hear my appeals for an audience. But if that is the case, then I must return and prepare."

"We can just ride over now, if you'd like," said the child naively.

"Certainly not! I beg your pardon, but I cannot appear like this." He gestured at his clothing—a plain sash, not of the highest quality, and his second-best trousers, and he wore no gold at all, except for his ambassador's ring.

Mitya shrugged. "Very well. I'll ride back with you."

They rode back across the huge expanse of the camp, which lay quiet under the midday sun. The fortress stood alone and isolated up at the edge of the hills. Jiroannes wondered how the city folk dared resist Bakhtiian, seeing how vast his army was and how no one had yet stood against him.

"Oh, look," said Mitya as they neared the ivory and emerald flags that marked the Vidiyan camp, "there's Aunt Sonia. What's she doing at your camp?"

Six jaran women waited at the edge of his camp. No, they did not *wait:* two stood, four sat, while they watched Samae. Samae! As bold as you please, the slave girl demonstrated a Tadesh dance for them. Her lithe movements, her elegant carriage, gave her an air of nobility and of utter self-possession. Her face bore a mask of concentration, but also an expression of peace. Mitya cast down his eyes to stare at his saddle. He was blushing furiously.

One of the jaran women looked back over her shoulder, hearing the horses. Samae, attuned to the slightest distraction, glanced up and saw Jiroannes. At once she broke off her dance. Her face shuttered, and she dropped to her knees, bowed her head, and clasped her hands subserviently across her chest. Her shoulders hunched, just slightly, bracing for a blow. Beyond, under the awning of Jiroannes's tent, Syrannus stood wringing his hands.

"Mitya!" One of the jaran women spoke. Her anger carried clearly in her tone, and she spun around, flashed an enraged glance up at Jiroannes, and gestured to the other women. "You will leave with us. Now."

"Yes, Aunt Sonia." So meekly, without even the courtesy of a good-bye, Mitya rode off with them. The boy's head was bowed, and he cast one anguished glance back over his shoulder at Samae, but she continued to stare at the ground.

How dare the woman speak to him like that? Jiroannes dismounted. A guard ran up to relieve him of the gelding. He walked across to Samae and slapped her. She rocked back, absorbing the blow, but did not otherwise respond.

"How dare you perform in public like that? Without my permission? And for a group of shameless women, at that, and out where anyone could see you?" She said nothing, of course.

"Eminence." It was Syrannus, still wringing his hands. He hurried out to Jiroannes. "I beg you—"

"Of course you warned me, Syrannus, but you should have had better sense than to even think of sending her out of camp, when you knew that something like this might happen. They will think I have no control whatsoever over my own slaves. How can they respect me?" Then, with a flash of irritation, he noticed that she still wore her coarse hair caught back in a braid. The black ends curled down over the collar of her tunic.

"Give me a knife," he said to Syrannus.

"Eminence!"

"A knife!" That even Syrannus should begin to question him was the outside of enough.

Syrannus quailed before his anger and ran to fetch him a knife. "But, eminence, surely the girl has not deserved any punishment—?"

Jiroannes grabbed the braid and pulled it out, tight. He held the knife against the base of the braid. And Samae jerked away from him.

He was so shocked by her rebellion that he did not at first react. She had resisted him. *She* had resisted *him*.

"Eminence," Syrannus hissed. "People are watch-

ing." For once, in the white heat of his anger, he remembered prudence. "You will come with me," he said
in a furious undertone. She obeyed submissively enough
now and followed him into his tent. She stood silent and
unmoving while he hacked off her hair, leaving it a ragged mess.

"Now," he said. "I need my emerald sash and my
best clothing. The brocaded boots." While she dressed
him, he called Syrannus in. "What else have we to bring
as gifts? Something small but delicate. The spinning
birds, perhaps? Yes." Thus fortified, he left Samae to
clean up the ruins of her hair and with Syrannus and four
guards as escort, made his way to the center of camp,
where Bakhtiian held audience.

Two soldiers stopped him outside the center ring of
tents, and he waited for what seemed ages. Even then,
allowed to proceed, he had to leave his own guards behind and go on alone, with only Syrannus as escort. The
ground lay clear before Bakhtiian's tent although a fair
number of people, many of them jaran, some of them
foreigners, stood along either side. An elderly man signed
to Jiroannes to approach, and he walked forward and
knelt about twenty steps out from the awning.

The prince sat on an overturned wagon, on a pillow,
with his chief wife beside him. The austerity of Bakhtiian's dress surprised Jiroannes, especially compared to
that of his attendants, both male and female, who wore
gold and riches in profusion and fine silk and brocaded
clothing. Bakhtiian wore what any common rider wore:
the red shirt, the black trousers and boots, with a plain-
hilted saber at his belt and a wooden staff bound together
with horse-tails across his knees. Deep in conversation
with the woman Jiroannes recognized as Mitya's "Aunt
Sonia," Bakhtiian ignored the ambassador. After a long
while, the elderly man tapped Jiroannes's leg and indicated to him that he should move to one side. So he was
not going to be recognized, but he was being allowed to
stay. After so long confined to his camp, Jiroannes felt
that this, at least, was a small victory. He settled cross-
legged on the ground to wait, uncomfortable without a
chair to sit on. Syrannus stood behind him, holding the
box with the mechanical birds.

A new foreigner was escorted in, a man in a gold sur-

coat with two unarmed soldiers in attendance as well as
an elderly woman in a plain dress. Bakhtiian looked up.
The man knelt before him.

"Bakhtiian." So the envoy addressed him, with no
other title than that, translated through the woman. "I
come from His Majesty, Aronal-sur, King of Habakar
and all its subject lands. His Majesty commands me to
tell you that he is merciful, and disposed to be kind in
this matter. He says this to you: Leave my kingdom and
my lands, and I will trouble you no further."

Bakhtiian said nothing. He simply sat, examining the
envoy without the least sign of fear. With contempt, perhaps. The envoy shifted restlessly under the fierce gaze,
looking nervous at first and then frightened.

"Indeed," said Bakhtiian at last, in such a low voice
that Jiroannes had to strain to hear him, "the king will
trouble us no further once he is dead. He made war on
us by his own actions. Does he not know that our gods
make easy what was difficult? That they make near, what
was far? I know what my power is, and soon he shall
regret that he angered me. Go. Do not come before me
again, unless it is to serve me."

Red in the face, the envoy retreated in disorder. A new
deputation was brought in, a trio of men dressed in similar robes. Habakar priests, they were, with a complaint:
evidently a Farisa wisewoman had come into Habakar
territories with the jaran army and was even now prose-
lytizing her religion among the peasants, especially the
women. Surely Bakhtiian would not let this outrage continue?

"I have brought this Farisa wisewoman here as well."
Bakhtiian beckoned forward a plain but intense woman
of indeterminate years. Then he sat back and, with the
barest glint of a smile on his face, he listened as the
priests and the wisewoman argued doctrine. Each side
appealed to him at intervals, they with righteousness, she
with rather more desperation, but he refused to intervene. His wife rose and left, escorted by Mitya's aunt.
When she returned a little while later, the debaters were
still going at it.

"Enough," said Bakhtiian after seeing that his wife
was settled in comfortably. "You will never agree, so I
will make a decision. You will not interfere with each

other just as I will not interfere with you unless you vi-
olate our laws. But I will say this.'' He leaned forward
and directed his stern gaze on the three priests. ''You
suggest to me that I have this woman whipped for her
presumption. For your presumption, I order you whipped.
If you ever suggest such a practice again, I will have you
killed. Take them off.''

They were led off. And if the Habakar priests looked
startled, the Farisa woman looked more startled still.

The elders of the city of Puranan came forward with
five chests of tribute. A party of envoys from another city
begged clemency for their citizens and offered to surrender. Three men—one no older than Mitya—were dragged
forward in chains. A sobbing woman trailed behind them.

''What is this?'' asked Bakhtiian.

''These khaja were caught stealing and killing two
glariss calves from the Vershinin tribe.''

''Why have you brought this to me? Of course they
must be executed.''

The woman dashed forward and threw herself prostrate
at Bakhtiian's feet. Sobbing, she spoke in bursts. The
plain-dressed woman translated. ''Bakhtiian, she says that
if you kill these three men, then she will have no more
family, because these are her husband, her son, and her
brother.''

''Indeed. Well, then, I do not wish to rob her of every
man in her tent. For her sake, one may be spared.''

The woman clasped her hands together, laying her
forehead on them, and spoke toward the ground.

''She says that she can find another husband, God willing, and that He may also provide her with more children, but for the brother there is no substitute.''

To Jiroannes's surprise, Bakhtiian laughed. ''It's quite
true, what she says. For her wisdom, I will spare all their
lives.'' The woman broke out sobbing all over again, and
the men cast themselves to the ground in gratitude.
''Gods,'' said Bakhtiian, looking uncomfortable, ''take
them away. And fine them for the calves. What is it,
Anatoly?''

Yes, it was he, the handsome young prince with the
golden-haired foreign beauty for a wife. But his aspect
was quite altered now from what Jiroannes had seen this
morning. He strode in looking grim, with a phalanx of

armed men walking behind him, escorting a dark-haired jaran man who went pale and flushed by turns. Behind them, escorted by two women, one foreign, one jaran, walked a very young foreign woman. The girl wore Habakar clothing, a shabby gown laced with coils of bronze sewn into an overskirt, and she was pretty, for her kind, if one ignored the terror on her face.

The one called Anatoly halted before Bakhtiian. He bowed his head. ''I am ashamed that I bring this matter before you, that one of my own men has brought this disgrace on our jahar. I ask that you punish me as you would him.'' Bakhtiian raised his eyebrows, looking curious, and nodded at Anatoly to continue. ''The woman accuses him of robbery, and of—'' he hesitated, clearly reluctant to say what came next. ''—of *forcing* her.''

Jiroannes could not help but smile. What could a woman expect? She was probably a whore trying to get revenge for not being paid. Surely she understood that a conquering army did not expect to pay for conquered women's services.

''Bring him forward.'' Bakhtiian spoke quietly, but the anger in his voice radiated like fire, scorching. The man came forward and dropped to his knees in front of the prince. ''What is your name?''

''Grigory Zhensky.''

''You have ridden with the army for—?''

''Four years, Bakhtiian. First with Yaroslav Sakhalin, and now with Anatoly Sakhalin.''

''What do you have to say for yourself?''

''Bakhtiian.'' The man threw his head back and looked up at his prince. ''I would never force a woman.'' He said it with distaste, and he looked anguished enough. Jiroannes was utterly confused. What were these men talking about, and apologizing for? ''She came to me two nights past, and asked if I wanted to lie with her. There's been nothing said—no orders have come down the line that we aren't to touch any khaja women—I thought since she came to me that—'' He faltered and lapsed into silence.

Bakhtiian sighed. He glanced at his wife. She shook her head. Then, as if to bewilder Jiroannes even more, *she* spoke. ''Bring the woman forward.'' The woman came forward and knelt in the dirt, shivering. ''What is

your name?'' Tess Soerensen asked, kindly enough.
"Can you tell me what happened?"

The woman spoke through the translator. "I am Qissa,
daughter of the merchant Oldrai. It is true that I came to
this man and offered him my—my favors, but he took
them and then refused to pay me. By the merchant's code,
which I learned at my father's knee, this is robbery, to
take goods without paying for them. And to cast me aside
then, that is—''

The girl spoke the word easily enough, but the translator faltered. "To force a woman. I do not know this
word in your tongue, Bakhtiian. I beg you will forgive
my ignorance."

"You are forgiven," said Bakhtiian's wife. "There is
no word in khush for forcing a woman against her will."
But the translator shook her head, not understanding her,
and Tess Soerensen sighed and returned her attention to
the Habakar girl. "You're a bold thing. Most women
would account themselves lucky to be alive. Why did you
bring this case forward?"

The girl clasped her hands so tightly in front of herself
that her knuckles faded to white. She looked very young,
younger than Mitya. She shuddered convulsively, but she
managed to speak. "I have young brothers and sisters.
My family lost everything, and now we have nothing to
feed them with. So I . . . we could think of no other
way—'' She faltered and suddenly, as if fear seized her,
she cast herself onto the ground and just lay there, awaiting her fate. The two young riders looked enormously
embarrassed; ashamed, even.

"Gods," said Bakhtiian. He cast a glance at his wife,
as if expecting her to untangle the situation.

She switched abruptly to Rhuian, and though her voice
was low, Jiroannes could still hear her. He leaned forward, listening avidly. "This is what you get, Ilya, when
you bring two cultures together. They will misunderstand
each other, and if you can't control it, then you will earn
chaos."

"Then what do you suggest I do? It is by right a woman's matter, and should be directed to Mother Sakhalin."

"Who, if she is wise, will throw it right back to you.
It is all very well to hold jaran to jaran laws, and to let

the khaja hold to khaja laws, but what will you hold them to when they mix? As they will.''

The principals waited, the two young men with resignation, the girl—well, who could know what she was thinking, with her face hidden in the dirt? And Jiroannes experienced a revelation: Bakhtiian was listening to his wife because he respected her opinion and might well act on it. Like an epiphany, or the climax of sex, it all poured out, all the little hints, the strange behavior, the things he had observed and ignored, all these months he had been with the jaran, and he saw now how thoroughly he had misunderstood them. They were worse than barbarians. As in the ancient tale where the Devil turned the world upside down, forcing people to wear their clothing inside-out, soldiers to till and farmers to fight, women to rule and men to serve them, they were an abomination.

''Where is the Vidiyan ambassador?'' Bakhtiian asked.

Syrannus had to nudge Jiroannes in the back before he reacted. Jolted out of his thoughts, he started up and stumbled over his own feet before recovering himself. Savages they might be, but his duty demanded that he deal wisely with them. And after all, Mitya was jaran. With dignity, he drew himself up and walked forward and, fastidiously, stepped around the prostrate girl to kneel on one knee before the prince.

''What should I do, ambassador?'' Bakhtiian asked. ''The man acted rightly, and yet the woman was wronged. The woman acted out of necessity, and with good faith for the exchange, and yet falsely accused the man.''

Jiroannes realized that his hands trembled. Thank the Everlasting God that the long dagged sleeves of his bloused tunic covered his hands to the knuckles.

Then a woman hissed between her teeth. She stood just behind Bakhtiian's wife, and it took a moment for Jiroannes to recognize her, all decked out in finery: it was indeed Mitya's Aunt Sonia. ''You ask this one to judge?'' she demanded of Bakhtiian. ''When he is the worst offender of all? He keeps a woman as a slave in our camp!''

Bakhtiian smiled, but Jiroannes did not find the expression reassuring. ''By his wisdom, so shall we know him. Ambassador, know this before you judge: by jaran custom, false accusation is akin to treason, and the punishment for a first offense is to be stripped of all rank and possessions and given into another family's camp, to act as their servant. As for the other—well—it is women's jurisdiction. Sonia, what would the punishment be for forcing a woman?''

Sonia smiled viciously. ''Death.''

Bakhtiian placed his hands on his staff, where they rested quietly, and he waited.

Jiroannes knew fear, stark fear, in that instant. A slave knew only his master's coercion, having no power of his own. The conclusion was obvious, read both by simple reasoning and by the triumphant and angry look on Sonia's face: under jaran custom, to lie with a woman slave was the same as raping her.

Here, kneeling alone before Bakhtiian, the power of the Great King seemed so distant as to be inconsequential. Jiroannes cast himself on both knees and bent his forehead down until it touched the dirt. No one struck him dead, so he lifted his head, although he did not raise his eyes.

''I would counsel mercy, great lord, by reason of their ignorance.''

Sonia hissed again, to show her displeasure.

''Bring the woman slave here to us,'' said Bakhtiian. ''As for these others. Zhensky, this time, I absolve you. I hope you have learned your lesson. Anatoly, you and your man will go to Mother Sakhalin, and you will accept whatever punishment she sees fit to burden you with, for your ill-advised conduct.''

They left. Jiroannes saw their boots pass him, but he did not dare look up to see their expressions, although he could not imagine they were anything but thrilled at their good fortune.

''As for the girl. By the gods, lift her up. It's indecent for a woman to grovel so. Here now, Qissa. Bring your father to me. We have need of merchants to serve us. What he has lost, we will restore to him and his family, so long as he remains loyal to us.'' The girl was led away by the two women who had brought her in. ''Gods, I'm thirsty,'' said Bakhtiian.

Jiroannes remained bent over in the dust, but he could smell the pungent aroma of fermented mare's milk, and of another, richer scent, something hot. The court waited. It was silent, except for the shuffling of feet, someone leaving, someone arriving, a messenger coming in with a dispatch which he recited in rapid khush to Bakhtiian. Jiroannes was too terrified to even attempt to understand it. He was going to die. He had flouted his uncle's direct order not to bring a woman in his party, and now he was going to die for it. Was the choice worth it, to have had a woman at his disposal all these months? By the Everlasting God, of course it was not. One year of continence was a small sacrifice compared to what he was going to pay now.

He was a fool, and a damned fool at that.

"Eminence," said Syrannus in an undertone, crouching beside him. "They have brought her. You must rise, eminence, or be thought a coward in your dying."

It was true. At least he would die like a man. He rose. It was a little hard to straighten his legs, because they were numb from kneeling for so long. Samae came forward, her face still. She hesitated, glancing first at Jiroannes and then at Bakhtiian, and then at Bakhtiian's wife, as if she did not know where to give her obeisance. When she moved at last, to Jiroannes's surprise, she moved to kneel in front of him.

"Furthermore," said Sonia clearly into the silence, "he sent the girl to Mitya, who all unknowing thought she had come to his tent by her own will." There was a gasp around the court, as if a heinous crime had just been compounded by something worse. "More than once," she added. "I just discovered that this afternoon. I don't blame the boy."

What method did they use to execute their prisoners? Was it slow? Quick? But hadn't the old crone said that prisoners ought to die quickly and bravely? The Great King's torturers were not so merciful. He had seen them at their work.

"Sonia," said Bakhtiian in a low voice, "because he is an envoy, I cannot kill him. By my own decree. But—" He forestalled her angry retort by raising a hand. "If I send him home a failure and request a new envoy from the Vidiyan King, surely that will be enough to ruin him."

Which it would. Disgraced, he would be condemned to the provinces and to a life of obscurity and poverty. Suddenly death did not seem so horrible an option.

"It will have to serve," said Sonia through tight lips, her voice hoarse. "What about the woman?"

"She will go free, of course. Syrannus."

The old man started, shocked to be addressed by name by the great prince. "Your eminence." He knelt.

"You may address me as Bakhtiian." He said it with a frown, as if the title of "eminence" annoyed him. "Tell the woman that she is free."

Syrannus looked at Jiroannes. "I am in no position to object!" muttered Jiroannes to the old man. Definitely, disgrace and dishonor was a worse fate than death.

Syrannus coughed. "Samae." He spoke in Vidyan. "The prince has granted you your freedom. You are free."

Samae said nothing. She remained kneeling at Jiroannes's feet, her hands folded in her lap.

There was a pause. No one moved.

Her stubbornness irritated Jiroannes. At least let this horrible episode end, which it could not until she left. "You are free," he snapped at her. "Do you understand?"

She shook her head. She did not otherwise move.

"Can't she talk?" demanded Sonia. "Is her tongue cut out, perhaps? I saw that done in Jeds. What are you asking her?"

"I have never heard her speak," said Jiroannes, angry that this woman doubted his honesty. "And she has a tongue. I know that well enough. I told her that she is free." Then, to emphasize it, he said the words again to Samae, in Vidyan, in Rhuian and, haltingly, in khush.

Samae shook her head. She did not move.

"She seems to be refusing her freedom," said Tess Soerensen.

"Gods!" exclaimed Sonia.

"I am tired," said Bakhtiian, "and I want to eat my supper. Go, all of you. Leave us in peace, if you please. Ambassador."

Reflexively, Jiroannes knelt, thus bringing himself onto a level with Samae. The effect was unsettling. He was aware all at once that his clothes were stained and mussed from kneeling and that dirt mottled his hands and cuffs. He felt the coarseness of dirt streaking his forehead. He stared at Samae's profile and at the ragged lines of her short hair. Her face was expressionless. No muscle on her even twitched, although Jiroannes would have said that it was impossible for any human to sit so still.

"Ambassador. You will in future refrain from sending this woman to my cousin, unless she chooses of her own will to go to him."

Jiroannes jerked his head up. "You are allowing me to stay?"

"A slave is one who has no power. She has the power to choose to refuse her freedom and stay with you. The gods know, I like it little enough, but it is her choice, not mine. So be it. But be aware that the women of this tribe will be watching you closely. They will not be so lenient again. Do you understand?"

"I understand. You are generous, Bakhtiian, more generous than the—"

"You may go."

Jiroannes left. But walking back to his camp, with Syrannus a step behind him to his left and the girl three steps behind him to his right, he felt, not elated, but burdened. Her presence evermore would be a reproach to him. Surely she could not have refused her freedom merely to afflict him with her constant attendance?

That evening he called Lal to help him undress. And though his blood was hot, stimulated by the fear and the tension of the day, he could not bring himself to summon Samae to his bed.

CHAPTER THIRTY-FOUR

The hills above Qurat had a torrid beauty dimmed and softened now in the cool light of dawn. Terraces angled down to the mudbrick walls of the city. Above the fields, parched trees and grasses grew along slopes alternately steep and gentle. Two riders negotiated a streambed dried out by the summer's heat and walked their horses at a sedate pace along a sere hillside. They rode alone, except for the three riders—one man, two women archers— riding about fifty paces behind them, and the ring of riders two hundred strong that circled them an arrow's shot away.

"It used to be," said Bakhtiian, reining his stallion around a dead log, "that I could take you out alone onto the grass and lie with you under the stars. Now—" He glanced to his left, where riders appeared and disappeared between distant trees, their red shirts a flag.

"When did we ever do that?" Tess asked. "Grass is an uncomfortable bed, if you ask me, and in any case, by the time we married, you were already well on your way to needing an escort whenever you left camp."

He smiled. "No, you're quite right. It wasn't you. I was much younger and more impulsive. It must have been Inessa Kireyevsky."

"*More* impulsive?"

He laughed.

"Kireyevsky," she mused. "I don't know that name."

"The Kireyevsky tribe is one of the granddaughters of the Vershinin tribe. Inessa was the only daughter of their etsana—"

"Of course. Was she married?"

"No."

"Did you think of marrying her?"

Kriye pranced as Zhashi came up beside him, and Ilya

reined him in. Zhashi flattened her ears, and for an instant Tess thought the mare might kick; instead, Zhashi ostentatiously lowered her head to graze. Ilya chuckled.

"Any man thinks of marrying, when he's young. But I hadn't been back from Jeds for that many years, and I had so much I wanted to do. I didn't have time to marry."

Tess studied him. Four years ago, she had been thrown together with him and his tribe. Four years ago, her life had changed utterly, and she did not regret what she had left behind. Not when he smiled at her as he did now. It was not that the essential core of restlessness, of ambition, in him was stilled by her presence: that had not changed in the least. But before their marriage a discontent, an uncertain temper, had worried at him constantly, wearing him away. That was gone now. Not muted, not faded, but quite simply gone. It had vanished the day he had marked her, and she had marked him. And to know that one had that effect on a person, especially on a personality as powerful as Ilya's—well, it would have taken a stronger person than she was to resist the urge to stay.

He was in a mellow mood. She took in a deep breath. It was time to test the waters. "Vasil still rode with your jahar, back then," she added.

His smile evaporated. "Vasil never learned how to let go of what was no longer his."

Encouraging, but not an answer. "How long have you known Vasil?"

His whole expression shuttered. "I do not wish—"

"To speak of him. I know." *And neither do I, but the truth has to be faced, by me, and by you.* "You're very like Charles in some ways, keeping things to yourself, never sharing them with others. Ilya, if you don't wish to speak of Vasil with me, then that is your right, but I think you ought to speak to someone about him. It's eating away at you inside. Dr. Hierakis—"

"Dr. Hierakis? I think not."

"Niko. No. I can see from your expression that he was too close to whatever happened. Do you know Vasil named his daughter after you?"

"Yes," he said. For a jaran man, he certainly knew how to construct formidable walls.

Tess sighed, having used up her stores of courage for

the day. She started Zhashi forward again. "What shall
we name this one?" Her fingers brushed her abdomen,
which had barely begun to swell.

His face relaxed, now that he saw she was willing to
let the subject drop. "If it's a girl, Natalia, after my
sister."

"Then Yurinya, if it's a boy."

"Agreed." His voice dropped. "Oh, Tess. I was afraid
we would never have a child. I have always wanted to
have children of my own."

Tess chuckled. "After lying with Inessa Kireyevsky
out in the grass, and God knows what other women, you
might well have some children."

He shook his head, looking puzzled, and reined Kriye
back as they came up to a stand of red-barked trees
crowned with a sprinkling of thin leaves. "How could I
have children, Tess? I wasn't married."

"But Ilya, you know very well that you *could* have
gotten a child on some woman."

"Yes, and in Jeds that child would be called a bastard.
But here, the man she was married to would be its father,
not me. And that is as it should be."

From here, Tess could see far below, in miniature, the
golden domes and minarets of Qurat, and the square citadel in the northwest corner of the city. "How much
longer do we wait here?"

He studied the terrain. Although they overlooked the
city here, they were much too far away to do any damage
even with missile fire. Beyond the city lay the plateau
and the huge camp of the jaran army, scattered out to the
horizon. A thin line of river shone in the farthest distance; above it, clouds laced the sky. Closer, to the west,
a narrow valley shot up into the mountains: the pass that
led into the heart of the Habakar kingdom.

"I had hoped to draw them out. With the strength of
the Habakar army still in front of us, I don't want to leave
this city behind untaken, not at such a strategic site. But
we have now taken control of every city on this plateau
but Qurat, and we must move forward." He shrugged.
"We shall see."

"Look there. A rider is coming up."

He sighed and reached out to grasp her hand and,
drawing it up to his lips, to kiss her palm. Then he let

her go. "It seems we have had our quiet for the day. Come, we'll go meet him."

The rider wore bells, and he was mounted on a fresh horse from the camp below. Aleksi and the two archers—Valye Usova and Anatoly's sister Shura—joined them, and the circle of riders closed in to form into ranks around Bakhtiian. They parted to let the messenger through.

"Bakhtiian! The Habakar king is marching with a large army through the western pass toward our position."

"Ah. So I did draw someone out. Good. How long?"

"One day. Two, perhaps. They're slow, on the march."

Ilya nodded. His expression closed up, becoming remote from Tess, from his companions, from everything except the matter at hand. "A council," he said to the messenger. "You ride to the Sakhalin camp. Aleksi, get me Vershinin and Grekov. All the dyans to my camp." The sun crept up ever higher in the sky, and Tess could see that it would be another hot day.

Another dawn. Two riders sat side by side on a slope overlooking a river and beyond it the far distant walls of Qurat and the hills and mountains behind. Where once had lain the camp of the jaran, filling the flat ground between as water fills a lakebed, now two armies moved, restless, falling into position. To the west, where the pass opened out onto Qurat's plateau, the last of a stream of wagons, the Habakar supply line, trundled in toward the city, which had opened its gates now that the jaran had given up the ground before its walls. To the northeast, on the other side of the shallow river from the armies, huge squares of wagons had formed, making a mobile fortress of the jaran camp. Behind the two riders, along the ridgetop, a thousand horsemen waited, watching.

"Anatoly is furious," said Tess. "He wanted to ride in the battle, not watch it from up here as part of my escort."

Aleksi glanced up at the line of riders a stone's throw above them. Because Anatoly's jahar was lightly armored, red was still the dominant color of the line, diluted with the dull gleam of armor and accented by red ribbons tied to their lances. Scattered within the red line, the archers wore many different colors. "Anatoly is a fine commander, but he has yet to learn that battle is not the only way for a man to gain honor."

"Aleksi, you can't be any older than Anatoly. How have you gained this knowledge?"

She grinned at him, but Aleksi pondered the question, frowning. He patted his fine gray mare on the withers. Bakhtiian had given him the horse when Tess had adopted him as her brother. The irony still amused Aleksi, in a black kind of way. Tess had quite literally saved him from death; she had stopped the Mirsky brothers from killing him for the crime of stealing a horse from their tribe, a crime which it was quite true he had committed and deserved to die for. And in return, he, who deserved nothing, had gotten everything: a sister, a tent, a family, and a tribe. And this fine gray khuhaylan mare, who was a finer horse than anything the Mirsky tribe had ever owned. Certainly she was a far finer animal than the broken-down old tarpan he had stolen after Vyacheslav Mirsky had finally died. He would never have stolen a horse, but he needed to leave the tribe quickly, before they took away from him—the damned orphan the old man had taken in—the few but precious gifts Vyacheslav had given him.

"Tess," he said finally, seriously, "though no one ever disputed how good I was with the saber, did that bring me honor? No, because I was an orphan. Even at Bakhalo's school, though I won every contest, still, I had no standing. It seems to me that fighting in a battle can only bring a man honor if he already has honor from his family."

Tess watched him, looking thoughtful. It was one of the things Aleksi loved about her. He had never been part of any tribe, not since he was very young, a little older than Kolia, perhaps, and his whole tribe had been killed by khaja raiders. The gods might as well have swept a plague over them, it was so sudden and so complete. All had gone, all but him and his older sister Anastasia. After that, the two of them had struggled along, always on the outside, sometimes tolerated, sometimes driven away, but Aleksi had learned to watch and guess and analyze, and in the end he had discovered that he did not see the world the same as other jaran did. But Tess never thought he was strange for that. Because Tess did not see the world the same, either.

"But Anatoly," said Tess, "has a burden to bear as well, being the eldest grandchild of Mother Sakhalin. He wishes to prove himself worthy of his place."

"It makes sense, in a way, that he married the khaja woman. That sets him apart, like it does Bakhtiian."

"Anatoly should have married a khaja princess then. He married to please himself. Certainly not to please his grandmother, who wanted him to marry Galina."

"Galina!"

"She's young, but in another two or three years . . . it would have been a good match, marrying him into Bakhtiian's family."

"It's true," said Aleksi, "that although Sakhalin is the eldest tribe, and first among all the tribes, Bakhtiian stands highest now."

"I wonder which of the daughter tribes your tribe descended from, Aleksi."

He did not want to think about it, but he managed a calm reply, to please Tess. "I don't know. I don't remember much of anything really, except that I had an aunt named Marina."

"And a sister, Anastasia." She said it softly.

Too horrible. It was too horrible to think of her. "Look," he said, pointing. "They're moving."

A moment later he realized his mistake. The color drained from Tess's face, and she clenched her left hand into a fist. Her lips pressed together. A single tear slid down her face. She had been talking to keep from thinking about what was going on below. Now he had hurt her.

"Why the hell," she said in a fierce undertone, "did he have to take the center for himself? Couldn't Sakhalin have commanded the center?"

"Tess. Look out there." Surely even in the face of her fear, Tess understood the demands of honor. "That is the Habakar king. Bakhtiian *had* to take the field personally."

The ground sloped down from the hooves of their horses to the river, and across the river the jaran army massed opposite the Habakar legions. Banners sprouted up here and there, marking units. To the rear of the Habakar center a veritable forest of pennons and flags marked the king's own guard, who all wore gold surcoats and who were mounted on gray horses harnessed with gold. Opposite the Habakar center massed the jaran center, which was distinguished only by a plain gold banner out slightly in advance of the front ranks.

"Gods," said Aleksi, "surely Bakhtiian isn't going to lead the charge?" Seeing Tess's anguished face, he lapsed into silence. There was nothing they could do from this distance, not now. But the gold banner simply rode along the jaran lines, surveying them and surveying the enemy, and came back again, and the center parted to let it through to the rear.

Drums beat. Like the sudden strike of a snake, the two flanking units of the jaran army sprang into action. They swept obliquely, swinging wide to hit the ends of the Habakar line with the middle of their units. The center moved forward to engage their Habakar opposites, and the jaran reserve, marked by Bakhtiian's golden banner, moved forward with them, but stayed behind the back ranks.

"I feel sick," said Tess.

On the left flank, Sakhalin hit hard. Immediately the Habakar line began to give way, shrinking back as Sakhalin's riders curled around the end. Stragglers trailed off from the back of the enemy line. But Vershinin was not so lucky. The Habakar flank shifted to receive his attack, and the engagement deteriorated into chaos. Sheets of arrows blurred the scene at intervals, like a cloud's shadow.

"They're all on foot in the middle ranks of the khaja army," said Aleksi, trying anything to keep Tess from making herself ill with dread. "What's that called?"

"Infantry."

"Yes. By their colors it looks like there are two units of them, green and blue, with the king and his mounted guard behind. Why aren't they reacting? Sakhalin is pressing, but I don't know if Vershinin can hold. What does Bakhtiian mean to do?"

All was confusion in the center, with the jaran lines and the Habakar lines intermingling. A pall like smoke hung over the battlefield, waxing and waning: dust thrown into the air.

"Look!" exclaimed Aleksi. "Look how their line is drifting." The Habakar green unit shifted, slowly at first and then with speed, drawing away from the center to drive against Vershinin's exposed flank. A gap grew, and grew, between the center units. Flags and pennons waved and bobbed to the beat of a resounding drum as the king's guard moved forward to fill the gap.

Bakhtiian's gold banner shifted. The jaran reserve moved. Like lightning, it struck forward, the gold banner first through the gap between the blue and green units. Bakhtiian's riders hit the king's guards, driving them backward. Other groups split off to attack the drifting infantry unit, leaving the blue infantry unit stranded and, soon enough, surrounded.

Chaos on the field. It was all Aleksi could make out, from this distance. The gold banner thrust in among the pennons and flags of the guard. Where the king was, where Bakhtiian was—it was impossible to tell.

"Oh, gods," said Tess, and then said it again, and then lapsed into silence. She went pale with fear. Tears leaked from her eyes, but she cried without sound. Zhashi, sensing her mood, remained quiet under her.

But the king's guard disintegrated under the force of Bakhtiian's attack. In a straggling line they fled backward, deserting their infantry units, racing for the city and for the hills.

The gold banner streamed out onto the deserted field and then stopped and, with deathly precision, the reserve re-formed into ranks and turned and hit from behind the Habakar line engaged with Vershinin.

After that, it was slaughter. Qurat closed its gates. A steady line of Habakar soldiers retreated toward the pass. Like a fainter echo, an uneven stream of jaran casualties forded the river, heading in to camp.

"Tess." Aleksi unhooked his water flask from his saddle and opened it. "You must drink something. It's almost midday. And eat. Here."

"I'm not hungry." Her voice was hoarse. She started, dragging her gaze away from the field. After a moment she accepted the flask and drank. Then, because he continued to hold out a strip of dried meat, she sighed and took the meat from him and chewed on it unenthusiastically.

The gold banner broke away from the battle and headed toward the river. Now Aleksi could distinguish individuals. Three riders separated from the unit and splashed across the river to head up toward Tess. Tess wiped at her face furiously, eliminating the telltale marks of tears.

Bakhtiian had not one mark on him, though he had been in the thick of the battle. Vladimir, at his right, had four arrows sticking out at angles from his cuirass but a broad grin on his face. In his left hand he held the banner pole, its end braced into a wooden cup tied to his saddle. The gold cloth stirred in the breeze. Another orphan, Vladimir was, who had found a home in the Orzhekov tribe: He was Bakhtiian's chosen banner bearer, and he was married to a woman of the tribes. No wonder he was happy.

Konstans Barshai had his helmet off, and a wicked-looking cut scored across his left eye and forehead and up onto his scalp, but the blood splashed down his face and on his armor did not seem to bother him, and his seat was steady. Anatoly Sakhalin rode down to greet them. He looked tense and angry.

"Well met," said Bakhtiian. His gaze had, first and most tellingly, focused in on his wife, but now he scanned the line of riders above and glanced back toward the field below. "A well chosen vantage point."

Anatoly did not reply for a minute. His face was flushed, and his lips set. "I wished to fight in the battle," he blurted out. "I would have done well."

Bakhtiian turned his attention to the younger man. His even gaze caused Anatoly to flush even more. "Is this not honor enough for you, Sakhalin, watching over what I hold most dear? Did I single out any other commander for this post? To serve my wife, who will forge the links that will allow us to hold together what we are winning now? Not every battle can be won out there." He waved toward the field, and the army mopping up, and swung back to glare at Anatoly. "Your uncle Boris is dead. Killed on the field."

Anatoly paled, and then color rushed back into his cheeks.

"But in time, if *this* jahar serves its purpose, we can use words to win our wars, not our own relatives."

"I beg your pardon, Bakhtiian," said Anatoly in a low voice. "I spoke rashly. I didn't think."

"You are young," said Bakhtiian, more gently. "Very well. I have no need of envoys right now. Yaroslav Sakhalin is forming up his army now to start over the pass. Anatoly, you will take your jahar and go with him. But I charge to you this duty: that you will be responsible for bringing back to me the head and coat and crown of the Habakar king. After that, I will expect you to serve my wife with a more level head."

Anatoly flushed a bright red, and Aleksi could not tell whether it was chagrin or excitement that most colored him. "Thank you! You honor me!" He paused and glanced toward the jaran camp, busy with the wounded. "May I say good-bye to my wife?"

Bakhtiian arched an eyebrow. "There is no time. I want the king. Go."

Without further hesitation, Anatoly nodded his assent and went back up to the ridgetop to order his jahar forward.

"Aleksi," said Bakhtiian, watching this movement with an expression of pained amusement, "I don't mean to slight you as well. Would you like to go with them?"

"I am content where I am, Bakhtiian."

"Ah." Bakhtiian turned his black and they started down toward camp, Tess between Bakhtiian and Aleksi, and the two young riders trailing behind, a discreet escort. "Tess, you haven't said one word to me. Are you well?"

"You didn't have to lead that charge," she said in a low voice. Aleksi could hear how drawn her voice was, taut and strained.

"But I did," he said, equally softly. "That man killed my envoys and blinded Josef."

Her silence was eloquent.

"Now do you see?" he asked, softer still. "Do you see why I was so reluctant to let you join Yaroslav Sakhalin's jahar? Do you think I doubted your ability to fight? Never that, Tess. I doubted my own ability to stand the sight of you in such danger."

"I never saw you actually ride into battle like this. Not until now. Gods." She lapsed into silence again, but she sounded mollified.

"In truth, it makes little sense for me to lead the army from the front ranks, or to risk myself in such an impulsive charge." He grinned. "I won't do it again, my love."

She chuckled. Weakly, it was true, but it was a laugh nonetheless. "Unless you have to."

"Unless I have to."

They rode into camp and immediately Bakhtiian was besieged. He excused himself and rode off with a trio of men: one of the Vershinin cousins, the Raevsky dyan, and Anton Veselov.

"Now what do I do?" Tess asked of Aleksi. "They have no need of me with the wounded. Mother Sakhalin runs the camp, and Sonia our tents. I don't have enough experience for any council of war. What use am I?"

Aleksi could hear how upset she was, as if she had turned her fear into disgust at herself. "If this was your brother's army, what would you be doing?"

Tess glanced at him, startled. She had not been expecting him to reply. Then she laughed. "You're right, of course. Let's see if there are any Habakar prisoners. I've got a start on their language, and I need to develop my understanding of their legal system as well. Let me see. Aleksi, go to—who is handling prisoners?"

"Raevsky."

"Well, that seems appropriate. We'll go sort out a few and take them to my tent. Josef and I can work on this together."

"You must not forget to eat, Tess."

"With you here, and Sonia? I won't."

On through the afternoon Tess and Josef sat side by side on pillows, under the awning of her tent. Five Habakar prisoners—two noblemen, three priests—knelt out in the sun in front of them, and ten archers and ten riders stood at guard around them. Tess was writing something down in her book when Dr. Hierakis hurried into camp and stopped ten paces away to survey Tess with a skeptical eye. The doctor strode over to Aleksi.

"Has she rested?" she demanded of Aleksi. "Eaten? Has she gotten enough to drink?"

Aleksi nodded. "Sonia and the children have brought us everything we need."

Tess turned. "Cara." She switched to Rhuian. "I've

made up my mind about the—'' She said a word Aleksi
did not recognize. "I want you to prepare the—'' She
stopped, glanced at Aleksi, and went on in her other
language, the one she called Anglais. Aleksi went very
still, and he concentrated. He was quick with language,
quicker than anyone suspected, even Tess, and he had
learned long ago that in order to survive he had to be one
step ahead of everyone else. Something about Ilya, and
a drink; something about growing old, or not growing
old—that was confusing; the doctor objected, Tess insisted, and between them they reached an agreement.
The doctor looked—not reluctant, but as though she had
to make a show of being reluctant. Tess did not look
triumphant that she had won out over the doctor's objections; she looked stubborn and defensive.

The doctor excused herself and left. Tess turned back
to her discussion of the general outlines of Habakar legal
doctrine. Josef, who wore his empty eye sockets as if
they were a badge of pride, brushed Tess's sleeve with a
hand, verifying her presence, and she edged closer to
him. Kolia brought them milk. The little boy stared hard
at the foreigners baking out under the heat of the sun, at
their outlandish clothing and their olive-dark complex-
ions and the sharp line of their black beards. It was a
drowsy heat, stifling and dry. Aleksi listened to the voices
of the priests droning on, punctuated here and there by
a question from Tess or Josef, or a monosyllabic reply
from one of the terrified noblemen. Eventually he dozed.

He started awake when Bakhtiian arrived.

"Send them away." Bakhtiian gestured toward the Habakar prisoners. "I'm hungry." He vanished into the
tent, reappeared a moment later with a pillow, and threw
it on the ground beside Josef. Then he sank down beside
the blind man and took one of Josef's hands in his own.
Rapidly and in a low voice, he began to tell him in detail
about the battle.

Tess rose and went to help Sonia and the children with
the food. It was getting dark. Aleksi got up and lit the
lanterns, hanging them around the tent poles so that they
gave off a soft glow of light that penetrated out beyond
the awning. Venedikt Grekov and his nephew Feodor
came by with an intelligence report about the pass and
the flight of the Habakar king. Sakhalin's jahar was hard

on the king's heels and they had overtaken so many khaja
soldiers that they had simply killed them rather than be
burdened with prisoners. With Grekov also came his
niece, Raysia. She offered to stay and sing for them.

Dr. Hierakis came back in time to eat with them, and
she brought with her the stocky khaja woman Ursula,
who was flush with accounts of the battle. Other members of the Orzhekov tribe came, Vladimir and Konstans
and other riders—some with their wives and children,
those who had them along—and Niko Sibirin and Juli
Danov and their grandchildren. Everyone was in a fine
humor, as well they might be.

Raysia sang. Between each song she looked long and
hard at Aleksi before beginning her next piece. He was
gratified by her attention, but worried by it, too. What if
Raysia Grekov told her mother that she wanted Aleksi to
marry her? A Singer did not have to concern herself with
pleasing anyone but herself. The gods had touched her,
everyone knew that, and with the gods' touch came not
only great responsibilities and burdens but great freedom
as well. Raysia was also an outsider, in a way. At the age
of twelve her spirit had been borne away by the gods to
visit their realms, and her body had lain for days, empty,
in her mother's tent. When she returned, she was a
Singer, her sight altered forever. She was shunned and
feared by some, but respected by everyone, and she had
the gift to see what was hidden from others. Aleksi
sometimes wondered if he had been touched by the gods
in that way, but the curse he had brought down first on
his tribe and then on his beloved sister Anastasia was
surely a punishment for his presumption. If Raysia Grekov wanted him, how could he refuse her, though it was
properly a man's choice in marriage? He did not want to
leave Tess, even to go to live with Raysia. He had lost
Anastasia already, those many years ago. He did not intend to lose his new sister, Tess. It would be better not
to marry, or perhaps to marry another orphan, one Tess
and Bakhtiian and Sonia were willing to admit into the
family. Valye Usova was a nice girl . . . but she would
bring her brother Yevgeni with her, a brother whose loyalty was still suspect, since he had ridden with Vasil Veselov for so many years.

It was too painful to contemplate. Aleksi shut off these

thoughts and tried to concentrate on the singing, but his heart was not in listening this night. Next to him, Tess shifted restlessly. She kept glancing over at Dr. Hierakis with a questioning gaze, and the doctor nodded each time, assuring her of something, Aleksi was not sure what. Bakhtiian listened keenly to the music, drank sparingly from the cup refilled by his wife, and spoke closely to Josef in the intervals between songs.

That night, after Aleksi had gone to bed, Raysia came to his tent and he let her in. Gods, but she was sweet. And yet, lying awake after she had gone, he knew that he could not leave Tess, and not just for his own sake.

In the morning a deputation emerged from Qurat to seek terms, but Bakhtiian refused to see them. Instead, he left Josef behind with the rearguard and the Veselov and Raevsky tribes, and told Josef to leave the Qurat envoys waiting for a few days and then strip the wealth from the city in return for its complete and utter submission to jaran rule. They broke camp and started up into the pass. Bakhtiian rode at the head of the army, next to his wife. He looked pale. At midday he called a halt and sat, just sat for a time, rubbing at his forehead with his hands. They camped along the road that night and set out again in the morning. This day Bakhtiian was clearly ill. Dark circles rimmed his eyes, and his skin had a mottled, pasty color. Once, and only once, Tess suggested he ride in a wagon. But he did switch mounts at midday, choosing a placid little bay mare for the rest of the day's ride instead of his restive stallion.

Late that afternoon they reached the summit, a broad, windy height. From here, Aleksi saw the hazy outlines of land far below, fields, a miniature city, and the endless spread of land out to the blue horizon. Up here it was clear and hot, and the wind buffeted Aleksi where he stood on an outcropping staring down, far down, to the Habakar lands. Smoke rose in patches scattered across the countryside. Evidently Sakhalin's army had already arrived.

He walked back to the front rank of wagons to find Sonia ordering that Tess's great tent be set up, although the rest of the army was on marching orders and sleeping under wagons or out in the open for the night. The cloth walls shook and rippled, torn by the heavy wind, and

Aleksi ran over to help. It took fifteen people to battle
the tent into place and secure it, and even then the wind
boomed and tore at the walls. They could not set up the
awning at all. The gold banner, raised on the center pole,
snapped loudly in the gale.

Bakhtiian watched the proceedings from horseback. He
was white and his hands shook, but he did not dismount
until Tess came to lead him inside. Her face, too, was
white, but with an agony of the heart not of the physical
body. They disappeared inside the tent. Dr. Hierakis
strode up soon after and went inside. Sonia followed her
in and emerged moments later.

"Aleksi! Set up your tent just beside here, and don't
leave camp."

"What's wrong with him?" Aleksi asked in a low
voice, aware of people milling around, asking questions.

Sonia shrugged. "Vladimir says one of the Habakar
priests cursed him. Perhaps it's witchcraft."

"Perhaps," said Aleksi. But what if it wasn't Habakar
witchcraft? He had seen Dr. Hierakis at work, had seen
that she knew how to heal wounds that even the finest
jaran healers would have given up on. Everyone got sick,
at times. Plagues might race through a tribe, and during
the siege of Qurat, many of the jaran had gotten fevers.
Children had died, as well as some of the men weakened
by wounds. Why should Tess look so anguished? Bakhtiian was strong. There was no reason to think a simple
fever would kill him. Unless this was not a simple fever.

Aleksi unsaddled his mare and hobbled her for the
night, and set up his tent alongside Tess's. At dusk, the
wind died down. Fires were built, but with night came
the strong winds again, ripping at the camp, at the tents,
at the fires. Most people hunkered down to wait it out.
Dr. Hierakis emerged out of the tent, alone.

Aleksi lit a lantern, shielding the flame with his body
until it steadied and then sliding the glass back into place,
and he offered to escort her back to her wagons.

She shook her head. "You stay here. Galina is waiting—there she is."

"Bakhtiian?"

"He's ill. But he seems stable. I think he'll have a few
rough days before he feels better."

"Is it the river fever?"

She glanced at him, measuring, curious. "No, I don't think it's the river fever."

"Ah," said Aleksi. "Neither did I."

The light spread a glow across her front, illuminating her face and the strong line of her jaw. Her black hair faded into darkness, and her plain tunic was washed gray. "You're a strange one. Sometimes I think you see more than we know you do."

"You speak khush very well now. You learned it quickly. The actors did, too. Have you noticed how many of their—what do they call them? Songs?"

"Plays."

"—*plays* that they've begun to say in khush?"

"No, I hadn't. I haven't seen any of their performances. Good night, Aleksi."

"Good night, Doctor."

She gave him a brusque but sympathetic nod and went off with Galina. Aleksi wondered how old she was. She did not look any older than, say, Bakhtiian, but she carried herself like an Elder. She carried herself like Mother Sakhalin or Niko Sibirin, and the Elders treated her like one of their own. Perhaps she, too, was a Singer, a gods-touched mortal, granted knowledge beyond her years. That might explain the Elders' respect for her, and her own strange way of carrying on, of looking at things from afar, of measuring and watching. Like he did.

He went to bed. As he dozed off, a voice whispered at the front of his tent. He inched forward to twitch the tent flap aside. It was Raysia. Though he could only make out the outline of her form, silhouetted against the incandescent stars, he could feel it was her, knew it by the shape of her hair and the soft, clean scent she bore with her. She slipped inside. The walls of his tent shuddered in the unceasing wind, but otherwise it was silent. He fell asleep afterward with her draped half over him.

Only to start awake, hearing his name.

"Aleksi!"

Tess, calling to him. She was not screaming, not yet, but panic swelled her voice. He eased away from Raysia, and she woke, mumbling a question.

"Stay here," he said, struggling to get dressed. He cursed himself for not sleeping with his clothes on.

"Aleksi! Oh, God."

He grabbed his boots in his left hand and his saber in his right and crawled out of his tent and ran to hers. Tess was not in the outer chamber. A single lantern lit the inner chamber, and he found her there, rocking back and forth on her heels, staring, rocking, gasping for breath.

"Aleksi! Oh, thank the gods. Get Cara. Please." Her voice broke.

Bakhtiian lay asleep on pillows, a fur pulled up over his naked chest. His face was slack, and his mouth half open. He looked rather undignified, sprawled out like that. Aleksi paused to pull on his boots.

"I can't wake him up." She choked out the words. Then she began to sob. "Oh, God, why did I do it? Why did I insist?"

"But, Tess—" Her complete disintegration shocked him horribly. "Here, let me try." He bent over her, daring much, and shook Bakhtiian gently. No response. Then, suddenly, losing patience and hating the terrible shattering condition Tess had fallen into, he slapped him. Bakhtiian's head absorbed the blow, moving loosely, but he did not stir in the slightest. And Aleksi understood: Bakhtiian's spirit had left his body. He had seen it happen once before, with his own sister Anastasia, some four winters after their tribe had been obliterated. Except his sister had never come back. Her spirit had stayed in the gods' lands, and her body had withered and, at last, died.

Like a black wave, fear and anguish smothered him. He could not move. He could not move.

"He's going to die, Aleksi. He's going to die."

Brutally, Aleksi crushed the fear down, down, burying it. Then he ran to get the doctor. Dr. Hierakis was fully dressed, sleeping wrapped in a blanket beneath one of her wagons. She rose with alacrity and hurried back with him, stumbling once in the dark. A thick leather bag banged at her thigh. The wind whined and blew around them. The walls of Tess's tent boomed and sighed as he went in behind the doctor and followed her in, all the way in, to stand silent just inside the inner chamber.

Tess talked in a stream of rapid Anglais. The doctor ran a hand over Bakhtiian's lax face, moved his flaccid limbs. She opened her bag and brought out—things.

Aleksi effaced himself. He willed himself to become

invisible, but neither of the women recalled that he was there.

Things. Objects. Aleksi did not know what else to call them, so smooth, made of no metal he recognized, if indeed it was even metal. Not a fabric, certainly, not any bone he knew of, this hand-sized block that the doctor palmed in her right hand and held out over Bakhtiian's head. Just held it, for a long moment, doing nothing. Then she swept it slowly down over his body, uncovering him as she went. When she had done, she covered him back up again and took a flat shiny tablet and laid it on a flat stretch of carpet and said two words.

If Aleksi had not honed his self-control to the finest pitch, he would have jumped. As it was, he twitched, startled, but he made no noise. The tablet shone, sparked, and a spirit formed in the air just above it. A tiny spirit, shaped with a man's form but in all different colors, wavering, spinning, melding. Until Aleksi realized that it was Bakhtiian's form, somehow imprisoned in the air above the tablet.

He must have gasped or made some noise. Tess jerked her head around and saw him.

"Damn," she said. "Aleksi, sit down."

He sat. "What is it? Is that Bakhtiian's spirit?"

Dr. Hierakis glanced up from studying the slowly rotating spirit hanging in the air. "Goddess. I thought you'd stayed outside."

"It isn't a spirit, Aleksi," said Tess. "It's a picture. A picture of his body. It shows what might be making him—ill—what might be making him—"

"But his spirit has left his body," said Aleksi. "I know what it looks like when that happens. That's his spirit there." He pointed to the spirit. It spun slowly, changing facets like a gem turning in the light, little lines hatched and bulging, tiny gold lights stretched on a net of silvery-white wire, brilliant, as Aleksi had always known Bakhtiian's spirit would be, radiant and gleaming and surprising only in that it emitted no heat he could feel. "I can see it."

"No, he's just unconscious. That's just an image of his body. The doctor is trying to find out why he's fallen into this—sleep."

"We know why," said the doctor in a dry, sarcastic

tone. "I'm trying to find out how extensive the damage is." Then she said something else in Anglais.

"Oh, hell." Tess burst into tears again.

"It isn't Habakar witchcraft," said Aleksi suddenly. "It's yours."

The doctor snorted. "It isn't witchcraft at all, young man, and I'll thank you not to call it that. But it's quite true that we're the ones responsible."

"*I'm* the one responsible," said Tess through her tears.

Dr. Hierakis shook her head. "What can I say, my dear? The serum has metastasized throughout the body, and for whatever reason, it's caused him to slip into a coma."

"You can't wake him up somehow?"

"Right now, since his signs are otherwise stable, I don't care to chance it. You knew the risks when you insisted we go ahead with the procedure."

Tess sank down onto her knees beside her husband and bent double, hiding her face against his neck. He lay there, limp, unmoving. The walls of the tent snapped in, and out, and in again, and out, agitated by the wind. The doctor sighed and spoke a word, and the luminous spirit above the tablet vanished. A single white spark of light shone in the very center of the black tablet. A similar gleam echoed off the doctor's brooch.

Aleksi jumped to his feet. "Where did his spirit go?" he demanded.

Dr. Hierakis let out all her breath in one huff. "Aleksi, his spirit did not go anywhere. It's still inside him. That was just an image of his spirit, if you will."

"But—"

"Aleksi." Now she turned stern. "Do you trust Tess?"

"Yes."

"Do you think she would do anything to harm Bakhtiian?"

"No."

"Aleksi. This slate, this tablet here, it isn't a magic thing, it's a—a *machine*. Like the mechanical birds that the ambassador from Vidiya brought but more complex than that. It's a tool. It can do things, show us things, that we could not otherwise do ourselves or see ourselves. It helps us do work we otherwise could not do, or work that would take much longer to do if we did it—by hand.''

Aleksi considered all this, and he considered how many times he had wondered why Tess seemed ignorant of the simplest chores and duties that the jaran engaged in every day. "Do you have many of these machines in Jeds?"

The doctor smiled. He saw that she was pleased that he was responding in a clever, reasonable way to her explanations. He knew without a doubt that she was telling him only a part of the truth. "Yes. Many such machines."

"Then why didn't Bakhtiian see them there, when he was in Jeds? I never heard Sonia or Nadine mention such *machines* either."

"Tell him the truth," said Tess, her voice muffled against Bakhtiian. "I can't stand it, all these lies. I can't stand it. Tell him the truth."

Aleksi crouched down and waited.

The doctor placed her tablet inside her bag and followed it with the little black block. "The truth is, Aleksi, that we don't come from Jeds, or from the country overseas, *Erthe*, either. We don't come from this world. We come from up there." She pointed at the tent's ceiling.

He shook his head. A moment later, he realized what she meant, that she meant from the air above, from the heavens. "Then you come from the gods' lands?"

"No. We aren't gods, nothing like. We're human like you, Aleksi. Never doubt that. We come from the stars. From a world like this world, except its sun is one of those stars."

She could be mad. But he examined her carefully, and he could see no trace of madness in her. The doctor had always seemed to him one of the sanest people he had ever met. And as strange as it all sounded, it might well be true.

"But. But how can Tess's brother be the prince of Jeds, then? If he—" Aleksi broke off. "May I see that thing again? Does it show other spirits besides Bakhtiian's?"

"So much for the damned quarantine," muttered the doctor.

"What are we going to tell them?" Tess asked. She straightened up. Tears streaked her face, but she was no longer crying. "When they come in and see him like this? How long, Cara? How long will he stay this way?"

"I can't know. Tess, I promise you, I will not leave him. But I'll need some kind of monitoring system. I'll have to set up the scan-bed in here, under him, disguise it somehow. I'll need Ursula." She glanced at Aleksi. "And hell, we've got him now. With the four of us, we can keep the equipment a secret. I think. Unless you want the whole damned camp to know."

"No!" Tess stood up and walked to the back wall and back again, and knelt beside her husband, and stroked his slack face. "No," she repeated, less violently. "Of course not. I just—" She looked at Aleksi. He saw how tormented she was, how terrified, how remorseful. "Aleksi." Her voice dropped. "You do believe that I didn't mean for this to happen. That I'm trying to help— oh, God."

She was pleading with him. Tess needed him. "But I trust you, Tess. You know that. You would never hurt him."

She sighed, sinking back onto her heels. Her face cleared. However slightly, she looked relieved of some portion of her burden. And he had done it. It was almost sharp, the satisfaction of knowing he had helped her.

"But what will we tell the rest of the jaran?" the doctor asked. "I hope I needn't remind you, Aleksi, that anything you've seen in here must be kept a secret. *Must* be."

"Will his spirit come back?" Aleksi asked.

"It *will*," said Tess fiercely.

"I don't know," said the doctor.

Aleksi rose. He shrugged. "Habakar witchcraft. They're saying it already."

The doctor grimaced. "I don't like it."

"What choice do we have?" asked Tess bitterly.

"Well." The doctor rose, brushing her hands together briskly. "There's no use just sitting here. Aleksi, can you go fetch Ursula? Then meet me at my wagons."

He nodded and ducked outside. A faint pink glow rose in the east. The wind was dying. Up, bright in the heavens, the morning star shone, luminous against the graying sky. Could it be? That they came from—? Aleksi shook his head. How could it be? How could they ride across the air, along the wind, up into the heavens? And yet. And yet.

His tent flap stirred. Raysia ducked outside, dressed and booted. She saw him and started. "Oh, there you are. Is something wrong?"

"Habakar witchcraft," he said, knowing that the sooner he let the rumor spread, the more quickly Tess and Dr. Hierakis could hide their own witchcraft. Their own *machines*. "The Habakar priests have put a curse on Bakhtiian."

"Gods," said Raysia. "I'd better run back and tell my uncle." She glanced all around and, seeing that no one yet stirred in the predawn stillness, she kissed him right there in the open. "I'd better go." She hurried off.

So it begins. He paused at the outcropping. The land was a sheet of darkness below, black except for a lambent glow flickering and building: Sakhalin had fired the city.

ACT THREE

"He, who the sword of heaven will bear
Should be as holy as severe"

—SHAKESPEARE,
Measure for Measure

CHAPTER THIRTY-FIVE

David ben Unbutu sat and stared at blank white wall. He sat cross-legged, with the demimodeler placed squarely in front of him, its corners paralleling the corners of the plain white room. He shivered because it was cold. The scan unit was on, but all the image showed him was the dimensions of the rectangular room, white, featureless, blank.

A footstep scuffed the ground behind him. "Anything?" Maggie asked.

He shook his head. The beads bound into his name braids made a snackling sound that was audible because of the deep stillness surrounding them. "Our scan can't penetrate these walls, and neither can we. It's got to be here. It has to be, but we can't find the entrance."

"Or the entrance won't open for us." She sank down on her haunches beside him. The heat of her body drifted out to him, and he shifted closer to her, as to a flame.

"Thirty-two days it took me, Mags, to survey this damned place and the grounds. Every way I turn it, the only space I can't account for is right there." He did not point. They all knew where it was, behind the far wall whose blankness seemed more and more like a mockery of their efforts. "That's got to be the control room, the computer banks."

"The place Tess got the cylinder. This matches the description she gave Charles. So what's he going to do?"

David blew on his hands to warm them. Maggie laid a hand on his. Just as the white wall emphasized the rich coffee brown of his skin, it lent hers more pallor, so that the contrast seemed heightened, dark and pale. "We're not Chapalii. Tess didn't find her way in by herself. She had a Chapalii guide. If Rajiv can't crack the entrance, then there's no human who can."

"Well." She released his hand and unwound from her crouch, standing up. "You may as well come eat. It's almost dusk." She offered him a hand and he took it and rose as well, bending back down to switch off the modeler and tuck it under his arm before he straightened to stand beside her. She grinned down at him. "I hear you're the current favorite of the spitfire."

"Damn you." David laughed. "You're trying to embarrass me. I think she just wanted to see how far the melanin extends."

"I hope her curiosity was suitably satisfied."

"Why don't you ask her?"

"Oh, don't worry. I did, and it was." She laughed in her turn. "You're blushing. You're such an easy target, David."

"I would have thought there wouldn't be any challenge in it, then. You're a heartless woman, Mags."

They crossed to the door and slid the panel aside to let themselves out. Immediately, warmth enveloped them although it stayed cooler inside the palace in contrast to the hot summer days passing outside. The ebony floors of this chamber gleamed, and networks of light pulsed in their depths, as if the flooring concealed a delicate web of machinery. Maggie broke away from David and paced out the meter-wide counter that stood in the room. It extended in an unbroken, hollow rectangle within the larger rectanglar chamber; she slid up onto it and climbed over to the smaller counter, a half meter wide but also unbroken, that stood within it, and then hopped that one as well to stand in the very center of the room. The two counters separated her from David. She looked at him, and he at her.

"What the hell do these represent?" she asked. "I don't see anything on here, no storage places, no controls, no patterns, no heat, nothing but the smooth surface."

David gestured back toward the door they had just come through. On either side of the door stood two tall megaliths. "Rajiv is pretty certain that those are transmitters of some kind. Maybe this is a power source."

"Damned chameleons," said Maggie cheerfully. She hopped back over the counters to return to David. They went on.

They no longer exclaimed over the palace. They had been here forty-three days and were as used to it as they ever would be. But still, for sheer size and the elegance and profusion of its detailing, it was magnificent. And it was theirs, the only Chapalii palace where humans had ever run free, unobstructed by protocol officers, by stewards, by the simple presence of any Chapalii at all. That it was thousands of years old did not lessen their victory. For all they knew, and from what little they had been permitted to see in Chapalii precincts now, Chapaliian architecture had scarcely changed at all in the last millennium.

Jo Singh had taken samples from every surface she could get a molecular flake off of, and Maggie had covered the same ground David had in his survey, recording every detail in three media for Earth's databanks. Charles walked the palace incessantly, as if by becoming intimately familiar with it he could somehow divine the intricacies of the Chapalii mind. After all, why should they have ennobled him? Why should they have rewarded him for his failed rebellion against them rather than simply killing him for the trouble he caused them?

"It's damned impressive," said Maggie. David started, feeling that she echoed his thoughts.

"Do you ever think," he said slowly, "that we might just be better off as subjects in their Empire?"

"They don't bear grudges, you know, or at least, not that I've ever noticed. Not that I'm much among them, of course."

"Not that any of us are," David said.

"Sometimes I think they're better than us. Less prone to emotional decisions. More concerned about peace, and peaceable living. About stability. They must think we're savages, the way we go on."

David grinned. "Yes, rather like we look at the natives of Rhui and pride ourselves on being better than them, because we've grown out of their primitive state. We live well. All of us, I mean, all humans, not just you and I and the rest of Charles's retinue."

Maggie paused as they went through an archway. She lifted a hand to trace a translucent spire of a glasslike substance that bordered the opening, lending its shadow to the pattern of tiles on the floor. At its core, fainter patterns mirrored the walls. "But it's a moot point, isn't it? Charles has already decided for all of us."

"Now, Mags, you know very well that the League Parliament voted full confidence in him. That is to say, that they'd follow wherever he led, knowing that he's got his eye on freeing us from the Empire somewhere down the line."

"Look. Here comes an escort."

Down the dimly lit hall came a white-robed priest—the ancient woman called Mother Avdotya—and a figure now intimately familiar to David. He hesitated and then walked forward beside Maggie, one hand tapping the modeler nervously. It looked like a plain black tablet of polished ebony, and he always carried parchment and quill pen and ink in the pouch at his belt, so that he might be thought to be using such instruments to conduct his survey and the tablet merely as a surface to write on, but it still made him anxious to meet any of the jaran when it was visible. Nadine, especially. Nadine always wanted to see the maps and architectural drawings he made. She had a clear grasp of maps and distances; she had just last night drawn him an astonishingly accurate—for its type—map of the coastline from Jeds up to the inland sea to the port of Abala. She had a fierce, impatient personality, overwhelming and breathlessly attractive to him, and he could not help but think longingly, for an instant, of Tess's more supple temperament. But Tess was as far out of his reach now as was the Chapalii control room. And Dina was here.

"What have you done for me today?" Nadine asked him, falling into step beside him. She spoke Rhuian precisely and without a trace of accent, as if she had learned the language through Tess's matrix and not by the laborious process of one word at a time. Even her uncle spoke with an accent, although his command of the language was equally impressive.

"A lintel," he replied, "from the southwest transept." He withdrew a rolled-up square of parchment from his belt-pouch and halted to smooth it open on the modeler.

Nadine studied it, frowning. "This pattern, here . . . isn't that repeated, but backward, on the northeast transept? And reversed, too." She stared as if she could puzzle out some vital information from the drawing. "You have a fine hand," she added.

"No doubt," said Maggie, with a smirk. David cast her a glare.

Nadine stepped back. Her lips quirked up, but she did not smile. "I want to add to my uncle's maps on the way back. We'll probably be riding far into Habakar territory, and eventually, riding south, the land route must come to Jeds. Someday I'd like to map both routes to Jeds, by ship and by horse."

"Would you, indeed?" said Maggie under her breath in Anglais. "No doubt your uncle would as well."

"If you will," said the old priestess, who had waited patiently through this exchange. "The prince and the other priests are waiting only for your presence to begin the meal."

"Of course." David rolled up the parchment and stuck it back into his pouch. They had to match their stride to the priestess's limping walk, so it took some time to wend their way through the maze of the palace and into the back rooms where the jaran priests lived. "How long have the jaran sent priests here?" he asked Nadine as she sat down next to him on a bench in the dining hall.

"Since we found it here. Surely you can see that the gods have touched this place, so we honor it."

"How long ago was that?"

She shrugged. "Perhaps Mother Avdotya knows. Perhaps my uncle guesses. A long time ago, in any case. But my uncle says that these zayinu from over the sea built this shrine, the zayinu called khepelli. Do you think this as well?"

"Yes, I do. But surely you know that, if you've spoken with Tess."

"There are many things Tess does not speak of," said Nadine cryptically. "And many things she speaks of without saying much. I will come to your bed tonight, if you wish it."

David felt heat burn in his cheeks and hoped that Nadine was still unfamiliar enough with his coloring that she could not tell he was blushing. "Yes." He managed to force out the syllable through a suddenly choked throat. Although the word was barely audible, Nadine smiled and returned her attention to her food.

Later, as they finished eating, Charles signaled to his crew, and they left together to go meet in the tiny room allotted to him. He sat on the edge of the narrow bed. Rajiv sat in the one chair, a hemi-slate resting on his knees, and Maggie on the edge of the wooden table. Jo sank down onto the floor with catlike grace. David remained standing with his back to the door.

Charles regarded them one by one. "What progress today?"

"I've got a tentative date on a ceramic sample," said Jo. "Ten thousand years, minimum. It's got to be that old. Ten to fifteen, by my best estimate. I incline to the later date."

"Does that surprise any of you?" Charles asked. He, of course, did not look surprised, but then Charles had become as adept at maintaining a blank expression as his Chapalii counterparts in the high nobility.

"Yes," said Maggie emphatically. "A thousand years, perhaps. But look at this place. Not here, but the rest of it. How could it have survived in such good condition? What does humanity have left from fifteen thousand years ago? That's Paleolithic times. Some obsidian blades and a few cave paintings?"

"Margaret," said Rajiv primly from his chair, "what you are not doing is thinking clearly. I cannot believe we know a thousandth part of the extent and sophistication of Chapalii technology. I will present you with an analogy. Take one of these jaran. Take a curious, intelligent one, such as the woman Nadine Orzhekov. What she knows and imagines of our life and technology is likely closer to the truth than what we know and imagine of Chapalii technology."

"Furthermore," said David, shaking a finger in front of his own lips, "it's the only reasonable window of opportunity for the human migration that was needed to populate this planet. If the Tai-en Mushai moved an entire Homo sapiens population here to work as his—slaves? for his amusement? for who the hell knows what reason?—then that time frame would be reasonable. Hasn't Tess found some correspondence between Rhuian languages and Earth languages?"

"I don't know why the Mushai brought humans here," said Charles quietly, "but I do know from the evidence in that cylinder that he was using this as a base to foment rebellion against the emperor. If that was fifteen thousand years ago . . . have things really changed that much in the Empire? Have they changed so little?''

Rajiv tapped his fingers lightly on the hard surface of his slate. ''We will not know how much additional information was hidden within the interstices of that cylinder unless we can install it on the original equipment it came from, the equipment here. The Keinaba house consoles could only access the top layer of information, and there was clearly more coded in underneath.''

''So.'' Charles said the word and then said nothing for a long moment. Through the small window set high up in the wall, David saw stars and the thick leafy crowns of trees. ''This we know. I think we have no choice but to call down an expert from Keinaba house.''

''Call down a Chapalii?'' Maggie asked. ''On planet? That would be breaking your own interdiction.''

Charles snorted. ''I'm already breaking my own interdiction. And they've seen Chapalii here before. Any other objections?''

Rajiv bent his head. ''You know my feelings.''

''What are your feelings?'' Maggie demanded.

Rajiv glanced up at her, his dark eyes glinting. ''I suggested it. There is one technician I have worked with. She is one of these *ke,* one of the nameless ones of their lowest caste, but she is an artist with this machinery. I cannot forgive a society that condemns such intelligence and promise to that kind of subjugation for no better reason than that her parents were born of parents who were born of parents . . . and so on.'' His eyes flashed with anger. His dark brows were drawn down, and a pulse beat in his jaw.

''A Chapalii female!'' Maggie exclaimed. ''I've never met a Chapalii female. I thought they were all in purdah or something. Restricted. Secluded.''

''It is true,'' said Charles slowly, ''that they are rarely together with Chapalii males. Beyond that, I have formed no sense of what their status is. But the Tai-en Naroshi offered me the services of his sister to design a mausoleum for Tess.''

''How morbid. At least you didn't take him up on it.''

''But I did.'' Charles smiled, not with amusement pre-

cisely but at some ironic joke. "They work at a slower
pace than we do, though. Cara believes they're quite long-
lived." He brushed his hands together briskly and stood
up with decision. "Then if there is no more discussion,
I'll send for a deputation from Keinaba."

"But Charles," said David, "can you trust them?
Surely asking them to uncover this information—the Tai-
en Mushai is almost a Lucifer kind of figure in their history, as far as I can tell. Or at least, that's how Tess
described him to me once. Will the Keinaba family agree
to help you uncover his past? To start in motion what
may prove to be another rebellion against their own emperor?"

"I think that they'll do anything I tell them to do. This
is one way to test that."

David just shook his head. "You're damned cool."

"Don't forget that I saved their house from extinction
by my intervention. They owe me everything. They are
bound to me like—" He shrugged. "Well, aren't there
any historians here who can provide me with a good analogy?"

David had known Charles for forty-five years now. He
and Charles and the other Charles—who was now
Marco—had gone to university together. David's path had
parted for a time from that of Charles after university,
but in the end he had come back to him, to the cause, to
the rebellion, to the endless struggle for freedom. David
felt more and more that he knew Charles less well the
longer they were together. As if the closer David got, the
more Charles receded, or at least that the force repelling
David grew stronger the longer he was exposed to it. Not
that Charles was in any way cold to him, that he didn't
trust him, listen to him, even joke with him now and
again in the way he used to when they were young, but
that Charles himself was retreating far down into the
depths of the Tai-en, the duke, the only human who had
any true power within the Chapalii hierarchy. David loved
Charles. He respected the duke, but he wasn't sure that
he liked him much.

"Where is Marco, anyway?" he asked, thinking of old
times. "I haven't seen him all day."

"Out scouting for a landing site, in the event we were
forced to this decision. But I expect him—"

Someone came running down the hall. A moment later the door burst open and Marco plunged into the room, pulling up short. "Just got a frantic message in from Tess. Christ in Heaven. She and Cara—" He swore fluidly and imaginatively in Ophiuchi-Sei. "She talked Cara into slipping Bakhtiian some damned serum or other to try for a temporary halt to his aging."

"What!" That was Jo. "But the physiological discrepancies could be lethal!"

"Exactly. That's what the message was about. Here, I'll play it back for you." He unhooked his slate from his belt and laid it on the table. With a pass of his hand over the shining surface, and a single spoken word, an image appeared above the slate, Tess's image. Her message was garbled and almost incoherent, but one fact came through clearly: Bakhtiian had slipped into a coma and Cara didn't know the likelihood of his ever coming out of it.

"Goddess above," swore Maggie. "Talk about breaking the interdiction."

"Well?" asked Marco after Tess's image froze and he keyed it to vanish.

"Did you find a good landing site?" Charles asked.

There was silence, while everyone else sorted out the sudden change of subject.

Marco blinked. He ran his left hand back through the thick shock of his hair. "Yes, in fact, I did. But what about—?"

"If Cara is there, then there is nothing further I can do. Now. I'll need a scrambled message, Rajiv, to be sent to Odys through Jeds and thence on to Keinaba. I want them to arrive as soon as possible. Marco, when is the new moon? I think we'll have the best chance of getting them in unseen then."

"But Charles—" David burst out. "What about Nadine? Surely she deserves to know. We don't even know what kind of rules for succession they have. Won't she want to ride back?"

Rajiv had already opened up a branching pathway over his slate, encoding a signal and encryption into it. Marco had a strange, almost disturbing expression on his face as he watched Charles.

"David," said Charles, "I would dearly love to tell

Nadine Orzhekov about her uncle's illness. How am I to explain how we got the news so quickly?''

"You're right," muttered David.

"It would be damned convenient for you if he died," added Marco in a low voice.

"It might be," said Charles. "In fact, it would be, and it's damned inconvenient for me that I find myself standing here hoping that he doesn't die. Because I rather like him."

"The Tempest," said Maggie suddenly. "That's the right analogy. Doesn't the magician Prospero save everyone's life? Aren't they all bound to him, the humans and spirits both?"

"What are you talking about?" David demanded.

Charles laughed. "Doesn't he play with all their lives? Thank you, Maggie. I'll take that as a vote of confidence. I think. Jo, let's go down to your room and you can show me how you reached your dating results."

They dispersed. Maggie following Charles and Jo out the door. Rajiv did not move, but he was well sunk into a working trance, manipulating his pathways in a shimmering three dimensions in the air above his slate. David sighed and moved to follow the others. "Aren't you coming?" he asked Marco.

"Which makes me Caliban," said Marco under his breath. "And of course *she* plays Miranda."

"What?"

Marco started. He shook his head. "Nothing. Never mind. Yes, let's go see Jo's results. So, David my boy, I hear you're the spitfire's new favorite."

David chuckled, since this was old, familiar banter. "You should talk. Wasn't her cousin—the blonde one—courting you the entire time we were at camp?" In charity with each other, they left Rajiv to his task, light glittering and spinning in the tiny room like the web of a sorcerer's working.

CHAPTER THIRTY-SIX

Tess kept vigil.

All that day, although in the afternoon Sonia made her walk outside. "You must keep up your strength, Tess," Sonia scolded. "It does a woman no good to weaken herself when she's pregnant."

Cara brought up one of her wagons in the late afternoon. That night she and Ursula, with Aleksi aiding them, set up a bed which would monitor Ilya's condition continuously. With some clever drapery of fabric, the doctor arranged an intravenous system to keep him in fluids; then she set up her cot out in the outer chamber of their great tent. The wind shook the tent walls incessantly, so that the noise became like a lullaby, monotonous and soothing. Tess slept, a little.

In the morning Sonia charged Aleksi with taking Tess for walks, one in the morning, one in the afternoon. Cara made some excuse about the bed, but since Sonia had been in Jeds, she accepted the excuses and was dissuaded from investigating too closely. In any case, she had the rest of the extended family to provide for, and the Orzhekov tribe to administer, and Tess to worry about.

Tess sat by the bedside, not stirring unless someone approached her directly. Katerina drew aside different flaps within the tent to let the wind through, to cool it down, but the air remained stuffy. In the afternoon, Aleksi came.

"Come." He took her hand and drew her to her feet. Ilya lay still and silent on the bed. "The doctor will watch. You must come outside and walk."

She went, because it was easier than protesting and because he was right. Outside was an armed camp. The gold banner whipped in the wind atop the tent. Vladimir and Konstans stood on either side of the awning, white-faced, like statues. Two rings of guards circled the Orzhekov camp, the great tent at the center. A stone's throw out, a line of unmounted men paced; farther, horsemen rode a tight circle. Sonia held court under the awning of her tent, and supplicants came forward one by one to address her. Beyond, the stark outline of the ridgetop shimmered against the blue sky. It was hot, and the wind was hot, and the sun beat down on the height like a hammer.

The light and the weight of her anguish bewildered Tess. "What's going on?"

"The rumors are spreading," said Aleksi. "Sonia is letting etsanas and dyans in one by one to assure them that all is well."

"Which it isn't."

"Tess."

"I'm sorry." She felt dizzy. She rested a hand on his arm.

"We'll walk," he said sternly. They made a circuit of the inner ring of guards, composed mostly of men from the Orzhekov tribe itself, who were also part of Ilya's own thousand. What was wrong? they asked her. Was he ill of a fever? Was it true that a Habakar priest had witched his spirit out of his body, and that they were even now battling in the gods' lands for control of the Habakar kingdom? Tess found meaningless words to reassure them, but mostly Aleksi talked. They walked one circuit around, and then a second. The second was easier, because the guards let her walk in peace.

"A third time," said Aleksi, "and then you must eat, Tess." He hesitated. She plodded on. She felt heavy and full, and her breasts were beginning to swell. She had a horrible irrational fear that she was going to get the child in exchange for Ilya, and she realized that she wanted Ilya more.

"If I could take back what I did—" she said, and an instant later realized that she had said it aloud.

"What did you do?" Aleksi asked.

"Dr. Hierakis is eighty-two years old."

He caught up to her and, with a touch on her elbow, stopped her. Then he looked once to each side, as if he thought the wind itself might be listening. "You mean that."

"It's true."

"But she looks no older than—Ilya. Perhaps a little older, because she carries herself like an Elder. How old is your brother, Tess?"

"He's seventy-seven. Fifty years older than me."

"How can you have the same parents?"

"Because we live longer."

"Are you zayinu? They say the old ones lived long lives and never aged. But they fled across the seas and under the hills long before the jaran came to these lands."

"No. Well, yes, in a way, but only because of our machines. We are like you, Aleksi. We're the same, it's just that our machines allow us to live longer and travel farther." She sighed. "You don't believe me, do you?"

But his face was quite still. She could not tell what he was thinking. "Can you make us live so long and stay so young?"

She hung her head. On this height, the wind had scoured the ground clean of vegetation and loose soil, leaving only a hard-packed earth surface and the rougher solidity of bare rock. "That's what I was trying to do."

"Ah." They continued their walk in silence.

"Tess!"

Her heart pounded wildly. She spun around to find the source of the voice. There he was: Kirill, riding through the lines. He swung down from his horse, threw the reins to a waiting guard, and ran over to her. She did not care that they were there in the open, where everyone could see; she hugged him hard and would have held him longer, but he disengaged himself from her gently. He took a single step back from her, to emphasize that they stood apart.

"Tess," he said more softly. "Is is true?" She nodded, but could not speak. "Gods," he said in a low voice. "But we have come so far." He shifted to stare at the tent, at the bright walls shifting in the wind, and Tess realized that although the sling still cradled his arm, his shoulder looked odd to her.

"Kirill." She grasped his withered hand, clutching the fingers where they peeked out from the cloth sling. And felt them move.

She shrieked, and then, for the first time in two days, she laughed, because she was so surprised.

He took hold of her shoulder with his good hand. "Shhh!" He glanced at Aleksi, but Aleksi only smiled enigmatically and looked away. "Don't say anything. Gods, don't cry, Tess." He stroked her hair, briefly, and dropped his hand from her. "Five days ago my arm began to tingle all over. It hurt. Yesterday my hand came alive. Tess." He stared at her earnestly, the fine blue of his eyes no less bright than the brilliant bowl of the sky. "If the spirit can return to my arm, then surely Ilya's spirit can find its way back to his body. Fight its way back, if I know him."

"Then he will be a Singer," said Aleksi quietly. "He'll be gods-touched, like Raysia Grekov."

"Gods," echoed Kirill in a muted voice. "Like his own father."

"Kirill Zvertkov." It was Katerina. "My mother wants to see you. You haven't paid your respects to her yet."

He grinned. "Of course, little one."

"I'm not so little anymore," she said tartly.

"Quite right," he agreed. "Tess." He walked with Katerina over to the other tent.

"Tess," said Aleksi, "you're rather free with how you act in public with married men, and you married, too."

"Oh, go to hell," said Tess in Anglais. He grinned, but she did not smile. "Let's go back." But even as she ducked inside the tent, that one phrase of Kirill's came back to haunt her: Like his own father. Ilya never talked about his parents. Never. His own father had been a Singer—a shaman, really, since the Singers of the jaran shared this trait, that they had fallen into a trance or a desperate illness at some stage in their lives and come back to tell about it. Their spirits had gone to the gods' lands and there wrestled with demons or consorted with angels, and then been sent back to this world; that is what the jaran said. Her first lover in the jaran had been a Singer. Fedya had been a little fey, as well as a fine musician, and he had also received a respect from jaran of every age that went far beyond his years and his family's status. How little she had known then, how little she had understood, to think he had merely been a quiet, perceptive young man and an amiable, unpossessive lover. He had been far more than that, but she had never known it until long after he was dead.

Aleksi halted in the outer chamber and let her go in alone. Cara, seeing her enter, rose and retreated. Tess sank down beside the low bed on which Ilya rested. She touched his dark hair. She traced his brows and the still centers of his lidded eyes and his fine cheekbones and the dark line of his beard. Damn him. Now and again he had spoken of his sister. But he never spoke of his parents. How dare he not trust her with that? Had he hated them?

She laid her head on his chest, her ear turned to hear the slow steady beat of his heart. His chest rose and fell, and if she ran her hand under the wooden frame of the couch, she could find the control panel for the scan unit hidden away beneath a carved wooden strut. Its surface was cool, but heat bled off from its edges.

No, he had not hated them. He had loved his family, he had loved them deeply and passionately because Ilya loved deeply and passionately. It was the only way he knew how to give his heart. Perhaps he had loved them too well, as he perhaps loved her too well. If she left him, would he cease speaking of her because the memory was too painful?

She kissed his limp fingers, one by one, and then she talked to him, just talked. She told him about her own parents, who were kind and quiet and humorous and loving. Although their only son could have supported them, they had continued their own work, she as a lab tech, he as a teacher. They liked to argue about religion and politics and the modern fashion of wearing only clothes grown from vegetable matter, and that last year they spent months debating the merits of the production of Shakespeare's *Henry V* they had taken Tess to see, the one in which all the setting and costume details, and all the business, were thinly veiled references to Charles and to humanity's hope that he would one day succeed in defeating the power of the Chapalii Empire. They were rude to people who tried to insinuate themselves into their lives or their house because of Charles. They spoke to Charles every day at noon, without fail. They protected and prized their privacy above all, and the privacy of their little daughter.

And they had died in a flitter crash when that daughter was ten years old. Once, when she was fifteen, Tess had

found a scan image of the crash site, and she had spent
one month poring over the image from all angles, trying
to make sense of what had happened. She had never managed to.

"Tess," said Cara softly from the curtain, "will you
come eat? It's dark. When did you last eat?"

It was dark. Tess sat passively while Ursula lit a lantern. The glow lent Ilya a corpselike color, pale and
waxy. Tess hurried out of the room, and there was Sonia,
with food. Sonia took one look at her face and hugged
her, just held her. They stood that way for a long time.

Tess ate. Later, she slept. In the morning, early, Sonia
woke her with a kiss and some milk. "Mother Sakhalin
has come," she said. "She wishes to speak with you
alone."

"Oh, Lord," said Tess, but she rose and straightened
her clothing and ate. Sonia left to escort Mother Sakhalin
in, and Tess rearranged the blankets over Ilya and
smoothed them out, and stroked his slack face. She could
see the imperfections in his face more clearly with him
lying here unconscious. He was a good-looking man, but
he was not blazingly handsome, not like Anatoly Sakhalin or Petya. Not like Vasil. It was his spirit that drew
the eye to him, that burned from his eyes and from his
face, that made him as glorious and as hot and as attractive as the sun. Now, just lying there, flaccid, lacking
any of the vitality that lit him, he looked rather ordinary,
and she could not recall why it was she thought him the
most beautiful man she knew.

"Tess Soerensen." Mother Sakhalin eased the curtain
aside and took four steps into the inner chamber. The
etsana stopped and stared at Ilya.

"Mother Sakhalin." Tess inclined her head, giving the
old woman the respect she warranted. "You honor me
with your presence."

Sakhalin circled the couch, examining Bakhtiian from
all angles. "I have seen this condition before. He has
been drawn away into the gods' lands, and we must wait
for the gods to send him back." She halted beside Tess
and considered the younger woman. "Or to keep him in
their lands. Who will lead the army after he is gone, if
he dies?"

"Your nephew," said Tess, without thinking. "Yaroslav Sakhalin. He is Ilya's chief general. His army has given Bakhtiian his greatest victories."

"My nephew is a brilliant general," agreed Mother Sakhalin. "A better general than Bakhtiian, and it is to Bakthiian's credit that he long since recognized that. But he does not have Bakhtiian's vision."

Tess put a hand to her eyes. "I'm sorry. I'm feeling dizzy."

"Sit down," ordered the etsana. Tess sank down. Mother Sakhalin sat down beside her, and now Tess did not feel as if she towered over the old woman. "You are pregnant, but there is no guarantee the child will also possess this vision, and in any case, the child will inherit through your line. Both Bakhtiian's sister's son and aunt's son are dead, which leaves only his cousin's son."

"Mitya? But he's only—what?—fifteen?"

"There are younger boys as well. Do any of them have this vision?"

"No one has the vision. No one but Bakhtiian."

"Then what is to become of us if he dies?"

Here in the tent, the air retained night's coolness. From outside, Tess heard Aleksi talking to little Ivan about milking the glariss. Katerina and Galina complained in loud voices about the lack of water to wash clothes. Tess could hear the tension in their voices; they knew what was going on, and they knew—not what it meant if Bakhtiian died, but that it meant that their world would be shattered.

It was too much to cope with. It was all her fault. "I don't know," said Tess. "I don't know."

"You are the sister of the prince of Jheds." Mother Sakhlain's face was creased and lined with age, and her mouth was pursed with disapproval. "You are the adopted daughter of Irena Orzhekov, who is etsana of the Orzhekov tribe. And you are Bakhtiian's wife. You must act."

"I don't understand," said Tess, feeling helpless and inadequate under Mother Sakhalin's eye, "how he became what he is. Where did it come from?"

"His father was a Singer. His mother was a proud and ambitious woman who became etsana very young, too young, I think."

"Like Arina Veselov?"

"Arina Veselov is not ambitious, nor is she proud in the sense I mean. And she married well."

"Ilya's mother did not marry well?"

"Alyona Orzhekov was marked by an orphan named Petre Sokolov, whom no one dared kill for his effrontery because he was a Singer. He said that the gods had given him a vision that she was the woman he must marry. Surely the gods must have known that they would have this child"—she gestured with a wrinkled hand toward the unconscious Ilya—"together. But Alyona Orzhekov loved another man. Everyone thought that this other man would marry her. He was a Singer, too, but he was also the dyan of his tribe, young, proud, and ambitious. And virtuous, and pious in his devotion to the laws of the gods." Tess had always felt overawed by Mother Sakhalin, who was old and wise and impatient with folly. Now Sakhalin smiled, and Tess caught a glimpse of what the younger woman must have been like: shrewd and patient and sharp-tongued. "I never liked him."

"What was his name?"

"Khara Roskhel."

"But he's the man who killed Ilya's family! Isn't he? How could he—? How could—? Yuri once told me that he was cruel."

"The most devout are often the cruelest. Yes, he was cruel, and he had visions as well. He never married, you know. They say he wanted no woman but Alyona. Such possessiveness is a very ugly trait in a man." She glanced again toward Ilya. Was Sakhalin thinking that Bakhtiian himself possessed this ugly trait? "They were lovers," the etsana went on, "always, through the years that followed, and openly so; what Petre Sokolov thought of this, no one ever knew. He was not a good husband for her. She needed a man who would rein back her worst impulses, one she could respect, one she would listen to."

"He did none of these things?"

Sakhalin shrugged. "What he did or did not do, I can't say, since I don't know. But an etsana ought not install her own son as dyan of her tribe, especially when that son is only twenty-three years old."

"Even if that son is Ilyakoria Bakhtiian?"

"Even so."

"I never had the honor of meeting your husband, Mother Sakhalin. But I feel sure that he was a good husband."

For this impertinence, Tess was rewarded with a smile and a brief, acknowledging nod. "Of course he was. My mother and my aunt chose him very carefully. He was the kind of man your brother Yurinya Orzhekov would have grown into, had he lived."

"Ah," said Tess. "Then he must have been a very fine man, indeed." She folded her hands in her lap and stared at her knuckles.

"It is true, though," added Sakhalin, musing, "that I never understood why Roskhel turned against them. He was one of Bakhtiian's earliest and strongest supporters. No one remarked it at the time; the connection between the two tribes was so close because of his liaison with Alyona Orzhekov. But it was at the great gathering of tribes in the Year of the Hawk that he turned his face against Bakhtiian, and later that year that he rode into the Orzhekov camp and killed the family. That is the mystery, you see, that he killed the two women and the child. He was a pious man—none more so—and it is against all of our laws, both of the gods and of the jaran, to harm women and children in the sanctity of the camp, even in the midst of war."

Someone was arguing violently outside. There was a shriek, then, closer, in the outer chamber, Cara exclaimed in surprise. A moment later the curtain swept aside and Vasil Veselov strode in. He stopped stock-still and stared, horrified, at Ilya. Mother Sakhalin rose briskly to her feet. Although Vasil stood a head taller than she did, she clearly held the weight of power. Tess stared.

"Your presence here is *most* improper," snapped Mother Sakhalin.

As if he were in a dream, Vasil took a step forward, then another one, then a third, and he sank down to kneel at the foot of the couch. His agony was palpable in every line of his body.

"He exiled you," said Mother Sakhalin. Her voice shook with anger. "How dare you walk unannounced and unasked into his presence?"

"Leave him be," said Tess suddenly, surprising even

herself. "Look at him." In the dim chamber, with his head bowed and his hair gleaming in the lantern light, Vasil looked like an angel, praying for God's Mercy. She felt his pain like heat, and it soothed her to know that someone else suffered as she suffered.

"I knew," said Sakhalin in a cold, furiously calm voice, "that the weaver Nadezhda Martov was Bakhtiian's lover. That she first took him to her bed soon after he returned from Jheds, and that he never refused her when our two tribes came together." Each word came clear and sharp, bitten off, in the hush of the tent. "Had I not known that, you can be sure that I would have forbidden my nephew to ever give his support to Bakhtiian's vision. Because of this one." She said the last two words with revulsion. There was no doubt what she meant by them.

Vasil's head jerked up. "I did nothing most other boys didn't try."

Mother Sakhalin strode across the carpet and cupped her hand back. And slapped him.

The sharp sound shocked Tess out of her stupor. True, and confirmed by Vasil's words and Mother Sakhalin's action, what Tess had only suspected. She stared at them, unable to speak.

"An adolescent boy ought to be wild and curious," replied Sakhalin in a voice both low and threatening. "Then he grows up to become a man. Which is something you never did, Veselov. Your cousin Arina is within her rights as etsana to allow you to remain in the Veselov tribe. But from Bakhtiian's presence you were long ago banished, and that is as it should be."

"I did not ask to love him," said Vasil in a hoarse voice. "The gods made me as I am."

With her left hand, Mother Sakhalin took hold of his chin and held him there, staring down at him, examining his face and his eyes. "The gods made your body and face beautiful. I have no doubt that your spirit is black and rotting. It is wrong, and it will always be wrong. Go home to your wife."

She released him. He bowed his head. Tears leaked from his eyes and slid unhindered down his cheeks. He rose and turned to go, slowly, as if the weight on him, compelling him, dragged him both forward and back. And there lay Ilya, perhaps dying, whom he clearly loved.

"Let him stay," said Tess in a low voice. Her anger welled up from so deep a source that she did not understand it. Vasil froze, but he did not look at her.

Sakhalin's gaze snapped to Tess. "Do you know, then, that Bakhtiian almost lost everything because of this one? That they said that the reason Bakhtiian never married was because of this one? That the etsanas and dyans were forced to go to Nikolai Sibirin and Irena Orzhekov after the death of Bakhtiian's family, and to tell them that they could not support a man who acted as if he was married to another man?"

Oh, God, not just that they had been lovers, but that Ilya *had* loved him in return. "But Ilya sent him away, didn't he?" Tess asked, feeling oddly detached as she replied, as if one part of her was all rational mind and the other an impenetrable maze of emotions.

"He chose his vision, it is true."

"Damn him," muttered Vasil.

"Shut up," snapped Tess. Vasil's anger gave her sudden strength. "And he slept with women? That is true, too, isn't it?"

"Yes."

"And the etsanas and dyans did support him. And he did marry."

"That is also true," agreed Mother Sakhalin. "For what reason are you assuring me of what we both know to be true?"

Tess lifted a hand and motioned Vasil to go to the corner of the room. He glanced at her, swiftly, and then sidled over to a dark corner, where he almost managed to lose himself in the shadows. As a human soul fades into death.

A shiver ran through Tess, like a blast of cold air, but she forced herself to speak slowly and carefully. "You just told me that a woman like Alyona Orzhekov needed a good husband, one who could rein back her worst impulses, one she could respect, one she would listen to. Isn't it also true that a man like Bakhtiian needs a good wife—one who can rein back *his* worst impulses, one he respects, one that he, and others, will listen to?"

Her gaze on Tess held steady. "That is true, and more

true yet, I suppose. There hasn't ever been a man like Bakhtiian among the jaran.''

"Has it not been agreed that I am that wife?''

Her lips quirked up. It was not quite a smile, not quite, but for all her outrage, Mother Sakhalin was amused. "Yes, it has been agreed. Not that the etsanas or Elders had a choice in the matter, but still, it is agreed that he chose wisely.''

"Thank you,'' said Tess demurely. "But if that is true, then you must trust me in this. You must trust me to deal with his . . . affairs in an intelligent and judicious manner.''

"You're well aware,'' said Sakhalin slowly, "of the power you have over our fate.''

"Oh, yes.'' *Oh, yes.* "I'm well aware of that.''

Mother Sakhalin inclined her head, once, with respect, with acceptance. "Then I leave this in your hands. May you judge wisely, and well.'' She took her leave.

Silence descended. Wind shuddered against the tent wall. Tess could just barely hear Ilya breathing, a shallow, steady rhythm.

"Why?'' Vasil asked, his voice scarcely audible above the bluster of the wind. When she did not answer immediately, he came out of the corner, his face a mask of light and shadow. "It's true, you know. Everything Mother Sakhalin said was true.''

"I'm not convinced that the truth can ever be that simple.''

"Tess?'' That was Sonia, calling from the outer chamber.

"It's all right.'' Then she laughed weakly and sank down to her knees beside Ilya's couch. "Oh, gods, no it isn't,'' she said, her throat choked up with sudden misery.

Vasil walked over and sank down next to her. He bowed his head. What did it matter who Ilya loved more if Ilya died? And *she* had killed him. Wasn't it better that Ilya live no matter what choice he made? No matter what choice he wished to make? And he had to live. He had to live.

Somehow, Vasil's presence was balm. No matter that she might fear Vasil's beauty, no matter that the jaran condemned him, still, a link bound the two men. As she

thought it, as if Vasil felt her thoughts, he touched her
on the hand. She caught in a sob and turned to him and
embraced him for what comfort he could give. It was
almost like being held by Ilya.

Then she heard footsteps in the outer room, and at
once, like conspirators, they broke away from each other.
Sonia came in and brought milk for Tess; she cast a skeptical glance toward Vasil and left again. Ilya breathed.
The day grew hotter, and the air inside the tent, stuffy.
Outside, the wind died down, only to come up again in
the early afternoon. Otherwise, nothing changed.

CHAPTER THIRTY-SEVEN

"Damn him!" swore Diana. The tent collapsed in a heap. She burst into tears.

A moment later Anahita strode by, her dark hair caught up in a loose bun. She adjusted her duffel bag on her shoulder. "Still hasn't come back, has he?" she asked sweetly. "Do you think he's going to? Or do you suppose he's out there looting and raping with the rest of them?"

"Shut up! Leave me alone!"

Anahita smirked at her. Diana knew that in one second more she was going to hit the black-haired woman.

"Do you need help?" asked Gwyn, entering just in time to avert catastrophe. He set down a chest—Joseph's disguised oven—and surveyed the ruin of the tent. Anahita flounced away.

"These tents just aren't meant to be taken down by one person, and everyone else is busy. . . ." And Anatoly was gone. Just ridden away sixteen days ago without saying good-bye, although he had sent a message back to her through his sister, Shura. Diana had not the least idea when he might return, or if he would return at all. She began to cry again.

Gwyn laid a steadying hand on her shoulder. "Now, Di, this won't avail you anything. Let's get that tent in order, and load it into the wagons. They don't wait for anyone, you know."

Between her sobs, she helped him fold up the tent walls and roll up the carpets and bind the poles together. The sun breasted the horizon and spilled light onto the trampled field of grain on which they had made their night's camp. On the march, she and Anatoly had done this together every morning, sometimes with one of the Veselov tribe's children to help out. They had worked out a system: this edge of the carpet to be rolled up first; the lantern to nestle in this corner of the finely carved wooden chest that had been one of the groom gifts from the Sakhalin family; Anatoly to bind up the poles and she to layer and fold up the tent. Then he would ride off, but she could be sure of seeing him once or twice during the day—indeed, Arina Veselov had once commented kindly that Anatoly was a little immodest in his public attentions toward her—and almost always at night.

"Do you think it's true?" she asked in a small voice. "About the looting and the . . . the raping?"

Gwyn shrugged. "I'm not about to tell you that war is pretty, Diana, and these last fourteen days we've seen how badly this land has been devastated since the news came about Bakhtiian collapsing. Still, they treat their own women with respect. I don't know."

Diana wiped her cheeks with the back of her hand, sniffing. "I'm sorry."

"For what?" Gwyn demanded.

"Why did he just go off that way?" She struggled to stop the tears, and failed. "Oh, I hate this. I just hate this. I don't know what's wrong with me. I hate this army. I want to go home."

Gwyn sighed and hugged her, holding her while she sobbed noisily on his shoulder. "It's been a difficult trip," he said finally. "I think Owen is the only one not showing signs of wear and tear. It's especially hard for you."

"It wasn't," she said into the cloth of his tunic. "Not until Anatoly left again. But I wonder sometimes—" She broke off and pushed herself free of Gwyn's embrace.

"What?"

"I don't know. Here, if you hand me the tent folded over that way, up on my back like—yes, that's right—"

"You can carry that?"

"It's not that far, and it's more unwieldy than heavy."

"That's what I meant."

They trudged across to the wagons and deposited their burdens in the bed of a wagon, and then returned to fetch the rest of Diana's things. "I wonder, though," she said softly as she knelt to pick up the chest where her clothes and his nestled together, "if we really had all day to spend together, if we'd have anything to talk about. Even on the march, before the battle—it was sixty days or

more, I think—still, most of what we did together was
things.''

"Things?''

"I mean daily things. Setting up the tent. Taking down
the tent. Sleeping. Eating. Helping with the chores at the
Veselov tribe. Watching the children. I'm not sure we
have anything in common.''

"Besides blond hair and handsome faces, you mean?''
She made a face at him. He chuckled. "Can't sharing a
life full of daily things be something shared in common?''

"Oh, of course they can. But . . .'' She swung the
chest into the wagon and watched as Gwyn hoisted the
poles and her carry bag into the bed as well. She piled
the pillows on top. "Sometimes I talk about acting, and
sometimes he talks about war. We listen politely to the
other one, but I don't care about strategy and how his
uncle sent the right flank, or was it the left flank—you
know. I don't think he cares that much about acting. I
think he thinks that it's some kind of mystery he's not
supposed to know the secrets of.''

One of the Telyegin sisters walked down the line of
wagons, checking the harness and the beasts—Diana
thought of them as oxen although they were called *glariss*—hitched to the tongue. Diana waved to her, and the
older woman waved back but kept walking. Ahead, at the
edge of the field, the first wagons started westward, the
rising sun at their backs. "Do you want to ride with
me?'' Diana asked as she clambered up to the seat and
took the reins.

"Honored, I'm sure,'' said Gwyn with a flamboyant
bow. "This will keep Anahita off my back. She's very
insistent about having an affair with me, and I'm getting
tired of it.''

"Oh, my. Is that an edge to your voice that I hear?
I've never heard you ruffled before, Gwyn.''

As he climbed up, they were hailed by Hal and Quinn.
"Can we come along with you?'' Quinn yelled from a
distance. They broke into a run and arrived, panting and
breathless, and managed to climb into the bed, scrambling on top of the pillows, just as the line lurched forward. "We're saving Hal from his dad. They got into a
roaring argument.''

Diana glanced back to see Quinn bright with the excitement of having witnessed the altercation. Hal looked morose and angry.

"He's so damned patronizing," muttered Hal. "He treats these people like they're experimental subjects—"

"We're all experimental subjects to Owen," said Gwyn.

"—yes, but we chose—well, at least *you* three chose—to participate in the experiment. I mean, look at what's going on around us. Does he even notice? People dying. Children starving. Cities destroyed. I swear he only thinks of it as a canvas for him to work on, and work against. Did you see what my mother is doing? She's recasting *Lear* with Lear as a jaran headwoman, and then the rest is pretty much the same, and rendering it all into khush."

"Oh." Diana felt a sudden, obliterating sense of discovery. "That's marvelous. I think it'll work, too."

Hal swore. "What gives us the right to tamper with their own tales, their sense of history? We've already performed Mekhala's story, and now we're working on the second one, which if you ask me is a damned sight risky."

"What?" demanded Quinn. "The old myth about the daughter of the sun who comes to earth? You can't imagine they'll ever suspect the truth, can you?"

"Isn't that patronizing? This is supposed to be an interdicted planet. We shouldn't be here at all!"

"They can't stay interdicted forever," said Gwyn softly.

"They haven't!" exclaimed Hal. He lapsed into a sullen silence.

The wagon bucked and heaved up over the line of earth that demarked the field from untilled earth. In the distance, a burned out village stood silent in dawn's light. A few walls thrust up into the air, blackened, skeletal. Nothing stirred in the ruins.

"And you know what else?" said Quinn in a low, confiding voice. "I think Hyacinth has a boyfriend."

Diana snorted. "According to Hyacinth, he has a thousand boyfriends, and as many girlfriends, too."

"Hyacinth does tell a good story," said Gwyn.

"Oh, come on," said Quinn. "Phillippe says that Hyacinth has slept in their tent every single night since we switched tent mates. Well, he said there were three nights that Hyacinth didn't sleep there, but he knows it was a woman Hyacinth went to because—well, anyway, he knows.''

"Because he was sleeping with her himself," muttered Hal.

"Oh?" asked Quinn tartly, "and you haven't been propositioned, Hal? Are you telling me that you haven't slept with even one jaran woman since we got here?"

Hal pursed his mouth mulishly and refused the bait.

"But anyway," continued Quinn, "Phillippe thinks Hyacinth has a real boyfriend."

"Isn't that dangerous?" Diana asked.

"Well, you have one. Hell, you have a husband."

"Quinn." Diana sighed, disgusted. "Don't you use your eyes?"

"I don't want to talk about it anymore," said Quinn, seeing that her audience was not prepared to amuse her. "And anyway." Diana glanced back again to see Quinn undoing her carry. Quinn looked furtively to each side, and once behind, and then drew out her slate. "I have the first act of the recast *Lear*. Do you want your lines?"

So as they advanced across the countryside, they studied their lines and exclaimed over the twists Ginny had worked in to the basic plot. They passed a second burned village, and a third. In the early afternoon the walls of a city loomed in the distance. Carrion smells drifted to them on the breeze. A pall of smoke obscured the horizon. Diana had to concentrate on her driving as the wagon bumped and pitched across a succession of trampled fields.

"How are these people going to eat if all their crops are gone?" Hal mumbled.

"Oh, Goddess," Quinn gasped. "Look."

There, a stone's throw away from the path of the wagons, lay a mound of corpses. A vulture circled lazily in and settled on a dead man's chest, and began to feed. Rats scurried across the tumbled bodies. Diana wrenched her gaze away and kept her eyes on the back of the wagon in front of her. A blond child lay on the pillows in the bed, blissfully asleep. But the two women in the front glanced only once at the corpses and then away, as if the sight did not interest them.

More bodies littered the fields, in heaps, mostly, as if they had been rounded up and slaughtered en masse, although now and again a single body could be seen fallen in the midst of trampled corn, an arm outstretched—defiant or pleading, Diana could not tell. Quinn had her hands over her eyes. Hal stared with haunted eyes at the destruction.

"It's been worse," said Gwyn softly, "these last fourteen days. They must be taking revenge for that curse they say the Habakar priests put on Bakhtiian."

Ahead, the city lay lit with fire, but as they came closer, Diana could see figures on the walls. She could see a pall like smoke sheeting the air between the walls and the vast army stretched out below. This time arrows shot out from the jaran side, too. A billow of black cloud rose up from inside the city, tinged with the stench of burning.

A crowd huddled out beyond them, in a field flattened by the advance of the jaran army. "At least there are some survivors," said Diana, and then she saw what they were doing: jaran riders were slaughtering their captives. Mercifully, it was too far away for her to see what they were doing in detail, and she averted her eyes in any case. The wagons trundled on. Ahead, the jaran camp grew up out of range of missile fire from the city walls, but they did not stop. Their line of wagons went on, circling the city at a safe distance and heading on. Everywhere was devastation. The army had swept through with a scythe of utter destruction, leaving nothing in its wake. Once or twice they passed a pitiful huddle of refugees, exclusively women and small, terrified children, but mostly they saw no one, as if this fertile land were uninhabited. Once a small troop of mounted women passed, herding a great mob of bleating goats and cattle and sheep—not the kind the jaran kept, but different breeds—and once again they saw a troop of riders killing prisoners. Mostly the land was empty, and emptied.

By dusk, the city was a glow on the horizon behind them. If it did not fall tomorrow, then it would fall next week, or the week after. They made camp alongside a sweetly-flowing river. Diana went down to the river to wash, as if she could somehow wash the day's horrors from her.

A number of jaran women had flocked to the river's

edge, and many of them simply stripped and waded into the water while others took clothing downstream to wash.

"Diana!" Arina beckoned to her from the shore, where she stood watching a naked Mira splash in the shallow water.

Diana stumbled over to her, catching her boots on rocks, unsure of her footing in the dim light, unsure she could face Arina with any friendship at all. Across the river stood a village. Well, what was left of a village: it was burned out, of course. A large scrap of cloth—a shirt, perhaps—fluttered in the breeze and tumbled down an empty lane as if some unseen spirit animated it. Otherwise, the village was deserted, inhabited only by ghosts—if even ghosts had the courage to haunt it.

Arina held Lavrenti. Diana could not help herself. As she came up to the young etsana, she put out her arms for the infant. Arina handed him over. Lavrenti had grown; he wasn't thriving, not that, but he was growing, and his tiny mouth puckered up and he gave Diana his sweet, open-mouthed, toothless smile. Diana cradled him against her chest and stood there, rocking him side to side and talking nonsense to him. He chuckled and made a bubble and reached up to grab for her silver earrings.

"A messenger came from Sakhalin's army," said Arina, "to his aunt. She sent her granddaughter to tell me that Anatoly sent a message to you."

"To me!" Diana flushed, feeling ecstatic and terrified at once. Lavrenti gave up on her earrings, which were out of his reach, and turned his attention to tugging on the bronze buttons at the neck of her tunic instead.

Arina frowned, looking very like a stern etsana, and then grinned, which spoiled the whole effect. "He said to say that he loves you, which was most improper of him. He should be able to wait until you are private." She paused. Diana could not help but wonder, bitterly, when that event was ever likely to take place. "He sent this to you." Arina drew a necklace out of her pouch.

Diana gasped. It was made of gold, and of jewels cunningly inlaid in an ornate geometric pattern, and it was as heavy as it was rich. Then Arina drew out and displayed to Diana a pair of earrings, and two bracelets, all done in the same alien, lush style, gold and emeralds and chalcedony.

Loot. Anatoly had sent her loot from some far palace where probably two-thirds of the inhabitants were dead by now, and the rest likely to starve when winter came. And did he have a mistress there, some khaja princess who had begged him for mercy? The spoils of war. For the first time it struck her: what if Bakhtiian died, what if the khaja army regrouped and conquered this camp? Would she become one of the spoils of war? Or would she simply be killed?

"Are you cold?" Arina asked with concern. "I hope you aren't coming down with a fever."

"No. Just tired." She did not want to say it, but she had to. "It was so horrible, today. Ever since we came down on this plain, it's been horrible."

Arina drew herself up. It was easy to forget that this pretty, petite young woman was headwoman of a tribe, an authority in her own right. "It is true that these khaja scarcely deserve as much mercy as the army has extended them. Not when their priests have witched Bakhtiian. But if he dies, I assure you that I will counsel the commanders to show no mercy at all."

At first Diana was confused because she thought Arina was rendering her an apology. Then, an instant later, she realized that it was true: Arina *was* apologizing, because Arina thought that what Diana thought was horrible was the mercy the army was showing. Which as far as she could tell was no mercy at all.

"But—" she began, and faltered. "Then there's still no word about Bakhtiian? He's still the same?"

"He is still there, up on the pass. Tess refuses to move him, and she is right. He will fight best when he lies closest to the heavens. Ah, Mira, are you done, then?" She called to an older girl to come dress Mira and turned back to Diana, dressing Diana with the jewelry much as Joseph helped her when she got into a particularly elaborate costume. The gold gleamed in the dusk. Lavrenti batted at the gold earrings while Arina tucked the silver earrings into Diana's belt-pouch. "You must wear these gifts often, Diana, so that everyone will know that your husband is fighting bravely and well."

"Damn him," said Diana under her breath, and she burst into tears.

CHAPTER THIRTY-EIGHT

Vasil woke before dawn. Every morning, now, he woke even before his wife, so that he could go to Bakhtiian's tent as soon as it was decent and stay there until dusk, when it was no longer proper for Tess to accept male visitors not of her family—not while her husband was there, at any rate. It was dim, in the tent, and warm. In her sleep, Karolla had thrown an arm carelessly across his bare chest, and he shifted just enough to slide out from under its weight. She opened her eyes.

And just looked at him. He dropped his gaze away from hers and rummaged for his clothes.

"It's wrong," she said in a low voice. "It's wrong that we didn't go on with the tribe. The children and I are alone here, Vasil."

He flushed, half with anger, half with shame. "They aren't unkind to you."

"No, they aren't unkind to us. But they all know that I am Dmitri Mikhailov's daughter. If Sonia Orzhekov is polite to me, it is only out of pity. I am tired of living with their pity."

He flinched away from her tone. He had never heard her so—not angry, Karolla never raised her voice—but so stubborn.

"If you will give all the burdens of being dyan into Anton's hands so that you can linger here, then you must by right give him back his authority. It's wrong." She hesitated. He turned back to kneel beside her, but her gaze did not soften. She sat up, and the covers slipped down to reveal her breasts and her belly. Her breasts were swelling again; he knew the signs—she was probably pregnant, although it was too early to be sure. "Everyone knows why you have stayed, Vasil. Have you no pride?"

He gripped a corner of the blanket and squeezed it tight into a ball. "I never lied to you, Karolla. Not before we married, and never afterward. You know that he must come first with me."

"You will be exiled again. Then what is to become of us? You have children now, a son who will neither speak to you nor obey you, and a daughter who will obey no one but you. Or can you even think of someone besides yourself?"

The pain hit then, the overwhelming, shattering pain of his fear that Ilya was going to die. Now. Today, perhaps, or tomorrow, or the next day. "I think of *him* every moment I am awake," he said in a choked voice.

She turned her face away and shielded her eyes from him with one hand. Her shoulders tensed. A shudder passed through her body.

"Oh, gods. Karolla, I didn't mean to hurt you." He flung his arms around her and pulled her down with him back onto the pillows. "My sweet, you must know that you are the only woman I care for. You're the only woman I ever wanted to marry."

She stayed stiff in his arms. "Because you needed the refuge my father could offer you. Because you wanted my father to kill Bakhtiian for you." Tears streaked her face. She had never been one of those women who cried well. Crying simply made her skin blotchy.

"Have I ever been unkind to you?" he demanded.

"No, not unkind. But you left us."

"To save my own life. And I came back."

She went still and ceased struggling to free herself from his embrace. "I know why you came back."

"Do you?" He hated seeing her like this, suspicious, bitter. She had always loved him so unreservedly before. He was the center of her life, just as he had been the center of his mother's life. He could not bear to lose that. He kissed her. At first she did not respond, but he knew how to persist. "Karolla. My sweet Karolla."

She murmured something deep in her throat, a curse or a prayer, and strained against him. He rolled onto his back and swung her up on top of him. There was a rustle at the curtain.

"Mama?"

"Valentin!" snapped Vasil. "Out."

"Won't," retorted Valentin.

"You get out of there or I'll drag you," said Ilyana from the outer chamber.

"Valentin," said Karolla softly. "Do as your father says."

"Yes, Mama." It was said sullenly, but the curtain dropped back into place and swayed and stilled.

Karolla's face had shuttered, and Vasil cursed his son silently for breaking the mood. Valentin resisted him every step of the way and grew more intransigent each day they stayed here. He should have sent the child on with the Veselov tribe and just kept Karolla and Ilyana with him.

Karolla sighed and pushed away from him. "You'd better go. They'll be expecting you."

But he caught her back. He could not, he would not, leave with her in this mood. He could not stand to see her devotion to him so shaken that she would begin to question him like this. And anyway, he knew how to make her love him; he always had.

"My heart, how can I leave with you hating me like this?"

She paled. "I don't hate you. You know that!"

"Look how you turn away from me. You're all that I have, Karolla, you and the children." Already she was melting, she hesitated, she turned back toward him. "And you alone, my own dear wife, you are the only person in all the lands who I can trust. I can give myself into your hands and know that you won't shun me, or curse me, or drive me away. But I have nothing to bring to you, nothing. That is my shame." And thus she embraced him, caressed him, to prove that it was not true. Although it was true: he had the right to be dyan but it was a position which he neither wanted nor was suited for.

"It isn't true," she insisted, laying him back on the pillows. "It was never true." She smoothed his hair back from his brows and kissed his perfect lips. Vasil knew they were perfect; he had been told so often enough. All that was left him was his beauty, and the ability to make people love him. For his beauty was still pure, and it was his beauty that Karolla had first loved. Just as Ilya had, those long years ago.

* * *

So it was rather later than he had planned when he approached the great tent in the midst of its ring of warriors. He knew they hated and despised him, the riders who let him through each guard post, but he could not muster up the energy right now to win them over. Even the women of the Orzhekov tribe, many of whom he had once charmed, hated him now, ignored him, and called their children away from his path.

He saw Tess. She walked at a brisk pace in a sweeping circle, accompanied by the sharp-faced orphan she had adopted. Vasil paused, waiting for her. The young man— what was his name? Vasil could not recall it—strode with the lithe and easy swing of a man who is entirely comfortable in and confident of his body. Arina had told Vasil that he had been the last and best student of the old rider Vyacheslav Mirsky, and that many of the older men said that he surpassed even his master in his skill with the saber. He had a hand cupped beneath Tess's elbow, and they spoke easily together, closely, like any brother and sister. Had Bakhtiian approved this relationship? Was he jealous?

Tess looked up and saw Vasil. Her expression closed, and she grew grave and troubled. Her brother shifted, without looking at Vasil, but his stance became protective, shielding. They came up and halted before Vasil.

Vasil stared at her. Out here in the open, with the light on her face, she looked tired and drawn and yet still handsome enough that any man might be excused if he fell in love with her. But it was Bakhtiian who had married her. That was all that mattered. He smiled. Her face lit, absorbing the heat of his regard, and she smiled back. The brother arched an eyebrow. Vasil could not read him, and it bothered him that he couldn't tell whether the brother liked him or despised him.

"Aleksi and I are going riding," Tess said. Her voice sounded rough from disuse. "But I suppose—" She faltered. "Well, Cara will be there."

The thought of going any longer without seeing Ilya made Vasil ache. But he dropped his chin in feigned obedience. "Of course, it's not proper—"

"Oh, go on," she said impatiently, as he knew she would, because he had discovered that she *was* in fact impatient with the disapproval with which everyone else treated him. The jaran knew that his presence here was improper. *He* knew that his presence here was improper. He was like a reflection of Bakhtiian, but a reflection that showed what Bakhtiian might have become: corrupt and self-serving. He knew what they thought of him, and he did not blame them for thinking it. But the gods had made him this way. Was he to fight against what the gods had wrought? And anyway, Tess Soerensen rebelled against their strictures. She disliked their censure, and she favored him because he suffered under it. He allowed himself a broader smile, feeling that he had scored a triumph. She touched his arm, briefly, warmly, and then excused herself and left, escorted by the brother.

Two young men stood on either side of the awning, Vladimir the orphan and Konstans Barshai. They stared at him as he walked up to the tent, Vladimir with enmity, Konstans with curiosity. He gave Konstans a brief smile and ignored Vladimir. He paused on the carpet. A moment later the healer came out of the tent, rubbing her hands together briskly.

"Konstans, where did—?" She broke off, seeing Vasil. "Ah, you're here. Well, I'll go in with you."

Vasil followed her meekly. Now she was a strange one. He found her disconcerting. As far as he could tell, she did not care about him one way or the other, neither to disapprove or to sympathize. He was not altogether sure that she cared about Bakhtiian all that much either; like Aleksi, her loyalties lay with Tess Soerensen. She led him in through the outer chamber, with its khaja furniture and a single scarlet shirt lying on the table, a shirt whose sleeves and collar were embroidered with Ilya's distinctive pattern. Vasil wanted desperately to touch that shirt, but he did not dare stop. They went on, past the curtain, into the inner chamber. There lay Ilya, looking thinner and paler and just as still. Fifteen days, it had been, and still his spirit wandered the heavens.

"Now," said the healer, turning to view him. "I can't leave you here alone with him. I hope you know that."

He bowed his head, acceding to her judgment. Of course she could not trust him. He had ridden for six years with the dyan who had tried his best to kill Bakhtiian. He had ridden as an outlaw these past three years.

Who was to say that he had truly given up his vow to see Ilya dead? The doctor settled down on a pillow and propped a book open on her knees.

"Can you *read?*" he asked, more to woo her than because he was interested.

She glanced up at him, as if she were surprised that he had addressed her. "Yes." Her gaze dropped back down to her book.

"Ilya tried to teach me, when he first came back from Jeds," Vasil continued. "But it's so much easier to learn things by hearing them. I don't understand how those marks can speak."

Her face sparked with sudden interest. "Here," she said. She turned the pages and then stopped. "I'll read this aloud to you, and then you see how much you can repeat back to me. Hmm. I'll have to translate it into khush, so bear with me." She spoke:

> "He, who the sword of heaven will bear
>   Should be as holy as severe;
>   Pattern in himself to know,
>   Grace to stand, and virtue go;
>   More nor less to others paying
>   Than by self offenses weighing.
>   Shame to him whose cruel striking
>   Kills for faults of his own liking!"

Vasil felt the heat of shame rise to his cheeks. "Are you mocking me?" he demanded.

She cocked her head to look at him, measuring. "Not at all. Should I be? I was thinking of someone else entirely."

"You were thinking of Bakhtiian," he said accusingly.

"No, in fact, I wasn't. Sit down, Veselov. You're looking rather peaked. Can you remember it?"

He snorted, disgusted. "Of course," he said, and reeled the speech off without effort.

"Here, let's try a longer one." But he managed that as well, and a third, and she harrumphed and shut the book. "Well, you have good memories, you jaran, which shouldn't surprise me, since you're not dependent on writing. Why are you here, Vasil?"

The question surprised him. "Surely they have all told you?" he said bitterly.

"I've heard many things," said the healer in her matter-of-fact voice, "but I'm curious to hear what you would say, given the chance."

Ilya's presence wore on him, standing here so close to him. He strayed over to the couch, half an eye on the healer, and just brushed Ilya's hand with his fingers. Ilya's skin was cool but not cold. The healer said nothing. Vasil slid his touch up to cup Ilya's wrist and just stood there, feeling the pulse of his blood, the throb of his heart. He shut his eyes.

"I remember," he said in a low voice, "when I first saw him. Our tribes came together that year—it was one cycle plus two winters past my birth year—"

"So you were fourteen."

"I must have been, I suppose. The Orzhekov girls all wanted to bed me. They even ignored some of the riders, the older men, because of me—but still, I grew into my beauty early. My mother always said so. She said there had never been a child as beautiful as I was."

"It might even have been true," said the healer in a low voice. Vasil could not tell if she was warming to him, or simply mocking him. But the memory dragged him on.

"But then I met Ilyakoria. He was born in the same year, the Year of the Eagle, but I was a summer's child and he winter's."

"Was he a handsome boy?"

Vasil felt how his skin warmed Ilya's, as if his heat, his presence, and his tale, too, might draw Ilya back from the heavens if only he told it truthfully enough. "No." He opened his eyes and grinned at the healer. She, too, was a handsome woman, not of feature but of dignity. "He was one of those hopelessly unattractive boys that no girl ever looks at. And he knew it, and they knew it. But he had fire in his eyes and a vision in his heart. No one saw it there but me. Well." He shrugged. "Perhaps his father did, but his father rarely spoke. I think his mother was disappointed in him."

"In her husband?"

"No. In Ilyakoria. But I had never met anyone like him. I loved him. He was like a blazing fire on a bitter cold night, that you cannot help but approach, to find warmth there.''

"Ah. And you were beautiful. Of course he would love you in return, at fourteen.''

"Of course.'' Vasil studied her, but still she did not seem to be mocking him.

"And then?''

"Then when my tribe moved on, I stayed with the Orzhekov tribe.''

"That was allowed?''

"Much is allowed, if you're still a boy, and you're discreet. Girls, too.''

"Is that so?'' A smile played on her lips and vanished. "Is it, indeed?''

Vasil withdrew his hand from Ilya's wrist. "Then he left for Jeds. I thought he was gone forever.'' His shame and his fury and his despair still burned through him, as he remembered. "I tried to find a woman to marry but I found that I could not forget Ilya, that no one, male or female, could replace Ilya in my heart. I hated him for that, all those long years that he was gone.'' He had to pause, the force of emotion was so strong in him. He had forgotten how long these feelings had lain there, buried, hidden, festering.

The healer regarded him evenly, and he thought he felt a little sympathy from her. "Then he came back.''

"Then he came back. I heard of his return many seasons later, and I left my tribe again to go to him. His own mother had already made him dyan of the Orzhekov tribe by the time I found him, so quickly had he worked. Like a Singer, he had left the jaran and returned to us gods-touched, except now everyone could see it, not just me. They called him Bakhtiian, 'he who has traveled far.' They said he had a vision in his heart, and they all vowed to follow him.''Without meaning to, he lifted a hand to trace the line of Ilya's brow, tenderly. He turned his hand over and ran the backs of his fingers down around Ilya's eyes and down the curve of his beard. Ilya's strong face was so wan and so lifeless. This was only the shell of Ilya, not Ilya at all, and yet Vasil could not imagine a sweeter sight. "He let me join his jahar, because of what we had once been to each other, but there were other boys, other men, who loved him now, too.''

"And he lay with them?"

"No." He drew his hand away from Ilya's face and clenched it around his other hand. "No." He could not help but say it triumphantly. "I was the only one. But a good dyan inspires love from his riders. Only if they love him will they die for him, you see."

"Yes, that makes sense."

"He didn't want to love me. He loved women, too. He'd discovered that in khaja lands, and now, of course, women wanted him, which they'd never done when he was nothing but an awkward, ugly dreamer. But still he did not marry."

"Why didn't he want to love you?"

He shook his head, wondering if she was stupid or simply ignorant. "Because he wanted to unite the tribes. I should have known from the first, you see." Oh, gods, still, after all these years, it was hard to say the truth out loud. "He loved his vision more than he loved me."

"Is that so surprising? Here." She stood up abruptly and blinked once, twice, three times, deliberately. "Veselov, move away from his couch."

Her tone was so sharp that he moved immediately. She went to stand next to Bakhtiian and she placed her hand on a wooden strut at one end of the couch. Then she shut her eyes and stood there for the longest time.

Ilya shifted on the bed. Slightly, barely, but his mouth moved and his right hand curled and uncurled, then stilled. Vasil thought his own heart would burst, it pounded so fiercely.

"Konstans!" called the healer. "Come in here." A moment later Konstans appeared, wide-eyed. "Send Vladimir to get Tess. You will watch Veselov in the outer chamber."

Konstans ducked out again. Vasil heard words exchanged and then the sound of someone running away from the tent.

Ilya opened his eyes. And suddenly, everything about him had changed. What had been a slack, limp form was abruptly invested with that fire—however dampened, however weakened—that characterized him. Vasil could not help but be drawn toward it, to the foot of the couch. Ilya stared for the longest endless moment at the billowing ceiling of the tent. The healer glanced at Vasil, then

passed a hand slowly over Bakhtiian's eyes. At first he
simply stared above. Belatedly, weakly, his gaze caught
the movement and tracked it.

"Oh, gods," said Konstans hoarsely from the curtain.
Vasil felt more than saw the young rider collapse to his
knees onto the carpet. Bakhtiian reacted to the sound. His
head moved and his right hand curled up into a fist.

"Bakhtiian," said the healer in a calm, even voice,
"you are in your own tent. I am Dr. Hierakis. I—"

But his gaze had tracked down his own body and
caught on Vasil. He stared at him. Vasil stared back,
drinking in the sight of him. Gods, Ilya was looking at
him, just looking at him. Was it possible that it was his
own presence, his story, his voice, that had brought Ilya
back?

Ilya's lips moved. A hoarse croak came out. Bakhtiian
shut his eyes, took in a difficult, shuddering breath, and
opened them again.

"Tess," he said. The word was slurred and thick but
perfectly understandable. "Where is Tess?"

"I sent for her," said the healer in that unruffled tone.
"She will be here soon. You have suffered an illness, but
I think you will be well now. You will be fine, you must
just rest and regain your strength."

Ilya tracked up to look at her. His mouth quirked, as
if he was trying to recall who she was. "Hand," he
croaked. "Can't move—hand." His right hand uncurled
and curled again. Down by Vasil's hips, his feet and legs
stirred.

"Rest for now," said the doctor sternly. "Rest here
until Tess comes. Let me give you a little water, to
moisten your lips." She turned away. "Konstans, don't
just sit there and gape. Go get Sonia. And Ursula."

"Of course." Konstans leapt to his feet and left, but
his face, his whole expression, transformed from gravity
to joy.

Tess. Ilya's first thought had been for Tess.

Ilya tracked down to stare at Vasil again. What did that
expression mean? That he was glad to see him? Furious
at seeing him? That he didn't recognize him at all?

"Left hand," said Ilya. "I can't move my left hand."
Which was concealed under a blanket.

"Don't try to move it," said the healer. "Here. I'll

just moisten your lips a little, and we'll see how you swallow.'' She softened his lips with water, and he managed to swallow, but he kept staring at Vasil. Outside, Vasil heard the sound of running footsteps. *Her* voice. The curtain swept aside and Tess stood there, just stood there, staring avidly and with sheer incredulous disbelief at her husband.

Ilya still stared at Vasil. He shifted his head slightly to the right, to the left, as if testing to see if his neck still worked. He did not see his wife, not yet. He saw only Vasil.

''Grandmother Night is laughing at me,'' said Bakhtiian.

''Ilya. Oh, God, Ilya.'' Her voice was low and husky with emotion. At the sound of it, Bakhtiian's attention broke utterly away from Vasil. The healer stepped away from the couch and the next instant Tess was there. She made a sound low in her throat and fell to her knees beside her husband, stroking his face with one hand and his hair with the other. His right hand fluttered and moved and he lifted it to touch her cheek.

A hand brushed his sleeve. Vasil started, he was so taken aback. He had forgotten anyone else existed, but the two of them—the three of them.

''It is time you left,'' said the healer kindly. By her tone, she did not mean to entertain any protests. Vasil bowed to the inevitable and walked to the curtain. He paused there, but neither Tess nor Ilya marked his going. The healer gestured, looking a little impatient. He ducked out.

In the outer chamber sat the adopted brother and Sonia Orzhekov, faces bright with hope. ''Is it true?'' Sonia demanded. ''He's awake?''

''It is true,'' said Vasil, suddenly heartened that he had this vital news to impart. ''He has returned.'' Like a messenger bearing good tidings, with this news he would be welcome everywhere. He smiled at Sonia and was pleased to see her smile back. He went outside.

A crowd of them had gathered here, in a semicircle beyond the awning; so quickly did rumor spread. Vasil paused to bask in their regard: not for him personally, it was true, but for what he had to tell them. Still, what did it matter? From now on, he would be associated with this auspicious moment.

"Papa!" There, isolated in one corner of the awning, sat Ilyana. She jumped to her feet and threw herself at him, and he caught her to him. He realized that he was crying from sheer joy, and he ducked his face against her blouse to wipe away the telltale tears.

"It's true," he said more loudly. "Bakhtiian has returned to us."

After that, for the rest of the day at least, no one cared who he was or why Mother Sakhalin disapproved so heartily of him; no one cared about the old stories that Bakhtiian had been forced to banish him or else lose the support of the Elders for his dream of uniting the tribes. With Ilyana at his side, Vasil spread the news and luxuriated in their unreserved and ungrudging attention. He made his way back across the camp to his wife's tent, and there he set up his own little court, with Karolla and Ilyana at his side—Valentin had run off somewhere—and received visitors until it was too dark to see.

CHAPTER THIRTY-NINE

The commotion broke Diana out of an unpleasantly gratifying dream, unpleasant because, snapping awake, she reached for Anatoly to continue, only to remember that he wasn't there and that she had no idea whatsoever when he would return. It seemed to her that the longer he was gone, the more she missed him. Her hand brushed the soft leather pouch in which she stored the finery he had sent to her. Nestled in among the pillows, it was a poor substitute for him, but it had touched his hands more recently than she had, and for that reason she kept it by her.

Outside, a woman spoke in a commanding voice. "Where is your mother?" Then, Diana realized that she knew that voice, and that Arina Veselov was asking for "Mother" Yomi—whom the jaran had mistaken for the headwoman of the actors' tribe, just as they thought of Owen as dyan.

"Hyacinth, what in hell happened to you?" asked Quinn, outside. She received silence as her reply, except for the muffled sound of crying.

Diana dragged a tunic on over her loose striped trousers and pulled on her soft leather boots. She twisted her hair back and, with a deft flip of her hand and a silver brooch, pinned her hair up at her neck. Then she ventured outside.

To be greeted by a shocking sight: her dear friend Arina Veselov, looking like no friend now, escorting a party of red-shirted fighters who guarded a disheveled Hyacinth. A bruise was forming on Hyacinth's right cheek. Tears stained his face, and his clothes were grimy, as if he had been dragged through the dirt. Quinn stood staring, with Oriana at her back; a moment later Hal came crawling out of his tent, bleary-eyed, to gape at the scene. Gwyn ran up.

"Arina," Diana began tentatively, but Arina merely glanced her way and shook her head fractionally, as if to say: I can't speak to you now.

So they waited. Hyacinth was still crying, but soundlessly now. He wiped his face with his sleeve. The men surrounding him did not look at him, looked anywhere but at him, but they remained aware of his presence nevertheless and alert to any move he might make to escape. The other actors arrived in ones and twos, curious, worried. Finally Owen and Ginny arrived, looking sleepy and puzzled, with Yomi and Joseph trailing behind. It was just light enough to see. Behind, in the main camp, activity already bustled at this early hour, and a fair crowd of jaran had gathered at a little distance to watch.

"Mother Yomi," said Arina formally, inclining her head with the respect of one peer to another. "It is my bitter task to bring this man back to you. He is no longer welcome in our camp, and perhaps will no longer be welcome in yours." She bowed her head briefly over her folded hands. "Although none of us will venture to interfere in how you judge this case among yourselves."

Owen and Ginny simply watched. Yomi glanced at Owen and then replied. "I beg your pardon, Mother Veselov, but please let us know what offense the boy has committed. He's scarcely more than a child."

Anahita tittered. Quinn slapped her on the arm, looking outraged.

"How dare you!" shrieked Anahita, tossing her black curls back away from her face.

"Anahita," said Gwyn in a low voice. "Shut up, or leave."

Anahita went red in the face. With a snort of anger, she walked away. But no one laughed at her discomposure. Hyacinth fell silent.

Arina Veselov looked grave. She looked so impossibly tiny, standing there with the weight of her authority on her, and yet she carried an air of implacability with her. Her chin quivered, and she set her mouth in a thin line, then spoke. "In the days before day existed, Mother Sun and Father Wind talked together, Aunt Cloud and Uncle Moon talked together, and from this congress came children. So did they, the gods, decree that when a girl becomes a woman, when a boy becomes a man, so will they talk together, that from such congress will come children. And so did the tents of the jaran grow from one tent to many tents, and the tribes of the jaran from ten tribes to a hundred hundred tribes. But this one—'' She opened a hand, palm out, to indicate Hyacinth. ''—has turned his face away from the gods' decree. Thus must we, in our turn, turn our face away from him.''

Quinn had sidled up next to Diana, and Diana felt that Gwyn had moved up behind her, like a shield at her back. Hal glowered at the jaran. Yomi looked perplexed, and for once, Owen appeared to be perfectly alert, absorbing every word.

''I don't understand,'' whispered Quinn. ''What does that mean? What did he do?''

''I thought,'' said Gwyn in an undertone, ''that Hyacinth was being discreet.''

Yomi sighed and stepped forward to extend a hand toward Hyacinth, but he ignored her. ''Mother Veselov, I'm still not sure I understand what you are trying to say.''

Arina set her lips even tighter, as if the entire conversation were distasteful to her. She glanced back once at Hyacinth and then at one of the men standing guard—her brother Anton, Diana realized. ''I beg your pardon for bringing such news to you, Mother Yomi. He was found consorting with another man.''

''And?'' Yomi asked, waiting for the explanation of the crime that had evidently followed this discovery.

Arina stared blankly at her. Yomi stared blankly back.

Diana took one step forward. ''Yomi,'' she said softly in Anglais, ''I think she's trying to tell you that same-sex partnerships aren't—ah—tolerated here, and certainly not when they become public.''

Owen swore loudly. Yomi hastened forward and took Hyacinth firmly by one elbow, dragging him away from his jaran escort. ''Mother Veselov,'' she said briskly, ''I thank you for bringing this boy back here. Now we will speak with him.''

It was a dismissal. Arina recognized it. She nodded, apologized again for the unseemly episode, and retreated, ruthlessly dispersing the distant crowd as she went.

''You damned fool,'' said Owen.

''Oh, hell,'' murmured Gwyn. ''He's going to lose his temper and antagonize Hyacinth at the same time.''

"Have you no self-control?" Owen demanded. "I *thought* I admitted only professionals to my troupe, but now I see that I've made an exception. Clearly you can't think any farther than your genitals extend."

Hyacinth burst into tears. He gulped out words that no one could make sense of, strangled in sobs.

"Owen," said Ginny quietly, going over to put an arm around Hyacinth. "Perhaps we'd have better luck in a softer and more private discussion of what happened."

But Owen was in a white rage by now. "I wash my hands of him!" He stalked off.

"Yes, let's discuss this in private," said Yomi. "Ginny? Joseph?" She glanced up. "Gwyn and Diana, you, too. Come." Hyacinth trailed passively after her. They went to the Company tent.

"Sit," said Ginny sternly, pressing Hyacinth down into a chair. "Now, what in hell happened, my boy?"

Hyacinth looked awful. His bright hair was mussed and tangled. Dirt streaked his chin. His left sleeve had a rip in it. He stared at his hands, which lay motionless in his lap. There was a long silence. At last Hyacinth spoke, his voice so low that Diana had to strain to hear him. "I met this man. I liked him."

"But, Hyacinth," said Diana, "by the way you talk, I thought you knew all about—I mean—" She faltered.

"I think what Diana is trying to say," said Yomi, "is how, if you're so experienced at this, did you get yourself into this mess?"

"Oh, Goddess," said Ginny under her breath, "what will Soerensen say when he hears of this? He was so insistent that we not break any taboos."

"Go on, Hyacinth," said Joseph gently. "You may as well tell us the truth now, since I think you've done as much damage as you can by—"

"By lying?" Hyacinth flung his head back. "Well, it's true, that I exaggerated. It's true I joked about sleeping my way through the camp, and sleeping with everyone, and, no, I never did. Oh, men looked at me in *that* way, a few of them, but they never did anything about it, except once, and then he was ashamed, and it was all so secret and quick and shameful that it was ugly instead of joyful, and it made me feel dirty since he clearly felt that way. Women propositioned me, lots of women, and they were fine and pleasant, those I went to. But you know I prefer men.''

''But then if you knew they thought it shameful, if you knew it was wrong as a cultural norm, then why did you go ahead this time?'' Ginny asked, shaking her head. ''Why? We're in *their* culture, Hyacinth. We can't just tromp around in our seven-league boots and trample wherever we go.''

''If it was *wrong?* You know it's wrong, how *they* act. Punishing someone for what's only natural.'' He was no longer sobbing, but tears leaked from his eyes again. ''Do you know what they're going to do to him? They're going to exile him. Ostracize him. You know what that means, don't you? He'll die.''

Diana stared. The truth was, she had never thought Hyacinth capable of thinking much about anything. He was a decent actor, with a chance to grow in time if he worked at it, but the rest of the time he was such a damned flighty, shallow, pretty boy that it was hard to take him seriously or even to believe that he could feel this deeply and understand this much.

Gwyn sighed. Yomi covered her eyes with a hand. Joseph shook his head.

''Then why did you do it?'' demanded Ginny.

''I didn't know,'' he said, anguished, and Diana believed him. ''I know they're savages, and I knew enough to know that the kind of primitive war they wage would be ugly—but you can learn to look the other way.''

''Oh, Goddess, maybe *you* can,'' whispered Diana.

''But I thought because they're pretty open about their sexuality that they wouldn't be so harsh. I knew I had to be discreet. And it was my fault. He said I ought to leave, and I said—well, and then we fell asleep. And then it was morning.'' He began to weep in earnest again. ''It isn't fair. His life has been hard enough. He and his sister were orphaned and sent to live with their aunt, but she didn't treat them well, and then he became an outlaw—I don't understand that part—and now they let him ride with the army again, but I think they'll be happy enough to see him go. It's a good excuse to get rid of him. He's worried about his sister.''

''Hyacinth,'' asked Yomi slowly, ''how long has this been going on?''

He shrugged. "A month? Right after that skirmish up in the hills we were caught in. Longer than that, I guess. A while."

Yomi turned to Diana. "Do you know anything about this?"

"No. It's not a subject I ever—discussed—with my husband. Or with anyone else, for that matter. Just with Hyacinth. But I thought he knew what he was doing!"

"You don't understand." Hyacinth stood up. "It's my fault. If we don't do something, he'll die."

"What do you suggest we do?" asked Ginny quietly. "We're traveling with them, Hyacinth, not the other way around. I remind you that we work under the duke's interdiction."

"Tits!" swore Hyacinth. "You know damn well we're breaking that interdiction anyway. All the plays. Theater. Everything. It's so much piss, if you ask me. We're influencing them just by being here—and his own sister is married to the king! I think it's for the better, too. They need to be civilized. Do you really approve of the way they kill? Slaughter wholesale? And now they're going to kill Yevgeni just because he loves men rather than women, as if that means anything."

"They're not going to *kill* him!" Yomi exclaimed.

"Do you think he has a chance, sent out into hostile countryside alone?" Hyacinth sounded disgusted.

"You're dependent on the tribe, here," said Diana softly. "Everywhere, here, whether you're in hostile country or out on the plains."

"Yevgeni said there used to be a tribe that was just men, just fighters, who had left their tribes because they—because they wanted that freedom. He was with a group of them when they came into the army, but he says that the last real group of them died." His beautiful, mobile mouth twisted down into a bitter grimace. "They died saving Bakhtiian's life. I told him that he should demand to see Bakhtiian. If men like that would save Bakhtiian, surely Bakhtiian owes them a favor, to save Yevgeni."

"Hyacinth." Gwyn shook his head. "But custom has to be strict in a place like this, in a society like this. Isn't it true that they have to be rigid to survive? Isn't inflexibility necessary in a hostile environment?"

"I don't know," said Hyacinth peevishly. "I just know

that Yevgeni trusts me, and I'm not just going to stand
by and let him be exiled.''

This fierce declaration brought only silence.

''What precisely do you intend to do?'' asked Yomi.
''I remind you that you are a member of this troupe, and
bound by its rules as well.''

''I forbid you to interfere,'' said Ginny.

Diana twisted her hands together. She had seen so
much suffering in the last months. So much of it had been
distant suffering, the suffering of strangers and it was true
that it was easier to ignore it, to displace it, to thrust it
aside; it disturbed her to know that she was learning to
do that. Perhaps one had to learn to do that to survive,
to make existence bearable, to make happiness tenable,
in a world so full of pain. But if offered the chance to do
one thing. . . .

''I could go,'' she said softly. ''I could talk to Arina. He
must be from her tribe, or in her tribe's jahar, if she has
jurisdiction. What did you say his name was, Hyacinth?''

The hope on his face was painful, the more so because
Diana knew very well that her pleas had only the force
of sentiment behind them, with no authority whatsoever.
Unlike, say, Tess Soerensen, she had brought nothing to
her marriage, no power, no ties, no value, and while it
was possible that Mother Sakhalin had forgiven her for
that, still, no one was likely to do Diana any favors for
the sake of her connections.

''His name is Yevgeni Usova. His sister's name is Valye. She's one of the archers. He's so proud of that, that
she's one of the women training to be mounted archers.
She's really assigned to Anatoly Sakhalin's jahar, but he
didn't take any women with him when he went because
they were going so far into khaja territory, and they didn't
want to risk it.'' Diana felt sick, suddenly, feeling that
she hadn't clearly understood how dangerous the mission
Anatoly had undertaken was, but Hyacinth went blithely
on, reminiscing about his boyfriend. ''So she was training with Kirill Zvertkov to begin with, so they remained
with the Veselov tribe until Sakhalin gets back. But they
didn't want to leave Yevgeni there, with the Veselov tribe,
because he used to ride with Veselov. The cousin. Vasil,
that's his name. They say he's very handsome, the cousin, and charismatic. I think Yevgeni is in love with him,

though he never says as much to me. But he rode with him for three years, and longer, really, before that. But they let him stay because of Valye—he's the only family she has. Now what will she do? They won't trust her either, or she'll do something stupid like try to follow him into exile. She's sweet but not very smart. But she adores him. She worships him. Oh, Diana, do you think you can do *something?*"

"I'll try," said Diana. "With your permission, Ginny, of course."

Ginny swore under her breath. "What are we supposed to do? Take him in? Take him back to Earth with us? Like a pet dog?" Hyacinth went red. "Oh, don't yell at me, young man. You've caused enough trouble. I want you to think clearly for a minute—if you can—about what it would be like for one of these people to be jerked out of the world they know and thrown headlong into ours. It won't be an easy transition, no more than it would be for us if we were really and truly abandoned here without any of the fail-safes and modelers and slates and medical supplies and equipment and weapons we brought with us."

"That happened to Tess Soerensen," said Diana.

"And let her be a lesson to you, Hyacinth! Now. Go on, Diana, and why don't you take Gwyn, too?"

"Let me go," begged Hyacinth.

"No," added Ginny. "Mother Veselov already gave you into our hands. They don't want you back. Owen's not going to take this at all well, my boy, if it means they'll forbid you performing as well. And we're supposed to do *Caucasian Chalk Circle* sometime in the next five days."

"You can even think of that? With a life at stake?"

"Hyacinth, we all have our limits. I can't save the world. I can't stop this war. Maybe, just maybe, I can communicate a few things through art."

He flung himself back into the chair and buried his face in his hands. The entire line of his body spoke agony.

"I'll go now," said Diana, more to be rid of this scene than because she desired the next one.

CHAPTER FORTY

Trouble came in the guise of a woman. It always did, Jiroannes reflected. The guards snuck two whores into camp and he caught them at it. He was not sure whether the guards intended to pay the women or simply kill them afterward, but the women looked desperate enough, thin and dirty and ragged. One had a child with her, a wild-eyed little creature with weeping sores around its mouth and a red rash on its arms. Once, Jiroannes would have left his men to it. They deserved some reward for their months of service in these God-forsaken lands. Jiroannes had not touched Samae in twenty days, and already even the sight of the whores' scrawny thighs and grimy abdomens moved him to lust. The guards had gone much longer without women.

"Syrannus," he said as the whores straightened their clothes and the guards rebound their sashes, "chase the creatures away."

"Yes, eminence. May I give them some food?"

"Give them food!"

"Eminence, in these lands, whores receive payment."

"Do what you wish. Don't bother me with it."

The next day, the guards mutinied. Politely, it was true, but they sent a delegation consisting of the captain and his two lieutenants to present their grievances to their master. This would never have happened in Vidiya.

Jiroannes received them on the carpet. Lal attended him, standing behind his chair with a large fan, which the boy worked up and down. Samae was out getting water from the river. She did the work Lal used to do, and the boy had quickly learned the more elaborate business of being a personal body servant.

"Your eminence." The captain knelt and bent to touch his forehead to the carpet.

"You may speak."

"Eminence, you must know that the jaran women will have nothing to do with us. They call us names, eminence, foul names, and scorn us, and there are none who will accept coin or cloth or food for lying with us. Now you forbid us congress with these women who are willing enough to come into our camp. This is unjust. The Everlasting God has also decreed, eminence, that it is improper for a man to pass more than ten days without knowing a woman, for fear he will succumb to baser lusts."

It was true, of course. Jiroannes sighed. "I will consider your grievances, captain. I will have an answer for them tomorrow."

The captain touched his forehead to the carpet again, rose, bowed, and backed away. His escort backed away as well, until they were far enough away from the tent that they could without deliberate insult turn their backs on their master.

"What are you going to do, eminence?" asked Syrannus.

Jiroannes smoothed out his trousers. The hot, stifling air made him sweat, even with the turgid breeze stirred into life by Lal's tireless fanning. "I have no choice, Syrannus. I must take this matter before the jaran."

"Ah," said Syrannus, and nothing more.

Jiroannes sat, brooding. Smoke cast a pall over the air, adding to the stifling heat. Although the Vidiyan camp was now situated at the end of ambassadors' row, in the least desirable site, still the tents of the jaran army spread out beyond his camp. Farther, at the eye of the storm, a city bled smoke into the heavens. Jiroannes could see its wall from here, a distant line. He thought there might still be some fighting going on there, but he could not be sure. Now that Mitya was gone, Jiroannes had no inside source of information. For twenty days he and his party had drifted along in the wake of the army, moving at the right time, camping at the right time, and otherwise utterly at sea. He did not know the name of this city, or which general was in charge of this assault. The guards had heard a rumor that Bakhtiian was ill, that he was dead, that he had been witched by the Habakar priests and that his spirit had left his body to do battle in the

Otherlands for this kingdom. It might be true, for all Jiroannes knew. He missed Mitya's information.

He missed Mitya's friendship.

What a strange thing it was, to think of having a friend. There had been other boys at the palace school whom he had liked, but one never trusted anyone at the palace. He sighed.

"Syrannus, you will attend me. Together with two of my guards." He rose. Lal dropped down to kneel behind the chair.

"Where are we going, eminence?"

"I don't know. We must find Bakhtiian, I suppose, or if he isn't here, then whomever is in charge." The two guards took their places at his back, and they walked together out of their huddle of tents. Syrannus went ahead to accost a pair of older jaran men who were repairing a shattered cart wheel. He spoke with them for a while and then returned to Jiroannes.

"Eminence, these men say that Mother Sakhalin is in charge of this camp."

"Mother Sakhalin? A woman?" Jiroannes sighed again, but these days he felt only mild shock at such tidings. "Where will we find her tent?"

"In the center of camp, eminence."

"Bakhtiian is not here, then?"

"Eminence, the men say that it is true that Bakhtiian was witched, that he lies as one dead up in the pass. They say that until he wakes again, the army will lay waste to the countryside."

Jiroannes shuddered. Fleetingly, he imagined this army trampling through the lush gardens of the Vidiyan palace, careless of the destruction they wrought to the fine architectural and decorative work that they certainly could never appreciate. But they could destroy it. It was easier to demolish than it was to build, especially for savages.

He hung his head and stared at the rings on his fingers. Topaz, that one, malachite, a thick band of plain gold, and a single diamond set in gold leaves bound with pewter. All along, it had been easier for him to scorn the jaran as the barbarians they definitely were than to try to understand them and build a bridge across which he and they could truly communicate.

"We will attend Mother Sakhalin," he said softly.

Syrannus looked surprised, but he bowed his head and led Jiroannes to the center of camp. In the jaran camp, in the late morning, things were fairly quiet. Dawn and late afternoon were busiest, what with milking and watering and meals. A couple of boys pushed a handcart filled with dry dung through camp. Crippled men repaired harness. Two older girls churned milk to butter. Little children ran here and there, attended by the elderly. If the besieged city on the horizon disturbed them they did not show it.

At the center of camp they found a ring of guards, but just a single ring, nothing as elaborate as the triple shield that had surrounded Bakhtiian's tent. They waited here while a messenger was sent in. Some time later a young jaran woman arrived to escort them. Jiroannes swallowed this insult with no change of expression and followed her in, Syrannus alone attending him now.

Mother Sakhalin held court in much the same way Bakhtiian did, but she was rather more ruthless, Jiroannes decided. He recognized her immediately: the ancient crone he had seen watching the mounted archers at practice, that fateful day, twenty days ago. He recalled now how scornfully he had thought of her then. Here she sat in judgment like a queen, seated on pillows on a dais with two other women, one very young and very pretty, one almost as old as the old woman, seated on either side of her. The escort motioned to Jiroannes to stand to one side. He stood and waited. Syrannus waited behind him. A cluster of women and old men argued in front of the dais. As far as Jiroannes could tell, they haggled over grazing and watering rights. One tribe had watered its herd too early, and in revenge the other tribe had grazed its herds on fields reserved for the first tribe. The old woman presided over this dispute with an expression of deep disgust on her face, and in the end she stripped both tribes of their current rights and assigned them worse rights—the last to go down to the river? the stoniest patches of grazing land?—than they had previously owned.

"You see," said Jiroannes in a low voice to Syrannus, impressed despite himself, "that will teach them to bother her with such trivial matters."

A troop of horsemen rode in and dismounted, all but

one of their number. This last, a dark-haired young man,
remained seated on his horse as if he were somehow in
disgrace. A girl armed with bow and arrows was called
forward to stand in front of the queen. She threw herself
down and began to plead in a high voice, but the queen
silenced her with a wave of a hand.

"The punishment is exile," said Mother Sakhalin. She
turned to the pretty young woman beside her. "Your dyan
will strip him of all that binds him to your tribe."

"My dyan is not here," said the princess. Her thick
black hair was bound back in four braids and overlaid
with a rich headpiece whose jeweled links hung to her
shoulders. She regarded the scene gravely. The audience
hushed. Glancing around, Jiroannes realized that in the
course of moments the number of people attending had
doubled. Stillness hung over them. "But my brother will
act for him in this matter. Anton?"

One of the jaran soldiers came forward. If he were this
woman's brother, then surely he was a prince, but Jiroannes could see no difference between him and the
other men by the way he dressed. He was much older
than the princess. Perhaps he was a bastard child of an
early concubine and thus not a legitimate heir to power.
He inclined his head respectfully to the two women and
then turned to the mounted man.

"You," he said to the man, "whom we once knew as
Yevgeni Usova, you will dismount."

The man obeyed. His face was white but otherwise
expressionless. The girl kneeling in front of the queen
began to weep. His wife, perhaps?

The captain gestured to one of his men to lead the
horse away. "This horse belongs to no man," he said.
He drew the young man's saber from his sheath and
handed it away as well. "This saber belongs to no man."
Then he drew his own knife. He laid it along the collar
of the young man's shirt and cut, down through the fabric. The silk did not cut easily, and it was messy work,
but with a grim face and an unrelenting manner, the captain cut the shirt off the offender, piece by piece, and let
it fall into the dust. The young man stood there, silent,
unmoving, and the sun beat down on his pale body.

"This shirt belongs to no man."

On the dais, the queen watched without the slightest

sign of mercy on her face. But the princess had averted her eyes, as if the sight pained her.

"Yevgeni Usova is dead to us," said the captain. He turned on his heel and walked back to his men. At this signal, all the watchers averted their eyes. Some actually physically turned away, to show their backs to the exiled young man. He hesitated, but only for one moment. The old crone glared at him. Her mouth was a tight line, her expression implacable. The man turned and, with his head high, he began to walk away into his exile.

"Yevgeni!" The girl sprang up from the ground in front of the queen. "I'm coming with you."

He stopped. He was close to Jiroannes now, and Jiroannes saw his face whiten at the girl's words. If before he had looked resigned, then now he looked terrified. He turned back. "No. I forbid it, Valye."

She cast a defiant glance toward the queen and ran over toward him. "I don't care. I'm coming with you."

"Valye!" This from the princess, who flung up her head. Her eyes looked haunted. "You have a place here. You know that. You must stay."

The girl stopped beside the man. She was young, very young, with dark brown eyes and black hair like his. All at once Jiroannes saw the resemblance: they had the same blunt nose and blunt chin and narrow foreheads, features that proclaimed them to be relatives. "I won't stay. It's death to send him out there with nothing, and you know it. At least with my bow we'll have a chance to stay alive."

"No," Yevgeni whispered harshly, under his breath. "At least I'll know you're safe."

The queen rose. She was not much taller standing than sitting, but her authority seemed to enlarge with the simple movement. "Valye Usova, your loyalty to your brother is commendable, but I forbid you to leave with him. He has condemned himself by his own choice. Let him go."

"Please, Valye," said the princess. "You know you must stay here. You know it's what your brother would want."

"No! No, I refuse. You all say one thing with your mouths, but you cover your eyes to stop from seeing what

you know is true. You know what your own cousin is,
Mother Veselov, and yet he still rides with the tribe.''

"He was banished once," said the queen sternly.

"Then why isn't he here with the tribe where he's supposed to be? He's still up there!'' The girl pointed up,
to the northeast, toward the distant mountains. Her voice
rose higher, and it broke as she spoke again. "You all
know why he's there, but you all pretend you don't know.
You all know that whatever Yevgeni might have done,
he's done as well."

"Young woman, you go too far."

The girl spun to face the captain. "Anton, aside from
this one thing, what fault has Yevgeni ever shown?'' The
older man only looked away and would not answer.
"None. You know it's true. He's an exemplary rider."

"He rode with Dmitri Mikhailov," said the princess. "For that reason alone, he is untrustworthy."

"And so did your cousin!" cried the girl triumphantly.
"But you acclaimed him dyan as soon as he returned.
Yevgeni was loyal to the dyan he followed, always. He is
now, too; he's loyal to Bakhtiian. But you're punishing
him because he was Vasil's lover once. But now Vasil
has Bakhtiian back—oh, yes, he told Yevgeni about that
and Yevgeni told me, so don't think you can keep it a
secret—so Yevgeni is nothing but an embarrassment to
you all—"

"That is enough!'' The queen stepped down from her
dais and marched over the dusty ground to confront the
girl. "You will be silent, or you will leave this camp
forever."

The girl lifted her chin. Unshed tears sparkled in the
sunlight.

"Please, Valye," begged the brother. "Please, for my
sake, stay."

"I'm going." With monumental disdain and appalling
rudeness, she turned her back deliberately and insult-
ingly on the queen. "Come, Yevgeni, let's leave." She
took him by the arm and he had no choice but to go with
her. The crowd parted to let them through and then, once
they were gone, burst into a wild roar of exclamation.

The queen marched back to her dais and, with assis-
tance from the two princesses, clambered back on. She
turned to survey the crowd imperiously. "Quiet," she

said. In a circle radiating out from her presence the audience quieted, ring by ring, until all were silent again. She settled herself down on her pillow. Her eyes searched the crowd. Her gaze settled on Jiroannes. He flushed, sure suddenly that he was about to become the next victim, a fitting close to the disaster he had just witnessed.

"Ambassador. What brings you to my camp?"

For a moment he could not move. Syrannus poked him in the back, and he started and walked forward to kneel before her. It felt very strange to kneel before a woman, and yet, at this moment, it did not feel degrading.

"Madam," he began, not sure by what title to address her.

"You may call me Mother Sakhalin."

"Mother Sakhalin. I come to you because—" He faltered. Without Mitya, he had no one to practice khush with, and his facility with the language had suffered for it. But Syrannus was there, kneeling behind him, and using him as an interpreter, Jiroannes felt able to go on. "I arrived in your lands with twenty guardsmen, of whom one died of a fever at the last siege. They have complained to me recently that it is difficult for them to endure without the . . . comforts of women."

"It is difficult for any man to endure that," said the queen. A few people laughed, but the atmosphere remained somber, and Jiroannes had a fair idea now of why the young man Yevgeni had been exiled.

"But I know," Jiroannes continued, more carefully still, "that your justice is strict. There are women of these lands, of Habakar lands, who would—ah—come to my men, but I did not know if this is allowed within the laws of this camp."

The old queen considered him. The young princess stared at her hands and did not appear to be paying any attention to this conversation. "If these men do not have wives, then certainly it is unreasonable to deny them this comfort. Certainly jaran women are uninterested in khaja men. But as you are all khaja, there seems no reason that you can't deal together well enough."

"Then my guards may allow *khaja* women into their tents?"

She watched him. He felt the baleful intensity of her stare, and he felt that she meant to play some horrible trick on him that only she would find amusing. "It is also true that the khaja women here no longer have husbands. They may well desire to be married again. That is how I judge it, then. If these men wish to take wives, they may." She paused and skewered him with a bright, malevolent glare. "You will see that they are treated as a wife deserves, will you not?"

Kneeling here at her feet, what else could he say? "Assuredly, Mother Sakhalin. You are kind, wise, and generous."

She snorted. "You may go, ambassador. Now, Mother Grekov, did you say there was a dispute over the stud rights of that bay stallion?"

Thus dismissed, Jiroannes rose and went back to camp, his escort at his heels.

"What do you think, eminence?" Syrannus asked.

"I think the old woman is no fool," said Jiroannes. "She must know that men will go to all lengths to find women, if they're kept apart long enough. So she has given me a way to keep my men happy."

"I meant, eminence, about the young man they exiled."

"He was caught fornicating with a man, of course. Although I don't know why the other man wasn't exiled as well."

"But the girl, she said—"

"She was overwrought, Syrannus. We must not listen to rumor. In any case, he will die, sent out alone like that."

Syrannus sighed. They had reached their tents, now, and Jiroannes sank gratefully into his chair and accepted a cup of hot tea from Lal. "But, eminence, what if Bakhtiian dies?"

"Then we wait. If a successor emerges, we deal with him. If one does not, then we ride for home and hope we make it there without being killed. Tell my captain to attend me."

He sipped at the tea. It was spicy, and it scalded his tongue. Lal really was very good, better than Samae had ever been, about making everything just as he liked it. Already, without being asked, the boy had begun fanning him against the afternoon heat. He recognized all at once that Samae had rebelled against him constantly, in subtle ways, primarily by never acting until he ordered her to act, so that her obedience was never a thing of her choosing but always a matter of her being forced to endure his commands.

The captain arrived and touched his forehead to the carpet in front of Jiroannes. "Eminence, you sent for me."

"Captain." He explained the terms that Mother Sakhalin had set them.

"But, eminence, many of us have wives, proper Vidiyan wives, at home. These foreign women are good enough for whores, it's true, but they aren't our kind."

"Captain, I understand your reservations, but I am presenting you with a solution. Keep whores, but treat them as if they were wives and all will be well. I will see that you have enough rations to cover everyone."

"But, eminence, what about their husbands?"

Jiroannes tilted his head back. Smoke rose in the distance. He wondered if the city had fallen yet. "I doubt they have husbands left. I doubt there are any men left alive in this land. I expect, captain, that many women will be grateful for such shelter as you and your men can provide them."

"If they bring children, eminence?"

"As I said, captain, treat them as you would your own wives. As long as we do not antagonize the jaran, you may keep them here. Do you understand?" And because the captain was wise enough to have risen up through the ranks to his current command, he did.

"Are you hungry, eminence?" asked Lal.

"Why, yes, I am." At the outskirts of his little camp, Samae appeared, trudging under the weight of two full buckets hung from a pole slung over her shoulders. Her face was still, bearing no expression. Why had she refused her freedom? The question nagged at him. It had bothered him for twenty days, now, but he could think of no answer.

"Eminence, here are some delicacies I made," said Lal, breaking into Jiroannes's reverie. He knelt before Jiroannes's chair and held out a plate of chased pewter on which savory looking pastries were arranged in an artful pattern. "I hope they please you."

Jiroannes wrenched his gaze away from Samae. He

accepted the food. "Thank you, Lal," he said. "These are very fine."

The boy beamed and padded away to fetch warm water and a cloth to wash his master's face and hands after he had finished.

At dawn, Jiroannes was woken by Lal. "Eminence. I beg pardon, eminence, but there are men here to see you."

Jiroannes started awake and sat up. It was dark in the tent. A man shouted outside, answered by a whoop. A troop of horses pounded past. The rush of fear that hit him astounded him. What had he done? Whom had he offended? Had his guards raped some woman? Did his people, with their fine, superior Vidiyan blood and up-bringing, treat their wives in a manner repugnant to the jaran? But they had no wives here, and no women in camp, not yet.

Lal brought him a knee-length brocaded coat and helped him into it, then tied his turquoise sash around his waist in a casual style—not too formal, for this kind of meeting. Hands shaking, Jiroannes went outside. In the half-light of dawn, he recognized two of the riders: one was Anton, the brother of the princess. One was the brown-haired actor, the man who took the most demand-ing parts of the dance.

"Ambassador, I am Anton Veselov," said Veselov. "I beg your pardon for disturbing you at this hour, but we are conducting a search."

Jiroannes blanched. He thought wildly about what items he possessed that might get him executed. Lal ap-peared in the doorway of his tent, and immediately Ji-roannes was convinced that they had come to accuse him of consorting with the boy, but no one remarked on the slave as he hurried off to wake Syrannus.

"One of the khaja Singers, the *actors*, has vanished. Perhaps you have seen him?"

The brown-haired actor chimed in. "His name is Hy-acinth. He has bright yellow hair, and he's this tall." He used an expressive hand to measure a space above his own head. "Surely you were at the performance of the dream play. He played the spirit who causes so much mischief."

"I believe I know which you mean." Jiroannes discovered that his voice was shaking with relief. This matter had nothing to do with him at all.

"I do beg your pardon for disturbing you, ambassador," continued Anton Veselov, "but we're asking at every camp, to see if anyone heard anything last night."

"He stole some things, you see," added the actor. "From our camp."

"And either he, or his confederates, stole horses as well."

"Ah," said Jiroannes, suddenly quite sure who his confederates had been. "No, I'm sorry, but I haven't seen or heard of him. But perhaps you'd like to question my people. They may have seen something I did not."

"Thank you," said Anton Veselov.

In the end, to Jiroannes's surprise, Syrannus provided them with the first scrap of information. The captain of the guards had asked Syrannus to ride with him down to the river, where a ragtag collection of refugees had gathered on a flat field next to an abandoned village, there to negotiate with the whores. While Syrannus had been waiting, with the unholy glare of distant fire and the luminous stars and the last gleam of the waning moon to attend him, he had seen three riders splash across the ford, riding north. At the time, he had thought nothing of it. Now, he recalled quite clearly that one had been a woman, and another very awkward in the saddle.

CHAPTER FORTY-ONE

Tess heard the altercation in full flower as she and Aleksi rode up behind her tent.

"No, damn it! I won't rest! There's too much to do. We must move on at dawn tomorrow."

"Bakhtiian, you aren't nearly strong enough to ride yet." This from Cara, sounding cool.

"I'll ride a gentle mare."

"Ilya, you're going too damned fast. You know better than to—"

"Out, Niko! Out!"

Tess dismounted and threw her reins to Aleksi along with a wry grin. Then she hurried around the corner of the tent to see Ilya, lying propped up on pillows under the awning of the tent, yelling at the combined forces of Niko, Cara, Sonia, and young Katerina. His personal guard stood with expressionless faces just beyond the carpet. Farther away, at the first ring of guards, Elders and dyans waited for their turn to see Bakhtiian. Like flowers turning toward the sun, Ilya's four victims shifted to look hopefully at Tess.

"Out," said Tess mildly. They left. "Vladi, Konstans, you too." They left. Ilya lay there glaring at her. He was pale and he looked exhausted. "You're going to bed," she said to him.

"I don't have time to—"

"I *said*, you're going to bed. Come on."

"Tess—!"

"You only woke up yesterday, my love. You were unconscious for fifteen days. You need to rest."

He heaved himself up to sit. His eyes flashed with anger, and his lips were white and drawn tight. "I need to order my army. According to the information I've received this morning, Sakhalin has given them orders to destroy everything. How are we to make use of a country that is ruined so thoroughly?''

She crouched and grabbed him around the back, under his arms, and hoisted him to his feet. ''Let me rephrase that. You *will* rest. Now.'' He was thin, much too thin, and he still wasn't eating much. Although he swore at her, he was far too weak to resist her marching him into the tent and back to their bed. She eased him down and he collapsed. Then, taking pity on him, she lay down beside him and stroked his hair and talked to him soothingly about whatever news she had gotten in the past sixteen days. His left hand came to rest on the swell of her abdomen. He fell asleep. She stayed beside him for a while, continuing to stroke his hair and his face, filled with such impossibly intense elation that she thought she might well burst from the strength of it. She kissed him a final time on the forehead and went outside.

''My favorite type of convalescent,'' said Cara, who had returned to sit in the shade of the awning. ''Irritable, unreasonable, and stubborn. You must stop him from pushing himself too hard.''

Tess snorted. ''Cara, he's going to push himself too hard no matter what any of us do or say. I'll do what I can. I wish we could get him to eat more.''

''That will come in time. His body is still recovering from its molecular catharsis. He'd be much weaker if we hadn't managed that intravenous connection to feed him through the coma.''

Tess picked up the pillows he had been lying on and shook them out. ''Did it work?''

''It affected him. As for what its effect was—ask me in ten years. Now, if he's asleep, I'll go run some more tests on him.'' She rose and went inside.

Tess strolled over to see Sonia, who was supervising a general cleaning in preparation for their move the next day. ''Are we really moving at dawn tomorrow?'' Tess asked.

Sonia shrugged. ''Unless you can talk him out of it. I don't think he's ready to ride yet.''

''I *know* he isn't. Sonia, who is Grandmother Night?''

Sonia's whole expression became stiff. She paled. Grabbing Tess by the elbow, she dragged her out away from her tent, away from the children and relatives, out to the gap between their two tents where they could speak in privacy. "Tess! Never speak Her name in daylight. It's bad luck."

Tess was astounded. "But—"

"Who's been talking to you? Vasil?"

"Vasil! No, I heard Ilya say her name. It was the first thing I heard him say when he woke up."

"Gods," said Sonia, looking grim. "Is that where he's been? In Her lands?"

"But who is she? Why have I never heard of her in all the time I've been here?"

Sonia glanced around. The movement was almost comical, it was so broadly done, but Tess could not laugh because Sonia's expression was so horribly grave. "She is the Old One, the First One. She gave birth to us all, to the world, to the gods, to the animals, and then brought death in a fit of anger. She's jealous and angry and very, very powerful. There. I've said enough."

"But, Sonia, what did he mean? He said—"

"Don't say her name in daylight!"

Tess gulped. She had never in four years seen Sonia in this combination of anger and terror. "He said, '*She* is laughing at me.'"

Sonia blanched. "Gods," she murmured again. "My mother once said that it was because of Her that his family died. But she's never spoken of it since. Perhaps it wasn't Habakar witchcraft that took him to the spirit lands. Perhaps She did. Perhaps he offended Her once. Gods, that would be an ill-omened thing. It all was, the death of his family."

"Is that why no one speaks of it? I've never heard you or Ilya talk about his parents."

"Tess, I will say this now, but never again. They died badly. But what is worse, is that the man who killed them, Khara Roskhel, was my aunt's lover, and had been for many many years. Perhaps my mother suspects why he turned against Ilya and his mother. I don't know."

"Perhaps Ilya knows why."

"Perhaps he does. Do you truly want to ask him?"

No. But there was wanting, and there was necessity. "I have to ask him. How long after their deaths was Vasil banished?"

"Vasil? A few months, not more than that. It was all

a great scandal. Roskhel hated Vasil. He thought it was an offense against the gods that a man would love another man so openly.''

''What do you think?''

Sonia shrugged, evading the question. ''Vasil was always charming to us. He wanted us to like him, and we did. I never saw the harm in him riding with Ilya's jahar.''

''Were they lying together, too? After Ilya came back from Jeds?''

Sonia flushed. ''I don't know. I—Ilya slept with many women. Everyone knew that.''

''But you think they were.''

Sonia stared away from Tess, at their tents, at the ring of guards out beyond, at the tents beyond them, the Orzhekov camp. Wind trembled through the camp, agitating awnings and pots. People were already packing, readying to leave the next morning. ''Everyone thought they were,'' said Sonia in a low voice. ''That's why he was forced to banish Vasil. Otherwise no one would have followed him.''

''Hmm,'' said Tess. The puzzle did not yet make a coherent picture.

Sonia stared at her. ''Don't you care?'' she demanded.

''Don't I care about what?''

''That he and Vasil might have—!''

''Of course I care! But what can I do about it?''

''Gods, Tess. I'm so sorry.''

''Sorry for what? That you think Ilya still loves him?''

''That he loved a man at all—'' Just saying it made Sonia flinch.

''What do I care whether it's a man or a woman? I can never be beautiful, not in that way. I haven't known Ilya since he was a boy, I didn't ride in his jahar for three years side by side with him while he united the jaran. I never believed in him when no one else did, because I didn't know him then. How can I compete with that? Or with the memory of that?''

There was a long silence. ''Sometimes,'' said Sonia softly, ''I forget you aren't jaran. I loved a man once, but he left to join the arenabekh. He loved men more than women. I could never forgive him for that. And why should I?'' she continued, bitter now. ''He turned his

back on his own tribe, and he turned his back on the
children he might have had. Such men are better off
dead.''

"I don't agree—'' began Tess, and then stopped. In
jaran society, where there was no place for them, perhaps
they were better off leaving, for the arenabekh, for death,
for somewhere else. Was that why Ilya had gone to Jeds,
at sixteen? Cara had told her yesterday evening what Vasil
had confessed to her. If Ilya had thought there was no
place for someone like him with the jaran, because he
loved another male, then he might have been willing to
risk such a dangerous journey, knowing he might never
return.

"Sonia,'' said Tess finally, "you must remember one
thing. When Ilya left your tribe to go to Jeds, he left
everyone behind. Everyone. Nothing, and no one, has
ever been as important to him as the vision that drives
him. Not even Vasil. Even if Ilya did still want him, he
can't go back to him now.''

"You're forgiving,'' murmured Sonia.

"What is there to forgive? I know Ilya loves me. Hell.''
She gave a wry, unsteady laugh. "He married me twice.
But I don't think Vasil has changed. Ilya must face him,
or he'll never heal.''

Sonia jerked her head up and glared at Tess. "Don't
let Vasil get too close to him! That would be idiotic.''

Tess laughed. "I'm not afraid of Vasil.'' But it was a
lie. She was afraid of Vasil. And she could not help it,
but she was beginning to wonder what it would be like
to lie with him.

"You should be,'' said Sonia, and for a wild instant
Tess could not tell if Sonia was saying that Tess should
be afraid, or should be wondering.

Ilya slept all afternoon. That evening he insisted on
taking reports out under the awning. After the stifling
heat of the daytime, the cool evening air proved refresh-
ing. Tess watched him eat and drink—not enough, but
more than he had managed before—and she sat beside
him as scouts and riders came forward and spoke with
him. Josef sat on his other side, listening, remembering
everything with that astonishing memory he possessed.
Now and again Ilya asked him for a piece of information

or to clarify something someone had said. Tess could see
how weak Ilya was: normally he would never have needed
to ask; he had a formidable memory himself. Now it was
all he could do to sit there and receive visitors.

And it was just as well he did, she soon realized, even
as their reports droned past her and she forgot every word
they said. Ilya wanted the reports so that he could feel
that he was in control of his army again. But his army
also needed to see him. It was no wonder the army was
laying waste to Habakar lands. They thought Habakar
priests had killed him. Now, these men could see he was
alive, and they would pass that message down the lines.
Their faces reflected their joy and their relief. Because
Ilya lay on pillows, they knelt, each one, to speak with
him, so as not to tower over him, but as the night wore
on, Tess felt that they were kneeling to Ilya out of duty
and love and fealty. And though he was exhausted, their
presence and their devotion gave him strength.

It grew late.

"Ilya," she said, when a scout made his farewells and
walked away into the darkness, "you should go to bed.
You must rest."

Ilya shut his eyes. "Yes," he said.

Josef nodded and rose, and little Ivan leapt up to escort
Josef back to his tent. Cara had gone to her own tent.
They sat alone under the awning.

"I traveled a long journey," he said in a low voice.
"I saw my own spirit. It is a thing of bright colors and
twisting lines. It is brilliant, Tess, like fire. The gods
touched it and made it burn, and I saw that they have
given their favor to my dreams."

"Of course they have, my love." She covered his
hands with her own and just held them, strangely moved
by his recital.

His voice slipped so low that she had to bend to hear
him. "How much more will She demand that I pay her?"

"Who?"

A guard hailed them. A moment later, a small party
was escorted out of the gloom. "Ilya." The guard was
Vladimir. "He insisted, but if you want me to send them
away. . . ."

Vasil stood before them with his family in tow. Karolla
looked nervous. Ilyana looked curious. Valentin trailed

behind, clutching his mother's tunic, his pretty mouth turned down in a sullen frown.

In the stillness, Tess heard singing coming from the farthest reaches of the camp, a cheerful noise.

"No," said Ilya softly. His gaze locked on Vasil. "Let them stay."

Tess rose swiftly and beckoned to Karolla and the children to come closer. "Have you met Karolla? This is Karolla Arkhanov. This is her daughter Ilyana." An awkward silence, while the man and his namesake regarded each other doubtfully. "And this is Valentin." Valentin peered out at Bakhtiian and then, after a moment, came out from behind his mother and sat down on a pillow. Tess offered him a sweet cake. He accepted gravely.

Vasil sat down. No one spoke.

Tess offered cakes to Karolla and Ilyana, and then to Vasil, and under the cover of this nicety they all passed a few more minutes.

"You must miss Arina," said Tess, to say something.

"Yes," said Karolla.

The conversation lapsed again. Tess passed around the cakes a second time.

"You're Dmitri Mikhailov's daughter," said Ilya suddenly.

"Yes."

Sitting next to each other, Karolla and Vasil were a study in contrasts: her soft, plain face next to his beauty; her resigned expression next to his bright one.

Ilya turned his gaze back to Vasil. Tess could not read his expression, except to see that he was very tired. "I banished you," he said quietly.

"Yes," agreed Vasil, watching him avidly. Tess wondered what Karolla felt like, sitting there, knowing that Vasil loved this man better than he loved her. Was Karolla wondering the same thing, about her and Ilya?

"Why are you here?" asked Ilya.

"I am dyan of the Veselov tribe now, and I am also married." Vasil smiled slightly, and he transferred his gaze from Ilya to Tess. The warmth and brilliance of his smile caught Tess quite off guard, and it rendered her breathless for an instant. She smiled back at him. She could not help herself.

Ilya looked white. One hand clenched tight around the

tassels of a pillow. "I mean here, now," he said in an undertone. "You know damn well what I mean, Veselov."

It was almost embarrassing to see Vasil as he absorbed Ilya's attention. What did it matter what Ilya said to him, as long as he said something? He glowed with it, but like the moon, Tess saw suddenly, his was all reflected glow. He did not have heat enough to burn within himself, not like Ilya. She felt all of a sudden that she teetered on the edge of an answer, about him, about them.

"You know why," said Vasil.

"You are forbidden my presence."

"Yet I am here." Vasil drew in a great, shuddering breath. He opened his hands. His eyes had a beautiful shape, rounded with a hint of a pull at their ends. His lips were as pretty as his son's, but on him, with all the life and mobility of expression he bore with him, all the features that might otherwise have seemed weak and effeminate were strong and bold instead. "Tell me to leave, to never look on you again, and I will obey."

"No, you won't."

"But I will." He said it so sincerely, but Tess knew he was lying. Everyone here knew he was lying, except perhaps Ilyana, who sat loyally at her father's side. He dropped his voice to an intimate whisper. "You don't want me to go."

Ilya shut his eyes. He was exhausted.

"Vasil," said Tess firmly, "he needs to rest. I must ask you to leave." She rose and made polite farewells to the children and to Karolla. She had to give Vasil a shove to get him on his way. "Go." Then she turned back to Ilya. He was already asleep. She found Aleksi and together they carried Ilya back into the tent and took his clothes off and laid him on the bed. Aleksi left, and Tess stripped and lay down beside him. He sighed and turned into her, draping an arm over her, tangling his legs in with hers.

"Ilya, why is Grandmother Night laughing at you?"

He did not reply. She thought perhaps he was still asleep, but a moment later his hand moved to rest possessively, protectively, on her belly. He stroked the swollen curve and sighed deeply into her hair.

"Why was Nadine spared?" she asked suddenly. "The

rest were killed, even her brother, who couldn't have been very old. Why didn't they kill Nadine, too?''

He stiffened in her arms. ''She wasn't there,'' he said hoarsely. ''She and my aunt's youngest daughter—the one who died—were like Katerina and Galina are now—as close as twins. She was with Anna, out doing chores, I suppose. Out getting water, probably.''

''What about Natalia's husband? Where was he?''

It took her a moment to realize why he had gone so hot so suddenly; he was sweating. ''With me, of course. With the jahar.''

''He rode with your jahar?'' she asked stupidly.

''Of course he did. He married into the tribe, of course he rode with my jahar.''

''What happened to him?''

''He left,'' he said curtly. ''I was glad to see him go. I hated him.''

''What was your mother like, Ilya?''

She didn't expect him to answer, but he did. ''Proud. Arrogant. Impulsive. Vain.''

Tess laughed a little. ''She sounds rather like you.''

''No,'' he said softly, ''I am like her. She never liked me, not until I came back from Jeds.''

''That can't be true!''

''You never knew my mother,'' he said bitterly.

''No, and I'm sorry I didn't.''

''Don't be. You wouldn't have liked her, and she'd have made your life miserable.''

''Ilya!'' The force of his anger and pain stunned her. ''Didn't you like her?''

''I loved her.'' He said it gratingly, as if he were ashamed of it.

She hesitated, but she had never found him in such a forthcoming—in such a vulnerable—mood before, so she went on. ''What about your father?''

He laughed. It was a fragile sound, brief enough, but it heartened her. ''My father was a strange man. He was an orphan. Did you know that? He was a Singer. He never said much. He never tried to counsel my mother, and she dearly needed counseling, sometimes. Not in all things. She negotiated with other tribes skillfully enough. They all said so, and it was true. But her own headstrong desires . . . those she never learned to control, and he never tried to help her. I'm not sure he cared. But he loved me. He only stayed because of me. He said the gods had told him that he would have a child who would have fire in his heart. He said the gods had told him that this child would change forever what the jaran were, that the gods would take the child on a long journey, a Singer's journey, to show him what he must do to bring the light of the gods' favor onto their chosen people.''

''And that child was you.''

''That child was me.'' His words were slurred, now. ''And now I have gone on the Singer's journey twice, once in body, once in spirit. That makes me a Singer, like my father.'' He lay heavy on her, where an arm and leg were draped over her, and he sighed and shut his eyes again.

''Go to sleep, my heart.'' She stroked his hair. A Singer. He was now a Singer. It seemed a doubly heavy burden to bear.

He slept soundly all that night. The next morning he insisted they start out down toward the Habakar heartlands. He rode a placid mare, but by mid-morning he was so exhausted that, given the choice between halting the train of wagons on the trail so that he could rest or riding in a wagon instead, he agreed to ride in a wagon. Tess sat next to him, one arm around him, propping him up. On his other side, Sonia drove. A constant stream of riders—women and men both—passed them, just to catch sight of him, just to see if it was true, that he had defeated the Habakar sorcery and come back victorious and alive.

By mid-afternoon he trembled as if with a palsy. Tess and Sonia overruled his objections and halted the wagons and made camp. He was so tired that Tess practically had to hand-feed him, and then he fell asleep before he could hold an audience. Vasil came by that evening.

''He's asleep,'' she said. She sat under the awning in the cool evening breeze, reading by lantern light from Cara's bound volume of the complete works of Shakespeare.

''You look tired,'' said Vasil. Without being asked, he sank down beside her. ''Karolla is pregnant, too.''

That startled her. ''A third child. You must be very pleased, Vasil.''

He smiled. "I love my children. Is he really asleep?"

She closed the book and set it to one side. "Vasil, what do you want? Or do you even know?"

All at once his expression lost its casual self-assurance. "Oh, gods, I thought he was going to die. I couldn't have borne that. At least, even banished from him, I knew he yet lived."

His vehemence shook her. "Why did you come back? You must know that he can't see you, that it will never be acceptable."

"I had no choice," he muttered. He dropped his gaze away from her shyly, forcing her to stare at his profile. The lantern light softened him, giving him the lineament of an angel.

Tess sighed. She had long since discovered that she was susceptible to brash men who hid behind modesty. She leaned over and took his hand. "Vasil." Then she faltered. She did not know what she needed to say.

Daringly, he lifted her hand to his lips and kissed her knuckles, and then turned her hand over and kissed her palm once, twice, thrice. She shivered, and not from the cold. "You'd better go," she said, and was shocked to hear how husky her voice sounded.

Without a word, without looking at her, he placed her hand back in her lap and left.

"Oh, God," she said to herself as she watched him walk away. As she watched him as any woman watches a man she is attracted to, measuring the set of his shoulders and the line of his hips and the promise of his hands. No wonder Sonia had warned her against him.

CHAPTER FORTY-TWO

Tess refused to go on the next day. Ilya raged at her, but she simply smiled and kissed him, and Sonia backed her up. So he rested. The day after, she agreed to go on only if he would ride in the wagon all day. Furious but trapped, he submitted.

That day they came down onto the Habakar plain, and scouts and patrols came by in increasing numbers just to get a look at him. The next day, and the next, and the next, he grew stronger in stages. They journeyed at a leisurely pace, attended by his jahar and visited by an ever-growing number of riders. Bakhtiian, they would say, pointing at him from a distance. Some came forward to pay their respects. He gave brief audiences in the evening. Tess always had to cut them short before he was ready to quit, but he was pushing himself constantly, and Cara shook her head and disapproved.

Tess was shocked at the wasteland the army had made of these lands. She could tell they had been rich, once, that they had been rich just a month before—before the jaran army had descended on them. They passed no village, no city, that was not torn by war or deserted. They passed no field that was not trampled into dust. Once they passed a pasture strewn with corpses rotting in the sun. Tess saw not one living person, except for the jaran. Ilya muttered to himself and that evening he sent messengers forward to prepare the main camp to receive him. He sent a messenger to Mother Sakhalin, asking that he and she hold an audience once he had arrived.

Riders lined the path of their train's progress, to watch him go by. The closer they came to the main camp, each day that passed, the more riders appeared along their route. Three more days passed. At midday on the fourth

day—twelve days after he had emerged from his coma—
they made their triumphal entrance to the main camp.

It was noisy, both the camp and their reception. Over
the protests of almost everyone, Ilya mounted his black
stallion and rode at the head of the procession, Tess on
his left, Josef and Mitya on his right. Tess knew well
enough that Josef's presence served to remind them all
of why they were here in Habakar territory, and Mitya's
to remind them that Bakhtiian had heirs. Vladimir, bearing the gold banner, rode behind, and after him came
Bakhtiian's personal guard, the members of the Orzhekov jahar, resplendent in their armor. After them came
Sonia, driving a cart in whose back sat the other Orzhekov children who were with the tribe. Then rode the rest
of his jahar, followed by the wagon train and the rearguard.

The members of the camp and the army had assembled,
making an avenue between them down which Bakhtiian
rode. The way was straight and clear through the huge
camp, angling in to the center where lay the Sakhalin
encampment and a broad empty field reserved for the
Orzhekov tribe. Sonia had sent a wagon ahead in the
night, with Aleksi and Ursula, containing the great tent.
Now it stood alone in the center of the field. Ilya was
glad enough to dismount and recline on the pillows lying
there for his use. He was tired, but not as tired as he had
been, and his face shone. Tess sank down beside him.
They watched as the wagons trundled in and made their
spiraling ring around the central tent. The camp grew up
around them.

Mitya and Galina brought them food and drink. Ilya
dozed a little. When he woke, he gazed at Tess with a
quizzical look in his eyes.

"What is it?" she asked. She smiled. She felt deliri-
ously happy. She had gambled, and it had paid off. It
made her feel reckless. He looked stronger already. In
another ten or twenty days, it would seem as if the entire
episode had not happened at all.

"I haven't seen you wear jahar clothes since—" He
shrugged. "Since I don't know when."

"Men's clothes don't fit a pregnant belly."

He smiled suddenly, "A child, Tess. Think of it."

"My bladder thinks of it constantly. We need better plumbing."

"What you wish, you shall have, my wife. But, ah, do you have any designs in mind?"

"I wish David was here. He's the engineer. He could design something simple and efficient."

His eyes narrowed. "David ben Unbutu. Tess." He hesitated.

"Yes?"

"Never mind." He shook his head. "I'm hungry."

"Still?"

But his expression changed, and an entirely new gleam lit his eyes as he examined her. "Just now." He reached out to take her hand, caught it up, and hastily dropped it again. "Tess. We'll go to our bed early tonight."

Demurely, she straightened out the folds in her tunic so that the brocade lay smooth over her crossed legs. "Whatever you say, my husband," she replied, smiling. "Are you sure you won't have some important audience to attend?"

"Quite sure." He propped himself up on one elbow. "There is Mother Sakhalin. You see, after I've seen her, then there's no one else I need see, no one but you." He got to his feet carefully and walked across to greet Mother Sakhalin and to escort her to a pillow next to him. She came attended by a huge retinue: etsanas, dyans, ambassadors, and even, to Tess's surprise, several members of the acting troupe.

"Bakhtiian," said Mother Sakhalin, acknowledging him. "Well met. It is with joy that I greet you this day."

He accepted her benediction with becoming modesty. Pleasantries, sweet cakes, and tea were passed around. "Most of the news of the army I have heard," he said, after a decent interval had passed. "Is there other news I ought to hear?"

Tess enjoyed watching Mother Sakhalin and Ilya together. They respected each other, and yet they remained wary, too, of the power the other one wielded. Mother Sakhalin had a vicious sense of humor and Ilya enough aplomb to match her. Tess suspected that they were the kind of pair who, had they been of an age, might have been lovers but never, ever, husband and wife. Sakhalin presented Ilya with various events, and he exclaimed over her wisdom and adroitness in handling them.

"The barbarian ambassador, the one with the slave, may yet learn wisdom," she said finally. "He has asked that his guardsmen be allowed to marry khaja women and bring them into camp."

"Has he, indeed?"

She considered him with amusement. "Of course, that is not how he asked, but he did his best to bring the matter forward modestly and with good manners. I told him that as long as they treated the women as they would treat their own wives, I might allow it."

"That was generous of you, Mother Sakhalin. But can you be sure they treat their own wives well?"

She looked affronted. "Surely any wife is treated with respect? Even savages must know such simple courtesies."

"Is this all that has happened in camp in my absence, Mother Sakhalin?"

For an instant, and no longer than that, the old woman hesitated. Then she went on. "There is nothing more that needs to be brought to your attention. Six horses were stolen. We have sent out a jahar to look for the thieves."

"Horses stolen? In the midst of this army? The thieves must be desperate souls, indeed."

But instead of answering, Mother Sakhalin took her leave, and her retinue departed with her. Except for the actors. They tarried. Tess waved them forward: an embassy of four, Ginny Arbha, Yomi Applegate-Hito, Diana Brooke-Holt, and Gwyn Jones.

"Well met," Tess rose to greet them, but their sober faces told her immediately that all was not well. "What's wrong? Has something happened?"

"Mother Sakhalin didn't tell you?" began Diana, and then broke off, looking embarrassed.

"Is something wrong?" asked Ilya in Rhuian. "May I help?"

Ginny turned to Tess. "There's been a disaster," she said in Anglais. "Hyacinth has run off with a man and his sister, and he stole things from our camp."

"Oh, God," said Tess. "What did he take?"

"His own gear, which included a little solar-celled

heating unit and his computer slate, a thermal blanket, some other things.'' She faltered and looked to Yomi.

''A water purifier. A frying pan. Some rope. A tent, which has heating coils in the fabric, as you know. One hundred bags of tea. A lantern, solar-celled. A medical kit. A permanent match.'' Yomi faltered as well.

''And a knife,'' finished Ginny, ''with an emergency transmitter and broad field stun capability built in.''

''Oh, God,'' repeated Tess. ''Have you let my brother know?''

''Immediately.''

''What did he say?''

''He said to contain the damage, if we could. He said to leave the problem in your hands for now.''

''I'll have to thank him,'' said Tess wryly, ''when I see him again.'' She glanced down and surprised a peculiar expression on Ilya's face. ''I beg your pardon,'' she said in Rhuian, and immediately all the actors begged pardon as well.

''Not at all,'' said Ilya, so softly and politely that she knew he was furious. ''I beg your pardon for disturbing your reunion.''

''One of the actors has run off,'' Tess explained. ''But you never did explain why,'' she added, glancing at Ginny.

''Tess,'' said Ginny, again in Anglais, ''evidently they have some kind of taboo on same-sex relationships in this culture. Poor stupid Hyacinth was caught with one of the young men, the young man was exiled, and his sister and Hyacinth ran off with him, to share his exile, no doubt. The Goddess knows, the only thing they'll share is an ugly death. We're heartsick about it, but what can we say? It's their taboo. Perhaps you would like to explain this story to your husband. Evidently Mother Sakhalin did not.''

Tess said, ''You'd better go. Let me know if you hear anything. I'll have to think about this.''

They made polite farewells and hurried away.

''It is one thing,'' said Ilya in a low, taut voice, ''to go to their tents and speak with them in their own tongue. It is quite another to speak it in front of me so that I can't understand what you're saying. Couldn't you have been more discreet? At least gone aside. Gods, Tess! How do you think I felt sitting here like a damned idiot? I'll thank you to treat me with more respect in the future.''

"Ilya." She sat down. "Now listen. You must recall that they come from another land, and they didn't know whether what we were discussing might embarrass or offend you.''

"Well? Surely Mother Sakhalin gave me the entire report. There was nothing offensive there. Why did the actor run off?''

She hesitated. "He was caught with another man.''

Ilya went red with anger. "So Mother Sakhalin has yet to forgive me for Vasil. We will see about this. I suppose they're the ones who stole the horses.'' He struggled to his feet.

"Ilya, I don't think—''

"By the gods," he said, brushing her hand away, "I'll lead the damned search party myself.''

"Ilya!'' She jumped up. "Don't be a fool. You idiot—!'' But he stalked off. "Aleksi!'' Aleksi appeared from around the corner of the tent, his hands grimed from greasing down an axle. "Send Mitya after him, damn it!'' He nodded and obeyed.

Ilya did not come back that evening. Mitya did. What had passed between Bakhtiian and Mother Sakhalin he did not know, but Bakhtiian had ridden off to see the nearby city which had fallen. The last remnant of its city garrison was holed up in the citadel and in the neighboring temple, still fighting. Bakhtiian, Mitya said, had been in a rare foul mood and had ordered his jahar to ride out with him to end the siege once and for all.

Tess felt sick. Physically sick. Her abdomen cramped all evening. Cara fussed over her and made her drink lots of tea and ran a scan over her, but her signs remained positive. The next day dragged by. Ilya did not return. They received no news except that renewed fighting had begun at the city, spurred on by Bakhtiian's arrival. Tess slept poorly. Another day dragged by; another night came. At Cara's insistence she went to bed, but now her back ached. She dozed. Then, starting awake, she heard him walk quietly through the outer chamber and push the curtain aside to come in to her.

"Ilya? Ilya, please don't be mad at me.''

He sank down beside her and reached, groping a little

in the darkness, and found her face, and kissed her. "I'm not mad at you."

It was not Ilya.

"Vasil!" She broke away from him. "Who gave you leave to come in here?"

"I heard that your back is hurting you." With no more invitation that that, he slid the blanket down off her bare back and stroked his hands along the curve of her lower back while she lay on her side.

"That feels good." Tess relaxed suddenly against his hands.

"I learned to do this for Karolla. Her back always aches her when she's pregnant, especially when there's a little one to be carried about. She said it helps."

"It does help." It did help. He worked without hurry, slowly, up her back to her shoulders and her neck. She sighed and shut her eyes—not that it mattered; it was pitch black, and he worked solely by touch—until he ran his hands over her shoulders and started down her front.

"Vasil."

"If you tell me to leave, I will leave," he said, and she knew he was telling the truth. In this one matter, she was certain of it.

"Vasil, you shouldn't be here." His hands had retreated to her shoulders.

"I'm alone in a tent with a woman whose husband is gone. What is wrong with that?"

"Well, I didn't invite you here, for one thing."

"Yes, but I'm sure you would have, if only I'd put myself in your way this afternoon. I do beg your pardon for forgetting to do so."

She chuckled. "Not convincing enough."

"Your back hurts. Admit I've made you feel better."

"You've made me feel better."

"Do you like sleeping alone?" he asked, curious.

"No."

"Well, then—"

"You have a wife," said Tess. "Does she like to sleep alone?"

"She has children to share her pillows with."

Tess laughed. "I'm not sure if this is any more convincing, but you're certainly persistent."

"Do you want me to leave?"

She knew she should say yes. She knew it very well. But she was cold, and lonely, and out of sorts, and, according to jaran custom, quite within her rights to entertain a lover in her husband's absence. Indeed, Sonia thought her rather odd for not having taken any lovers since her marriage, but then, much was forgiven her because of her khaja birth and upbringing. "I don't know," she said at last, unwilling to say no, unwilling to say yes.

And then, of course, she heard voices outside and footsteps through the outer chamber.

"You bastard," she said softly, "you knew he'd just come back tonight, didn't you?"

The curtain swept aside and Ilya appeared there, holding a lantern. In the glow, Tess saw that Vasil was smiling.

The silence drew out so long that at last Tess sat up, drawing the blanket up to cover her breasts. The dim light made Ilya seem as pale as wax. He did not speak, he only stared. Vasil simply sat, a half smile frozen on his face. Tess watched them.

Ilya's voice was low and sharp. "If you try to steal her from me, I promise you, Veselov, I will kill you. Get out."

"I was not aware," said Vasil, even softer, "that it was your tent to order me about in. *She* has not asked me to leave."

Ilya did not take his gaze off Vasil, as if he feared that once he did so, some disaster would occur. "Tess, tell him to leave."

"No," said Tess. She saw how Ilya started, how his gaze leapt to her. He was astonished. "No," she repeated, and drew in a breath to tell him—to tell him that she was tired of watching him run away from his fear, whatever his fear was, whatever he feared Vasil for. That she had to know, finally, what Vasil meant to him.

"Damn you," he said. "Damn you." But he wasn't talking to her at all. He was talking to Vasil. "This is how you revenge yourself on me, isn't it, Vasil? By stealing her love from me. Did you think I doubted that you could do it? Of course I did everything in my power to keep you away from her. But you waited until I was helpless, didn't you? And now . . ." He was shaking, and

Tess realized to her horror that he was about to start weeping from sheer, hopeless grief. "Grandmother Night is laughing at me. Gods, how bitter her bargains are. She means to take everything from me that I love except what I was willing to give to her in the first place."

"Ilya," Tess began, horrified that she had forced him to this. She started up to her feet.

"He's drunk," said Vasil, stopping her with his words. She sank back down. "He never goes on like this unless he's drunk."

"And he'd know," said Ilya in a hostile voice. "You'd know, wouldn't you, Vasil? You've seen me drunk often enough."

"I've never seen you drunk," said Tess. "Never." Except once, when Dr. Hierakis had gotten him drunk— but she'd seen him more under the influence of anesthesia than alcohol.

Ilya took one step and then another, and Tess could not tell whether the steps were unsteady because he was indeed drunk or simply because he was exhausted. He fumbled with the lantern, hoisting it up to tie it to the thong dangling from the pole above. Vasil rose at once, to stand next to him, close to him, and took the lantern from his hands and deftly hung it up. Then he turned and caught Ilya's face between his hands, and kissed him on the lips. For an instant, an hour, no more than two seconds, they kissed. Then Ilya twisted away from Vasil and stumbled over his own feet and collapsed beside Tess on the pillows.

A strange mood enveloped Tess, that outside this ring of light cast by the lantern nothing else existed.

"You *are* drunk," she said finally, smelling the distinctive aroma of fermented milk on him.

Vasil towered above them. "Rough work, that battle?"

"Miserable," said Ilya. He stared at his hands, whether because of what they had done at the battle or because he did not want to look at her and Vasil, Tess could not tell. "Five women were killed."

"Women!" Vasil exclaimed.

"We had to bring in the archers. It would have been slaughter otherwise."

"Did my dear sister fight, then? She's been mad for it, ever since that skirmish."

Ilya laughed harshly. "Gods, she'll make a commander yet. She's a terror on the field."

"I'm not surprised."

"A better fighter than you."

"She's a damned sight more vicious than I am. As you know."

Ilya looked up at him. Was there the briefest softening of his expression? Tess could not be sure. "Vasil, you know damn well you can't be found here."

Vasil crouched, so they were all on a level. "Why not? You were gone, Tess was here. Why shouldn't I have come in?"

Ilya rounded on Tess. "Did you invite him? Did you? I'm not sharing you with *him!*"

"Ilya, why did you get drunk?" she asked, stupidly stuck on this one point.

He jerked his head away from her and stared at the far wall.

"Because he's mad at you," said Vasil. "And anyway, isn't an ugly battle excuse enough to get drunk?"

"Aren't all battles ugly?" Tess demanded.

"There were children in that citadel," said Ilya under his breath. "Children. They slaughtered them, rather than let them fall into our hands. Gods. There was a baby, a tiny baby. And a pregnant woman." He covered his face with his hands. He shuddered.

"Oh, Ilya." Tess embraced him. The blanket fell down from her as she pressed against him. Almost as quickly, Vasil moved and crouched down on his other side, running a hand up Ilya's arm, up his shoulder and neck, up to the luxuriant mass of his dark hair.

"No," said Ilya. But he did not move away.

"You do love him," said Tess, amazed by this revelation. Amazed that, faced with the truth, it no longer frightened her.

"You don't understand," Ilya said into his hands. "I love you, Tess."

"I know you love me," Tess said. And he trusted her. He trusted her to see this. She felt such a rush of confidence and joy that he must have felt it as well, because he sighed audibly and turned his face into her hair.

So close, across Ilya's body, Vasil smiled at her, and she was struck by a second revelation—that she desired him in part because Ilya desired him. "You see," Vasil said to her, "how much you and I are alike. I love him. You love him."

"And *he* is gods-touched by a vision in his heart. This is all very well, Vasil, but the bitter truth is that no matter how he feels, he already chose his vision over you."

"But I'm a respectable married man, now," said Vasil. "So is he. There's no reason we can't live in the same camp. Not any more."

"Stop discussing me as if I'm not here," said Ilya into Tess's hair. "Given the choice, you must know that I'd choose Tess over you without hesitation."

"Did I ask you to make a choice?" asked Vasil.

Ilya went quite still.

"What are you suggesting, Vasil?" Tess asked, astonished and appalled and abruptly intrigued.

Vasil leaned close across Ilya and kissed her. It was a lingering kiss, and his hand slid caressingly up her bare back—except it wasn't Vasil's hand, there, on her back. It was Ilya's.

"Do you want me to leave?" Vasil murmured.

"No," said Tess, surprising herself, because it was the truth. Ilya said nothing. Neither did he move away from them. They took his silence for assent.

CHAPTER FORTY-THREE

The monitor implanted in David's ear buzzed, stirring him out of his drowsy lassitude. The candle had burned out, leaving the little room in darkness. Even the high window, paned with a transparent substance stronger than glass, let through only the light of stars, not enough to illuminate anything more than dark shapes against darker background. The dark of the moon.

"Oh, hell, I've got to go," he said, sitting up.

Nadine yawned and pulled her legs up so that he could scoot past her. "Umm," she said, and fell silent, undisturbed by his nocturnal comings and goings. She ought to be used to them by now, he thought, glancing back at her as he struggled to get his clothes on. He swore as he got his trousers tangled up. He shook them free and tried again.

"David." He felt more than saw that she raised herself on an elbow to peer at him. "You aren't married. Do people think you ought to be?"

"No. I don't think it's any of their business, anyway. Do people think you ought to be married?"

"Of course." Her tone was caustic. "I even have a suitor, who would mark me in a moment if he didn't know that I'd cut him to ribbons if he tried."

"You don't like him?"

She shrugged. "I like Feodor well enough. He's a pleasant lover. But he doesn't care about Jeds or anything I learned there. He doesn't care about maps. He doesn't wonder about anything, he just rides in his uncle's jahar and acquits himself well in battle, and is a good son to his mother and a good brother to his two sisters. He doesn't have any imagination, David!"

"And you have enough for two people. A trait I'm rather fond of." She smiled at him, and David grinned back. It was one of her great charms: he was fond of her, and she of him, and yet there was no possessiveness in their relationship. They shared what they shared while they shared it. Beyond that, they had their own lives. "But if you don't want him, then what is there for people to complain of in your behavior?"

Her voice darkened to match the room. "Because women aren't supposed to have any choice in marriage. Because every woman ought to be married, so that she can have children."

"Do you want children?" He gave up trying to get his trousers on standing up because he couldn't manage to keep his balance. He sat down and slid them on one leg at a time.

"No. I want to ride."

"With the army?"

"I like the army. I'm a good commander, too. I'd rather explore, though, like Marco."

"Like Marco!" He chuckled and stood up, fastening his belt on. "Yes, you and Marco would make a good team."

"Thank you," she said. "I admire him. He reminds me of Josef Raevsky, but perhaps you don't know Josef."

"No, I'm sorry. Listen, Dina, I have to go."

"Why? I know the prince is expecting a party to arrive from the coast, but surely they won't arrive until daylight. How can you know which day they'll arrive, anyway?"

David sighed. He was growing annoyed with this constant slippery sliding he had to engage in to get around her tireless, curious questioning. It would have been easier if he'd never taken up with her, but he liked her, damn it, and as the days passed he found his irritation being directed more and more at Charles. Charles should never have proclaimed the interdiction if he didn't mean to hold to it. Damned hypocrite. It wasn't Charles who had to dance the delicate dance of truth and lie to avoid giving away privileged information, to avoid the betraying slip of the tongue, to avoid telling this stubborn, affectionate spitfire that her beloved uncle was unconscious and possibly dying.

"I'm sorry." Nadine lay back down. "It's none of my business."

Which only made him feel worse. He went back and

kissed her, and left, thankful that she was both sensible and understanding. He padded down the hallway to Charles's room. The door was latched shut. He knocked twice, a pause, and twice more. Jo opened the door. He slipped inside. Inside, Cara Hierakis's image stared at him without seeing him.

"—preliminary signs show that he's no worse for the wear. He's weak, as might be expected after almost sixteen days in a coma, and he's a damned difficult convalescent, if you ask me, but I don't at this time expect a relapse."

"How is Tess?" asked Charles.

"She's ecstatic. Hello, David." The image raised its eyebrows and glanced behind itself, toward nothing they could see. "Her health is fine. I must go."

"Off here," said Charles. The image snapped and dissipated into nothing. A cold light illuminated the room, a steady gleam that seemed alien to David's eyes after the flickering lantern light he was growing used to.

"What happened?" David asked.

"Bakhtiian came out of the coma and seems fine, if weak."

David put a hand to his chest. He felt—relieved, and was surprised to find himself so happy. Certainly he had no reason to care about Bakhtiian and perhaps good reason to wish him dead. "That's good news to give to Nadine," he began, and then remembered that Nadine didn't know that her uncle had even been in a coma.

"We've got the landing scheduled for three hours from now," said Charles, dismissing the momentous news as if it was of trivial importance. "We'll split the party. Marco and Rajiv and Jo to the landing site. Marco, you'll stay with the shuttle for as long as they stay on-site. Rajiv and Jo will escort the technicians back here. David, you'll run interference with the jaran, since you have the best excuse to be able to speak khush well. Did you come up with any ideas on keeping them out of the way?"

David sighed. "I'll run a survey tomorrow of the north and west walls and gardens, a real old-fashioned kind with string and survey markers, and I'll ask for help. I can use quite a few of them doing that, and perhaps keep the rest entertained."

"Maggie?" Soerensen asked.

"Mother Avdotya has already agreed to let me observe the worship services and also I have her and a few of the older priests willing to let me interview them tomorrow about their myths and the history of the palace as they know it. I'll make it all last as long as possible."

"That will have to do. I'm most concerned about Mother Avdotya and Nadine Orzhekov, since they seem consistently to be the ones who are most likely to notice anomalies in our behavior. Do your best."

"Nadine will be interested in survey methods," said David. He glanced at Marco, who lounged casually against one wall, arms crossed on his chest. "She said she admires you, Marco, because you're an explorer."

Marco chuckled. "What? Does she want to join me?"

"Yes. I rather think she would, if she could."

Marco shrugged. "And why not? She's quick on her feet, a better fighter than I am, smart, and curious." He cast an inquiring glance toward Charles. "Why not?"

"One bridge at a time," said Charles. "She is also Bakhtiian's niece, and I believe his closest living relative. She has a duty to him."

"A woman's duty in this kind of culture," said Maggie, "is usually to get married and produce heirs. Neither of which I see her doing. I like her. I wish we could take her back with us."

The comment produced silence that was sudden and uncomfortable.

"Fair trade," said Marco with a twist of his lips that wasn't quite a smile. "The sister for the niece."

"I don't think so," said Charles smoothly. "Now. You'd better go. You've got a long ride, and it's dark out there."

Rajiv gathered up his hemi-slate and the six long tube-lights they were going to use for trail lights and landing markers. Marco shrugged on his cape. Jo pulled a second, heavier tunic on over her clothing and belted it at her waist. Without further ado, they left. Maggie went with them, to escort them down to the stables and run interference, as Charles called it, in case anyone came investigating this nocturnal exodus.

"Is there a problem, David?" Charles asked abruptly.

"A problem?" The question took David aback.

Charles sat down on his bed and considered David with

that level, bland gaze that had come to characterize him. However busy he might be, however many pans he might have frying in the fire, he never did two things at once. If he spoke to a person, singling that person out, then all his attention focused on the conversation. Even his hands sat at rest, folded neatly in his lap. David knew how deceptively mild his expression was.

"You're upset about something," said Charles, "and I don't keep sycophants around because they don't do me any good."

Thus neatly forcing David to speak his mind, even if he was reluctant to. "It's this damned interdiction. It's hypocrisy and you know it. I'm tired of lying to Nadine—well, to all of them, if it comes to that, but to her in particular. Don't you think they know we're holding things back? Aren't we harming them more by being here than—?"

"Than if we hadn't come at all? No doubt about that. But Tess came here, and so here we are. Think of it as damage control."

"It's not damage control," said David. "Oh, Goddess, you mean that message that came in this morning."

"About the actor running away? Yes, in part that."

"What are you going to do about him?"

"Rajiv is hunting down the code on that transmitter. We'll likely get a fix on him within five or ten days. If he's still alive by then."

"You're cool about it."

"David, you know me better than that."

"You've changed, Charles. I say that as one of your two oldest friends."

Charles regarded him evenly. "What choice? No choice. I do what I must." He gave a short laugh and grinned, looking for an instant so much like the young man David had met at university that David might almost have thought they were the same person again, and that the gulf that had grown between the old Charles and the new one had suddenly closed. "Bakhtiian confided in me before we left the army that he couldn't tell what he could and couldn't believe out of all the things Tess had told him."

"If he expected you to enlighten him, then I'm sure he was disappointed."

"You *are* angry."

"It's disrespectful, beyond anything else," said David. "Treating them like children—as if we know better, as if we have to protect them."

"The interdiction did protect them."

David sank down into the single chair and rested his forehead on a palm. "Which is true. Oh, hell, Charles, it's just an untenable situation."

"Yes," Charles agreed without visible emotion. "Remember as well, David, that this is the only planet we have any real control over, because of that interdiction. Chapalii can't come here without my permission—or, if they do, as that party that Tess fell in with did, they must do it covertly. We can't afford to lose that power. Cara can run her lab in Jeds precisely because the Chapalii can't investigate it at their whim. This is our—our safehouse. Our priest hole. Our hideaway. Not to mention the entire philosophical issue of whether it would be ethical to ram our culture and technology down their throats in the name of progress. So it's to my advantage to keep the interdiction in force."

"Even if you break it yourself."

"Even so. I'm not a saint, David."

"However much you try to be?"

Charles chuckled, a refreshingly and reassuringly human sound. "I only try to be because I know that whatever I do wrong will come back to haunt me tenfold. I don't like this situation any better than you do. If we took Tess away, we'd be quit of it."

David lifted his head off his hand. "Would you force her to go? Could you?"

"Of course I could. I control this planet, David. Would I?" He thought about it. The little room the priests had given him to sleep in mirrored him in many ways: simple, plain, without obvious character. But David knew that behind the plain whitewashed walls ran a complex network of filaments and power webs and ceramic tiling for strength and the Chapalii alone knew what other technological miracles and contrivances, hidden from sight but always present, there where they couldn't be seen. "I don't know. I haven't been forced to make that decision yet."

"Goddess help them both when you do."

"Both?" asked Charles.

"Both Tess and Bakhtiian. And his people. And the countries in the path of his conquest. He's a madman. You could stop him."

"I could kill him physically. I could tell him, show him, the truth, which Tess believes would kill him spiritually. What's so strange about him, though? Earth has had such men in her past."

"Does that make it right? Knowing we could intervene?"

"I don't know. Is intervening right? Will it make any difference in the long run? Does this argument have anywhere to go except around in circles? He's better than most, David. He thinks, he's open-minded and curious, he cares about law and legal precedence, and I believe he cares enough about what Tess thinks of him that he'll temper brutality with mercy."

"Like that man he executed for rape? He did it himself, and he didn't look one whit remorseful about the act to me."

"Who knows? Perhaps killing him on the spot like that *was* a merciful punishment, compared to what he might have received."

"Without a trial?" David demanded.

"He had a confession. But I can't help thinking about the actor. Three of them alone in hostile territory."

"And horse-stealers, too. That must be punishable by death, under nomad law."

"Do you think their deaths will be easy, or quick?" Charles asked.

"Don't forget, the actor has a weapon with him—one of our weapons. And other equipment. That gives him an advantage."

"And it breaks the interdiction in exactly the way I did not want it broken," Charles added.

"In fact, it might well be easier if the poor boy did die, and his companions with him."

"It might well. But then there'd be all that equipment out there to be recovered. Either way. . . ." Charles shrugged.

David felt suddenly heartened. He chuckled. "You know, Charles, I don't envy you. I'm perfectly happy to be sitting here, and you sitting there."

Charles's pale blue gaze met David's brown one. His lips quirked up. "As well you might be. Now, I'm going to get some sleep."

David realized that that was as close to a confession of the burdens weighing on him as Charles was ever likely to give him, or to give anyone. Perhaps Charles could no longer afford to be vulnerable. Perhaps Charles regretted what he had lost but knew well enough that the loss was permanent, that there was nothing of his old self that could be recovered, even if he wanted to.

"Yes," said David on a sigh. "That's a good idea." He stood up and left Charles to his solitary state. Back in his own tiny room, he managed to nap on the hard bed for the few hours until dawn. He woke when the first light bled through the window, and he rose and dressed quickly and hurried downstairs to the eating hall in order to make it in time for breakfast. Maggie was there, although Charles wasn't. She signaled with one hand—"all okay, going as planned." That meant that the riders ought to come in mid-morning, escorting their "party from the coast." What would the jaran make of this Chapaliian visitation? Mother Avdotya had mentioned the khepelli priests who had visited four summers past. Their stay had been short and uneventful with a single exception: they had left with one fewer member of their party than they had come with. This mystery had never been solved, nor had any remains been found of the missing priest. The jaran knew of blood sacrifices, both human and animal, but as far as David could tell, they did not indulge in them except under the most pressing need. He had asked Nadine about it, but she seemed to think such an act shameful, although he could not tell whether that response came from her jaran upbringing or her Jedan education.

What would they think of a Chapalii coming in with Soerensen's escort? With his blessing? Under his authority? Nadine would be sure to be suspicious, and she would give a full report to her uncle. David did not for one instant doubt her loyalty to Bakhtiian, or doubt that she put her loyalty to him and to her people above all else, however much she did not follow their customs in other ways.

Well, it was hopeless. As Charles had said, the argument could run around in a circle and never get anywhere. He saw Nadine and went to sit beside her. She greeted him with a smile and he set to work on the food while discussing with her his plans for a survey of the north front.

"But tell me, David," she said after he had told her of his plans, "I see how you can use this method to measure accurately the dimensions of the shrine. Is there a way to measure greater distances, using the same methods? I can draw out a map with rough accuracy—Josef Raevsky taught me how to do that, and I learned more about maps at the university in Jeds, but still, there must be more accurate methods. Mostly, the jaran measure distances by how long it takes a rider, or a wagon, to get from one place to another. But that's not a good measure. How fast is the rider? Is it a jahar that's foraging as it goes? Is it a wagon train? Is it a messenger, who changes horses frequently and so can ride as far in one day as wagons cover in ten?"

"I'll show you some more about that today," replied David. "If you have two angles and one side, you can calculate the rest of the triangle. That's why I use a staff that's a set length; in my case two *meters*."

"Yes, I know about triangles. They're one of the gods' mysteries."

David chuckled. "Yes, there is a certain magic to them. Now, look." He took his knife and held it point down, perpendicular to the table. "If you know the height of your measuring staff—this knife—and you know the angle—"

"But I understand that," said Nadine impatiently. "I helped you survey the grounds of the shrine. But what about really long distances? Do you have to measure each stretch of ground you ride over? Add them together, perhaps? How can you reckon distances off to each side, as well? And bring them all together to make an accurate map?"

You put satellites into orbit. You use aerial photography. You use computer-driven navigational instruments and beacons and . . . "At sea you use a sextant and the altitudes of celestial bodies," said David instead. "On land maybe you don't really need a truly accurate map, because you can use landmarks to guide your travels."

"Yes, but what if you *want* one?" Nadine insisted. That was the trouble with her; she wasn't content with what just worked.

"Orzhekov!" One of her riders burst into the room, breathing hard from running. "Messenger, riding in."

She jumped to her feet but hard on the man's heels came the messenger himself, wind-blown, pale, looking exhausted. He wore a harness of bells strapped over his shirt. The bells sang as he walked.

"Feodor!" exclaimed Nadine. She froze.

The young man strode across to her. By Nadine's expression, David could guess who it was: the young man named Feodor Grekov, the one Nadine had mentioned with scornful affection. The young man of princely family who wanted to marry her. And David's first thought, unintended and embarrassing, was to wonder if now that Feodor was here, Nadine would throw David out of her bed in favor of her jaran lover.

The bells chimed and brushed into silence as Feodor halted before Nadine. He was good-looking; David could see that even through the young man's fatigue. He looked competent. He looked like exactly the kind of man Nadine had made him out to be: reliable, stolid, and pleasant.

"What news?" she asked, looking worried. "Have you come from camp?"

"Your uncle," he said. The words seemed choked out of him, either from suppressed anguish or from exhaustion; perhaps from both. "He's—" It all came out: Bakhtiian had fallen ill. His spirit had been witched from his body by Habakar priests. No one knew if he was dying, or if he was coming back to them. No one knew.

Nadine stood there dead still. Her mouth was drawn tight, and David could see the pulse beating under her jaw. She looked half in shock. And he couldn't say a thing. He couldn't even reveal that he understood their conversation perfectly, now that he understood khush much better than he dared let on.

"You must return," Grekov finished. "You're his closest living relative."

"I must return," she echoed, but the voice had no force of emotion. Only her drawn face did. She stared out the huge windows onto the gardens, brilliant with summer flowers. David felt sick with guilt, seeing how she suffered with fear for her uncle. Knowing she didn't have to.

Grekov drew his saber. A murmur ran through the men standing around them. Nadine's eyes went wide. She began to draw her own saber. She looked furious. "Grekov, this is no time to—"

But Grekov's aspect had changed, and David mentally added 'stubborn' to the young man's list of attributes. "Mother Sakhalin came to my mother and my aunt and my uncle. They agreed between them that I should set aside my—scruples and mark you. Bakhtiian must have heirs."

Nadine had her saber half out. She seemed suspended, unable to move one way or the other, unable to act, unable to accede. "Our cousins have many fine sons."

"That's true," said Feodor, "but it's properly through his sister's line that Bakhtiian should have heirs. You know it's true. You know it's your duty to marry, if your uncle dies. He may be dead already. Who will the tribes follow then? They would follow your child." He brought his saber to rest on her cheek.

Nadine had gone so pale that David thought she might faint. But, of course, Nadine would never faint. Her saber did not move. Neither did Feodor's. David wanted to tell her, Goddess, how badly he wanted to tell her. But he could not.

Her mouth worked, but no words came out. She shut her eyes, briefly, and opened them again, as if disgusted with herself for trying to hide from what was facing her. Then she slid her saber back into its sheath.

Feodor marked her. She submitted meekly enough, but her eyes burned. Like her uncle, her spirit showed in her eyes, and it was a strong spirit, even in defeat. Blood welled and coursed down her cheek, dripping off her jaw. A drop caught on her lips and, reflexively, she licked it off. Feodor had the grace to look ashamed, and yet, at the same time, he managed to look jubilant, as at an unforeseen victory.

David turned away. He could no longer stand to watch.

"Give me the bells," said Nadine. "I'll ride to my uncle's bedside. You'll stay with my jahar, here at the shrine, until the prince of Jeds is finished with his work here, and then you'll escort him back to the army. Yermolov will act as your second.''

It was a trivial revenge; it might be months until they saw each other again, but Grekov did not look disheartened. Why should he be? As far as David could tell, marriage was for life in the jaran. The young rider slipped out of the bells and handed them to Nadine. She slung them over her shoulders and turned to go. Her glance stopped on David, and her mouth turned up in a sardonic smile. She knew he knew and understood what a bitter blow this was to her.

What she did not know was that he could have prevented it.

''I'm sure he'll be all right,'' David said, impelled to say it. He wanted to shout it: *He is all right. He's alive. He's recovering.* But it was too late. Perhaps the time would have come inevitably, the pressure for her, Bakhtiian's sister's daughter, to marry and have a child who could inherit through the female line closest to Bakhtiian. It was some consolation. Not much.

''Good-bye, David,'' she said. He felt as if she were saying good-bye not so much to him personally, or to him as her lover, but to what he represented, the knowledge, the curiosity, the urge to explore and range wide. It was pretty damned difficult for pregnant women and women with small children to range wide.

''Good-bye,'' he said and watched her go. Grekov watched her go. Her jahar watched her go. The priests, those who were there, watched her go. Yermolov escorted her out to the horses.

Charles walked in by the other door. ''Is something wrong?'' he asked.

About two hours after Nadine had left, Rajiv and Jo rode in with the Chapalii party. The tall, thin figures of the Chapalii looked doubly alien to David after he'd been so long on a planet where Chapalii did not set foot. David saw them ride in from his vantage point at the northwest corner of the palace, but they were far enough away that he couldn't see them as more than distant shapes. In a frenzy of self-flagellation, he had designated Feodor Grekov to assist him personally in the surveying, with most of the other riders strung out at intervals along the space. He didn't need them, of course, but it served to keep them busy. Feodor was quiet and helpful, and he seemed good-natured. He even asked a few questions, and he seemed interested in the concept of using triangles to measure distance. But he had nothing like Nadine's bothersome, nagging, wonderful curiosity.

David was relieved when dusk came and he could excuse everyone and go inside to eat dinner, to pretend to go to bed. He crept out through the shrine, which he knew like the back of his hand by now, having mapped it twice over, and made his way to the room which hid the control room.

The room sat blank, white, cold, and empty, and as impenetrable as every other time he had been there. Then, a moment later, the wall exhaled and Maggie stood in a dark opening.

"Quick," she said, beckoning. "Come in. It's amazing."

He hurried over to her. A narrow tunnel fell away before him. He followed her back into the blackness. The wall shut behind them and a bright light shone ahead. They came out into a chamber lit with screens and lights and stripes of color. The garish light illuminated five figures: three of the tall, angular Chapalii figures that were as familiar to humans as any ubiquitous authority figure is, and two shapes that seemed squat and thick in comparison: that would be Charles and Rajiv. Maggie took hold of David's arm and dragged him forward. David stared. How could he help but stare? Two flat screens and three holo-screens flashed information past at a dizzying speed. Charles acknowledged David with a nod. Charles stood between two Chapalii, one resplendent in mauve merchant's robes, the other dressed in the tunic and trousers of the steward class. Rajiv was oblivious to anything except the console at which he stood and the Chapalii standing next to him, with whom he conferred in a low, intense voice. Maggie lifted her eyebrows and looked at David, grinning, waiting for him to react.

A Chapalii female! In shape he could not have told any differences between her and the two males. But the skin . . . Unlike the two males in the room, whose skin was pale, almost dead white, whose skin flushed colors betraying their emotions, the female's skin was dark, a kind of tough-looking, all-purpose gray. It seemed scaly, without being scaled. She wore a lank tail of hair hanging from the slight bulge on the back of her skull. In dim light, he could not have told them apart, except for her thin hank of hair, and that might have been a class difference. But in bright light, she looked alien. The males might pass by some far stretch of the imagination for human, or humanlike, creatures. She had the same build, but her strange coloration, her thick, dry epidermis, betrayed her fundamental otherness. She was weird; she was eerie. And David was used to the idea of unearthly beings.

"So?" David asked, when he found his voice.

"So once we got into the room, Rajiv and the ke—the female servant there—got inside the system within one hour. It's all there, David. The contents of the Mushai's computer banks."

"We knew that."

"Yes, but we never got past the surface layer before. And there's more, much more than was on the cylinder Tess brought. They've spent the last five hours figuring out how to translate the information off this system and on to some transferable media. Evidently the cylinders only work off the consoles they come from. Like matched sets. Information is so valuable a commodity that it's hoarded just like—like the jaran hoard gold."

"They don't hoard gold," corrected David, "they wear it."

"I think the analogy still holds."

"What if they can't transfer the data off."

Maggie shrugged. "How should I know? Rajiv will probably come live here for the next ten years and transcribe everything manually onto his modeler. But even so he'd never get the hundredth part of it that way. Still, that ke is a brilliant engineer, according to him, and his standards are high. They ought to be able to work something out together."

"David." Charles came over, the merchant at his side. "You have met Hon Echido, I believe."

"Honored," said David, recalling his polite Chapalii. He gave a brief greeting bow, which Echido returned exactly.

"Let's leave them to it," said Charles. "I have no doubt they'll be up all night. And the next day, as well."

Charles gestured to Maggie and David to precede him. Echido waited behind Charles. The steward stayed where he was, presumably to aid Rajiv and the ke, who were oblivious to this desertion. They left the room and walked back through the quiet palace by a roundabout route. Their path took them to the vault of the huge dome. They halted there. The cavernous depths of the hall and the height swallowed them, muffling the sound of their footsteps on the marble floor, making whispers of their voices. In the darkness, the thin pillars that edged the distant curved walls gleamed a pale pink, like a hint of sunrise to come. Above, far above, the dome seemed splintered with stars and luminous cracks and amorphous blots of utter darkness, like a portal onto the depths of space.

David held Maggie's hand, finding comfort in the heat of her skin, in her proximity. Farther off, Charles stood and stared up. Echido stood slightly in front of Charles. In the darkness, his robes, too, seemed luminous, as if fibers of light were woven into the purple fabric. The Chapalii lifted up his left hand. He spoke a sentence.

The dome lit. Everywhere, everything, lights, blinding, scattering, crystal sparking in a thousand colors and rainbows arching in vivid, astonishing geometric patterns so high above in the vault of the dome that they seemed unreachable. Across the marble floor light fragmented into colored patterns, animal shapes intertwined, plants interlaced, helices and chevrons, so bewildering in their profusion that it staggered him. All perfectly placed to create a web of light, a latticework of color, a net of brilliance, that seemed to David's eyes to represent everything and nothing, order and chaos at once. It was glorious. It was uncanny. It was beautiful.

David gaped. Maggie gaped, gripping his hand. Even Charles gaped, for once shocked into speechlessness.

"The Tai-en Mushai," said Echido in his colorless voice, his Anglais fluent and uninflected, "became so notorious that although his name is obliterated forever from the emperor's ear for his rashness, his title lives on nevertheless. Not least because of his sister, who is known as one of the great artists of my people. It is she who designed the Grand Concourse leading from Sorrowing Tower to Reckless Tower to Shame Tower. I am grieved that this achievement here must rest in obscurity.''

"End it," said Charles suddenly, startled out of his stupor by Echido's calm voice.

"As you command, Tai Charles." He spoke another sentence. Glory vanished, to leave them shuttered in a darkness which seemed as endless as the void. Silence descended. After some minutes, David could make out the traceries in the dome again, distinguish the faint gleam of the pillars along the walls. He understood Echido's sorrow, that such beauty must be concealed. A moment later he realized how astounding it was, his sympathy with Echido's sadness.

"I humbly beg your pardon, Tai-en," Echido added, "if I have by my rash action troubled you. I recall that this planet is under an interdiction of your making and the emperor's approval."

"No," said Charles, "no, I don't mind this once. I've never seen anything like that. It was . . ." His voice betrayed his awe. ". . . beautiful. But it must not happen again, here or elsewhere in this palace, not as long as there are natives on the precincts."

Echido bowed. "To have given you pleasure, however brief, Tai-en, is a great honor to me."

"I am pleased," said Charles, acknowledging Echido's gift. "David has a map of the palace, and I would dearly like to know what other—art—is hidden here, and how it might be brought to life. How did you do that?"

"But surely—" Echido hesitated. "Tai-en, every princely and ducal house holds to itself a *motto,* I believe you would name it in your tongue. Said thus, it illuminates both the noble lord himself and what his family has created in his name."

"Ah," said Charles. "Of course. How did you know the Mushai's motto? Surely it has been a long time since his name was spoken in the halls of the emperor."

"Uncounted years," said Echido. "Tai-en." He bowed. "But all know it, still, because its very words are—as reckless as he was. So it remains with us, over time uncounted and years beyond years. 'This hand shall not rest.' That is one way it might translate into your language, although I am sure the Tai-endi Terese could render a more accurate, fitting, and poetic translation.''

"I am sorry," said Charles, "that she is not here to see this."

"I, too, Tai-en, am saddened by her absence. Our acquaintance was brief, but I count myself favored that she dignified my presence with her attention." He folded his hands in front of him. David knew that the arrangement of fingers and palm had meaning, that it signified an emotion, a statement, a frame of mind, but he could not interpret it. Tess could, but Tess wasn't here. No wonder Charles refused to let her go. She was invaluable to his cause.

"We must go," said Charles. "I hope no one was awake to see this display, however much I am pleased to have seen it myself. Otherwise there could be awkward questions." He started to walk. Maggie let go of David's hand and paced up beside the Chapalii merchant. David fell in next to Charles. They paused at the buttressed arch that led into a long hall lined with alternating stripes of pale and black stone. Echido and Maggie kept walking, but Charles turned to look back into the vast hollow behind them. From this angle, no lights shone, not even faint ones. It was as black as a cave. Only the immensity of air, palpable as any beast, betrayed the cavernous gulf beyond.

"So what will your motto be?" David asked, half joking.

"I've been reading *The Tempest* lately," said Charles, his voice as colorless as Echido's. "After what Maggie said. There's a little phrase the sorcerer Prospero says to the spirit Ariel, who serves him." Here in the darkness, David felt more than saw Charles's presence, familiar and yet strange at the same time, here, where he might learn what lay now at Charles's heart. Charles still faced the huge chamber of the dome. His breath exhaled and was drawn in. On the next breath, he spoke.

" 'Thou shalt be free.' "